"Yeah," Sal the Cacophony said, narrowing her eyes at Ozhma. "Is that for me?"

Ozhma froze.

Oh no, is what *for her? Is that Vagrant slang? Is she about to shoot me? All of us? Is she going to steal my face? Can she do that? Do the... Oh, hang on.*

She hadn't even finished thinking before the tankard was out of her hands and into Sal's. The woman tilted her head back, guzzling the liquor like it was water. It dribbled from the corners of her mouth, down the slope of her collarbone, across the muscle of her body to mingle with the sweat and blood and scars.

The scars.

She was covered in them, elegant strands of knotted flesh to answer the chaotic ink of her tattoos. And none of them presided over her body with the same majesty of ruin as the thick one that wound its way from her collarbone to her belly.

"Thanks." Sal let out a belch, sucked in air through her teeth. "Tastes like shit." She wiped her mouth with the back of her hand. "Anyway, sorry for the threats, but it's important that you hear this." She lowered the tankard, took a long breath, composed herself. "It began like this, right?"

Praise for

SAM SYKES AND THE GRAVE OF EMPIRES TRILOGY

Seven Blades in Black

"Sykes is a master at taking familiar elements of fantasy and stirring them to a wicked, wholly original churn. In Sal the Cacophony, Sykes has crafted a protagonist for the ages. Ludicrous, wicked, delightful." —Pierce Brown, *New York Times* bestselling author

"*Seven Blades in Black* offers villains that are as memorable and unique as the heroes. Action, magic, romance, and humor mingle well in this mammoth tale. It's an immersive read in a well-realized world." —Robin Hobb, *New York Times* bestselling author

"Exciting and inventive. I never realized how much I needed wizard-hunting gunslingers in my life."

—Peter V. Brett, *New York Times* bestselling author

"*Seven Blades in Black* is terrific. The tale of Sal the Cacophony is delightfully sarcastic and deeply sorrowful."

—Nicholas Eames, author of *Kings of the Wyld*

"Gunslingers and mad mages and monsters, oh my. Sykes's latest is a brutal and vulgar epic yet still fun enough that—and I say this as the highest of compliments—makes me wish like hell it ends up with an adaptation into a role-playing game."

—Chuck Wendig, *New York Times* bestselling author

"Sykes's writing is full of heart, hilarity, and the frank understanding that as humans we are all disasters. Come for the adventures, stay for the weirdos." —R. F. Kuang, author of *The Poppy War*

"By the end of the first page, you'll know Sam is in love with his characters. By the end of the second, you'll know you are too."
—Myke Cole, author of *The Armored Saint*

"With skillful worldbuilding, unexpected humor, and characters real enough to touch, this is easily Sykes's best book to date."
—*Publishers Weekly* (starred review)

"Compulsive from start to finish." —*Kirkus* (starred review)

Ten Arrows of Iron

"Reunites readers with the magnificently complex heroine Sal the Cacophony in a hair-raising adventure packed with action, wit, and feeling.... This an unforgettable epic fantasy."
—*Publishers Weekly* (starred review)

BY SAM SYKES

The Grave of Empires

Seven Blades in Black

Ten Arrows of Iron

Three Axes to Fall

The Gallows Black: A Grave of Empires Novella

The Iron Dirge: A Grave of Empires Novella

Bring Down Heaven

The City Stained Red

The Mortal Tally

God's Last Breath

The Aeons' Gate Trilogy

Tome of the Undergates

Black Halo

The Skybound Sea

An Affinity for Steel (omnibus edition)

THREE AXES TO FALL

THE GRAVE OF EMPIRES: BOOK THREE

SAM SYKES

orbitbooks.net

Cover design by Lauren Panepinto
Cover illustration by Jeremy Wilson

Map by Tim Paul
Author photograph by Libbi Rich

Orbit
Hachette Book Group
1290 Avenue of the Americas
New York, NY 10104
orbitbooks.net

First Edition: December 2022

Orbit is an imprint of Hachette Book Group.
The Orbit name and logo are trademarks of Little, Brown Book Group Limited.

Library of Congress Cataloging-in-Publication Data
Names: Sykes, Sam, 1984– author. | Paul, Tim, cartographer.
Title: Three axes to fall / Sam Sykes ; [Map by Tim Paul].
Description: First edition. | New York : Orbit, 2022. | Series: The Grave of Empires ; book 3
Identifiers: LCCN 2022007652 | ISBN 9780316363525 (trade paperback) | ISBN 9780316363532 (ebook)
Classification: LCC PS3619.Y545 T57 2022 | DDC 813/.6—dc23
LC record available at https://lccn.loc.gov/2022007652

ISBNs: 9780316363525 (trade paperback), 9780316363532 (ebook)

Printed in the United States of America

LSC-C

Printing 1, 2022

If it still hurts in the morning, this one's for you

Borrus Valley
REVOLUTION OFFENSIVE
Ocytus
Jerks
DICKS
Six Walls
DOPES
Bitterdrink
These guys are OK!

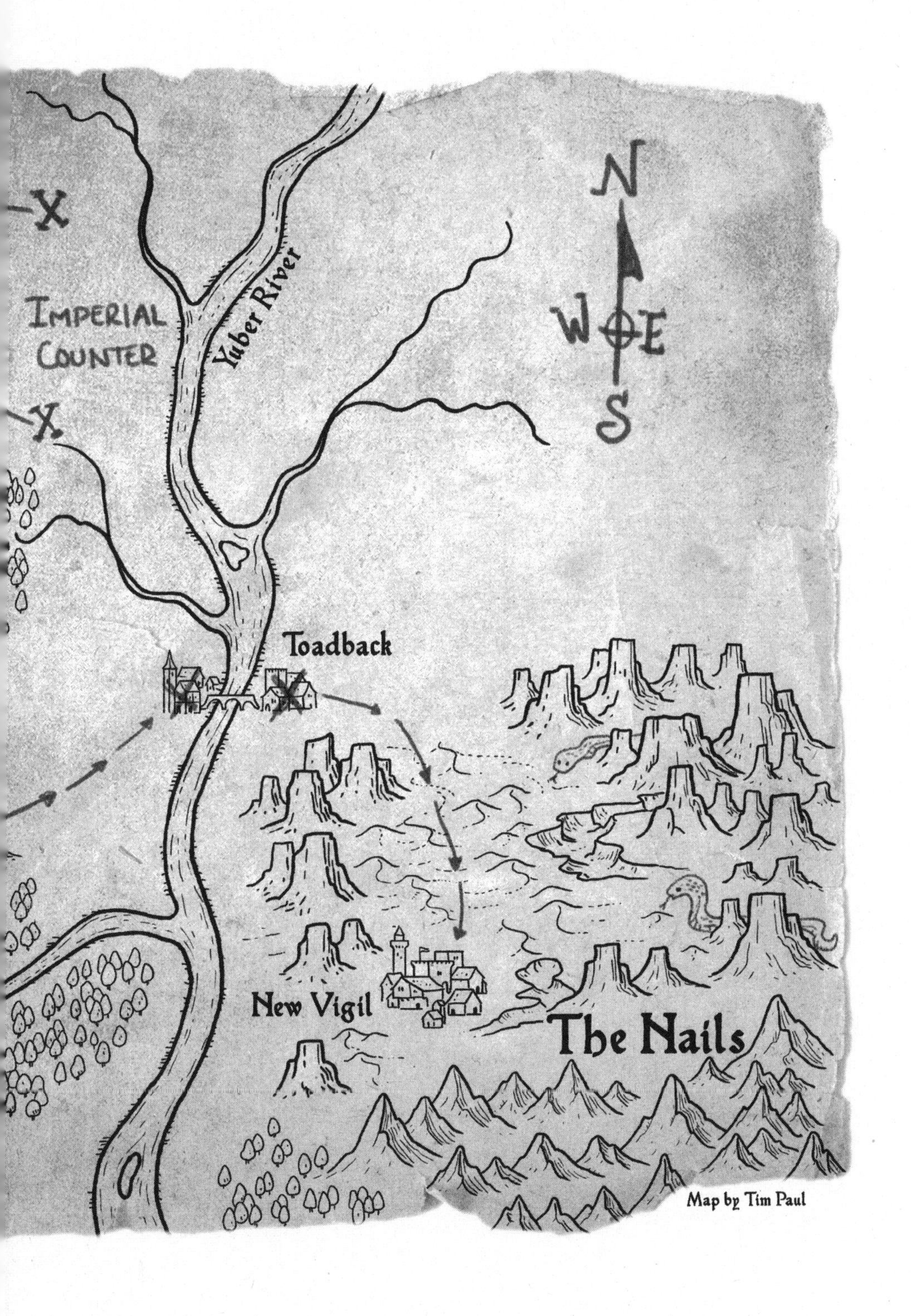
N
W
E
S
Imperial Counter
Yuber River
Toadback
New Vigil
The Nails
Map by Tim Paul

FOR THOSE RETURNING TO THE SCAR...

All right, bear with me. A lot happened and not all of it is my fault. Just keep that in mind as we talk.

Some know me as a meddler, others as a bad dream, and a few as an excellent taste in whiskey. Sal the Cacophony. Vagrant. Oathbreaker. Wielder of the most terrible weapon in existence.

Pleased to meet you.

It wasn't so long ago I went by another name, though. They called me Red Cloud. And my magic was like nothing the world had ever seen. Those I thought I could trust agreed—they stole my magic from me. And in exchange, I put all thirty-three of their names on a list and started looking for them.

I was doing fairly well at it, too.

Until I started a war.

Now, it's not technically me *that started the war. Or at least, I wasn't the only one there.*

I followed the name of one of my betrayers, Darrish the Flint, to the Borrus Valley: a cold little place where the Imperium and the Revolution, two nations with quite *a lot of weaponry to spare, had designs on each other.*

In the midst of my hunt, I was recruited into an operation for what I thought were noble purposes. Or, at least, purposes that were so self-serving that I wanted to call *them noble.*

Two Lonely Old Men, inventor and architect, plotted to hijack a great weapon from the Revolution's legendary fleet of airships, the Ten Arrows. A suitably motley crew of colorful Vagrants and myself signed on for the plan. And, after a reasonable number of things going wrong, managed to make it onto the airship itself.

And that's when I learned everything at once.

I learned Liette, the woman I couldn't give up my revenge for, was aboard the airship and working with the Revolution to solve the mysteries of the great weapon we were there to steal.

I learned that Two Lonely Old Men had betrayed us all without knowing it and that what we did to the airships actually made them drop their bombs upon settlements, forcing an Imperial retaliation.

And I also learned that Culven Loyal, one of the most trusted and powerful lieutenants of the Revolution, was actually an otherworldly being inhabiting a husk of a human.

That seems important to note.

The weapon itself turned out to be the prison of another such being, a Scrath. Rather than allow Loyal to devour it, it chose to inhabit the closest vessel to hide in.

Liette.

We survived the airship. We escaped the Valley. But we couldn't stop the war.

And now she and I make our way across the Scar, trailed by the ruin of the war as we head east, trying to escape the conflict and find a way to get the Scrath out of Liette before Loyal finds us.

Or before the war consumes us.

Or before the thing inside her assumes control of her.

Or before the—

Actually, maybe I'd better just stop there. This is getting a little depressing.

ONE

THE SCAR

Ozhma was not having a good day.

The inn had been out of breakfast potatoes. She'd had to change a wagon wheel an hour out of town. And *now* she was being asked to prevent thousands from dying needlessly in a hellstorm of flame and fury.

She hadn't even worn the right shoes for it.

Her nice little red boots were made for dazzling buyers, charming customers, and not—as she *specifically* said when she joined Avonin & Family Whiskeymakers—trekking her magnificent ass up an incredibly steep cliff.

Maybe not *specifically*, but she was sure that cliffs were covered in the reasonably long list of places she would not haul her ass. But then, she reasoned, she was pretty sure she'd never have agreed to be escorted up a cliff by the threat of painful death should she not.

"Listen, you want to sit still back there?"

And yet...

She glowered up from beneath her hat—her very, *very* sweaty hat—at the back of the man's messy head of hair. *Man* was as close a descriptor as she could decide on for him—he was male, tall, and with the lean fighting muscle she liked so well, but the rest of him was a mystery.

His clothes were an ill-fitting shirt and baggy trousers, cinched in some vague attempt at the Imperial style by a thick cloth sash. An immense amount of skin, marred by scars and a tattoo of a thick tree trunk, was on display—which she didn't mind—but his long brown hair was a greasy mess, a match for his stubble-caked face—which she *did* mind.

He looked like a bandit. She'd have been happy to call him one. But bandits rarely smelled so strongly of silkgrass, and the pipe dangling from his lip positively reeked. And no bandit she had ever heard of carried a thick piece of wood at their hip instead of a sword.

"Not to complain or anything." The man exhaled a cloud of smoke that coiled over the crown of his head to blow back into her face. "Actually, a lot of people—including me—are going to die if you fuck this up. So I guess I do mean to complain a little."

"Wow, what amazing advice," Ozhma replied, her breath heavy with nerves. "This entire time, I've been wondering what I could *possibly* do to make *your* life easier." She glowered at the back of his head as hard as she could—he couldn't see it, but she damn well hoped he would *feel* it. "Need I remind you, sir, that *I* am doing a service for *you*."

"You're doing it because we're dead if you don't."

"That doesn't make it *not* a service. And, if you hadn't noticed"—she gestured to her own short, chubby, and impeccably dressed self—"I'm not particularly *built* for this."

"I had noticed, actually." He struggled to cast a glare over his shoulder at her. Which, considering their position, was difficult. "Why the fuck do you think I agreed to carry you? Your perfume isn't *that* nice."

Ozhma furrowed her brow. "It's not like I enjoy this, either. I left a lot—and I must stress a *lot*—of whiskey back with my wagon that I would hate to lose while I'm doing this favor for you."

"I told you I'm good to cover whatever you lose." The man snorted twin plumes of smoke out his nostrils. "Your war profiteering won't suffer."

Despite everything else about him, Ozhma had actually been rather close to liking him before he said that. But the words did not so much cut her as fashion themselves into a huge fucking axe and embed themselves in her back.

It wasn't the first time she'd been accused of that. How could it be? Once the Borrus Valley exploded, the rest of the Scar wasn't far behind. There wasn't a freehold, a town, a hamlet, or even a fucking hovel between here and the Valley that hadn't been wracked by the Imperium's and Revolution's latest cock-measuring contest.

Nor was there anything new about that. Being crushed between the two powers was something every Scarfolk expected.

Normally.

But that had been before. Before the Valley and the Ten Arrows. Before the Imperial retaliation. Before the Revolution started conscripting every civilian they could find and forcing them into battlefields their bones would decorate and before the Imperium started burying entire towns alive.

And normally, she could let his words slide.

Normally.

"NO!"

But not today.

Her hands curled into fists around his clothes. Her thighs squeezed around his middle. Her entire body shook so hard upon his back that he had to stop and find his footing again.

"Take it back," she said.

"Huh?"

"I am not a war profiteer. Take it back."

"Look, we don't have—"

"Take it back," she said, making to hop off of his back, "or I'll leave. You can do whatever you want about that, but neither you *nor* I will go one step farther unless you take. That. Back."

There were many, many important lessons one learned in the Scar and almost all of them revolved around not angering things that could kill you. Not angering a tall, muscular, drug-addled son of a bitch with a weapon was number six. But there were also many, many things a woman like Ozhma was ready to get angry over.

And one of those things was letting someone else tell her what she was.

"All right, fine. I take it back." He sighed, adjusted her on his back. "You're a fucking saint for doing this. I'll erect a damn statue of you and tell my grandchildren of your grace. Fuck me, sorry."

Ozhma beamed, her mouth falling open in delight. "I didn't know you were a grandpa!"

"I'm not. Can we go?"

"Oh, sure."

Immediately assuming someone's sincerity was not necessarily a hard lesson she'd learned, but it just made her life a little easier and also he *was* a tall, muscular, drug-addled son of a bitch with a weapon.

"And *not* that I'm trying to bring it up again," he said, "but there's a lot riding on us getting to the top of this mountain soon, so I've got to ask... is there anything that *would* make it go faster?"

She paused, thinking. "I always find trips seem shorter with a little pleasant chatter."

"Are you fucking serious?"

"Well, why not? You're asking me to help with a task whose exact nature you can't tell me but which has a lot riding on it. I can accept that, but it seems just plain rude for you to ask that of me and not even tell me your name."

Ozhma had only recently been promoted to representative-at-large in the company, but she'd found a truth that spanned across the many townships and cities she'd visited: be it Revolutionary, Imperial, Haven, or worse, people bought things the same way. The currencies changed—sometimes it was whiskey, sometimes it was trust, sometimes it was patience she asked for—but the sale was always the same.

And it started the same way in the man's bristly face. Reluctance melted away into a sigh of smoke and exhaustion and—dare she hope—just a *little* kindness.

"Rudu," he said.

"There," she began to say, "now—"

"Rudu the Cudgel."

Her lips puckered as those last two words sank into her.

The Cudgel.

The tattoos. The weird clothes. The bizarre weapon.

Holy shit, she told herself as her eyes widened and her brow glistened, *holy shit, he's a fucking Vagrant.*

"That make you nervous?" Rudu asked.

"*NO, WHY WOULD IT?*" Ozhma shouted nonchalantly.

"If I wanted to hurt you, I wouldn't be carrying you, would I?" He grunted, adjusted her on his back. "And if you didn't want to hurt *me*, you could sit up a little, for fuck's sake."

"Right, I... I trust you," she said and somehow believed it, a little. "It's just... you weren't kidding, were you?"

He took a deep drag of his pipe. "I wasn't."

"People are in danger?"

He held his breath. "They are."

She swallowed, afraid to ask. "Vagrant danger?"

Rudu exhaled a shimmering cloud, pointed skyward with his chin. "What do you know about what's on the other side of this cliff?"

She followed his gaze. The horizon of the Nails' towering cliffs and mesas was stained dark here and there, the sound of distant earth shifting a bare whisper from this far away.

"It's... New Vigil, right? The city?"

Rudu let out a bleak chuckle. "Yeah, it might have been that, at one point. Before people decided it was worth fighting over, anyway."

Ozhma wrinkled her nose. "Fighting over? Really?" She glanced around the desolate cliffs. "Isn't it out in the Nails? The place people very specifically avoid because it very plainly is *not* worth killing over?"

She herself had only traveled this close to the forsaken land because it cut a few hours off her journey. And because no one—a broad group including bandits, armies, and herself—thought it was worth fucking much. Ideal traveling, if you kept your eyes open.

"I didn't say it was worth killing over." He sucked on his pipe, let out a cloud of shimmering pink smoke. "I said it's worth fighting over."

Ozhma grimaced a little. "Uh, can you...maybe explain the difference?"

"Many years and wizard drugs ago, I could have."

Ozhma's chest tightened. She swallowed something bile-bitter. She tried to take a deep breath and tasted only the rancid reek of Rudu's pipe smoke.

And for the first time since she'd taken this job, Ozhma began to think that, perhaps, things were getting out of hand.

It was a chilling thought. She hadn't exactly lived a dangerous life—her parents had died horribly *after* she'd moved out, which by the standards of the Scar was considered lucky—but she'd never before felt that there was something she couldn't handle. She'd learned how to run the family business, how to fend off debtors, how to stretch a piece of metal to its utmost limit, all before she was fifteen.

Honestly, even when her wagon had been stopped by a scruffy-looking weirdo who reeked of drugs and looked like he'd just mugged a beggar for his clothes, she hadn't panicked. This was, after all, the same Ozhma who'd been waylaid by bandits three weeks ago and walked away having sold them some very fine whiskey *and* not had her head chopped off.

That was it, wasn't it? she asked herself. *That was the moment you thought you could handle anything, be it bandits or debtors or...or...* Her eyes drifted toward Rudu. *Or a fucking renegade mage high off his fucking ass on silkgrass asking you to handle a city—a whole fucking* city*—of people who are about to die and...and...*

She glanced down the long and winding path that led back to the road, back to her wagon she'd carefully hidden, and back to Miss Malice, the ornery bird who pulled it that she'd left grazing on seed. She could make it there, she thought, and maybe pretend this hadn't happened. She could force herself not to look back or think about it or ever acknowledge it. She could return to the office, tell them it was just another boring delivery, take a week of vacation to drink enough that the entire thing would one day be a vomit-soaked blur. All she had to do was run.

Well, not run, she told herself as her body began to sweat at the very idea of it. *You could... I don't know, tumble down? Roll? Jump?* She squinted. *Actually, no, all those would probably end in... like, dying. And there's no guarantee that—*

"You all right back there?" Rudu interrupted.

She didn't know how to answer that. Not anymore. She didn't know how to talk to a Vagrant. She'd never met one; she'd heard stories and they all ended the same way.

There were two outcomes to an encounter with a Vagrant: you either gave them what they wanted or you gave them what they wanted *and* they ripped your soul out, imprisoned it in a skull, and carried it around as a toy for all eternity.

That last one probably wasn't true. But maybe it was? She had no idea. She'd never even met a *legal* mage, let alone a Vagrant. She wasn't ready for this. She wasn't *capable* of this. She was a sales representative! In the *deep* Scar! She sold whiskey to hicks! She couldn't have this many people relying on *her*.

How many people were they even talking about? A hundred? A thousand? How many people were in New Vigil? How many hicks and drunks and shopkeeps and merchants and... and...

And people just like Mom and Dad.

A worm of a thought. It burrowed into her brain, that thought, made her think of the hard times. The times when sales were slow, when shipments were lost, when they had to come together and think of what keepsake to sell next.

The times when, somehow, no matter how bad things got, they still managed to feed her and give her nice clothes that she asked for, and that one week where they'd had Dad's terrible dumplings because she loved them so much...

She didn't know how many people were in New Vigil.

But there were probably a lot of them that knew hard times.

And, with a resigned sigh, Ozhma knew what her answer was.

Ozhma had seen exactly one weapon of war in her life.

Plenty of weapons—swords, hand cannons, the odd eviscerator-spoon here and there—but only one weapon made specifically for killing a lot of people in a short amount of time.

They'd called it the Journey of Four Thousand Indefatigable Strides. But that was really hard to remember, so most had just called it by the name she would hear often, spoken in the same hushed reverence one speaks of monsters.

Tank.

A great beast of metal armor and belching severium smoke, iron crab legs picking through the hills beyond her home, a horror of a cannon attached to the top of it. She remembered its great metal shudder when it came to a stop, the smoke-tinged hiss as it settled down and its iron hide split open to release soldiers into her city. They'd only come to restock, the gun had never even pointed in her direction, the whole affair had taken only an hour.

One hour with a tank had given her nightmares for years.

"Oh, my sweet heavenly fuck."

Dozens of them sprawled before her.

She had the fleeting idea that they looked like toys from so high up here, iron soldiers scattered across the plains far below. Yet the blackened scars where their still-steaming guns had fired and the pall of severium smoke that hung around them, mantles on a war god's shoulders, was thick. Some lay splintered into metal shards and smoldering wreck, the charred remains of their crews scattered like ashes.

It was a sight that made her breath catch in her throat. A horrifying sight. An awful sight.

And they were by far the least alarming thing.

She couldn't call the marching flatlands a battlefield. Rather, the sight reminded her of a butcher's shop: a mass of tangled iron machines and red meat and odors.

The scars of battle had worn away the land, the grasses chewed up beneath the treads of tanks and the churn of machine wheels, the trees sundered by gunfire. The sky fared no better, colored by smoke and the crackle of lingering lightning, decorated here and there with weapons and projectiles that hung lazily in the air and drifted idly by, punctuated by a blast of unearthly flame or the glow of violet eyes beneath.

She'd never met a mage before today. But she knew what magic looked like.

She just never thought it would be this horrible.

At the center of the disaster stood a great towering Marcher tank mounted upon treads, smoldering like a colossal torch. Across the stained and ruined land, the bodies lay: their uniforms and corpses indiscernible from flame, soldiers lay twitching beside smoldering machinery, purple flames burned impromptu pyres. Looming over it like a morbid specter, an airship—a horrific mass of wood, metal, and engine—hung over the battlefield, its engines filling the sky with the sound of locusts and its cannons poised at its railings.

Her mind went numb at the sight of it. The *smell* of shit and blood and metal and severium powder on the breeze. She didn't even notice that the bodies of the two armies weren't pointed toward each other.

Their aggressions were turned to the looming shadow at the edge of the plains, the great city of fire-scarred walls and ominous iron gates, whose battlements trailed smoke and were painted with dried blood.

"Is that..." Ozhma craned to get a better look. "Is that New Vigil?"

"Yes," Rudu grunted, glaring up at her. "You fucking mind?"

"Oh!" Ozhma looked down at him and smiled sheepishly. "Sorry."

She scooted back down to a comfortable position, draping her arms around his neck as he readjusted his grip on her legs and pulled her a little firmer onto his back. With a grunt of complaint, he continued carrying her up to the top of the cliff.

She didn't take offense at his ire, but it did surprise her. Grassheads, in her experience, tended to be fairly relaxed after two bowls and catatonic after four.

Rudu had just finished his eleventh.

And he was *still* stressed.

She couldn't blame him, she supposed. If she had previously seen the wreckage of the plains below, she'd probably need to smoke a lot, too.

Hell, it was probably only because she was downwind from him and his pipe that she wasn't completely losing her shit over the span of their trek.

"What happened?" she asked, breathless. "What the fuck happened?"

"What's it look like happened?" Rudu asked.

"Like hell took a shit on earth."

"Whoa. That's pretty good." Rudu puffed on his pipe. "I was going to say that the Imperium and the Revolution both want that city bad enough to attack it at once and divide it up later, but I like yours better."

"What do you mean? The Imperium and the Revolution have been trying to kill each other for longer than I've been alive. What could make them do that?" She blinked. "Hang on, the Imperium *and* the Revolution? Guns *and* wizards? Pointing in the same direction? How the hell is that city still standing?"

"They called a ceasefire last night," he replied. "The dumb bastards behind those walls won't give up. But the dumb bastards in front of those walls won't stop killing each other. So now a bunch of dumb bastards, including you and me, are going to try to sort this shit out." He exhaled a large cloud of smoke. "One day is all anyone is willing to wait. Come tomorrow, if negotiations don't work, they'll just level it and fight over the crater."

"Well, *that's* just ridiculous. You can't have a 'leveled' field and have a crater, since a crater is a depression."

"That is not helpful."

"Grammar is *always* helpful," Ozhma said, without pausing to ponder why she didn't have many friends. "But, anyway, that's good, right? Negotiations? Negotiations are good. Negotiations means people at least *want* this to end well."

"Maybe. But 'well' for you and 'well' for two nations with enough guns and magic to wipe their ass with civilization are two very different things."

"Okay, yes, true, but let's... try to stay positive," she said, wincing. "If people are willing to talk, then people are willing to listen. And if you can do both, then you can get done whatever needs to get done."

"Huh. That's pretty insightful."

"Thank you. My mom used to say it," Ozhma said, beaming. "So if they're willing to talk, then you just need an envoy who's willing to talk. Who are you sending?"

"You."

"Oh! Neat."

The next few seconds before Ozhma, blissed out on secondhand silkgrass, realized what he had just said would be some of the happiest of her life.

"Wait, what?"

"We're here."

It had either been the drugs or the sheer, desperate denial she was using to keep herself together, but without realizing it, they'd arrived at a camp. The road sharply leveled out onto a flat cliff that overlooked the plains, providing a view of the carnage. Military tents had been erected—self-serious blue of the Revolution a wary distance from the gaudy violet of the Imperial pavilion—and the air was alive with activity.

Messengers and clerks in Revolutionary uniforms rushed to and fro, delivering documents to a small fleet of overworked scribes who busily translated them into scrolls to be sent by messenger birds. Imperial mages sat in deliberate circles, their eyes aglow with their power as they stared into pools of water in which images of cityscapes and blood-soaked fields flashed. Multiple people with multiple medals of distinguishment argued, red-faced and furious.

But no one was killing each other.

Which, while ideal so long as she was in the thick of this, was nonetheless bizarre. She could fathom, with a little creative thinking, a cause that would convince the Imperium and Revolution to choose not to attack each other. But the idea of the two actually setting up camp together to talk damn near broke her brain.

Just like the fall from Rudu's back damn near broke her ass.

"*Hey!*" She clambered to her feet, rubbing her amazing rear end. Rudu seemed to neither notice nor care, waving for her to follow as he entered the camp.

She hurried to stay close to him. As menacing as she'd once found him, Rudu now seemed like a big, sweet, drug-addicted puppy in comparison to the people surrounding her. Revolutionary commanders wielding bizarre weapons snarled at Imperial mages, glowing eyes impassive beneath their cold metal masks. These were people used to killing, used to not being bothered by killing. And, one by one, each and every one of their cold, appraising eyes fell to her.

Silence followed her through the camp, the heated arguments and the concerned chatter dying as the camp's inhabitants watched her go. It unnerved her to be watched by people carrying steel. Always had. People like that had a way of looking at you—you caught it, if you paid close enough attention—like they were considering all the ways they could take you apart.

She abandoned any thoughts of running, then and there. She couldn't bear the idea of even turning around. She couldn't see their eyes; she couldn't know what they were thinking.

"You're late."

But in another second, she did anyway.

She came to a paralyzed halt beneath a stare hewn and sharpened to cold iron knives. A hard-faced woman, features sharp enough to carve the skin off a serpent, with a proud jaw framed by black hair cropped in military fashion. A match for her short-cut blue coat adorned by stylish medals affixed to the lapel. The dried grime of battle lay upon her like it would on a blade: fittingly.

The arcane command structure of the Revolution made Ozhma's head hurt to even think about, but she knew an officer when she saw one. They didn't give big, fuck-off swords like that to just anyone, after all.

"Can't be late if I didn't tell you when I'd be back," Rudu replied.

The woman narrowed her eyes. "You informed *my* aides that you were going out to"—she paused to cringe—" 'find some turd to flush down this particular shitter.' "

"And I found one," Rudu replied.

"*HEY!*" Ozhma snapped.

Ozhma swallowed hard as the woman leaned over her, her terrifying face made even more terrifying by the hard shadow painting it.

"And you are prepared to accept this duty?" she asked, her voice as severe as her stare. "To accept the burden of negotiation and the lives that shall endure or end by your decisions?"

Ozhma blinked. "Um..."

The woman glared at Rudu. "You did not tell her?"

"Didn't have time," Rudu replied as he lit another bowl. "Gave her the basics: city, killing, lot of people dying because of you, that sort of thing. If I told her any more, I didn't think she'd come."

"Imbecile," the woman hissed. "You *dare* bring a civilian into this without being *clear* to her of the dire nature of—"

"I want to help." Ozhma tried to sound how she thought boldness ought to sound like. "I... I heard enough. If there are a lot of people..." She stood as imposing as someone of her stature could muster. "Then I want to try."

The woman's gaze softened, if only just a little. But beneath the iron layer of anger was a steel layer of discipline. She stood rigidly for a moment and offered a deep, formal bow.

"You have the gratitude of the Glorious Revolution of the Fist and

Flame and of its Great General, madam," she said. "And you have the honor of addressing Cadre Commander Tretta Unbreakable, servant of the Great General and his will in these circumstances."

"Uh...hi?"

Tretta spun on her heel, began stalking toward the center of the camp and a wide pavilion set up there. She didn't even bother to gesture to follow; she merely kept talking and left Ozhma scrambling to catch up to her.

"I will be as brief as I am able," Tretta said. "The city of New Vigil is presently under the occupation and control of forces hostile to the Revolution. Revolutionary citizens are held within."

"Among others," Rudu added from behind.

"Others?" Ozhma asked.

"We have knowledge of Imperial, Scarfolk, and various freehold citizens behind the walls, as well," Tretta replied, "but the bulk of the population is made up of Revolutionaries."

"Lapsed Revolutionaries. Deserters." Rudu offered a bored shrug to Tretta's bare-toothed snarl. "You said she needed to be informed."

"There is no such thing as a *lapsed* Revolutionary, merely Revolutionaries waiting to be returned to the embrace of the Great General." She sucked her anger in back behind clenched teeth. "Regardless of affiliation, the citizenry present is unarmed and vulnerable. Our attempts to decisively take the city ended...un-ideally."

Ozhma glanced back over the cliff to the horror on the field below. "I'm sorry to hear that."

"In the interests of reducing further casualties, we called for a ceasefire and the enemy agreed," Tretta said. "We are not so naïve as to believe that treating directly with the enemy would result in anything other than carnage, hence mutual terms have been decided upon that envoys shall act in our stead, such as yourself."

Ozhma's head bobbed along, heavier with every word that sank into it. "Right. Okay. So I'm...an envoy. Okay. An envoy is a representative. I'm a sales representative. That's basically the same thing. Basically the same *thing*. *Basically* the same thing." She smacked her lips, wondering which word she would have to emphasize to believe it. Instead, she settled for looking to Rudu. "Right?"

"Oh. Yeah, no, just think of it like a sale except instead of making money, you're trying to keep a small city full of people from becoming a pile of ash." He tapped his bowl out on the heel of his sandal. "But yeah, basically."

"Right. Good. We agree. Good. Great. Good, good, good."

"It would be difficult to overstate the danger you're walking into," Tretta said as she came to a halt outside a lavish Imperial pavilion. "Only in the direst circumstances against the vilest of foes would we override the Revolutionary Mandate." A grotesque centipede of an expression crawled across her face. "I truly never thought there would be such a day. Or a foe."

She pulled back the pavilion's curtains, exposing a decadent interior of exquisite furniture and hardwood flooring. The military accoutrements—the maps pinned to tables, the scattered documents and open manuals, the minuscule troops on the table—only served to heighten the room's wonder. It was as though someone had simply magically transported an entirely furnished war room into the middle of nowhere and—

Oh, right, Ozhma thought suddenly. *Mages.*

If anything *could* diminish the room's splendor, that distinction belonged to the pavilion's sole occupant.

A woman, short and spear-slim, stood at its center. Her Imperial military coat and the longsword at her hip suggested she belonged there, but only just. Her hair, Imperial ivory, hung in greasy tatters, her figure stood slouched and defeated, her uniform looked as though she hadn't taken it off in days. Bruises and scratches that had yet to be healed—or cleaned—dotted every inch of skin.

"The Three's representative has been selected." Tretta gestured to Ozhma, who stood trying to squint into the war room. "You represent Imperial interests here. Do you have any questions before she departs?"

The white-haired woman turned around and Ozhma cringed.

Exhaustion colored every inch of the woman's face a ghastly pale. Her chapped mouth and tear-stained eyes both hung slack, resignation exploded across her expression, as though exhaustion, horror, sorrow, and anger had battled it out and her face had simply collapsed under the weight of them all.

Whatever war this woman had fought, she'd clearly lost.

"This woman?" she asked, weary voice a match for her face. "You want to send a civilian in there?" She managed a glimmer of incredulity for Tretta and Rudu. "To *her*?"

"Hey, your envoy had a dick-nose but I didn't say shit, did I?" Rudu snapped back.

Some fragment of emotion, some edge gone dull, scraped across her face, desperate to come loose. But it, too, fell beneath the weary weight on her face and disappeared.

"Send whoever, do whatever," she said, turning her back to them, "I don't care anymore."

Ozhma didn't realize she had been holding her breath until the curtain fell. The chill that slid over her was hard to shake off as Tretta turned and began to lead the way once again.

"She seems..." Ozhma struggled to find the word. "...Nice?"

"Our Imperial counterparts in this plan are less optimistic than we are," Tretta said, her voice hardening. "Their leader has yet to arrive. Their commanding officer will not even deign to speak with us directly. Her shortsightedness remains her weakness. The enemy feeds on our anger, takes everything from us with it."

"You're exaggerating," Rudu sighed.

Tretta came to a sharp, sudden halt. She whirled on Rudu with such ferocity that Ozhma almost cried out, terrified of the swords she was certain were about to come out. Tretta stood an inch from his face and spoke between clenched teeth.

"She is a killer," Tretta said, "a danger to every being that has ever breathed the air of this land. I will *not* permit her to do to this city what she's done to the rest of the Scar, no matter who I have to cut through or into how many pieces. Whether you choose to be behind my blade or in front of it when that happens, I leave to you. Am I clear?"

Rudu took in the threat in one long, unblinking stare of stunned silence. Or what *appeared* to be stunned silence, anyway, until he exhaled a cloud of shimmering silkgrass smoke into her face.

"Relax," he said, "I'm here for my employers' interests. Not hers."

Tretta curtly waved the smoke from her face. "Good."

At the very edge of the camp, where the tents gave way to scrub grass, a man lingered. Newt-like and clad in Imperial silks, he leaned upon a cliff face, beside an immaculately drawn square of chalk, not sparing the approaching trio so much as a glance up from the fingernails he was focused on cleaning.

"The final envoy has been selected," Tretta barked. "Open the portal." Upon the man's distinct lack of motivation to move, she hissed. "Did you *hear* me?"

"I did," the man replied in a refined Imperial accent. "But I didn't hear 'please.' Nuls have the manners of animals."

He turned away, eager to end this conversation. Violet light flashed behind his eyes; he rapped his knuckles upon the chalk square.

A light blossomed across the rock face, bursting to violet life. Veils of twisting light coiled, spun, and danced around each other in a miasma of light and movement. Ozhma was forced to turn her face away, shield it with her hands, yet she could still *feel* the twisting light. Like it was looking at her.

"Magic," Tretta said, sneering. "Detestable, yet necessary. Time is of the essence and the enemy cares nothing for the lives beneath their heel. It falls to us to care more for their people than they do. Our top priority is getting as many people out of there alive as we can before daybreak tomorrow. After which, we will be forced to act. Do not permit the enemy to claim ignorance of that fact. Or the fact that our action shall be swift, overwhelming, and final."

Tretta affixed her with a spearhead of a glare, one that punched straight through her ribs. Her mouth ran dry. All the tanks, all the mages, every bloodied edge of every bloodied blade on that battlefield... and *she* was responsible for holding them all back? How? How could she? How could *anyone*?

"Man, she's *my* fucking envoy," Rudu grunted, smoke wisps leaking through his teeth. "If you want to terrorize someone, go yell at your own people and at least get saluted for it."

Tretta's eyes sharpened to points upon him so cruel that Ozhma almost felt herself bleeding. But for as much as those eyes made her cringe, she didn't truly panic until Tretta's *very* big sword came out of its sheath.

"Do *not* suffer from the delusion that I will permit you *or* your vile, withered employers to interfere in this. If the Three *dare* to interfere, I will—"

"You make a lot of threats, lady," Rudu interjected without looking up from his pipe. "Enough of them were funny that I let them go, at first, but now all this talk about shoving things into other things, well." He took a deep drag. "It's starting to seem a little unprofessional. I can't say as I think my vile, withered employers would want to work with anyone unprofessional." He looked up, pointedly exhaled in Tretta's face. "What do you think? Should we ask?"

Tretta's body shook with barely restrained rage. Her grasp on her blade tightened, the silk of her coat stretching against the muscles desperate to unleash the steel. And her eyes—those hard, savage eyes that it hurt to be under—burned forge-hot.

And she did sheathe her sword, turn on her heel, and storm away.

"What the fuck?" Ozhma whispered urgently, seizing Rudu's sleeve like a giant child clinging at her drug-addled parent's arm. "What the *fuck*? Did she say the Three? Like the Ashmouths the Three? Like the *criminal fucking killers* the Three?"

"I'm going to level with you, lady," Rudu replied, "I'm not a very nice guy. No one here is. And *definitely* not the fucking maniac squatting in New Vigil."

He looked down at her. And in his eyes, she saw an ugly honesty, the kind that comes before you learn how badly you've fucked up.

"I didn't tell you everything. But I didn't lie to you, either," he said. "You can help a lot of people, but..." He frowned. "Her, me, everyone here—we're not the kind of people who have things work out very often. I don't want you to turn back. But if you want to..."

"I don't," Ozhma replied before she even realized it. And by the time her brain had caught up to her heart, her head was already nodding. "I'm... I can help. I can do this."

He nodded. But he didn't smile. Maybe, even though he'd asked her here, he'd wished she'd taken the chance to run.

She would never know. Not for sure.

"All right." Rudu looked back toward the door of light. "Ever used a portal before?"

"No. Never. Not once. I'm... I'm a little terrified, if I'm honest."

"Understandable. Ever walked through a door before?"

Ozhma found enough relief to smile. "I have. Are they basically the same thing?"

Rudu put a hand on her shoulder.

"Nope."

And pushed.

"*Holy shit.* Took them fucking long enough to send someone, didn't it?"

Ozhma could hear the voice. But she couldn't see who was speaking. Or at all.

"Oh my goodness! Look, she's not moving! Was she hurt? Tortured? Did those maniacs... *impugn* her?"

The moment she had stepped through, the portal was absent from her, as was anything that had happened after it, along with basically all of her memories, sensations, feelings, and possibly—she couldn't be sure—the entirety of her digestive tract. Other than that, though, it seemed like it had worked.

"Nah, this is just her first time through a portal."

"You can tell that?"

"Yeah. Look at her twitch. Like a fucking newborn piglet pushed all glistening and raw out of a sow's ass. Miracle of life. Thing of beauty."

Her mind slowly pieced itself back together, word by word. Ozhma. Rudu. Tretta. Negotiation. *Enemy.*

And bit by bit, everything else began to come back: the flow of blood through her body, the feeling of the hot ground beneath her...

"Until I am *absolutely* certain whether your description or your abhorrent understanding of anatomy offends me more, could you possibly stop with the grotesquery? Our guest requires aid."

"Well, just hold on for a second. She might be dead and we don't have to do anything. Sometimes happens. Check to see if she shit herself."

"You *cannot,* in any conscience let alone good, ask me to do that."

Ozhma's vision, finally, caught up to the rest of her. She found herself flat on her back and staring up at two faces.

A woman and a man. Twins, by the look of it. Both of them had the same long features and the same scrutinizing, shrewd eyes, both of them wore their black hair in braids. But the man's face was nervous and timid beneath his hood. And the woman's... well, it certainly wasn't fucking timid. Her brows were knitted in a permanent scowl and her chin was adorned with tattoos depicting the twisting bars of a portcullis.

The decoration lent her smile an unsettling quality matched only by the coarse cut of her voice as she grinned over Ozhma.

"Congratulations!" she said. "You didn't shit yourself! It's a fucking miracle."

"*Rude,*" the man chastised before reaching down to help Ozhma up. "Apologies for Yria. For all her talents, she can be a little..." He hesitated as he stared at her arm, removed a cloth from his belt, wiped her sleeve clean, and *then* assisted her. "Tactless."

"Oh, listen to Diplomat Dickwipe here," Yria grunted as she took Ozhma's other arm with less delicacy and more effort. "Talking about tact like we aren't in the middle of a fucking war zone."

Together, they gently raised Ozhma to her feet. Or tried, anyway. The woman's arm was weak, her body stiff as she lifted.

Ozhma stood, swaying, on earth flattened and baked by searing heat. The smell of metal and powder filled her nostrils. Behind her, a second sun burned, the immense pyre of the Revolutionary tank continuing to wail to the sky through a mouth of flame and smoke. The corpses were arranged around it, petitioners bowed in worship before a macabre god.

The field. She was in the field. In the blood, in the guns, in the bodies.

Ozhma inhaled a breath of ash and stale blood. Her head wobbled on her neck, unwieldy and heavy with sights she hadn't been ready for. She kicked up plains dust as she swayed on unsteady feet.

"Easy there!" Yria cautioned. "Don't fucking go tits over on me, woman. I don't think I could manage lifting your ass twice in one day."

Ozhma twitched. And for one hot second, she was able to put the horrors she had just seen out of her mind long enough to remember the lesson she'd learned so many years ago in Mom and Dad's shop.

Never regret a sale. Never take anything for free. And never, *never* let them talk shit.

"Yria, was it?" she asked.

"Yria the Cell." The woman made a crude mockery of a bow. "At your service."

"Ozhma. Charmed. Vagrant?"

Yria grinned a big, tattooed grin and elbowed her brother. "See? She noticed."

"I can't imagine I'm lucky enough that your magic power is the ability to choke on your *own* ass." Ozhma paused in the midst of dusting off her skirt to cast an appraising look at Yria's narrow hips. "Nor could I guess where you'd find any in that mockery of a backside. But if you could muster the strength to kindly shut all the way the fuck up of your own volition, I'd be grateful."

The twins' faces, in stunned unison, fell. Their mouths hung open, their eyes went wide with shock. Then they looked to each other.

"Oh, I like her," the man said.

"Fuck off, I liked her first," Yria snapped.

"Let's hope she doesn't end up killing us all after that. *That* would be awkward." The man waved a hand and moved to drape his sister's arm over his shoulder, gesturing Ozhma to follow. "If you wouldn't mind? We've only got a day, after all. My name's Urda, by the way... *not* that you asked, despite my giving you multiple obvious openings and, oh, never mind, you're not even listening."

Had she been, she probably would have felt a little embarrassed. As it was, though, she could only manage enough sense to follow numbly along as the twins led her across the plains.

From afar, the carnage on the field had seemed awful, but comfortingly abstract—a frightening portrait, something that would give her a few nightmares and then blissfully fade from her mind.

But this close, here among the reek of shit and blood and the broken metal, it was something real and something impossible. She couldn't bring herself to see the details: the blood staining the ground, the shattered barricades and broken machines, and the bodies that lay with their backs turned in retreat and painted by gun and arrow wounds.

To see them, their faces screwed up in fear that had twitched out of their corpses, would be too much. But her eyes wouldn't let her look away. It all became a singular blur, a monster of twisted metal limbs and a crown of corpses and eyes full of blood, one that she knew would never fade from her mind, blissfully or otherwise.

And still, impossibly, that creature was easier to look at than the survivors.

Them, she couldn't help but see the details: the glassy emptiness of their eyes, the wounds that painted their patchwork uniforms and the cuts that they'd stopped binding when they'd run out of supplies, the weary shake of their bodies as they dragged the corpses and helped the wounded heading toward the distant walls. The closer they got, the more there were, until Ozhma found herself just one drop in a tide of suffering flowing slowly toward the walls of New Vigil.

"This is... horrible," Ozhma whispered, breathless.

"Is it?" Yria muttered. "I didn't fucking notice."

Ozhma felt her cheeks flush. The obviousness of the statement hadn't even occurred to her. She had just had to say it. The truth of it was too heavy to hold in her head.

"Sorry, but...," Ozhma said. "They didn't tell me much about what happened here before they...you know. I'm still not *totally* sure what's going on?"

"Well, if you did, that'd make you a popular fucking girl, wouldn't it?" Yria spat. "You probably know more than any of these sad fucks here."

"I know that the Imperium and Revolution both want this place bad enough to..." She winced as a man dragged one end of a stretcher with two bodies on it, the other end dragging through the dirt. "To do this."

"The situation is slightly more complex than that," Urda said, pointedly searching for any space to stare at that wasn't covered in blood. "Theoretically, anyway. It's not *precisely* clear what the Imperium and the Revolution want with New Vigil, but they're willing to kill for it."

"You know fucking well as I do that the killing *is* what they want," Yria spat. "They aren't going to stop until we're choking on our own ashes."

"*Please* stop saying things like that. You're making me *very* nervous. They wouldn't have sent envoys if they just intended to kill everyone."

"They would if they know this place is worth dying for."

"Is it?"

Ozhma hadn't become aware of the question that had tumbled out of her mouth until the twins looked over their shoulders at her. Yria managed a long sneer.

"This shitburg?" Yria asked. "What do you think?"

Yria turned away, but the movement was awkward. So was her entire gait, Ozhma noticed. The weight of her body was off, like she wasn't used to walking with all of her limbs. Her eyes drifted toward the woman's arm, to the blackened spider's web of veins against the pale skin. It hung at her side, completely paralyzed.

"Some would say it is, at least," Urda offered. "You see, due to the intricate nature of our, shall we say, *attendants*, we—"

"Cram your fucking craw, you talky twat," Yria snarled. "We aren't fucking supposed to talk to them."

"If *that's* the case, I must once again renew my objection to your *abhorrent* treatment of her."

"Well, if they wanted someone treated all yes-madam-may-I-lick-your-ass, why the fuck did they send *me* to make the fucking portal?"

"See? *See?* You *know* the way you talk to people, including me, is terrible, but you refuse to stop! Given the delicate nature of this circumstance, you need to—"

"What circumstance? The fucking armies about to blow our cunts out of our skulls? *That* fucking circumstance?"

Ozhma kept track of the twins' bickering only as long as it took to be stunned by it. How anyone could act so... so *normal* in this, it hurt her head to wonder. And yet, looking at the soldiers felt worse.

The closer they got to the city walls, the more intact the defenses became. Craters from cannon fire stood alongside newly deployed barricades and dug-in ballista nests. Soldiers in patchwork armor and various stains of blood manned stations with autobows, blades, spears, anything they could get their hands on. Ozhma cringed to see some soldiers wielding kitchen knives as weapons. And once she saw how small and young the hands that held them were...

She looked away. But that didn't help.

Behind her, across the sprawling plains, the armies of the Imperium and the Revolution stood.

They'd looked terrible enough from the cliff, the toys of a particularly cruel child. But here, on the ground, with the violet glow of mages' eyes peering out between veils of dust and the tanks looming out of a sea of half-buried bodies...

All the bodies...

There was nowhere to look. Nowhere her eyes could rest that wasn't stained with blood or decorated with corpses. Even the living carried the same haunted, glassy stares as the carcasses of their comrades, only the mechanical rhythm of their weary movements distinguishing them from so much flesh rotting out on a rotten field on a rotten earth.

She wanted to throw up. She wanted to scream. She wanted to collapse.

But she couldn't even bring herself to close her eyes. She forced herself to take it in, to swallow the bile and hold back the tears. Whether she'd been asked, ordered, or threatened, she was here to try to help these people. To try to get them out of here okay. They needed it. They needed *her*.

She had no idea if she could do it.

Only that she had to do it.

The world inside the fire-scarred walls of the city was little different than the world outside. There were fewer bodies and bloodstains littering the dirt roads, but to call it welcoming would be a lie. Hell, she didn't even feel right calling it a city.

The bombed-out ruins of homes stood charred alongside the skeletonized, half-dead houses that had escaped the fire but not the soldiers. All along the unpaved streets, she saw houses destroyed or scavenged to make defenses. A few landmarks stood out—an opera house in the distance, a few larger buildings that served as storehouses and barracks—but everything else looked like the city hadn't even gotten started before people had begun blowing the shit out of it.

Wagons pulled by heavy draft birds plodded up and down the street, transporting the wounded and cowering deeper into the city before returning with a burden of siege weaponry or armaments. Soldiers—old and young, hale and weathered—lined up to receive weapons, tools, secondhand medical supplies. Some seized their steel and raced off to reinforce the front, some accepted it and trudged off with weary resignation, and some simply had it thrust into their numb hands to let the tips of their blades fall and drag in the dust, staring glassy-eyed out at some blood-and-char horizon that they hadn't stopped seeing just yet.

There was no such thing as priceless, Mom and Dad had told Ozhma once. Everyone got what they wanted, so long as they were willing to pay for it. The obsessive mutterings of a pair of charming old tightfists, that advice had seemed, but it had seen her through a life in the Scar. Death and suffering, the two staples of the Scarfolk, were easier to handle if you could believe that they were the natural consequence for seeking out riches, living on one's own terms, whatever led them to that morbid end.

It was a timid truth. The kind that falls apart if you look too long at it.

And Ozhma hadn't blinked since she set foot past the walls.

Where was the choice in this? Where was the meaning in this suffering? What had these people done to deserve this? What could *anyone* do to deserve these hollow-eyed stares and muted, broken voices?

And what, she wondered, could she do to stop it?

"Hold on a second, assholes, we're here."

The twins came to a halt. Yria jerked her thumb over her shoulder.

"You want to hurry the fuck up and get inside or you want to take another look at my ass?"

Ozhma glanced up at the building looming over them. A dingy, one-story affair with a thick door, boarded-up windows, and a dirty sign swaying overhead that portrayed what Ozhma couldn't be sure but on closer inspection mostly certain was a pair of rothacs engaged in furious intercourse.

"A tavern?" Ozhma squinted at the sign. "This really isn't the time. And it looks like it's out of business."

"Well, now, do you see anywhere *else* that we could use as a headquarters, Lord and Lady Fuckmouth?"

Ozhma looked up and down the dirt streets. Everywhere else was either skeletonized, bombed-out, or currently on fire, it was true.

So she merely sighed, followed the twins to the thick door, and prepared herself for whatever scene of misery awaited on the other side.

"DO I FUCKING LOOK LIKE I KNOW WHAT A BATTLE SQUARE IS?"

She was not, however, prepared for the sheer wall of sound that bowled her over.

"Fires are still going in the Dirtmouth neighborhood! Where the fuck is our water?"

"Am I seeing this? They brought a fucking airship *to a fight?"*

"Beat the shit out of anyone who runs. I don't care how old or young. If we lose one more to desertion, we're as good as dead."

There were certainly more voices than those—many more—but those were the only words she could make out. The rest was lost to the rush of noise pumping through the arteries of the cramped tavern.

What tables hadn't been used to barricade the windows were laden with briefings, maps, leathery covers of old war manuals stained by overturned inkwells. A steady stream of messenger birds alighted on the windowsills to deliver tiny scrolls before being sent back off. The tinny, machine screech of mechanical apparatus that belched out paper scrolls with illegible markings on them punched through the noise.

Against the chaos of their own making, the people seemed almost insignificant.

They ran from table to table, carried sheaves of papers and news through the choked walkways of the tavern, frantically scribbled down messages to be fastened to overworked birds before hurrying them back out, screamed at each other and argued over what the sigils on the paper coming out of the machines meant.

Ozhma guessed, by the cleanliness of their green coats and the relative lack of blood on their clothes, that she had found the leadership.

Men and women in varying degrees of emotional breakdowns milled about, numb from exhaustion and fear. The air reeked of desperate panic. A sufficiently loud noise could have killed a good half of these people, they looked so run-down.

This was the enemy? These terrified men and weary women? These people in ill-fitting coats running around like headless birds? They didn't look capable of keeping a stone inside this city, let alone a population.

"Sorry, can I help you?"

A man had stopped in the middle of the rush. Dark skinned, his hair natural and thick, he stood in a green military coat far too big for him and carried a sheath with no sword at his hip. His smile was strained, but his was the only face she'd seen thus far that wasn't either miserable or dying.

"Oh. Um, yes, we're here to..." She glanced behind; in all the chaos she hadn't even seen the twins slip out. "I mean, *I'm* here to..." She paused, thinking—*to do what? To fail? To suck and die? To... no. Pull yourself together. You can do this.* "I'm an envoy?"

"Oh! You're the last! The others are already downstairs. If we hurry, you can..." He caught himself, smiled and extended a hand to her. "Sorry, things are a little..." His lips pursed, unable to find a word he was comfortable with. "At any rate, I'm Meret." He caught himself again. "Sorry, *Tactical Officer* Meret." And again. "Damn it, wait, no, I'm Field Officer Meret." And again. "No, sorry, I was right the first time. Meret. Tactical Officer Meret. Sorry, I'm not... it's really... I don't..."

Ozhma seized his hand in both of hers. She gave his arm a tug—not a lot, just enough to make him turn his weary eyes to her. She gave him the warmest smile she could think of and gently patted the top of his hand.

"Ozhma," she said. "Ozhma Tenstead. It is my utter pleasure to meet you, Meret."

He blinked, as if she had just punched him in the mouth. Then, like ice off the thaw, the strain seeped out of his smile and left behind something more relaxed, if only a little.

Every part of that gesture—the use of both her hands, the tug, the choice not to call him by the title he wore so poorly—was deliberate, a practice honed over years in her parents' store. The tweaks had taken time to figure out, but it had all come from the same lesson.

Nothing was going to get done unless everyone felt good about doing it.

"You, too, Ozhma," he said. "And... thank you. For coming here. I... had some reservations about the envoys the Revolution and Imperium sent." He blinked. "Oh! Yes, we should probably get you to them, before..." He chuckled nervously. "Before everyone dies."

She winced. Normally, they were relaxed for more than three seconds. Then again, she told herself, they *were* all about to be incinerated, so...

"I don't want to ruin your day," Meret said as he guided her through the human frenzy, past the tavern's bar and toward a door in the back, "but negotiations haven't been going *that* well." He paused, thought. "Well, that's not fair of me. No one's been shot yet, so they could be going worse." He stopped, hand on the door, and looked back at her. "Do you want a drink, by the way? Sorry, I should have asked earlier."

She blinked. "A drink?"

He gestured to the tavern's bar. It was, like every other surface, laden with papers and documents and maps. But, unlike every other surface, there were more than a few half-drained bottles and upturned glasses. One would have thought that people facing down the two strongest armies of the Scar would ask people to be more sober... then again, Ozhma reasoned, facing down the two strongest armies of the Scar would also be a pretty good reason to drink.

"I think I'm fine," she said, all the same.

"Right. Good. Okay. Understandable." He moved to open the door, but clenched his teeth, like he couldn't bring himself to open it. "Actually, you should really take a drink with you."

He made a gesture. A man rushed over with a sloshing tankard of brown liquor and thrust it into Ozhma's hands.

"Oh," she said. "Um... thanks?"

"Sure, sure." Meret opened the door, leading down to a cellar. "Just keep moving forward. You'll find the general in the back, with the other envoys."

"You're not coming?"

"Sorry, I kind of... have to make sure we don't *all* die, you know?"

That *was* a good reason to stay behind, she had to admit, but as she stepped out onto the stairs and followed the dim lamplight into a dark room smelling of earth and old bricks, she was still more nervous without Meret by her side.

His had been the only face that wasn't haunted by the violence. Hell, she already missed that nervous, soft-spoken voice of his. Without him, in the dark, the other faces—the glassy eyes, the slack jaw, the numb horror—seeped back into her memory, nothing to keep them out but the tankard in her hands.

It turned out Meret had been right to give her a drink.

She brought it up to her nose and sniffed it. The pungent scent of whiskey filled her nose, made her want to vomit, always had since she was a kid. Outstanding, she thought, they'd sent her into this mess and she couldn't even be a *little* drunk for it.

"Are we all going to fucking have to die for this?"

Which was unfortunate because, though she didn't know it then, it would have been very useful to be shit-faced that day.

"It's not about you! It's not about your problems!"

She followed the sound of voices.

"Don't you fucking throw that in my face!"

Or rather, voice. Specifically, a male one. Specifically, an *angry* male one.

"I'm telling you that there is no way out that doesn't end like this. You can't be the one to make this decision alone. You CAN'T."

She couldn't make out who he was talking to and the reasoning became clear as soon as she reached the end of the cellar. Another door, thick wood and mounted on the brick with heavy iron hinges, stood there, stoically trying to hold back the angry shouting within.

"No. Fuck you. FUCK you."

Ozhma heard the muffled voice of someone replying. She squinted at the door, tiptoeing closer and pressing her ear against it, trying to make out that other voice.

"I'm sorry."

Was that... a woman?

"The last envoy they caught eavesdropping, they broke both her arms."

Ozhma started, nearly dropping her tankard of whiskey. She composed herself in time to remember the two other envoys. One of them, tall and reed-thin and wearing Imperial purple, stood leaning against the cellar wall, a contemptuous look on his face. His Revolutionary counterpart, a young lady with a short-cropped hairstyle and a long diplomat's coat, offered her a nod.

"Oh. Sorry." Ozhma scooted away from the door, clutching the tankard against her chest as she extended a free arm to the Imperial. "Ozhma. I'm the third envoy."

"Galatatian ki Zanzora, Imperial emissary granted the honor by Her Highness, Empress Athura the Fourteenth." He glanced at her hand, didn't take it. "Charmed."

"Oh, um." Ozhma glanced to the Revolutionary woman. "And... you are?"

"Cadre Agent Insightful," she replied tersely.

"How long have you been waiting here?"

Insightful didn't answer. Nor did she even bother looking down at Ozhma. Her pose was rigidly at attention, her eyes locked straight ahead.

"Don't bother, madam," Galatatian said. "Until she sees the enemy, she refuses to speak. Possibly for the best. Negotiations take a certain amount of authoritative verve. Ill-suited is this art to the brainwashed masses." He smiled down his nose—which, Rudu was right, did look a lot like a dick—at Ozhma. "Or the unwashed, if you'll pardon."

Ozhma wouldn't, in better circumstances. But then the door slammed open.

Looming out of the frame was an imposing man. Or, Ozhma corrected herself, a man trying to appear imposing.

His frame was broad and corded with lean get-shit-done soldier's muscle that even his weathered green coat, trimmed with harsh-looking fur, couldn't hide—and in fact, only accentuated. His long black hair was done up in an afterthought of a tail, framing a hard face that had scars, beard, and mustache in all the right places to be a man you shouldn't fuck with.

And yet…

His hard face couldn't hide the wrinkles where he smiled too much and laughed too easy. His long body couldn't hide the parts where he'd gone a little softer, a little broader, a little warmer. And his eyes, ravaged by fear and fury as they were, couldn't dim the kindness.

There were very few people Ozhma liked right off the bat.

But this man was one of them.

"*You're* the envoys? Fucking *great.*"

A little.

"Apologies." The man attempted to rub sleeplessness from his eyes, failed. "That was uncalled for. Thank you for coming out here. We appreciate the effort to end this without additional violence."

"Without violence *or* dignity, apparently," Galatatian interjected snidely. "No wine, no food, no accommodations; has your little art project of a city *ever* received properly the emissary of a true power?"

The man stared at Galatatian's nose. "You ever blow your nose and find spunk in your handkerchief?" He ignored the furious stare the envoy sent him, pointedly glanced over Agent Insightful, and looked down at Ozhma. "And you're the envoy of the Three?"

Am I?

"Er…yes?" Ozhma forced the nervousness out—confidence, she chided herself, confidence, knowledge, and patience were how you made any sale, be it for money or lives—and forced a smile on her face. She held out her hand awkwardly. "Ozhma. Sir."

"Cavric," he replied, taking her hand. And her smile became a little less forced. "Cavric. Leader of New Vigil."

"Oh! You're the general?" She smiled at her good luck—she'd been baffled as to how to even *begin* negotiating, but here she was, already warming up to its leader. She pulled herself up, stood tall and straight as she could. "I'm here to ensure the safety of the people here, sir. I can only hope that we are both open to doing what's necessary."

Cavric's face fell. Something cold and bitter as the ice on dead crops crept across his scowl.

"I hope so, too, Ozhma." He pulled his hood up over his head, stalked away. "But it's not me you're negotiating with."

"What?" she shouted at his back as he stormed up the stairs of the cellar. "Then *who*?"

"Me."

A voice from behind the door.

The *other* voice.

It came crawling out of the darkened room like a spider: low, dark.

"You can come in here or I can go out there, but if I have to fucking get off this chair, I'm breaking it over someone."

Galatatian narrowed his eyes in an unconvincing attempt to steel himself. Agent Insightful tensed up, like she was walking to a fistfight and not a negotiation. Both of them pushed forward past the door, leaving Ozhma to scurry behind them like a child.

The dank earth of the cellar opened up into something…the opposite of that.

A room. An expertly polished, exquisitely furnished, and extremely impossible room opened up into the earth. Hardwood floors, walls, and ceiling made a perfect square, adorned with rugs, chairs, beds, and shelves brimming with books and beautiful things—even the pavilion she'd seen back at the camp was pathetic compared to this room.

This amazing room…buried underground…in a city that was plainly starved for resources.

Ozhma squinted, trying to work it out in her brain. How could a city so strapped it could barely defend itself have a secret room this luxurious? What was it? Some form of decadent bunker so that the city's rulers could wait out in comfort while their people died? Had she been wrong about Cavric? About Meret? Was this *truly* the enemy?

She looked to her fellow envoys to see if they also struggled with the luxurious sight. But their eyes were fixed in dread on the center of the room. On the grand velvet chair in the middle.

And the bloody figure draped across it.

Illuminated by the faint light of a lantern overhead, the shadows swirled too deeply around the figure for Ozhma to see more than a few shattered fragments of a human: white hair drenched in sweat, corded muscle under skin painted with scars, a long hand at the end of a long arm colored with ink, raised in request.

"One moment, if you don't mind," the figure said, their voice raw with exhaustion. "I told you if I got up off this chair, I'd break it over you and I don't intend to be called a liar. And since I've killed a lot of people today and I'm just a little hungover, before I get off this chair and we get started, indulge me as I make this perfectly clear.

"I don't want any prestigious introductions, any verbose threats, any wordy demands like 'methinks you must consider the recompense' or shit like that. I know who you are and I know who you work for. I know what your bosses want." The voice grew colder. "And I know what they're willing to do to get it.

"So if I get up and hear any fancy wordplay intended to sound ominous, threatening, or anything I deem unacceptably dramatic, I'm going to break the mouth it came out of. That's rule one. Rule two is that you don't say shit until you've heard what I've got to say. You so much as sneeze while I'm talking, I'll break... break..." A frustrated sigh. "It's been kind of a long day, can you just pretend I said something threatening there? Thanks."

Ozhma's grandparents had once said she was too nice to go into sales. Ozhma's great-grandparents had once said she was too nice to be alive. And, without quite realizing it, she proved all four of them right as two words politely came tumbling out.

"Anything else?"

Ozhma clapped a hand over her mouth with a gasp. The two other envoys went rigid, their expressions horrified. From the armrest it was draped across, the figure's head looked up.

And a pair of eyes, blue and cold as a river at the end of winter, looked over her.

She swallowed hard as the figure rose off the chair. Her heart hammered in her chest with every weary fall of bootsteps. Her breath ran so short she almost fainted before the figure stepped out of the shadows.

And became something much, much worse.

A woman. Tall, corded with muscle left generously bare by what could be generously called an outfit of leathers and cloth, a sword hanging heavy with use at her hip. Her long arms were painted with tattoos, writhing cloudscapes of thunder and wings illustrating a chaotic portrait across her flesh. Dried blood adorned her skin, along with a number of cuts, bruises, and outright wounds. Rudely cut hair, Imperial white in color, hung around a face decorated with scars, a long one running the length of her right eye.

Ozhma's heart fell.

She hadn't seen the scars, the tattoos, the face ever before in her life. But she knew them.

Ozhma had lived a lucky life: good parents, comfortable upbringing. But one thing she had never appreciated until that moment was how much of the world's horrors were stories to her. Tales of ravenous beasts, of dangerous weather, of the wild and unkillable Vagrants had been just that to her: tales.

Until that moment, Sal the Cacophony had been no different.

Ozhma had heard some of them: the one about her killing a thousand men in one night, the one about how she'd destroyed Paarl's Hollow to deny bandits the joy of it. What was supposed to be the usual birdshit. What very well *might* have been the usual birdshit.

But what wasn't the usual birdshit was what was happening in the Scar.

The destruction of the Borrus Valley, the bombing of the Blessing, the tens of thousands upon tens of thousands decorating the Scar in bloody heaps because of the resurgent war between the Imperium and the Revolution—Ozhma had heard of that, too; she had seen it with her own eyes. And she had heard, from every lip that could bring itself to stop sobbing long enough to speak, that the fire that ravaged the Scar had all been sparked by one woman.

And her terrible, terrible gun.

"Yeah," Sal the Cacophony said, narrowing her eyes at Ozhma. "Is that for me?"

Ozhma froze.

Oh no, is what *for her? Is that Vagrant slang? Is she about to shoot me? All of us? Is she going to steal my face? Can she do that? Do the... Oh, hang on.*

She hadn't even finished thinking before the tankard was out of her hands and into Sal's. The woman tilted her head back, guzzling the liquor like it was water. It dribbled from the corners of her mouth, down the slope of her collarbone, across the muscle of her body to mingle with the sweat and blood and scars.

The scars.

She was covered in them, elegant strands of knotted flesh to answer the chaotic ink of her tattoos. And none of them presided over her body with the same majesty of ruin as the thick one that wound its way from her collarbone to her belly.

"Thanks." Sal let out a belch, sucked in air through her teeth. "Tastes like shit." She wiped her mouth with the back of her hand. "Anyway, sorry for the threats, but it's important that you hear this." She lowered the tankard, took a long breath, composed herself. "It began like this, right?"

"That is *enough.*"

It was Galatatian that swept forward, hot on the heels of his own outrage. His face twisted into a dick-nosed mask of authority, he strode in front of Ozhma, sweeping an arm out as though he could sweep aside the entire city with it.

"Scourge of the Innocent, Harbinger of the End Times, Oath-breaker and Violator of every Imperial Code!" Galatatian thrust a defiant finger in Sal's face. "Do *not* dare to seek to threaten an emissary of Her Majesty with such vile crudity. We shall entertain none of your coarse pageantry and demand, under the wrath of both the Imperium and the Revolution, that you release the people of this city and immediately submit to—"

Ozhma guessed that was inappropriately dramatic, because that's when the violence started.

Sal seized Galatatian by his collar, hauled him off his admittedly *very* nice shoes, and raised her drained tankard like a headsman's axe. It hung in the air for a long, terrifying second.

Ozhma's eyes were locked on the metal bottom of the tankard. She let out what she considered to be a very reasonable plea for calm.

No one could hear her. Not over the sound of the envoy's face breaking.

The tankard came down. Galatatian's outrage choked on Galatatian's teeth as Sal slammed the bottom of the tankard into his face. Blood spattered her knuckles as she raised it and brought it down again and again, filling the room with a wet, crunching music. She released his collar. Galatatian slumped to the floor, moaning.

Sal stared at him there for a second before turning, her cheeks painted with his gore, to face Ozhma.

"It began like this," she said, "right?"

"Right," Ozhma, sweat beading on her brow, agreed.

TWO

THE SCAR

Only three people had been eaten that morning, so things were looking up.

Yes, of course, *ideally* no one would be devoured messily by an incredibly temperamental dragon. *Optimally*, only one person would have been scooped up into its talons and swept into the sky, if only for dramatic effect. *Preferably*, only two people would have been shredded by tooth and claw to rain viscera down upon horrified onlookers.

But six months in, I couldn't hope for any of those things anymore.

Ideals had been abandoned the minute after eight of us came crawling out of the ruins of the Borrus Valley and put its smoldering hellscape behind us. Optimality was abandoned almost as quick, four months ago, when we became sixty. And now that we were almost four hundred, preference had gone from "escape the raging war devouring the Scar" to "try to avoid being eaten by the huge fucking flying lizard."

Just like the third guy hadn't.

Brannoc, I think his name had been, one of those small village heroes—you know the type, the kind that grew up brawny and tough and thought that made them a badass. When the skies had gone black and the cry had gone up to make for the ravine, he'd picked up the maul he'd been using and turned to make a heroic last stand to defend everyone else.

But here's the problem with heroic last stands.

Sometimes they worked.

Its scales and feathers a shimmering amethyst against the noonday sun, the sight of the great dragon was made hardly less majestic by the gore spattering its jaws. It wheeled lazily across the sky, possessed of a certain feline mischief as it amused itself by dropping a brawny corpse out of its mouth, only to swoop back down to catch it before it fell.

If the dragon's rider was bothered by its mount's morbid amusement, she didn't show it. But why would she? She hadn't minded when it had done the same thing with the other two, either.

I peered up through a gap in the rocks, squinted against the sunlight as the dragon wheeled around again.

"Well?" someone asked from behind me.

I rolled out my shoulder. I felt a muscle pull out of place, winced.

Fucked up a parry three days ago fighting off Revolutionaries. Hadn't healed properly.

"It's not leaving," I sighed.

"Oh." A nervous swallow, the kind that cowards think will make them bold. "Well, we can just wait a little longer, can't we? *Eventually*, it'll be called toward another mission and we can make a break for it."

"This *is* its mission," I snapped, whirling around. "It's not out here to scout or negotiate or do *any* of the other things you think it is. It's out here to kill people. Because this is a fucking war between a lot of assholes with a lot of weapons and we're the unlucky fuckers caught between them and no amount of pretending is going to make it not that."

Meret's smile fell at my harsh words. In better circumstances I would have felt bad about that. As it was, I couldn't afford to indulge the horror and exhaustion battling behind his spectacles over which one of them he should be.

Meret was a good person. Good enough to still think you ought to treat people nicely, even in war. Good enough to keep sticking his nose into places it ought not to be, no matter how many times it got slapped. Good enough to stay with this little mess we'd gotten him into and keep using his dwindling apothecary skills and supplies in service of a thankless, faceless mass that could offer him no pay or gratitude beyond the knowledge that he'd done the right thing.

The kid was going to get himself killed out here if someone didn't say something.

"You're right," he whispered. "We're all going to die if we don't do something."

The way he looked at me, that wary and desperate need for reassurance that everyone looks for before they do something terrible, almost killed me. But I met those eyes and, quietly, I nodded at him.

I drew in a breath, winced at the pain in my lungs.

Took a hit to the chest three weeks ago, hadn't given it time to heal. But I bit it back, forced my thoughts away from pain and back onto good old reliable guilt.

I shouldn't have done that to Meret. I shouldn't have yelled at him. I shouldn't have had to. A man like him shouldn't be out here. He was an apothecary, not a field medic. He should have been in a backwater town making a living brewing teas for old women with joint problems, not out here cramped in a ravine beneath a jagged crown of crowded rock.

And he had been.

Until I blew that backwater up.

And every other backwater between me and the crater that had been the Valley.

I'd done right by him since. He was under my protection and that didn't count for nothing. But I would spend many nights wondering what I could do, what anyone could ever do, to make up for stealing a life like that.

But then, I thought as I looked over the great gash in the earth, *what else is new?*

If I squinted, I could almost pretend they weren't hundreds. Their numbers were alternately illuminated and cloaked by the sun creeping through the crowded rocks overhead, and if I pretended that only the ones in the light were real, if I could ignore the ones hidden in darkness, I would feel less like shit.

And for the briefest of seconds, it worked.

Then my eyes adjusted. And I saw them, huddled together in the shadows. Children, alternately wailing or staring, numb, at the ravine walls. Men and women, arguing bitterly or trying to stay calm or not bothering to speak to anyone but the ghosts of those they had left behind. Grandmothers and grandfathers, sharing smiles that had begun as warm and encouraging and had been chipped away by road and death to the tight press of pained lips they shared now.

I had known their names once. Brannoc. Everise. Mathorlis.

Then we'd met more. And I started calling them by their professions: the blacksmith, the bartender, the seamstress.

Then we'd met more. And I could only remember them by their faces: Broken-Nose, Lips-I'd-Kiss-Under-Better-Circumstances, Beard-Face.

And more. And more. And I couldn't remember them anymore. But by then it was just as well, since they kept dying.

The people of those backwaters. Of Littlebarrow. Of Clef's Lament. Of House of Regrets. Of Ten Troughs, Whisperwhile, Cragstown, Zukk's Fevered Hope, Cruelriver, and on and on and on. They'd had towns once, squares where they bartered, taverns where they celebrated, homes where they lived. Now they had the burdens on their backs, the wagons pulled by weary birds, and their many dead in their dreams.

Sometimes, we met a lot of them in a group where most of a village had gotten away before it was annihilated by Revolutionary cannon fire. Sometimes, we met only a few that had managed to escape the flames and thunder and terror unleashed by Imperial mages. Once, we met just one man standing in the ruins of his village, digging neatly lined graves for the neatly lined corpses before him. We called to him. He didn't answer.

The Scarfolk came from many different places and many different lives. They were a strong people, a tough people... but not this tough.

It was never rare to see trickles of refugees leaving a home ruined by bandits, beasts, or disaster. But trickles were easy to manage. The Scar, barren and harsh as it was, could absorb a few trickles.

What had come out of Borrus Valley hadn't been a trickle.

What had come out of Borrus Valley, where the fighting had begun, where the bombs had fallen from airships that droned an iron song through the sky and mages had ringed towns one by one and buried them beneath the earth, had been a flood.

No, I caught myself. Not a flood.

These were the rats, the vermin that felt the rumbling in the earth and fled shrieking through the dark, heralds of the flood to come. And it had come. Out of the Valley and across the Scar, it had come. Drowning villages and townships and freeholds under tides of thundering cannons and sparking magic and firing lines and flaming hands and tanks and dragons and every other terrifying weapon the Revolution and Imperium had been spoiling to use on each other.

There was no warmth between the huddles of people cramped together in the ravine. They weren't together because they liked each other. They were together because a herd made it easier to escape predators. They were together because their horror seeped into each other, became part of everyone else's traumas, and formed into the same mute, numb march. They were together...

Because of me.

Well, that's not entirely fair. It's not like the Imperium and the Revolution were cuddly before this—any spark could have lit the fuse to their war.

But I had been there.

When the bombs fell from the Revolution's air fleet. When the Imperium's attack birds painted the clouds red with gore. When powers no one knew, nor should ever know, fought among the peaks of the Borrus Valley. I had been there to see the sparks lit. I had been there to strike a few of them. I had been there to stop them.

And I hadn't.

And now the spark was a world on fire, steadily pushing the hundreds and hundreds toward something terrible, something I couldn't stop, something—

Easy. The thought punched its way through my crowded skull, beat down the others. *Easy. Don't fall down that hole again.* A pause, then another, solid hit. *She can't afford for you to.*

That thought—those last, echoing words—almost shook my head apart with its weight.

First, you kill the dragon. Then, you get her to Ocytus. Dragon. Then Ocytus. The thoughts became mechanical in my head, repetitive and comforting. *Ocytus. Ocytus first. Guilt later. Just keep going. Just keep going until there's enough room between her and the Valley that you can sleep. She deserves that.*

Or maybe I was talking about me. I don't know. I was two nights deep into an ongoing experiment to replace the need to sleep with whiskey, and while I thought it was a good idea, my aching scars and sinews did not.

A body jostled into me. I bit back a shot of pain as my foot began to throb.

Rolled my ankle fleeing from the Imperium three months ago. I'd get around to fixing it.

"So, uh," Meret asked as I pointedly ignored the pain in my leg, "what are we going to do about the, uh, you know... dragon?"

I only bring up the condition of my mind and body so that you can see why I might have thought my response would seem reasonable at the time.

"Well, fuck, guess I'll kill it."

"What?" Meret's eyes widened in that way I thought was kind of cute when I wasn't about to go die. "How? Hey! *Wait!*"

I wasn't about to let him make me aware of the likelihood of bringing down a flying reptile the size of a house, so I kept walking.

I pressed my way through the crowd of refugees as I headed toward the rear of the ravine. Or rather, I *tried* to press through them—truthfully, I would have been happier if I had to. I would have been happier if they had crowded inconsiderately around me or clung to me asking for help.

Hell, I would have taken anything other than the sunken silence that greeted me.

The burbled conversation of the crowd fell to a hush as I passed. Knots of refugees silently cleared from my path as I walked. A boiling-kettle noisy churn of humanity died softly with every stride, until the only sounds echoing off the cramped walls of that ravine were my footsteps and their stares.

No hate in those eyes. Hate I could deal with. Anger, too—those were sharp feelings, feelings made for cutting and fighting, and the Scar was littered with bodies testifying to how well I handled hate and anger.

But this... this empty, hollowed-out, animal terror in their eyes, I didn't know what to do with. I didn't know how to handle being the thing that kills them.

They'd heard. In fragments and in whispers, they'd heard what happened in the Borrus Valley. And in fragments and whispers, they talked. They shared stories of the vicious woman who had started the war, whose gun breathed fire and drank blood, whose every step meant another mother died and another city burned.

Rumors. Legends. Outright fabrications. I'd heard them all. And because I'd heard them all, I could barely remember which ones were true and which ones were false.

Once there are enough of them, words stop being words. They stop being stories and tales and legends and start being more solid things: whispers become the last weapons of the desperate, muttered fears become bricks to build walls with, screaming becomes the torch you cling to in the night. And when they're all hurled against you at once, when people clutch them so hard they bleed before they throw them at you... well, maybe you just stop noticing which ones are real and which ones only feel like they are.

It didn't bother me, I told myself. Not the stories, not the stares. I couldn't let it. I couldn't let myself be weighed down by their fears, no matter how badly they needed that.

Fear later, I let my thoughts go mechanical again. *Ocytus first. Fear later. Ocytus first. Fear later.*

And if I listened to it long enough, I could *almost* ignore that hollowed-out terror in their faces as it followed me through the ravine and to the jagged rent that let out onto the fields.

"I don't fucking care if your bird needs to graze," a voice growled ahead of me. "And frankly, I don't fucking care if you get devoured, either. But *everyone* else seems to have this insane idea that getting eaten by a dragon is bad, so if you could kindly maintain that illusion by getting the fuck back inside, I'd appreciate it."

It actually *is* possible to move a lot of people across a great distance with some semblance of order. But it takes a lot of goodwill, a lot of muscle, and at least one person who's more pissed off at everyone else than everyone else is pissed off at them.

"But it's been *days*. My bird is going to wither!"

"So shoot it and eat it now before it gets skinny. Now get the fuck back inside."

I had one of those.

The refugee, a harried-looking man with a bridle in one hand, scurried back into the ravine, muttering curses that promptly fell silent when he shuffled past me. And in the gap stood what passed for security among our little caravan.

"Problem?" I asked as I approached the woman.

Sindra shot me a sneer that was somehow deeper than either the scratches *or* the years of stress-induced wrinkles decorating her face. "Only if you consider a complete shattering of the human soul to be a problem."

"I do."

"Well, then we've got several hundred fucking problems, don't we?"

She staggered inside the ravine, cursing over the sound of metal creaking as she limped in. Her prosthesis groaned, its spellwritten sigils sputtering. She'd damaged it breaking up fights in the caravan. The same fight during which someone—I won't say who, but it was almost certainly someone incredibly attractive and possessed of a rugged, nay, capable charm—threw something at someone that *may* have been the tools used to fix her limb.

"That man, though," she said as she leaned against a rock, knuckling out stiffness in her back, "will not be a problem."

"He looked a little pissed."

"He looked a little pissed because he's a grown-ass man being told he can't go outside," she muttered. "And now that he's vented at me, he'll be fine for another day. Same with the rest of them that'll come snarling at me today."

"You'd think the flesh-hungry reptile would be a natural deterrent."

"Yeah? You'd also think that people would have gotten tired of killing each other, too, but you'd be a fucking imbecile, all the same."

"That's a good point," I replied, "unless you meant I, specifically, would be an imbecile, in which case, fuck you."

"I don't have time to worry about you," Sindra groaned as she removed her coat, tattered and bloodstained, and shook dust out of it. Her bare arms were decorated in cuts over hard, lean soldier's muscle. "No one does. They aren't thinking of you, or the dragon, or even the fucking war. They're thinking about the place."

"Which place?"

"The bathhouses of Cathama. Where do you think, idiot?" She gestured a weary arm out somewhere. "They're thinking of an empty shack or a campfire or any spit of land big enough to lie down where they won't be killed. People don't get *less* human in a crisis. They need to walk and sleep and eat without being afraid, otherwise they're not humans. They're just another beast crawling across the dirt. They know that. And it eats at them worse than a dragon does."

I tried not to think about that. Tried not to think about that terror gnawing its way through the crowd. How it would eventually reach her and this whole thing would be blown to shit.

"Fought the Revolution's wars for years," she muttered. "Men and women breaking themselves, building themselves back up, surviving almost anything." She reclined, closed her eyes. "I like to think, out of all those years I threw away for someone else's battles, I at least came out with more patience and compassion than I had."

"Yeah, same." I snorted, hocked a thick glob of snot, and spit onto the floor. "Anyway, I'm going to go shoot the shit out of a dragon. If they're making barbecue tonight, can you save me some? Thanks."

Sindra and I did not have what you might call a friendly relationship. She, a hard-nosed Revolutionary from a law-abiding background. Me, a more free-spirited, go-with-the flow, accidentally-destroy-the-only-home-you-ever-knew type. Our relationship was workable. So when I told her I was going to go do something to get myself killed, I expected a grunt or maybe a request to have my flask before I went.

I was not expecting a lot of joints popping and metal creaking as she rousted herself to put herself in my way.

"No," she said curtly.

I paused, met those flints she called eyes. "I didn't know you cared."

"I don't."

Well, I *had* been flattered.

"Thanks for letting me know. Move."

"No."

She imposed herself again between me and the exit. This time, I was less flattered. In fact, I was a little insulted. Sindra was a tough woman—I'd seen the big men she'd put on the ground. But a tough woman was the same as a tough man: they both are a poor match for a giant fucking gun that spits magic.

She knew it as well as I did. Because I *let* her know it as my hand rested upon the black hilt jutting from my belt. The heat crept into my arm immediately, flooding through my hand with a burning indignation. Who was this woman, the gun demanded through his burning brass, to think she could stop the Cacophony? To think she could even *inconvenience* us? I was a patient woman, but I had an urge. An urge to just draw him and solve this with an explosion of brass and an eruption of sparks.

Only one thing stopped me.

I didn't know if that was my urge flooding through me...

Or his.

"I don't care," Sindra repeated, visibly deflating with the breath. "Because you don't."

"Oh, I don't? Fantastic fucking news. I'll just go back and sleep for another few hours, then, won't I?" I grinned. "Seriously, though. If you want me to break your face apart, there are easier ways to ask."

"You don't care about the dragon," Sindra reiterated, pointedly swallowing my threat, "just like you didn't care about the beasts, the bandits, or anything else that's plagued us this entire godless trip. You don't care about the enemy." She pointed over my shoulder. "It's them."

I didn't look. I didn't want to. I didn't want to see the accusing stares dropping, the hushed conversations stopping, the fear in their eyes again battling with the hatred for the woman who'd burned down everything they'd ever known.

But I felt them all the same.

She sighed, put a hand on my shoulder. "Look, I don't have a fancy fucking gun or a pretty name, but I've killed. And I've seen what's left over after the killing. I know you..." She paused, bit back frustration. "I know you want to run from them. Even if it means running straight down a dragon's throat. But...you can't. You can't run from them. And you can't die on them."

My eyes focused on a patch of dirt to her right. My lips hung numb. The words bled out onto the ground.

"They wouldn't mourn."

"Wouldn't mourn the woman who burned down their homes and sparked a war, probably not." Sindra squeezed my shoulder.

"Wouldn't mourn the only thing keeping them from getting crushed by a war? They'd bleed tears."

My brow furrowed. "That doesn't make sense."

"You don't fucking say? People don't make *more* sense when they're in the middle of a war? I take it back. Go. Spread this revelation with the world. They have to know."

I never knew exactly *why* Sindra left the Revolution. She claimed she didn't have the stomach for the killing anymore, but I privately suspect it was because she was this much of a dick with everyone.

"It doesn't make sense to them, either. None of this does," she continued, "and it's not going to for a long, *long* time. But the only way they're going to live long enough for them to figure it out is if we get them out of here. And the only way that happens is if Meret keeps everyone calm enough to move. And the only way *that* happens is if I'm here to remind you not to be an utter moron. It's a great fucking wheel and it's noisy and it's scary and it's bloody and it doesn't fucking make sense, no, but the only way it keeps turning is if we move it."

Sindra was not a woman for words. Not usually, anyway. Before this, the most verbiage she'd spent on me had been red-faced and *extremely* vulgar. These words, this speech, I think it should have made me inspired. Or at least, feel less horrible.

And if I had only *merely* sparked a world war that displaced thousands, it probably would have.

But Sindra hadn't been there in the Valley. Sure, she'd seen the end, but she didn't know what we'd done before it. She didn't know just how badly things had fucked up.

She didn't know how many people I'd hurt.

And I couldn't tell her. I couldn't say it. I couldn't even *think* of it without... without...

Guilt later. Ocytus first. A long, tired breath. *Guilt later. Ocytus first.* A pair of eyes narrowed on the woman before me. *Ocytus. Get her to Ocytus. Nothing else matters.*

"Whatever they need," I whispered to her, cold as the wind crawling across the stone, "the only thing anything in my way is going to get is the Cacophony. That can be the dragon. Or that can be you."

Sindra held my stare. Hers was a soldier's stare, the type that big, strong men crumbled under. But mine was a killer's stare.

The type that soldiers know not to press.

"You know I'm right," she muttered as she stalked out of the way. "If you want to go be a big fucking spectacle, be my fucking guest. But if you want to be a big fucking spectacle and come back alive, get your ugly friends."

A surge. Panic. Guilt. Horror. Welling up in me. Coiling at the base of my neck. It was heavy. Too heavy. I was going to...

Later.

A breath.

Ocytus.

"I'm not talking just to hear my own damn melodious voice. You want to keep running, you stay alive," she called after me. "Hell, could be you'd even get far enough to figure out how you fucked it up. I managed it, for a while."

"Yeah?" I called after her as she vanished into the darkness. "What happened?"

"You did."

THREE

THE SCAR

I'll level with you. Of all the types of operas out there, I like ensemble pieces the least. You know, the ones with a bunch of characters playing companions or entangled lovers or heroes brought together 'neath the stars of fate, dumb shit like that.

Don't get me wrong, I see the appeal: you've got plenty of characters to choose your favorite from, there's all this sexual tension going around, and before it's all done, *someone* is going to make a speech about drawing strength from friendship right before they stab someone else and that's always great to see. I love all that shit. I adore it, even. But something keeps me from enjoying them the same way everyone else does.

"Fuck me, no wonder you've never pleasured a woman. Your fingers're deader than mine."

They're completely inaccurate to real life friendships.

"I know you're simply speaking out of frustration. I'm not bothered. I am not irritated. I am calm."

"Well, hello, Not Bothered, Not Irritated, and Calm. Could one of you introduce me to someone who knows what they're fucking doing? You're putting them in too shallow! Use some fucking muscle."

I followed the voices—the cursing, the meekness, the additional cursing luring me like the song of a particularly vulgar, confused siren. At the edges of the ravine, the tough and withered plant life conspired with the rocky outcroppings to form a series of coves hidden between the stones and the thorns. As far as cover from a dragon went, it wasn't bad.

If you didn't mind the possibility of it becoming kindling.

"I don't have to do this, you know! I could be back with the weavers, making blankets! Where *my* talents are *appreciated*."

"Woe—and I mean fucking *woe*—to any circle of any kind that requires *any* use of hands that takes you in because I haven't seen this much fumbling since I lost my virginity in a fucking *barn*."

Which my associates clearly did not, given all the fucking noise they were making.

I rounded the corner, saw them squatting around the hasty campfire and bedrolls that they'd staked out as their own. A pair of them, brother and sister, each the same skinny, sharp-eyed, dark-haired echo of each other. Save where his leanness made for shy smiles and gentle words, hers made her rather like a hatchet: straightforward and best used for dismembering people.

"I am your *brother*," Urda gasped. Though his voice was breathless with indignation, his eyes were focused on her skinny arm lying in his lap. "And in addition to being vulgar and inappropriate, you're also being unhelpful. This procedure takes time."

"It always fucking takes time," Yria snarled in response, her mouth curling around the portcullis she had tattooed on her chin. "It takes more and more time every fucking day because it takes more and more magic every fucking day and that's more and more Barter that I don't fucking have protecting every smelly fucking pukemonger and artisanal shitstain calling themselves a refugee that finds their fucking way into this mess and it's *never* going to get fucking better."

Those were harsh words for the refugees, honestly. And I might have objected, had it not been for two things.

One, some of them *did* smell.

And two, this is what the operas about companionship never get right.

I'm sure friends do rely on each other's strength, from time to time. Just as I'm sure, sometimes, long-winded dramatic speeches about the power of friendship *do* inspire people to greatness. In better circumstances, I could have done something with that.

But I wasn't in better circumstances. Or inspirational circumstances. I was in get-by circumstances. And speeches aren't how people get by.

During the good times, everyone's got speeches. When the drinks are flowing and the laughs are loud, everyone talks about how they're going to change the world. During the hard times—during the blood-on-the-dirt times, the wake-up-screaming times, the get-by times—they sound different.

"I know it doesn't seem like it will," Urda whispered, "but please try."

"I can't, you son of a bitch. Can't you fucking see that? I *can't*."

"I know. Please, try, anyway. For me."

They don't make speeches or plans. They don't inspire or stir great emotion. They pick a direction, they put their head down, they start moving until they can't anymore.

"All right," Yria sighed. "For you. You soft fucking loser."

They exchanged a slight smile—or rather, *he* smiled, she made a masturbatory gesture—and he returned to his work. The needles, tiny slivers of green and silver, trembled in her skin. Beneath the shade of a tree, I could see the sigils on the needles—impossibly tiny—begin to glow and hum in her arm.

Urda's work. Spellwrights were always as impressive as someone who can make a sword explode with a few lines of script could be—that is, always—but his work was on another level. He'd spent days painstakingly carving in infinitesimally small scale on the needles, wrighting the sigils he needed onto the tiny pins.

Sigils *she* needed, rather.

He said they were designed to stimulate muscle response. That they could, with a subtle enough command line, persuade numb limbs to awaken. I hadn't found any fault with that logic, but I didn't think it was going to work.

And from the look on her face, neither did Yria. The irritated boredom on her face suggested this was mostly for his benefit, not hers. She viewed her arm, lying numb and limp in his hand, with the same resentful resignation one looks at a broken wheel on a run-down carriage: unfortunate, but inevitable.

See, Yria was a Vagrant, same as me. But instead of having a magic gun and dashing good looks, she was a Doormage. The Lady Merchant that governed every mage's strength and every mage's price had given her the ability to leap between portals with ease not seen outside the Imperium. And in exchange, she took life. Movement. Energy.

From Yria, specifically, the Lady had taken her arm. The limb spent more time than not paralyzed, the nerves inside gone dead, leaving her with nothing but a lump of skin and bone. A decent Barter. A fair Barter. Yria had gone for a long time without paying one.

Until she met me.

I knew in my bones that, one day, I would have to take account of all the heavy pains I'd laid on the twins' shoulders.

But on that day, I came only to deliver them one more.

I knocked on a nearby dead tree trunk in an approximation of a door. A quartet of wary eyes looked up.

"Well, well, well." Yria regarded me with a crooked, unpleasant grin. "If it isn't Princess Peepingpants. You missed me undressing, if you were hoping to get a heaping helping of voyeurism, but if you give me an hour and a sandwich, I'll take a shit in front of you for a pound of metal."

"Oh my goodness, that's... I'm going to..." Her brother's words disappeared into a dry heave. "Why would you put that image in my head? Why would anyone *pay* for that?"

I took the implication that I would ever have to pay to watch someone take a shit the same way I took her vulgarity: without complaint. Six months and a few unbearable days with the twins had taught me their limits, as well as mine. Urda was a sensitive soul, requiring a kind touch and patience and other qualities you wouldn't ask someone named the Cacophony to provide. Whereas Yria?

"How the fuck would I know? Ask the mayor of Shit-for-Pay here."

Yria just needed to be an asshole. Any setback—starvation, injury, sickness, or exhaustion—she seemed to be able to clear up just by spewing a few foul words.

Ordinarily, anyway.

But ordinarily, I didn't hear desperate malice behind her swears, the wounded animal fear that slipped out in every talk. Ordinarily, Urda didn't look like he was going to fall to pieces just by breathing. But the strain was there, worse in them than it was in the others.

Which made sense. It'd been her magic and his spellwrighting that kept broken wagons moving and opportunistic bandits off our trail. But all that had a cost. They weren't in any better shape than I was. I couldn't begrudge them a little vulgarity.

Also, I had just called her a bowl of fucksoup the other day, so it wasn't like I had room to talk.

"Dragon's blocking the way," I said, gesturing over toward the sound of distant roaring. "It'll eat every last refugee, if we don't—" I paused, considered. "If it isn't stopped."

"Sounds like a self-solving problem to me," Yria muttered. "Just pick the weakest and slowest and leave them behind as a distraction. Or the ugliest. I don't fucking know, I don't talk to them."

"You're truly robbing yourself of a unique experience," Urda replied. "My horizons, aesthetic *and* cultural, have expanded monumentally since I made the pleasurable acquaintance of the weavers' circles and the chefs' society. My life has truly been improved beyond measure by the joy of knowing these people." He paused, sniffed, continued tapping needles. "Now, all that said, if I *was* going to feed one to a dragon to escape, I'd choose that dreadful oaf with the keg."

"Barnabor?" Yria snapped, incredulous. "What'd he ever do to you?"

"Nothing, aside from expel gases wantonly with no regard for others. But he's also the largest person and would keep the dragon occupied for longer."

"Oh, you're sniffing your own gases if you think I'm letting you kill my drinking buddy. He isn't even an asshole. We've got *tons* of assholes we could throw to the lizard before we—"

"We're going to kill it."

I didn't realize I had spoken the words. I didn't realize I had been afraid of saying them. They just came out. And they fell, like a severed head, onto the ground and stayed there, rotting in the silence that followed.

"Or fuck it up so bad it doesn't come back after us," I continued, hand on my belt. "Ocytus isn't far. We don't need to do anything more." I grunted, made a gesture with my chin. "Between your powers and mine, we stand a chance. How soon can you be ready?"

"Yeah." Yria's eyes remained locked on her arm as her voice drifted off. "My powers..."

She didn't want to say it. Her eyes did, her face did, but her mouth refused.

"No."

It was nice of her brother to do it for her.

"I'm sorry, but no." Urda was on his feet now, pulling up all one hundred ten pounds of his frame as tall as it would go. "My sister's used too much of her magic. Her arm is suffering from limited mobility, her Barter keeps growing and she...she..."

His voice went soft under the dirt crunching beneath my feet. When I stood before him and stared down at him through my scars, when his skinny frame disappeared in my shadow, I expected him to shake himself to pieces. The nervous lump he swallowed looked big enough to knock him over from the weight.

"Sal."

And yet...

"Please." He shook. He licked his lips. He didn't move. "She can't."

Can't.

A knife in my ear, twisting. The word sounded strange in his mouth. Strange in my ears. Something about the way he said it, so soft and gentle. It didn't sound right. I knew the word only in my head, a hard and heavy sound.

I can't fail again. It came back. Anvil heavy and hammer hard. *I can't let her down again. I can't keep failing her. I can't... I can't...*

My muscles tensed. The old wounds and aches vanished under a wave of heat coursing through me. My jaw ached from clenching and my hands curled into fists so thick they trembled with their own weight.

I can't let anything stop me.

"It's all right."

A hand appeared on his shaking shoulder.

"It's okay."

It slid down, took his hand. His eyes, wide and tremulous, turned to ones wide and calm.

"We're going to be okay," Yria said to her brother. She sighed, looked back to me. "I don't know... maybe I can help a little. Or something. I don't know."

"It's not smart," Urda hissed in her ear. His body continued to shake, even as she held him. "Your magic isn't sustainable like this. Your body's going to... to..." He swallowed something sharp. Tears welled up in his eyes. "I can't lose you, Yria."

"Come with me," she said. "Keep an eye on me. Make sure I don't do anything stupid." And she looked back up at me with a sneer that was bereft of tension or scorn. Just her usual sarcastic, asshole self. "Unless that'll fuck up your grand plan to be a grand fuck-up, Queen Queeftaster?"

And hey, she gave me a higher rank this time.

I let that go with a grunt and a nod. I didn't need them respectful. I just needed them. Because she needed me.

And so I needed them all.

"So, where's Agne?"

At my question, the twins' eyes went wide. They shook their heads and hands at me, as if they could make me take back the question.

"Agne is," Urda said softly, "enjoying some time to herself to collect her thoughts and prepare for the—"

"Last time we interrupted her tub time, she shoved me down a hill, then carried me back up the hill and shoved me down again." Yria wiggled the only fingers that worked, demonstratively. "With one fucking hand, mind you. We don't bother her, unless—"

"You're bothering me now, aren't you?"

A voice, delicate like the tinkling of a piano's ivories, came down from the hill at the back of the grove. I could see there, nestled among the trees, a folding changing screen of polished teak and taut paper. Trails of steam, scented with flowers, wafted from behind it. The light of a lantern glowed, illuminating a silhouette behind the screen: an image of a woman in a tub, elegantly and dutifully scrubbing at her body, extending a long and shapely leg.

Even in silhouette, Agne the Hammer was a sight that made some part of my heart ache in a tender way.

"Though, I suppose the tranquility was already ruined by the dragon."

And the fact that she could break me over that leg with just one hand didn't hurt, either, if that doesn't scare you.

And if it does... well, I don't want to tell you how to live your life, but you're missing out.

"It won't stop following until we give it a reason." I watched the curve of her silhouetted muscle, some part of me wishing that I could admire them for reasons other than dragon-killing. But needs must. "So, we'll fuck its shit up a little and... and... sorry, where'd you get the changing screen? It's nice."

Well, it *was*.

"From Madame Covoi, that lovely grandmotherly type from Quill's Respite. Traded it for my tea set."

"But you loved that tea set."

Agne paused, sitting still in the tub for a moment. I could see the cut of her jaw and the slope of her neck, taut as she stared at something.

"There are many things I love that I no longer have," she whispered.

Water sloshed as she pulled herself out of her tub. A pair of glittering eyes peered over the top of the screen, all six and a half feet of her easily looking down at me as she retrieved a towel and began to dry herself off.

And I tried not to think about how her eyes glittered a little less that day.

"Be that as it may, I'm quite fond of Madame Covoi, as well," she said. "And I'd prefer for her not to be digested. If I can help with that, I'd like to. Just..." A crystalline moment of hesitation—the kind that only people who are about to break your heart know how to do. "What, exactly, will I be doing to assist?"

"Nothing much," I replied. "I figured we'd hit it hard, get it riled up, see what it does, and then come up with how to take it down as we—"

I was interrupted by the shifting of earth under my feet. The twins cried out as they were knocked over. I seized a nearby tree to keep steady, my eyes drawn to the space beneath the changing screen, to the pale, perfectly pedicured foot that Agne had just stomped down.

And uprooted a few saplings with.

"I really must insist you tell me."

I didn't blame her. For that, for the stomp, for any of it. The Barter Yria had to pay was bad enough, but even if her magic left her paralyzed, she'd be the same unrefined, unpleasant, and frankly, unwashed lout she would always be.

A Siegemage's Barter was different.

And it was one I was loath to ask of anyone.

"Yeah," I said, forcing iron in my voice. "I can do that."

But I was going to, all the same.

"No one nation controls the stretch of land between Ocytus and the Valley." I squatted down, traced shapes in the dirt in a vague approximation of a map. "But the Revolution has fortifications here." I drew a circle in the dust. "Six Walls is a post not far from here. Big enough that it'll have guns better equipped to deal with a dragon than what we've got."

"What we've got is a shitty plan and a shittier map-drawer... person," Yria muttered.

"Cartographer," Urda offered.

"Yeah, fuck you, too." Yria snorted down at my very good effort of a map. "You realize, of course, that the Revolution aren't exactly keen to help people who blew up their airships, right? They aren't fucking around anymore, Sal. They're conscripting every last person on two working legs they can find and using the ones with one leg to do paperwork."

"I'm not proposing a political marriage here," I growled. "We don't need to do anything more than get the dragon near the fort. While they fight it out, we get moving and leave it all behind."

"Sounds... spontaneous." Agne's frown deepened. "Not that I'm unaware that slaying something so large requires some improvisation, but... Sal, so much of this seems to rely on it going exactly as you think, on the dragon chasing you, on Six Walls retaliating..."

"So much of this relies on me being able to piss off a dragon and cause monumental amounts of collateral damage," I snapped back, glaring up at her. "Do you really expect me not to be able to handle that?"

"Bitch has a point," Yria said in agreement.

"Okay." Agne nodded, sighed, repeated the words. "Okay, yes. Yes, I can do this. I can do this." Her eyes closed, her breath softened, she whispered words I wasn't meant to hear. "I'll still be me."

What the fuck am I doing?

When you're a Vagrant, you end up asking yourself that question at least three times. Once when you break your oath to the Imperium, again when you choose your name, and for the final time when you kill someone for no reason other than your own personal gain. After that, you either never ask it again or you ask it every day.

You can guess which one I was.

I never asked myself when it was just me. When it was my blood being spilled, my revenge getting done, my steel making my own way. No one got hurt but me and the idiot standing in range.

But now that it was my blood and theirs, now that it was my revenge that got us here, now that it was my steel that wasn't enough…

No one ever sang a song about Sal the Cacophony that said she was guilty. No one ever said she turned down help. No one ever said that the knowledge of people spilling blood for her miserable hide would ever feel this unbearable.

If they had, maybe I would have stopped after the first time I asked that question.

"Get dressed and ready and meet me at the ravine in half an hour," I said as I pulled myself up and dusted off my leggings. "We'll get everyone in position and take care of this." My body ached with the strain, my exhaustion settling into my bones in the time I'd stopped moving. "This is the right thing to do. Trust me."

"Yeah, trust you," Yria sneered. "Not much other choice, is there? The associates of the woman who blew up the Valley don't exactly get to go back to *petty* crimes, do they?"

I'm not sure how it happened. Whether it was something she'd said or something I'd felt or something else entirely. I didn't know how she managed to get me so angry so quickly. But before I knew it, she was shaking in front of me, just like her brother had. And my fist was embedded in a splintering hole in the tree's trunk two inches from her head.

"You leave, leave," I said, low and cold like a winter storm creeping under the door. "You stay, stay. You do either, though, you shut your fucking mouth and get out of the fucking way between me and Ocytus. Got it?"

It wasn't supposed to be quiet like this. Deathly still and painful. She wasn't supposed to look at me like that, all wide-eyed and terrified. I wasn't supposed to do that. Not to someone like her.

"I got it," she said.

I felt their eyes, their stares trying to bore into my back as I left, trying to figure out what had happened that we'd ended up like this, where I made threats like that. Truth be told, I was trying to figure it out myself, sometimes. Somewhere between the Valley and here, we had lost the luxury of cooperation, of politeness.

Maybe I could have gone back and found it.

But the concern didn't last long. The thought even less. As my head returned to that place of iron and machines, that place that kept me going.

Ocytus. Dragon. Her. I told myself. *Ocytus. Dragon. Her.*

If I had to die to make her safe, I would. I'd known that from the day I met her.

I don't think I realized until then, though, that if everything had to burn to make her safe, I would also do it.

But then... what else could I do?

This was all I was good at.

FOUR

THE SCAR

If you ever end up on the wrong side of society, be it in an organized or spontaneous manner such as befitting a Vagrant, remember to make one good, disgusting story about yourself. Say you like to eat the skin off people's faces or make up some shit about keeping the viscera from your defeated enemies in jars. The specifics are up to you—just make sure that the story is about some inappropriate, unfathomable, or otherwise unpleasant love of gore.

It won't make life any easier, but it will make sure no one goes rifling through your shit.

I found my stuff where I'd left it—positioned right next to a jar of mysterious brown liquid I'd been leaving out to dissuade the curious from finding out if the stories about me were *really* true. I found my satchel and my sword belt, slung both of them around my waist.

I'm not ashamed to say that the weight of a sword on my hip made me breathe a little deeper. In the Scar, you can't be ashamed of something you're likely going to need before the end of the day. Rather, it didn't make me feel good *enough.* A sword was supposed to make you feel like you're in control, like the world will look out for you if it doesn't want to get cut. But this sword was...too heavy. Too weary. He already knew the work I had in mind for him and was preemptively resigned to ending up lodged and rusting in someone's right lung.

You might be wondering why I talk about my sword as if it's a person. Well, Eric is just that kind of sword.

You might also be wondering why I named my sword Eric, but if you went through the heartbreak of losing Jeff, Geoff, and Joff in the span of two months, you'd understand.

I rifled through my saddlebags, nestled in the little part of the ravine I used for myself and those around me. My fingers wrapped around cloth, sent my lips curling into a smile. I pulled the scarf free in a crimson ribbon, the tiny sigils along its border winking themselves awake before contentedly fading to a barely noticeable glow.

Luckwritten enchantment. Handy in a fight. Does not make you less of a hopeless bastard in any other aspect of life.

I fished back into the saddlebags and felt cold metal jingling around my fingers. They were always cold, I noticed lately. No matter how long they'd been in a hot saddlebag, they always came back cold and hollow in my palm. The shells, thick silver slugs, rattled around in my hand as I looked over the sigils etched onto their sides. One by one, I counted them out: Hellfire, Hoarfrost, Discordance. My classics.

I pocketed six of them into the satchel at my hip, feeling them clink softly as they settled. I already felt heavier with them. Maybe that's why I hesitated before reaching down to my belt.

Or maybe I was just scared.

My fingers found that black wooden hilt. I wrapped my hand around it and felt the heat seep through the leather of my glove and into the flesh of my palm and up the bones of my arm. And I pulled him out of the leather of his sheath and into the harsh light of day and, not for the first time, I regretted doing it.

His brass glimmered with a hellish light. Steam peeled off the length of his barrel. The thick chamber clicked into place as a pair of metal eyes leered at me from the grinning dragon carved into its barrel.

The Cacophony was happy to see me.

He always was.

I felt the heat coiling off of him. I heard him shudder to life in my hand.

"Where?" he asked.

"Out," I muttered as quietly as I could. No one needed to hear me talking to my gun. "There's a dragon we need to take care of."

"Large?" he asked.

"Very."

The steam cooled a little as he contemplated.

"Bring that one," he whispered to me in a voice brimming with cinders.

"Not now," I muttered.

"Now."

"We don't need it—"

"NOW."

Heat seared up my arm. Fiery fingers brushed past my ribs and lapped at my heart. I gasped, felt my breath go hot in my lungs. That was new. He always burned me when he got angry. And he always stopped before things got that bad. But he wasn't.

Not this time.

And not anymore.

I clenched my teeth to hold back the scream as I reached back into the saddlebags and pulled loose the shell. The one he wanted to use so badly lately. And the instant I did, the heat dissipated, shot out of my chest, back down my arm and into his brass. Happy again. His brass grin bigger. His eyes full of something that metal shouldn't be able to express.

All from one tiny little shell.

"Steel Python?"

I stiffened at the voice behind me. But I didn't turn around. I could feel her eyes boring into my back, the curiosity magnified behind her glasses. I could feel the concern, the worry, the accusation in her eyes. The desperation for me to talk to her about *any* of it. I could feel it.

I just couldn't bring myself to look at it.

"Just a precaution," I replied, after a moment.

"Steel Python is not a precaution," she replied firmly. "Steel Python is a war crime."

"Only when you're fighting people," I said. "When you're fighting a dragon, it's a precaution."

"Against a *dragon*? Against a fire-breathing, flying reptile that carries on its back a veritable *quiver* full of mages?" She snorted. "While your confidence remains, as ever, inexplicably and ruefully attractive, even that... that *weapon* can't bring one down."

"No, he can't," I agreed as I buckled the sheath around my waist and slid the Cacophony in. "But he can get its attention. We're not far from Six Walls."

"That's a Revolutionary fort."

"It is."

"The same Revolution that wants to kill you."

"Yup."

"And you want to fight them *and* a dragon?"

"Okay, look, there are some plans that make *so* much sense that you don't go thinking through them or they don't make sense anymore, got it? Like an opera plot." I checked my belts, felt the weight of my weapons. "Six Walls has cannons. Cannons can bring down a dragon. If I can lure one to the other, hopefully they'll fight each other while everyone else fucks off."

"There are..." She did that thing where she struggles to find the right word for how bad of an idea this sounds. "*Multitudinous* things wrong with what you're proposing."

Multitudinous, huh? It was going to be that kind of conversation.

"I know," I said.

"The dragon might not attack, or Six Walls might not retaliate."

"I know."

"Or you might lure the Revolution *back* to the refugees and every last one of them could be conscripted into their firing lines."

"Well, did I just say I fucking know or didn't I?" I snapped.

It's funny, the way people become like weapons. You learn how to handle them over time, figure out which way to point them to make them work the best, get a sense for how they fit in your hands, and most importantly, you learn the sharp and pointy parts of them that hurt.

And you almost come to miss those parts.

I wanted to feel her glare again. I wanted to feel those analytic eyes narrow and explode as they gave up trying to control their anger. I wanted to feel the tightness of her mouth as she struggled to keep her ire in check long enough to figure out the right words for it.

I wanted to feel angry, to shout and yell and scream and threaten.

That would at least be different from... everything else.

Instead, I got a weary sigh that came quicker and quicker every time we talked. The anger had kept us going, the irritation and the arguments and the little sharp parts that both of us were too stubborn to let go of. I once put milk in my tea and we argued about it for ten days. I just told her I was about to go try to kill a dragon and she... she...

Maybe it was the road, the constant running and fleeing that had stripped that anger out of her.

Or—a bitterly fearful thought crept into my head—*maybe it's something else that took it.*

Without knowing, without *wanting*, my stare drifted to her eyes. To those brown orbs behind those bright glasses. I studied them, searched every last inch of those eyes. Were they a little darker today or was that just the shadows of the ravine? Did they recognize me like they used to? Were they...

Were they still hers?

"Did you tell the others?" she asked. "About Ocytus?"

A pregnant, guilty pause.

"They know we're heading there," I muttered, rolling out a pain in my shoulder. "Nothing else."

"Meret, too?"

A longer pause. Heavier. Harder.

"Meret," she pressed. "Does he know?"

"He doesn't fucking know we'd get there faster without him."

She merely grunted. We both knew I wasn't going to fucking tell him he was on his own. Not after what I'd done to him.

"He knows they'll be safe there." I swallowed hard, tried not to make it a question. "And they *will* be safe there."

"For the better, I suppose," she replied. "Not like we can exactly tell them to come follow us to a city that doesn't officially exist, can we?"

Ocytus's existence was a matter of debate. Between the legends and stories and half-drunken rumors about the fabled, mechanized, wondrous city of the Freemakers and the official, impenetrable, six-hundred-page preamble that the Freemakers responded to any inquiries *about* their fabled city, people hadn't gone much further than agreeing that it might possibly exist somewhere at some time for some people.

Which, as far as hopes of salvation went, was slimmer than a turd on a three-week diet of dirt and cabbage.

But, as anyone being pursued by a flesh-hungry dragon will tell you, you don't get to choose which hope you cling to.

As far as the refugees knew, we were heading to salvation. And for all I knew, that might be true. The farther east we went, the farther from the fighting we were. And, if Liette's plan could be trusted, our journey there might just end this whole fucking war.

But since Liette's plan relied on getting the Freemakers—an organization that once, and this is a fact, blew up a man's tomb so they could pry the gold out of his corpse's teeth to collect the money he owed them—to lend their considerable talents to ending the war, I didn't think it wise to tell the others. Somehow, I doubt they'd be soothed by the idea.

But that was fine. They didn't know what we were planning. It was better for them, I told myself—no false hope, no disappointment. And once I told myself that, it was easier to tell myself the other lies. I told myself we could do this. I told myself we would be okay. I told myself...

I told myself that she didn't need to know why I wanted to go to Ocytus, either.

Ocytus. A word hammering in my ear. *Ocytus. Dragon, then Ocytus. Dragon, then make sure the refugees are safe, then Ocytus. Make sure they don't get any diseases, make sure bandits don't tear them apart, make sure the Imperium doesn't burn them or the Revolution conscript them, make sure they don't ever fucking look back over their shoulder and remember how much you fucked up everything for them, their homes, their families, their...*

A touch.

Not a word. Not a voice. Not the sound of soothing whispers, but the feel of warm fingertips on my skin and coarse leather on my body. It was her touch, her hands sliding around my waist and her head pressed against my back, that broke the thoughts. It was her though, the heat behind those fingers, that made me stop and breathe deeper and cleaner than I had in days.

"Liette," I whispered, my hand falling onto hers.

"It's going to get easier," she whispered, directly into my back. I felt her voice, felt it in her chest pressed against me, felt it sink into mine. "There will be fewer people. There will be less fighting. It's going to get easier."

"You're just saying that," I muttered.

"Is it helping?"

"I didn't fucking tell you to stop, did I?"

Her hands slid up my sides, found my arms. They trailed over the curve of my bicep, alighted gently upon my scars, traced the feel of my tattoos. Those fingers, those hands that had made hundreds of machines, potions, scripts, acids, and explosives that had rattled this world down to its core.

Had they always been this soft?

"And I would think you should know by now, through my most *vivid* demonstration of my capabilities, that I do *not* 'just say' words." I couldn't help but grin at the ire tingeing the edge of her voice. "It's a perfectly observable fact that doing any task over and over results in an increase in skill, hence, even if circumstances do not improve, your ability to handle them will have. Hence, *easier*."

"Didn't you once tell me that all creations eventually unravel into entropy?"

"I take two exceptions to that," she replied. "First of all, I told you that while you were reveling in your victory at a whiskey-drinking contest—which is the whole reason I brought it up—so I had no intention of you remembering that. Second, I am *trying* to be supportive, you ungrateful fuck."

"And I told *you* that I express and receive affection best through physical actions instead of words." I took her hand in mine, kissed her fingertips. "Which is why I'm about to go blow a hole the size of the sun in a dragon's skull for you. See you at dinner. Love you."

I tried to move, but couldn't. Her arms had ceased holding me in a loving embrace and had begun holding me in a loving chokehold.

"Look at me."

I turned. I did.

My neck was stiff, but it didn't hurt to look down at her. My eyes were bleary from sleeplessness and stress, but those brown eyes behind her spectacles were as real and solid as a brick to the head. And even after miles of road and leaving behind half-finished graves and walking past the burned-out skeletons of homes, she still smelled like flowers.

Without realizing, my hand drifted numbly to her ear, pushed a lock of black hair out of a face that wasn't used to smiling and tucked it behind one of the myriad writing quills arranged in her hair. She smiled. Soft and fleeting as a snowflake in summer. But she smiled. And I breathed a little deeper.

Fuck me, had she always been that small? Or did she just look that way, pulled up against me, the softness of her skirts against the dirt and grime of my skin, because of how many people I knew wanted to kill her? I tried not to think about it as she rested a hand upon my cheek.

I failed. But I had to try.

I owed her that much.

"You can't help anyone if you're dead," she told me. "Not them. Not me. Not anyone."

"I know."

"I am telling you this because you do not know." She took my face in her hands, forced my eyes on her. "But I *do* know. And I know you're trying to think of how to get out of this by killing, or fighting, or blowing things up, or just dying, but I am telling you now that this won't work. And if..." She glanced down at her shoes. "If you die, I can't make it."

They say never lie to your partner.

I don't know who the fuck they are, but I bet they're lonely.

Maybe in opera, that works. Maybe in stories, only wicked people lie. But, like I said, real people aren't like that. Real people have burdens, traumas, terrors that they can't even look at, let alone name. Lies—little lies, like this one—are what keeps us going.

She wasn't just Liette. She was Twenty-Two Dead Roses in a Chipped Porcelain Vase, one of the most infamous Freemakers in the Scar. She'd been fine before me, she'd be fine after me. She was only telling me this to make me come back.

And it was going to work, too. Sneaky little shit.

She didn't ask me to promise to come back. We weren't people who believed in promises. She simply let her hands slide down from my face, across my chest, and rest on my belly as she stood on her toes and kissed me. As gently and cleanly and softly as I'd ever been fucking kissed.

Better than any fucking promise in the world.

The embrace—and the mood—was broken by a faint growling sound. Liette's eyes drifted down to my midsection and the rumbling beneath her fingers.

"Let me make you something."

She released me suddenly, took off, and started rooting around in her bags. I sighed as she fished out a pot, water, and a package.

"I don't have time for food," I muttered.

"Oh, so you have time for dying of scurvy, then?" she asked without looking up as she arranged the pot on a stone slab and removed a quill from her hair. "If the answer is yes, bear in mind I won't lie to people and say you died in a more impressive way."

"*You promised you'd—*" I caught myself, gritting my teeth. "Look, there's a dragon out there."

"*Yes.*" Her voice didn't so much cut me off as cut me off and cauterize the wound. She slammed her hands down and stared at me through those eyes, aggravated to big angry brown by the lenses of her spectacles. "There's a dragon out there. A huge, fucking flying lizard that you're going to fight and because as brilliant as I fucking am I have never *once* figured out how to stop you from doing some dumb shit and while you're *out there* almost getting killed, I will be *in here*, utterly powerless to help you and terrified of what's happening and what *could* happen if you're gone, so if you would *kindly* indulge me in permitting me to assuage my massive—and I must emphasize, *massive*—anxiety over what the fuck is going on right now by contributing just the *tiniest* bit to your well-being, I would greatly fucking appreciate it, you stupid fucking asshole."

This, too, was not the first time one of her long and angry sentences had left me a little intimidated and a little turned on. And after what happened the last time, I decided to wait.

"Fine," I sighed, sitting down. "What have we got?"

She didn't bother glancing up as she etched a series of small symbols in a ring around the pot, pouring water in with the other hand. The sigils glowed a bright red, the slab growing bright with heat as the water came to a boil. After she'd taken a moment to admire her own spellwrighting work, she grunted.

"Field noodles."

"Field noodles," I groaned. Cheap, practical, and utterly devoid of flavor since the day a Freemaker invented them and promptly made a fortune selling them to soldiers. "What the fuck happened to real noodles?"

"Real noodles are in a restaurant somewhere civilized people don't solve their problems with magic and swords," she grumbled as she dumped the brick of dehydrated noodles into water.

"Fuck me, though, how long has it been since I've had noodles?" I leaned back, moaned inwardly. "The *second* we find a city that isn't on fire, I'm going out to find some. All thick with broth as warm as a baker's snatch."

"That's vile."

"All right, Madame I'm-Too-Good-to-Compare-Food-to-Genitals, what the fuck are *you* having when we reach a city?"

She leaned back, closed her eyes, thought. "Dessert. Specifically, an Imperial flatcake."

"Fancy." I whistled.

She smiled as her mind drifted off. "Coated in powdered sugar, *alive* with fresh fruit..."

My eyes drifted down to the pot, widened. "Liette," I said.

"Drizzled with wine cordial, garnished just so..."

"Liette!"

"With a candied mint leaf and—"

"LIETTE!"

She opened her eyes. Her nostrils quivered. She looked down and saw what I saw.

The pot was gone. The noodles were gone. The water was gone. In its place was an ivory-plated, beautifully assembled Imperial flatcake. Right down to the candied mint leaf.

"No." Liette gasped, stepped away. "*No!* I didn't mean to...I wasn't trying that time. I wasn't trying! It was doing it on its own... it...it..."

Her voice rattled itself silent and into her body. Every inch of her started shaking; she hugged herself to try to make it stop.

I know what you're thinking and, yes, it is very odd to conjure desserts out of nowhere. And I promise you I'll address that, but at that moment, I wasn't even thinking.

I was up. I was moving. I was grabbing her by her shoulders, I was pulling her against me, I was breathing in her flowers, and she was breathing in my fire. Her blood was racing beneath her clothes, her body twitching in ways a body ought not twitch, but I didn't let her go. I held her tight. I whispered.

"It's not you," I told her as I stroked her hair. "It's not you doing this. It's not you, Liette."

I took her by the chin. Her eyes were shut tight behind her spectacles.

"Look at me," I whispered.

She held her eyes shut, shook her head, refusing.

"Please."

She swallowed hard. Tilted her head up. She opened her eyes.

And I had to stop myself from swearing again.

Stars.

Swirling. Innumerable. Bizarre constellations and uncharted rivers of light and dark. Glittering in a void darker than night, alive with brightness that burned my eyes, all of them drifting aimlessly in her head.

It's not her, I told myself. *It's the thing inside her. It's not her.*

It took me a moment to remember: the airship, the monster we found inside it, the light that had left its body and entered hers. Every time I tried to recall it, it made a little less sense, warped my memory a little more. I started remembering conversations I hadn't had, stories I'd never heard.

"Blink," I whispered to her. "Blink."

She did.

And her eyes were brown once again. And full of tears.

"Sal," she whispered. "Sal... I can't control it. It's getting too hard to hold it back. I can't... I don't know... I..."

Brilliant people are weak. They build these beautiful worlds in their head and then see *one* thing they can't explain and it all comes crashing down. This is why stupid people rule the world. We see something we don't understand and we start headbutting it until it collapses.

Which wasn't *quite* what I was doing here, but you get the idea.

"Ocytus." I pulled her close to me, until I felt her heart stop racing. "Ocytus." I looked into her eyes. "I am going to kill this dragon. I am going to come back. We are going to Ocytus. And we are going to fix this. Okay?"

And she nodded. And she pressed herself back against me. And she breathed out.

"Okay."

Now, I don't particularly think of myself as dumb—or at least, not especially. But compared to a Freemaker? Compared to *her*? I, along with the vast, vast, *vast* majority of the world was an imbecile.

But that's what made us work. Same as any stupid and brilliant person. She would be the one that would fix this, the one that would figure out how we got out of this, the one that would think about and figure out what it would take to get that thing inside her out of her. I would just be the one too stupid to consider that it might not work.

As you might have guessed, I have a talent for that.

"But now," I said, "I'm going to go do something incredibly dumb." I released her, swung my attentions back toward the plains as I stalked out of the ravine. "Tell everyone to get ready and wait an hour. Then start running. I'll have enough of a lead by then."

"Wait."

I turned and grinned. Call me a sentimental sap, but I lived for these moments. The moments right before I left for danger, where I turned to her and saw those big eyes and those tiny lips and heard the words she couldn't risk me not hearing…

"Are you seriously going to take that cake?"

I blinked, looked down at the plate in my hand. "Well, you made it for me, didn't you?"

"*I* didn't, no," she replied. "The reality-warping horror *inside* me did."

"Yes, but it was your noodles that had their laws of time and space violated, so it still counts as yours."

"That doesn't..." She scrunched up her face. "What if it's not safe to eat?"

I blinked, took a bite, chewed, swallowed, grimaced.

"You're right," I said as I turned, shoveling the rest of it into my mouth like a fucking animal. "Wine cordials taste like shit."

FIVE

THE SCAR

Believe it or not, there was a time when dragons actually weren't considered all that impressive.

Ancient and rare enough to warrant the Empress's decision not to waste them on mundane warfare, the vaunted Imperial dragons were relegated primarily to parades and other social functions. Formerly reserved to be the mounts of Imperial Prodigies, their rarity had since led to a decline to their legend and a rise to any number of jokes about how much of the Imperial budget goes to the Empress's expensive aviary.

Some of them were really funny.

And then the dragons were actually returned to the fields and everyone remembered how they could breathe fire and swallow people whole and such.

They got less funny after that.

This one looked positively not funny at all.

The great beast, scales shimmering with the scant sunlight filtering through swirling clouds overhead, lounged atop a butte. It surveyed the ravine with a decidedly feline grace—its claws neatly folded over each other, its tail flicking back and forth, its eyes sharp, focused upon the tiny cracks between the rocks crowding the ravine, watching the tiny shapes of people scurrying in and out of shadows.

With predatory imperiousness, it bided its time, enjoying the anticipation. Its bored rider, absently polishing her gauntlets, could not be said to share the enthusiasm.

But fuck, what are you going to do to make a dragon go? Yell at it?

From my hiding spot beneath a crowded copse of dried-out trees, I studied the dragon. And the miles of terrain that lay between us.

"Sun's going down, but it's cloudless," I muttered, pulling my scarf lower over my eyes as I looked skyward. "That's not good. Not much cover, either." I paused, considered. "Not much *noncombustible* cover, anyway." I snorted, spat. "No wind for it to ride, on the upside. It'll be nice to have a running start, at least."

My partner took in the same sight I did. And, with gritty silence, arrived at the same conclusion.

"Six Walls is two and a half miles that way." I looked to the east, toward the rocky hills woven together with the ash-gray skeletons of dead trees. "Good location for a fortress, honestly. Next to impossible to mount a foot assault through the hills. Imperial assault, bandit raid, Havener war party—it doesn't matter, everyone ends up the same way." I pulled a flask out of my belt, popped its cork. "Dead, rotting corpse lost to the tangle of the wilds. Terrible way to go. Awful." I sloshed a mouthful of whiskey, swallowed, smacked my lips. "We'll probably be fine, though."

My partner twitched, clearly unconvinced. But I was used to that. We both were.

"So, here's what I'm thinking." I took another swig. "We grab that thing's attention, then make for the hills. Stick to the rocks instead of the trees, since that thing will light anything not made of stone on fire. Squeeze off another shot at the edge of Six Walls to keep it interested, then let the Great General's boys and their big fuck-off guns handle it. It's rough terrain, but given the twistiness of it all, we're looking at about six effective miles of dodging a fire-breathing lizard. But you can do it." I leaned over and patted my partner's neck, cooing gently. "Yes, you can. *Yes, you can, you big beautiful dragon-dodging baby.*"

My partner bristled, fixed an angry yellow glare on me, and bit my hand before stiffening up, letting out a sound of displeasure, and taking a massive shit on the ground. That could be construed as criticism of my plan.

Then again, given she was a giant fucking bird, that might just be how she was.

I bore the complaint silently. After all, it wasn't *my* ass that was going to be running from a giant flying explosion. Even as I put a foot in the stirrup and swung myself over the saddle, she bristled uneasily.

Now, a Badlander bird like Congeniality, that's normal—you don't ride a bird that eats you the minute the carrion runs out if you like things easy. But what the breed lacks in manners, it makes up for with courage, as fearless as it is mean.

And Congeniality was so mean I once saw her kick an actual kitten into the trash. Seriously.

So to feel her shifting restlessly under me, to hear the hesitant quarrel in her chirp...well, it didn't make me feel *better* about our prospects for survival. But I knew it wasn't the lizard that she was worried about.

Because I was scared of the same thing she was.

I eased the Cacophony out of his sheath, grimaced at the sensation of the heat pouring off of him. This, too, was not unexpected—a foe as big as a dragon was one he'd been looking forward to for a while and I couldn't begrudge him his excitement.

Normally.

But this time was different. This time, he burned too bright. Cinders danced in the teeth of his dragon grin. The brass of his barrel caught the light in just such a way as to suggest, unnervingly, that it was rippling. Alive.

That big brass eye of the grinning dragon seemed to fix on me as his voice coursed red hot in my veins.

"Shall we?" he asked.

I met that brass stare for a long moment. "Almost," I replied. I flipped open his chamber, loaded a shell. "We have to get its attention first."

"Steel Python?" he asked.

"Not this time," I said, slamming the chamber shut. "Sunflare. Blind it first, make it harder to see us when it's in pursuit."

He seethed. *"Too small. I deserve a grand entrance."*

"Later," I said.

His brass twitched. The heat from him began to blossom, pushing through my glove and into my skin. I drew a breath through clenched teeth, whispered in pained words.

"*Later,*" I gasped. "It's a dragon. It's not going to go down in one shot. There'll be opportunities for grand entrances after we set the stage. I promise." The heat spiked. I almost shouted out. "*I promise.*"

The heat stilled, dimmed, abated. Satisfied, his grin reflected my own clenched teeth.

"If you like," the Cacophony hissed. *"I would hate to be accused of being unaccommodating."*

You might think that, upon accepting the madness inherent in the proposition of a talking gun that shoots magic, it would be difficult to be unnerved by what it said. But you'd be wrong. No matter how much creepy shit I'd seen in a career that gave me considerable opportunity to do so, the Cacophony could still be creepier.

He just had to try harder.

Soothed by the promise of imminent carnage, he allowed me to aim him as I drew up straight in the saddle and stared down the sights. The dragon loomed, a big black target stark against the sun. My finger curled around the trigger, hot through my glove. The scar on my face ached as I squinted.

I had a moment, maybe a reflex or maybe a vision. I saw a world where I dropped this weapon, went back for her, and just kept on running. I felt it. And how badly I wanted it. And how much it hurt that I couldn't do it.

And, like I would do so many times instead of confronting uncomfortable feelings, I pulled the trigger.

The rattle of metal and the sound of thunder echoed across the stretch of land between us. The dragon glanced up before it knew what to think. And before it knew what was speeding toward it, Sunflare exploded.

A flash of light, the kind so painfully bright it makes you feel like something wicked in you is shriveling up, erupted across the sky. Clouds and shadows were swallowed, shape and color were consumed—the plain and the dragon and all of creation disappeared into the light, the only sound to escape the terrified shriek of a suddenly blinded dragon.

I squinted, shielded my eyes—even at this distance, I could barely stand to look sidelong at the eruption without feeling like my eyes were cooking in their sockets.

Sunflare wasn't supposed to do that. Sunflare was supposed to be a bright burst of light, but not this big. And not this bright. What blossomed across the sky that day was not my shell, nor the spell written on it.

It was a malign light, not a flash that robbed sight but a spiteful glow that plucked eyes out one by one.

Maybe I was being paranoid. Or maybe I wasn't being paranoid enough. And if I wasn't about to be killed, devoured, and shat out by a giant lizard, I probably would have thought more about just how the Cacophony had done that.

But I already told Liette I'd come back, so...

The dragon's roar shifted from terror to fury, clawing in confused frustration at its own snout. Already cursing the time I'd wasted, I jerked hard on Congeniality's reins and put the spurs to her. With an irritated squawk and another snap of her beak, she nonetheless took off at a sprint toward the twisted hills.

The rocks and dead trees came swooping up before us as we tore across the plain, but not nearly quick enough. I cursed myself, my bird, my luck, and then myself again—I'd misestimated the distance, wasted too much time, I didn't fucking know how but I already felt the great rush of wind behind me as the dragon's wings carried its pursuing shadow across the plains.

I spat curses that degenerated into frustrated sobs as I scrambled to load another shell. But my fingers were numb and the terrain made for bumpy riding. I had barely wrapped my hand around another shell when I heard the great shudder of air behind me as the dragon drew in a deep breath. I winced, shielded myself with the scarf as best I could, and tried to ignore the knowledge that it wouldn't do shit against the fire to come.

A surge of heat. A searing flash of light. A red scar opened up.

Flame poured out of the dragon's mouth, stark and vibrant against the gray and cloudy skies as spittle fell from its maw and burned cinders on the grass. The dragon's flame carved a wound in the clouds as it sailed overhead. The sight was majestic. Stirring.

Awfully nice of the dragon to leave me alive to witness it.

The beast's fire painted across the sky a good mile away from me, a haphazard spray of flame and cinders that swallowed up stretches of grasslands in fields of flame, but not much else. Maybe it was aiming or maybe it was just panicking, either way I wasn't exactly mad about not being cooked alive. Though I hesitated at the edge of the hills—this plan only worked if it chased me and if it couldn't see me, that wasn't likely to happen.

So I pulled Congeniality to a halt and I waited for it to notice me.

And, not that I claim to be an expert in such things, I noticed it was taking an *awfully* long time for this flying helltoad to come down and kill me.

It continued to wheel about the sky, lighting up the clouds with its fire aimlessly while setting more patches of grass ablaze. Had the Sunflare shell really hit it so hard that it was *still* blinded? Was it just fucking with me? Was it...

Wait.

I caught it. Three short bursts of flame in the sky. One long patch of burning earth. From afar, it'd looked mindless. Up close, it looked like...

Son of a bitch, I thought, *is that thing calling for reinforcements? What the fuck does a dragon need with reinforcements?*

Hair whipped across my face. Tall grass lashed against Congeniality's ankles. The wind had changed. When had the fucking wind changed? Smoke came roiling toward me, a black and billowing halo from the great wall of flame. I cursed, jerked on the reins and put my spurs to Congeniality's flanks.

The bitch didn't need the encouragement, I'll tell you that. I could barely hold on to her, struggling to keep my scarf from flying off my head as she wildly tore into the hills. Jagged stones reached out from hard-packed earth, claws and crowns that we darted around and ducked beneath. Timber crumbled beneath her claws as she leapt over water-starved trees and launched herself off of desiccated logs. We ran wildly, thorns tearing at us and sitting red-stained and satisfied in our wake.

And still the fire came.

Smoke coiled over us, ahead of us, taunting us as it closed in on our eyes and in our lungs. The heat of the flames lapped at our scratches, boiled the blood beneath feathers and flesh. I spat through coughs, winced against the cinders grasping for my eyes as I rummaged through my satchel.

"Hoarfrost?" I asked through hacking coughs.

"Agreed," the Cacophony answered.

Chamber open. Shell in. Shut, hammer, turn, and...

Boom.

The Cacophony shuddered, his brass rippling as he disgorged the shell. It streaked into the smoke and flame behind us, erupted in a blinding blast of white and blue. I shielded myself as an ivory cloud came rolling up, trampling smoke and flame beneath it. It passed over us, left Congeniality's feathers rimed with frost and a thin layer of ice clinging to my skin. It shattered and fell from me in twinkling shards as I beheld the hills.

Ice covered the rocks. Frost coated the timber. Every patch of blackened earth was smothered beneath a grip of cruel cold and every spark of flame had been swallowed in a great freezing grasp. The hills hung, quiet and still before us—in other circumstances, it might be beautiful.

"Do you like it?" the Cacophony asked, evidently pleased with himself.

I looked over the cruel serration of the shards of ice, the jagged thrusts of their tips, the way that even something as trivial as frozen water could look malicious when it came out of him.

"Fire's out, at least," I muttered.

"Yeah," a voice from above answered, "thanks a lot for that, asshole."

The clouds parted overhead. A figure came descending from above, a wisp of whirling hair and silks at the center of a gale. I recognized the scanty Imperial uniform of a Skymage and I recognized why the wind had changed so suddenly. And when she got a little closer, I recognized the face.

"Shenazar," I growled. "Here without Captain Tight-Ass and the rest of the Magic Morons? She let you out of the yard today to go burn off some energy?"

"The *captain* requested my presence, thank you very much," the Skymage replied, snapping her fingers. "Granted, I wasn't supposed to be the one to find you."

The dragon's shit made a little more sense now. "Been looking for me?" I asked, as I loaded another shell into the Cacophony.

Shenazar's face fell. Her eyes went dark. "I have, Cacophony. For months, every Empress-loving citizen has been looking for you. The Butcher of the Valley. The Endless Howl. The Warbringer."

"Is that what they're calling me now?" I asked, secretly pleased—I *liked* "the Endless Howl." "I feel like I should apologize, getting all the credit for starting this whole thing while you guys are out there doing the hard work of killing helpless people." I raised the gun. "Hey, hold still a second so I can shoot you in the face. That's how I apologize."

"I wasn't supposed to be the one to find you," Shenazar repeated, "but we're all very glad it turned out this way."

I hesitated. Like an idiot. "Who the fuck is *we*?"

What's the old saying? Ask a question that'll get your head staved in, get your head staved in? Something like that? Anyway, shit got bad in a hurry is what I'm trying to tell you.

The air shimmered. The Lady's song rang out. I pulled the trigger. Shenazar swooped away, fleeing as the shell streaked after her, impossibly fast. The shell disappeared into a flash of light as a great circle of purple, twisting brightness was violently born in the sky.

The portal opened and closed in an instant, just long enough for a trio of shapes to fall out of it and land upon the ground. The earth shuddered with the impact, punching through ice and stone and withered tree to send them hurling out in a halo of debris. Congeniality chirped warily, forcing me to fight to keep control of her.

When the dust had cleared and the light had faded, I saw the shell I had just fired. Smashed against someone's chest like a tiny silver gnat. A pair of gauntleted fingers, ebon metal rattling, plucked the shell out and held it up thoughtfully for a moment.

"I heard you were using fancier stuff now," the voice that owned the hands muttered.

The gauntlet clenched into a fist. It shuddered as the shell exploded beneath metal fingers, flashes of flame and steam peeling out between riveted knuckles. The gauntlet opened again to drop the shattered fragments of a Hellfire shell to the ground, where it lay beside a pair of matching ebon metal boots.

"But a gun, Salazanca? What kind of two-curtain opera nonsense is this?"

Neither of which you'd expect to see on a four-foot-nothing woman, her stark black hair done up in a tight military braid and the pristine press of her Imperial uniform only mildly rustled by the magic bullet full of fuck-you I had just shot at her. Hell, you probably wouldn't even think to find a woman that short on a battlefield.

If you'd never heard of Riacantha ki Camathusula, I'd call you ignorant.

And if you'd never heard a tale of the woman they called Bad Neighbor, I'd call you lucky.

Sadly, I'd met them both, so I guess you could call me both dumb and unlucky.

"Ria," I greeted her indifferently.

The coolness of my voice was just a flimsy disguise for the coil of my muscle. My heart hammered, begging me to put spurs to Congeniality, to start running and never look back. But I knew that to be a bad idea.

Running only made it more exciting for her.

"I hadn't expected you to hear anything of me or of the Scar, for that matter," I said. "Aren't you retired?"

"I was," she replied, sneering. "Thirteen campaigns, forty-six battles, and Lady knows how much Barter I've given to her, but I finally managed to get my medal of service and go quietly to live a distinguished lady's life of tranquil reflection." She snorted, spat onto the ground. "So you can imagine the knot in my taint when I got redeployed out here to deal with your shit."

"*My* shit?" I hadn't meant that to sound quite so nervous, but you don't raise your voice to Bad Neighbor without pissing yourself at least a little. Out of respect. "Listen, woman, it's your fucking Imperium that's out here setting everything and everyone on fire. Take it up with them."

"They offered me compensation." Ria grunted in reply. "And I took it. But it's a long fucking trip across the ocean, Salazanca. Long enough that I heard what you'd been up to out here. The shit you'd blown up. The cities you'd set on fire. The people you killed." Her eyes narrowed. "My people, Salazanca. *Our* people."

I didn't respond. I couldn't.

I wouldn't be called a liar.

We were different people back then. She was Bad Neighbor. I was Red Cloud. And we were hell on four legs. I bled red with her in the battlefield and bled whiskey with her on leave. Between us, there wasn't a Revolutionary regiment in the Scar that wasn't pissing themselves at our names. The battles were ours. The victories were ours.

And so were the people we buried out here.

"Whatever they told you, Riacantha," I replied, forcing my heart out of my throat, "I didn't go looking for this one. I didn't pick this fight."

"That's *not* according to our research."

A pair of slender shapes—the other two from the portal—approached from behind to take up positions on either side of the little woman.

"All collected intelligence points to the actions of one"—the first one, a young man with red hair as neatly kempt as his clean-pressed uniform, paused to look over some papers in his hand—"Sal the Cacophony as the perpetrator of the Valley War." He squinted at the papers, cleared his throat. "Contributions from other malefactors notwithstanding."

"The rank and file can handle the Revolution's latest little tantrum." The other one, a youth as dark and sullen-looking as his counterpart was cheery. "The madam's duty is to handle you, specifically. Which means that's our duty, too." He spun a slender finger in a circle. "Whee."

"The madam," I repeated, my sneer drifting back toward Riacantha. "These are your new assistants, then?"

"These are my *compensation*." Riacantha grinned, holding out her gauntleted hands gently. On cue, each of the young men laid a hand gently in hers. "Altrocus and Simivo. The only two mages with demeanor and aesthetic enough to get me to haul my ass out here." She took their hands in hers, squeezed lightly. "Gentlemen?"

"Charmed," both mages replied, bowing in unison.

"Allegedly," the sullen-looking one muttered under his breath.

I bet that one was Simivo. He looked like a fucking Simivo.

Congeniality stirred beneath me. She sensed the trouble to come, just as keenly as I did. Don't get me wrong—we'd both faced our fair share of Imperials before and neither of us had flinched. But those had been different: rank-and-file slobs and cocky mage pricks looking to lose some teeth.

Those weren't Bad Neighbor.

I hadn't fought alongside those before.

"So, what's the dramatic introduction for?" I glanced, as obviously as I dared, toward the trees—if the twins or Agne were ready to intervene before shit got hot, I hope they realized that it was boiling now. "A courtesy? Or do you just like doing things the old-fashioned way?"

"I don't hold off an Imperial dragon for a courtesy." Riacantha's face fell as much as it could. Years of war and Barter had stripped away her most prominent emotions, but she could muster enough disappointment to make me pause. "This is a plea, Salazanca."

My grip loosened on the Cacophony's trigger. Riacantha held her gauntleted hands out wide, gesturing to the broken landscape around us.

"You and I fought on this land, once," she said. "But not for this land. You and I did our duty, as we were told. We fought the Revolution here. We died for the Imperium here." Her frown deepened. "We said farewell to our friends here. Malhavosh, Friendly Dumar, Algumbraq..."

"Tharava, Ellissrien, Onokori," I finished. "Good mages."

"Good mages who turned to Dust on this sad, broken earth," Riacantha continued. "We saw too many of them lost on the wind here. It was for them we fought. Not the Imperium. Not ourselves. Each other."

She pulled something from her belt, extended a gauntlet.

"There doesn't have to be any more, Salazanca," she said. "Not you. Not me. Not any of us. No one has to die here."

She unclasped her fist.

"You don't have to suffer anymore."

My breath caught. My blood went cold. My body went slack.

I'd been around the Scar. I'd seen shit that made brave people's water splash cold on the earth. Never before, in all the monsters and murderers I'd met, had I ever seen something like what I saw in her hands.

A scroll. A simple, yellow scroll. No different from any other scroll, save for the silver band securing it. Even as far away as I was, I could see the glint of the purple gems that marked the wings of the great bird upon it.

The seal. The seal of the Imperium.

"The Empress gave me a request," she said, as soft as a voice like hers could go. "Before I left. And then she gave me this." She held the scroll up in two thick metal fingers. "You know what it is."

I did. Every Vagrant did. Some Vagrants lost sleep dreaming of it.

"A letter of pardon," Riacantha said. "For everything. Every drop of blood you've spilled, every splinter you burned, right down to every mean joke you've ever made about her. The Empress will overlook it all, ask for no apology or show of remorse. Keep whatever you took, live however you like. She only asks two things: put your sword down and return to the capital."

I sat there, staring, silent. Like it was a joke I was too dumb to get. Like she couldn't be serious.

I didn't ask her if she was. She'd never been one for lies, even before she lost the ability long ago. She stood there, holding that tiny little scroll in her massive fist, not needing to say another fucking word.

She knew what she was offering.

Pardon. Amnesty.

Home.

Once a Vagrant went Vagrant, that was it. The moment they broke their oath was the moment they started running. Any Imperial, from the highest Judge to the lowest servant, would know them as a foe to be killed on sight. Whatever else a Vagrant gained, they lost their nation, their people, their home.

You're not supposed to lose those kinds of things. They're as much a part of you as your heart and lungs. And when they're gone, you can feel it as keenly as any wound. There wasn't a Vagrant in the Scar hard enough to convince you they didn't miss home.

Including me.

Yes. I missed it. I missed comforting fires and parties with nice whiskey. I missed a house with a garden and a bed with real sheets. I missed the esteem, the favor, the *love*—even if it was for what I did for the Imperium instead of me, I missed it. I was tired of being hunted, tired of being hated, tired of running a road that just got longer the more I ran it.

And I was tired of losing her.

Riacantha didn't know about Liette. Or the thing inside her. If she did, we'd be having a different conversation. But she didn't need to know for me to see the possibility.

The Imperium. The mages. One of them, hell maybe even *all* of them, could pull that thing out of her. Summoners had tamed Scraths before, after all. And even if there wasn't one in Cathama, there were a hundred other nations in the Imperium I could go to. *One* of them would know. *One* of them could save her. All I needed was one out of millions.

And she'd be saved.

And she'd be herself.

And we wouldn't have to run anymore.

"Salazanca?"

I blinked. The images I'd had in my head—the moments of fires we'd built, meals we'd cooked, fights we had in our own house—slipped into the fog of my mind. Ghosts of dreams, imploring me to release them.

"Are there..." I dried my lips. "What's the catch? What else does she want?"

"Nothing." Riacantha grunted. "That was my other price. I told them you wouldn't surrender, you wouldn't recant, and you wouldn't apologize. You're Red Cloud, Salazanca. Thousands of us are alive today because of you. The Empress can eat a little bit of indignity in exchange for you laying down your weapon." She grinned. "And if she doesn't, she can eat a little bit of my ass and I'll happily tell her so."

She held out her hand, took ten deliberate steps forward. Her assistants tensed, but she waved them down. She stood there, in the clearing, in full view of me and my terrible weapon, facing us with nothing more than a scrap of paper.

And a promise.

A promise that the running was over, the fighting was over, the hurting was over, and I could just be with her again.

"I don't want your blood, Salazanca," Riacantha said. "And I don't think you want mine, either. And you and I both know that everyone we lost to this savage earth and its upstarts wouldn't want us bleeding each other. It can end here. I promise. To Salazanca, to Red Cloud, to whatever name you want me to promise to and to however many times I have to say it. You can come home." She drew a breath. "All you have to do . . . is put your steel away."

My eyes lingered on her, on that short little woman with the big fucking gloves and boots. She'd barely changed at all. No scars, no wounds, not even a gray hair.

And when I looked at her, I still saw the woman who broke down the gates at Obstinance alongside me and covered me as I went in. I still saw the woman who let me win in arm-wrestling one time because I had a bet going. I still saw the woman who stayed up with me, closing out the drink halls after every battle, whether we lost or won.

She was the same old Riacantha.

And maybe I was different now, but . . .

"Salazanca?" She spoke, soft and urgent. "Please?"

I looked down at her. And I saw that hopeful little grin. The same one she'd given me when she pulled rubble off me and when she was about to go try her luck with a fellow at the bar. Riacantha. As much my friend as she'd ever been.

And in that moment, I knew my answer.

I looked down at her. I met her smile with one of my own.

Riacantha ki Camathusula.

Bad Neighbor.

The Empress's finest Siegemage, hero of the Scar Campaigns.

My dear friend.

Broke my heart to shoot her.

SIX

SIX WALLS

The first time I met Riacantha, we were on the same ship bound for the Scar. We hit it off, after we hit each other, over the last remaining bottle of Avonin & Sons whiskey. The days we spent drinking and laughing before we landed were magical.

The days after, less so.

We could hear Revolutionary cannon fire ten miles from the beach. And an hour later, they were beating down the gates. Two hours later, our defenses consisted of two overworked Wardmages struggling to keep the doors up against the pounding fire of tanks and machines. By noon, half our mages had been taken out by Revolutionary weapons and our entire company was ground under the wheels of their tanks.

Bad way to go.

Less bad than what happened next, though.

Riacantha arrived first, just before the Wardmages were spent. She waved them down, the only people standing between her and the massive mess of steel and powder on the other side. When they left, she sat and waited for the doors to break.

But when that took too long, she did it herself. The Revolutionaries were stunned—both from the fact that the gates had fallen and from the fact that the gates had just fallen on them. Riacantha leapt atop the doors, met their tank barrel-first. It unloaded, an eruption of fire and carnage that washed over her like a tide.

When it passed, she stood, unfazed but for the hair that had been singed from her head and a slight look of annoyance across her face. And before they could flee, let alone reload, she took up those big gauntlets and...well...

I don't know if you've ever heard what sound people make when they're crushed inside a metal shell, but I don't recommend it.

Either vengeful or just annoyed, she dragged the mangled, bloodied mess that had been the tank all the way across the plain to the Revolution's base.

And broke down their door with it.

The day after she earned her name, Bad Neighbor would earn many more legends: the Battle of Thon's Sorrow, the Battle of Claybowl, each one with its own stories and atrocities.

But for me, I don't think I knew her until that day when the doors came down and the tank started firing.

It was a Resolute Jaws of Purifying Flame, a new piece of technology we hadn't even seen. A barrel of bombs and fire that could punch through steel gates. The fire that belched out of it was so intense, burned so bright I had to shield my eyes. The nul staff we had on hand fled, lest they be incinerated by even looking at the thing. When it cleared, the gates had been melted down and the ground had been cooked and the sky had been painted black.

And Riacantha had just stood there. Small and delicate at the center of that devastation. And all she wore was that little, irritated expression.

Kind of like the one she was giving me now.

Altrocus and Simivo looked up from the cover they had sought, expressions aghast. The earth where the Cacophony's shell had struck was torn apart, sundered by sound and force. Trees were split apart. Rocks were pulverized. The dirt of the earth had been rent away in a great gash.

Riacantha stood at the center of it. Her clothes were ragged, having almost been torn off her back. Her hair was a frizzled mess, damn near shredded from her scalp. Her face was contorted in mild ire.

"Fine." She sighed, let the scraps of the letter of pardon fly out of her hand and into the breeze. "Fine. We'll do it your way."

She held out a hand.

"Simivo?"

The sullen lad—I fucking knew he was a Simivo—stood up. His eyes flashed purple. The distant song of the Lady, grating and discordant, filled the air. From the devastation, the massive, shattered trunk of a tree levitated unsteadily into the air. Simivo's outstretched palm guided its huge, splintering weight to Riacantha's hand.

A Graspmage. She had a fucking Graspmage.

Should have shot him first.

If I came out of this with my spine intact, I'd make a note about that.

The little woman's shape disappeared beneath the tree trunk as she hefted it over her head in both gauntleted hands, spread her legs out in a stance, aimed it like a spear, and—

Oh, right, I thought. *Should probably be running.*

I spat a curse, wheeled Congeniality around, and gave her the spurs. She didn't need the encouragement, tearing off into the twisted labyrinth of the hills and leaving the mages far behind us.

This wasn't good.

I know that seems fucking obvious, but it's one of those things that's *so* not good that it warrants remarking from the regular not good.

Shenazar. Riacantha. Mages upon mages upon fucking mages. If there was anything that could have been worse than a dragon, it was this. The way they'd signaled, organized—this wasn't an accident. The dragon hadn't been a random woe on the road. It had been waiting for us.

For *me.*

Now it and every fucking Imperial in screaming distance knew where I was.

But not her, I told myself as I pressed low against Congeniality's back, the dead trees whipping around us as we tore through the labyrinthine hills. *They don't know where she is. And they're not going to fucking find out.* I narrowed my eyes on the rock-strewn, branch-choked trail. *Six Walls. Same plan. Get them there. Start a fight. Get the fuck out. You can do that. You just need to make sure nothing else—*

Sound in my ears. A distorted song. The Lady Merchant's.

Now why in the fuck did you have to go and think that?

I saw a flash of purple. Altrocus, smiling like he was just so damn happy to see me, appeared in a burst of light atop a nearby hill. His eyes locked upon mine for a second, his brow furrowed in calculation. With a glance, he looked farther down the road and extended a hand. Purple light swirled as a portal opened in the sky overhead.

Right in my fucking path.

Lovely.

Riacantha fell out of the sky like a meteor, gauntleted fists hammering into the earth as she struck. The earth vomited, choking on bile of pulverized stone and shattered roots that came sweeping over me, a cloud of strangling horror. I fought to keep control of Congeniality's reins and my breath alike as I scrambled to pull something out of my satchel.

"Ah," the Cacophony lamented, his chuckle hot and painful in my ears. *"Rather makes one contemplate what would have happened had we simply gone with Steel Python, does it not?"*

"Hoarfrost," I choked out, coughing. "*HOARFROST.*" I slammed a shell into the chamber, aimed it into the cloud. "Go for the heart. She'll shrug off anything else."

"If you insist."

I pulled the trigger. The hammer clicked. The cloud flashed blue as the shell struck out, gathering frost from the air and coalescing into a savage icicle. Jagged, it tore a freezing scar through the cloud as it shot into the dust and landed with a heavy, painful *thunk*.

"You got her?" I gasped.

I shouldn't have hoped.

The dust dissipated. My icicle stood, twinkling and glistening in the fading light, perfectly impaled in something that was *not* a dangerous Siegemage I wanted to kill. The tree hovered before Riacantha, nearly folded in half by the icicle jutting through it. Simivo, beside her, waved a hand and tossed both the tree and my last chance at ending this nicely away.

"All your fucking promise, Salazanca," Riacantha growled as she started stalking toward me. "All that we went through together. And you'll throw it all away for what? Money? Fame? *Power?*"

I froze, eyes fixed on the woman approaching me. My brain scrambled for something—a joke to stop her, an explanation to soothe her, a threat to make her pause for *just* a little bit.

And in all the time I spent looking for a lie, the truth slipped out.

"Love," I said. "This is for love."

She paused, looking for a moment like that answer might have just—

"Birdshit."

My mistake.

I scrambled for another shell. She burst into a sprint. The earth shuddered with every stride she took. Congeniality flailed beneath me as the earth shifted beneath her. I couldn't get my fingers around something. The Cacophony burned in my hands. The Lady's song burst out.

"Altrocus, enough." Riacantha waved off the purple portal that blossomed into being beside her. "I don't need a portal."

Altrocus appeared beside Simivo, furrowed his brow. "That portal's not—"

There was a great cracking sound. A surprised cry. Riacantha's form went hurtling into a tree. And then through it. And then two more before she skidded to a stop against a colossal boulder.

"Mine...," Altrocus finished, eyes wide.

Agne stepped out of the portal, sparing a glance for me and for the two wilting mages before looking to the fist that had just put one of the Imperium's legends through a pair of oaks.

"*Tch*," she sighed. "Scuffed my knuckles. I knew I should have worn gloves." She paused, glanced to Riacantha's quivering associates and quirked a brow at their uniforms. "Dear *me*, but is *that* what the Imperial fashion is these days?"

"Agne," I sighed, spurring Congeniality forward.

"Classy, colors match, just a *hint* of tastefully exposed skin—absolutely gorgeous," she continued, studying their garb as they cringed away. "Ugh. How unfair. Before I went Vagrant, we all wore the same dreary, menacing black thing. Terrifying, I'm sure, but no individuality. Now, if the Imperium had been handing out uniforms like *these*, I might not—"

"Agne."

"Oh, excellent." Agne acted like she just now noticed me, perking up. "Unfortunately, the twins are unable to join, as they're experiencing a *touch* of difficulty farther behind. They wanted you to know that—"

"I don't fucking *care* right now," I snapped. "It's not just a fucking dragon, Agne. They *knew* we were here. I have to keep moving and *you* have to get the hell out of here."

"Yes, I'm sure it's all very scary," she said in the way that only a woman who can take a sword to the face without blinking can. "But I did promise the twins, and I would absolutely love to find out where these two gentlemen got their—"

A shriek. A crash. A burst of earth.

Riacantha came flying out of the underbrush, hurling into the sky and falling upon Agne with a crash. Agne let out a shriek as she went falling to the ground for the first time in Lady knows how many years. Riacantha's gauntlets worked mechanically, shuddering as they pummeled the taller woman, making the trees shake and the rocks stir on the earth.

With a snarl, the little woman seized Agne by her ankle and, with both hands, spun and hurled and...

Well, I don't know if you've ever seen a six-and-half-foot-tall woman be thrown into the sky by a four-foot-nothing woman, but under different circumstances, that might have been noteworthy.

Under the current ones, however...

I put the spurs to Congeniality, sent her speeding back down. Riacantha glanced up as Congeniality took a flying leap over her. I took the opportunity to put a boot in Altrocus's face as we rushed past—anything to slow that fucker down.

I couldn't stop to finish him. Either of them. I had to keep going. Had to keep them on me, off Agne, off Liette, off everything.

I spurred Congeniality forward, ready to pivot once I broke out onto the open fields that led to Six Walls. There was no way their lookouts hadn't seen this carnage; their cannons would already be trained on us by the time I emerged.

I gritted my teeth. I clenched the reins. I roared as we tore out onto a flat, featureless plain.

And if I'd had the breath for it, I would have screamed.

No grass. No rocks. No trees. Just a vast circle of soft earth. No walls. No towers. No cannons. Where I had hoped to find my salvation—and the ass-ton of guns and soldiers that came with it—I found only earth.

No.

How the fuck? My fevered mind raced against itself for answers. *How the fucking* fuck *did I fuck up the directions? I was* sure *that Six Walls was here. I was* certain. *Where is it? Over there? Where?*

I searched the horizon of the hills. No towers or cannons peered over their crowns, no banners flew against the gray skies. I couldn't see so much as a fucking cottage. The only decoration that broke up the endless beige of the earthen circle was a single banner, impaled in the earth and flapping against the breeze.

And it wasn't Revolutionary.

The Imperial flag flew here, solitary and smug, denoting no place of import and celebrating nothing save for the utter joy of how fucked I was.

Breathless and boneless, I slid out of Congeniality's saddle. I rummaged numb fingers through the saddlebags, grabbing a handful of metal and sliding them into my satchel. I swatted her on the thigh, gasped out into the wind.

"Go. Go now."

She warbled, chirruped, but didn't hesitate before she took off running into the hills. She and I had an understanding, one that kept us together all this time. We weren't going to be able to outrun them on open ground and no one in the world had ever said "fuck Sal the Cacophony's bird, specifically."

This was going to end here. No need for both of us to be around to see it.

She vanished into the grass. I breathed in the cold gray. I closed my eyes, fumbled a shell into my gun, and turned to meet them.

And they were many.

Smoke came roiling out of the hills, memories of the carnage I'd tried to flee catching up to me. Light flashed in the gloom, portals opened as sores on reality. And from it, they emerged.

Veiled Embermages, steam and cinders trailing off their shoulders. Graspmages, their panoplies of weapons wielded by phantom grips forming halos around their heads. Doormages, their belts laden with divining tools. Siegemages, dead-eyed and empty. They filtered out of the smoke, coming to assemble in military order behind a great swirling portal.

Riacantha emerged, her pets at her side, to affix me with a glare. The wind whistled overhead. Shenazar, skies swirling around her, came swooping out of the clouds, herald for the great reptile that followed. The dragon's wings beat away smoke and debris as it landed at the head of the mass of mages, folding its wings neatly and craning its head aloft to regard me with terrible animal ire.

The Imperials stood at attention as a wisp of a woman ascended the horned crown of the beast's head.

Slim as a stiletto, face sharp as a sword, wit like a hammer—she stood, white hair cropped so short and severe around her angular face and purple eyes, draped in her military garb. She folded her hands behind her and stared down at me contemptuously.

Velline ki Yanatoril.

Decorated Imperial warrior, captain of the Hellions squadron, recognized by the Empress herself for valor and loyalty. We actually might have gotten along famously, except she somehow acquired the ludicrous idea somewhere along the line that I was a threat to peace, stability, and life itself for some weird reason.

"Velline," I said, looking up at her as I wrapped the Cacophony's hilt in both hands. "No imperious demands for surrender and lists of my crimes?"

Velline shook her head slowly. "No last curse of defiance in a pathetic bid to bide time?"

I glanced around the empty field. "No, I think I'm pretty much fucked here." I clicked my tongue, raised my gun. "You want to just do it?"

She didn't answer except to slide into a stance, hand on the hilt of the black blade hanging from her belt. Her eyes were focused on me, flashing purple as the magic flowed through her and the song called to mind.

Theater. Pageantry. We both knew it. She was a Quickmage. The Lady Merchant made a deal with their kind, granted them superhuman reflexes, the ability to move faster than the eye can connect and clear immense distances in the blink of an eye. And in exchange, the Barter she takes...

Well. I guess it doesn't matter.

Point was, we both knew how this was going to end. Even if I could pull the trigger faster than she could move, there's no way I'd hit her before she was upon me. The only reason she was hesitating was because she wanted to know where I was going to aim; I could see in the tension of her stance. After that, I'd hear the Lady's song once more and then...

Maybe that doesn't matter, either.

But I was tired. Tired of running. Tired of trying and failing. Tired of fighting. Tired of hurting. If this was where I had to die, I wouldn't fight it. I wouldn't have it said that Sal died begging or flailing. Instead they'd say that Sal the Cacophony held her gun out, closed her eyes, and heard the song of the Lady Merchant...

"Oh, fuck. OH, FUCK."

And when Sal the Cacophony realized that last bit hadn't been her, she opened her fucking eyes.

An Embermage with a truly impressive set of lungs was currently shrieking, flailing wildly, and struggling violently. Which made sense.

If I was also in the process of being pulled eight feet off the ground by a gigantic puppet, I'd be upset, too.

The creature emerged from a nearby copse of trees, its lacquered, skeletal limbs unsettling camouflage for the surrounding deadwoods. Its body awkwardly bobbed this way and that as it swept silently forward, the Embermage in its grasp struggling to free a limb. The captive leveled his arm at the puppet's leering face, a harlequin nightmare of clownish color and empty glass eyes, and unleashed his power.

Flame swept out in a torrent over the thing's face, a gout of fire under which the puppet's face disappeared. Rather than collapse, the great mannequin made a rattling sound, a disembodied echo I only barely recognized as human.

"Rude."

The puppet seized the Embermage's offending limb, snuffing out the flame. Its harlequin face seared black by the fire looked all the more unsettling, its makeup molten and in greasy streaks across its wood. It took the mage's other arm in its free hand.

"I didn't even get to introduce myself." The puppet hoisted the screaming Embermage in both hands, held him aloft before the enraptured assembly of Imperials. *"Now I've got to be all fucking dramatic."*

The puppet's wooden digits creaked as they clenched together.

And pulled.

The shrieking ended in a spray of red. The Imperials who were still capable of horror recoiled away from the grinning harlequin face, glistening with the insides of their former comrade, as it turned toward them.

"Poneir the Curtain." The puppet made a morbid imitation of a bow. *"At your service."*

"A Vagrant!" Velline shouted to be heard over her troops' own panic.

Worse.

"A Dollmage."

I muttered that part. No one else heard me. Not that it mattered.

A Siegemage leapt forward, a massive spear in her hands. She hurled it at the colossal puppet. The mannequin shuddered as the spear burst through its chest in a spray of splinters. But all it succeeded in was making the morbid marionette look even more unsettling.

"I just *said to let me introduce myself."* The puppet seized the Siegemage in one hand, hoisting her up. *"Do they just not teach manners in the Imperium anymore? No wonder everyone fucking leaves."*

Dollmages, see, have an interesting power. They can project their consciousness and energy into almost anything that isn't alive: weapons, machines, one time a book of dirty poetry. Which doesn't *sound* too interesting compared to mages that shoot fire and lightning.

But I guess that's why she had the giant puppet made.

"Attack!" Velline shouted. "Destroy it!"

"Unsporting."

Another voice. Another verse of the Lady's song.

Another fucking Vagrant.

Velline was forced to whirl, faster than human eyes could catch or human reflexes could move. Her blade shot out, narrowly shearing the frigid icicle that had been aimed for her chest. She glared at the roiling cloud of frost that blossomed out of the nearby woods.

And the fur-clad, masked Frostmage that emerged. Her grin was lazy. Her skin was pale blue. Snowflakes had been tattooed across her arms, the only skin visible beneath layers of frost-rimed furs.

"We worked hard on our introductions," the Vagrant said, crystals of ice swirling menacingly around her fingers. "Now there is no time for even Grini the Scalpel to introduce herself." She pouted. "Mean."

"Stay out of this, Vagrant," Velline snarled back. "This is Imperium business. We have no quarrel with you."

"Damn shame, that," the puppet rattled. It hefted the Siegemage like a mace. *"Because I've got a quarrel with you, your fucking Empress,* and *your fucking army that took my life from me."*

And brought it down.

Two bodies disappeared in a spray of red.

"Ah, but we can talk about that later."

"Yes, yes. Introduction time is over, I think," Grini the Scalpel said.

She threw her hands into the air. Frost burst out in a bright spray of cold and white. The Imperials froze, waiting to see what kind of attack this was.

I, however, being able to recognize a signal the *second* time I saw one, was already limping away.

My validation came a second later. With swords, war cries, and foul leathers. Bandits streamed from the woods and the hills, shrieking wildly and waving their weapons as they came crashing into the ranks of Imperials to join their leaders.

Flames erupted from the crowd before Embermages were dragged beneath hacking steel. Doormages vanished, reappearing behind bandits to skewer them with short blades. Riacantha cursed as she struggled to fend off the massive puppet currently swinging her own comrades' corpses at her like they were clubs. Bandits swarmed over the dragon, roaring and hacking at its wings and throat and any soft part they could find as the rider desperately tried to fend them off.

Ordinarily, I'd have called a bandit clan insane for attacking an Imperial regiment, Vagrant-led or no. But this wasn't your average clan—their hides were reinforced by metal, their weapons sharp enough to cut through armor and scale. Where they fell, they got back up. Where they cut, they cut cleanly. And where they killed, they wasted no time before moving on to the next.

They were everything you didn't want bandits to be: organized, equipped, and terrifyingly sober.

Through the brawl, Velline struck. Her eyes flashed purple, her steel flashed silver, as she disappeared, inhumanly quick, to reappear elsewhere, striking down bandits and relieving her comrades. She was a whirlwind of destruction, a storm contained within another storm. Breathtaking. Magnificent. Ferocious.

I assumed, anyway. I was about three hundred feet away by then. Not like I was going to fucking stick around.

Don't get me wrong, this was still bad. Tangling with Vagrants strong enough to command bandit clans never ended well. And the Imperium wouldn't be stuck messing with them forever. And if I'm honest, whoever is still alive at the end of this is still going to want to kill me and the hills will be alive with them looking for me later, along with anyone I happen to be with.

The Scar is a terrible, dangerous place. But it's a terrible, dangerous place for everyone and sometimes that works out for even the unluckiest asshole.

"Holy shit, is that Sal the Cacophony?"

Sometimes. I said sometimes.

A quartet of bandits, laggards from the brawl, moved to stand between me and the hills I needed to get to. The leader of them, a young lady with a bright smile and what I *think* was a severed foot hanging from her belt, smiled at me from behind her swords.

"Wow!" she said. "You destroyed my village when I was a kid! It was amazing! I always wanted to meet you."

"Yeah, well," I grunted. "Here I am." I hefted my gun, tried to hide how much my arm shook holding him. "Kid, you don't want this."

"She's right." One of her companions put a hand on the bandit's shoulder. "Poneir and Grini said that she was off-limits if we found her."

"Poneir and Grini said a lot of things," the bandit growled. She hefted her weapons; others did, too. "Poneir and Grini say too many things..."

The ground shifted. My arm shook. One of them took a step

forward. My arm dipped a little. Her smile grew wide with recognition. She hefted her blade, started running at me. The Lady's song filled my ears. I could see myself in her steel. The sword came down.

So did her arm. Unattached to her body.

The bandit paused mid-charge, looking dumbfounded down at her limb, still clutching her sword, lying in the dirt. Severed so neatly at the joint of her shoulder, it barely even bled.

Not that it stopped her from screaming.

She screamed, flailing her stump of an arm for as long as it took her head to be severed along with it. Her body hadn't even hit the floor before two bandits started fleeing, getting narrowly away before a pair of deep gashes appeared in their backs, their muscles cut so harshly they folded in half where they stood. The last remaining bandit looked at me, then at her suddenly dead comrades, and dropped her sword.

"You're right," she said, "I don't want—"

The Lady's song rang out. The wind whistled. She fell to the ground, pawing absently at the wound in her chest that hadn't been there a moment ago.

Magic. Some fucking mage. Some fucking Imperial. I didn't know.

I kept my gun up, searching the air for whatever assailant had just struck the bandits down. Magic? A new weapon? I couldn't afford to think what it had been. I kept my guard up for a moment longer before I fled.

Beaten. Exhausted. Bloodied. Bruised.

But alive.

Alive as I ran into the hills.

Alive as I limped into the brush.

Alive.

If it mattered at all.

SEVEN

NEW VIGIL

"What's a Dollmage?"

Sal glanced up from the spot on the floor she'd been glowering at. "Huh?"

"You mentioned a Dollmage." Ozhma shuffled some papers. "A... Poneir the Shawl?"

"Poneir the Curtain," Sal replied.

A muttered curse, a few scratches. "Poneir... the... Curtain. Okay. And what does a Dollmage... do, exactly? It involves dolls, I gather."

"Sometimes, yeah," Sal replied. "A Dollmage can pull their own consciousness and energy out of their bodies and into inanimate objects. The ones with foresight and money like to have their effigies custom-made. And Vagrants have plenty of both."

"Terrifying... but also that's really impressive."

"Right?" Sal paused, squinted across the table. "Are you taking notes?"

Ozhma paused, glanced up from the scribbled-upon papers in her hands. "Uh... yes?"

"Why?"

Ozhma furrowed her brow, offended in a way she didn't know she could be. "I've been asked to act as envoy and I take that seriously, thank you very much. Any job worth doing is worth doing well, after all." She held up a hand pointedly. "*Especially*, I'd like it emphasized, when the threat of imminent annihilation and mass death is a lingering possibility. We haven't lost sight of that goal, have we? I hope? Right?"

Sal held her stare for a moment. A grin spread across her face, imperceptibly slowly. Ozhma tensed at the chuckle that ensued—*typically*, when people capable of massive destruction start laughing, it's not for a good reason—but the dry laugh that came out of the woman was...weary. Remarkably, relatably weary. The Vagrant leaned over and elbowed the person next to her.

"Where'd you fucking get her?" she asked. "She's adorable."

Galatatian ki Zanzora, Imperial emissary, looked up from the fourteenth bloodied handkerchief and gaped at her beneath the ruin of his shattered nose.

"Are you not aware," he uttered contemptuously, "of the grievous insult and injury you visited upon my person?"

"Fuck me, are you still hung up on that?" She reached down beside her chair and pulled out a bottle of brown liquid, thrusting it toward the Imperial. "Have a drink and forget about it. Wait, hang on." She pulled it back, uncorked it, took a hasty few swigs. "Okay, now you can have it."

Galatatian sneered at the bottle, causing his ruined nose to start bleeding again. She shrugged and glanced across the room, to the Revolutionary agent standing immobile in the shadows, eyes fixed and ears open.

"How about you, sadpuss?" She winked, waggled the liquor bottle suggestively. "I know it's against Revolutionary Mandate, but we're all going to die anyway. Do you really want to get blown to pieces having never gotten shit-faced before?"

"*Do you mind?*" Somewhere inside her, Ozhma knew it was probably not a wise idea to take that sort of tone with a woman who'd just finished telling her about how many people she'd killed, but manners were manners. "The severity of this task is *enormous* and

I'm sure we would all appreciate it if you could at least *feign* concern for it."

"I *just* said we were all going to die, didn't I?" Sal shrugged, took another swig. "What the fuck do you want from me?"

"Acknowledgment," Ozhma said. "Acknowledgment that this is serious."

"I never said it wasn't." Sal yawned, sprawling out across her chair. "This is how I deal with serious situations."

"You're drunk."

"And you're all pissed off and flustered. But when we all end up dying in a sea of carnage, *I'll* still be in a good mood."

"How can you talk like that?" Ozhma shot out of her chair, clutching her notes before her like a shield. "How can you make this seem so... so..."

"Effortlessly attractive?"

"Awful."

"Okay, see, I knew it was one of the two."

"*STOP THAT!*" Ozhma's objection came out breathless and belabored. "The Revolution has its guns poised on this city. The Imperium has its mages at its gates. The *Ashmouths* are in this. People will live and die based on what *we* do in this room and I don't think it's unreasonable to ask that you put some fucking effort into..."

She had the words, excoriating and insightful, right there on her lips. But they wouldn't come out for some reason. Her mouth tasted too dry, all of the sudden. Her breath was...

Gone.

I can't breathe. Poison. She fumbled for the water cup she had been offered, saw it still untouched. *Wait.* Urgency punched through desperate thoughts. *There's no air. There's no fucking air!*

Ozhma's eyes, now wide with terror, darted from Sal to the envoys. Each of them wore looks of strain, struggling with the same lack of air. But as none of them had been in the middle of screaming, her situation felt slightly more desperate. She clawed at her throat, gasping and struggling for breath.

But it wasn't there. And neither was sound. The noises she made, the desperate and breathless pleas for aid, were silent in her ears. Air had vanished. Sound had disappeared. When she fell to the floor, she did so noiselessly. Her hands scrabbled against the wood in her desperation to claw herself to the door and escape. But the pressure inside her chest made her feel like she was about to explode. Everything was smothered beneath the sensation of her lungs being crushed. Everything but a thought.

No, she thought. *Not yet. I still have so much to do.*

Darkness crowded her vision. The world went black, along with silent. And Ozhma slid into a void.

Then. Cold. Damp. A noise, distantly heard though heard all the same.

"Hey. Stay with me."

And then, the breath.

So clean and cold that it damn near sheared her lungs. She drew in a flurry of desperate breaths, hungry to hold on to them before they were snatched again. A hand lay upon her back, rubbed her gently.

"Easy. Easy. Slow breaths. Deep breaths. Like that."

Funny thing.

There weren't any stories about it. No one told tales. Hell, maybe no one even knew she could. But when Sal the Cacophony, killer of men and bringer of woe, held Ozhma gently and helped her to sit up, it felt...

"What happened?" Ozhma gasped, suddenly aware that she could hear herself—along with the other two envoys, who lay gasping on the ground. "We were talking and you were being an asshole."

"All right, you ingrate," Sal grunted, "just die next time, then."

"And then... and then..." Ozhma rubbed her head, now pounding as breath stirred it awake. "No air. No sound. I couldn't..." She shook her head. "How did that happen?"

"A reasonable question." She glanced over at the envoys as they struggled for breath. "Dick-nose, you got anything to tell her on that?"

"The Imperium does not...does not..." Galatatian managed *some* form of indignity, to his credit, before descending into a coughing fit and hurrying for the door.

"No?" She glanced at the Revolutionary Agent Insightful. "How about you, friend? Do you want to tell her?" Sal stood up, held her hands out wide. "About Culven Loyal? About the weapons *you've* got?"

The agent glowered at her but said nothing. Sal sneered back at her.

"That's the ugly part, isn't it?" she chuckled. "All your fancy Revolutionary propaganda, all the speeches of your Great General about liberation and freedom from the Imperium, but you don't even need an *excuse* to start dropping bombs on people, do you?

"And *that*," Sal said, spitting pointedly toward the feet of Ozhma, "is why I don't take this shit seriously. Because they sure as hell aren't and neither should you. Negotiations, diplomacy, decorum—all the same fucking shit. Foreplay from a bunch of people with a lot of weapons and money justifying why they're about to fuck everyone."

The agent opened her mouth to retort, but settled instead for a scowl as she skulked away and out the door, followed by a litany of curses.

"That's what I fucking thought," Sal roared after her. "Ask the kitchen to loan you some oil so you can grease up before you crawl back up the Great General's asshole. And when you get there, tell him *and* his fucking Revolution to come back when they're fucking serious."

The door slammed. The room shuddered. Ozhma, now conscious enough to feel disgust, winced as she tried to get up.

"That was not helpful," she groaned. "They aren't going to cooperate if we keep alienating them."

"They aren't going to cooperate..." A hand seized Ozhma by her arm, hauled her swiftly to her feet. "Because they aren't here to negotiate."

Sal took a long swig of whiskey as she helped Ozhma find her balance. She then glanced warily at the door before thrusting the liquor into Ozhma's hands.

"Drink this, sit down, and shut the fuck up," she muttered. "They'll be gone, but not for long enough."

"What?" Ozhma, too confused to resist, allowed herself to be sat down into a chair. "Wait, what are you talking about? How do you know they'll be gone?" Her eyes widened, realizing for the first time who she was alone with. "Will... will they be back?"

"No, dumbass, they're the kind of messengers that leave a room where sound and air disappeared and *don't* tell it to their superiors. It'll take some time for them to figure out what the fuck just happened and who to blame for it, but they will." Sal took a seat, grunted at the cup in Ozhma's hands. "Drink."

Without thinking, she took a sip of bitter liquor and felt it settle like a cinder in her belly. "But you said it was them who caused it, right?"

"I didn't say shit. I *implied* it was them because they don't know neither of them has something that *can't* do that."

"Oh. Wait, what? So you lied?"

"Fucking drink," Sal growled, provoking another sip. "I wasn't lying, either. *None* of us are getting out of here alive if *either* the Revolution or the Imperium gets an opportunity. The only reason they *haven't* is because they don't have what they want yet."

"They want an end to the violence," Ozhma said, taking another drink instinctively. "Why wouldn't they? I saw what happened on the battlefield. It was carnage like I'd never seen before."

"Carnage *you'd* never seen before," Sal replied. There was something different about her voice—urgency smothered her previously flippant tone, her words as hard and cold as her eyes. "You really think nations get as big and rich as theirs by caring about how many people have to die? They could turn us into ash from a hundred miles if they felt like it."

"You're exaggerating," she scoffed. "I've known plenty of Revolutionaries *and* Imperials and they're just like anyone else."

"Fucking *drink*." Sal groaned, running her hands over her face. "Yes, I'm sure you *have* known a lot of good ones. Yes, great, you're an icon of rational diplomacy and I swear to the Scions I'll sing your praises and go between your legs after all this is done if you'll just *listen* to me."

"I'm trying, but..." Ozhma glanced over the Vagrant, her many scars and fearsome tattoos. "Like, you *know* what people say about you, right?"

"Yes, I..." Sal paused, narrowed her eyes. "Wait, what do they say about me?"

"That you're a killer."

"Okay, just checking, I—"

"That you're a destroyer."

"Yes, I get it, but—"

"That you caused this whole fucking war, all these fucking Vagrants, all this...this *blood* just as easily as you brush snow from your shoulders. There are *no* stories about how reasonable and good at *not*-killing you are." She met Sal's gaze. "And frankly, I believe them."

Sal sneered. "Birdshit."

"I assure you, it's not—"

"It is." The furor slid from Sal's face, revealing an unsettlingly confident grin. "Because if you really thought I was a liar, you wouldn't have come here." She leaned forward, the shadows making the crook of her smile all the more unappealing. "And if you really thought the Imperium and Revolution *wouldn't* kill everyone, you wouldn't have agreed in the first place."

"I'm *here* because a dangerous Vagrant is threatening thousands," Ozhma snapped back. "I'm *here* because even if I hadn't heard the shit you've done, I've *seen* the shit you've done. I've traveled all over this forsaken spit of earth and worked with everyone under its sun and *none* of them have ever done *anything* half as violent as you."

"None of them? *None of them?*" Sal snarled back, leaping out of her seat. "I am *one* woman. One woman with a big fuck-off gun, sure, but just one woman. I don't have armies. I don't have states. I don't have cannons or magic or tanks or dragons. You can call me the most violent person you've ever met." She leaned forward, her sneer curling her scars into briars. "But I'm just the only one whose name you know."

Ozhma was not *necessarily* a confrontational woman. Her parents had always encouraged her to find a solution that made everyone happy—or at least, less mad. And though she knew life would never be easy enough for that to work all the time, she prided herself on three things: her calm, her wit, and her ability to handle conflict.

"Oh *yeah*?" she slurred as she staggered out of her chair. "Well, *you're* a huge bitch and I'm fucking leaving!"

She did not pride herself on her alcohol tolerance.

Sal shouted something back at her, but the whiskey was boiling behind her eyes. She staggered unevenly away, pushing the door open—or trying to, before she realized it opened the other way—and storming out.

Cold air seeped through the dirt walls of the cellar. Beads of sweat became clammy on her face—she hadn't realized how hot it was in there. She hadn't even stopped to notice why that room had been so gently warm and this room had been so . . . so . . .

She paused, looked back over her shoulder. The door hung ajar, glimpses of the room and its furnishings and charming lighting shining bright behind it. She glanced back to the dingy, dirty, lightless cellar before her. In all the energy and anger and almost-getting-her-head-bashed-in, she hadn't really stopped to wonder . . .

It wasn't possible.

None of it. None of this.

A city being simultaneously attacked by both the Revolution *and* the Imperium? An exquisite room fit for a Freemaker in the middle of a dirty cellar? A city *surviving* a simultaneous attack by both the Revolution and Imperium?

The thoughts had struck her, here and there, like hail on a tin roof. And between everything else, she'd let them simply slide off of her, convinced herself she could get answers, convinced herself she *wanted* answers. But only now, with her brain stewing in a pool of liquor and the collar of her dress tightening around her neck, did she start to realize.

I shouldn't be here, she gasped inwardly. *I'm a fucking booze seller. I'm a fucking girl from the townships. I'm not... I can't...*

The pressure built inside her, grew terrible claws and teeth. She could feel it gnawing on her spine, bending her head low, sending her vision swimming. It was hard to breathe.

The Cacophony. She was caught between the Revolution, the Imperium, and the fucking Cacophony. *All* of them wanted something—what, she didn't know—and *all* of them were willing to kill people—how much, she didn't know—if they didn't get it, and all of it relied on her—*her*, short and fat and small and weak—learning exactly the right thing to... to...

Actually, fuck this.

The only thought left.

Fuck this, fuck that, fuck all of it.

In between the hurried sound of her footsteps as she rushed for the stairs.

Fuck her, fuck them, fuck it.

She grabbed the door, threw it open, stumbled forward, and collided face-first with someone's groin.

So things *could* get worse. She knew that now. That was good to know.

The figure that had appeared in the doorway moved swiftly out of the way, allowing Ozhma's drunken stumble to complete itself gracefully by collapsing to the floor in a gasping, sweating, drunken heap.

Somehow, this was *always* the moment pretty people started talking to her.

"So." Cavric, with his square jaw and kind eyes, looked down at her as she lay there, panting. "It's going well down there?"

"Yes. Good. It's great. It's well. It's perfectly well." Ozhma managed a single manic smile before exhaling. "Uh... am I going to die?"

"At the moment, no. Sal's a lot of things, but she's not the type to kill someone like you. In the long term..." He looked over his shoulder, to a trio of people hurrying a grievously wounded woman to a cot. "We'll see."

He extended a long arm to her. The sleeve of his coat had been rolled back, exposing a long length of dark-skinned, muscular forearm. He held it there, expectantly, as she quietly took in its calluses, its weathering.

Its size.

But before it could get *too* weird, her hand shot up and took his arm. He hoisted her to her feet with just one hand, but she could feel the weariness in his grasp, and hear the exhaustion in his sigh.

"That first part is good to know, I suppose," she said, dusting her dress off. "How did you meet... er... Madame Cacophony?"

"I tried to help her and she put her gun in my face."

Ozhma's smile fell. "And you consider *that* to be a good gauge of her character?"

"Well, give me a break, it was a long time ago," he replied as he turned and trudged off. "At the very least, she didn't kill *me* when she kidnapped me."

"That... wait, what?" She hurried after him, neither willing nor really all that able to return to the room below. She shouted to be heard above the bustle of the command room, pulled her body in and out of people's way as she followed the tall man through the crowd. "She's a kidnapper, a murderer, *and* a Vagrant?"

"Really, that last part covers the first two, but yes," Cavric sighed, the sort of sigh that suggested he had anticipated this to be a one-or-two sentence conversation and was sorely disappointed.

Which Ozhma might have felt bad about, under normal circumstances, but he had nice forearms and she had no desire to return to the lunatic woman below. And, she had to admit, she had a *real* nice whiskey buzz going.

"I really hate to criticize plans of actions established prior to my arrival," she said, "especially since I'm *sure* that so many people worked hard on it, and I really, *really* don't want to be seen as someone who can't handle the task set before her but..." She winced. "Is... that woman *really* the person best suited to handling negotiations?"

"No." Cavric's answer was terse and worryingly straightforward. "In what I would call a reasonably informed opinion, I don't think Sal the Cacophony should be handling any productive task more complicated than stirring soup." A pair of soldiers rushed forward, seizing his attention with a hushed conversation. With a nod, he clasped their shoulders, whispered something in return, and sent them scurrying off. "Even then, I wouldn't be surprised if she ended up using the pot to kill someone."

"All right, so..." Ozhma dabbed at sweat that was no longer there. "Can I ask then, why—"

"Are you serious?"

He froze there, tall and rigid in the middle of the tumult. And beneath his eyes, wide and wild with exhaustion and stress, the chatter and outbursts of the command room seemed to go quiet. Or maybe it was just her.

Her eyes were fixed on him. For the first time. Past the handsome face and strong arms, she could see something else. Shoulders that had been stronger now slumped beneath his coat. Hands that looked so capable trembled at his sides. And even though he was tall and big, she could see by the fit of his clothes that he had been much stronger, much less tired, once.

He'd buried himself beneath his stresses and his fears. It was all he could do not to disappear beneath them entirely.

"Because she's the only thing *they're* afraid of," he said, pointing toward a door in a vague gesture. "Thousands of Revolutionary soldiers. Mages so thick it looks like a fucking cheap opera out there. Birds and tanks and beasts and monsters and *all* that's holding them back is her."

"Surely, the soldiers here—"

"Are farmers. And hunters. And carpenters and bartenders and fucking butter-churners," he replied. "New Vigil isn't..." He caught himself, drew in a breath. "We're not idiots. We all knew that the Imperium and Revolution wouldn't tolerate us building a new city with their leftovers. But I thought we'd have more time. This place was just a bunch of villages before we started building walls and... and..."

He teetered a little. She swept forward, concern overriding drunkenness, standing uncomfortably close to him. She seized his arm, pulling it onto her shoulder, steadying him right before he collapsed.

He weighed much less than she thought he would.

"Easy," she whispered intently, pulling him close. "Easy. Lean into me. Don't let them see you fall down."

He nodded, the wisdom apparent to him as she helped him lean against a table. This was an old trick, one taught to her over and over by the wealthy and the strong she served. Powerful people couldn't be seen flinching. Not bandit kings, not rich collectors, and certainly not him.

"Sal is... not my first choice for handling this. But how the fuck was I to know there would be a *this*?" He rubbed his eyes, drew in a deep breath, and turned to a tin kettle on the table. He gave it a test, nodded at the sloshing sound within. "I'm irritated at her, but she's not the one pointing a thousand cannons at my city. *They* are."

"Sir, forgive me, but—"

"Just call me Cavric, please. I don't want to get used to authority."

"Okay. Cavric." She fought to keep the delighted squeal from her voice. "Forgive me if you've already thought of this, but... that's Sal the *Cacophony*. It certainly seems to me that having that *weapon* of hers inside the walls is just as dangerous as a thousand outside."

"Yeah?" He glanced at her, his face too weary to be curious. "Have you seen it doing anything?"

The air. The sound. The room.

The thoughts pattered against her head, slid off, and were discarded. She had no idea what that was. It might not have been the gun. It might not have been anything. And frankly, she didn't feel like it would benefit her, him, or the people he was protecting to add that burden to him.

"You're right," he said with a sigh as he poured himself a cup of visibly old and stale coffee, either not realizing or not caring as he sipped. "I know you're right. Everyone here who's heard even a *little* bit about her knows you're right. That weapon is unholy. It shouldn't be within six miles of a decent family, let alone inside the walls of a city."

"Then why?" Ozhma asked. "Surely, limiting her role would appease the Imperium and the Revolution."

"It would."

"And that would save more lives, wouldn't it?"

"Very likely, yes."

"Then..." She winced. "Can I ask?"

Cavric's finger returned to the cut on his cheek. He thumbed it thoughtfully for a moment, stared at his bloodstained fingers before rubbing them together. They smeared, the blood turning to a thick brown, sludgy as his coffee.

"Because Sal can only kill us," he said. "They can do worse."

She blinked. Her memory scrambled against his words, flooding with memories of the regal smiles of Imperial buyers and the earnest grins of Revolutionaries. Hard people, she remembered, as she had known many hard people. But kind, as she had hoped everyone was beneath that hardness.

"Sir... Cavric," she said, "I don't think I can agree; I've known *many*—"

"I know you have. So have I." He pushed back his long mane of black hair in a vague imitation of a military cut. "Deserter here. Left the Revolution some time ago. I served with some men and women I thought were the greatest soldiers I'd ever seen. Hell, I still think they are.

"But that's not what's fighting us. We aren't fighting good people. We are fighting the Imperium. We are fighting the Revolution. They have more weapons, more magic, more people, and more money than we do. We can't hold out. And everyone here knows it. Just as they know that if we fall, it won't be death that awaits us."

She swallowed a dry, painful breath. "It can't be that bad."

"It can and it is," he replied. "They didn't come here to kill us. They came here to take us back. They came to dismantle our homes and our bodies until we agree to do things their way, to keep serving them so they can keep fighting. They'll spare most of us. Maybe all of us. But we won't be who we are anymore. We'll be back under their control."

His gaze grew distant. His face grew tight.

"And the story of New Vigil, how we stood against them and it was all for nothing," he whispered, "will be another story they use to break everyone else. The Imperium and the Revolution can take away our history, our homes, our ideas. Sal can only blow everything up." He sighed, knuckling the small of his back. "And the story of how New Vigil cast itself to ashes instead of agreeing to go politely into the fire? Well, it's not great, but it's better."

The door burst open suddenly. A shout, something between a command and a plea. A body draped between people, bleeding and motionless. Someone caught Cavric's attention. He shoved the mug of coffee into Ozhma's hands, took off running toward the commotion.

She could only stare at him as he left, unable to comprehend what she had just heard.

He's insane. She swallowed another painful, nervous breath. *He wants to die.* She glanced around the command room, saw all the people there embroiled in their tasks, not an ounce of fear on their faces that she could see through her heavy breathing. *They all want to die. They're going to die. I'm going to die.*

Her eyes were pulled toward the open door. And without realizing it, she felt herself walking toward it. No one noticed. No one even looked at her.

Just leave, she told herself. *Just go. Tell them you made a mistake. Tell them you're not feeling well.*

She made it halfway across the floor. No one did anything more than run around her.

Tell them you can't do it. Make up something. Or don't make up something. Do anything, please, just do anything. Just leave.

She made it to the threshold, licked her lips.

Tell them there's nothing you can do. That's the truth. You can't do anything. You're in way over your head. You can't do anything. This isn't where you need to be. You can't do anything.

And she froze. A cold blast of air hit her. An uncomfortable thought.

Right?

She stared down into the coffee. A distorted face looked back at her.

Ozhma. Plump and happy merchant's daughter. Saleswoman extraordinaire. Quivering, scared little girl. Helpless. Useless. Incapable. Too scared. Too small. Not enough.

She stared at her face. She brought the coffee to her lips, took a sip.

She smacked her lips. Blanched. Threw the rest of it out the door.

And then she turned around. And started walking. And she made it to the cellar stairs and the hall and the door. Until she finally found herself sitting in that room once again, across from Sal, who regarded her calmly.

"Ready?" she asked.

Ozhma closed her eyes. Nodded. Opened them as she felt the whiskey cup being pushed back into her hands.

"Oh, um," she said, "I'm ready to hear you, I don't need to—"

"I know you don't. *I* do." Sal grunted as she took a swig herself before returning it. "Trust me, this will be easier if we're both a just a *little* shit-faced."

Ozhma opened her mouth to object.

But then . . . if Cavric trusted her . . .

She sighed, threw her head back, drained all four fingers remaining, and tossed the cup aside.

"All right," she said, pausing to belch. "Go on."

EIGHT

THE SCAR

The adrenaline wore off. The pain set in. These legs didn't seem so strong anymore and this body felt so damn heavy.

I didn't know how far I had run. I didn't know if I was safe. I didn't know a fucking thing except that I couldn't go another fucking step.

I stood there, swaying unsteadily on legs turned to jelly and breathing ragged breaths through overworked lungs, waiting for the blow. The dragon's breath. The sword in the neck. The fireball from a mile away. Whatever Imperial or Vagrant or bandit was going to kill me.

It didn't come. They weren't going to kill me.

Pity.

I collapsed. I fell to my knees. I fell to my hands. I tried to keep the salt out of my eyes and the pain out of my back and just get the fuck back up on my feet and just pick the fucking gun up and just get to Liette and the others and try, fucking *try*, to make things get better.

But I couldn't.

I couldn't run anymore. I couldn't try anymore. I couldn't even breathe.

I opened my mouth to take a breath, but all that came out was a choked, wet sound. A noise born of a pain with no language, a wound with no treatment. It tore itself out of me, spilled itself onto the air as I let out a long, slow wail.

And I wept.

I'm not a person who cries often.

I don't mean that I'm tough or something, I just mean that I don't cry. I've seen so many things, taken so many hits, pulled so many triggers that I somehow forgot how to do it somewhere along the road. And it wasn't anything I saw or touched or felt that made me collapse and let the tears fall out and stain my fingers.

It was what I knew.

This was it, wasn't it? This was everything in my life now, right?

More running, more pain, more waking up wondering if the knife that I can feel waiting for me in the dark is real, more nights spent looking at the horizon wondering how far I'd have to run before I could forgive myself for leaving them all behind, more time wondering how the fuck I'd fucked up so fucking hard that I did all this and it was never going to get better and everything I did and everything I wanted to do would end with me broken and wheezing and dying on the fucking earth, just as fucking alone as when I started.

Alone. But for him. But for the thing that keeps killing. The thing that I brought with me. The thing that I couldn't even put away without it hurting.

"We must go."

Him.

"There is nothing left here but ashes."

The brass thing in the ground next to me. My tears sizzling as they dripped off my face and onto his. He looked at me through that brass. Steam began to rise along with his anger as he saw me, dirty and broken and weeping.

"Must I repeat myself?"

And I felt his heat seeping into my skin. And I felt his anger crawling into me. And the tears didn't stop, even as I tried to force them.

The Cacophony doesn't have pity. Or remorse. What little he had that was human got burned away, bit by bit, day by day. So I didn't know why he stopped himself, why he retreated back into his brass and the heat left me. I didn't know. I didn't care.

"Perhaps we can rest. For a bit."

All I did was roll onto my side and cry. Cry for what was never going to end. Cry for all the things that had gone wrong. Cry for the fact that his heat had died down and, just for once, something didn't hurt.

If only for a little while.

I couldn't get up. I couldn't keep getting up. I couldn't keep getting up and keep falling down and keep fucking up and keep ruining everything and keep doing it over and over and over with no end in sight.

I couldn't.

So I made the decision. I felt the cold, hard earth under my body. The skies swirled cold overhead. This was fine. It was cold here. Quiet. If they buried me here, no one would come to visit, no one would get ideas, no one would get hurt. It'd be over.

And so I closed my eyes. And I stopped trying to hold back the pain. And I waited to die.

Hours. Minutes. Days. I didn't care how long I'd waited or how long it was going to take. I wasn't going to get up this time.

When I heard the heavy footsteps crunching in the distance, I thought about calling out to them—but what would be the point? When I heard them getting closer, I thought about getting up—same thing. I didn't even bother opening my eyes until I heard them right on top of me.

And felt the big beak nudging me awake.

Badlanders are good for a lot of things. They can run for miles on very little water, they can eat and digest anything, and in a fight, they do to other birds what forty-pound spenders do in five-pound brothels. But they're not exceptionally good at sympathy. Which you could tell by how much she kept nudging me despite my attempts to die peacefully.

And when I finally cracked open an eye and beheld the big *where the* fuck *is my dinner* expression on her face, all I could do was weakly try to swat her away.

"I found her wandering the outskirts of the forests," her voice came ahead of her footsteps, tiny feet crunching on sand. "She was acting hungry, but refused to eat."

I didn't open my eyes to look at Liette. But I felt the cringe scar itself across her face anyway.

"I even tried offering her some..." A pause to swallow a gag. "*Entrails.*"

"Those are supposed to be a treat for her," I muttered. "And you're supposed to be with the caravan."

"I am supposed to be where I need to be."

"Meret needs you."

"Obvious lack of confidence aside, he's demonstrably capable."

"Go back to the caravan."

"I invite you to get up and try to make me."

I sneered. "I am not getting up."

"You cannot get up."

"I am *choosing* not to get up."

A pause. "May I sit down, then?"

"I don't own the land, do I?"

"You do not." She daintily brushed away the earth beside me before smoothing her skirts beneath her and sitting down. "But I'm sure if you did, you'd have built a tavern here by now."

The silence that hung between us was the worst kind. Not the tense silence before steel is drawn or the solemn silence when it's put away. This was the silence of the blow to be struck, the wound to be carved, the pain that's yet to come.

"Imperium's gone," I muttered.

"I noticed," she said. "You succeeded."

Doesn't feel like fucking success.

I wanted to say that. To tell her that this didn't work, that this wasn't worth it, that none of it was. But I didn't.

We're never going to make it to Ocytus. This is not going to end.

I wanted to say that. Just to hear her call me stupid and list all these amazing reasons why that thought was completely mistaken and of course we'll make it. But I didn't.

I'm sorry.

I didn't want to say that.

But I did.

"I'm sorry."

The tears came with my voice, the strange and misshapen pain coming back into my throat.

"I'm sorry." I wiped them off my face with the back of my hand. "I'm sorry that I fucked up and got us into this. I'm sorry that I keep fucking up. I'm sorry that you're stuck here with me instead of… of…"

"Of what?" she asked softly.

"Of being happy. Of having a nice little shop somewhere and making clockwork mouse toys for neighborhood kids or something, I don't know."

"Your vision of my circumstances without you is offensively saccharine. Children would never be able to appreciate my craft."

"You should go to Ocytus," I said. "On your own."

"No."

"You could make it there yourself. Probably easier, even."

"I don't dispute that."

"I'm weighing you down. As long as I'm near you, I'm going to burn you, Liette."

A pause. "I don't dispute that, either."

The earth shifted. I felt her warmth pressed up against me. I felt her hand on me, fingers delicately tracing the jagged curve of my scars and frayed edges of the dressings on my wound. I felt her breath on my throat, warm, as she wrapped an arm around my neck and pulled herself into the hollow of my throat.

"Then," I started to breathe out, "why don't—"

"Don't ask me that," she whispered. "Don't ask me why. I'm not going to know why for a long time, and even then, I might not be sure."

I could feel the close of her eyes. That long, slow breath she took in and held softly, like she did whenever she was about to solve a problem or get a present. But the sound that left her lips was new. It was a breath—as hot with exhaustion as any of her others—but it was a different kind of exhaustion, a different kind of tired. The kind of tired that came not from fleeing and from pain, but of long days with warm drinks at the end and long nights of sleep. And lying there, my arm around her, her skin against my scars and her head on my shoulder…

Well, shit, I could almost feel it, too.

"I choose you," she muttered, "instead of why."

It happened slowly. Shapes blooming in the dark around me. Nature ordering itself beneath us. The dirt sorted itself, gave way to hardwood floors bedecked with carpets that weren't possible. From the dark and the fog, walls were born, arranging themselves into a gentle square and sprouting bookshelves, a hearth and more, furnishings growing like thorns from a flower. A roof. Windows. A door.

A home.

It had come from a dream—hers, mine, the thing inside her, I didn't know. It had assembled around us in the long slow draws of our own breaths. A house for a life we'd never had, a home for a future we'd never thought about.

The ground stirred beneath us. The floor shifted once again, gave way to something soft. A bed with silk sheets and vast pillows rose up beneath us, the bed we always wanted to wake up in.

It was our life. What it could have been. If we were different. If I was better.

"Liette," I whispered, too tired to say more. "You're doing it again."

She didn't answer. Her breathing was quiet and deep. She slept peacefully against me, dreaming of a world I could never give her, a home we could never build. And that thing inside her…

The Scrath...

Eldest.

It made it into reality.

I should have woken her up, stopped her. But I was exhausted, and she was warm against me and... and...

Fuck.

Maybe I wanted to know what it felt like, too.

Just for a little bit.

We lay there. The sound of Congeniality rustling in the underbrush as she searched for bugs outside. The swirl of clouds, heralding faraway storms to come. The feel of these four walls, this soft bed, this dream...

It was still the Scar. Still the worthless land that was always worth killing over. Still full of monsters, human and otherwise. Still the field of the war that would burn us all.

But that land, that small patch of earth and sky and dream on that night, that was ours.

And I held on to it.

Until my eyes grew heavy. And I drifted away, following her.

And we both disappeared.

"Cacophony."

A splinter of a voice.

"Are you dreaming, Cacophony?"

Embedding itself in my skull.

"I cannot tell from here."

And tearing open a hole from which my dreams drained.

I stirred to consciousness at the beckoning of my throbbing head. It felt like... an out-of-tune flute, a sharp whistle of an incomplete note, ringing out behind my eyes. I rose to my rear, crept from the bed Liette had dreamed into reality, and left her sleeping there.

My eyes were locked upon the door. My body tensed. My hand drifted down to the floor, to the leather belt that lay there.

"Come outside."

The words. I heard them. I felt them.

"Let me see for myself."

Not for the first time.

I couldn't explain it. It was a voice like a scar. A pain came from listening to it, a stretch of skin and a spark of ache. I knew it. As keenly as I knew my own scars. As keenly as...

Steam filled my nostrils. Heat pricked at my fingertips. My hand wrapped around a black hilt, pulled his glimmering brass free. He looked at me through his metal eyes, his joy gleaming in them.

Whatever was happening, he didn't want to be left behind.

I crept out of the house that shouldn't be, pushed the door open. The night air hung still and humid, damp with the clouds roiling overhead. Grasses swayed gently in the breeze slowly pushing the storm toward me. Only the most determined moonlight could make it through the cloud cover. I loved nights like this.

Only...

Normally, there was sound. The insects and birds that usually bantered through the night were quiet. But even the distant hills and woods were silent, as though not a beast in creation wanted to draw the attention of the predator that walked that night.

Can't say I blamed them. I would have gone quiet and run for it, too.

But that would be rude.

After all, this predator had invited me specifically.

It took me a minute to see her, the old woman standing amid the tree line. She stood so thin and humble, just another pale and withered trunk among the many dead things, that I didn't see her at first.

But once I did, I couldn't stop looking. I saw her feet, bloodied and dirty and shoes hanging off in scraps of leather from the miles she'd walked without rest. I saw her body, haggard and thin from sweat, wrinkled skin rippling like water with every wheezing breath. And I saw her eyes...

But she didn't see me. Her neck was bent, her head wobbling bonelessly backward, mouth open and eyes fixed blankly on the cloudy sky overhead.

"Apologies," she rasped, with that voice...that splintering, sharp voice that sawed through me. *"I am to understand it is considered rude to interrupt one's rest. I confess, it is difficult to understand the limitations of your vessels."* Her lips curled up into a smile as her knees shook. *"As you can see, this one is almost spent."*

I wanted to scream. I *needed* to scream. You don't get used to seeing shit like this, people worn like costumes, skin like clothes. But I swallowed that fear, forced it down into the pit inside my belly.

She—actually fuck, I can't call it a *she.* Whoever I was talking to, it wasn't her—this woman was dead, this shell wasn't her. *It* lolled its head around, contemplative.

"Ah. I can barely feel it," the thing inside her rasped, its voice echoing in my sinew. *"Your revulsion. Your horror. But you struggle to hold them back. Perhaps it is you who are being rude now."* Withered lips curled into a broad smile, so wide the skin at the corners of its mouth began to crack and bleed. *"Is it not custom to offer food to people you know?"*

"It is," I replied, at last, "but not for you."

"Do you not know me?"

"I know what you are." I narrowed my eyes at it. "But Scraths aren't people."

It smiled.

It smiled so damn big and so damn long that blood wept from the corners of the mouth of the body it stole and its gums pulled back over every ancient tooth.

It was enjoying this.

I still remembered it. I remembered this thing and its voice that peeled back my skin. I remembered it, on the decks of the airship that started this whole mess. I remembered it and the body it wore back then. That suit of flesh had been called Culven Loyal, adviser and loyalist to the Great General, leader and founder of the Glorious Revolution of the Fist and Flame.

But the thing inside it...the Scrath...had called itself something else.

"Leave, Wisest," I said. "I liked your old outfit better."

Blood wept down its face. *"I have not been called that name by anyone other than siblings. To hear it in your voice is unsettling. Do you intend to force me to go?"*

I didn't answer it because we both fucking knew I couldn't. There's power, there's *real* power and then there's a fucking Scrath. Existence looks away from them. They wear people like suits. They are incomprehensible, unbelievably powerful, and one of them was currently shit-talking me.

"Do you know why I am here?"

"Do you know how cold it is out here?" I growled in response. "You don't get to have mastery of reality *and* play dumb, you fucking shit. I know you're here for her."

"Not her." Its head rolled to the side again. *"My sibling inside her. I know Eldest is here."*

With a horrifying pop, the woman's head righted itself. Her eyes were sunken to black, empty pits. And within them...

Stars. Endless skies of stars.

"This is their work. Their creation. Their presence is made manifest." The vessel's empty eyes surveilled the tiny cabin. *"I had hoped I would have had enough time to handle this disagreement with the Imperium before that had happened. But perhaps it is good that I came when I did."*

"No part about you is good," I said, hand on my gun, for all the good it would do—even the Cacophony couldn't do shit to a Scrath. "Not you, not your presence, and not your fucking war."

"Our war," it corrected me. *"We made it together, you and I."*

My jaw wouldn't unclench enough to let me respond. The guilt came boiling up, white hot in my throat, and burned me like a fever behind my eyes. The scars and the pains and the memories of that day and all the days that followed churned in my gullet. I couldn't open my mouth to call it a lie.

But it didn't matter.

It knew, all the same.

"Ah." It craned its neck backward again, face delighted. *"You blame yourself. For all of it. You radiate it. I feel it as surely as you feel the sun."* Its mouth tore further. *"Eldest does, as well, you know."*

That guilt slid away suddenly. Left behind was the fear. As cold and naked as a blade in my spine. It coiled around me, choked me, forced the words to my mouth.

"Do not talk about her," I snarled, my hand curled around the Cacophony's hilt. "Don't you even *look* in her direction."

"Their long exile has worn away Eldest's senses," it continued. *"They feel you, but through her. They do not understand. They merely react. She houses a consciousness without awareness, a mind without fetters. It shall consume them both and—"*

"All right, fuck," I interrupted, rubbing my temples. "You're a Scrath. A being beyond comprehension. You do *not* get to go on like an opera villain. What the fuck do you want?"

"I wish to assist you." Its withered arms hung out wide. *"Permit me to collect my sibling, Cacophony. I shall remove them from their vessel, remove them from your concern entirely, and leave you in peace."*

I furrowed my brow. "Just like that?"

"As effortlessly as I describe," Wisest's voice rasped out. *"Eldest's thoughts are scattered, afraid. They crave safety. I can shepherd them, guide them toward clearer consciousness. Their thoughts shall be added to ours, their knowledge to ours, and the vessel shall be unharmed."*

"That 'vessel' is *mine*, you shriveled sac," I spat. "And birdshit she'll be unharmed. I've seen Scraths. I've *fought* Scraths. There's not an ounce of sanity in you, let alone mercy."

"Mercy is irrelevant to the procedure. Eldest's presence compromises the vessel's integrity. She will maintain neither form nor consciousness with prolonged exposure." Thin limbs stretched out. *"I am capable of extracting Eldest with no harm to the vessel."* It paused. *"Your vessel. There shall be no damage, you will not require even a moment's thought on it."*

"Yeah?" I sneered at it. This thing. "The last skin suit I saw you wearing was Culven Loyal's, one of the Great General's right hands. You're in the fucking *Revolution*, asshole, feels like you getting ahold of your sibling would probably end up being my problem, eventually."

"No more than usual, I conclude." The grin grew broader, bordering on genuinely amused. *"Are you laboring under the delusion that my influence dictates the Revolution?"*

"Are you denying it?"

Its head swiveled. *"Not entirely. I am merely part of guiding it on its way. More than capable of guiding it far away from you, Cacophony, if that remains a concern."*

"Oh, well when you put it like that, I am *much* less worried about handing more power to a reality-fucking, mouth-flapping piece of shit who's whispering in the ear of the guy with the most guns in the world. Thanks and fuck off."

"I am incapable of the desire needed for duplicity," Wisest responded. *"Though even were I, it would prove unnecessary. You have borne witness to my potential. You are aware of what I am capable of. I could acquire my sibling by force, if necessary."*

I squinted. "Then why haven't you?"

The Scraths are unknowable. Even the most coherent among them is so bizarre in their thinking that they're difficult to listen to for long. They don't act like humans do.

But the tense, timid silence that came from Wisest was about as close to human as they got.

"Why not kill me? Tear me apart? Make me disappear and reappear in the ocean or whatever the fuck you things can do?" I canted my head, as if I could see the logic if only I could find the right angle. "Why are you trying to negotiate?"

"Courtesy."

"Birdshit. You just said you weren't capable of desire; you expect me to believe you're capable of *courtesy*?" I kept my eyes locked on the vessel. "You may be beyond comprehension, but you're a shit liar." I took a challenging, and thoroughly unwise, step forward. "What are you *really*..."

My voice trailed off as the vessel jerkily backed away suddenly, gangly limbs flailing to put distance between us. I stopped, stared, and smelled the reek of burning in my nostrils...

I glanced to my hip, then to the vessel. Slowly, I raised the gun, leveled it at the vessel. His brass eyes gleamed, teeth broad and shining in his barrel. I felt him tremble in my hand—eager, excited... *alive.*

And the vessel scrambled backward again.

"You're fucking with me." My grin was low, slow, and not at all happy. "You're *fucking* with me." I couldn't help but laugh as I stepped forward, forcing the thing another step back. "All this you've put me through, all this stupid 'unfathomable' shit..." I held up the Cacophony. "And you're just as afraid of him as everyone else."

Wisest didn't deny it. It didn't have the capability to.

"What is it about him?" I wondered aloud. "Are you suddenly afraid of bullets? Fire?" I narrowed my eyes at it. "Or have you heard how hungry he is these days?"

He trembled in my hand. His brass rippled, shuddered, like he took a great breath in and exhaled a cloud of steam.

He knew. He knew I was talking about him. And he loved it.

"I am aware of your weapon, Cacophony." Scraths aren't capable of much emotion, but I liked to think there was just a bit of petulant spite in Wisest's voice. *"Though, it would seem you are not."*

"I'm aware he's making you look like a huge bitch."

Here's a point I'll come back to later.

If you ever get the chance to call an unknowable horror from beyond a bitch, resist the temptation.

"I can feel the weapon's anger. I can feel the weapon's consciousness." Wisest's head lolled back and forth on a shriveled neck. *"Yours has grown strong. Wise."* It paused. *"It is rare to see such a consciousness deign to receive orders from someone less potent."*

Okay, I know it's hard *not* to call them names, especially when they're acting like it, but trust me—

"Shut the fuck up and use whatever powers you have to fold yourself entirely up your own asshole."

—it'll come back to haunt you.

"I don't care what you want, I don't care what you have to say, and I sure as shit don't care to keep having this conversation," I snarled, as loud as I dared—I couldn't have Liette seeing this, *knowing* this. "And I don't fucking care which part of him you're afraid of, but so long as you are…" I raised the weapon, clicked his hammer back. "You come back here again, you come to me or to her or to anyone I so much as shake hands with, I will tear apart whoever you're wearing that day until I pull you out and let him slurp you up like a fucking noodle. Am I clear?"

No response. Not so much as a twitch.

"Am I clear?" I repeated.

Nothing. The body stood frozen. Not a breath, not even a twitch of muscle. It simply stood there, as if time had stopped for it and it alone. Was it thinking? Worrying? Or just fucking with me?

"AM I CLEAR?"

"I am aware of your intentions, Cacophony," it answered finally, still frozen. *"I am aware of your past and your future. All things that are and ever will be. As is Eldest. You cannot stop either of us."*

"I told you I'm not giving you—"

"Apologies for the miscommunication. I am neither requesting nor demanding. If you do not wish for me to take Eldest now, then I shall simply wait for the moment in time you beg me to."

"Fuck off."

"I have seen it. I have felt it. I am there right now. I can see the tears on your face, the broken body in your arms. I feel the pain… the rage… like a dream. Ah. But insubstantial. When I am able to experience it in the present, in person, I shall—"

I warned her.

It, sorry.

Hammer clicked. Bullet sped. Hoarfrost leapt from the barrel and formed an icicle, jamming through the vessel's chest and sending the withered form flying, ending with a spray of bark and splinters.

The vessel hung there, pinned to the tree. No pain. No screaming. Not even a flutter of lips as it spoke.

"Consider it."

The vessel's head swung backward, its eyes toward the sky. Its mouth, ragged with wounds and dried blood, craned open. From the old woman's throat, a great flash of light blossomed. An unsettlingly pale glow, undulating and writhing like a living thing, emerged from the vessel's mouth and trailed into the night air.

That light, alive with malign intellect, slowly ebbed this way and that. Contemplation? Or was it mocking me? I couldn't tell. And I sure as shit wasn't going to ask it to stay to explain.

The light slowly coiled off into the night, disappearing between the stars, and vanishing. Leaving me alone.

With the body.

I had to convince myself to approach it—

No, I reminded myself. *Not it. The Scrath was the* it. *The vessel was a person.*

I shouldn't have looked into her eyes. I wished I hadn't seen the wild fear in her stare, her skin stained with the salt of tears that had dried on her cheeks. Had she felt it? I wondered. Had she known? Had she been aware of the thing inside her, wearing her like a suit, helpless to stop it as it tore her body apart?

Is that what it'll look like, the thought crept, intrusive and impossible to stop, *when it happens to Liette?*

I didn't want it in my head. And I wish I could tell you I shook it out, like dust from my shoulders. But it stayed there, hammered itself in, as the Scrath's offer stung my memory.

Wisest could free Liette of the Scrath. Or so it claimed. I'd seen what that thing was capable of; I had no reason to doubt it. But... if a thing is unknowable and unfathomable, how *do* you know what it's going to do? And when I thought about it, about the power that Liette held inside her, in the borrowed hands of Wisest and its endless Revolutionary armies...

Well.

Some thoughts you have to make your mind an anvil against. No matter how hard they hammer, you have to force your skull thick and your thoughts slow and your hands busy. It's the only way to survive, sometimes.

And so I let that thought and that fear hammer my mind. And I let them bounce off my head as I sheathed the Cacophony and set to work removing the woman from the icicle.

No real point in it, I supposed. I didn't have it in me to bury her and burning her was only going to draw attention. I told myself it was to keep my hands busier than my head, to give myself something to worry about that wasn't a Scrath.

But looking back, as I made a hasty cairn for her in those hills, I can't help but wonder if it was maybe something simpler.

Maybe I needed to know that Sal the Cacophony, killer, warmonger, Vagrant, would not let a body so thoroughly abused languish without rest.

Maybe I needed to know that, whatever happened…

I could set things right, afterward.

Or at least, as close as I could get.

NINE

OCYTUS OUTSKIRTS

Ask the Freemakers how long they've been around, they'll tell you, "For as long as humanity has been gifted with imagination and burdened with an inability to realize it."

Ask them again after you've punched them in the mouth for being a pretentious twat and they'll tell you only for about a hundred years.

Their answer isn't necessarily wrong, mind you. Those who would pursue creation without regards for primitive notions of morality weren't uncommon back in the Imperium. Machinists who sought to replicate a mage's power, alchemists who used their arts to make intoxicating drugs, and Spellwrights who sold their respected craft to the highest bidder were active in the reaches of the Imperium.

It's just that it's terribly difficult to operate illegally in a nation where the authorities have scrying pools that can see anywhere. Crafters who didn't bow deeply enough for Imperial Law's liking were sniffed out, smoked out, and stamped out.

Except the alchemist drug peddlers. We just stopped at sniffing and smoking with them.

Get it? It's a drug pun.

I shouldn't joke, actually—thousands were killed.

Until the Revolution, anyway.

Once a power had been established that could not just stand up to the Imperium, but actually repel them, the renegade creators of the world got bold. They came to the Scar to practice their arts free from Imperial regulation—and later, once the Great General got tired of the secrets of his machines being pilfered, Revolutionary regulation.

Now, you might imagine it would take an awful lot to get a bunch of self-interested, highly intellectual, and emotionally stunted scholars to work together, but it turns out the ire of two world-crushing powers counts as "a lot."

Hence, Ocytus. Legendary city of the Freemakers.

Well, let me correct myself.

Hence, Ocytus. *Theoretical* city of the Freemakers.

Freemakers were disunited by intent and by principle. Each one of them was, by virtue of being a member, free to pursue their own goals without hindrance or contribution. This made it difficult for those who might want to know the location of Freemakers, such as one or two tyrannical governments, since no Freemaker knew of any other Freemaker's location or activity. As they were reclusive by nature, the idea of them gathering into one spot sounded insane to me.

Liette, of course, insisted that it was real. Not only was it real, it was hidden with such expert technique that no Imperial Scrymage or Revolutionary agent could ever deduce its location. Ocytus, she said, was a city so profoundly advanced in technology that anyone not in possession of a Freemaker's intellectual capacity—that is, approximately everybody in the world except for a handful of smarmy smart shits—would even be capable of imagining its existence.

Which was impressive and all, but Liette also once sent me an *incredibly* passive-aggressive ten-page essay after a discussion we had about which side of the basin the soap should go.

So what I'm saying is that she can be the slightest bit prone to exaggeration about certain subjects. *Particularly* subjects regarding the vast intellects of herself and/or her colleagues. Now, I know you're thinking that after all this time, surely I *must* know by now when Liette has the right answer.

There are plenty of geniuses in the Scar. Just like there are plenty of swords in the Scar. You can't survive out here without steel or wit, after all. But here's the thing about swords: most of them break. The only difference between a good sword and a bad sword is whether it's in you or not, after all, and they all end up littering the Scar's fields anyway. But there are a few good ones, here and there. Good not because of how many people they've killed or how much blood they've spilled.

A good sword, a *truly* good sword, is the one that's in your hand exactly when you need it.

Genius—Liette's genius—works the same way.

I truly believed that.

Right up to the point she led me to a giant pile of birdshit.

I placed my hands on my hips, surveyed the humble buildings that sprawled over a barren patch of land that broke like a boil on the edge of a vast sprawl of forest. The birdshit pile, one of many, courtesy of the various riding birds milling around, was merely one part of the artistic whole. The reeking stains on the earth were splendidly complemented by the rickety corral tended to by bored-looking stablehands and tied together by what appeared to be a large, splintering, inexplicably moist house masquerading as an inn.

I idly scratched a scar on my cheek, sniffed, got a big inhale of the scent of bird poop.

"You know," I said, "I'm not saying I *did* imagine Ocytus looking like this, but I *do* have the imagination to conceive of a corral full of birdshit."

I didn't look to see the glare Liette shot up at me. I could *feel* it.

"The fact that you believe a corral summates the whole of Ocytus is vocal proof that you, in fact, do *not* possess the qualities necessary to find it." She adjusted her glasses, looked back at the corral. "Furthermore, while I don't dispute the corral's *hasty* need for fecal control, it would physically be impossible to, as you suggest, literally fill a corral of birdshit."

"Uh-huh." I pulled my flask out, took a sip of pungent whiskey, handed it to her. "Here. You only get pedantic when you're nervous."

She crinkled her nose. "I do not drink whiskey."

"In a war, everyone drinks whiskey."

"Not when they require their wits about them." She rubbed her temples, took a deep breath. "I am going to say something, and under threat of my turning around and immediately leaving if you do, I am going to ask you not to comment on it."

"Sure," I said, taking another swig.

"I mean it."

Mouth full of whiskey, I rolled my eyes and gestured for her to hurry. She sighed, started walking toward the inn, then uttered the most profane thing I had ever heard her say.

"Not all Freemakers are as nice as I am."

I could feel a retort boiling in my throat and, being the nice person I am, made the immediate decision to attempt to drown it.

"While the occasional creator is moved to leave their impact on the world, to wit"—she paused to gesture to herself—"the vast majority of Freemakers are motivated by greed, vanity, and ego, in that order, caring for nothing else but satiety of those hungers."

"Am I allowed to comment on this part?" I asked. "Because you have taken many, *many* jobs for money."

"*In my spare time*," she hastily interjected, thrusting a finger in my face for emphasis. "The objective of my research has always been to improve the world, hence..." She caught herself, swallowing hard. "Hence my association with the Revolution."

Was that what she told herself? That it was about changing the world?

She'd sought to assist the Revolution in their unearthing of a Relic, an object of power that she and I would discover actually housed a being of inestimable power called a Scrath... the one currently living inside her, in fact. That's where the war had started, where all the trouble had begun.

And changing the world hadn't been the reason she'd given me.

"The past being the past and the present currently being on fire, I maintain that the intervention of the Freemakers could shift the tide to a stalemate. Long enough for sanity to reimpose itself and for the common people of the Scar to get clear, at least."

"And I maintain you'd have better luck asking a Cathama madam for a free fuck," I replied. "Appealing to the better nature of the Freemakers is like trying to drink a stone."

"For you, yes," she replied. "For one of their esteemed colleagues, it's..." She sighed. "It's worth a try."

I disagreed.

Like I said, Liette was a genius. And like every genius she occasionally forgets that everyone else, myself included, is the same terrified, greedy, violent dumbfuck we've always been. And the Freemakers were the smartest dumbfucks around. The chances of them being of any use in the war—on our side, anyway—were so slim you wouldn't bother eating them if you were starving.

So I disagreed. But I kept that to myself. Not just because I had no chance of convincing her, but because whatever plan she had to attempt to stir the charities of the Freemakers would keep her busy enough not to notice what I would get up to in her majestic imagination city.

Like I said.

I had two reasons for going to Ocytus. Both of them were to make her happy. But only one of them would get that thing inside her out of her.

"So what do you think they'll do?" I asked as we neared the inn's front door. "Build an Unfucking Machine?"

"First of all, that's not a thing," she replied. "Second, if it was a thing, it would have to run on some sort of fuel source dedicated to unfucking things, which does not exist. Third, if it *did* exist, there would not be nearly enough of it to unfuck everything that has been fucked so why the *fuck* would I bother building it in the first place?" She caught her breath, composed herself, took the doorknob. "I don't know. Hopefully I can at least convince them to stay out of the war. Maybe take the refugees in."

"That's what we came all the way out here for? To make the

refugees safe?" I grinned. "Why, my darling, I never knew you cared so deeply for them."

"I don't," she replied flatly, looking up at me from behind an appraising glance. "But you do."

My mouth pinched shut to keep me from swallowing my own tongue.

She was doing this for me.

For my guilt. For my fuck-up. For me.

Why the fuck couldn't she be awful like everyone else?

"Now, kindly maintain that image of quiescence for the next few minutes, if you please," she said, straightening her hair and glasses. "The way into Ocytus is fraught with peril and hair-thin paths, a single error is fatal and the very first step we take is behind this door."

I let the seriousness weigh upon me. I nodded once. The door opened and I followed her in, ready for anything.

"Welcome to the Rutting Sow!"

Ready for most things, anyway.

In what I was suddenly aware was a running theme in my life, I stepped into an extremely dingy excuse for a tavern. The common room was bare of everything but a few sorry tables with a few sorry dishes on them and an ancient voccaphone in the corner blaring out opera with such alarmingly poor quality that I was half tempted to shoot it and put it out of its misery.

But as sorry as the furnishings were, the people were worse. A young lady languidly wiped down a bar in the back. An older gentleman sat on the stairs leading up to what were presumably rooms on the second floor. Neither wore a hospitable grin, and the dowdy woman that had invited us in already looked bored with us.

"I'm afraid we have no rooms," she said as we approached. "You're welcome to rent out the stables for an evening, though. Assuming you don't mind the smell. But if you do, there's always . . . a . . ."

The woman trailed off, lips pursing in alarm as Liette stopped right in front of her. Which was understandable, considering Liette's face was about half an inch from her own. Her eyes narrowed, face hard and set in searching the woman's face for something. Apparently having found it, she stepped back, folded her hands behind her back and announced loudly.

"I do not require a room," she said, "but I would like a bottle of wine."

The young lady looked up from behind the bar.

"I'm afraid we do not carry wine," the older woman replied, cool and measured.

Ah, I realized, rolled my eyes. *They're doing some kind of password birdshit conversation.*

This sort of thing was exciting in operas, but dreadfully tedious in situations you could just as easily solve with threats and swears.

"There must be some mistake," Liette responded in deliberate fashion. "The grapes in this region are thick and they grow on steep slopes."

The older gentleman glanced up, pointedly.

"Ah, but I'm afraid the mistake is yours," the woman replied, just as deliberate, making me wonder what the point of a secret password was when everyone was going to be so fucking obvious about it. "This is a hop-growing region, famous for its ales, its lagers, its port."

Liette's brow furrowed. "Port's a type of wine."

The woman blinked suddenly, as though slapped. "What? No, it's a beer. This is a hop-growing region. I *just* said that."

"*No*," Liette insisted. "A port is a dessert wine. Port*er* is a kind of beer."

"Some people call it port," the young lady chimed in, then looked puzzled. "I'm... *pretty* sure I heard that somewhere?"

"Yeah, see?" the woman said. "Some people call it port."

"I've drunk the Scar dry," I offered, "and nobody I've met calls it that."

The air of the inn went dead silent. Every face in the room, Liette's included, looked at me with aghast expressions, like I'd just farted during an elegy. Sensing that I had intruded, I quietly raised my hands and backed away.

The woman looked back to Liette. "Is she with—"

"Yes," Liette said.

"And did you tell her we were going to be doing a password?"

"Oh, for fuck's sake, Daurine," the young lady groaned, "why do you keep *saying* it's a password?"

"*Don't try to change the subject,*" Liette interjected harshly. "Now, I don't know how you do password execution four hundred and seventy-one out *here,* but if you're going to say it's a hop-growing region, you damn well better have your terminology in order."

"Now wait a moment, wait a moment." The older gentleman chose this instant to interject, producing a large book and a pair of bifocals. "According to *Thalamann's Guide to Brewing, port* is a perfectly acceptable term for beer."

"Is that the first edition or the second?" Liette asked.

"What difference does it make?"

"The second edition had updated statistics on fermentation," Daurine offered.

"No, that was the *third...*"

All four of them, now adjusting spectacles that three of them had produced out of nowhere, descended over the open book, bickering and sniping and correcting each other with the linguistic precision of a lawyer with a gun.

"So, uh." I leaned close to Liette, whispered as loud as I dared, "When do you get to the password?"

"This is part of it," she replied without looking up. "Don't worry, these people are operating off of *vastly* outdated terminology. We should be done in an hour."

"Possibly two," the young lady offered. "Feel free to make yourself comfortable."

There was only one situation in which I wanted to see a bunch of intellectuals fight, and since I didn't see anywhere to place a bet, I waved her off and turned toward the door.

"Think I might take a piss instead."

"Oh!" The woman, Daurine, looked up as I stalked away. "Would you mind doing it on the north side of the building? It's looking suspiciously tidy over there and it might blow our cover."

"*Damn* it, Daurine!" the young lady snapped.

Now, keep in mind that I said the Freemakers were geniuses. I never said they were smart.

In fact, I'd say that they're the epitome of the ancient principle that keeps us from getting anywhere: the smarter you are, the dumber you sound.

For example, you might be smart enough to be part of an organization of the most brilliant minds in the Scar and still be dumb enough to ask a perfect stranger to piss all over your cover for authenticity.

I'd chosen a tasteful little spot between two flowerpots. I think Daurine would have appreciated that. Against the idle racket of the birds in the corrals and the hands tending to them, it almost felt peaceful. So peaceful I almost didn't notice the footprints.

Two perfectly shaped outlines of bootprints were painted in dust on a box that stood just beneath a tiny window. A window that peered into the room I had just been in, where the Freemakers were still arguing.

Someone had been curious.

And under ordinary circumstances, I might just leave it there.

But hell, I was in a good mood. So I hiked up my breeches, slapped on my belt, and went to look for someone to hurt.

I squinted, searched the dirt around the walls. I picked up the trail in short order and followed the tracks around the inn and toward the corral. But between then and there, the tracks got mixed up with dozens of others, disappearing into a fog of foot traffic. I glanced up. Around the corral, I saw the various disinterested-looking stablehands tending to their charges: watering and leading the birds, combing them down, distributing grains and seeds and animal scraps into their buckets.

Now, I'm sure these people, no doubt part of the farce that was the Rutting Sow, had plenty of good reasons to be listening in on the conversation in the inn. But I was also sure that they probably also had one bad one.

And, call me curious, but I wanted to know which.

I walked slowly through the corral, being certain to pass as close to the stablehands as I could. And once I did, I could sense it: their darting eyes, the nervous swallows, the palpable tension radiating off them. Each of these "stablehands" tensed up as I passed, more than any practiced hand would at the sight of a killer in the Scar. As I'd thought, they were the same as the three inside: smart people well unused to violence posing as normal Scarfolk. Charlatans. And obvious ones, at that.

Most of them, anyway.

It wasn't until I cleared the corral that I noticed him. Hell, I might not have, had he not moved. A young man, skinny and pale and with a mop of untidy hair, mechanically shoveled birdshit into a bucket. He didn't look at me, not so much as a stolen glance. He was perfectly calm around me and all my scars and steel.

That's how I knew.

I stood behind him, folded my arms across my chest, stared him over with a studying gaze. It's always good to let people you might end up killing know you're present—it's not just polite, it gives them a chance to do the smart thing and make this easy.

Which this fellow clearly was not.

But he also wasn't doing the dumb thing and trying to run. He simply kept shoveling, pretending I wasn't even there, like the most important thing in the world really *was* shoveling birdshit.

Honestly, if I ended up maiming a perfectly normal stablehand over this, I was going to feel really bad, maybe.

"If you need something, the inn's got food and drink," he said without glancing up. "I've kind of got a job to do here, if you don't mind."

"I don't mind at all," I replied, pointedly not moving. "And I don't doubt that you've got a job to do. I just have to wonder, though..." I narrowed my eyes. "Who are you doing it for?"

He tensed suddenly. Then he sighed, his shoulders slumping in resignation. He dropped the shovel and shuffled around slowly. He was doing the smart thing. I was impressed.

Until he suddenly broke out into a run, anyway.

He was quick, but he was frenzied, panicking. It wasn't hard to see where he was bolting, so it wasn't hard to cut him off there. He tried to twist past me and out the gates of the corral when I caught him by the collar. I swung him around, smashing his face into one of the gateposts. He let out a wail and, when I turned him to face me, a wet red stain painted his face.

"*FUCK!*" he screamed, going limp in my hands. "Fuck, fuck, fuck, my *nose*!"

"Shit, is it broken?" I asked.

"I don't think so."

So I headbutted him. There was a popping sound.

"How about now?"

"FUCK!"

"Yeah, I notice you keep screaming 'fuck' and not 'help,' like someone might if an incredibly attractive woman was about to beat the shit out of him." I took his right hand in mine, seized his little finger. "You're working for someone and I'm very tired. We can help each other out. Just tell me who."

"*Fuck you!*" he snapped.

" 'Fuck you'? I've never heard of any boss named 'Fuck You.' Does Fuck You have a guy who's good with broken bones?"

And then I snapped.

Or rather, he did. His finger, anyway. Fuck you, I said I was tired.

"*SHIT!*" he shrieked.

" 'Shit' is not 'fuck,' so we're getting somewhere." I took his ring finger. "The littler the finger, the easier it is to heal. You sure you want to do this the hard way?"

"FUCK—"

"Just say 'yes' next time."

Snap.

Another wail. This time, he didn't even curse. Good for him. I took his middle finger.

"Revolution or Imperium?" I growled, bending his finger threateningly. "Haven? The freeholds? Talk to me, friend, I'm on to the fingers you use to masturbate."

He just bit his lip, shut his eyes as tears bled onto his face. So be it.

Snap.

A scream. A formless, agonized noise of a scream. No confessions, no begging, no bargaining. And it was only then, only when I took his last finger in mine, that I began to worry.

"Talk," I growled. "Tell me who you're working for. *TALK.*"

Nothing. Not a damn thing except the sound of that last finger.

Snap.

And the scream that followed. Four fingers. Four screams. No answers. And I felt my blood run cold.

There was only one organization in the whole fucking Scar that someone feared enough to take four broken fingers rather than snitch on.

"Holy shit," I whispered, releasing him. "You're an Ashmouth."

He slumped to his ass, clutching his shattered hand. But when he looked back up at me, a grotesque grin was on his face.

"Bet you wish you figured that out four fingers ago, shithead," he said through a pained smile. "You scared now, bitch? You scared of the Three?"

"A little, I won't lie." I slid a hand to my belt, produced something hot, pointed it at him. "But tell me how you feel about this."

The man froze, staring with horror into the Cacophony's grinning barrel. Steam coiled off his brass, the metal shivering in anticipation. I squatted down, pressed it to his brow, the sweat sizzling off the barrel.

"We understand each other now," I growled. "What do the Ashmouths want here? What do the Three want with the Freemakers?"

"The Freemakers?" the man giggled, red bubbling in his mouth. "No. They're not interested in Freemakers. Not all of them, anyway."

Cold blood in my veins. Heart clenched in my chest. I couldn't remember how to blink or to breathe or to do anything but pull the trigger and splatter his skull across the dirt.

Liette.

My finger curled around the trigger. The gun shuddered with delight. The man's lips puckered.

Wait, I thought, *I didn't hit him in the mouth.*

And then I just saw fire.

Something sticky and hot splattered across my eyes. My vision went bright red, heat radiating across my face in painful waves. I screamed, clawed at my eyes with one hand as I blindly lashed out with the Cacophony in the other.

The fucker had been chewing some kind of alchemic, some searing sputum that burned my vision, blinding me. My hands argued with each other over whether to grope for my sword, claw the shit out of my eyes, or just keep snarling and flailing around with my gun.

Not like this, I screamed inside my head. *Not done in by some asshole with fancy spit.*

Hands seized me. I screamed. More hands grabbed me, held me down, shouting things I couldn't hear through the blinding pain. Something cold, thick, and uncomfortably viscous splashed across my face. My eyes went from blinded with panic to *nearly* blinded with how puffy and weepy they were right now.

It was enough of an improvement to see the chorus of stablehands encircling me as I lay on the ground in a puddle of thick stuff. At their center stood Meret, wielding a small bottle dripping with some manner of... of...

Well, I don't know what it was, but I know what it looked like.

"Sal!" he gasped. "Are you all right? What happened?"

"What happened is someone *spat* hot *shit* in my fucking *eyes,*" I muttered, clawing the substance off my face. "I am not all right, Meret. It is it physically impossible to be all right in this situation."

"Well, it can't be that hot if a simple alchemic neutralizing base could wash it off," a suspiciously intelligent-sounding stablehand said. "We keep it around for...well, not for stuff like *this*, but close enough."

"I set out ahead of the refugees," Meret said as he helped me to my feet. "I'd only just met these fellows when I heard you scream. Who *was* that person who ran off?"

"Aldondo?" one of the stablehands asked. "He's recent. He just came in from...from..." He furrowed his brow, looked to his companions. "Wait, which Freemaker did he say he worked under before us?"

"Uh, he was with...," another stablehand said, scratching her head. "I actually don't know if he told us."

"He didn't tell you because he didn't work under any Freemaker." I paused to press a finger to my nostril and launch something vile and phlegmy out the other. "He's a fucking Ashmouth."

Silence. The bad kind. And everyone's eyes went so wide it was as if they were terrified to blink, lest they should open them and find themselves looking down a blade.

To call the Ashmouths *criminals* is an understatement in line with calling getting stricken with gout, set on fire, and savaged by wild animals *a bit of bad luck*.

Except the wild animals would stop once there was nothing left to eat. The Ashmouths will pop your eyes out of your skull and make you watch your own face getting sliced off.

That's not hyperbole. They really did that, once. They had him carry his eyes and his face in his hands to the edge of a roof before shoving him off. Allegedly, it was because he had crossed them, but that's the thing about Ashmouths: you don't know you've crossed them until you're already dead.

"*Here?*" one of the stablehands said. "We've got to warn Ocytus! The Ashmouths are vicious! Violent! They'll cut our arms off and sew them onto each other and—"

"It's your job to shut the fuck up and let me handle it," I growled. "They're after *me*, not the Freemakers."

"Oh." The silence was broken by a chorus of relieved chuckles. "They're only trying to kill *her.* I thought for a second we were in trouble." A stablehand clapped another on the back. "I mean can you even *imagine*? My brother got in debt to an Ashmouth for *three* pieces of metal and they hacked off his hands. Right in front of him! I know! They're absolute monsters." And then he glanced back to me. "Anyway, good luck!"

The stablehands dispersed back to their duties. Meret remained. And he looked more terrified than ever.

"Ashmouths? *ASHMOUTHS?*" he gasped. "The *Three* are fucking after you?"

"No, idiot," I replied, wiping more shit off my face with the back of my hand as I attempted to blink the last pains out of my eyes. "That was just a lie I made up to get rid of them."

"You... what... I..." Meret drew in a breath, attempted as much composure as people like us could manage. "Okay. That's one hell of a lie, but so long as it's not—"

"They're after Liette."

"WHAT?"

"Keep your voice down," I muttered. "I haven't figured it all out yet. But since I'm not a complete fucking idiot, I'm going to guess a power-hungry gang of murderers is probably looking to seize control of the thing they'll think will give them more power."

"You mean the—"

"Don't say it." I looked up at him, deadly serious. "Don't you say the word."

"I... but then we have to tell her. She needs to know." He turned to go. "Where is she? We have to—"

Don't get me wrong, I love violence. I love solving complex problems quickly and sometimes with a brick. But that's because most of the people I use it on aren't like Meret. They're killers, not healers. They're cruel, not concerned.

So when I lunged after him, seized him by the collar, and slammed him against the wall?

Well...those are the times when I wished I was smart enough to know a better way.

"*We* need to keep our mouths fucking shut," I whispered harshly. "We don't know how much the Ashmouths know. We tell her, that thing inside her goes crazy in *full* view of every assassin watching this place—and I guarantee you there are—and suddenly they know *everything*."

"But...but..." He swallowed down his nerves, lowered his voice. "Sal, we *can't*. We just *can't*. Something like this, at a time like this, if she *doesn't* know..."

"She isn't going to have to," I said. "The Ashmouths aren't going to try anything drastic on the Freemakers' territory and once we're out of Ocytus, our problems will be solved."

He furrowed his brow. "How?"

I clenched my teeth. "I can't tell you."

"Of course."

"*YES FUCKING OF COURSE*," I all but roared, pressing him against the wall. "I can't tell you because I don't have time to tell you because, in case you haven't noticed, we are dealing with some weird shit right now. Whatever piffling knowledge you *thought* you had about the shit we're in, you need to let the fuck go of right now because you have no fucking idea, Meret. And I only barely have more of an idea, but it's still more than you. So maybe, *just* maybe, you can trust, this one fucking time, that I maybe know what I'm doing."

There are three reasons why I don't like working with idealists like Meret.

One is, as you've noticed, they actually tend to talk a lot of sense. It *would* be smarter to tell Liette if only because Liette was the smartest person in the room, if the room was the world.

But the second is that an idealist doesn't know people. They love people, want the best for them, but all their plans to do so begin and end with people making sense like they do—they've got a hundred ideas on how to make a land full of people who agree with each other better, but no actual clue how to get that first part working. And that doesn't work any better here in the Scar than it does in any of the other cities full of people turning indifferent ears to people screaming themselves hoarse that there's a better way.

But the real reason I don't like idealists?

"I... okay."

They believe you.

"Okay," Meret said, sighing. He laid a hand on my shoulder. "Okay, I trust you."

They believe that you can be better. They believe that you *want* to be better. They believe you when you say you know how to do that.

"The rest of the refugees are just behind me, so I should get back to them." He squeezed my shoulder, smiled. "We're going to get out of this, right?"

And somehow, these idealists, these stammering imbeciles with no idea how people work, no idea how people hurt themselves, no ideas at all beyond the hope that somehow things can be better are the ones you can't bring yourself to disappoint.

"Right," I lied.

He headed back toward the distant dust cloud signaling the march of the refugees, back to tell them that I had everything under control, back to tell them that things wouldn't be this bad for so long this time. They'd believe him. They'd keep walking because they believed him. And they'd keep believing him until they couldn't any longer.

I tried to tell myself that what they believed was their problem. I tried to tell myself that I could only look out for myself and Liette and that anything else would be a pleasant bonus, at best. I tried to tell myself this was true.

But then, I also tried to tell myself it wasn't my fault their homes were destroyed.

And maybe I was just too tired, too beaten up, too bloodied to realize I was full of shit.

I couldn't afford to think about it. I heard the inn's door slamming and hastily mopped at my face, hoping to remove any traces of the Ashmouth's spit and whatever that not-bird-semen-but-also-maybe mixture had been. When I turned around with a mostly clear face, Liette was walking out of the inn with the air of someone who had just left sixteen broken bones and a destroyed alehouse in her wake.

"We may proceed." She gestured with her chin toward the distant tree line as she removed her glasses and began to clean them. "My credentials proved adequate for purposes of entry. Word has been sent to Ocytus. We are expected."

"No shit," I said, whistling in appreciation. "How'd that argument in there go?"

And that woman.

That beautiful woman.

That woman with the eyes that got big whenever she got a new book, with the hands that tightened into little fists, with the smile that came so rarely and with such effort that I would eagerly burn this whole damn world down over and over, as many times as it took just to see it...

Well, she looked at me. And she put her glasses back on. And she gave me this little triumphant grin and said proudly:

"I used footnotes."

And I smiled back. And I put my arm around her.

"That's my girl."

And with her, I walked off to burn it all down once more.

TEN

OCYTUS

So, I admit, from my description of them, you might believe the Freemakers to be a ridiculous society composed chiefly of intellectualists so desperate to prove their imagined superiority over each other that they'll erect contrarian, puzzling nightmares of logic and conversation impenetrable to anyone who isn't so steeped in the perfume of their own shit to the point of being utterly incapacitated by high-minded foppery.

I'm not saying that the description is inaccurate, there's just a little more to it.

Liette wanted to see Ocytus for the same reason the Freemakers were very vested in people *not* seeing Ocytus. Their inventions routinely, and usually literally, shake the world to the point that any one of their members with sufficient free time could possibly shape the future of warfare on a whim. Usually for the worst.

But the idea of Freemakers using their genius to neuter the war wasn't too far off, either—clever leverage of their collective clout had persuaded more than one army to see things their way, after all.

However, for all their brilliance and inventions, the Freemakers were, by nature, an exclusive organization. So if you were to point out that the Freemakers were a tiny organization of egoists who, collectively, had seen possibly forty minutes of physical exertion put together, they wouldn't say you were wrong, they'd merely call that a feature of the design.

And they might be right.

But, genius or no, that left them in a poor position to resist the various armies, guilds, and organizations that wanted them subjugated or dead.

For all the weapons they could make, all the innovations they could discover, Freemakers had little hope of standing up for themselves militarily. They could make better machines than the Revolution, but the Revolution had millions who could use them. They could spellwright just as well as any Imperial, but they couldn't muster a squadron of mages to protect it. They could dissect the philosophy of the cultists of Haven to pieces, but it wouldn't stop said cultists from putting a machete through their skull.

Strength of arms was unreliable to Freemakers for purposes of defense. And thus, the strength of their own creations was likewise inadequate. So, with both those purposes out, they relied on the last possible defense that smart people had.

"Wait, didn't we just come through here?"

Making every fucking thing so pointlessly complicated that everyone else just gives up.

I put my hands on my hips, surveyed the meadow we had arrived at. Was I exhausted? Or drunk? Or both? I looked around the trees: same old trunks surrounding the same pile of dead thistles and wood that covered the meadow. Hell, it even had the same damn owl sitting in the branches and napping.

"We came through here, yes, but only on the *first* leg of the journey." Liette extended her hands wide over the meadow. "The way to Ocytus is *through* this meadow once, then around and through it again, then one or two more times, depending on which day it is, and it is..." She squinted, counted in her head. "Okay, *three* more times. Then a quick loop around the trail there"—she pointed to the other edge of the meadow—"and we're almost halfway there."

An intellectual's intellect is only their second-most-potent weapon.

Their first, of course, is everyone knowing their intellect. Because if everyone *thinks* you know what you're talking about, they tend to trust you, even if you say something incredibly insane like what just came out of Liette's mouth.

"Well, hang on," I said. "If the trail is right there, can't we just go toward it?"

"If you'd like to end up dead, be my guest."

And if neither renown nor intellect worked, the third-most-potent option available was painful, painful death.

Or at least, it was for the Freemakers.

The forest that made up the outskirts of Ocytus was about like any you'd expect in this region of the Scar: tall trees bristling with leafy crowns, rocks, snickering rodents running up and down the canopy. *Any* of these things would be a good place to hide an automated repeating gun or a potent gas trap or... or... a squirrel with a knife? I don't know.

And I don't know if they had any of *those*, either. But that's where their first-most-potent weapon comes back in: it's not about whether they have squirrels with knives, it's about whether I *believe* they have squirrels with knives.

Yes, I know how that sounds. Fuck off. I'm tired.

And that tiredness kept me following, compliantly and silently, as Liette led us back through the forest and into what seemed like a numb, quiet gauntlet of climbing rocks, navigating trees, and crawling beneath logs.

I didn't want a fight. And I *definitely* didn't want to be bisected by theoretical armed rodents, so I kept my mouth shut.

Frustrating, I admit. I wanted to talk. Even though her mind was on Ocytus. And so was mine.

Reason being, of course, that it's harder for me to realize what a fucking asshole I am when I've got some banter.

It's true that both our minds were on Ocytus. But it's not true that we were of the same mind. A mind like hers, with all those convictions and the intelligence to believe in them, was thinking of what Ocytus could do for the world, of all the intellects in there turned toward a single purpose.

But a mind like mine looks for something else. Not that I'm unintelligent, of course, no matter what my decision-making thus far has led you to believe. She was returning to Ocytus to save the world. I was returning to Ocytus to save her.

...Ah, yeah. I lied about not having been to Ocytus before, didn't I? I'd tell you that's a rarity, but the truth is I kind of do that a lot.

But it's not *technically* a lie—I also do this a lot, too, but fuck you, it's my story—since I'd never been to the city *proper.* Only to the part underneath, which doesn't exist, and which I didn't actually visit.

Suffice it to say, the Freemakers have been around for a long time. But Ocytus has been around for longer. And if that sounds overly complicated, confusing, and outright insulting to your intellect, then you've figured out how Freemakers work.

"Here."

After the endless turns and twists over rocks, under logs, between trees, backtracking and retracing and backtracing and *un*-tracing, Liette finally announced that we had arrived.

At the meadow we had just left.

Nothing had changed. Not the trees. Not the sun. Not even the fucking owl in the tree.

"What?" I asked, looking around, wondering if maybe there was something obvious I couldn't see or maybe if she was on drugs and why hadn't she shared them with me? "This is the same fucking place."

"It is!" she said excitedly, beaming like that made sense.

I blinked at her. I sighed. I reached for my gun.

"Look, it's fine if you've forgotten the way," I said. "I'll just start setting fires and we'll see if that works."

"*NO!*" She complemented the force of her objection with a rather severe adjustment of her spectacles. "Your extremely peculiar association of flammable materials with problem-solving is, I would argue, damning proof of your inability to perceive the nature of our journey."

"Those are a lot of big words for 'I'm an annoying prick,'" I growled. "You just led us in a hot mess of a hike and brought us back to exactly where we started."

"Precisely," she said, smirking. "The location was irrelevant. The *process* was important." She glanced toward the trees. "Am I incorrect?"

She was right that trying to solve all my problems with fire was insane, but she was also talking to trees, so that, to me, wasn't a reason to not at least *try*. But before I could object, let alone touch the Cacophony, I noticed movement in the tree she had just asked a question of.

The owl sleeping there stirred to life. Its head twisted around in that freaky way they do, then it quietly ambled to the edge of the branch it had been on, angled its body toward Liette, and opened its eyes.

Sorry. Its lenses. Not eyes.

"You're not *technically* incorrect," the owl said—or rather, the owl screeched through a crackling mechanical blare that emanated from its beak, like a voccaphone. "But since the protocol indicates that the process *should* take roughly another ten hours to arrive back here, you are also not technically correct."

"While I accept the letter of your assessment," she said to the owl as I stared, slack-jawed and maybe a little offended by the scene going on here, "I object to the nature of it. The actions we've taken over the last hours are *clearly* indicative that we're meant to be here. No one *but* a member in good standing of Ocytus would know the way to get as far as we have, rendering further dedication to the process of navigation a pointless expenditure of energy."

"Be that as it may," the owl crackled back, "there are *countless* unacceptable circumstances that may occur if we relax the protocol for even a moment. You could have memorized the route only this far, for example."

"Then how would I have known to talk to the owl?"

The owl went silent for a moment. "Maybe... maybe you thought the owl was magic and would show you the way out."

"That's ridiculous."

"It's been known to happen."

That *was* technically true, but the magic talking owls you meet in forests are not helpful—trust me on this. I wasn't about to tell her that, though. I *was* about to interject into this whole insanity, with words first and then with fire.

But then it hit me, as soon as I opened my mouth.

"Just a moment." Liette narrowed her eyes. "I recognize your voice. Sixteen Sorrowful Songs, is that you?"

"Indeed, Twenty-Two Dead Roses in a Chipped Porcelain Vase, it is me," the owl replied. "I'm managing residential operations for the previous four years and the next six years. As you *well* know."

"I knew it," Liette replied. "You're permitting your bitterness at our wager to interfere in your duty, Sixteen Sorrowful Songs. *You* were the one that bet ten years of research."

"I was *owed* ten years of research, you little asshole."

"Don't take that tone with me, you insufferable piece of shit."

"Oh, that's rich, coming from someone who killed two informants in pursuit of a potion that didn't even end up working."

"That's more than I can say for you and *your* body count, you wanton maniac. At least stuck in research, you can't kill anyone else with your garbage creations."

The pointless protocol. The pettiness. The personal insults.

"Motherfucker."

"*Father*fucker."

This was it, wasn't it? This *was* the password. This was how they *truly* proved they belonged in the Freemakers: by knowing enough about each other to prove it by flinging personal insults.

"Just open the door already, you miserable excuse for a scholar," Liette snarled at the owl. "You have no right to make this so complicated."

"*Fine*," the owl screeched back. "See what I care. Just don't track the stench of *failure* into *my* clean halls. Oh, and would you mind stepping back? This thing is kind of tricky."

"Oh, certainly." Liette took my hand, squeezed it as she led me away. "Okay, we're clear."

"Excellent. Stand by... you dick."

Further argument was lost in a deep groaning noise, as though the earth itself had been unsettled out of a long and comfortable position. Metal whistled, whined, and screeched beneath a carpet of dead forest that suddenly began to vibrate to life. A great blast of steam erupted from the floor, followed by another, and another, a wall of white mist spitting out nettles and dried leaves as it formed a perfect square.

The rattle of iron shattered the tranquility of the forest as the earth split apart to allow metal doors to slide open, a peculiar carriage of metal and gears, fueled by pumps and vials and devices I couldn't begin to name, rose up to greet us. It shuddered to an ominous stop, looking for a moment as though it might go plummeting back down the iron shaft it had just emerged from. And when it had shed enough important-looking pieces to come to a stop, a tiny woven gate opened with a little chime to invite us in.

"Mind you, this particular egress is not well-maintained," the owl blared at us as we approached the carriage. "They keep telling me I need to send someone out to this elevator to fix it up, but then people I dislike keep trying to use it, so as you can see, I'm in a real bind here. Anyway, it *shouldn't* collapse, but if it does, death is near instantaneous."

"Come on then," Liette said as she stepped onto the platform, shooting me an impatient look when I hesitated to follow. "What are you waiting for?"

"You heard the bird," I said, eyeing the rickety contraption. "It doesn't *look* safe..."

"I can give you three reasons why it is," Liette replied with a sigh. "Firstly, even the shoddiest of Freemaker machinations are infinitely safer than the unsophisticated heights of ordinary craftspeople's talents. Secondly, I remain perfectly capable of assessing the possibility of mechanical failure and, while I *do* detect enough here to be concerning, I furthermore remain perfectly capable of either reducing chances of said failure or ensuring that death goes from *near* instantaneous to almost certainly instantaneous."

"Uh-huh. And the third?"

"I once saw you compete in a raw bird–eating competition and refuse to believe you have even a moderately working sense of self-preservation. Now come along."

I did, but I wasn't happy.

She acted like I hadn't even given her the trophy after I'd won.

The door to the carriage snapped shut as soon as I walked aboard. It swayed unsteadily beneath me, held up by rickety gears and cables that showed a little too much wear for me to be comfortable. The chill that's normally reserved for moments where I have a blade at my neck crept back into me as the elevator rattled, whirred to uneasy life, and began to descend.

Steam hissed overhead as the metal hatch slid back into place, plunging the shaft into darkness. For a moment, anyway. In another breath, light sparked. And multiplied.

I winced twice. First for the eerie greens and blues and purples lighting up in a neon miasma. And again once I saw the sigils the light radiated off of. I'm no stranger to Spellwrights—I mean, obviously, otherwise I wouldn't be going through all this trouble for one—and I'd long grown accustomed to the weird and unsettling sigils they made with their weird magic inks. But the sigils lighting up the elevator shaft, glowing faintly as their magic aided the machinery in sliding jankily down the shaft, were...offensive to look at, full of angles that didn't make sense and going in directions that hurt the head to ponder.

"Old sigils," Liette muttered, perhaps sensing my unease. "The machines that built Ocytus were from before the Freemakers even organized. We've studied them for ages and still aren't sure what their functions are." Their pale light reflected off of her spectacles, hiding her eyes behind a white shine. "Unusual, though. They almost..." Her voice went soft, distant, an echo dying on the horizon. "Make sense."

There.

At the very last breath of the very last punctuation on the very last word of the very last sentence. I heard it. Just like I heard it whenever her eyes went distant and her voice went quiet and she stared at something with that look in her eye like she knows in an instant how to take it apart.

Those were her words. But that wasn't her voice.

I caught it in the breaths. In the blinks. In the long and ancient sighs that crept upon her, heavier and older than the last time. It was that thing. Eldest. It was inside her. Peering out from behind her eyes, testing out her voice. In the moments I caught it—in those fleeting breaths between us—I could tell I wasn't looking at her anymore.

And I wondered, as the elevator began to slow, how long it would be before she couldn't recognize me, either.

The elevator came to a halt with the soft *ping* of a chime. Alchemic globes sputtered to uneven light as the carriage doors opened, emptying out into a...a...

Honestly, I wasn't sure what the fuck you'd call it.

A tunnel? There were plenty of burrowing beasts in the Scar—remind me to tell you how I escaped Burg's Atrophy one day, by the way—and this was easily big enough to be one of their nests. But the walls were too smooth. And I don't know any monster that goes to the trouble of constructing a cute little waiting platform, complete with bench and alchemic lamppost.

Long, twisting metal tracks ran the tunnel's ceiling and floor, vanishing out of the platform's light and disappearing either way down the tunnel. Liette seemed unconcerned about this—or about any of it, really—her attentions were on some...metal...slate...thing.

I don't fucking know how to describe it. It was a big metal sheet—dull as dirt one minute and the next—

"Ah, here we are."

Liette removed a quill from her hair, daubed it into a pouch at her hip, then pressed it to the metal. The sigils blossomed across the sheet, an elegant network of glowing lines and symbols I didn't understand. But Liette, apparently, did—she scratched her chin, studying the map... thing... with a troubling understanding.

"Mm, this is aggravating." She gestured to a pair of crimson lines. "Our most direct route to Ocytus has been altered. Must be a cave-in or something." She traced her quill across the sheet in an elaborate series of sigils drawn in a line from one sigil to the next. "Not to worry, though." She paused. "Not to worry about *this* particular instance, I mean. In general, you should be very worried about everything else."

"I figured I'd just go ahead and be worried about all of it," I muttered, gesturing to the sheet. "What's this thing? More dead-guy graffiti?"

"Old. Sigils," she responded, annoyed. "And yes. This one, we understand enough to manipulate. But not to maintain. One day, it'll all crumble and we'll have to navigate with the inelegance and discomfort of your typical biped." She finished her scrawling with a punctuating tip onto the metal. The lines glowed an appealing blue. "But for now, I thought it'd be nice if we traveled in style."

There was a distant stir of air, a rush of wind that came up from the tunnel. The sound of machines whirring, shrieking, roaring followed. The twisted lines of metal across the ceiling and floor began to shudder, squeaking uneasily as a faint light appeared around the tunnel.

And with a sudden burst of light, rushed toward us.

I shouted, grabbing Liette and pushing her behind me as I drew my sword, ready to fight off whatever beast had found us. And yes, I will wholly admit to overreacting in hindsight. But if you had been there to see it, you'd have tried to kill it, too.

Another carriage. A few of them. Shining brass metal tarnished with age and use, sigils glowing dimly across their surfaces, each one linked together with a complex rig of cables and chains.

And within . . . chairs. Quite tasteful, actually. Velvet-lined benches ran the length of each carriage, a delicate seating area arranged for multiple travelers around spaces intended for larger luggage to transport.

I'd never seen anything like it before. My breath caught in my chest. My blood shifted under my skin the way it does when something's wrong. This machine was incredible. This machine was amazing. This was—

"Calm down," Liette chided, pushing past me, "it's just a tram."

"A what?"

"A tram." Liette found a small lever on the side of one of the carriages, giving it a flick to send a door sliding open. At my slack-jawed gaping, she sighed. "A tram is a system of tracks designed for transport to—"

"I can obviously tell what it is," I snapped back as I uneasily followed her into the carriage. "It's just . . . you call it a tram?"

"What else would we call it?"

"It's a speeding hellfire shot of a train. Why not call it the helltrack?"

"That's stupid," she said, sitting down on one of the benches and motioning for me to join her.

"Hellengine, then."

"No."

"Hellwheels."

"What is it with *hell* and you?" she asked. "Do you only know the one descriptor?"

"I know the ones that sound impressive." I leaned back, sprawled my arms over the bench. "Why, what would you call it?"

"I don't know. Something understated, I suppose." She looked out the window as the tram sputtered back to life and began to slither down into darkness. "Something like Elegance. Simplicity."

"You won't let me call it the helltrack, but you'll call it Simplicity?"

"It's just an example." A yawn crept into her voice. "Comfort might also be nice."

"Comfort?" I chuckled as the lights went out and we disappeared into the earth. "Well, if anyone was capable of picking a name less interesting than 'tram,' it would be you. Tell me what the fuck is supposed to be comfortable about—"

I didn't see her.

Not her distant stare or her tired eyes. And I didn't hear her or the voice that I swore wasn't hers sometimes.

But I felt her. I felt the weariness through her clothes. I felt the collapse of her body. I felt the flutter of her eyelids as she rested her head against my chest, pressed her nose into the hollow of my throat, and closed her eyes.

I didn't know how she could sleep. Not while we were on the Mighty Helltrack, not while we were going to Ocytus, not while a war was raging over our heads. I envied her for it. And resented her for it.

And more than anything, I wanted her to keep sleeping.

I wanted this warmth. This weariness. This slow rise and fall of her body as she drew in slumbering breath. I wanted her to stay like this, here in the dark.

Because here…I knew it was her.

For now.

And as we went deeper into the earth, I felt that itch. The same cold pang of certainty that comes when my body knows blood will spill before my brain does. My scars knew why we were going to Ocytus. My scars knew we were going there to get that thing out of Liette.

And if it didn't work…my scars knew what would.

ELEVEN

CENTRAL OCYTUS

Don't get me wrong, even if I wasn't romantically involved with one of them, I'd still like the Freemakers.

They keep things interesting. Unbound by any nation, law, or desire beyond becoming great at whatever it is they decide to do, they have schemes that shape the Scar as surely as the Revolution or the Imperium does. There are a thousand warlords, murderers, and Vagrants who owe their careers to a Freemaker.

Myself included.

You've probably heard a story or two about them, yourself. And if you've heard of the Freemakers, you've heard of their defiant, mysterious city.

Ocytus.

City of Wonders. The Halls of Intellect. A world beneath worlds made of pipes and machines and whirring gears and sliding halls. A place where the brightest, most ambitious, and cleverest meet to debate, to invent, to create beneath spellwritten sigils whose glows never dim. A city full of machines that walk and talk as people, of cannons that level mountainsides, of potions that can make you older, younger, someone else entirely.

Eventually, the stories get so fantastic no one can even believe them anymore. Ocytus and its wonders fade from minds as stress and worries take their usual spots, like all stories. But the fantasy...

Well, the fantasy is nice.

"Now listen here, you miserable little twat."

But the reality is way, *way* more fun.

"I got no problem with you coming out here, pretending you know what you're talking about," the woman known as A Dire Hag Laughs at Cruel Jokes said as she walked slow, stiff circles around the arena. She paused, glaring at her foe across the floor. "And if you were just talking about shitting your pants, I'd trust your expertise. But you're talking armored mobile explosive delivery here, and that"—she rapped her knuckles on the tank's iron hide—"is where the boys call me Mommy."

The tank, a compact little thing humming away on earth-chewing treads and spewing severium smoke from its exhaust released a happy little roar of its engine, spinning its turret around like just the *cutest* little weapon of mass destruction. In response, the crowd—some forty-odd people looking the kind of wealthy that's so wealthy it just looks insane but you can't say anything because they're wealthy—roared their approval, waving coins in their hands and barking wagers.

A Dire Hag Laughs at Cruel Jokes' opponent, tall and slim and dark-skinned with perfectly coiffed hair to match his perfectly polished spectacles and perfectly fastidious suit, seemed unimpressed.

"I gaze upon your trivial offering and see nothing but a devotion to efficiency," the man, Black Wine for a Funeral, replied, sneering down his nose at the tank. "Practical. Sensible. Utterly devoid of heart or flair. Destined for the same ignoble scrap heap of perfectly reasonable and unimpressive ideas, like the doorstop and the paperweight. Whereas I..." He gestured to the giant man beside him, bowing deeply. "I like to think aesthetically."

The giant man made of iron—a body of rattling weapons and severium fumes cobbled together in the sleek design of a suit of armor—rumbled. To look at it, I'd have called it a Paladin, one of the Revolution's weapons, but this one was... gorgeous. Carved into a many-limbed man of perfect musculature and features, its arms moved with mechanical precision, each one ending in a different but equally horrific killing implement.

"I'll see your fucking aesthetic if there's anything left of it, you sniveling elitist," the older woman snarled, shaking a fist at her foe.

"You'll see me make a *throne* out of the ruin of your rubble, you backward hick!" the other man shouted back.

"LIGHT IT UP, LADS!"

I couldn't be sure who yelled that: her, him, or the crowd. Actually, it might have been me who did it. The mood swept through the crowd as those assembled around the arenas howled in anticipation for the coming slaughter, waving sacks of jingling money as they placed bets.

The excitement exploded, along with part of the arena, as the mechanical man and tank waded into each other. The tank opened up with a salvo of turrets, blowing two of its foe's limbs off. The mechanical man retaliated by digging hook-like appendages into the tank's shell and hammering on it with a mighty mace of a hand.

"Ha. See?" I nudged the person beside me. "How the fuck is that thing going to fight a *tank*?"

The Freemaker—I hadn't caught his name, something about Two Turgid Owls or something—cringed at my nudge, wiping his suit clean. "Boast while you can, knave," he said. "Black Wine for a Funeral's creations are works of art, peerless in design that *never* fails to inspire."

"We didn't bet on whether it would inspire, motherfucker, we bet whether it would beat a tank." I snorted. "You ever seen a still life painting beat a gun?"

"The demonstration is not over yet," the Freemaker said, pointedly wincing as another pair of arms were blown off. "We agreed."

"You agreed. *I* agreed to go get shit-faced with someone with *my* winnings that *you* owe me, you flaccid worm."

"Apologies. *Which* Freemaker did you say you were again?"

I met his eyes, smiled. "They call me... A Dour Tune to Dance To."

The Freemaker was a wealthy man. Fine clothes, snobby attitude, dripping with arrogance. I didn't start to feel the urge to hit him until he sneered at my fake Freemaker name, though.

I had put *thought* into that.

My arm tensed, my eyes locked on his ears, already picking out the spot I'd slap him to knock the stupid out of him. So it was probably a good thing someone grabbed my arm.

"Would it inconvenience you *too* much," Liette hissed as she pulled me away from the crowd and my potential assault, "to act *slightly* more subtle here?"

I blinked. I looked over her head.

The halls of Ocytus sprawled out, hewn from the earth with impossible precision and bedecked with glistening halls of brass and chrome. Mechanical servants whirred alongside golems—paper, wood, metal, everything—as they hauled ever-increasing barrels of liquor to laughing intellectuals. Impromptu bets over whose acids could burn faster or whose explosions could ring out louder filled every avenue with noise and ensuing cheers. Alchemic lights flashed alongside spellwritten sigils, illusionary dancers of impossible beauty beckoned people into beautiful parlors, the smoke of a thousand pipes of a thousand drugs filled the air in a near-constant cloud.

"Sure," I said, "I guess I can tone it down. Wouldn't want to offend anyone."

"Quaint. You are quaint, Sal," she said in that I-want-to-call-you-something-worse tone of voice. "And while I am certain that will affect some charm here, I would be considered derelict in all definitions of the word *duty* were I not to point out that the clientele here are heavily concerned with money, explosions, and pursuing petty pleasures." She drew in a breath, exhaled. "Do you understand?"

I opened my mouth.

"Do you understand in a way that is *not* about to result in you saying 'but I like those things'?"

"Then no, I don't." I scratched my head. "If they're as bad as that, what makes you think they'll intervene in this mess?"

She hesitated before answering. I saw the doubt weigh down her eyes, draw them away from mine. It had been one thing to dream of the Freemakers' aid outside of Ocytus. This close to their decadence, their spending, their sheer *power*…

Well.

Who the hell would give that up if no one could make them?

"Well." I put a finger under her chin, tilted her eyes back toward me. "If anyone's smart enough to pull it off, you are."

"We are surrounded by genius intellects, each one capable of a multitude of feats of brilliance unfathomable to minds that have yet to be born," she responded calmly.

"Yeah, but you smell nicer."

I leaned down, found her lips, her scent, her warmth. I held her there, as long as I dared to, before she gently pushed me away and adjusted her spectacles.

"Your attempts to varnish the severity of the situation with overtures of affection are obvious." She cleared her throat. Her face flashed a gratifying shade of crimson for a single instant. "But… appreciated. Thank you. I trust you can keep yourself entertained."

An explosion rang out behind me. I whirled around to see the arena, bathed in a cloud of smoke as the mechanical man stood triumphant over the smoldering tank, their two creators raking in the scorn and accolades alike while money changed hands.

"Well, fuck, I was *going to*," I sighed, "but yeah, I can—"

I turned back. She was gone.

And I leaned against the cold metal wall and let out a breath I'd been holding for six months. And I hated myself for it.

Just like I hated myself for kissing her like that. Part of me thought she'd have caught on by now, realized I was full of birdshit. Part of me hated her for not doing that, for trusting me, for making me admit to myself.

I hadn't come here to stop any war.

A tap on my shoulder. I looked around. Two Cats Shit in a Drawer or whatever I had named the foppish Freemaker I'd made a bet with stood there, palm outstretched.

"Madame...A Dour Tune, was it?" he asked smugly. "I believe you owe me something?"

"A Dour Tune to Dance To, you ass." I took his palm, held it steady. "And yeah, she does owe you something."

I snorted, pressed one nostril shut and...well, back in the service we used to call it "nature's crossbow." I spat the glob of glistening phlegm into his palm, took a moment to savor his horror, patted him on the cheek.

"I'm not her, though."

I stalked off before he could raise protest. No one came after me. I suppose the indignity of being paid in personal fluids was more overwhelming than the need to collect a debt. And in a few moments, it didn't matter. I disappeared into the veils of severium-tinged steam, beneath halos of spellwritten light.

The wager, anyway, had only been something to keep me from getting bored while I waded into that crowd for a different reason. A few greasy compliments and *just* enough feigned flattery and the crowd of Ocytus had managed to tell me exactly what I wanted to know.

Three streets up. I recounted their instructions in my head, counting the slick metal avenues and the pale lights dancing off their streets. *Take a right. Left at the second alley. And then it's at the far back.*

"*Dreadful little shop, if I'm honest,*" one of the crowd, a lady with a hat that had commanded authority, had directed me. "*Antique technology might be quaint in the cities, but this is Ocytus, darling. If you're there to collect a debt, you'll get it paid in junk.*"

Fortunately for me, I wasn't there to collect a debt.

"We're closed," someone—a bored-looking young woman with unwashed hair to complement her unwashed clothes—called from behind a counter crowded with haphazard pieces of outdated salvage. She didn't bother looking up from the novel she was thumbing through. "We open again next week. Maybe. Or not. Whatever you— *HEY!*"

I didn't blame her for being upset. I had, after all, just shoved a bunch of crap off the counter. When she shot to her feet to grab it, I caught her by the wrist, hauled her forward.

"I'm here to see him," I growled.

"*Who?*" she replied. "Lady, I'm not like one of these brains. I'm just trying to—"

"I buried him under a dead tree," I interrupted. "Its last leaf fell in autumn, two years ago."

The young lady didn't react. But she didn't struggle.

"Did you get another?" she asked.

"Never again. There will never be another."

See?

That's how you do a fucking secret password.

"All right, fine." The young lady shoved me off of her. "Don't see why you needed to mess up my counter to tell me that. I work hard trying to make this place look like shit. Go lock the door."

I grunted, returning to the shop entrance. The bolt clicked with a heavy snap. A well-maintained lock in a dirty, run-down slab of wood. I doubt anyone had noticed.

I followed her to the back of the shop, where she was moving multiple stacks of old paperwork and musty wares aside. After a small eternity of shuffling, a tiny door in the wall was unearthed.

"It's tinier than I thought it would be."

"Yeah." She collected an ancient-looking lamp that was suspiciously full of oil, sparking it to life. "It's a real pain. I have to bend down to get in there."

I grimaced, noting that she was several inches shorter than me. "What's the point of that?"

She kicked the door; it opened stiffly. "Well, would *you* want to go in here? Come the fuck on. I want to go home."

We crawled through, emerging into a dank cellar beyond. Between even more piles of debris, the floor opened up into a narrow staircase spiraling downward. I followed the dim glow of her lantern as it led me to the bottom of the earth.

"Hang on," she grunted, setting the lantern aside. "This part's always such a fucking pain."

She walked to the edge of the chamber, nothing more than a stone square at the bottom of a hole, and grabbed what looked like a brick. With a grunt, she dug her heels in and started to pull on it.

"Come on," she said, wincing. "Come on, you stupid—"

She was interrupted with the groan of metal relenting. With heaving grunts, she began to walk backward, dragging the brick with her. It gave way, along with the rest of the wall, sliding out to reveal a thick slab of metal.

And on it...

The man I'd come to Ocytus to see.

A sarcophagus greeted me, lying in the hidden compartment, roughly two men wide and just as tall. The metalwork was horrific to look upon: ribbons and seams of metals of purple and red and shades I'd never even seen, all arranged in an offensively structured array of sigils. It hurt my eyes to look upon.

I wanted to turn away. But someone else didn't.

Heat at my hip. My hand was drawn to his hilt. Steam slipped out between my fingers as I drew him from his sheath. His metal rippled. His voice slithered into my ear.

"I sense him now. I could not before."

"I imagine he has good reason to hide," I said. I glanced down at the Cacophony. "You ready for this?"

And I felt him smile.

"Oh yes. It's been too long."

TWELVE

ELSEWHERE

There is a story.

It's known to only a few. The people who made dark deals in dark places. The people who found the blood on the stone.

It begins down in the dark, beneath the Imperial Palace of Cathama, where thirty-four people met to bring down an empire and one of them limped away. Down there, where a woman grasped a crown made of brass thorns in her bloodied hands, red life whispering from wounds that would one day be scars. Down in the deep, where the woman who had once been Red Cloud and would one day be called the Cacophony, emerged from the gloom as neither of them.

But this is not that story.

This is the story of the metal in her hands. A crown, brass and twisted into thorns, sitting in a place of foreboding honor in the Imperial crypts, down there in the dark. It was meant to fade from memory, along with the emperor who had worn it upon his fevered brow.

But the crown refused to be forgotten.

It simply waited. Waited until bloodied hands grabbed it. Waited until a fevered mind heard it. Waited until a shattered heart held it.

And then, it spoke.

And she had listened.

The woman, her uniform unable to stanch the blood, thought only of the pain, of the betrayal, of the agony that had brought her here. A pained mind cannot reason—reason is the first thing you give up when you get hurt. And a mind that cannot reason cannot argue.

And neither did she.

She followed a guiding voice. Whispered promises in her heart. They would give her everything she needed to make the pain stop, if only she would give them what they needed.

And she wanted to give it to them.

They brought her down the dingiest, darkest alley in Cathama. They brought her past the dredges and nul outcasts who lurked in its barrows. They brought her to a small shop in a small building on a small street in a small part of the city.

She raised her hand to knock.

The voice told her not to.

The voice told her she was done asking to enter.

And she didn't argue. She shoved the door open, leaving a bloodied handprint on its window. She stumbled inside, the blood falling out of her and onto the shop's hardwood floors. She looked up through darkening vision, to the man standing there in the middle of the shop.

Tall. Dark skinned. Gangly as a scarecrow and with a head of black hair as big and vast as the night. He stood there, a cup of tea in his hands, his mouth hanging open with a word he couldn't say, his eyes unblinking with a thought he didn't dare do.

"Your name," the woman gasped, "is a Dead Dog Buried on a Black Hill."

"I..." The man looked like he was about to deny it. He sighed, instead. "Yeah. That's me."

The woman held up the crown. The man stared at his reflection warped in its thorns.

"He says," the woman said, "it's time to pay your debt."

And she fell onto the floor.

And did not rise.

Sharp, stabbing hours turned into long, anguished days. The man tended to the woman without a name as best he could—brilliant as he might have been, his mind had always been focused on things less practical and more aspirational than medicine. She healed with alchemics, with time, and with as much whiskey as she could fit between the two.

It took time to become accustomed to it. The absence of her magic. The great emptiness inside her where her power had once flowed. The silence within her where she had once felt a beautiful song meant only for her.

She wept often.

She bled occasionally.

She was silent frequently.

But she healed.

In the corner of the man's dingy workshop, recuperating upon a dingy cot, as the man paced around his dingy workbench, his long dark stare fixed on the thing it held.

And if she looked close enough, she could almost convince herself the crown of brass thorns stared back.

"Fuck me," A Dead Dog Buried on a Black Hill muttered as he paced. "Fuck me, fuck me, *fuck* me. I was *this* close to convincing myself this day would never come. This damn close to forgetting about this shit."

He put his hands on his knees, leaned forward. He squinted, scrutinizing the crown, peering at it from every angle he could imagine, as though there were some perfect way to look at it that would take away the unsettled look on his face. He reached out, hands trembling, terrified to touch.

His fingers rested upon the brow of the crown. His breath caught.

"It's warm," he whispered. "Holy shit, it's warm." He swallowed a painfully dry breath. "Did he actually fucking do it?" He looked to the woman without a name. "Did he actually fucking *do* it?"

"Wouldn't be here if he didn't," she responded faintly. "He told me to find you."

A Dead Dog Buried on a Black Hill's face grew long. "How much do you know?"

"He told me," she said, "everything."

"It didn't tell you everything," he said. "It couldn't have. How long have you had it?"

"A few hours."

"A few hours is *not* enough time to understand what—"

"I understand," the woman without a name interrupted. "Wouldn't be here if I didn't. He's told me what he can give me, told me what it's going to take." She took a sip of sour whiskey, felt the pain in her jaw dim to a throbbing ache. "I can do it."

"No one can do it."

"I can do it," she responded, less faintly this time. "And so can you. He told me of your deal." She looked to him. "Is it true? Did he take away your pain?"

The man smacked his lips, nodded. "I've been around for a long time because of him."

"Then you owe him," she said. "And you're going to hold up your end of the bargain."

His brow furrowed, incensed at being spoken to in such a way. But the moment he started to speak up, he felt something tugging at the edge of his consciousness, an errant pull demanding his attention.

The crown. It sat there. Twisted brass briars reflecting his own slack-jawed horror back at him.

It looked at him. It spoke to him.

And he was compelled to agree with it.

"You understand the magic this is going to take, right?" he asked. "We're talking old magic. The Oldest Magic. Before the Imperium. Before the first Emperor. The libraries don't even know this shit *exists*."

"But he did," she replied. "He knew. And he told me. An oath. A bargain. A deal. Same as the Lady Merchant. I get it."

"No, not the same. This isn't a transaction, this is a contract. It—"

"Shut the fuck up," she uttered, turning her one good eye toward him, "and pay your debt."

A Dead Dog Buried on a Black Hill frowned, but did not protest. He turned to the crown, tentatively picked it up. He held it, looking at it from every angle he could again, though this time with less trepidation and more curiosity.

"Exactly as he described," he whispered, "unbelievable. He knew all the materials we'd need for this." He shook his head, muttered to himself. "Not enough metal in the crown, but he *did* say we were going to need more. I can get the alloy. I can make him into a sword that can kill kingdoms."

"No."

He looked up at her. "No?"

"No," she replied, looking at the crown. "He changed his mind."

And the crown looked back at her.

And smiled.

"He wants to be a gun."

Days passed long and slow and painful. The woman without a name learned new lessons she never wanted to: how to walk instead of fly, how to feel the limitations of a human frame, how to heal without magic.

Harsh lessons, as any lesson worth knowing is. But she learned them, there in the dingy workshop, hidden away from a world that continued to turn without her. The hours under the floorboards were spent mostly hurting, sometimes reading, frequently crying.

And writing.

Always writing.

Names. Faces. Laughter in the dark. Eyes that had turned away from her suffering. Smiles that grew longer as she bled.

She dedicated them to memory, wrote down every name she

could, every detail she could remember. Wrote until her quill tore her paper to pieces and she reached for another one and tore that to pieces, too. The names became seared onto her mind, into her skin. Moments that weren't spent blinded by agony were consumed by anger instead.

The man, for his part, did not object to this.

He dutifully continued to uphold his end of the bargain. He provided what medicine and comfort and treatment he could. He provided her paper sometimes, books other times, whiskey each time.

But he, too, was consumed. By his work. By his bargain.

His workshop was ablaze. A forge to melt metal to exact specifications. A set of specialty tools to construct tiny mechanisms for a weapon. Inks of bizarre origin to be penned in painful sigils, layer upon layer, each one vanishing into the brass as soon as it was dry.

It was long work. Painful work. Monotonous work.

"Hey."

So much so, that they found themselves in a sort of pained rhythm.

"You hear about your friends?"

Muttering to each other to pass the time. Remind each other of the existence of other humans.

"They're not my friends," the woman without a name said.

"Whatever," the man replied, not looking up from his work. "Imperium went hunting for them after they figured out what you all were up to down there. They tore ass out of the city and slipped out of the entire Imperium before the Empress's trackers could pick them up."

She paused. "Did any die?"

"Nah. The Empress is the Empress, but she chose each of those fuckers for a reason. None of them were caught. All of them escaped."

She wrote something down. "Where did they go?"

"Same place anyone goes to escape the Imperium, I would bet," he muttered. "Not a province or prefect that isn't searching for them." He held up the piece he was working on, squinted at it, chided himself at some imperceptible flaw before returning to it. "But last I heard, they don't have those in the Scar, do they?"

"They went Vagrant."

"Looks like. Feels like a waste, you ask me," he grunted. "Go through all the effort of trying to overthrow the Empress only to go play opera hero in the Scar. Could have saved us all the effort and just done that to begin with."

She was silent for a long moment. "That wouldn't bring them what they wanted."

"Sure it would have," he replied, hammering something into place with a delicate glass mallet. "They'd be far away and be free of the Empress, the Empress would have them out of her hair, everyone's happy."

"They wanted the throne."

"Nah."

"I was there."

"I know."

"No, *I* know. I *know* what they wanted—"

"Yeah, what was it again?" He scratched his chin. "To overthrow the crown? Be their own Imperium? Rule over this one?"

"They wanted power. Control."

"Freedom. Same thing."

"You don't know what you're talking about."

"Yeah, sure," he muttered. "I'm a fucking nul running an illicit workshop in a city full of magic bastards who can set me on fire for looking at them wrong. What the fuck would *I* know about power and freedom? Clearly, your magic bastard problems are far too complex for *me* to handle. Hey, by the way, I emptied the bucket you piss in. You're welcome."

She said nothing to that. He continued talking. Not necessarily to her.

"People don't change," he said as he continued to work. "Trace a king and a peasant back to their roots, you find the same quivering pile of shit desperately hoping to be free. He'll do it any way he has to. Even found an entire fucking Imperium. You look at an emperor and see a powerful man, but what you get is a cock who thinks stomping on people is the same as being free."

There was a faint hissing sound. The metal on his workbench twitched, gave out the slightest note of steam.

"Don't fucking take that attitude with me," he muttered to the metal. "This is a contract. I don't owe you flattery." The metal simmered. He continued. "Freedom's the only thing anyone wants. Freedom to run, freedom to hurt, freedom to die as you think you deserve."

She stared at her hands and wondered if that was true.

Those hands that used to command reality. Those hands that had leveled five hundred foes in a single day. Those hands that used to taste the wind and feel the sky upon them.

That was freedom. Had been freedom. No one could have touched her up there, no one could have made her feel weak, wounded.

Useless.

The woman with no name wondered if that was what she truly craved. She looked inside herself, into all the memories of flame and of shadow, and all the wounds and lashes she had borne. She looked past her dreams and her lives she imagined she'd one day have. She looked past the agony in her body that crept into her brain on spiderweb strands. She looked.

And she knew what she wanted.

"What did he give you?" she asked the man, almost as an afterthought.

And the man paused. And the man stared into emptiness.

"He gave me what I asked for," he answered.

And then continued his work in silence.

Time passed. Blood dried. Scars knit.

And, day by day, their work finished.

Until the day she pulled herself from her bed on legs that ached to run again and came to the worktable. The man stood there, thinner and paler than he had been when he had started, and laid trembling hands upon a black box.

She looked down at his hands. The scar across her right eye twisted as she scowled at him.

"Open it," she said.

"I will," he said, with a voice that indicated he might not, "but I need to tell you something."

"You've told me a hundred times before."

"And I'll tell you a million times if I have to because I can't open this box unless you know damn well what's inside."

"Power."

"Not power. Magic." His voice turned deadly serious. "The first magic. The oldest, strongest, and most terrible kind. There was no other way to make him whole again." He inhaled sharply. "Before the Imperium was even a dream, this is what they used to make magic. No Barters. Just an agreement."

His fingers alighted upon the box again. Faint wisps of smoke peeled out from between the hinges.

"A bargain," he said. "What you ask of each other, what you *give* to each other... you won't be able to get back, understand? Not until it's over."

"Until what's over?"

He frowned. "He'll tell you. You sure you still want to do this?"

She nodded. No hesitation. She had asked herself that question the day she crawled out of that dark place and every day since and the answer was always the same.

The man sighed, disappointed in her answer. Slowly, he creaked the lid to the box open. Slowly, hissing steam and heat alive with anger rose from within. Slowly, she took him in—his brass eyes, his long grin, his dragon's head.

He had wanted to be a dragon.

She reached into the box. Her fingers stopped just short of his metal, her body sensing something she couldn't. But the scars on her skin were too heavy, the pain was too fresh.

She took him by the black hilt.

And inside her blood, she could feel a voice.

It introduced itself, politely and properly. It sympathized with her agony. It proposed a solution.

It offered a deal.

And she took it.

And on that day, they both found their new name.

THIRTEEN

OCYTUS

Bear with me, these are a real pain in the snatch to work."

"Do you need any help?"

"No, you'd only fuck it up. Just . . . hang on . . . and . . . fuck, no, not that way. No! *No, no, no, no* . . . okay, shit. That was close. And . . ."

The last cylinder clicked into place. Five tubes of hardened glass, each one swirling with a different alchemic mixture—this one tarry and viscous, that one bile green and writhing—stood at five points surrounding the sarcophagus. The young lady—Themeter, she'd introduced herself as, eventually—mopped her brow as she knuckled out the small of her back.

"*Fuck* me, this isn't worth it," she groaned as she limped around the sarcophagus, to a mechanical apparatus situated at its flank. "Pays well and it's easy enough except for the times I have to do this shit."

"But you *can* do this shit," I half asked, half threatened. "I didn't come this far to leave without answers. And if I have to tear them out of—"

"Okay, let's just take a moment to breathe here," she replied as she busied herself over the apparatus, adjusting a few dials and beakers of fluid. "Whatever answers you want, you'll get them from him, okay? I'm just the staff. Getting mad at me won't make this go any faster."

"I—" My indignation caught in my throat, tempered itself into a frustrated sigh. "Sorry. You're right. I've just had a rough couple of days."

"*Thank* you. See? Was that so hard? Wasn't it nice to treat each other with respect?" Themeter smiled at me. "Maybe if you tried that more often, you wouldn't be such an ornery dickwipe." She reached for a large plunger, paused. "I wasn't going to tell you this, but since you apologized...you might want to look away for this part."

I grunted. "Do it."

She sighed, pulled the plunger down.

The sarcophagus groaned, machinery of ancient metals beckoned to life by the song of the apparatus's clicking, whirring, buzzing language. The veins of metal across it glowed faintly, the spellwritten sigils between their lines responding in kind. The lights blossomed in nauseating tones, vibrancies, and colors that human eyes weren't meant to bear.

There was a gasp of dust and air that had been trapped for ages as the sarcophagus's lid slid open. The interior had been lined with black silk that had begun to show signs of age, despite the coffin's best efforts to preserve it. The material hung thin and threadbare, the stuffing leaking out in places.

A fine match for the corpse inside.

He was smaller than I remembered. Not the long-limbed, powerful fellow whose hands had worked so diligently. Gaunt, his skin clinging to him so tightly that the crests and valleys of his skull were visible. His suit, still immaculate despite the ravaging of time, hung off his frame. He was withered and weak.

Which I guess made sense. No one said you get prettier when you die.

There was a grotesque sucking sound. The five cylinders shuddered to life. The fluids drained out of them, traveling through a network of coiling copper pipes that embedded themselves in the corpse's skin, each one affixed by a surgical graft. I watched his body contort and twitch as the fluids flooded into him, making his skin bulge and engorge in places. Saliva tinged with black bile bubbled out of his mouth.

She was right. I should have looked away.

But fuck, it wasn't like I was going to look any better when someone dug me up.

The body shuddered. Twitched. Spasmed violently for a moment, rattling the pipes infiltrating its skin. And then lay still. Themeter and I exchanged a look before she leaned closer.

"Boss?" she whispered. "Did it work?"

"Mmf."

The corpse let out a muffled groan.

"Huh?"

"MMF."

"*Oh!*" Themeter hastily produced a handkerchief and held it to the corpse's mouth. "Sorry, boss. I always forget. Ready."

His lips parted. Black liquid, thick and shimmering with human oil, bubbled out of his lips and onto the fabric. Themeter diligently cleaned it all off her employer's mouth. The corpse smacked its lips, rasped out with a voice that was thin and withered.

"Themeter."

"Boss?" she asked, looking up.

"Notation."

She hastily pulled a notepad and pen out of her pocket. "Ready."

"Awakening number four thousand sixty-six," the corpse began.

"Sixty-seven," Themeter corrected softly.

"Sixty-seven, thank you, Themeter," he continued. "Dreams again. Frustratingly bereft of answers. Every time I begin to get close, I awaken. Thought I heard her speaking this time. Can't remember what." He paused, his lips twitched. He spat out a lingering glob of bile. "All right, to business, then. You've got my investments ready, I hope. How's my money in Avonin and Sons doing? Last I checked, the blight had—"

"Uh, boss," Themeter interrupted. "Sorry, but two things. They're

Avonin and *Family* now, and, uh..." She looked up at me. "You have a visitor."

"A visitor?" The corpse's face twitched, distressed. "Themeter, I *told* you—"

"You did, boss. I didn't forget. But...you said..."

The corpse's face stilled. "Ah. Yeah. The exception."

"A Dead Dog Buried on a Black Hill." I stepped forward, making certain to use his full name. You don't call a Freemaker anything else unless you want to never work with them again. "How's the profane, unholy science business?"

"Sal the Cacophony," he rasped. "I thought I'd be dead before seeing you darken my doorway again."

"Yeah, well." I glanced his withered frame over. "Looks like you were."

"I won't insult you by pretending to understand your business, Vagrant; don't insult me by pretending to understand mine." A Dead Dog Buried on a Black Hill eased back into his sarcophagus, the machines and tubing feeding his body shuddering briefly before resuming a normal hum. "I'm looking for answers to questions we don't even have the intellect to know we're thinking of. I'm seeking the tailors of reality. If you know a better way to do that, go ahead and let me know."

I didn't. I mean, unless you just did a lot of drugs at once and hoped for the best. But I digress.

"I guess I shouldn't ask how you're doing, then," I muttered.

"I am as I always will be." He managed the weakest, saddest of grins. "You don't hook yourself up to this thing unless you're ready to commit to it." Beneath his sealed eyelids, I saw twitching. "But unless it's been longer than I thought, you didn't come here for that."

There was a quiet malice in the silence that hung between us. The same laboring, tortured stretch of quiet that came before uttering the name of the people who hurt you and after whispering the name of the person you love. It was an acknowledgment between us, him and me, that whatever we said next...

It was going to hurt.

"Did you..." The Freemaker paused, his voice shuddering. "Did you bring... *him*?"

A coil of steam hissed from the sheath at my hip.

He did so like it when people talked about him.

"Yeah," I said. "He's here."

A longer, terrified silence this time. The moment right between making a bad choice and making it worse.

"Let me see him."

I eased my hand down to the black hilt. "He's... different. Stronger. Are you sure?"

"Yes. I'm sure." His withered body shuddered, the cylinders of his machine whirring. "Let me feel him."

I winced.

I had kind of been hoping to avoid this part, honestly.

I could feel the heat as soon as my fingers wrapped around the hilt. Even through my glove, it felt like putting my hand in boiling water. The smell of it—that acrid, reeking stink of burning air—polluted the chamber. The air shimmered around him as I held him out in both hands, presenting him to the corpse.

The Cacophony's brass twitched, shuddered, rippled.

Pleased.

And he spoke searing words.

"Hello, old friend."

Three words. That's all it took.

And the world exploded.

The notepad in Themeter's hand ignited; she dropped the flaming pile of papers with a screech. The metal of the cylinders began to swell and bulge with the heat. The pipes inserted into the Freemaker's withered frame rattled dangerously. The fluids inside bubbled. And across his desiccated flesh, char appeared in thin black patches.

A Dead Dog Buried on a Black Hill's scream came out on coils of smoke that snaked their way out of his throat. His wail was long, loud, agonized.

And not the least bit scared.

"*Enough!*" he screamed, after a few moments stretched into searing eternity. "*ENOUGH!*"

I sheathed him.

In the absence of the weapon, a strange chill set in. It was as though the Cacophony had drunk the heat from the room, leaving a freezing, shuddering void of warmth as he slid back into the leather.

When the fuck had he learned how to do that?

"Incredible," A Dead Dog Buried on a Black Hill gasped. His body was painted with char marks, his machinery was twisted and warped, steam still coiled off his skin. He was a mess and he hadn't looked that great to begin with. "Amazing. I never...I didn't have the capacity to imagine what he would become. There is no language for it. There are no words."

"He's just showing off for you," I muttered, not believing it myself. "He hasn't seen you in a long time."

"Incredible," he kept gasping. I don't know if you've ever seen a corpse orgasm and, in fairness, I don't know if that's what I was seeing, but whatever it was, it was unpleasant. "The things he must have seen. The lives he must have tasted. Tell me..." His voice grew fevered, completely oblivious to the ruin of his body. "How many?"

"How many what?"

"How many has he tasted? How much has he fed? How many? Do you remember? Tell me of them. Numbers. Ages. Sex. Did you notice any variance? Any anomalies? Any—"

"I don't fucking know, and if you finish, I'm going to turn you into jerky and shit you out on the road." I hadn't meant to sound that angry, especially toward someone I needed a favor from, but fuck me, if you had seen the look on his face. "A lot. Many. Too damn many. I don't know. You felt him. You know how strong he is."

"Strong," he groaned. "Stronger than I could have imagined. To see what he could have done, what he's brought low. How is he firing? Are you having trouble acquiring ammunition? Describe your stance when you're firing him."

"He's fine, the shells are fine, and fuck off," I snapped. "I didn't come here to show you the time of your life."

"Ah, the agreement." He sounded disappointed, but that was better than the alternative. "I wouldn't have been in such a hurry to achieve immortality if I knew I'd be dealing with bureaucracy even after I'd died. But a deal's a deal. What does he need?"

"Information. And I need it. He doesn't need anything else. He's eaten enough."

I paused. The words lingered behind my lips, the last moment I had before I opened my mouth and ruined everything. And, like I did every time, I went ahead and did it anyway.

"Almost enough."

The Cacophony seethed in his sheath. Themeter paused, looked up nervously from the machines she tended to. A Dead Dog Buried on a Black Hill, through eyes sealed shut, still stared at me too damn intently.

"I need you to tell me," I whispered, "if the Cacophony can pull something out of a living person."

Beneath his sealed eyelid, something twitched. Withered lips curled faintly.

"A living specimen?" he rasped, musing. "Interesting."

"Person." I laid a hand on one of the *very* delicate-looking pipes sticking into the Freemaker's body. "I said a living person. And you're going to tell me if I can draw something out of a *person* and leave them intact." I drummed my fingers demonstratively, sending the machinery shuddering. "The next time you say 'specimen,' we're going to find out how well you function with only *four* of these shitheaps keeping you alive."

Now, the information necessary to saving the life of the woman I loved was held by the man I had just threatened and insulted, so I can't say it was a *smart* move. But it *did* smear that creepy smile off his face, so it's hard to say whether it was good or bad.

The corpse's lips trembled. His body shuddered a little. As though he'd not so much had a thought as passed one like a kidney stone.

"Depends," he said.

"On what?"

"On a lot of things," he said. "The extraction process is complicated. Only he really knows how to do it. But the energy he tears out of a mage doesn't leave anything behind."

"I'm not talking about mages," I muttered, leaning in close. "I'm talking about..." I furrowed my brow—the precise words to describe shit of this magnitude escaped me. "Something else. Like..." I didn't want to think about it. I didn't want to say it. I didn't want it to be real. But it was. And I did. "Think of a tavern. The nicest tavern you know with the meanest drunk inside it. Too drunk to be thrown out, too sober to be talked out. He refuses to leave. I need to know, can the gun..." I caught myself. "Can the Cacophony throw the fucker out?"

"He is the most ferocious weapon to have been imagined in any mind of any nation. If you want someone out of your house, just pull the trigger and count to one."

"If this could be solved by blowing the shit out of things, I wouldn't be here, now would I?" I spat. "Can the Cacophony pull the drunk out?"

You ever been looked at with suspicion? Like you'd done something wrong, but you know you didn't?

You ever been looked at that way by a corpse?

It's fucking weird.

"What kind of drunk," he rasped, "are you talking about, Sal?"

"I'm talking about—"

"And, just for a moment, pretend you haven't forgotten I'm the smartest fucking man, living *and* dead, in this entire shitheap of a city and talk to me," he interrupted. "You're asking a specific question. I need specific details. If the next words out of your mouth aren't precise, then just go ahead and put me back in the wall and quit wasting my time."

And so I did.

I told him everything. Everything I could. Everything I dared. I told him about Culven Loyal and the Scrath inside him. I told him about Eldest and Liette. I told him how far we'd come and what it could do and what I was afraid of and the only thing I thought could help.

The only thing I didn't tell him was how desperately I hoped there was some other way.

"Now that *is* an interesting question," he said, after all the talking had been done. And the enthusiastic curiosity in his voice was unsettling. "*Could* the weapon extract a Scrath?"

"*Without* damaging her," I snarled. "Keep that bit in the front of your rotting brain, you got it? Not a sinew out of place, not so much as an eyelash touched, or I bury him in the ground and forget this whole thing."

"Of course, of course, the"—he paused for an unwholesome length—"person must be left intact." A longer, less creepy pause. Then a contemplative hum. "Theoretically, it could be done."

"It could?" I hated how much hope was in my voice—I was just begging to be disappointed.

"Theoretically," he said.

"What does that mean?"

"It means that the extraction process is entirely within the control of the weapon," he said. "Killing his ordinary fare—the mages you've killed while you were out being a pain in the world's collective colon, for example—merely presumes, correctly, in most cases, that the subject is unwilling to surrender its essence to the weapon."

Made sense to me. I hadn't met a mage yet that had been voluntarily devoured by this gun.

Of course, I hadn't asked. Who would? *How?*

"So, if you've got a subject that's willing to let the weapon..." His lips stiffened for a long moment. "I'm struggling to find the words that won't provoke a thuggish retaliation from you."

"Just say it. I promise I won't hit you."

"I don't believe you." He sighed. "But fine. If you've got a subject that's willing to let the weapon slip inside and have a metaphorical look around... there should be no reason he couldn't simply take the Scrath with him on his way out."

He was wise to make me promise. That was definitely an awful way to put it. But I wasn't bothered. I had only barely heard that part. The moment I heard the last part, the part about how it could happen...

How she'd be left unharmed.

Fuck.

I didn't realize it until then, but it felt like I'd been living with a knife in my chest. It'd plunged into me and punched through my lung back in the Borrus Valley and every step I'd taken since then had driven it in deeper. And now, with those words, with this chance, this insane plan... well, fuck, even if it was only out an inch...

I could breathe without it hurting so bad.

Fuck.

We could do this. I could do this. I could fix this.

All I had to do was convince Liette to let the weapon she loathed and feared look inside her—and all the horrific implications that statement carries—and extract a terrifying being beyond consciousness from within her.

So that was neat, too.

But I could do it. If I could save her, I'd convince her. I'd let her call me every name, scream at me until she was hoarse and breathless, weep and rage and beat me down until she could see it.

I'd carry this knife in my chest, every last knife in the Scar down to the fucking hilt, if that's what it took to get her out of this.

I could stand her hating me for a while. Maybe forever.

And if I didn't think too hard about it, I could almost believe it.

"Curious, though."

Nothing much could have dampened my mood just then.

"To think what the weapon would be capable of if he were to consume a Scrath."

But wouldn't you know it.

"With the power he already has..."

That fucker had to go and say something horrifying again.

"Scraths." The smile on the corpse's face was dreamlike, pleased at the unwholesome images twitching behind his eyelids. "Every last drop of information we have on them, even after all these centuries, and we still don't have enough to fill a thimble. To think they can occupy a host without consuming its consciousness. Fascinating.

"I wonder, then"—his voice drifted darkly, lilted into a rasping lullaby that hurt to hear—"what would become of the Scrath's consciousness? Would it overwhelm his? No...no, the weapon is too strong for that. Too strong now." His smile curled painfully wide again. "Ah, I can still feel him. How strong he's grown. How strong he *could* grow.

"I sleep so long these days," he mumbled, as though he were drifting off even now, "in my dreams, I hear them. Sometimes, I even see them. At the corners of my eyes. Intrusive thoughts. They showed me once a vision of flames. Everything ablaze, people trapped in tombs of burning ice, of steel raining from the sky and a chorus that split the clouds apart. I thought them warnings, merely there to ward me off, but what if..."

He drifted off. I leaned closer. "Dog? Hey." I resisted the urge to shake him. "Freemaker. Don't die on me now." I paused, looked up at Themeter. "Wait, *can* he die like this?"

"He made me promise not to tell, sorry," she muttered. She glanced from him to the machines. "He can't stay awake for long. Normally, he can go longer than this, but that..." She froze, cringed at the memory as she wiped soot from her brow. "Whatever the fuck that was, it tore the machines apart. If you've got anything to ask him, I'd do it now."

"Listen." I leaned in, whispering urgently. "Think as hard as you can, Freemaker. Specific question, specific answer." I breathed in. "How strong will the Cacophony be if he eats a Scrath?"

"Strong." A Dead Dog Buried on a Black Hill's smile was perverse in its serenity. "And why wouldn't he be? The Scraths have heard his name. They were the ones who—"

He paused. Shuddered. The machines whirred, sputtered, sloshed liquid. I glanced at Themeter, who shrugged helplessly as she continued assessing the machine's damage.

"Ah," the corpse rasped. "I can't remember. But he will be strong."

"How strong?"

And the piping rattled. And the machines groaned. And desiccated flesh stretched and snapped as the corpse's stiff neck turned and he stared right at me. His grin gnawed through my rib cage and sank its teeth right into my lungs.

"You know," he said, "how strong."

I swallowed hard. I wanted to scream at him, to demand he explain that. Or, failing either of those, to punch him so hard I forgot what he said. But I didn't do any of those. Why would I?

He was right.

"Ah." He returned his neck to its position. His body, ravaged and charred as it was, settled back into the sarcophagus with some semblance of composure. "I'm tired. How long until the next awakening, Themeter?"

"It'll be a year, at least, boss," Themeter replied, looking up from the machines with a frown. "This is going to take a *lot* of metal and time to get working again. Some of these pipes, we don't have backups for. And the cylinders..." She winced, shook her head. "I don't know, boss. Was it worth it?"

The corpse smiled. The parched skin around his lips, cracked with heat and blackened with char, pulled back and exposed long teeth, black gums receded all the way back into his head. And, as the last coils of smoke slithered out between his teeth, he answered.

"Absolutely."

FOURTEEN

OCYTUS

People don't celebrate in the Scar. Not like other places.

Sure, there are still songs to be sung, laughs to be had, drinks to be enjoyed, same as anywhere. But in the Scar, these are as many mournings as celebrations. The songs are joyous because they're frequently your last. The laughs are either too strained to be credible or too dark to be funny. And every drink that comes as a welcome relief eventually comes back as a burning need.

We cope in the Scar. We don't celebrate. But sometimes, we get close.

I had gotten close that day, as I left A Dead Dog Buried on a Black Hill's shop and departed down the winding, glimmering avenues of Ocytus. Close as I could ever remember coming to celebrating.

I had a plan. I had reason to believe it could work. I had a way to fix everything. The weight bearing down on my neck since I'd gotten that thing put into Liette was lessened, just a moment, and I was ready to laugh, I was ready to sing, I was ready to break down and cry over how close I was.

And I should have been doing any of that.

"Hey."

But I wasn't.

"What the boss said about your gun... is that true?"

Her voice still rang out in my head. Those last few moments before I'd left the shop, when she'd come hurrying up the steps after me to catch me, breathless, with fear in her eyes.

"*Could it do*"—she had struggled, between her wind and her terror, to find the words—"*what it did to us in there... what I felt... could it do that to others?*"

He could and he did, I told her. She had to know its stories. And she did, she told me. And she hoped they hadn't been true, the look on her face told me.

"*Down there, when it... the gun was...* burning," she had whispered, reverent and terrified, "*I heard something. Felt something. It burned in my head. It told me things that...*" She winced. "*Does it always do that?*"

I didn't know, I told her.

"*Is it going to do that to others?*"

I didn't know that, either.

"*Is it going to hurt?*"

Her questions had kept coming. Desperate, scrambling things, crawling out of her mouth and falling over me.

"*How are you going to keep control of it? What did the boss mean by 'extraction'? Please, tell me, what is that thing going to do? Please! How do you stop it? Is there something wrong with me now? Why does it keep burning? Please, my family is out there! Is this going to happen to them? Please! Please! PLEASE!*"

It'd ended only when the door slammed. Or it should have, anyway. But her words turned to lead in my head, bent my neck low, kept my eyes at my feet. Which, in a city full of every pleasure imaginable, I was *real* pissed about.

I wanted to hate Themeter for that. For the fear in her eyes. For the desperation in her voice. I wanted to resent her for tarnishing my hope, for taking that knife in my chest and jamming it right back into my rib cage. But I didn't hate her. Not for that, anyway.

I hated her for being right.

I should have been more cautious, I told myself. I shouldn't have trusted the eagerness in the Freemaker's voice. His excitement made me almost forget the cost of my plan. Until Themeter had reminded me.

The Cacophony.

The gun who drank the ruin of a thousand Vagrants. The gun who scattered a hundred cities' ashes to the wind. The gun whose story stretched farther, bloodier, and crueler than mine could ever hope to.

With the strength of a Scrath.

I thought about that. I thought about his brass rippling, about the cindered malice pouring off of his metal, about the way he seared in my hand and in my head. And I thought about fires. Climbing so high that they became the sky.

And I tried to tell myself that, if it came to it, I would not put that burden on the world. I tried to tell myself I'd make peace with my failures before I inflicted the Cacophony with that kind of power upon it.

And I stopped where I stood. And I counted for as long as I could.

I clicked my tongue. Eight seconds before I realized I was full of shit. That was longer than I expected.

I tried to distract myself by searching my memory for Liette's instructions. She'd pointed out earlier where the central chambers of the Freemakers had been; we'd agreed to rendezvous there, but I couldn't quite remember...

Was it before or *after* the brothel-arena-buffet combination?

"Pardon me, madam." I flagged down a woman wearing an elaborate dress that resembled something like a wearable guillotine. "I seem to be lost. Could you direct me to the central chambers?"

She furrowed her brow, the metal of her hat rattling as she did. "What?"

"The chambers. The place where the Freemakers meet. The Room of Enlightened Fuckers or whatever you call it."

"There is no such chamber; the only place Freemakers meet is at an orgy or an arms sale, and you are *clearly* lost." She paused.

"Or high. Are you high?" She leaned in, whispered conspiratorially, "Will you sell me some?"

Had I not been so struck by her words, I would have struck her.

"No such chamber?" I muttered to myself.

"Darling, with all due respect to my colleagues, have you *ever* known Freemakers to collaborate in something that wasn't a criminal conspiracy?"

"No," I muttered. "I haven't."

And I hadn't. I'd known. I'd fucking *known* there was no damned sense in trying to get the Freemakers on our side. And hey, looks like I hadn't been the only one to know.

Liette had never planned to meet with the Freemakers, I realized then. Meaning she'd come here with an ulterior motive. Which, I suppose, any ordinary woman might be upset about.

But shit, I'd come here to talk to the corpse that made my magic gun and hadn't told her. What the hell was I going to say?

"Hang on," I said, shaking my head. "We passed it. It was a huge square tower jutting up into the ceiling. Old stone."

"Oh, you mean the library? I suppose some people do gather there still." She paused. "*Mostly* for orgies. I hadn't heard of any today but if there is, you go on ahead—those things are never as fun as they say they are." Apparently no longer interested in me, she started walking, making a vague gesture as she did. "Head down this street and take the fourth left. It'll get you there quicker."

I took off as indicated. My mind started racing. First with suspicion—she must have known I'd figure it out, so she couldn't have meant for me to stay ignorant forever. Then with curiosity—but why? Not that she wasn't capable of duplicity, she just... never seemed to need it. And, being totally honest with myself, it's not like I'm the least gullible person out there.

And finally, with fear, a realization settling over me like a cloak of ice and regret.

What if she came here to do something about the Scrath?

What if she came here to try something dangerous to get it out of her?

What if it was so dangerous she couldn't even have told me?

My feet and my breath were heavy with alarm. How the fuck hadn't I seen this coming? I knew she was smarter than me, but fuck, I didn't realize I was this fucking stupid. Of course she'd had another plan. Of course she'd realized I'd never question it. I never do. I never fucking pay attention and then this shit happens.

I had no idea what she was down here for. And not knowing made my breath grow short and my chest clench tight.

Of course, the thought came as my eyes wandered across the street, *you could just fucking ask her, couldn't you?*

I'd stumbled across a cross section of businesses. Wedged between a butcher advertising a variety of exotic and a few highly illegal meats and a bar that appeared to be served entirely by a brass statue of a woman with fifteen tits dispensing beer into patron's gaping maws, a humble shop sat unassuming.

A tasteful display of windows revealed an expansive series of lockboxes set in the walls of an elegantly decorated office. At the center of its understated peculiarity was a simple desk, managed by a simple-looking man in a simple suit. In hushed tones, he communicated with a head I knew the back of well.

Liette's head bobbed along with the conversation. The quills in her bun rattling with each attentive nod. My eyes drifted up to the signage hanging over the shop's display.

BURLITH & MENZHI: CONTRACTS, LOANS, SAVINGS, LIQUIDATIONS

I wondered which one this asshole was.

"...and of course, Freemaker notes bearing our sigil are authorized for immediate compensation and exchange." I caught the hushed whispers of the man as he slid across a sheaf of papers to her. "A map of locations to all contracted brokers is included with your notes. We recommend committing it to memory and then destroying it. Preferably before you leave our offices."

"Naturally," Liette muttered back, sipping at what appeared to be a complimentary cup of tea. "And all my assets will be available? Your fees considered? I'll need them at a moment's notice."

"We're able to authorize that, certainly," the man—Menzhi, or Burlith—said. "Reliant, of course, on your willingness to dedicate your assets to our concern. We will be happy to make funds available. Though we'll be unable to relinquish them in totality to you should you have a change of heart. Contract standard, you understand."

"I do," she said after a tense pause. "And it's not an issue. I won't be changing my mind. I won't be returning to my operations."

"We're sorry to hear that, Twenty-Two Dead Roses in a Chipped Porcelain Vase." The man extended and shook a hand before glancing over her head at me, loitering in the doorway. "Though you can rest assured that your assets are safe in our hands for as long as you require them to be." He slid out of his chair, pointedly looking at me before turning. "If you'll pardon me a moment while I get everything in order?"

He disappeared into the back of the offices, the sound of multiple heavy doors opening and closing following him. I stood behind her as she sat at her chair, pointedly picking her tea up and stirring it with its tiny spoon—presumably for effect, since I know she hates the taste of sugar.

"Shall I ask how much you've figured out?" she asked without looking at me. "Or would you consider that an insult?"

"As much as I need to be irritated," I replied. "Though I wouldn't consider it an insult, since chances were good it was going to end with me irritated anyway."

"It seems a little hypocritical, doesn't it?" She took a long sip. "How many convenient lapses of memory compelled you to withhold events from me that I eventually forgave?"

"That's different."

"How?"

"Because you're the smart one," I growled. "Every lie I could come up with, you saw through. Every half-truth I offered, you completed. Every misleading statement—"

"I find the end of, eventually, true," she finished for me. "Am I to understand that you resent my attempt at subterfuge because I'm better at it than you?"

"*Yes*, motherfucker," I snapped. "I resent it. I resent us carving a path out here, leaving bodies in our wake, and being chased by assholes whose admittedly colorful personalities I stopped feeling charmed by long, *long* ago based on a lie."

A moment. A long pause. A soft sip, followed by the clink of empty porcelain as she set her cup back down.

"So. Do you resent that I lied," she whispered, "or do you resent that you believed me?"

"Huh?"

She slid out of her chair. She stood. She looked up at me over the rims of her spectacles. The faint light of the offices glistened off her eyes.

"Do you hate me because I told you something that wasn't true?" she asked, her voice halting briefly. "Or do you hate me because you thought I had a plan and I don't?"

"Liette, I—"

"Twenty-Two Dead Roses in a Chipped Porcelain Vase," she retorted, her voice quavering. "Down here, I'm Twenty-Two Dead Roses in a Chipped Porcelain Vase. I am one genius among many, in a city full of machinery, alchemy, and thought so advanced that it renders magic almost primitive in comparison, and with every, *every* ounce of brilliance in this fucking city, I can't *think of a single thing better than this*?"

I furrowed my brow. "What are you saying?"

It's hard to watch a genius try to lie. They've never had to, even though they think they can. Their mouths fall open as they get ready to spin a tale as effortlessly as idiots make it look like—like hers did. Then their brows furrow and their lips purse and they swallow hard as they realize it's harder than it looks—like she did. And then their hands ball into fists—like hers—and their bodies tremble—like hers—and they struggle to figure out any way of coming out of this without looking like an emotional idiot…

"I MEAN I'M FUCKING TIRED OF BEING THE SMART ONE!"

They never do.

She didn't, either.

"I'm tired of being the one to figure things out, I'm tired of being the one with an idea, I'm *tired* of being the one that's supposed to hold everything together because everyone else is so fucking stupid, greedy, evil, violent, or *all fucking four in such excruciating abundance that I and only I can approach anything even remotely resembling a fucking plan and... and...*"

No more words. She had millions of them and none of them were good enough. She looked away from me, held herself, pulled her glasses off, wiped her eyes, tried to find something, *anything* to do with her hands that would somehow distract her from this great and awful silence between us.

"Ocytus was never going to help," she said softly. "I didn't even bother asking. Everyone here is making money from the war—weapons to Revolutionaries, intelligence to Imperials." She sniffed, held up the sheaf of papers. "These are what I really came for."

I glanced over them. Alchemically treated paper, banded and demarcated, each one affixed with a number value and a tiny, artistic interpretation of the Freemakers' many laws. The closest thing they got to something they cared about more than money.

Freenotes.

While every Freemaker extolled the importance of accumulating wealth, the burdens of carrying around enough metal to suit their ambitions would be costly and risky. Freenotes, rarely exchanged outside of their own circles, were what they used as money outside of Ocytus.

I'd never even seen them before now. The sight made me uneasy.

"This is my plan," she said, her breath coming hard. "All my assets, all my metal, every drop of financial strength I have. They're considerable. They'll..." She paused, swallowed hard. "They'll help us."

"Help us," I asked slowly, "with what? What's the plan?"

"I told you. The plan is the money. It's enough to get the refugees somewhere safe. It's enough to get them help and for you to feel like we aren't abandoning them. It'll get us clear of this war, as clear as we need to be, and then..."

The silence between us stretched too long.

"And then?" I asked.

"And then...and then..." She stared at the floor. At the dark stain on the carpets where her tears fell. "And then I've spent every second of every day of these many months with this thing." She held a hand over her chest. "This thing inside me. I've heard its thoughts. I've felt it. And I..."

She looked up. She smiled softly at me. And sobbed.

"And I don't think I'm going to get out of this one, Sal."

I saw her knees shake before I heard her speak. I swept toward her as she pitched forward. She fell into my arms—lighter than she normally was, or had she always been this small? This frail-feeling? She pressed herself against me. I felt her sobbing, hot and wet on my skin.

"I'm sorry," she whispered, "I'm sorry, I'm sorry, I don't know, I don't know. I don't *know* how to get rid of it. I don't know how to leave it behind. I can't figure anything out and I've tried so hard and everything I think of, I realize won't work, and I think of more and then that won't work and I think and I think and I think and nothing...nothing is working, Sal. Nothing. I can't do anything. I can't fix anything. I can't...I can't..."

I held her. I stroked her hair. I let every hot tear fall on me and felt each drop boil on my skin. I could do nothing else but hold her, I told myself.

But as it turns out, I'm not as great at lying as I thought I was, either.

Tell her.

"It's a Scrath," she whispered. "It doesn't follow any rules of magic or nature or...or anything. I hear it in my head, I feel it in me, plucking away at my memories, slithering through my thoughts. Everything I think of, every ritual or magic or technology, it can't...

it won't..." She winced, shook in my arms. "It's going to tear me apart. It's going to eat everything in me. My heart, my brain, my... me. Every memory. Every feeling."

Tell her, my thoughts urged me. *Tell her about the Cacophony.*

"So... this is what I'll do," she said, after a long moment of tear-soaked silence. "I'll use my money to help. I'll use everything I have to help you, to fix things for you, to do everything I can." She found my hand, squeezed it. "For you."

Tell her it can pull the Scrath out of her.

"Liette...," I whispered.

"Please," she sobbed. "Please, let me do this for you. Please, Sal. I can't leave you like this."

"Like what?" I asked. "Liette, you're not—"

"You blame yourself for the Valley," she said. "Like you blame yourself for everything you do. To the Valley. To the people. To me."

"That's not..."

Tell her.

"It is. It always has been. You can't stop fighting and you can't stop hurting and you can't stop hating yourself for it."

Tell her about the Cacophony.

"It's okay," she said. "It's okay. I can't fix that. I know that. I never could. I'm fine with that." She wiped her eyes. "I can't fix the war, either. I know that now."

Tell her he can eat the Scrath.

"But we can help the people. I can help them. I can help *you*."

Tell her he can take its strength. Like Loyal wanted its strength.

"We can do this. We can get them to safety. Or something close to it. We can make it okay again."

Tell her you don't know what he'll look like with that power.

"And then..."

Tell her you already can't control him anymore.

"And then, I suppose... we'll see."

Tell her what's going to happen, the thought rang cold and quiet in my head, *when she's not there. And all you have left is the gun.*

I needed to tell her. I needed this knife out of my chest. I couldn't stand the pain anymore. But when I spoke, I could feel it. Sawing through my ribs, carving into my heart, my throat.

I had to tell her. But how could I? After all that, how could I tell her...

...that I'd burn every last inch of this world down to ashes for her?

I didn't know how. But I had to try.

"Liette," I whispered, "I—"

"Apologies."

The interruption came with the sliding of the heavy door. Menzhi—or Burlith—returned, with another sheaf of papers clenched in his hands.

"Normally, we're a little more leisurely with our paperwork so as to give people more time for..." He paused, looked at me, covered in wet tears and snot, and her. "Well, not *this* specifically, but things like this."

"It's fine." Liette composed herself with flashes of handkerchief and hasty combing work. In a hot breath, she stood before him, the perfect picture of a Freemaker. "We're in no rush."

"Normally, no, but we just received a notice from our outskirts observation." He unfolded a parchment at the top of the papers, adjusted his glasses. "Do either of you know a...Mertur? Merton? They included a description...short fellow, dark skin, big head of hair, and glasses?"

"Meret," I interrupted. "Yeah, we know him."

"Oh, *Meret.* That makes sense." He chuckled to himself, removing his glasses. "I swear, you pore over papers all day and you don't even *think* your eyesight can get any worse, but I suppose even a Freemaker needs new glasses from time to time, hm?" He laughed as he turned over the papers to Liette. "Anyway, he just sent for you. Says he and everyone else is about to be killed by the Revolution. Have a lovely day, madam and madam, and please feel free to help yourself to more tea on the way out."

"Wait, what?" I asked, stunned, as he turned on his heel and left. "*What did you say?*"

"I said the tea is free," he replied as he slipped back behind the door. "Jasmine, I think it is."

"No, about the—"

"The Revolution? Yes, I know. I thought it was clear by my obvious misdirection that I'm not actually interested in that part. In fact, I find the whole process rather uncomfortable."

He cleared his throat, took the door handle.

"So... best of luck. Or not, if you don't like him."

The door slammed.

And behind it, the doors continued to slam.

The sound of heavy metal closing shut, growing fainter, until we were left in silence.

FIFTEEN

OCYTUS OUTSKIRTS

Okay, so.

Yes, in theory, honesty is best for relationships. In theory, it would be wiser to stop, think, compare notes with Liette about what we both knew and try to figure out a way forward. And, in theory, from there, we could have worked out a more effective solution.

In theory.

Three things, though.

First of all: How? How do you be honest when honesty is what happens at the *end* of relationships? How do you find the time between being terrified you're going to lose her and terrified you're going to lose everything to explain it? How do you say something that might scare her off when she's the only one keeping you together?

Second of all: When? When am I supposed to find the time to do that? When is the best time to really *sell* her on the idea of tearing the deranged entity enmeshed in her sinew out of her with the help of my magic, ever-hungry gun who she's always hated and who I can no longer keep totally under my control? When do I decide to do that? Before or after we lose another refugee?

Third of all: Fuck you?

Sorry, that wasn't supposed to be a question.

I meant it as *fuck you*. As in *fuck you, I'll figure it out and I've got bigger problems right now.*

"I understand that this is not a trial asked lightly."

Specifically, I had problems about a thousand people, a thousand gunpikes, and a thousand stunted, propaganda-glutted brains bigger than what I should have been handling.

"Nor would I ask it of you, had I any other choice." A voice—familiar, thick and heavy as a maul—swept over the huddled refugees, sending them cowering beneath it. "But Imperial aggression, which has already cost you everything, has already taken so much from you, cannot go unanswered. The safety of the Scar, not merely the Revolution but all of its people, rely on me asking this service of you." A hard mouth curled into a hard frown. "And you making the difficult choice to uphold it."

I had to hand it to her—for a woman who has tried to kill me multiple times and come closer than most, alongside hurling every insult and curse at me she could possibly think of, I had a certain admiration for Tretta Stern.

Sorry. Tretta Unbreakable.

She got a promotion. Good for her.

The woman stood tall before the refugees, their lowered heads and bent backs arranged in a quivering line, her shoulders back and hands folded authoritatively behind her. Her face, framed by severely short-cropped black hair, was a little more weathered and a little more scarred than I remembered. But no injury was enough to keep the anger from weeping out of her face like sores.

A firm body held itself rigid beneath her elaborate uniform. A thick officer's saber hung menacingly at her hip. Heavy epaulets atop a heavier coat, brimming with medals—more than a few of them earned in conflicts *I'd* started, but do I get any thanks?—shuddered as she took in another breath and bellowed.

"Understand that the Great General, in his infinite wisdom, has made this decision. And in his infinite mercy, he has not made it lightly." She raised a hand. The crowd flinched away. "Nor do I expect it to be followed lightly. But I do expect it to be followed."

That.

That right there. *That* was what I admired. That total hard-eyed, stiff-shouldered way she carried herself. That complete confidence of the inevitable she wore when she addressed the refugees. *There* was a woman who did not agonize, who did not sit up at nights worried what she'd done wrong.

I couldn't help but envy that.

"The One Hundred Seventh Regiment of the Glorious Revolution of the Fist and Flame will resume its implacable march in two hours," she said to the crowd. "And when it does, a minimum of four hundred of you will be marching with it."

Of course, if I had a small army behind me, I'd probably be a badass, too.

In perfect order behind her, the ranks of the Revolutionary soldiers teemed. A thousand blue coats stood rigid at her back, their gunpikes held at attention and their eyes vacantly fixed across the refugees. Plumes of smoke rose from rattling machines behind them—tanks and transports rumbling idly nearby.

Must have been following them for a while, I thought. *Keeping the refugees in sight until they stopped here to rest. Scoop them up while they're too tired to fight back. Then give them food and rest and trust them to realize it's not so bad.*

I clicked my tongue. I had to admit, the Revolution was way better at conscription these days. It used to be that a low sergeant would just bust into a bar and order everyone into the army at gunpoint. It's nice that they get fed before they're forced to die in a war not their own.

But pointing something like that out when you've *caused* the war in question felt just a touch too hypocritical.

Not that I could do much beyond petty judgments, at the moment. I squatted in the bushes at the outskirts of the woods, watching the scene unfold. By the time we'd made it out of Ocytus, there were already more soldiers than I could hope to handle on my own.

Fabulous as I've made myself out to be, I'm still only incredible, not invincible.

"You can't do this!"

Or stupid. Like some others.

I would have picked out Meret even if he *hadn't* just shrieked an order at a platoon of heavily armed assholes. He came rushing out of the crowd of refugees in his threadbare coat and dirty glasses, holding his hands up in a plaintive plea that he seemed to believe was every bit equal to the many, many, *many* weapons arrayed against him.

"These people aren't soldiers! They're farmers, barrel-makers, *drunks*!" He shouted himself hoarse, flailed his arms around—made a spectacle of himself to keep eyes off the refugees. Not a bad idea. Fewer eyes on them, fewer ideas about them. "They aren't made for combat, for riding, for marching, for *anything* you need them to do."

"Within the heart of every free citizen lies the power and need to do what is right," Tretta replied, staring him down through narrowed eyes. "With the power of the Revolution and the Great General fueling them, they shall be—"

"Corpses. Corpses burned, broken, and destroyed," Meret interrupted—not without consequence, if the rigid tremble of Tretta was to be believed. "They could barely fend off bandits. They won't last a *second* against mages."

"If they can hold a weapon, they can hold a—"

"It doesn't matter what you *think* they can do, it just—"

"—I have overseen *countless* recruits—"

"—you don't know the first thing about these people, and further—"

I couldn't make out what they were saying after that. And truth be told, I kind of lost interest. Admiring as I might have been of her, Tretta's gift for conversation was not something I missed. And Meret's was only slightly less tedious.

Still, I couldn't help but murmur to myself.

"Smart."

"Is it?" At my observation, Liette finally deigned to crouch down beside me. She adjusted her spectacles, squinted. "He seems to be... annoying her? Satisfying as that might be, I hesitate to call it 'smart' when used against someone with considerably more firepower."

"He's annoying as he ever was, sure, but you don't see her firing, do you?" Sindra spat into the bushes next to us—she, at least, had been able to get to cover when she saw the Revolutionaries swarming. "He's challenging her. Stalling her. Drawing out time. If she wants to end him now, she'll have to kill him."

"That would seem expedient," Liette concurred.

"Not for a Revolutionary," she replied. "She needs these people fighting for her. She's not going to get that by shooting him." Sindra paused, considered. "Of course, she's not *not* going to shoot him, either. She's not leaving without the refugees." She glared at me. "Neither am I, for the record."

I rolled my eyes. For the record, I only suggested leaving them behind *once.*

"Yeah, yeah." I scratched my scar. "Give me a minute. I'm thinking."

"Of what?" Sindra asked.

"Of a plan to save them, *obviously.*"

"How much of this plan involves shooting?" Liette asked, pointed.

I thought, hummed, sniffed. "About... eighty percent?"

"So you're just going to start shooting?" Sindra shook her head. "Any idiot could come up with that."

"Well, not any idiot has a big fucking gun that shoots magic, do they, Madame Negative Thinking?" I didn't look at the offense on her face—which, you must believe, was hard for me to avoid doing—my eyes were drawn to the back of the line of Revolutionaries. "I haven't ruled out shooting, just so we're all clear. But humor me." I gestured with my chin. "How much would it take to take out *those* mean-looking fucks in the back there?"

Both of them followed my gaze. Neither had to look far for said fucks.

The line of soldiers was a disheveled line of blue coats and gunpikes. Three rows of soldiers shifted uncomfortably, sneezed, scratched themselves when they thought no one was looking. But the fourth row…

Fuck, I couldn't even tell if they were alive.

Each one of them stood tall and rigid. Their bodies were wrapped in thick black leather coats, shining and dotted with metal plates. Their faces were hidden behind heavy black masks, their eyes shrouded behind shaded lenses set inside them. Long tubes ran from their masks down to their chests, where curious apparatuses of machinery were affixed: cold, polished metal arranged in compact, whirring designs.

"No clue," Sindra muttered. "Never seen those in any unit I served in. Could be new."

"Fascinating," Liette whispered, adjusting her glasses. "What are those devices on their uniforms? I've never seen any machinery like that. I would *dearly* love to study one."

"Maybe for your birthday." My eyes narrowed. "I've never seen weapons like that, either."

Each one of them carried the same kit: a gunpike in their hands, a heavy combat knife at their belts, an autobow strapped to their backs. Which, by itself, might not be cause for concern. But I'd never seen gunpikes like that—black-hafted and ending in wicked saw blades, accompanied by a small chorus of built-in cannons. Or autobows like that—compact, polished, equipped with pristine firing machinery and a full complement of angry-looking bolts. And I couldn't see their knives very well, but I bet they had some weird birdshit going on, too.

"All right, fuck." I rubbed my eyes. "Two shots, then. One to disorient those mean fucks, one to disorient the regular fucks, you and Meret get everyone else out. Easy."

Sindra met my plan—which I thought was quite good, considering the circumstances—with a sour frown like she always did whenever she didn't like my ideas and shook her head.

"You're looking at the wrong soldiers." She pointed toward the rank and file. "Look at *them*."

It took me a moment, but soon enough and sure enough, I saw the same things she did. Soldiers were idly spitting, some muttering among themselves, others looking around warily. Only a handful of them held themselves tall as their weaponry. The vast majority of them...

"Those are conscripts themselves," Sindra muttered. "New ones, I bet. Mages chew through recruits like birds through seed. They aren't ready to fight the Imperium. *Or* a Vagrant."

I took her meaning. The Cacophony did, too, his pleasure emanating from the sheath in short, excited gasps of steam.

"You have anything that can break them?" she asked.

I didn't want to answer. "I have one."

Liette went quiet. The Cacophony seethed. Only one of them dared to say it to me.

"Steel Python?"

I nodded to the whisper meant only for me.

Steel Python.

"Can you spot their sergeant?" I asked as I fished something out of my satchel.

"Huh?" she asked.

"Look at them. Tell me which one of those fuckers the other fuckers like best."

Sindra furrowed her brow but looked anyway. She eventually picked out a taller, more confident-looking man walking slowly among the ranks. His age and scars were display enough of his rank, and more than a few of the conscripts tried their best to ape his posture and poise.

"Him," she said. "The one with the mustache. The other ones look to him."

I nodded. He was toward the end of the row closest to us.

Which was lucky. Or unlucky, depending on how you consider what happened next.

"All right." I slid the gun from his sheath, loaded a shell, slammed the chamber shut. "In a few minutes, the shit's going to be served. When it happens, grab Meret and as many people as you can handle and get moving. Liette, get back to the lift and get it ready. When they come chasing me, we'll disappear and they'll be left with nothing."

"Are you sure they'll chase you?" Sindra asked.

"I am."

I didn't answer. Liette did. I glanced over my shoulder at her, saw the concern etched across her face. I knew what she was thinking, I knew how talk like this made her. I knew that I was only ever one trigger pull away from that concern turning to horror on her face.

Would she do that, I wondered, when I told her what A Dead Dog Buried on a Black Hill told me about the gun?

Without another word, she turned and headed back toward the lift to Ocytus.

"All right, then." Sindra eased back to her legs, knees and prosthetic alike popping. "I'll head toward that gap in the trees over there. If at least half of them are smarter than your average rodent, we should get a few out." She glanced toward me. "You going to give a signal?"

I glanced at her. She rolled her eyes.

"Yeah, fuck me for asking, right?" she muttered as she stalked off.

And left me to my business.

I kept low, moving only when Meret or Tretta started shouting, making sure no eyes were wandering as I edged closer to the massed soldiers. The closer I got, the more I could make out of my target—tall, experienced enough to flout the no-facial-hair rule. But not particularly strong-looking. He didn't need strength. He laid hands on shoulders, muttered encouraging words, cracked the right kind of joke at the right kind of time to keep everyone's fingers off the trigger as he made his way through the ranks.

I could see why they all liked this fellow.

Made me regret what I was about to do to him.

"Your plan?"

"Him," I replied, nodding at the mustached fellow. "We take him out in suitably spectacular fashion, bait the rest, whittle them down as they come."

Steam slithered into my ears. He'd only heard one of those words. *"Spectacular?"*

"Spectacular," I reluctantly muttered in agreement.

His heat grew warm, affectionate. The steam peeling off him slithered around me, a delighted feline coiling around my legs.

"Steel Python," the Cacophony hissed.

I hated it when he was happy.

Or at least, I should have. But truth be told, even if I didn't say it at the time, I almost agreed with him. This—sneaking, hunting, planning, fighting—felt good.

This wasn't thinking. This wasn't worrying. This wasn't going down a list of all the people I hurt, had hurt, would hurt. This—the heart beating slow, the blood going cold, every part of me slowing down as it readied itself for the blow...

This felt good.

From the moment I put my hand on the Cacophony to the moment I saw my target drift just a little too close to my hiding spot...

Right up to the moment I grabbed him.

It happened quick. Too quick for anyone but the closest soldiers to notice me leaping out of the bushes and smashing their comrade across the jaw with the Cacophony's hilt. A stir went up, the situation coming together in flashes: a cry of alarm, a glimpse of teeth and blood on the ground, the confused rattle of gear clattering on gear. Their eyes searched the scene fervently, hands on weapons, and by the time they figured out what was happening...

Well, my arm was already around his throat and my gun was already at his head.

"Easy, now," I said to the numerous, *numerous* gunpikes now arrayed against me. I tapped the Cacophony's grinning barrel against the poor fucker's temple. "I only just met this fellow. I'd hate for you to rush our introductions."

Most of them froze. A few of them cursed, impotently. Many, gratifyingly, slunk to the back of the mob surrounding me. But the ones in black—the mean ones—they...didn't move. They simply turned their heads toward me in unison, black lenses taking me in through masked faces. Ready. Rigid. Attentive.

Movement caught my eye. One of the soldiers attempted to rush forward. I took a step back, whistled.

"Well, shit, you should have told me you were in a hurry." I drew the hammer back. My hostage froze. The sound of the brass clicking echoed through a suddenly silent clearing. "I can be quick."

"Attention! *Attention!*" a voice bellowed as a short, sturdy, very pissed-off frame barreled her way through the crowd. "For fuck's sake, when I say 'attention' that means you..."

Tretta emerged from the throng of soldiers, led by the tip of her drawn sword. Her face was painted red with anger, her wide-eyed scowl sending her conscripts shrinking before her. War and scars had done nothing to temper her fury.

And I had to admit, I felt kind of flattered that I could.

Because as she took in the situation and forced her breath slow, I watched that red-hot fury ebb away into something cold and hateful, sharpened to a razor edge and aimed squarely at my neck.

"Lower your weapons," she uttered, her voice drained of anything warmer than a snowstorm. "Eyes on the refugees. Ensure none of them leave and no harm comes to them." As conscripts awkwardly lowered their weapons and shuffled to surround the refugees, Tretta's eyes remained locked on mine. "Talk to me, Therel. Has she hurt you?"

"I'm fine, Commander." My hostage—Therel, apparently; nice name—grunted, making a half-hearted pull at my arm locked around his throat. "Don't worry about me. Take her out. She can't—"

"I really hate to interrupt dear Therel here," I announced, "considering I so inconsiderately made him the center of attention." I pressed the gun to his temple. "But I really must ask you to reconsider this whole 'she can't' line of thinking. I guarantee you I can." Steam peeled between my fingers. The Cacophony seethed, excited. "And I guarantee you I can make it messy."

A chorus rose among the conscripts. They'd seen the gun. They'd seen the scars. They were starting to put things together. A ripple ran through the crowd, an unsteadying that made men and women glance around nervously and shuffle their feet under them.

A warning glare from Tretta—and that big fucking sword of hers—stiffened their resolve for a moment. But I'd already seen it.

And I made sure she knew I did.

"Running down refugees, Madame Stern?" I chuckled. "Pardon, Madame Commander *Unbreakable*. You'd have thought your new promotion would give you better troops." I glanced at the mean-looking fuckers—had they moved? *Were* they going to move? "Or has the mighty Revolution faded so much that it needs to round up children and grandmothers to fight its wars for it?"

"You *dare*—" Therel had a habit of saying things I interrupted a lot, I noticed.

"Kitten." I pressed the gun against him warningly. "Mommy is *trying* to have a conversation."

"I had soldiers," Tretta replied, visibly biting back anger. "Good ones. I lost many of them in Borrus. I lost more of them at Six Walls. I lost the rest to Vagrants, bandits, and every other monster on this dark earth after your war."

"I'm one woman, Commander," I replied. "It takes armies to start a war."

"Armies or one sufficiently motivated monster." A pause, a narrowing of the eyes. "What business does a Vagrant have with a pack of refugees, anyway?"

I swallowed hard.

Fuck me, when did she start thinking things out? This used to be so easy—I said some charmingly obnoxious stuff, she'd take the bait, I'd figure a way out. That was our *thing*. That was what made us *work*.

"Not a damn bit of it, I'm afraid," I replied. "But a pack of Revolutionaries dogging my heels? That, I take issue with. I figured I'd come attend one of your little propaganda parties and see what all the fuss was about."

She stared at me, considering. I really didn't care for that. "Dogging your heels? Are you being pursued"—she paused—"Madame Cacophony?"

Fuck me. This wasn't good.

Something was different. She wasn't taking the bait. She wasn't getting angry. She was waiting, studying me.

And the mean-looking fuckers... they were studying her.

"Our intelligence reports that the Imperium's Hellions were after you," she said. "Is it true they even brought Bad Neighbor out of retirement for it?"

"I wasn't aware you were keeping apprised," I muttered, more irritable than I wanted to sound. "If you'd wanted to keep in touch, you could have visited."

"You have many visitors these days, it seems."

"I can handle the Imperium."

Her eyebrows quirked. Her face hardened. "Then you don't know."

I furrowed my brow, asked without thinking. "Know what?"

She shook her head. "I'll not make life easier for any enemy of the Revolution, let alone one that's caused as much strife as you have. You and these refugees aren't ready for the storm of shit bearing down on you, Cacophony." Something earnest and dire appeared on her face. "It isn't like the other times, Sal. The people after you are going to come down on you like a hammer and everyone near you will be crushed."

She extended a hand.

Not a sword. Not a threat. A hand.

"Surrender. Spare these people, this land, what's going to come as a result of your actions."

Just like that. No drama. No threat. Not even a fucking *glare.* She looked at me too earnestly, too honestly, too... *sincere.* There wasn't enough hatred in her eyes, not enough anger to make me write it off. This asshole, this absolute *fucker* of a woman, was acting like she was doing *me* a favor.

Had it really come to that? Had I finally carved so much blood and war out of this land that she couldn't bring herself to look at me as a foe anymore? When she looked at me—when *any* of them looked at me—did they see anything besides a monster?

Funny thing about people, though.

You can call yourself a beast, a murderer, and every kind of bad name you can think of. You can stay up late cursing your choices and fall asleep wishing for better ones. You can go every breath of every day hating yourself, thinking you're a monster...

...but the minute someone *else* does it...

"The thought had occurred to me," I said, and I didn't lie.

It was more tempting than I'd like, the thought of putting down my weapon, letting someone else handle it. Had I left it there, I'd probably not have caused so much trouble for myself. But my jaw wouldn't clench, my teeth wouldn't shut. The words came from me. And they came cold, angry, and sharp.

"But then what?" I muttered. "You cut my head off, stick it on a pike somewhere, and go back to the war. And time would pass and you'd collect more and more heads and lose more and more heads. You'd come up with a new monster to blame and a new reason why killing it didn't fix everything."

I could only barely hear the words coming out of my mouth. I didn't know where they came from. I didn't know when my arm tightened around Therel's windpipe or when my finger had inched a little tighter around the Cacophony's trigger.

Maybe the stress and the running and the wounds had gotten to me. Maybe Tretta's words cut deeper than I thought and I was bleeding anger.

"Just the same as I've been doing."

Or maybe I just didn't have the strength to keep up the lie.

"These refugees are nothing to me," I said, and again, I didn't lie.

"Just the cost of war." I narrowed my eyes, clenched my jaw. "*My* war. My gun. My sword. My fire. And I'm not done with it yet."

I tightened my arm around Therel. The soldiers stirred, looking alive with alarm. The black-clad ones flinched, stilling only at a glance from Tretta. I didn't care. I didn't fucking care.

I was out of words.

"And though we both agree it's my war, I don't fucking recall inviting you. Or the Imperium. Or any other fucker that wants to kill me."

What escaped my mouth wasn't words. It was the exhaustion. It was the blood. It was the nightmares and the scars and the cold mornings I woke up shaking with the fear that I was never going to fucking solve this.

"And you can tell them and all the other shit coming my way," I shouted, loud enough to be heard by conscript, comrade, and commander alike, "what you saw here. And when you do, I encourage both you and them to take a good, long think..."

I shoved Therel away from me.

"And all of you can decide together..."

I aimed the Cacophony at him. A scream went up. I didn't hear it.

"How bad you motherfuckers really want this."

I pulled the trigger.

The scream was taken up. Over and over, across soldier and refugee alike. They collapsed at the sound of brass clicking, covered their heads. I had the barest moment to see Therel's eyes—to see the image of everything he'd fought for in this fucking war coming at him down a brass barrel. I saw them widen, saw his mouth fall, as the waste of his life flashed before his eyes.

I didn't like the expression.

Reminded me too much of someone.

Silver spat from the Cacophony's maw. Streaked across the sky in a painful blur. It struck Therel square in the chest, knocked him to his ass. He gasped, retching for breath for a moment as he rolled around, flailing for purchase and for air, before finding his feet.

He stood back up. He touched the wound where the shell had struck and took in a deep breath.

"Therel?" Tretta asked, her arm held aloft, holding any action at bay. "Are you . . . all right?"

He certainly looked it.

But that's what makes Steel Python so nasty.

Everyone who gets it looks all right.

"I don't . . ." Therel shook his head, took in a deep, gurgling breath. "I don't feel right, Commander."

At first.

"Something's in . . ." His breath became ragged, sour, desperately ill. "Something's inside of—"

Then it gets messy.

"Therel? *Therel?*"

Tretta's words went unheard. Therel wasn't listening. He was scratching at his cheek madly, skin coming off under the fingernails. A red and glistening mass bubbled beneath his fingers. It swelled. It trembled.

And burst.

A gray metal spike poked out of his cheek, no bigger than a large sewing needle, red and glistening with his own life.

"I feel it," Therel gasped, staring at his own blood-covered hands. Another boil bubbled across his palm. "I *feel* it. It's cold, Commander. It's . . . so . . ."

"What did she do to you, Therel? Talk to me!"

He started to answer. It became a scream as another spike, bigger this time, punched its way out of his palm. Blood burst out of his hand, pattered thick and fat on the earth. Another wail tore out of him, another spike bursting out his shoulder blade.

"Commander! *TRETTA!*" the soldier screamed, poking at the protuberances and wincing. "Am I . . . am I going to . . ."

He was.

And he did.

A bursting sound, like a wet sack popping. Strips of pale, papery human flew through the air like confetti. Sky and trees painted morbid colors with the spray of bile and humors. A hundred glistening spikes, brimming and polished and trembling as they solidified.

A silhouette stretched long across the ground. A silhouette of a dozen spikes and a mess that had once been a man—his glistening parts strung from tip to tip, his firmer parts adorning long metal shafts like decoration. A silhouette of red glistening metals and sinews, sundered and fluttering in a stale breeze.

Every eye was on Therel.

The gore that had once been Therel.

They saw him. Every refugee. Every soldier. And Tretta. And I.

And him, warm in my hand, exhaling with delighted steam.

A moment of stunned silence. A dying wind. A breath, collectively held in half a thousand chests. A single, satiated hiss of steam.

"Beautiful."

And then.

The screaming.

"THAT'S THE FUCKING GUN!"

"I TOLD YOU THE REVOLUTION COULDN'T PROTECT US!"

"Therel? THEREL!"

A chorus of fear and pain went up, each voice clamoring to be the one to have their terror heard before the others. Yet, through the ruckus of motion and sound, it was only two words, shouted in haste, that anyone bothered listening to.

"Fuck this!"

I didn't know the woman who shouted it, the thin-looking country girl in a conscript's coat too big for her. I didn't even get a good look at her as she turned around. But when she hurled her gunpike to the ground and tore off running into the bush, well...

She *might* have been my favorite person.

"Resolute! Resolute, stop where you are!"

Tretta shouted. Resolute, if that was actually her name, didn't listen. Neither did the others that threw their weapons down and took off running. Or the refugees, who saw their chance for an escape. And there was a moment of tension as the conscripts fled into the woods. And then, there was only one voice.

"RUN!"

Screaming. Pushing. Fleeing. Conscripts cursed and fought against the others to escape, even as their commanders hauled them bodily to the ground, trying to keep them from retreat. Refugees tore off into the woods, the lucky ones following Meret as he waved them furiously toward an escape route—the unlucky ones...

...well, fuck, I did for them what I could.

Or so I told myself.

Through the panicked carnage, Tretta had the presence of mind to catch one last glimpse of me as I started stepping into the woods. I tipped my gun, shot her a wink.

"Anyway, think it over."

I disappeared into the foliage, took off running back toward the lift. I tried to put the sounds of carnage behind me, tried to ignore the glimpses of people rushing past as deserters and travelers alike tried to vanish into the woods.

Did what you could. You did what you could. They have a fighting shot now. You did what you could.

I tried to tell myself that. And a lot of other things. Because I tried like fucking hell to put the thought of what I'd just done—the image of Therel flensed and flayed and dangling like human bunting across Steel Python's tines—out of my head.

I tried.

I failed.

I couldn't help it. I couldn't keep it out of my fucking head. I couldn't keep the last sight of his face, the last thing he said, the faces of everyone who saw him from flooding my mind.

I'd known the fucker for five minutes.

And I put him down like a sick bird.

This is what they meant when they heard my name. This is what they meant when they heard about the Valley. It wasn't legend or spectacle or story they'd remember. It was how Sal the Cacophony, one woman with one gun, was more horrible than the entire fucking Revolution.

Is this what Liette, I wondered, *is trying to fix?*

I stopped running. My breath was loud, the sound of the panic less so. I leaned over, breathing hard, struggling to catch my wind. A scent reached my nose—a scent of smiling embers and laughing ash and steam coiling like the innuendo at the end of a sentence.

I looked down to the weapon in my hand. His brass trembled, burned excitedly. He shook in my hands.

He enjoyed that.

He was enjoying this.

And how much fucking more would he enjoy it, I wondered—though I tried so fucking hard not to—if he ate just a little more, got just a little stronger?

What would that look like?

I tried not to think about it.

I failed, again.

"Company."

My ears pricked up at his hiss. In the foliage behind me, I could hear the metallic clink of machinery activating. I heard whirring metal, caught a glimpse of sparks through the dense underbrush.

The metal turned into a shriek as a whirling saw blade at the end of a thick haft punched through the wall of leaves. Two more joined in. Black metal flashed as the saw blades chewed through the brush, spitting out branches and debris. The saw blades lowered, their wails diminishing to machine growls, as the woods fell clear.

I stared at the sudden opening.

Forty mirrored lenses set in dark mechanical masks stared back at me.

"Ah, right," I said. "You guys."

That was rude, I know, but I didn't know any better name for them. What was I supposed to say? *You mean-looking motherfuckers?* Ask them for an introduction?

Honestly, I would.

But they gave me one.

Twenty of them, in fact.

And after their saw-blade-spear-thingies all whirred into one shrieking symphony, *mean-looking motherfuckers* was fairly appropriate.

Not that I was going to stick around to tell them.

I took off at a sprint again. They followed. I darted through underbrush, over logs, tried to make the trail harder. Failed. Their saws tore through the bushes like butter, crushed branches underfoot as they came charging after me.

I tried to put distance between us, counted that they wouldn't be as quick in that heavy gear. But no sooner did I start pulling ahead than I heard the whirr of autobow motors. Bolts punched through the sky, whistling past as their crossbows launched machine-powered missiles at me.

I slid behind a tree. A heavy bolt punched through, stuck in the trunk, my own wide-eyed shock reflected in its black metal head.

Couldn't bring them to Liette. Had to shake them.

My hand went into my satchel, searched for a shell. I didn't need to kill them, just to slow them down.

"Sunflare," I muttered to myself as I slammed it into the chamber.

"I hate Sunflare," the Cacophony whined, dejected.

"So will they."

I whirled out from behind the tree. They were close enough now I could see the light reflected off their lenses. I held my gun up, pulled the trigger back, aimed as much as I dared.

Sunflare flew. Exploded. I looked away. The bright gasp of light incinerated the woods, devouring shadows and shape and color in a great burst of white-hot brightness that swallowed the carnage.

I turned away, shut my eyes, waited for it to clear. I could slip out while they were blinded, I told myself.

I didn't lie. That was a good idea.

But when I opened my eyes again, they weren't fucking blinded. They weren't even fucking slowing down.

No breath to curse. No thought for anything but running. My mind went blank, smothered by the fears running through it and the sound of boots closing in behind me. Had to get another shell. Had to keep them off me.

I found one, fished it out, slammed it into the gun's cylinder. I whirled, pulled the trigger.

Hoarfrost shrieked, bursting in a spray of freezing mist. A cloud of white and blue swept outward, banishing the sun and sky beneath it. I clenched my jaw as the cold swept over me, freezing my sweat to my skin.

Fuck me. I thought I'd been a good range away, too. Had I been closer than I thought? Or was the gun just that strong now?

The mist dissipated, chased away by the weary sigh that came out of my lungs. The mean-looking motherfuckers, whoever they had been, all stood rigid in place. Their black coats glistened like obsidian beneath the thick sheet of rime coating them, their bodies and weapons frozen mid-swing by the thick ice.

"Fuck me," I gasped, taking a moment to breathe. "Fuck me, you're persistent." When I had finally caught my breath enough to stand upright, I glanced at my frozen foes. "Who the fuck pays you guys enough to do this, anyway?"

I dared to inch closer to one, squinted. Their masks were hideous—inhuman lenses seated above a macabre apparatus of tubing and cylinders that formed some manner of mouth. Their armor was thick, featureless black, bereft of detail aside from the mechanical shit strapped to their chest, the fur trim of their coats, and…

"There we are." I squinted at the Revolutionary badge pinned to their chest, read out the dull iron letters as best I could. "Twenty-Second Mechanized Infantry Battalion? Are there any names that *don't* sound incredibly overwrought in the Revolution?"

I actually was lying that time. Mechanized Infantry Battalion sounded way, *way* better than *mean-looking motherfuckers*. But whatever, if I hadn't been running for my life, I'd probably have come up with something more exciting.

"Apologies. I don't mean to shit on your name." I grinned, raised a hand to rap my knuckles against the ice. "Seems you've got other problems at the moment, so I'll be on my—"

I rapped.

The ice cracked. A jagged white scar split across the rime. I staggered backward, eyes wide as the cracks spread. I glanced across the frigid field—they were *all* starting to thaw, squirming in their ice as tiny coils of steam peeled off their shoulders and the mechanical apparatus on their chest...

It glowed bright red. Heat poured out of its metal, flowed into their coats, bade the ice to shatter and melt.

"Shit," I muttered.

An arm broke free.

"Shit."

Then a leg.

"Shit, shit, shit."

And, assuming by the cracking sounds that followed, the rest of them started breaking out, as well. Not like I was going to check, though, what with me running and screaming like an idiot.

"Liette!" I screamed as I tore through the underbrush. "*Liette!*" I burst into a clearing. "*Where's the fucking lift, Liette?*"

I found her at the center of it. The disguise of earth and grass that had concealed the lift's entrance was sliding away at an alarmingly slow pace. Liette glowered concernedly at me as I came forward, gasping for air.

"It's coming. What's the matter?" she asked.

"Make it come faster, I'll explain later."

"For one, I cannot, as I am not in control of the lift beyond simply summoning it. For two, as I could clearly explain that, we obviously have time for you to—"

"*My bullets don't work on them, woman!*" I spat, wide-eyed as I tried to find the breath and the words at the same time. "The ones in black with the masks. They've got these... and these..." I futilely gestured around my face and chest. "Some kind of hot... heat... melty-ice thingies. Hoarfrost barely slowed them down."

"Hot...heat..." Her eyes narrowed, then snapped open. "Personal temperature regulation? The Revolution *has* that?"

"Yes, sure. Make the lift come."

"Well, did you get one?"

I stared at her, vacant-eyed.

"I'd like to take a look at it, is all—"

"THE FUCKING LIFT, LIETTE!"

"*Oh, right,*" she shouted back. "I'm *the unreasonable one here. Clearly.*"

She produced her quills and inks and knelt down, beginning to work. I didn't know what spellwrighting needed to be done to make this shitty machine move and I didn't care. I kept my gun up, loaded with whatever the fuck I hoped could stop them, and aimed at the direction the noise was coming from.

The sound of saw blades grew louder, joined by the shrieking rattle of metal.

"Almost," Liette muttered as her quill scrabbled across the lift's hatch. "I swear, they make this so unnecessarily..."

She trailed off into her own mutter. The machinery of the lift whirred steadily behind me. In the woods, the sounds of saw blades were joined by boots thundering.

"Liette," I muttered.

"Just another moment."

The machine whirred faster. *Did* it whirr faster or was I just imagining that? I clenched the gun tight, felt him grow hot in my hand. Black shapes blossomed through the foliage. I could see their lenses fixed on me.

"Let them come," the Cacophony whispered to me. *"I'm sure we can handle them. We'll make a game out of it."*

"Later, *later,*" I snarled. "Liette, are you fucking—"

"As a matter of fact"—she tapped her quill in punctuative definition—"I am."

The machinery of the lift sped to life. The hatch shuddered as it smashed into the earth with the force of its opening. The lift shot up with such vigor that it nearly flew off its machinery. Bolts and other important-looking bits of metal launched into the air. Liette adjusted her glasses, hummed.

"Oh, I see now. Too much speed will compromise the machinery." She chuckled. "Honestly, why didn't I think of that before? It's a simple law of—"

"Later." I took her by the shoulder, shoved us both into the lift. "Later."

"No, but I should mention, when I say 'compromised,' I mean—"

A motor whirred. A crossbow bolt shrieked past us, split a narrow tree in twain.

"FOR FUCK'S SAKE, LIETTE!"

She hastily finished scribbling something on the metal. The lift whirred back to angry life, stirred beneath my feet. For a brief moment, I could feel a surge of relief, an intense lightness that coursed through me.

Then again, that might have been the floor dropping out.

Liette screamed, clung to me. I very valiantly and dignifiedly cried out, clung to the lift, steadying us both. The hatch overhead began to shudder and stir, struggling to close itself just a *touch* too slowly for my liking.

I slammed another shell into the Cacophony, fired upward. Shockgrasp sped up the lift's shaft, erupted into a dozen arms of twitching electric light. They seized the metal of the hatch, pulled it shut with a shuddering slam and a shower of metal shards.

All right, I told myself. That was one problem solved, at least. Now all that was left was the—

The lift slammed into the floor, ejecting us out of its cage like so much offal. I pulled Liette into me, tumbled with her across the floor of the platform we had called the tram from. I felt bruises blossom across my skin, scrapes carve themselves into me alongside my scars, pain and exhaustion sweep over me.

But I felt her against me. Whole. Warm. Safe.

Decent trade. Not the best I'd had, but still.

"Are we..." Liette looked up from having buried her face in my chest. "Alive?"

"You are," I groaned. "I'll get back to you on me."

She pushed herself to her feet, hurried to the apparatus at the edge of the platform. The summony-spellwrighty-thingy, I don't fucking know. She pulled her quills free, began to go about her work.

"I can summon the tram presently," she said. "Are they following?"

I got to my feet, as well—*push* was slightly too ambitious a mode of movement, so I settled for kind of limping toward the shaft. I glanced up, saw only darkness. Shockgrasp had done its job—the force of it slamming the hatch shut had mangled the metal irreparably.

They wouldn't be getting through that without an explosion.

Which, I recalled at that moment, was something the Revolution had frequent and easy access to.

So, you know.

That was fun.

The shaft rocked with a sudden jolt. Spears of angry daylight came sweeping down the shaft as red-hot eruptions punched holes through the hatch's damaged metal. I saw the Twenty-Seconds swarming at the top of the shaft, affixing some manner of hook and wire to it and rappelling down like spiders, black carapaces glistening.

"I assume that explosion was not good for us," Liette observed without looking up.

"Most of them aren't," I replied, backing away from the shaft.

"I'll hurry, then."

"That'd be nice of you."

Light and sound came rattling up the tunnel. The tram was close enough to hear, damn near close enough to taste. Yet, as I heard boots landing on ground, I knew it wasn't anywhere near close enough.

No room here to use the gun. I slid him back into his sheath, ignored the dejected hiss of vapor he let out. My sword came to my hand with reluctance, my body aching and muscles screaming at the thought of fighting.

And it wasn't like I was thrilled, either.

But I was much less thrilled with the idea of being eviscerated by a whirling saw-bladed murderspear, so here we fucking were.

A Twenty-Second came leaping out of the darkness. Their polearm's engine roared angrily, the twisting blades lashing out, seeking to catch me at the waist. I parried the blow, felt the saws damn near tear the sword out of my hand.

The soldier slid back on their grip, lashed out more and more, put distance between us even as they drove me to the edge of the platform. A single scratch from that thing would tear me apart, but they didn't try to go for a killing blow.

Why bother, I thought, when they could just stall me and wait for the rest of their little friends to show up?

Another pair of lenses flashed in the dark, another polearm whirred to angry life, another soldier came lashing out. I struck back what blows I could, aiming for the haft of their weapons, hoping to knock them off balance—I couldn't think of anything fucking else.

"*Liette!*" I shouted as a third soldier landed in the shaft.

"Here! Here! *GET THE FUCK ON!*"

The tram came screeching to a halt, narrowly pausing long enough for me to turn and follow her as she went leaping into one of the cars before it wailed back to life and sped off.

"It's faster," I growled as I tried to keep my footing. "Did you do something to it?"

"No, asshole, it's just going faster because I asked it nicely," she growled back as she warily got to her feet and clung to the seating for purchase. "I'm just that much of a fucking *gem* of a person."

"And I love you for it," I sighed, clawing my own way back to my feet. "I can't imagine Ocytus will, though."

"Ocytus won't know."

"Why not?"

"Because *I* don't know. The sigils I wrote to summon it were... hasty. I have only a vague idea where this tram is going or whether we're going to— *LOOK THE FUCK OUT!*"

I whirled, twisted, saw my blurred reflection in the whirling saw blades as they punched through the air two inches from my torso.

The soldier's lenses flashed as they tried to pull their weapon back for another strike.

I couldn't let that happen. It'd be stupid to let them get the distance. And it'd be more stupid to break off and let them think.

So, I did what I always did when I was caught between a stupid idea and a more stupid idea.

I did an insane idea, instead.

I clamped my arm down on the shaft of the weapon. I felt my clothes rustle with the wind of the saw blades' motion as I pulled the soldier closer toward me, their weapon trapped under my armpit. They jerked forward, their masked face bobbing toward me.

And the feeling of the hilt of my sword smashing against their face, of the shock running down my arm, of watching their lens fragment and fly past me in shattered, twinkling glass?

Well, not *every* memory can be special. But this one was.

I struck. I struck again. I struck until shards of metal and glass were embedded in my forearm and my grip was slippery with blood. The fire that had kept me going all this time pooled in one arm, kept pumping my hilt against their face until their knee caught me in the belly.

I staggered backward. The fucker wasn't down. The fucker was, in fact, still quite the opposite of down, while my arms felt like they were about to fall off. I wasn't going to outlast them. I wasn't even going to be able to beat them down. The longer this went, the poorer it would go for me.

The soldier clawed at their face, struggling to pick shards of glass from it. Soundlessly, they settled for simply pulling their helmet free and hurling it to the ground. A woman, face bright red from the shards embedded in her cheek, pulled free of the helmet with a gasp. She threw it aside, turned to face me.

"Ah," she said, *"I see."*

That's all I heard out of her. She didn't curse or scream. Her face, savaged as it was, was pristine—free of pain and fear, even as her blood wept freely. She held that serene expressionless look.

Even as I jammed the saw blades through her chest.

Red and white flew in fragments. The apparatus attached to her chest was shredded, cast apart. The many layers of a human were peeled back in gory rending, flying out the windows of the tram and painting the tunnel in swiftly vanishing red streaks.

My arms shook with the force of the weapon's motorized blade, went bloodless and numb. My breath left, my vision was bathed in red and black. I pushed. And I pushed. And I pushed until there was the sound of sputtering and whirring and the saw blades jammed upon something hard and unyielding. The polearm went silent. Still.

I released the shaft. I heard a body fall. I wiped sweat and blood from my face.

She lay there, the soldier. She lay there, a red mess from the neck down, body opened like an envelope in an overeager lover's hands. She lay there. Dead. Motionless.

Still looking at me.

And smiling softly.

"I will look forward to our next meeting, Cacophony," she said. In a voice that I felt in my scars that I knew.

From its rapidly bleeding-out vessel, Wisest smiled at me.

"Consider what we talked about."

Her head slumped.

Her eyes rolled back.

And the faintest wisps of light trickled out of her lips to vanish into the darkness as the tram sped deeper into the earth and carried us far, far away.

SIXTEEN

BOOTY HAUL

"Fuck me, Sal." Poneir's voice was punctuated by a sharp, appreciative whistle as she looked at the weapon in her hands. "What'd you do to get the Two-Twos on your ass? Talk shit about their uniforms or something?"

I let out a grunt of a nonanswer. The slight woman—diminutive body swaddled behind thick robes and a headdress of antlers from an animal I didn't know—held up the saw-bladed spear, glancing down its shaft, narrowing weathered eyes on the tiny motor attached to the head.

"They're the Great General's bastards," she said. "I mean, they're *all* the Great General's bastards, but these are the Great General's own handpicked bastards. We fought with them back when I was in the army, near Weiless. Mean motherfuckers. Fancy toys. Cut through two regiments before we retreated." Her fingers fumbled around the weapon's grip. "How do you get them working again? Is it—"

It was. She pulled a lever. The spear roared to angry life, the saw blades shrieking and spewing out sparks and smoke, threatening to come apart at any moment. The woman's eyes, astonished, ceased to blink as she eased the weapon back to its fitful slumber.

"Oh, this thing is *real* messed up," she said. "You've fucked up all this mechanical stuff. This thing's as liable to explode in someone's hands as kill anyone." She clicked her tongue, glanced back up at me. "Still... it's pretty hard-ass, isn't it? Makes a lot of noise and fire. You sure you want me to have it? Seems kind of like your style."

I waved, noncommittal. Poneir nodded, and from the towering pile of weapons, metal, and materials she sat upon, she tossed the spear into the masses. A pair of immense, lacquered wood hands reached in, her puppet pulling out a wad of weapons and holding them out above the head of a shouting, clamoring throng of bandits.

"Here it comes, kids," the puppet—who was affectionally named Impiero, I'd learned—bellowed in an echoing voice. *"New toys for eager boys, new worlds for eager girls. Keep killing for me and you'll never be afraid again."*

The assembled bandits, gathered in a thick knot around her pile, roared with delight as the puppet opened its limbs and let the weapons fall down into eagerly waiting hands. They tussled briefly over the best ones before each of them emerged, drunk and waving a shiny new sword.

That explained why so many of them had been well-armed back when I first met them, at least.

"Look strong, don't they?" Poneir said, grinning. "I should have gone Vagrant years ago."

"What made you decide?" I mumbled, only half listening.

She laughed a veteran's hollow laugh. "Two decades using Impiero to put down rebellions, stomp on farmers, and kill Revolutionary nobodies and all I've got to show for it is aches that are there in the morning and friends that aren't. The Imperium can fight their own fucking wars and pay me back for the time I wasted fighting mine."

"Mm," I hummed, only half-conscious.

"Well, fucking excuse me for boring you," Poneir growled.

"I'm sorry, I'm sorry, I'm listening." I waved a hand. "It's just... new Vagrants are always the same. So dramatic and shit. And besides, I can't really concentrate." I gestured to the pair of hands massaging out my shoulders. "You know?"

"Ah." Grini the Scalpel made a disapproving sound, though crucially did not stop her magnificently cold hands from rolling out my stiff muscles. "Rude to say such a thing. Especially when you are a guest at someone's treasure pile."

"Seriously," Poneir said, gesturing over the clearing. "If you don't like mine, you can find another pile to hang out on."

The clearing—which, before massive applications of fire magic, had been a lovely little meadow—stood host to several glistening heaps of loot, not unlike Poneir's. Some were more weapon than money, some were more money than metal. But each of them stood in an ungainly, disorganized mess.

And atop each one was a Vagrant.

Kalt the Whisper, shrieking as he fired bolts of lightning in the air. Frinlo the Stair, as she teleported around her heap, talking to various people. Torono the Open Hand, standing silently atop the small arsenal of weapons he'd stolen from the small town he'd destroyed by himself.

They shouted and screamed and threatened. They postured and flexed and boasted. They hurled magic and shook grisly totems and wrought carnage and destruction every which way *except* at each other.

You just didn't do that sort of thing at a Booty Haul.

Now, if you've spent any time at all in the Scar, you've probably met a bandit—rubbed shoulders with one at a bar, bought furs from one in town, maybe even been accosted by one, if you're unlucky. And if you've spent more than a few years in the Scar, you've probably had to fight a bandit—fend off a raid against your town, your caravan, your camp, whatever; they aren't picky about their targets.

And, if you've spent as much time in the Scar as I have, knee-deep in blood and stolen steel, you've probably wondered where the fuck do all these bandits keep coming from?

A fair question. It's dangerous work, after all. The Scar is full of monstrous beasts that the average bandit has no real chance of escaping outside a town's walls. And between peacekeeper mercenaries,

Imperium and Revolutionary forces, and other bandit clans, there's a better-than-average chance of dying. And really, the most ideal outcome for a bandit is to start working under a Vagrant and hope you survive their moods and complete disregard for nul lives until you can get rich enough to escape.

A fair question.

And a Booty Haul was the answer.

See, there's only one thing the Scar has more of than monsters, armies, and Vagrants, and that's legions upon legions of disaffected, pissed-off, terrified, or otherwise-suggestible villagers who've lost everything to one of the above monsters, armies, or Vagrants and desperately, desperately want to strike back at the world that's hurt them so much, even if they die in the process.

In a good world, they'd get someone who told them that hurting people won't heal them.

In a perfect world, they'd never even have to be told that.

But since we live in the Scar, they get this.

Around each Vagrant's heap they gathered. Villagers, farmers, merchants—some as young as fifteen, some as old as fifty. They gathered in rings around each heap. They gathered in throngs in the pathways between each heap. They gathered together in thick clumps of sweat and panic and fed off each other's anger like miserable, starving animals locked in a cage together.

And slowly, without saying a word, without even trying, really, they convinced each other that picking up a sword and fucking someone else up was a good idea. Maybe the best they'd had in a long time.

The Vagrants certainly weren't going to stop them. Everyone who took one of their uniforms and signed up with their clans was immediately rewarded with a fistful of treasure from the pile, a new weapon to hit back against the world that hit them first. And it's not like anyone else was going to stop them, either.

Merchants of dubious characters, caravan brothels, and a *truly* impressive number of barrel-rolling, backswamp moonshiners would brave wilderness and war for miles to get a chance to sell at a Booty Haul. Emotionally unsettled people with lots of money tend to make rash decisions, after all. And it was the *only* time that you could get within a mile of a Vagrant and not be killed.

A Booty Haul was a place of business. A violent, loud, wine- and sweat-soaked place of business, but still. Posturing was encouraged, boasting was mandatory, but outright fighting was forbidden until the Booty Haul was declared over.

Waking up drunk, penniless, and working for a new Vagrant was something of a Booty Haul tradition. But eventually, the piles would disappear, the booze and drugs and intimate artists would run dry, and the new clans would venture out with new leaders to kill themselves in hopes of finding some more.

It was a gathering of murderers, thieves, and every breed of vengeance- and violence-consumed lunatic, in both magical and non-magical varieties.

Usually, that was an entirely bad thing.

But after a day of wandering where the tram had dumped us out, it was only a *mostly* bad thing.

"Of course, of course. I'm sorry. Your pile is beautiful, Poneir," I sighed, rubbing my neck as I leaned forward in my chair. "I've just got a lot on my mind." A sudden pain pinched at my neck. I glared over my shoulder. "And my fucking *spine.* Would it kill you to be more careful?"

Grini the Scalpel folded her arms over her chest. She'd doffed her fur hood, revealing a rather charmingly aged face, her wrinkles and white hair a pleasing accompaniment to an astonishingly warm pair of eyes. She looked down at me with a frown.

"You pay to be healed," she grunted. "This is how you are healed when you come to me. Massage. Alchemics. Bandage. You want to bitch, you pay extra."

She took my head, eased me forward onto the massage chair—which, credit to Grini, was an amazing thing to remember to loot. I'd probably fight an Imperial regiment to get one of these, too.

"Until then, do not burden Grini with your birdshit."

"Sorry, Grini."

I would have happily paid extra, just to be clear. But I wasn't the one footing the bill.

It may have been me who found our way to Booty Haul, but it was Liette that paid for our way in. If you're not coming to Booty Haul to be recruited, after all, it's customary to bring tribute. And if you don't, it's customary to turn you to a pile of ash.

"I had heard you were an asshole," Poneir chuckled. "But I also heard Agne say she'd been traveling with you. How do you manage to spend time with a sweetheart like that and still come out this pissed off?"

"Just naturally charming, already, I guess." I groaned, winced, let out an uncomfortable noise. "Fuck me to Dust, Grini, if you keep working on that spot for another ten minutes, I'll call you sir." I melted forward in the chair. "And if I'd known Agne and the rest would make it here first, I'd tell them to say something more flattering about me."

"Plenty to be flattered about already," Grini said, her hands gliding down to my lower back. "We are rich because of you."

"It's true." Poneir yawned, lazily rolled off her pile and into her puppet's giant hand, where she luxuriated. "Since this war kicked off, I go through fortunes like I go through people."

"Imperium fights Revolution, Revolution fights Imperium, Vagrant eats well on leftovers," Grini agreed. "Loot, recruit, and scoot."

"Personally, I don't know how much of that is thanks to you. But if it's even a little, I figure I owe you at least a drink."

Something rose in my throat, caught there. My words tasted of bile. "Yeah. You're welcome."

I reached down to pluck up the tankard of moonshine that could best be described as…well, no one drinks it for quality but you expect it to at least fuck you up proper. I was improperly fucked. Unobtrusively fucked, *at best.*

But, as the old army wisdom went, whatever couldn't be solved by quality could be solved by quantity.

I waved over a nearby lad toting a tray of sloshing tankards of moonshine. I reached for my metal to pay him.

"No need, Cacophony." Poneir plucked a trinket from her pile, tossed it to the lad. "Leave the shine, kid. Buy yourself something sharp and dangerous."

"Feeling charitable?" I chuckled as I grabbed another tankard, took another sip, tried a little harder to forget. "Or am I going to have to go down on you later?"

"Can't I just be nice?" Poneir asked, grinning through the fingers of her puppet. "You've got the Twenty-Second after you, along with..." She paused, suspiciously long. "You know, along with everything else."

"Everything else," I repeated flatly. I'd caught her hesitation and I let her know.

"Well, yeah," she said, coughing. "I mean, if I had the shit coming down on me that was coming down on you—"

"You're the second asshole to have said that in as many days," I said, staring at her over my tankard. "You know something I don't?"

"Everyone knows," Grini muttered as she adjusted one of my shoulders. "I ask the Vagrants, they know. I ask the Imperials, they know. Bird flies, sun shines, Sal the Cacophony is about to be killed."

"They've been saying that for a while," I grunted. "I've heard six different stories between my first one of these and my second one of these."

"Those are stories, though. Everyone's got stories," Poneir said. "*I've* got stories."

I smiled. "Not like my stories."

She did not smile.

"They're talking about your list, Sal," Poneir replied, low and dangerous. "*Vagrants* are talking. They hear about the people you've killed. They start wondering if you're going after them next. Or, if they're not on your list, if you're going after them to get to the ones who *are* on your list."

"Vagrants kill each other," I said, shrugging. "Vagrants kill each other all the fucking time. *You've* killed Vagrants."

Poneir smiled. "Not like you."

I did not smile.

"Vagrant kills Vagrant," Grini muttered, taking out a needle and replacing it elsewhere. "Sal the Cacophony does not just kill. She burns. A Vagrant kills a Vagrant, the Vagrant merely dies. Sal the Cacophony kills a Vagrant, no one speaks the Vagrant's name again."

"What she said," the Dollmage agreed. "You don't think nobody's noticed? You don't think nobody's figured out you're going to make your way to them eventually, and they might take things into their own hands?"

There were implications. And there were threats. And then there was whatever the fuck Poneir was trying to do.

"Something you want to tell me, old friend?" I asked. "Something you maybe wouldn't want to tell me if I unsheathe this brass at my hip?"

Poneir and Grini exchanged a nervous glance over my head. The Dollmage managed a weak smile. The Frostmage gently rubbed my shoulders.

"Apologies," Poneir said. "I got excited. It's all the fighting lately."

"Uh-huh." I took a long, pointed swig. "I didn't want to bring this up, since we ended up getting along so well, but some of your boys and girls tried to pick a fight with me not long ago. They mentioned something about me being off-limits. It might be a nice gesture to let me know." I licked my lips. "Since you're apologizing and all."

Another glance. Quicker. Briefer.

"This cannot be done," Grini said. "We apologize for the insult, Cacophony. It cannot be helped." She sighed. "Redfavors."

I grunted—annoyed, but amenable. That made as much sense as anything, I supposed. Redfavors—the currency of grudges, vendettas, blood oaths, and promises we Vagrants exchanged with each other—was a system simultaneously insubstantial and immutable. I couldn't ask them to impart more without asking them to renege on a Redfavor.

And that just wasn't done. Anywhere.

"Make it up to me another way, then," I said. "You see any refugees around here, you leave them alone. They have nothing you want."

"Sal. You wound me." Poneir, and her puppet, both clasped a hand to their chest in mock offense. "Why would Poneir the Curtain stoop so low as to terrorize victims of war?"

"Refugees are already past Bitterdrink, anyway," Grini muttered, dejected. "No fair."

"Bitterdrink?" I glanced at her. "The Revolutionary fortress?"

Fuck me, had we really gone that far east?

"Yeah, we saw some refugees," Poneir sighed. "And we... *debated* seeing if they wouldn't mind loaning us some strapping youths for our merry little band of killers. But then they got within range of Bitterdrink's guns, and the Revolutionaries were on high alert, and it was going to be a whole... *thing*."

"High alert?" My heart raced. Those absolute fucks—don't tell me I saved them from conscription just to have them walk back into it. "Why the fuck would they do that?"

"This is what I said," Grini hummed. "Why not round them up? Why not turn guns upon them? Why not at least have some target practice?" She dabbed oil on her hands, went back to my shoulders. "Ah, well. I suppose this is why I am not a Revolutionary. Too nice."

"Which means the Revolutionaries are on high alert, but *can't* spare the forces to round up some refugees," Poneir chuckled. "Which means they've got bigger problems than us. Which means we're here, drinking it up, and your refugees are probably in pissing distance of Toadback by now."

Relief isn't what I felt. I'd forgotten how to be relieved about a thousand miles back. But when I heard Toadback's name uttered, I at least unclenched a little.

Toadback was a fliptown—one of those freeholds that changes its allegiance from Revolutionary to Imperial and back again, depending on whoever happened to be closer and have more weapons at the time. And while it'd be a stretch to call a place like that "safe," fliptowns were at least considered too valuable by either army to devastate outright.

Of course, that was before the Valley.

Before the new war.

Before everything I did...

Stop it. I shut my eyes, tried to smother the thoughts. *They'll be safe at Toadback. Safer than they are out here, at least.*

"Might not be a bad place to be," Poneir mused aloud. She glanced over Booty Haul, taking note of the diminishing piles of loot and the increasing throngs of freshly recruited bandits. "I'd give it another day or two before this pig's bled dry."

I didn't miss the implication. Violence—at least, violence done without sufficient theater—was forbidden at a Booty Haul. But when the kegs ran out, the piles were no more, and everyone was drunk, rich, and sporting shiny new weapons...

Well, it'd be a good idea for *anyone* to be gone at that point, let alone someone like me.

The thought turned over in my head, sloshing along with the alcohol that failed to keep me from arriving at the same point.

Where the fuck was I supposed to go now?

Somehow, between the stress and the attacks and the huge fucking dragon, I'd only managed to think as far ahead as Ocytus. I'd hoped whatever I'd need to do would be there. And for all I knew, it still was, but fuck if they were going to let me back in there after I'd led Revolutionaries to their tram.

Liette said I'd be lucky if they didn't retaliate against me, even with her smoothing things over.

Which, in better times, might have been intimidating. In times like these, though? Where everyone was clamoring to crawl up inside my ass? Well, at least the Freemakers would kill me with visual flair.

And even then, the increasingly diverse cast of people motivated by seeing me torn to pieces was only, like, *third* on my list of problems. Second had always been just surviving long enough to make it to the next day.

And first was boiling at my hip.

Heat poured off the Cacophony, radiating with every shudder of the brass inside his sheath. Even as uninterested as he was now, barely paying attention, he burned so hot I could feel him in my chest.

The images of what had happened in A Dead Dog Buried on a Black Hill's chamber, of the fire searing and the metal warping and the fear on Themeter's face when she saw it flashed through my head.

And beyond those memories, darker thoughts bloomed. Thoughts of shadows and fires. Thoughts of hands reaching out of a sea of flames, blackening and withering to cinders and disappearing back beneath searing waves. Thoughts of cries and pleas vanishing beneath the cackle of fire.

I'd had these thoughts before. I'd dreamed of them. Of the sights I'd seen from so up high, when I used to fly, when I had another name...

But when I dreamed of them this time, when I saw the great font from which the fire poured... it wasn't Red Cloud I thought of.

Could I really do it? I wondered, for the thousandth time that day. Could it even really be done? Could the Cacophony pull Eldest out of Liette and leave her unharmed? Could he truly take the Scrath's power?

And could I do that to the world? To everyone? Could I give the Cacophony that kind of strength, that kind of freedom, and call it even?

Thoughts like those, I tried my best to think of as little as possible.

Because I already knew what the answer would be.

But how could it even be done? And where? Whatever chance I had of figuring that out would be difficult to do in the middle of a war.

"What's out there, anyway?"

"Huh?"

"Out near Toadback. It's just marsh from that point, isn't it?" I asked.

"Worse," Poneir grunted. "It dries up the closer you get to the coast, turns into rocks and shit. Nothing out there except the Nails. Dirt, monsters, more dirt and more monsters."

"And that town," Grini put in.

"That's not a town," she countered, "that's a joke."

"There's a town out there?"

"More like a coagulation of the desperate and swinish," Poneir answered, waving a dismissive hand that was echoed by her puppet. "A bunch of deserters, fittingly, fled out into the desert. Refugees keep trickling eastward, gathering in a bunch of shacks. They're calling it a town now."

"Maybe waiting out the war?" I wondered.

"Why bother?" Poneir chuckled. "Someone's going to win this war. And whoever does is going to go out there and take them back over and make them citizens of the Imperium or the Revolution or whoever. Fuck, I'm half tempted to take a crack at it myself."

"What's the name?" I asked.

"New Vigil." Grini plucked the last needle from my skin. "Nice name, no?"

That name...

That name brought me no comfort.

"Okay, you are good to go." Grini slapped me hard across my back, nudging me out of my chair. "I push the crap back into you, now you can go get it kicked out of you again."

I stood up, stretched. I ached. But fuck if I didn't feel like being alive wasn't so terrible right now.

Good enough.

"Happy?" she asked.

"Happy," I said.

"Okay, good." She turned her cheek to me, tapped a finger to her flesh. "Now give me a kiss."

I rolled my eyes, leaned in, gave that freezing skin the tenderest smooch I could muster.

Weird fucking price. But that had honestly been a pretty great massage, so who was I to question an artist?

I took up my tankard. Then I drained it, threw it aside, and picked up another tankard. And once I had drained *that* one and was about halfway through my next, I got to walking.

Not that it did a lot of fucking good. You want three things out of liquor: confidence to do the things you want to do, taste to make you feel the way you want to feel, and enough of a hit to dull the impact when you don't get either. This particular swill was usually good for one of those. But not tonight. Tonight, all the liquor did was fill my brain and make the questions and worries slosh around, bouncing off each other and shattering against my head.

The conversation with Poneir and Grini had left me unsettled. That, in itself, wasn't too surprising—if you *aren't* unsettled by a Vagrant, it's typically because they're a shit Vagrant. Nor was the fact that people were after me all that alarming—even if I *hadn't* had proof in the form of the Twenty-Second, people coming after me was just a typical afternoon.

What bothered me was just how many people knew.

When you're in shit up to your ankles, you're typically the first and only one to ever know it. When there's shit up to your waist, then you're usually the first of many to know. Only when you're in so much shit your feet can't even touch the bottom does *everyone* know it before you do.

Puzzlingly—or maybe it only seemed that way because of the booze—it was their evasiveness that had told me the most.

They mentioned Redfavors. Which meant they were compelled by the Vagrant code to silence. *Which meant* another Vagrant out there wanted to catch me off guard enough to make people swear to it... *or* it meant another Vagrant who they owed a favor to was aiming for me and they were bound to honor that by not helping me too much. Or... maybe it meant they were just full of shit and making it up?

Okay, so a Redfavor can mean a lot of things. But almost all of them are bad. A Vagrant looking for me was manageable, so long as I knew the Vagrant.

But I didn't know the Vagrant. And I didn't know the Twenty-Second. And I didn't know why Poneir *and* Tretta both knew more about the shit I was in than I did. And I didn't know if them knowing that meant they also knew about...

Liette.

The thought I couldn't drown with beer. The thought I couldn't smother with drugs. The thought that came to me before I knew my scars hurt in the morning and carried me to sleep when I could find it.

I glanced at the gun at my hip. The Cacophony peered back. Don't ask me how.

However he could do it—if he even *could* do it—was not something I could even contemplate, let alone see done, with an ambush hanging over me night and day. I needed somewhere—somewhere to think, somewhere to talk, somewhere to... to...

To figure out how to tell her this. Any of it.

My mind drifted to the other part of our conversation. To that rumor. That dismissive grunt of a name. Deserters in the desert. Out to the east.

New Vigil.

The second city to bear that name. I couldn't hear it without thinking about the first.

That city had been bright. Vibrant. Full of people and their problems. That city had known blue skies and green earth. That city had known love.

I know because I burned it to cinders. I know because I burned *them* to cinders. I know because... because...

"*Eres va atali,*" I whispered to myself.

Because I'll never forget the way a young man whose name I tried to keep far from my thoughts looked at me when he had learned that city had burned by my hands.

New Vigil.

A fantasy. A nightmare. Or it might as well have been.

Something rose in my throat. Something that rose every time I thought about that name, that face, that man. I spat it, and that name, out onto the ground. I wiped my mouth with the back of my hand and left them both in a puddle behind me.

I wended my way through the throngs of fresh recruits, dodged the imploring hawking of the merchants and the dancers and the brothels, waved off other Vagrants' calls for me to join their crew and the riches they promised. Booty Haul was safe for the moment, but that wouldn't last long.

I needed a plan. I needed a *good* plan. I needed a drink that wasn't piss, too.

I managed one. I'd work on the others later.

In the first stroke of unambiguously good luck since I'd managed to avoid going blind by drinking this shit, an attractive-looking serving girl for one of the local taverns came walking by, a tray on her hand and a blissfully full-looking bottle of Avonin & Family whiskey seated proudly atop it.

That wasn't piss. But if it was, I'd still have fucking drunk it. And if you'd had it, you would, too.

"Hey!" I called after the girl as she wended her way through the crowd of bandits. She didn't answer, necessitating me to shove the nearest asshole out of the way and shout louder. "*HEY, TRAY-GIRL!*"

She pressed through the crowd, unnoticed by the bandits who were embroiled in consuming much cheaper liquor. Which made it a real pain in the ass to push them out of the way. But some things in life, you don't give up on.

Snarling, spitting, and swearing, I forced my way through the crowd in pursuit of the woman. She slithered effortlessly through the throngs, disappearing into one of the tents at the outskirts of the clearing. I followed.

If she was bringing it to a boss, this could get ugly. If she was bringing it to a lover, this could get awkward. If she was bringing it to a dying man with a dying wish... well, I was about to look like a real asshole, wasn't I?

I entered the tent. Found no one but the girl. That should have been my first warning something was off.

"All right," I gasped. "I know this is sudden. I don't know where you got that bottle and you don't know what I'll do to get it. But I'll tell you the one that ends with both of us happy."

She didn't respond. She turned and smiled. And her face quivered, distorted, and disappeared into mist.

Which should have been my *second* warning.

As it was, the shit didn't hit me until a good minute after the alchemic lanterns flickered to life. A dozen shapes—frail and wrapped in black feather-lined leathers—surrounded me, hands on cruel-looking edges and twitchy-looking hand crossbows. Their faces, enshrouded behind crow-like masks with long, spearing beaks, leered at me.

Somehow, I'd managed to stumble into an ambush of deadly Ashmouths, most feared assassins in the land.

So, I take it back, that backwater moonshine shit *did* fuck me up.

SEVENTEEN

BOOTY HAUL

So, remember the thing I said about shit?

No, the other thing.

No, the *other* thing.

The part about it being directly related to how many people know about it. I stand by that advice, just so you know, but it occurred to me then—in that tent, seated beneath that lamp, with about a dozen-odd hand crossbows leveled at a dozen-odd parts of my body that I preferred unperforated—that there is a glaring, yet critical, addition to that advice.

If, at any time, should the people who *do* find about the kind of shit you're in turn out to be a Scar-wide syndicate of thieves, assassins, and criminals: stop worrying about the shit you're drowning in and *begin* worrying about the shit you're about to have forced directly down your throat.

See, shit coming down on you isn't anything new in the Scar. Everyone's got someone gunning for them, after all. But shit that the fucking *Ashmouths* consider interesting? That's... that's...

Well, let me put it this way.

"Sal the Cacophony," a voice grated against my ears. "It is my extremely unfortunate obligation to inform you that any thoughts you might have of your capability for dealing with the amount of pain we are prepared to visit upon you are erroneous, hubristic, and grievously, *grievously* misinformed."

Actually, that was a way better way to put it.

A pair of pointy elbows wrapped in a suit worn far too long landed on the table, thin fingers wrapped in painfully tight gloves steepled. Above them, a face ragged with exhaustion and stained by a pair of blood-rimmed eyes, leered into the halo of light cast by the alchemic lamp.

"Understand that we are already well aware of the situation you find yourself in," Necla the Shroud—Nightmage and Ashmouth crony with a lovely singing voice the one time I heard him—spoke through teeth clenched tight enough to hurt. "As we are already well aware of the forces arrayed against you. Our spy network is denser than a stone wall. We know *everything*, Sal."

I held his gaze in my own, kept my lips tight and my hands on the table. Though his threats made something bitter rise in my craw, I didn't show him a reaction. I gave him nothing to bargain with, nothing to threaten me with, nothing to use against me.

There's only one way out of an Ashmouth noose, and it's slowly and carefully.

"Understand, too, that if we desired you dead, you already would be." Necla made a vague gesture to the Ashmouths around him. "Given that you aren't, it would be safe to assume that the wisest course of action would be to listen carefully, speak carefully, and above all, *think* carefully. Life can become very good or very bad for you after you leave this tent, Sal. Which it is depends on your actions." He leaned back, took me in through his bloodshot eyes. "Any questions?"

I sniffed. Rolled my shoulder. Smacked my lips. Spoke.

"How are you doing, Necla?" I asked. "Getting enough sleep?"

Necla, I could tell by his face, was not happy about that crack. By his face, actually, I could tell he was not happy to see me. Or to be here. Or to be alive, really.

Not that I could blame him. He was drained of color and any

emotion more positive than *murderous*. His eyes were bleary, bloodstained pits in a visage more skull than skin. And his frown was so thick and heavy, I worried it was about to break his neck.

Someone, I could see, had been busy.

A Nightmage pays his Barter for his magic, like any mage. The Lady Merchant gives them the power to manipulate minds and eyes. And in exchange, they give her their dreams—the good ones, specifically. What's left behind after she takes those is so horrific that most of them simply choose to forgo sleep.

The more magic they use, the more dreams they lose. The more dreams they lose, the more sleep they fear. The more sleep they fear... well, I don't know if you've ever stayed up too late and gotten cranky the next morning, but if you can imagine that a thousand times worse and with mind-altering, hallucination-inducing magic attached, you'll have a reasonable idea.

"I am not getting enough sleep, Sal." Necla's voice was a needle pushed through leather. "I am not getting enough sleep because I am using a lot of magic. I am using a lot of magic because my employers are keeping me busy. My employers are keeping me busy because an extremely irritating buffoon with a magic gun decided to cause a war."

"I thought the Three loved wars," I replied. "The Ashmouths always make money in them."

"They do. And they do. I, however, do not. I, however, am capable of thinking further than my coffers. I am capable of thinking what happens when this war grows big enough to stop being polite—of everything that will come after and everything that will fail to come back." His bloodshot eyes widened. "And I am capable of thinking about that because it is all I see whenever I drift off for even a second.

"Bodies ground beneath tank treads. Entire cities disappearing into eternal night. Forests upon forests of corpses." He rubbed his temples. "And at their center... you. Always you, Sal the Cacophony. Even in my dreams, I can't escape you. I have drowned mothers in front of their children and slept like a baby, yet somehow *you*"—his voice sharpened—"*are capable of such reeking foulness as to penetrate every fucking facet of my brain.* Were we not here on official business, I would torture you to death. And even though we are, I am strongly considering it. Now. I ask again. Any. Questions."

My eyes slowly drifted to the man sitting next to him. Rudu, arms tucked into his loose shirt and folded across his chest, looked back at me through eyes likewise rimmed with red. Though, in this case, for an entirely different reason.

I glanced at the long pipe hanging from his lips, the coils of silk-grass smoke swirling around him like affectionate serpents. I gestured at it with my chin.

"Give me a hit?"

Rudu looked for a moment at Necla, who shook his head. He scratched his stubble, sighed, then removed the pipe from his mouth and handed it across the table to me. I took the deepest inhale I could manage, breathed a cloud of smoke across the table. I handed the pipe back to Rudu, who regarded Necla's glare with puzzlement.

"What?" he asked. "You said we were here to talk."

"Unbelievable," Necla snarled. "Need I remind you we are Ashmouths? Feared? Absolute in conviction and skill?"

"I'm still all those things," Rudu said, tapping the ash from his pipe and starting to load another. "But there's being feared and absolute, and then there's just being an asshole."

"Look," I said, trying as best I could to let the smoke seep into my senses. "If I promise to find you very scary, can you maybe get to whatever shit you want to talk about? I promise I'll even cry a little."

"There's no need for that shit, either," Rudu said, turning back to me. "We aren't here to make any more threats than would be professionally expected."

"Then what *are* you here for?"

Necla opened his mouth to answer. Rudu held up a hand to silence him. He stared at me, a frown deepening behind the veil of smoke slipping from his lips.

"We're here to help you. And Liette."

The Ashmouths around me twitched, raised their crossbows a little higher. Even though I couldn't see their faces, I knew they were bristling. And I knew that because *I* was fucking bristling.

"I'll tell you what I told him." I spat toward Necla's feet. "You say whatever the fuck you want to me and we'll all be happy. You ever put her name in your mouth again, and I'll—"

"Blow my head off," Rudu said, "with the Cacophony. Yeah. He told me." He glanced around at the various assassins. "And shit, I bet you could. But I bet it would end messier than either of us want to deal with right now." He exhaled another cloud of smoke, shrugged. "After we talk, though? Who knows?"

I held tense for a moment before relaxing, letting the Ashmouths follow suit. That was as good an offer as I was going to get right now. And besides, he *had* just let me hit his silkgrass. It'd be rude to start shooting.

At this point, anyway.

I seethed. "So talk. Or shoot. Either way, make it quick. I've got shit to do."

"Lives to ruin," Necla whispered more than hissed. It wasn't hate that made his eye twitch like that. "Civilizations to destroy. People to crush like—"

"All right, then," Rudu interrupted, nudging Necla out of his seat. "Take a walk, Necla." He handed his pipe to a nearby Ashmouth. "You all go with him. See if you can get him to relax."

Necla staggered awkwardly toward the door, the assassins reluctantly filing behind him. "I was *hired* to ensure that she listened."

"And you did." Rudu gestured to me. "She's listening. Now, let me do what *I* was hired to do, which is make sure you don't fuck this up by being you."

A few hisses, a few curses for professionalism's sake, but they left all the same. And once we were alone, I couldn't help but observe Rudu.

"I've never seen you without your pipe."

"I've never seen me without my pipe, either. This is that serious." He leaned forward. "Necla's twitchy. He's not the only one. Every Ashmouth in the Scar is on edge."

"Fuck you. You're making money hand over fist, like you do in every war."

"This isn't every war, Sal. I haven't been told everything yet, but the Imperium isn't fucking around this time. There's talk of Prodigies arriving. There's talk of..." He grimaced, afraid to say it. "They say there's going to be a Recivilizing."

His grimace became mine, accompanied by a cold pain in my chest I was damn sure was in his, too. You didn't hear a word like *Recivilizing* and not worry. That was the whole point of a Recivilizing.

The *official* point of the rarely invoked right of the Empress was peaceful in nature. A Recivilizing was a flooding of a "troubled" area with Imperial merchants, Imperial food, Imperial theater, and crucially, Imperial money, effectively turning a freehold into an Imperium city in a matter of weeks.

The unofficial point was what came before: the vast, vast, *vast* amounts of resources poured into slaughtering, terrorizing, and torturing whatever local forces might resist or resent the Imperial way of life. A list that included: local criminals and warlords, surrounding bandit clans, Revolutionary operatives, freehold barons of insufficient loyalty or lineage, peacekeepers who might be suspected of treason, bards and poets who spoke too much and sang too little, tavern keepers who lacked sufficient Imperial wine, merchants who looked at an Imperial soldier funny, regular-ass people who didn't look at an Imperial soldier funny but had something an Imperial soldier wanted, and then, of course, anyone who may or may not resent the Imperials for killing all their families.

Just to make sure.

I'd never seen one. Though I'd studied it, same as every mage in the army had. I knew how it worked. And I knew the body count.

Recivilizing a rebellious city carried a body count so high you'd weep to know the number of it.

Recivilizing the entire Revolution would be…

"So, yeah," Rudu sighed. "War is good for the Ashmouths. Massive, crushing execution of lawbreakers? Not so much. We've already lost ten Crow Markets, with *all* their assets, to the Imperials. If this keeps going, there won't be a war. There'll be a winner. And the Three don't want that to happen."

"Yeah," I replied bitterly. "The Three prefer their murders a little more casual, don't they?"

Rudu held up a hand—either to stop me or whatever he was about to say. After a moment, he let out a weary breath. "In another month, the war will have lost us so much money the Three won't fucking care if they get executed. They're determined not only to survive this war, but to find a way to recoup their losses."

"And let me guess," I said. "They've found a way to do it."

"Yeah."

"And it involves me."

"Uh-huh."

I rubbed my temples, made a sigh in that I-know-I'm-about-to-get-fucked-I-just-don't-know-how kind of way. "All right. What do they want me to do?"

"Let them take care of you."

I blinked. "Take care of, like…"

"Like whatever you need. Whatever home you want, in whatever region you want, with however much silks, wine, drugs, servants, or even a fucking duck pond, if you want it. The Three will hide you from any retribution from any adversary. Kill whoever you want. Remove whatever trace of yourself you want gone. They'll kill the Great General *and* the Empress the same fucking day, if it'll make you happy."

"All right, well, I admit I wasn't going to guess that. But the Three have asked for the Cacophony before and the answer is still—"

"They don't want the gun. They don't want your lover." He stared at me intently. "They want the thing inside her. They want the Scrath."

Heart in my throat. Blood in my ears. Fingers twitching.

Not good.

"I don't—"

"Just. Please." Rudu interrupted. "Don't pretend. We know everything. I'm not trying to intimidate you. I'm trying to inform you. The Three want the thing inside Liette. They're willing to give you anything and everything you want—for her, for you, for anyone you want—for a chance to extract it."

"We have money. We have—"

"Not like we have money. We know about the Freemaker's assets, too. They're not even a fraction of the Three's. And even if they were, money can hide you from the Imperium and the Revolution only until it runs out. The Three can hide you from them forever. The Three can make sure any mouth that speaks your name ends up dead in an alley. They can give you..."

He trailed off.

"Give me what?"

He looked at me again. His smile was soft. Sad. Painful.

"Don't you want to rest, Sal?" he asked. "Because I fucking do. I want to stop using my magic to do shit for other people. I want to stop worrying if the people who want to kill me today are the same people who will want to kill me tomorrow. I want to grow things in the ground. Or make books. Or... or... I don't fucking know what, but *something* other than this... whatever it is the fuck Vagrants do. I hate this life. And if the Three were offering *me* a new one, I'd fucking take it."

I stared at my hands. "And if they were offering someone... someone like Liette a new life?"

He stared at me. "If I had a different life, maybe I'd have someone like Liette, too."

Everyone has a reason for going Vagrant.

Some, like Rudu, didn't want to kill in someone else's name. Some, like Poneir, didn't want to die in someone else's name. Some, like me, didn't want to die before we were ready to. Everyone knows a Vagrant's reasons—it's in their stories, in their underlings, in their targets.

But a Vagrant has a reason to give it up, too.

It's tiring work. Not just the fighting. The being okay with the fighting. The waking up and knowing in your scars you won't go back to sleep without a new one. The drinking to escape the violence, the violence to escape the drinking. The stories, the swords, everything—it builds up, it gets bigger. And then one day, it's so big you just can't fight it anymore.

And when that day comes... that's when you don't have a reason to stop being a Vagrant.

I never thought I'd have that problem. Damn near every waking and every dreaming began and ended with me thinking I'd die same as I lived. That didn't change when I met Liette. I still had too many memories of arguing in the dark and leaving in the middle of the night to keep chasing my revenge, my list...

But that was before.

That was me dying. Me fighting. Me killing. Not her. And when I left, it was me who was going into the blood, the corpses. Me who was cleaning off before I came back to her. Me keeping the blood off her skirts, me keeping her safe, me not worrying her about what I'm doing to who and where. I did it. All of it. And more, before...

Before the Scrath. Before the Ten Arrows. Before I fucked up.

And now... I wasn't thinking about my reasons, anymore. I wasn't thinking about being a Vagrant or not being a Vagrant. I was thinking about her.

And what I'd do to make it right for her.

"How?" I asked.

"How, what?" he replied.

"How would you extract it?"

He stared up at the lamp for a moment before sighing. "I'll be honest. I don't know. I've seen ideas. I've seen the mages and Freemakers and Spellwrights they've got on hand. But I have only half a clue as to what a Scrath actually *is* and no clue at all how to get it out."

"Then what makes you think they can?"

"When have you ever known the Three to not get something they want?"

Once, I thought, glancing down to the sheath at my hip. *His* sheath.

Only once.

I don't know how long I stared, how long I sat silent, how many times I ran over how wrong this could all go in my mind. But each time I worried about each disaster, each problem, each way the shit could sweep over my head and into my lungs and drown me...I came back to one word.

Her.

"Anyway, you don't have to answer now," Rudu said. "And I wouldn't ask you to. Not now. But I will ask you again." He crossed his arms. "And after that...well, I don't fucking know what the Ashmouths will do, but I know they told me not to ask a third time."

He slid off his chair, wandered to the tent flap.

"We'll be in Toadback, Sal. For as long as we can be. Meet us there. We'll make it right."

And then he was gone.

And in his absence, I was left alone with the questions. How the fuck could I trust them? How could I believe they could do what I needed them to? How could I even think about working with them?

But every question had an answer. And none of them were as insane as I needed them to be to write the whole thing off.

I *couldn't* trust the Ashmouths—and they knew that, otherwise they wouldn't have offered terms to me. A criminal is, above all else, a merchant too honest to make it in business, after all. I couldn't believe that they knew how to save Liette, either. But neither was Rudu wrong—if there was such a thing as a possibility of taking it out of Liette, the Three would know who could do it, where to find them, and which family member to kill to make them work.

As for why I could even think about it?

Keeping the Scrath *out* of the Cacophony would be a good enough reason to consider it. But I wasn't thinking of that. Or the Ashmouths, really. I was thinking of her.

Find a person who makes you breathe a little cleaner, like she does, and you might also do some pretty fucked-up things not to lose them.

Eventually, I found my legs. And the energy to move them. I found my way outside. I found my way back toward my little corner of Booty Haul.

But then someone else found me.

"Sal the Cacophony?" a voice from behind me asked. And I would have been concerned, if it hadn't been quite so prepubescent.

"Yeah?" I turned to the lad with the serving tray.

"Don't go to Toadback."

I blinked. "What?"

"Toadback. Don't go to Toadback. It's not safe."

I narrowed my eyes. "Who the fuck are you, kid? And what the fuck do you know about Toadback?"

He shrugged. "Heviri. And nothing. I was only paid to say it."

"By who?"

"By a Mister 'Fuck You, I Didn't Get Paid to Do Extra Work, so Give Me Metal or Fuck Off.'" He glanced me over. "So, you got metal?"

"I've got a slap across the mouth you might get along with."

"All right, well, pleased to meet you, Miss 'Broke Asshole.' I'll be off now."

Now, don't go getting worried about what I said. I wasn't *actually* going to slap him unless he kept talking for, like, ten more seconds. And when he took off, I didn't feel the urge to chase him. I couldn't do much with what he'd just told me, after all.

Toadback *was* dangerous. Any place a gang of assassins tells you to meet them is dangerous. I didn't need telling.

But someone wanted me to know, all the same. Someone wanted

to make the effort to warn me. Someone wanted me alive. And, in this business, that's almost as bad as someone wanting you dead.

Was it Poneir? Or Grini? Rudu, with a pang of consciousness? Or someone else? Who the fuck had paid that kid?

I glowered over the crowd at him as he collected another tray and got to work. He talked to no one else that wasn't buying moonshine. I could still catch him, make him talk.

But honestly? Why bother? Someone wanting me alive, while concerning, was not so pressing a concern as the *many* someones wanting the other thing. And besides, it wasn't like I had a way of making him talk—I wasn't going to have it said that Sal the Cacophony threatened children. *Or* paid them for birdshit reasons.

Still, I thought as I walked away, he was a nice kid.

He'd be a great killer someday.

EIGHTEEN

BOOTY HAUL

When you do this as long as I have, you don't get to pick what comforts you anymore.

Wait, no. Not that. More that you find yourself able to find comfort in things that you didn't before. Sleeping on the ground is a shit way to live, for example, but it makes you appreciate grass a little more. You don't think of trees often until it rains, but then you're pretty happy to have one.

Point being, do this as long as I have, you find yourself taking comfort in some pretty unusual things.

"Well, well, well, if it isn't Queen Cuntface herself, come to share her regal wisdom with us piss-poor peasants."

Like that.

I genuinely never thought I'd be happy to hear that.

"You don't usually call me cuntface, Yria." I approached the makeshift fire and pile of logs and salvaged tents that had become our camp and doffed my scarf and belt, letting them fall in a gratifying thud. "Everything okay?"

Yria, her usually pleasantly hatchet-shaped face twisted into an unusually unpleasant sword-shaped face, sneered up at me. Seated across the fire, I got the distinct impression she might have leapt up and attacked me were it not for the patient ministrations of her brother, carefully sketching out sigils upon her arm with a quill.

"Yeah, as you can clearly see, I'm doing fucking great." She gestured to the cuts and scrapes across her face, the dirt on her clothes. "The bruises I got fighting all the people who want to kick *your* ass were lonely, so I went and got them some friends. I wanted to show you them earlier, but you were off tonguing ass in the bush somewhere."

"I was being pursued by Revolutionaries," I sighed, taking a seat myself and kicking off my boots. "I told you."

"And when did I say I didn't fucking believe you? But why were they pursuing you, Princess Peepants? Because you pissed them off. Because pissing people off makes you happy. Just like tonguing ass makes you happy. How the fuck is it you aren't keeping up with this?" She glanced to her brother. "*You* get it, right?"

"You're implying that all our current hardships are the result of Sal's obvious-yet-unembraced love of carnage, similar to an act of carnal dexterity, suggesting a poetic correlation between love and violence," Urda replied without looking up. "I thought it was obvious. Hold still, please. This is delicate work."

I peered as close as I could at the sigils—not sure why, since I couldn't understand them at all. "What *are* you doing there?"

"Delicate. Work. As I said. The type that would be rendered *indelicate* by you asking me questions while I'm trying to do it," he replied tersely.

I paused, cleared my throat. "But not by you saying all that shit?"

"Sal, *please.*"

You ever hear a polite person snap? They have a tone, like even the nicest thing they say to you will cut you deep. I'd never heard Urda talk like that. I had to admit, it didn't *not* make me feel like shit.

"These sigils, as you can see, are being applied directly to Yria's skin. I heard that these sigils can help delay a Doormage's paralysis and we've had some success with them."

"My fucking nethers went numb for six minutes," Yria muttered.

"Some *moderate* success with them," Urda corrected himself. "But it's still delicate work. Sigils aren't meant to go on skin. This could go wrong. This could go very wrong."

"Sure," I said. "But not for Urda of the Wild Quill, right?" I grinned. "The same Urda that can forge a spymaster's writing can handle some skin-sigiling, right?"

Urda didn't answer.

Yria just glared.

In hindsight, I probably shouldn't have brought up the war we started like it was a happy memory. That's something *I* could work on.

Silence fell over our camp. The kind I didn't like. The kind that gave me a good, long, uninterrupted opportunity to look at what I'd done.

I could still remember when I'd met the twins—in the room where the plan that made everything go to shit was concocted. I'd been unimpressed, even annoyed by them. But we'd worked together. I'd watched them grow from ungrateful, overly hostile amateurs to ungrateful, overly hostile professionals.

But looking at them now... I wondered if maybe, at some point, I'd stopped paying attention to what they became after that.

They were tired. Thin. Pale. Their clothes hung ill-kempt on their bodies, their eyes were deep in their skulls. The portcullis tattoo on Yria's chin was barely visible against the bruises and shadows that painted her face. Urda's fingertips were rubbed red and raw, ink staining the wounds.

When had this happened to them, I had the gall to wonder. When had they started breaking down like this? When...

I didn't have the energy to finish the thought. I knew the answer.

And I knew who had done it to them.

"You find out anything while you were out greasing your anus?" Yria asked. "Because I can see you didn't bring anything fucking back for your old friend Yria."

"Some, yeah. I learned people were after me—"

"I asked if you found out anything, not if you thought of a good reason to tell me something I already fucking know, didn't I? What'd you find out about things that affect *me*?"

I just then found out I had a lot of patience for Yria. But I chose not to say that part.

"We're close to Bitterdrink."

"The Revolutionary fort?" Urda asked. "We've been there once."

"We were *paid* to spring some asshole from its prison," Yria corrected. "We saw the inside of it for all of two minutes."

"Well, yes, but we studied it—" He paused, reconsidered. "*I* studied it extensively as a prelude to our caper. It's the Revolution's power in this region. Nothing but plains and swamp for hours in any direction. Plenty of room for their guns."

"Meret and the others made it past a few days ago."

Yria groaned. "I can't piss out the left side of my snatch because of what I did protecting those assholes and they can't be bothered to not get their asses conscripted? I fucking *told* you we should have killed a few to keep the others in line. But does anyone listen to me?"

"They weren't conscripted."

Both the twins looked alarmed. More than I thought they were capable of looking.

"*Weren't* conscripted," Yria repeated.

"Poneir said that the refugees have probably made it to Toadback by now. Bitterdrink, for whatever reason, didn't go after them."

"Fuck," Yria groaned, rubbing her temples. "Fuck, fuck, fuck, fuck, *fuck*."

I was concerned.

Not because of the swearing. But because of the single word swearing. This was bad.

"What's the matter?"

"We fought off Imperials on our way here," Urda said. "Agne and Yria and I, we..." He licked his lips. "Well, we won, anyway. I was looking for spellwritten objects I could salvage ink from, and while I did, we looted—"

"We didn't loot shit," Yria growled. "We *insisted* on compensation after they made me chase them."

"We *found* some messages. Coded in sigils I could barely identify, let alone read."

"All right, I admit that's alarming," I said, "but I'm not sure a bunch of unreadable messages are worth the shit you're about to drop in your pants."

"I didn't say I *couldn't* read them, I said I could *barely* read them," Urda responded, bristling.

"And what he did read was enough to make *you* shit yourself so hard your feet would leave the ground," Yria growled. "The Imperials are moving forces into the region."

I clicked my tongue. That was more alarming, of course, but—

"I couldn't make out numbers or specific directions," Urda said, his voice going soft. "But I caught a name. A big one."

My heart caught. "How big?"

They exchanged a glance. Yria looked away when she said the name. "Torle of the Void."

She was right. If I hadn't been full of nothing but moonshine and smoke, I would have shit my pants.

And so would you, if you knew anything about that name.

The Imperium has an array of weapons: dragons, legions, spellwritten arms, and of course, its mages. With such power, the Prodigies feel almost decadent. A mage that pays no Barter? That can perform any magic they can think of? That can fly with a thought?

I felt a pang. Tried not to think about flying. Not again.

But I digress. Point being, the Prodigies are capable of such immense destruction that there's almost no point in bringing them out unless you want to do something incredibly severe.

Like a Recivilizing.

I'd never seen one.

But Torle had.

Torle of the Void wasn't just a Prodigy. He was a hero of the Imperium: Her Majesty's Answer, the mage who led the counterattack to establish Imperial presence on the Scar's shores after the Revolution had briefly ousted them. He'd overseen the Imperial efforts to tame the region. Including Recivilizing a few cities. He served admirably, earned his retirement, and returned to the Imperium.

And that was when Red Cloud arrived to take over his work.

We'd met briefly, once, at his retirement ceremony. I recall he spoke little of his time in the Scar, disinterested in feats, tactics, discussions. Our mutual love of brown liquors led to a charming little discussion wherein he mentioned a few hobbies, subjects of interest: whiskey distillation and aging, bird-feather collecting, a bunch of other shit I couldn't remember.

And one thing I did.

Scraths.

Torle liked old magic. Knew more about it than many people should. And their presence on the Scar intrigued him, he had mentioned. That was long ago, though. Who knew if he even remembered anything about Scraths? What if it had just been a passing interest?

It was a flicker of a hope. Hell, not even a flicker. It was a desperate spark in the dark, there and gone. But the memory of its brightness gnawed at me, sat unwell as my brain struggled to smother my heart.

It was stupid. It was *beyond* stupid. Even thinking of a Prodigy was dangerous—the bastards could be listening, for all you knew. When I had been Red Cloud, I tore the Scar apart and I still dream of it. I had no idea what dreams Torle of the Void had learned to sleep through. It was stupid, I told myself. Stupid and futile.

And maybe that's why I couldn't get it out of my mind. Maybe that's why I wondered if I could speak to Torle. Or maybe that's why I felt the gun's weight at my hip and wondered if I could make him talk.

I couldn't. My brain knew that. My bones knew that. Everything but the tiniest, stubbornest, stupidest fucking part of me knew that.

So why the fuck was that part so loud?

"Torle of the Void," I muttered. "Fuck."

"Yeah," Yria sneered. "That's what I said."

The silence fell again. Deeper, this time. And in it, the twins seemed even more hollow than before. Weaker. Smaller.

I'd opened up something in them. Somewhere along the road, I'd pushed them too hard, said something the wrong way, I don't know. I cut them and they'd been bleeding out ever since.

How much further could they go? How much further could I *ask* them to go? They were Vagrants. Like I was. They were no better suited to protecting refugees and running away from fights than me. And my body was mine to destroy. But theirs weren't.

One day, I'd wake up and they'd be gone.

And I'd be hard-pressed to blame them.

But until then, I rolled myself back to my feet, grunted a general good night, and began to trudge toward whatever roll I had managed to turn into a passable bed. My brain was too full for words or apologies or worries. Too full of smoke and liquor and bad ideas to think about—

"Um. Excuse me?"

Urda. Without Yria.

"I hate to bother you about this, but..." He paused, swallowed hard. "Well, no, actually, I *don't* hate to bother you about this, but I want to know..." He held his breath, looked like he was trying to summon his courage. Or puke. Maybe both. "I *need* to know where we're going next, Sal."

I squinted at him. "Yria wants to know?"

His eyes kept trying to find somewhere else to look. "I didn't say that."

"You didn't," I agreed. "And I guess we keep going east. Toward Toadback. Follow the refugees."

"And then where?"

"What do you mean 'and then where'? We go until we can plan our next move."

"We've been doing that for months now." Urda's voice escaped in frustrated gasps. "Toadback is our next move. Just like this place was our last move. Just like Ocytus was the move before that." He gritted his teeth. "There is never a next move, Sal. We don't..." He caught himself. "*I* don't know if there is one at this point."

I narrowed my eyes. The liquor made me surly. Or his attitude made me surly. Or the fact that he was talking a truth I really didn't fucking want to hear made me surly.

"You want to go, you go," I growled.

"We *don't* want to go. Or...maybe we do want to go. But *go* somewhere. Not flee somewhere. Not run somewhere. I need..." He swallowed hard, looked down at his feet. "Yria isn't doing well. She's never used this much of her magic before. I can't keep treating her as we go. She needs somewhere to—"

"Fuck me, Urda, does it look like I know where that is?" I swept my arms over the sprawling marsh colliding with the sprawling Vagrant pageantry. "Would a woman who knows where someplace is be out here? Where it's just fucking dumb luck we ended up alive and together? Do I look like I have *any* fucking idea how to fix this, Urda?"

"But...but..." He quavered—the kid wasn't good with talks like this, I tried to remember. "But you're...you're *Sal*!"

I blinked. "Urda, what the fuck does that even mean?"

"I don't...it's...you're supposed to know, right? We're here because of you."

My face dropped. Fuck me, when he said it like that, it hit me like a damn brick to the jaw.

"Yeah, you're here because of me. And you can not be here because of me, too." I turned, stalked away. "Next time tell your sister to talk to me herself. Or to pick someone else."

"I'm...I'm sorry," he said. "I shouldn't have brought it up."

He should have brought it up. He had every fucking right to bring it up. And if I'd been a little more sober or a lot more drunk, I'd have told him that. But I didn't want to hear it. I couldn't.

I kept walking. Walking like I could just leave the thoughts gnawing at my brain behind me—Torle, the twins, the shit I was doing to them. They swirled into something, like the shit that comes out of a wrung-out bar rag, and it made me sick to think about.

I needed something. Some air. Some water. Someone to fight. Something to break myself against. Something to—

"Hey! Sal the Cacophony!"

Well, I wasn't expecting Cille the Cannon, but it'd do.

The man, tall and lean, dark skin painted at the edges with the ashes of an Embermage's work, came swaggering toward me. The muscles of his broad chest, seared with the tattoo of an exploding firearm, twitched as he approached. The muscles of my hand twitched in response. Specifically, toward my gun.

"Cille the fucking Cannon," I snarled. "You've got fucking balls coming after me here. If you think I'm going to apologize to you *or* your sisters, you're fucking insane."

"First of all, take it fucking easy, it's Booty Haul." He snorted. "Second of all, you broke *both* their hearts, so you better fucking apologize, eventually." He rolled his shoulder. "But last time I saw them, we got to arguing and then the magic came out and someone took someone's eye. I don't know, I was pretty drunk. So, you know, maybe don't apologize."

I understood the first part of that, anyway.

"Then why the fuck are you here?"

"Because I was invited?" He looked at me like *I* was the drunk, belligerent asshole. Weird. "When Agne the Hammer asks you to pay her a visit, you come fucking running, you know? Woman's got thews on her to crush a man's head."

I glanced over him toward her tent. A soft lantern light flickered behind the canvas, illuminating Agne's broad silhouette. But I only recognized her by her size—the proud chin, the strong bearing, the perfect poise I'd come to love from her was gone. She was bowed, head in her hands.

"She... asked you?"

"All right, well, the surprise in your voice hurt me a little more than I thought it would," Cille sniffed. "But this honestly might be the best Booty Haul of my life and I refuse to let you bring me down." He winked, walked off. "You have yourself a good night, Sal. I did."

I fucking hated Cille the Cannon.

Asshole couldn't do anything right. Even fight me.

That bothered me less than the sight of Agne did. It's not that I thought Cille did anything, or could do anything to her—even though I fucking hated him.

Or fuck, maybe I *was* worried. I didn't stop to think.

"Agne?" I asked, making a vague approximation of knocking on her tent flap before peering in. "I just saw a giant turd walking out of your tent. He says you invited him, but I thought I'd check if you need help cleaning the stains out."

Her back was to me. She wore a loose robe. Her hands were on her knees. Her eyes were staring at something I couldn't see.

She did not respond.

"Agne?" I asked, edging closer. Something about me wanted to hesitate, to turn away and leave. And yet. "Agnestrada?"

No answer. No sound. Nothing but a distant, tearless gaze affixed on some sorrowful ending to a story meant only for her. That was worse than a wound. I knew what to do about a wound.

"Cille," I muttered, "did he—"

"Nothing," she said softly. "He didn't do anything."

"Oh." I rubbed my neck. "Well, sorry for intruding, then. I'll..." I winced. "I'll let you be."

"I didn't do anything, either."

Her voice caught me, the little waver of weakness that I would write off in anyone else. To hear such a tone coming from a woman that strong...well, it made me nervous. But I stayed. I sat down on the cot beside her. I tried to see whatever it was her eyes were fixed on.

"I was..." Her voice drifted off, following her gaze. "We fought Imperials, Sal. On the way here."

"Yeah. Urda told me."

"There were a lot of them."

"I bet."

"They were strong."

"Mages?"

She didn't answer. "I had to fight them. I fought them all. I was terrified when they ambushed us. They closed in, with magic and with weapons, and I kept thinking 'not now, not now, not like this.' I was scared. And then . . . I wasn't."

I pursed my lips. I knew what that meant.

"And then . . . it just got easy," she said. "I didn't care about their weapons anymore. Or their magic. Or them. They kept hitting me and I didn't feel it. They kept coming and I just kept punching them and . . ."

Her voice fell low, painfully low.

"I don't know how many there were at the beginning. But at the end, there were none. I'd killed them. All of them. And I wasn't afraid anymore." She swallowed hard. Tears formed at her eyes. "I wasn't afraid, Sal."

"Agne," I whispered, "I'm sorry. Do you want me to . . . ?"

My voice fell. Her hand found mine. I held hers, as best I could.

"We found this place later. Before you. We thought we'd stop and recover before we tried to find you and the refugees. And I've been . . ." Her hands curled into fists. "I asked Cille over. I wanted to know if I could still . . . still . . ."

"Still what?"

"Still love." She wept. Not the tender-eyed tears she deserved, but the wide-eyed tears of someone terrified. "But then he came over. And I tried. I tried everything I could think of. All the things that made me feel . . . feel *something* before. But with him, it was . . . nothing. I felt nothing."

I licked my lips, breathed hard. "Well, that doesn't mean you've lost your emotions yet. Not necessarily, anyway, right? You might just not like him as much as you thought you did. That happens."

"It does happen."

Her hand tightened around mine.

"But what if that's not what happened?"

Her eyes trembled. Her fingers clenched. I felt the bones of my hand start to bend.

"What if I can't feel it anymore because I don't have it? What if I've used too much of my Barter? What if I'll never feel it again?"

I made a cry of protest, tried to free my hand as her grip crushed it. But she wasn't listening. Wasn't seeing. Her eyes were full of tears, watching that thing far away.

"Will I care that it's happening? Will I even *know*? What if it's already happening and I don't know it? What else am I losing? What do I have left? *What do I even—*"

"FOR FUCK'S SAKE, AGNE, PLEASE!"

She released my hand. I fell backward with the force of my pull. I rolled out my fingers, felt the bones pop back into place. Another moment and I'd have lost it all at the wrist. Bruises began to blossom across my hand.

And she hadn't even been trying.

"I'm scared, Sal," she whispered. "I'm scared to keep going. And I'm also scared to stop. I'm scared that leaving you and the twins will make me lose everything else all the quicker. I still feel for you. I... I think." She swallowed hard, blinked away a tear. "And I'm afraid to find out if that's true or not."

This is where I was supposed to say something. The part where any decent person would. But that wasn't me—I knew how to fight with words. I knew how to use them to goad, to intimidate, to hurt. But this...

What the fuck was I supposed to say? How was I supposed to fix this?

"Is there... anything I can do, Agne?"

All I can do is break shit.

"I just... need some time by myself, please."

I tried to talk, tried to try again, to say something better this time. I settled, instead, for biting back the scream that my throbbing hand forced up to my lips. I grunted something equally impotent, walked out.

She hadn't even apologized for my hand.

Was that her panic at losing her emotions? Or had she actually lost the ability to feel remorse? Had the twins noticed? Fuck me, why would they? They were so fucking battered and beaten, they barely noticed their own wounds, let alone whatever was or wasn't going on with Agne.

I tried to walk faster. Tried to focus on the pain in my bruised hand. I tried anything to keep the thoughts from catching up.

And I was almost successful.

"Welcome back."

Until I stopped.

Liette looked up from an appropriately offensively thick book as I approached our corner of the camp. Her smile was somber, but it was there. The thing I'd wanted to see all night.

"I trust you managed to have a fruitful outing?" she asked as she stood up and approached me. She eased my belt and my burdens from me. My arms hung numb at their sides. "I, myself, was less successful in reconnaissance, to my chagrin. The coarse nature of the festivities somewhat prohibited my efforts."

I held still. I'd meant to say hello to her. I'd meant to kiss her. I'd meant to do anything but sit there and let the thoughts catch up with me.

You're going to ruin them.

But they came, all the same.

"Though, I do confess that I managed to reconnect with an old..." Liette blushed a little. "Well, to be perfectly honest, she and I were rather romantic at some times. To a different extent than you and I are, of course, just to be perfectly clear. I believe you made her acquaintance at some point? Suveli the Wound?"

Agne. The twins. You'll burn through them. You'll burn through all of them.

I tried to tell her something. But I couldn't hear the words out of my own mouth. My ears were numb. My lips felt empty.

They won't even have the chance to leave. You'll kill them just by being around them. Because you can't fix this. You know you fucking can't.

"I apologize if the recollection brings you any discomfort, though

I assure you that she and I have well and truly concluded our business. She does this thing with gristle that I just cannot bring myself to . . . Sal?"

You're in such fucking shit, the Ashmouths *took pity on you. How is it obvious to everyone that you can't do this? How the fuck are you supposed to fix this?*

"Sal? What's the matter?"

She was talking. I couldn't hear her. Or see her. My eyes were hazy. My lungs were empty. I couldn't even feel my scars anymore.

You can't save her, either.

"Sal? Talk to me."

You're going to burn through her, too.

"Salazanca. Please. Please, look at me."

You can't save her. You can't save anything. You don't do that. You don't know how. That's not what you do. You can't stop it. You can't fight it, you can't, you can't, you can't

"SALAZANCA!"

I fell forward. No blood in my legs to hold me up. No wind in my lungs to keep me breathing. Everything was in my head, all my blood, all my breath, all of me. Wind hit my face as I fell to the ground. Shock ran up my knees, didn't feel it. My head was made of iron, my neck made of straw. Too heavy to hold up. All the thoughts became one.

I can't do this.

Tears on my face. Fingers clutching her skirts. Clinging to her like she was the last piece of a shipwreck in an ocean. Breath came back slow. Feeling, slower. But it came. I felt a hand under my chin, fingers in my hair, cradling my head against her belly.

She hadn't run. She hadn't left me.

I hadn't burned through her.

"Sal," she whispered to me. "Tell me what's wrong."

I looked up to her. Tears fell out of the corners of my eyes, slid into my ears. I swallowed something salty and bitter.

"Can I tell you something?"

NINETEEN

NEW VIGIL

For no particular reason, Ozhma recalled the first time she'd ever left her little village.

When she'd been asked to accompany her parents on a resupply run, she'd been ecstatic. She could barely believe that she would be so lucky as to go see a world beyond her own. She'd stayed up all night, thoughtfully pawing old adventure books—the trashy kind—and wondering what might happen? Would they see monsters? Have to flee from pursuing bandits? Would she encounter a stranger on the road who would shape her destiny? Maybe even find love?

Of course, later, when it was revealed they were taking a cart and an old workbird to another village four miles down the road, she had felt just a little silly.

But the feeling had lingered. The excitement would come back in those moments of drudgery when she yearned for a world outside of accountancy books and shipping lists. It had been a good feeling. A comforting feeling.

This feeling she had in her chest now, that was not a good feeling.

Sal's words, her story, *that* lingered in a bad way. The Twenty-Second, the Recivilizing, all the killing and all the ways the killing could be done—saw-bladed spears, fortunes that destroyed societies, magic that destroyed civilizations, *Scraths*—all the thoughts flowed into one another, became a river pouring down upon her. She felt like she couldn't breathe, couldn't think knowing the world was that big, that horrific.

But...she couldn't run.

The thought came. Held briefly for comfort, then discarded.

She couldn't leave. Not now.

"Then what happened?"

Ozhma hadn't realized how long she'd been holding her breath, or when she'd scooted so far forward in her chair it was only barely clinging to her ass. She smacked dry lips, reached for a drink that smelled the most like water among the truly impressive number of half-empty and drained cups around them.

Sal glanced lazily up from her own drink—which smelled very unlike water. "What do you mean 'what happened?'"

"You talked to her."

Sal looked into her cup. "Yeah. I did."

"And?"

"And what?"

"And you could have done that this whole fucking time!" Ozhma shouted, leaping out of her chair. She furiously flipped through her notes. "I have jotted down *countless* times when you could have solved things through basic communication! What did you talk about? What did you say? *What happened?*"

"What happened was a lot of words that felt like pulling knives out of my mouth and trying not to choke on the blood that followed. It was hard, it was painful, and it was private." She scowled over the rim of her glass, taking another swallow. "And you're full of shit on that part about it being basic."

"Birdshit."

Sal paused mid-drink. The scar around her eye wrinkled. "Excuse me?"

Ozhma's brain caught up a second later. She clapped a hand over her mouth. "Oh! I'm sorry. I didn't—"

"No, go on. Whatever you didn't, you've done it now."

"I...uh..." Ozhma swallowed spit. Then swallowed something not water. "I mean...you heard me. Where I come from—I mean, you know, running a business—communication is necessary. And when you have a common goal, it's at least easier to put aside your feelings and talk things out."

Sal stared at her. "Put aside your feelings," she repeated.

"I mean, I know it can be hard, but—"

"What if you don't have a common goal?"

Ozhma choked. Just a little. "I'm sorry?"

"What if you don't have a common goal?" Sal said. "What if you have something I want that you don't want to give?"

"Well, then...we could negotiate, maybe? I'm sure we could—"

"I'm not interested in negotiation."

Ozhma gritted her teeth, catching on to Sal's game. "Yes, well, I see. But if you just take the time—"

"Why take time?" Sal threw her cup. The sound of its shatter cut the room. "I want it now."

"W-what do you want?"

"Guess."

"What?"

"Guess what I want," Sal said. "And if you don't guess right..." She hummed, let her eyes drift down to Ozhma's hands. "I'll break your fingers. Like that guy at the corral."

"Okay, I get it," Ozhma muttered, holding up a hand. "But I'm serious. You don't need to joke."

Sal held her gaze for a moment. And then, she rose from her chair. Sweat and whiskey slid down in sticky droplets, her muscles taut and trembling beneath them. Her scars bunched with each step, twisted into angry snarls of flesh. She strode toward Ozhma. Fast. Too fast for anyone, let alone a woman that drunk.

Before Ozhma could get to her feet, Sal's fists slammed down, pinning her wrists to the chair's armrests. Sal tore a hand free, wrenched it in a ferocious grip, seized a chubby digit in leather-wrapped fingers. She leered, whiskey breath roiling out of her mouth.

"Bitch." She pushed the finger backward. "Do I look like I'm joking?"

"S-Sal," she gasped, "wait! *Wait a minute!*"

"What the fuck did I say about waiting?" Sal snarled, bending Ozhma's finger back a little more. "Now give me what I want."

"What do you want?" Ozhma shrieked.

Sal pushed the finger a little farther. The pain shot in angry lances through her arm. "I told you. Guess."

"Sal! I'm a messenger! You can't—"

"*GUESS.*" Sal roared, pulling Ozhma's finger back so far her wrist threatened to come off with it. "*NOW.*"

"*I DON'T KNOW!*" Ozhma screamed. "*I DON'T KNOW! I'M SORRY! I DON'T KNOW!*"

And Sal released her.

"Not so easy, now, is it?" she asked, weary and tired.

Sal trudged back to her large chair, flopped out in an exasperated heap. Her arm hung limply over the armrest, fumbled for a drink, picked it up, and drained it in one swig. She looked back up to Ozhma, folded so far back into her chair she almost disappeared into it, and frowned.

"Sorry about that," Sal said. "And for calling you a bitch."

A long, uncomfortable moment. Ozhma gasped out a lie. "It's fine. But you could have found another way to say that."

"I agree. I could have."

Ozhma squinted. "So why didn't you?"

"Because I didn't," Sal said. "Because I've drunk too much. Because I'm too tired and too pissed off. Because there's some shit in this world I'd break people's fingers to keep." She waved a hand. "Take your pick. Honestly, they're all true. And somehow." She spun a finger lazily around her head. "Up in here, they all start to sound the same sometimes."

"I don't understand."

"Me neither, but I'm trying," Sal sighed. She stared wistfully into the distance. "I don't know. I guess...when there's something you really want, want bad enough to fight over, you start seeing all the ways it could go wrong. Then those become all the ways it *will* go wrong. And then you can't stop thinking about it."

Ozhma frowned, rubbed her sore finger. "I understand that. A little."

"And you just keep trying to keep those things from going wrong," she said. "But you can't. But you can't *not* try. So you end up just..." She held her hands out, tried to grasp the words she was searching for in them, gave up. She looked back to Ozhma. "You ever wanted anything like that?"

"I... think so?"

"This isn't an 'I think so' question."

"Well, I mean, I've loved someone before."

"That isn't what I asked."

Ozhma thought, took another drink of... something. "I've always worried about... about not being anything."

She looked back up. Sal watched, silent. She drew in a breath.

"I guess I wanted lots of things. *Do* want lots of things. I want a home that feels like mine. I want to have someone with me in that home. I don't know who, yet, but I want them. I want the things from stories. From opera, you know? Well, of course, you know."

Ozhma laughed nervously. Sal didn't.

"I guess," she sighed, "I guess that I want to want those things more than I want what I have now. And every day, I wake up and don't think I'm going to get them. And every day, I wake up and feel a little less bothered by it."

"Why don't you get them?"

"I don't know. Where would I even start?"

Sal shrugged. "I don't know, either. I mean, obviously, I don't fucking know." She chuckled, tossed a cup aside, looked for another. "Fuck, maybe we could just solve each other's problems. I can buy you a nice house."

"I can't fend off two armies, so I'm not sure I can help," Ozhma laughed, momentarily shocked that she had.

"Yeah, well, I can't make anyone fall in love with you, either. Ah, well. Good try."

"Birdshit."

Sal cocked an eyebrow. "Didn't we just go over this?"

"No, this is a different birdshit. You absolutely could make someone fall in love with me. Anyone, if you wanted to. You wouldn't have to even use violence to do it."

For the first time since they'd met, Sal looked surprised. Ozhma tried not to savor that. Too hard.

"Well, I'm flattered, don't get me wrong," the Vagrant said, "but unless you're frisky for someone who likes people who know incredibly attractive women with big guns, I don't think I could help."

"*Birdshit*," Ozhma spat. "You *just* told me about the twins, about Agne, about all they gave for you. You can convince two outlaw criminals to follow you because you're you, but you couldn't convince someone tall and handsome to love me?"

Sal's expression soured. She drained her drink. Then the next one. And the next one.

"They didn't do that for me," she paused drinking long enough to say.

"They followed you. They fought for you."

"For their own reasons. Not for me."

"Their own reasons *are* you, Sal. Isn't it obvious?"

"It isn't obvious," Sal growled.

"Well, it should be, because—"

"It isn't obvious because it's not fucking true," she said over her cup. She took a swig, swirled it around in her mouth, spat whiskey on the floor. "Because that's not the kind of people we are. We don't fight for each other. Vagrants don't do that."

"Vagrants don't protect refugees, either, but they did it for you."

"For their own reasons," Sal grunted, again.

"No, but—"

"*FOR THEIR OWN FUCKING REASONS.*" Sal leapt to her feet, the cup trembling in her hand. "It wasn't for me because they know better than that. The shit that's happened to them, they did it for their own greed, their own legend, their. Own. Reasons. They didn't fucking do it for me because I'm not—"

She froze. Trembled. Her jaw clenched, her fingers wrapped so hard around the cup it threatened to shatter in her hand.

"Because it's my shit," she spat, taking a drink. "And I'm fucking taking care of it."

"Okay, well..." Ozhma forced her gaze open, resisted the urge to stare down at her feet. "I don't know them, but it's clear they thought enough of you to fight for you. So how is that different... than..."

Ozhma's voice trailed off as Sal's eyes snapped up. Terrified, she leapt behind her chair, wary of what might come after that. But Sal merely looked into her cup, swirled it around, sniffed it. She held it out, upturned it.

A small puddle of wine fell out and upon the floor.

"Fuck." She threw the cup aside, stalked past Ozhma, seized her by the collar as she did. "I've got to do something. Come back in a bit."

"What? Wait! Wait!" Ozhma protested, but didn't dare resist as Sal escorted her toward the door. "I'm a messenger! They said to—"

"And you will." Sal opened the door. "Give me a bit."

"I'm sorry if I offended you, but... what am I supposed to do?"

"Grab a drink. Take a walk. See the sights." Sal shoved her out the door. "This city won't be around much longer, after all."

Then slammed it in her face.

"Fucking asshole," Ozhma cursed to herself as she stomped upstairs. "Fucking... stupid... asshole... *asshole*!"

The frustration in her voice was multilayered, like all the fine things in life. She was pissed off at Sal, at Sal's obstinance, and at Sal's vocabulary. Sal the fucking Cacophony could string curses together like sausages while Ozhma the fucking Fat Girl Who Sells Booze was scrambling for a third cuss.

What was the point of all the posturing? All the secrecy? Didn't lives hang in the balance? Hers included? *Liette's* included?

She stood by her earlier observation: somehow, a Vagrant as ill-mannered, offensive, and belligerent as Sal *had* managed to acquire the suspiciously stalwart loyalty of multiple people, though she still had no idea why.

The woman displayed concern for none of them, not even herself, if her tales of self-destruction were credible—and Ozhma had many reasons to believe they were. In fact, Sal barely even seemed to know what she was doing most of the time. How had she collected these people? How hadn't they seen through her yet? How—

"Fuck, hang on, boys," a voice, feminine, burbled from up ahead. "It happened again. I've got wine now. You?"

"Apple juice, I think." Another, this one she recognized—Meret, had his name been? "I had cider, though, so I really don't mind."

"I had vodka and now I have... water." That one was Cavric; she remembered the depth of the weariness in his voice. "Fuck me. Anyone want to trade?"

"I will." She was surprised to hear Rudu's voice among them—startled, even. "But in good conscience, I can't identify it. I don't know what it tastes like. And it might have looked at me."

"Do you know me to be a picky man?" Cavric asked.

"I've known you for an hour," Rudu said.

"So, 'no,' then. Hand it over."

Ozhma emerged from the cellar into an ominously empty command center. A few people remained, here and there, tending to minimal tasks—mostly letter writing, sometimes sobbing. They worked by dim candlelight, save for one table, lit by the pale light of an alchemic glow.

"Uh, excuse me?" Ozhma announced herself, timidly approaching. "Did I miss... that is, did something happen?"

Four faces looked up from the table. Three, she recognized. One, she didn't. Ensconced at the far end of the table, a woman with dark red hair in tangled, unwashed knots glowered up from beneath a hood, face twisted in a frown.

"You lost?" the woman growled. "Or are you the Scar's shittiest spy?"

"Ah, fuck me." Rudu winced, holding up a hand. "Ease off there, Ketterling, huh? This is my fault." The Vagrant puffed idly on his pipe as he slid a tankard across the table, exchanging with Cavric. "Sorry, kid. I was supposed to go pick you up, but then I met these guys drinking and talking and I thought, 'You know, it's a lovely night, and everyone's going to die, anyway, why not share a cup?' "

"Excuse me?" Ozhma glanced, worriedly, to Cavric. "*Excuse me?*"

"He's talking shit, madam, if you'll pardon the language." Cavric took the tankard up in a thick hand, downed the reeking sludge, and winced. "Fuck me, that's awful, but it's liquor." He held up a finger. "Pardon that language, too. You and this degenerate are going to be fine."

" 'Degenerate,' " Rudu scoffed. He leaned over, elbowed Meret in the ribs. "Can you believe this guy?"

Meret, jostled, readjusted his glasses and brushed apple juice off his cloak. "Yes, well... admittedly, I haven't known you long at all. But you *do* strike me as a tad unsavory, given that you work with the Ashmouths and all."

"You can come right out and say it," the woman, Ketterling, spat. "This guy's leaving us to fucking die while he gets stupid on grass."

Rudu puffed out a cloud from behind his pipe. "Well, I was going to share, but now you've gone and hurt my feelings."

"I'm really sorry, but..." Ozhma pulled a chair up to the table as Cavric scooted aside to make room. "Can I ask what this is about? And..." She winced, feeling nauseous. "Can I have some water, please?"

"Ah, hell. Which one was water?" Cavric held up a cup. "This one?"

"That one *was* water. It's soup now." Ketterling slid her a tankard. "This one is water. For now."

"All right, so, not to sound ungrateful, since I asked and all—and thank you, by the way." Ozhma took several deep gulps before gasping. "But you all kind of said... *multiple* fucked-up things, so could I maybe get an explanation on the whole 'everyone dying' part?"

Cavric stared into his cup, sighed.

"The Revolutionary and Imperial diplomats have departed," he said. "They said they didn't need to hear more."

Ozhma swallowed hard. "Then . . . that means . . . we failed?"

"That would imply that they ever intended on honoring negotiations to begin with." He downed the rest of his drink. Winced. "In all likelihood, this was just a delaying tactic for the two armies to figure out what the other one was doing."

"So that means . . ."

"It means we're fucked," he said, "but that doesn't mean we failed."

"Oh. That makes . . . sense?"

"Well, there are two ways to look at it, as I see it." Cavric picked up another tankard, walked to a nearby keg against the wall, tapped it. A thick, syrupy goo slipped out. "We *could* dwell on how much of a chance we never really had against two militaries infinitely stronger and wealthier than we are." He slugged it back, blanched. "Or we could just keep drinking until we're stupid."

Ozhma frowned, took another sip of water. A thick, sour foulness assailed her mouth. She spat out a glob of syrupy sweet . . .

"Is that . . . molasses?"

"Fuck, did it change again?" Ketterling looked into her cup, grinned. "Ha! *Mama's* got vodka now, lads."

"What is this?" Meret smacked his lips. "Mango? I've never had mango."

"Then you can't know it's mango, can you?" Rudu looked to Ozhma. "Give it a few minutes. The drinks keep changing. I've got . . ." He tasted his, spat it out. "Vinegar. My fucking luck."

"What? By themselves?" Ozhma stared into her cup. "That's impossible."

"Impossible? You don't fucking say." Ketterling took a swig. "Between all the mages and tanks and imminent doom and all, I thought I was losing perspective."

"Madame Ketterling," Meret interjected. "I believe you should at least be introduced before insulting our guest." He gestured. "Ketterling. Commander of the Bant Knights."

"A pleasure." Ozhma offered the sweetest smile her sweaty, half-drunk face could remember. She glanced around the empty command center. "I didn't... miss something, did I?"

"When the envoys left, morale started falling." Cavric stared into his drink. "They saw it, plain as we all did. They knew what was going to come." He took a swig of... something. "And then the drinks started changing, so I figured why bother. I sent them to be wherever they felt they should be tomorrow morning, when it—"

He caught it, the way strong people always catch it and other strong people politely ignore it. But Ozhma was not a strong person, so she saw the way his wrinkles twitched, his frown deepened. He tried to force another smile through his beard, just as they tried to force themselves not to notice the flash of heartbreak across his face.

"Anyway," he muttered. "This is where we all agreed we needed to be. So here we are. Except for him. I don't know why he's still here."

"I stayed for the drinks." Rudu put down a glass of tart-looking juice, picked up a cup of tea. "Where else can you get this sort of experience?"

"Anywhere that fucking Vagrant and her magic gun go, for one," Ketterling muttered into her cup. "You don't think this shit always happens in New Vigil, do you?"

"Sal?" Ozhma chimed in. "Sal is doing this? *How?*"

Meret exchanged glances with the others. "It's... potentially wise not to ask questions with regard to the... the weapon."

"Fuck, are we not even going to say it?" Ketterling interjected. "Are we *that* fucking scared of it?"

"I am," Cavric replied solemnly. "And I'm not afraid to admit it because I'm not an imbecile. I've seen it. I know what it can do." He tried to finish his drink, gave up, and poured out a damp, croaking frog onto the floor. "I'm terrified of that gun."

A small chorus of muttered agreement, and then, almost as an afterthought:

"And I'm terrified of her."

Silence. Averted gazes. An intense, animal soundlessness fell, like cricket song falling quiet as a beast passes by. Ozhma felt almost in violation by whispering.

"Can I ask something?" She glanced between them. "If it's... I mean, if she's like you say she is. Why are you here? Why are you helping her?"

A different silence met her, a more unhallowed silence. The kind that made people fear to speak at funerals or avoid looking at dark stains on the earth that couldn't be scrubbed clean. A knowing silence—they had an answer, but speaking it was more painful than they could handle.

"Well, I'm fucking out, then."

Ketterling drained her cup, slammed it back down, belched. "I didn't want to help her in the first place and, frankly, if I hear why you dickwipes are doing it, I might lose my sunny disposition."

She wearily sauntered off. Cavric called after her. "Where are you going? We're all going to die tomorrow."

"To bed," she replied. "If I'm going to die, I might as well be well-rested for it."

When the room stopped shaking from the slam of her door, Ozhma looked back to the table. The silence was unbearable now, the discomfort on their faces plain.

"I... it's hard to say." Meret spoke first, his eyes glued on the table. "When I met her, months ago, I was terrified of her, too. She was a story..." He winced, reconsidered. "More than a story, really. Well, more like a cautionary tale. I lived my life in fear of her, same way I lived my life in fear of everyone and everything that I didn't know.

"Then she came to Littlebarrow. To the Valley." He sighed. "And I realized she wasn't a story. She was just... I don't know. And I don't know how to explain it, what I saw in her face, what we spoke of back in Littlebarrow. But at the end, I didn't see a story to be terrified of. I saw a woman. I saw Sal."

He took a long, slow sip of his drink. Ozhma leaned in.

"And then what happened?" she asked.

"And then the war happened," Meret answered. "And Littlebarrow was . . . and Sindra . . ." He swallowed something bitter and painful. "And then I realized it was one woman who had done that. Just one woman. Just Sal." He took his glasses off, rubbed at his eyes. "And then I was terrified of her again."

He shoved away from the table so suddenly, you'd think it was on fire. He muttered something hasty as he pulled his coat tighter around him.

"Would you excuse me? I think I need to be somewhere."

Ozhma tried to call after him and apologize. But he drew away from her voice, as surely as he drew away from the few left here that tried to ask him what the matter was. Maybe she had touched a nerve.

Or maybe he just needed to go be broken for a little bit.

"He'll be all right." Cavric reached across the table, pulled Meret's abandoned drink over to him. "People like him know how to recover. I envy it, honestly. In a better world, he'd be a thousand times more important to this city than I would. But here we are." He chuckled. "In a way, maybe that's why Sal's here, too."

"What?" Ozhma asked. "Just 'here we are'?"

"No, not like that. More like . . ." He considered, shrugged, drank. "Actually yes, exactly like that. People like her . . ." He considered again, shrugged again, drank again. "Actually, just her. Sal is like a tornado. She happens to you, then you figure out what to do with it."

She scratched her head, tried to contemplate that. "That—and I'm sorry if this hurts your feelings—sounds a little fucking insane, sorry again. No one *enjoys* having a tornado hit, let alone helping it."

"Well, I didn't say I *enjoyed* it, now did I?" Cavric managed a smile—soft, but not weak, like a joke he just thought of. "Then again, maybe I do. I did open my city to her, after all. I did agree to have her here."

"I'm having a little trouble keeping up, sir," Ozhma said, rubbing her temples. "You said she's a tornado. As in, she fucks up most things?"

"I can't deny that."

"But she's here, and you're not happy about that, or what she's doing."

"Also true."

"But you also *are* happy to have her here."

"Correct."

Ozhma blinked, squinted, bit her lower lip. "So... what the fuck? Respectfully. Sir."

Cavric chuckled—the joke only he knew was getting funnier. "Maybe I feel bad for the tornado."

"Sir. I'm being serious."

"As am I, madam, I assure you. When I defected from the Revolution, I knew I'd have to fight them one day. When I traveled with Imperial defectors, I knew I'd have to fight *them* one day. When we made New Vigil, I knew I'd die in its walls one day." He shrugged. "Sal just made those happen a little sooner than I thought."

Cavric grunted as he pulled his thick self up from the table. He swirled the last of his cup, drank it, set it back down. He rolled his shoulder out, tucked a thumb into his belt beneath his belly.

"Whether I want a tornado to be here or not, a tornado is here," he said. "And so long as it is here, I'd rather be behind it than in front of it."

Ozhma nodded. "I think I understand now."

"Good, because I'm too fucking drunk to explain it any clearer. Now, if you'll excuse me. Pleased as I am to have met you, neither of you are who I want to be with come morning." Heavy boots thudded across the floor. He paused, glowered over his shoulder at Rudu. "No Ashmouth tricks. No fuckery. You get her clear of this mess."

Rudu grinned behind his pipe. "Or else?"

"Or else I crawl out of whatever hole these shitheads put my corpse in and drag you back down into the earth with me."

To look into Cavric's eyes, you would never guess that such a thing wasn't possible, let alone that he couldn't do it. Ozhma swallowed hard. Not nearly as hard as Rudu did.

"Wow," he said. "Yes, Dad, I promise. Listen, you and the Ketterling girl, are you—"

"Good night, Rudu. Madam."

His slamming the door damn near shook the room to pieces. Ozhma had to hold on to her chair to avoid falling off. Or maybe it just felt like that. But as the room fell to hushed murmurs and sobs in the corners, she found her nerve. And found her eyes drawn to Rudu.

He emptied his pipe, packed another bowl, lit it without looking up. "What?"

"You know what I'm about to ask you."

"I do. I kind of hoped that 'what' part would have made you ask something else." He took a deep breath, stared into the cloud of exhaled smoke thoughtfully. "I don't know why I help Sal. Maybe I just don't have enough friends."

"That doesn't make—"

"Here's a better question," he interrupted. "Why are *you* here? You did what you were supposed to do. No one's going to blame you for it going to shit. You can be paid and on your way in an hour." He glanced out the window. "Hell, we should have been back *three* hours ago."

"I can't just leave!" she protested. "Not while there's still... still..."

"Still what?" He shook his head. "The big boy is right. The Imperium and the Revolution were never going to agree to spare the city. They probably never even intended to."

"But then... why were envoys sent?"

"Appearances? So the people with the big guns can shrug and say they tried and hope the other cities take the hint? Some statecraft shit I'm not high enough to understand?" He puffed on his pipe. "That's why *they* were sent here. You were sent here because certain parties are interested in how this all turns out."

She frowned. "Criminals."

"All right, madam, maybe relax with the judgment, eh?" he said. "It's only because I work for certain interested parties that this city is still standing. The minute I leave, the Ashmouths' interests are clear and they're free to turn it into a pile of ash." He gestured to her with his chin. "And I'm not leaving without you. So I ask you... why are *you* still here?"

People who smoked so many drugs, Ozhma decided, ought not to be able to ask such difficult questions.

Why was she here? The powers assailing this city had already made their decision. She could do nothing to stop it, do nothing to save the people here. Even if they *were* going to honor their word, how could she tell them what was happening? How could she explain what Sal was doing?

Hell, for that matter, how could she explain *Sal*?

The woman seemed hell-bent on destroying everything around her, starting with her. Ozhma, in her long history of dealing with obstinate, aggressive assholes had never met such an obstinate, aggressive *asshole*. Sal refused to help this situation, refused to even *consider* the people around her.

What would that even look like? Ozhma wondered. *Does she even know how to do it?*

Ozhma felt something cold in her heart. Cold and painful and unpleasant and she wished it would go away.

She felt bad for the tornado.

"So?" Rudu asked. "Got an answer?"

She shook her head, numbly. "No."

"You think you can actually do anything here?"

She held her eyes shut. "I don't know."

"Then... do you want to leave?"

Ozhma looked up, felt the tears hot on her face. "No."

She sniffed something wet back. Rudu sighed, reached into his sleeve, produced a silk handkerchief and handed it to her. She wiped her eyes, ignored his visible wince as she blew her nose. She swallowed salty tears, looked up.

"Are you going to make me leave?" she asked.

"Eventually, I'll have to."

"Are you going to do it now?"

Rudu glanced around the dismal, funerary command center. His eyes drifted across the huddled people and their muffled miseries. He took a long, thick drag of smoke and exhaled it, painting ghostly lights across the lantern. He kicked off his sandals, propped his feet up on the table.

"I like the atmosphere here, could stick around for a bit, I suppose," he said. "At least until my smoke pouch runs out." He gave it a shake in his pocket. "Probably a couple of hours, if I'm slow."

"Are you sure the Imperium and Revolution won't attack?"

"I'm not sure of anything." He lazily glanced toward her. "Are you sure you can do anything here?"

She had an answer for him. And for herself. And it came without words.

It came with her hopping off her chair, smoothing out her skirts, and holding out her hand. Rudu handed his pipe to her. She took the hardest drag she could, felt her lungs sear inside her, hacked out a wet, wheezing cough, then handed the pipe back.

She wasn't sure that was going to do anything, either.

But for what she intended to do, as she turned and headed back down to the cellar, she was going to need it.

TWENTY

THE SCAR

Anyway, if memory serves, I was about to do something incredibly stupid.

"Are you certain?"

I looked up from my sack of meat.

"About what?"

Liette, to her credit, didn't mention my greasy, bloodied hands or the various bits of offal I'd been tossing over my shoulder for the past mile or so. Her eyes were hard and dark behind her glasses, her face heavy with concern. She walked in hurried, hushed steps, leaning conspiratorially close to me.

"About this," she said, "about whether it will work or not."

"Oh. That." I fished out what appeared to be kidneys, threw them over my shoulder. A beak snapped shut somewhere behind me. "No. Not in the least."

"I..." She did that thing that smart people do when they have ten different words to call you stupid but can't do it—a moment of constipated explosion followed by a tired breath. "I understand. What you told me, about how we could...address the situation with Eldest."

"The situation?" I muttered. "You mean that fucking *thing*?"

"It is *not* a thing, it is..." She fumbled for the words, looked away, embarrassed that she couldn't find them. "It's hard to explain. I want it out of me. I can feel it... taking." She rubbed her throat with numb fingers. "It's like I can feel Eldest, its presence, observing me... but from within. I've known it so well, I can't think of it as a thing. I feel it hearing my thoughts, I see it peering into my dreams, and when I speak, I sometimes..."

She bit her lip, turned her face down, said no more. I didn't push her.

I meant what I said. It was agony talking to her about this. The same way it would be agony to see anyone you loved in shit like this, compounded with the agony of having to face how few options you had and how shitty they were, and topped with the agony of wondering how many ways you could have stopped this.

So, yeah. I wasn't any keener to press than she was.

"So... Eldest, then. Has it... told you anything that might help?"

But I was sure as shit less keen to lose her.

"I am not certain," Liette replied, rubbing her throat again. "It's hard, Sal. I want to help, but every time I look at Eldest, *feel* Eldest, I feel..."

"Like it's taking more?" I asked.

"Yes," she said. "But also... like it's not just taking. Like it's... trading." Her eyes widened, her fingers quickened as they stroked at her neck. "I catch only glimpses of Eldest, but when I do, I see seas of innumerable stars, I see the marvels of human imagination, I see all the ways to turn a single pebble into an entire world. I see cities that can't possibly exist, could *never* have existed with how amazing they were, and yet... I know they exist."

Her pupils contracted. Then, they expanded. Eclipsing her irises, the whites of her eyes. Her fingers went from stroking to scratching.

"They exist because Eldest has seen them," she gasped. "And if I look at them, if I look long enough, if I let it take just a little more, I can make them again. They're incredible. Buildings that move with a thought, stone that becomes water. I could make it for you, Sal. Miracles. They were *miracles*, impossible to explain! I could make it for us, Sal. If I just let Eldest in a little more, I could do so many—"

I grabbed her hand, prised her nails from reddening skin, slid her fingers into mine, and squeezed them gently. I brought my lips to her fingers, pressed them to each tip, each knuckle. And slowly, her eyes lightened. And it was her looking at me again.

"I can live without miracles," I said, "not without you."

She smiled, squeezed my hand back, before politely taking out a handkerchief and wiping her fingers clean. And I, impolitely, slid my hand back into the bag and produced several feet of entrails, letting them dangle in the road behind me.

"Thank you, Sal," she said. "For what you said. For... for doing that. I am aware—that is, I *know*, that these things are not easy for you. These things being emotional validation and conversations of—"

"Not to be rude, but you're no fucking great dialogue yourself," I interjected. "But thank you. I appreciate that."

"Still," she said. "Are you certain that this *particular* course of action is wise? While—you'll forgive my bluntness, of course—I wouldn't say that there are *many* that love you in the Scar..."

Ordinarily, I *wouldn't* forgive that, but lately that sentiment was hard to argue against.

"But the Imperium remains particularly unforgiving of Vagrants," she said, "and you are a Vagrant of particularity."

That sentiment, too.

And the truth was, I *didn't* know if this was going to work. But I did know that, of all possibilities laid before me, Torle of the Void was the only one that I felt good enough about to pursue.

True, the Imperium and I didn't have a good relationship—what with me shooting so many of them. But they at least didn't hate me enough to burn the whole thing down. Riacantha had offered me a return to the Imperium. I had to assume that meant I could push my luck enough to get Torle's attention.

And if I did, the knowledge he could tell me about the thing inside Liette could solve everything. Or at least, get me closer to solving it on my own.

Together, I reminded myself. *We're doing this together. She and I.*

And that was the sole reason we were going here. If Torle could offer us even a fragment of knowledge, Liette might be able to figure out the rest on her own—she was, after all, *painfully* intelligent. I wasn't certain about this plan, about the Imperium or Torle or Eldest or anything else but her.

Her, I was certain of.

"I guess you'll just have to trust me," I said, offering a smile that I *hoped* was reassuring.

"I do trust you."

And I don't know if you've ever heard four words that made you feel like you could cry in a good way at an inopportune time, but I had a hell of a time with it.

"I just remain unclear on certain motivations behind the finer points of your plan." She observed as I threw a liver out that was, I had been assured, not human. "Such as why there is a sack of meat involved."

"What else was I supposed to do with it?"

"A superior question would be why you have it in the first place."

"There was a guy selling sacks of meat at Booty Haul." I winked at her. "Thanks for buying me one, by the way. You're so sweet."

"And I respectfully did not ask questions at the time, such as why that person had so much meat," she said, "but I feel that, given it was my metal that bought it, I have a right to know."

I *tried* not to look at her like she was stupid, but she wasn't giving me a lot of choice here. I upended the sack of meat, let the remnants fall out onto the ground in a greasy, ugly heap.

"I think it's pretty fucking obvious." I jerked my thumb over my shoulder. "Or do you expect her to do this without any motivation?"

Congeniality let loose a keen of agreement. Or possibly indignation—hard to tell with her, really. She slurped down the last piece of entrails dangling from her beak before diving face-first into the remaining bits of carrion sweating in the sun.

She'd picked up our trail shortly after we left Booty Haul,

returning to me fat, happy, and smelling faintly of shit. Thanks, in no small part, to the bag of offal I'd been leaving behind me to lure her away from whatever poor fucker she was devouring.

You hear stories of faithful birds—noble mounts who are so bonded to their owners that they are there in the thickest dangers and at a moment's notice. And that might be true of some birds. But for Badlanders like her, you didn't get that kind of loyalty without a *lot* of fucking rotting organs.

The operas don't tell you that, do they?

"I choose to trust you on this, as well," she said, "though I want it noted that you have not put forth the most persuasive evidence."

I wiped my greasy, bloodied hand on my ass. "Noted."

I expect she wanted to say more to that, but at that moment, a sharp whistle caught our attention. Yria and Urda stood high upon a nearby hill, waving to grab our attention. I whistled Congeniality forward, pulled up onto her saddle, reached down, and seized hold of Liette's hand.

She slid behind me. Her arms wrapped around my waist. Her head rested on my shoulder.

I breathed that moment in as I spurred Congeniality forward: the rhythm of the bird's stride jostling her body against mine, the feel of her breath on my skin, the way she gasped when we went over a big obstacle. I savored them more, these moments, since we'd talked.

Deep down, maybe I worried I didn't have many left.

Congeniality darted around streams and brooks. This far east in the Scar, flat green was hard to find. Marshland battled hills for supremacy, with only a few miles of square plain breaking through the collision of the encroaching marsh and the resilient hills. Sun broke through the clouds in radiant shafts, setting rivers shimmering and painting macabre shadows with looming, bowing trees.

Here and there, I saw signs of people: campfires left abandoned, belongings left behind when they grew too burdensome. I wondered if any had been Meret, or Sindra, or the refugees. But only for a moment.

They were on their way to Toadback. Out of danger.

Me? I was going somewhere else.

"Our earlier opinion was correct, *as usual*," Urda said, beaming as we reached him. He pointed down the other side of the hill, to a rolling plain—big enough to move on, though worryingly small for escape purposes. "We've *ascertained* that Imperial surveillance is on this area."

"Quit fucking showing off for the glasses-wearer," Yria snarled. "We just fucking saw some bird scouts around here. Imperium's got eyes on this spit of green. You want their attention, you fucking get it. My leg's still fucking asleep."

I grunted, reached down, and laid my hand on Liette's. She leaned close, tightened around my waist for a moment.

"Be careful," she whispered.

She slid off Congeniality, joined the twins. Yria glanced toward me.

"Listen, I'm still up for this shit," she said. "But I can't... I don't..."

"You can't push her too hard," Urda interrupted. "Just... try not to make our aid too necessary. We're with you, but—"

"She'll handle what she can," Liette cut him off. "We'll handle what we can."

That was one of those answers that didn't really satisfy anyone, but it was as good as we were going to get. I spurred Congeniality forward to where Agne stood, arms crossed as she watched that long stretch of green.

"Worried?" I asked.

"No," she replied—whether she meant that or not, I didn't ask. "I'm here if things go awry, as usual. I was just... contemplating, I suppose." She scratched her chin. "The offer the Imperium gave you, about returning... do you think they'd..."

She frowned. Waved a hand.

"Never mind, Sal. I apologize. You've got problems of your own." She exhaled. "Just... try to—"

"Yeah. Urda told me." I looked down at her. "You really think I can do this?"

She looked like she didn't. And yet. "I do."

"All right." I leaned down in the saddle, licked my lips at her. "How about a little good luck tongue, then?"

Agne looked toward me, eyes wide with shock. Slowly, an impish, amused grin spread across her face. She pushed me away—damn near out of the saddle, honestly.

"I abhor you," she giggled. "Go be dangerous."

I returned the smile, pulled my scarf up around me as I kicked Congeniality forward. She could still smile. She could still laugh. She could even be offended. I liked reminding her of that, however briefly. It made me feel good.

Not necessarily good about what I was going to *do* just then, but what does?

Congeniality took me down the hill. We hit the plain at a trot. I could feel the eyes on me almost immediately—shadows of great scouting birds flitted over me through the cloud cover.

The Imperium *did* have eyes on this land. Made sense, I supposed, if the talk of them besieging nearby Bitterdrink was anything to be believed. I hadn't seen any Revolutionary force to challenge us out here, either. Which meant that there would be nothing to distract the Imperial riders from me, out alone on the plain, defenseless.

So, already, this plan was going great.

It had been some time when I finally made it out to the center of the green spit of land. An hour, at least, of Imperial riding birds swooping overhead. Never attacking. Never even challenging. Simply observing, disappearing, reappearing later.

I shielded my eyes, looked up at the sky, counted as many as I could.

Six.

Six chances for this to go either very good or very, very bad.

"Salazanca ki Ioril."

I'll give you a guess which it was.

I took my time in turning to face Velline. If she wanted to kill me before addressing me, she would have. Maybe she was still too classy for that.

Or, I thought as I looked at her, *maybe she's just too damn tired.*

Her uniform was pristine, but ill-fitting—she'd gone through all her best-looking ones. Her stance was spear straight, but with the intensity of someone who'd forgotten how to stand any other way. Her ivory hair was longer, less kempt, and almost as pale as her face.

"Do you know why I am an Imperial mage?" she asked.

"Because you were born into it," I answered. "Like I was. Fuck off, Velline. You're not who I'm here to see."

She did not fuck off. She stepped forward. Her sword dragged behind her.

"I could have gone Vagrant," she said. "I could have been excellent at it. Quickmages often are. But how could I have turned my back on the people that brought me here?"

"Hundreds before you found a way." I steadied myself on Congeniality as she chirruped under me. "Go ask them."

"I was starving. Impoverished. Filthy when my powers manifested," she said. "I'd been abandoned by everyone I ever loved. The Judge who found me nurtured me to health. The academy I was enrolled in gave me family, safety, well-being. The Empress I serve has given me, my soldiers, and *everyone* I have ever served with a life."

Another step forward. There was no sheath on her sword. A naked blade cut through the grass.

"I can understand why you would turn your back on that, much as I might disagree," she said. "I have thought. I have asked myself questions no one should have to. And I understood you, just a little, or so I thought. But what I can't understand..."

She raised her blade, leveled it at me.

"Is how you could hate the family that raised you so much that you would kill so many of them?"

"They aren't my family, Velline." I slid my hand to my waist. "And if you don't fuck off, I'll—"

"No, Sal."

Her voice was soft as her blade.

"Don't reach for your gun. Don't try to escape this. You know what's going to happen."

"And what," I said, keeping my hand steady, "is going to happen?"

"I am going to kill you. I am going to end this. I am going to cut out the source of all of this." She smiled softly. "Because if I don't, you'll cause another war. And another war. And another war."

"Can't say I fault that logic," I replied, cool as I could be. "But it's taken you a lot of friends to kill me before. Where are the rest of your—"

"Dead."

Tears. Cold and painless. They slid down her bloodless face.

"Shenazar, dead. Dalthoros, dead. My Hellions are dead. Or injured. Or abandoned. Or deserted to go Vagrant." She swallowed hard. "We were the finest in the Imperium. I was destined to protect them. And instead, you... you..."

She gave up. She blinked the water from her eyes.

"It doesn't matter now, Sal. I can move faster than you can blink, let alone raise a gun." She held out her hands. "There's nowhere to go. Nowhere for either of us."

"Velline, listen. Riacantha had an offer of amnesty for—"

"I know."

There was the briefest chord of the Lady Merchant's song. I blinked. There was a gust of wind behind me.

"You don't deserve it," Velline whispered into my ear.

Her blade flashed. I narrowly turned in time to keep it from carving me apart as it raked across my ribs, cutting me open. I struck out with the grip of the Cacophony. Too slow. She disappeared from sight, reappeared ten feet away, leveled her sword.

I kept my eye on her, hand on my bleeding side. I watched her as she stayed there, unmoving. I watched her as my eyes burned and filled with tears until I could take it no longer.

I blinked.

I heard the Lady's song.

And she struck.

Some operas say that, before you die, your life flashes before your eyes and you take the regrets and the joys with you to the black table. I don't think that's true—my life flashes before my eyes all the fucking time. But I do think that you can feel when you're about to die.

I think it feels like a rush of wind. Like noticing the stir of grass. Like taking a deep breath and not letting go of it.

Or maybe that's just what I felt.

If I unfocused my eyes, I could almost see her: shapes on the wind as she sped toward me, blade in hand. For a moment that hung, painful and taut, between us, I could see her before me, her blade thrusting toward my throat. A sliver of a second, sheared off and gone before I could even raise a finger.

And then.

Sparks.

A flash of steel. A spray of light sputtering across my face. I flinched. I blinked. I gasped.

I was still alive. Somehow.

And, somehow, Velline reappeared, skidding to a halt some distance away. She looked at her blade like it was broken, then at me, face wild with bewilderment.

Like I was somehow supposed to know what the fuck just happened.

But she didn't wait. The Lady sang a note. The wind rushed. I felt the echo of a blade behind me, heard the killing thrust coming.

Metal rang out against metal. Sparks struck my back. She skidded away, rolling across the ground. She leapt to her feet, searching the empty air as though she could pluck her frustration out of the sky.

"Show yourself!" she shouted into the wind. "Who are you to defy the will of the Imperium?"

I didn't know.

I wasn't going to ask.

And I sure as shit wasn't going to stand still for her to try again.

She vanished into the air. I spurred Congeniality to a sprint. The Lady's song rang out in discordant notes around me, clashing off each other. I could feel the wind rushing in against itself. Steel echoed. Congeniality's feet thundered beneath me. Sparks danced in angry bursts, unseen blades striking.

Velline appeared before me, struck with her sword. I pulled Congeniality up short, turned her away, sped off. She appeared beside me, flinched away and vanished as something rushed toward her. I pulled the bird this way and that, struggling to get away from her. But everywhere she appeared, she didn't stay long before vanishing again.

It was only when I got a chance to listen did I realize what was happening.

I wasn't hearing the Lady's song.

I was hearing two Lady's songs.

There was another mage here. Moving as fast as her. I was seeing only the briefest of sparks of a duel moving too fast for the human eye to track.

A scream rang out. Velline reappeared in a burst of red. A wound carved her sleeve in twain, a vein of crimson painting her arm. She pulled a small alchemic vial from her belt, hurled it into the sky. It exploded a moment later, erupting in a flash of bursting light.

And suddenly, the Lady's song was everywhere.

Doormage portals opened up across the field. Imperial mages flooded out into the field. Her reinforcements, maybe—she hadn't given up the dream of killing me herself. How nice for her.

From the last portal arrived a short silhouette, dominated by hulking fists and feet, flanked by two slender shapes. As if this couldn't get any worse.

"Salazanca?" Bad Neighbor herself landed out of her portal with a heavy *thud*, her pet mages following her. "The hell are you doing here?"

"*Vagrants!*" Velline shrieked in response, appearing in flashes of steel and blood across the field. "*Two of them! The Cacophony has a Quickmage with her! Assist me!*"

"Wait, a Quickmage?" Riacantha scratched her chin with a big gauntleted finger. "What's going on with—"

"DIE, VAGRANT!"

It was a Sparkmage that screamed. She sounded tired, hoarse from exhaustion and pain. She was a new recruit, maybe, unused to seeing so many people die. Or maybe she was a veteran who'd just hit the number of tragedies you can see and still stay the same person you were.

I don't know. I try to wonder what made her do what she did, how it all got fucked up. Maybe I feel bad for her.

Is that weird?

She thrust a pair of fingers forward. The Lady's song rang out discordant. Electricity danced down the length of the mage's arm, fulminated in a bolt of lightning that streaked across the sky toward me. I pulled Congeniality up short, saw the animal terror in her eyes as feathers sheared off her breast, blackening the skin beneath.

Another second and she'd be dead.

And maybe that's why I did what I did. And how I fucked it up worse. Because when I heard Congeniality's shriek, I also heard a voice whisper in my ear.

"Revenge."

And I listened.

I found his hilt hot in my hands. The heat seared through my glove, compelled me to draw him. And it's easy to suggest that maybe the Cacophony was the one that made me do that much. But pulling the trigger?

That was all me.

Discordance shrieked out, exploded. A wall of sound erupted, cast the assembled mages aside like so many toys hurled from a child's crib. They skidded, tumbled, caromed off rocks and fallen logs. Some staggered back to their feet, slowly. Some did not.

One hadn't even flinched.

Bad Neighbor glared at me out of a mildly disheveled uniform. "That wasn't wise, Sal."

She snapped a pair of gauntleted fingers. Her pet Doormage, still tragically moving, limped forward. She held out a hand; he waved a few fingers. A portal opened overhead, dropping a truly impressive ballista bolt several times her size into her hand. She drew her arm back, grunted, threw.

I spurred Congeniality, pulled her out of the way as the ground shattered behind us. Earth and stone and metal shrapnel licked at our backs, cut scratches into our skin. I kept running.

"That was actually pretty fucking stupid, *SAL*!"

Bad Neighbor roared as she held her hand out again. Her Doormage opened an even larger portal, an immense bolt falling into her grip. She snarled, took aim. With both hands. I wasn't going to make this one.

Not sure why another portal opened over her. Was she going to throw *two* of them at me?

But when I saw what came out of it, it all became clear.

Agne plummeted from the portal, arms high, feet low. The bolt splintered into metal and wood, flying off in shards as Agne came down on Bad Neighbor's head with both heels. She sank into the earth, continued to sink as Agne stomped the back of her head.

"I. *Told.* You. To. Be. Careful!" she snapped each word between each stomp.

"This wasn't *my* fault!" I shouted. "The Imperium, they—"

"Then why didn't you *think of this*?" Agne roared, brought her foot up high.

A gauntleted hand shot out of its shallow grave, caught her by the heel. Agne went flying, slammed face-first into the ground as Riacantha pulled herself out of the sodden earth. She took Agne's leg in both hands, swung her the other way, smashed her against the ground again.

Agne grunted, roared, bucked her leg up. The Lady's song rang out. Bad Neighbor went flying, her grip torn with the force of the strike.

"Just handle it," Agne said as she rose.

No anger in her voice this time.

I growled, pulled Congeniality into a sprint, got to handling it. I fired shots where I could—Hoarfrost to smother the Embermages, Shockgrasp to harry the Sparkmages—but they were getting up. Mendmages walked the battlefield, calling their comrades back to consciousness with their magic.

Until another portal opened.

And a slender shape darted out behind one of the Mendmages.

Liette produced a piece of parchment with strange writing on it. She slapped it against the Mendmage's back, then disappeared back into the portal, which winked out of existence. The mage glanced up like he had just felt a mosquito bite him.

Which, in better circumstances, might have been pretty funny—because he burst into flame shortly after.

The sigils on Liette's parchment activated, swallowing his uniform in a sudden combustion and turning him into a flailing pyre. A nearby Frostmage saw him, moved to intervene. Another portal opened behind him. Urda rushed out, peppered the mage in small, sigil-filled papers.

"Oh fuck oh fuck oh fuck sorry sorry sorry oh fuck oh fuck oh fuck."

He gasped as he fled back into the portal, disappeared. Yria's magic. The Frostmage froze suddenly—I don't mean like he did some magic shit, I mean he went rigid. He toppled over, paralyzed.

Yria. Urda. Agne. *Liette.* They were here. They were helping me. Just like they said they would.

Why did that make me feel like shit?

I kept running, kept loading, kept firing. But the mages kept coming—Yria couldn't open portals fast enough to keep them down. And Agne wouldn't be able to outlast Bad Neighbor. And that was all without wondering what the fuck happened to—

"MONSTER!"

Velline reappeared in front of me. Her foot caught my chest, struck me off my saddle. Congeniality kept running, driven by anger and fear, leaving me tumbling in the dust. I scrambled to my feet, struggled for my sword and my breath.

A blade from behind. The sword was struck from my hand. I turned, staggered backward in time to avoid her swing.

"Everything you do hurts people!" Velline screamed. "*AND YOU'LL NEVER STOP!*"

I would have replied, but I didn't think I had time, since she was about to kill me.

The wind howled. I saw her shape in fragments as she came rushing toward me. I saw the fury and pain on her face for a split second as she manifested like a bad dream, her blade leveled at my heart.

I didn't see my life flash before my eyes this time, either.

I saw the blade coming. I saw the twist of Velline's snarl. I saw the wind stir in front of me, a dark shape appearing.

And my eyes remained fixed on those sights. For a moment that felt like eternity.

And then, it stopped feeling like eternity.

I couldn't move. Could barely breathe. And I wasn't the only one. Velline hung, frozen in the air. Bad Neighbor and Agne were rigid, locked in a tumbling grapple that had suspended them mid-roll. Everywhere I looked—which wasn't far, as I couldn't move my eyes, either—mages were locked in place getting to their feet, in the middle of casting their magic, or flying from some unseen force.

And before me, interposed between my flesh and Velline's steel, was a person.

A man? A woman? I didn't know. Their back was toward me. Their body was wrapped in dirty traveler's clothes. Their hair hung long, unkempt and black behind them, frozen mid-flutter. They held a length of unpolished, featureless steel in their hands.

The one who had fought Velline. The other Quickmage.

But who were they? Why were they here? All questions I could have easily found the answers to, if I wasn't *fucking frozen in time like an asshole.*

Now, don't get me wrong.

All magic is pretty fucking annoying.

But there's something incredibly invasive about magic that fucks with time. It's one thing to render someone paralyzed with, say, a magic gun that shoots that sort of thing. It's quite another to paralyze an entire section of reality.

And many things, as you can imagine, can go wrong with it. It was dangerous magic. Horrifically dangerous. Attempted only by the strongest, most learned mages in the Imperium.

Which meant my plan had worked.

"To witness a war is to behold humanity's unflinching dedication to unhappiness."

A voice, soft and elderly, drifted down from above like thoughts from heaven.

"To witness a war between one's own, to see family opposed to family, is to behold the absolute surrender of love to fear."

And a soft, elderly man followed.

He was shorter than you'd think—back bent by too many years and too many books, barely any wisps of white hair left on his head. His hands were folded delicately behind his back. His simple, unassuming coat fluttered about him like a butterfly's wings as he touched polished, humble shoes to earth.

"I return to this place of carnage and sorrow not out of fear for what this war might become, but of love for humanity." The old man began to walk the field delicately, observing the suspended battle as one might take in an attractive shrubbery garden. "No life is lost senselessly out here. Yet when I see mage battling mage, Vagrant or not, I cannot help but feel a deep pain in my chest that I wish were not there."

He came to a stop beside me. He looked into my face with a warm smile, wrinkles pulled up around generous cheeks and tiny, shining dark eyes. If he weren't capable of killing me with a thought, I'd have asked him to be my grandfather.

Fuck, I still might.

"When my moment of calm ends, as all things must, I would insist on a world that did not disrespect my efforts to preserve the lives of all mages. Can you agree?" He looked slowly around the battlefield. "Well? Why don't you all say something?"

A moment. And then he chuckled to himself.

"Only joking. Only joking. I apologize for the fall."

He waved his fingers. And just like that, time became unfucked.

I fell hard to the ground, dizzy by the sudden reassertion of gravity upon me. I panicked, groping the ground for the Cacophony, struggling to regain my footing before Velline could kill me.

But when I looked up, she was gone. Vanished.

Along with the other Quickmage.

Had they continued their fight elsewhere? Was someone out for Velline? Or—

"Salazanca."

That warm voice caught my ear. A weathered hand extended to mine. A formality. The Lady's song rang out one of the purest notes I'd ever heard—a note I'd once loved hearing every day—and I was lifted to my feet with a thought.

I looked around. Mages all over rose to their feet and took a low bow, their bloodlust overwhelmed by duty. I looked back into the man's old eyes as he smiled and placed his hand over mine.

"I am so pleased to see you again, my friend," Torle of the Void said. "Now, may I ask that you inform me what goes on here?"

TWENTY-ONE

BITTERDRINK

In truth, I find Velline tragic." Glasses clinked as a deep green liquid fell steaming into the cups. "To her, the Imperium is a hand outstretched and benevolent. It gives her food when she is hungry, it offers her comfort when she is distressed. When it asks of her everything, she sees no reason not to oblige it."

A servant carried the tray with expert poise, performing a brief ceremony of benediction in the old Imperial style before offering me a cup, head bowed in tradition. I accepted one.

"She was blessed with skill in warfare, cursed with victories in it. She believed they made her strong. When, in fact, they merely numbed her to how much of oneself war can claim. Even in peace. Perhaps especially so."

The canopy fluttered overhead in the breeze. Imperial banners flew high over the pavilion that had been erected. A voccaphone in the corner blared out crisp Cathama opera lyrics. A table littered with notes, maps, and half-written poetry dominated the center.

"I cannot ask you to forgive her, as I can ask of no one such a burden. Yet I offer you this, freely, as a man who has studied not merely the tactics of warfare, but the intent—you and she both have pains and loss enough without each other's. The music of your silence apart shall be the sweetest you hear in your life. This, I promise you."

I sat respectfully through the wisdom, nodded where I could, tried to hold back sneering where I couldn't. I took the cup of tea to my lips, turned out to look over the cliff.

"Anyone ever tell you you're a pretty weird guy, Torle?"

Torle of the Void—Prodigy, Imperial, killer—smiled back at me from across the tea table that had been quickly erected upon our return to his camp. He turned to look over the cliff, stared wistfully at the field below.

"I believe that one cannot be unchanged by life. Personal curiosity merely becomes another means of measuring change." He raised his glass to mine. "Though, I confess to you beneath the Empress's banners, I am very happy to see you remain yourself, Salazanca." He paused. "Or do you prefer Sal?"

I grinned, clinked my glass to his. "You can call me Piss-Face, if you want, Torle. It's good to see you again."

I wasn't lying. Even if Torle's presence *hadn't* saved my ass, I'd have been happy to see him. But as it was, his insistence on calm and his offer to escort us to the hospitality of his camp was pretty fucking nice, so I wasn't complaining.

Not that there hadn't been complaints, of course. Bad Neighbor didn't love the idea, for one, but respected the rank enough to put up with it. The twins hadn't been thrilled, but chose to come if only to loot the buffets, and Agne...

Agne didn't say anything.

Liette stayed with them while I came to Torle's tent. Normally, that might have made me leery. But honestly, if you'd have been there, you wouldn't fucking believe me if I told you it was a war camp.

Barracks and armories were totally absent. In their place were pavilions for relaxation and study. Tiny libraries of scrolls and books had been portaled in from his home in Cathama. A miniature opera stage—which, he informed me proudly, his staff used to put on a showing of *I Loved That Lad*—tied everything nicely together.

I couldn't trust many things in this world. And a killer mage with limitless power was one of those things I absolutely *shouldn't* trust. But...

I trusted Torle.

"Sir?"

I just didn't trust his boss.

A servant flitted forward, scroll in hand. Torle unfurled it, read it over leisurely, then rubbed the bridge of his nose.

"They continue to stubbornly adhere, these nuls and their Revolution. Perhaps this conviction is the madman's appeal. The longer one goes, the fewer victories there are, replaced by inexorabilities." He sighed, handed the scroll back. "But I would ask none to share this burden. Vernirn, would you kindly deliver my third strategy to the front?"

"At once, sir." The servant bowed lightly, smiled. "May I get anything else for you or your guest? Water? Refreshments?"

Torle politely waved him away and the man took off at a leisurely stroll, as though he hadn't received an order in the heat of battle so much as he had just received a lunch order. I didn't bother to hide my befuddlement, which Torle received with a smirk.

"You question my methods, old friend?"

"I would question anyone who dispatched a war order to the same person who delivers the drinks," I replied—terse, I admit, but he had been the one to offer tea and not whiskey, so it's not like I was totally at fault here. "What's your third strategy?"

He sighed, almost looking disappointed, and waved down toward a basin swiftly drowning in carnage.

"Is it not apparent?"

The walls of Bitterdrink, the Revolutionary city whose guns were legend, stood large in the distance. The long cannons atop its battlements rotated this way and that, tracking the mayhem beneath its eyes of stone and metal before fixing on a target. The basin would shake with the force of their firing. A swath of earth would be bathed in flame and smoke, leaving behind a craterous grave.

The fighting below was no better; in fact it seemed downright unimpressed with the cannon fire. Revolutionary squadrons rallied in tight battle squares, heeding the barking orders of their sergeants and defending against the waves of purple flame that came roiling over them.

Covens of Embermages sped across the field, leaving blazing violet trails behind them. They vanished beneath wreaths of flame as the Revolution's guns fired upon them, reappearing elsewhere to strike at another flank. To the unobservant, it would seem there was no end to them—shrouded devils in Imperial uniforms, belched from the flame itself, undying and innumerable.

"I think I see," I said, as I followed the battles from high above. "You have Doormages dressed as Embermages, teleporting your squadrons around."

"Necessary for flanking."

"Poor for sieging, though," I grunted. "Before I was—"

A knot caught in my throat.

"Before you were betrayed," Torle helpfully offered. "Before you were robbed of your strength. Your destiny."

"Yeah." I smiled. Way bigger than I thought I would at the memory of it all. "Before that. During my time in the Scar, Revolutionary forts would eat our Embermages alive." I scratched my scar, thoughtfully. "But you're not pressing the city itself. You're pressing the squadrons, right?"

"Mm," he offered, settling into his chair. "You notice them? The small people?"

I was hoping I hadn't. But now that he'd called attention to them, I couldn't not see them—Revolutionary civilians went fleeing through the flames, darting among patches of fire on their way to Bitterdrink's gates.

"Your mages aren't attacking them," I observed. "Hell, for Embermages, they're downright restrained."

"You seem surprised."

"A little, yeah, if I can be blunt."

He smiled. "I would detest your existence were you demure."

I *really* liked Torle of the Void.

"You treat your servants kindly, you spare refugees. I haven't heard a word of reproachment uttered since we got here," I said. "A mage who treats nuls well is rare. A Prodigy who treats nuls well?"

"Mad?"

"A little."

"Great power has a way of teaching one not to expend it lightly. You would not be the first of my comrades to doubt this." His smile turned impish as he gestured toward a nearby ridge with his chin. "But to you, I say: look first, then speak."

Settled on the ridge, a small team of servants assembled around what might be called a fleet of ornate-looking telescopes. They carefully adjusted them this way and that, peered through them observantly, then wrote down their observations. Servants nearby bore messenger Shekkai birds, a steady stream of wings bringing messages to and from the cliff.

"Yeah, I was meaning to ask about that," I said. "But I also figured they might just be... what's the word for people with telescopes?"

"Astronomers?"

"Boring." I snapped my fingers. "But are they?"

"Indeed. Spend time among your nuls and one begins to appreciate their talents. These ones, I noted, spent their leisure time observing the stars. Hobbies, they called them. But in them, I saw application. From here, they observe the battle, they know where our foe goes, where our forces need aid."

"So, you're whittling down the Revolutionaries," I said. "I suppose that makes sense. But what's the purpose of driving them back to Bitterdrink? Once they close the gates, all the Embermages in the army won't be able to do shit."

"Would you permit *me* bluntness this time, Sal?" Torle asked, though rudely didn't wait for me to answer. "I fear that age may take me before we arrive at more interesting conversation."

I chuckled, sipped my tea. "Not a lot of people would find a war boring, Torle."

"We are not people, you and I. Not as the nuls are. Nor even as the other mages are. We are *Prodigies*." He held up a hand, frowned. "I misspeak, apologies. Our natures, our gifts, do not hold us above our comrades, but apart from them. Powers such as ours do not allow for the same views. Would you not agree?"

My eyes felt heavy at that point, so heavy that they pulled the rest of my face toward the earth. There were days I almost didn't think of it—who I used to be, what I used to do, how far I used to fly—and those days were merciful. But then there were days like this, when I couldn't help but remember Red Cloud.

And maybe it's wrong of me, but I missed her.

"Torle," I whispered, my voice choked. "Listen, I don't know what they told you, but I'm not like you anymore. I don't have my magic anymore. I lost it to... to..."

"To scoundrels who betrayed the very nature of their beings. I am aware of the Crown Conspiracy, Salazanca. As I am aware of your circumstances." He leaned forward, placed his hand over mine. "It is not merely power that makes us different. To have only held it even for a little while has changed us. I am aware of your past, your burden..."

He held my hand to his forehead. An old Imperial sign of mourning.

"And the great pain its absence must cause you."

The Imperium was easy to hate. Why wouldn't it be? They assumed their power granted them the right to rule and dared anyone to challenge that. And, in several thousand years, no one had been able to. The Revolution was the only one that had managed a response and look what assholes they had to be to fight even bigger assholes.

So, maybe I was a little embarrassed that it felt so good to talk to Torle. He was everything I said he was. But he was also a lot of things I hadn't said he was. He was kind-natured, he was gentle, he was understanding...

Or... fuck, maybe I was embarrassed because I didn't really care about any of that and it just felt nice to have someone speak to me without cussing me out.

"And I will consider it a great displeasure," he added, "should Sal the Cacophony have come so far solely to speak of military strategy. I am told she is quite accomplished, after all."

Fuck me, was he really this nice or was he about to sell me something? "I've seen a few things." I glanced sidelong at him. "A few things even you might not have seen in your time here."

"I sense you are baiting me. Fortunately, I am famished."

"You ever see a Compass Beast? A thousand feet tall and crushing cities under its feet?"

"Twice."

"You ever see the Ten Arrows? The Great General's legendary fleet of airships?"

"I have, yes. Very noisy. I did not care for the eleventh."

I smacked my lips, drained my cup, smirked, and leaned close as I could and still appear decent.

"Ever seen a Scrath?"

Torle of the Void was an intimidating man, in many ways. Even if you knew nothing about him as a Prodigy, he had a quiet, unassuming menace about him—a sort of contract you sign just by looking at him, wherein he agrees to be polite and you agree not to say anything stupid. You know the type. I, however, *did* know a lot about him. Enough to know that I should be more intimidated than I was.

But I wasn't truly scared of Torle of the Void until I said that word.

His eyes narrowed and his pupils shrank, an animal that had just caught the scent of blood. He leaned far closer than was decent, his voice heavy with disquieting desire. His warm, weathered hand tightened to a viselike grip around my wrist.

"Scraths." His smile grew unwholesomely broad. "Yes. I do know something about Scraths."

He eased his grip slightly, holding up a hand. "Apologies. I so rarely get the opportunity to discuss the subject. The Imperium, as you know, frowns on looking too closely at such... provocative studies." He settled back into his chair, still smiling. "But there are many things they cannot deny the Empress's Prodigy. Knowledge was the only treasure I asked for my service, and it was the one that she was most loath to give."

"The Imperium doesn't want people to know about Scraths?" I asked. "I suppose that makes sense."

"Why?"

"What do you mean 'why'? They're nasty fucking monsters that warp things around them and wear people like skin suits. Seems a pretty fucking decent reason to me."

"Why should we fear that which is dangerous to us? Why should we be forbidden to know the truth of our origins?"

I held up a hand. "Torle, I don't mean to sound ungrateful, but I *do* want to sound confused because what the fuck are you talking about?"

"I trust you completed your courses on magical theories while at the academy?"

"I did."

I had been high and drunk for some of them but I did complete them, so it wasn't *technically* a lie.

"And they taught you the same lessons they taught me: Barters, the Lady Merchant, all the pillars of our Empress's strengths. And, for a time, I was content with that knowledge." He peered out over the basin, staring at something beyond the battle. "Until I wasn't. I was unsettled by the Scraths, as anyone might be. But I overcame my revulsion and saw something within them."

Torle glanced at his teapot, picked it up and, without ceremony, hurled it to the ground. It smashed into shards soaking in steaming tea. He reached out a hand toward the tea, wiggled his fingers.

I heard the Lady sing a faint note.

The shards and liquid separated into two distinct spheres. They floated in the air, dancing at the direction of Torle's fingertips. Carefully, they reassembled themselves in midair to create a diminutive human-shaped creature that plopped down upon the tea tray.

A little teapot-person, a perfect ceramic recreation of an attractive opera singer—Thalacio ki Matauli, if I recognized my divas—who bowed low, doffed a lid from their head, and poured out steaming liquid into my cup.

"A trick. Nothing more than a diversion to brighten my day. Yet it is still an alteration, is it not?" Torle smiled. "I have taken reality as it was, and with but a little effort, it is something more pleasing to me. Something closer to me, as a human."

He clenched his fist.

"And the Scraths do this with no effort at all."

The teapot-person froze, stunned, shattered back into shards and steam. He flipped his hand over, the shards reassembled into another person, this one less attractive, painfully thin and bristling with jagged points.

"There are theories," he continued. "They are wrought on scrolls sealed with metal and buried in the Imperial Palace's deepest corners. Their authors are rotting in cells beneath the streets, never to die until every last drop of knowledge can be wrung from their shredded minds. I have read these theories. I have spoken to these people."

I took a drink of my tea, tried to hide my face behind it.

My instinct about Torle's knowledge had been correct. In ways I didn't want to know. He knew about Scraths, sure enough. But he also was fascinated by them. That was dangerous. If he knew about Liette before I was sure I could…

Don't, I warned myself. *Don't panic now. She needs this.*

"What do they say?" I asked.

"They do not teach the Oldest Magic in the academy." Torle's eyes grew distant, vast. "Our greatest scholars know nothing of it beyond stories. Yet some believe they are linked. That there was a magic before Barters."

He looked at me, smiled.

"A bargain. A promise made. A promise kept. Something given, something received. This is the Oldest Magic."

My mind raced back, back to the days after Red Cloud had died and the girl with the scars limped into A Dead Dog Buried on a Black Hill's shop. A bargain had been made that day, too. And with it, the impossible had happened.

I felt something, then. A heat blossoming at the base of my neck. I'd left the Cacophony with Liette—I couldn't let Torle know too much about him, not yet—but even now I could feel him. He reached out, from so far away, felt my thoughts with his fiery embrace.

He remembered the same bargain.

"Revenge for ruin" had been his terms.

"Eres va atali" had been my answer.

"It exists in some distant corners of the Imperium as mere legend, but there are theories that say the Oldest Magic created the Barters, that the first emperors traded away their people for generations in exchange for magic." He waved a hand, made a *feh* sound. "But this is where truth meets legend and legend meets propaganda. They are a bitter people in that part of the Imperium. An old man such as me has a hard time keeping up with—"

"Can they be removed?"

I don't know why I did that. Don't know why I interrupted, why I told him so much with that question. Maybe the pressure was getting to me, the knowledge that I was running out of time to fix this for Liette. Or maybe that burning pain at my neck went deeper than I thought.

But I'd asked it. And Torle had heard it. And he furrowed his brow at me.

"A Scrath," I said, my breath growing heavy. "It's not a... not a creature. Not a monster. Not like other things out here. It's a... a feeling, a..."

"A light?"

I closed my eyes. I saw myself on a stone in a dark place, watching a purple light coil out of my wounds and into the darkness to become...

Something else.

"Yeah," I said. "A light. I've seen them, Torle. The real them."

"I have, too. Once." Torle fell quiet for a moment. "Would you believe... Salazanca... that I have spoken to one? Once?"

I looked at him. My blood ran cold. My heart thundered in my ears. Every word I spoke felt dangerous, but I was so close.

"I would."

"They are painful to listen to. Their words are... without language or structure, merely thoughts that become..." He looked away. "I will speak no more of it. What we shared is of a personal nature. But they are merely a voice in a vessel. An echo in a jar. And you are asking, can they be released?"

The teapot-person-turned-teapot-monster froze. Then collapsed.

His eyes turned to me, his gaze unsettling. His face that had seemed so warm before now seemed... distant. Indistinct. I couldn't tell if he was looking at me curiously or if he was looking at me like he must look at so many other things: tiny, insignificant, breakable?

Red Cloud had seen such things, once.

"Or," he whispered, "are you asking me for help?"

I recoiled like he hit me. Like he hit me *hard*. My mouth hung open. I blinked back tears.

"Torle?"

His hand found mine again. It was tender this time. Warm. Something I dearly wished I'd had long ago.

"All that I know is yours, my old friend," he said. "I have studied your sacrifice greatly. And though I grieve that it was not of your own choosing, I am eternally grateful for the knowledge you have given me. Scraths are wondrous, dangerous beings. If you have need of my help with them, you have it. Even... releasing one."

"It can be done?" I gasped. I couldn't believe it. "Torle, *can it be done*?"

"It can," he answered. "I cannot tell you how I know this. Not yet. But it can be done. And if that is what you require, then my resources shall be at your disposal."

"That's..." I couldn't find the words, even the thoughts. "But I'm a Vagrant, the Imperium will—"

"The Imperium will honor the debt it owes to you. To *us.* I will see to it." He squeezed my hand the way I wish someone had a long time ago. "If you will but request it."

They still wouldn't come. The words. The thoughts. Everything was stuck in my throat, choked up behind something heavy and salty and bitter.

I couldn't believe it. Any of it. My luck. My instincts. That this was happening to me. That my problems were about to be over. That I finally didn't fuck it up. That I... that I...

I'm going to fix this for her.

My lips quavered. I swallowed the thing in my throat. I drew in a breath.

"Torle?"

His eyes went toward his pavilion as his servant returned, at the head of a small group of men and women in featureless work uniforms. Their faces were painted in dust and eagerness. They carried a myriad of surveyor's tools, charts, graphs, and notes under their arms. More servants. Nuls. And each of them beaming toward Torle.

"As requested," his servant said, stepping aside, "your report."

"Ah."

Torle rose, smiling.

"Apologies, Salazanca. We shall continue this conversation soon. The matters of our Empress's wars can be a tiresome, but necessary thing." He approached the nuls and, shockingly, embraced them warmly. "My friends. You seem to have been busy."

"We absolutely have, sir," one of the men chimed in.

"Your plan went off flawlessly, Torle," a woman said. "Our presence wasn't even noticed. We encountered no resistance whatsoever."

"You see?" Torle looked at me, smiled impishly. "Small efforts yield larger rewards." He stepped to the side, gestured to them. "May I introduce the members of my Geologist Appreciation Society?"

"Charmed," I said as I finished my tea and got to my feet. "More of your weaponized bookworms?"

"That is an *incredible* team name for us," one of the men—the one I decided I liked, because he was right—spoke up.

"Merely people whose enthusiasms intrigued me," Torle laughed. "I nurtured their love of the earth, gave them all the knowledge I could. And in return, they have served me well." He clapped his hands, beamed. "Tell me. Have the generals reported?"

"They have, sir." Nuls weren't typically trusted to carry orders, but this woman apparently was. "They report all Revolutionary forces have withdrawn to their fortress, as you predicted."

"Excellent. And in three weeks, we shall celebrate this day."

"Three weeks?" I chuckled. "Buddy, you brought Embermages to a siege. You'll be here for years before you can even think of a toast to make."

"Actually, that's incorrect," another woman spoke up. "Thanks to our surveillance of the foundations, Torle will only need a minimum of three weeks of bedrest."

I paused. Something cold lodged in my chest.

"For what?"

"Well, we tried to shave it down to two," one of the men laughed. "But our tools only go so far."

"Three weeks of relaxation will be perfectly acceptable," Torle said. "This sort of thing used to stress my body such that I would require months of recuperation. Even in my prime. Do you remember, Salazanca?" He looked at me, caught himself. "Ah, but I forget. This was before you came to the Scar."

That cold thing crawled around my neck, coiled like a noose. "What are you doing?"

The mood fell. As if I had just pointed out a stain on his coat. The nuls frowned at me, reproachful. Torle himself looked a little puzzled.

"I am doing my duty," he said. "The Empress has commanded that this fortress fall this day. My dear friends have looked hard at the earth here, shown me where it is weak. Together, we shall see our great lady's proclamation fulfilled."

The noose tightened. Blood pooled in my head. Thoughts rushed at me. The legendary battles that had been waged before I arrived on the Scar. The patch of smooth earth bearing an Imperial banner where Revolutionary fortress Six Walls should have been.

The reason Torle of the Void had his name.

"Torle, you can't."

The mood did not so much fall as collapse into a shallow grave and bury itself. The nuls regarded me with open hostility. Torle paused, like he was being patient with a stupid child.

"I can, Salazanca."

"That's too... there are rules, right?" I asked. "The Imperium has terms of engagement. You can't do something like... like *that* without a Re—"

"I am aware, Salazanca." His face had fallen completely. An empty, unfeeling vessel void of warmth. "The Recivilizing has already begun."

My heart caught. My mouth snapped shut. My eyes forgot how to blink.

"I understand your abhorrence," he replied. "I, too, once flinched at the idea. But, as I said, war has no more glories. Merely inevitabilities. Today is one such inevitability."

My body went bloodless. Like the noose had tightened so much that everything in me was in my head. My thoughts raced, my body staggered. I had to stop him. I couldn't stop him. I had to do something. I couldn't do anything. I had to... I had to...

"Let us speak again, soon, Sal," Torle said as he turned and left, his adoring retinue following him. "I apologize for how long this might take."

I had to get out of there.

TWENTY-TWO

BITTERDRINK

I am not a philosopher.

I've never been great at solving my problems with thinking.

If you want me to be completely honest, I can't even remember the last time I finished a book.

So, if you wanted to call me a hypocrite for the way I staggered away from Torle of the Void's pavilion, making my way down the hill to where the rest of his camp lay, I would accept that. If you wanted to say it was stupid of me, knowing even a fraction of the shit I'd done, to tremble at the thought of anyone else's violence, I'd accept that, too. And if you asked me how I could possibly be shaken by what was about to happen, given my hand in starting this shit, I don't know if I could answer you.

Like I said, I wasn't thinking.

I was feeling.

I was feeling the fear twisting in my belly, a cold knife in my guts. I was feeling the bloodless limbs carrying me down the hill. I was feeling that, despite everything I'd done to get here, how close I'd come to it all...

I'd fucked it up again.

"Well, well, well." Yria's voice, typically the equivalent of three cats fighting over a frog, was subdued—merely aggressive instead of outright hostile. "If it isn't Queen... Shit... ah, fuck it, I can't think of anything."

She lay stripped to the waist in a massage chair, her arms spread wide with a masseuse working on each one, a broad woman taking her shoulders in powerful hands. Urda sat nearby, idly plucking at an Imperial lap harp.

"I've never seen her so relaxed," he said. "And I never knew I could play harp so well. Ha! No, that's an exaggeration, I always knew I could play harp so well. I've read about it enough."

"I admit it," Yria muttered, "sometimes, you do good work, Sal. I might even be close to liking you."

"Thanks," I replied. "We have to go."

"I fucking knew it!"

She shot out of the chair, scattering the masseuses. Tits out, she stormed toward me and thrust a hand whose fingers didn't quite work in my face.

"You had to ruin it, didn't you?" she snarled. "You just *couldn't* stand to see me so happy. I knew you were cold, you smelly bitch, but this is..."

I couldn't think of the words to tell her. I couldn't think of words at all. My mouth hung open numbly. I just stared at her. Her voice trailed off, her eyebrows furrowing.

"No! No, I really must protest!" Urda said, rushing forward. "I've tried to be understanding, but this sort of thing is *good* for Yria! She *needs* this and—"

Yria grabbed him. Not violently. She just reached down with her half-numb hand, took his in it. They exchanged a look. A flinch. A conversation.

"I don't like this." Urda frowned, releasing her. "I do *not* like this."

He stalked away. Yria started to pull her shirt back on, paused, looked at me. "How bad is it?"

"Very bad," I said. "Torle is... it's very bad."

"Fuck. I was hoping it was the kind of bad that didn't need me to put on a shirt, but fine." She tucked her shirt into her belt, pulled her jacket back around her. "If it's bad as that, we should find your glasses-wearer. You should find Agne."

"There's not enough time," I said. "I'll find—"

"*You,*" she interrupted, forceful, "should find Agne."

She held me in a glare for a moment before turning and stalking off. Her gait was stiffer now than it had been. The fight on the field had taken more out of her than I realized.

Or had I even cared?

The terror in my chest gratefully smothered the guilt gnawing at my throat. There would be time enough to feel bad later. There was only time to get as far away as possible now.

A Recivilizing.

Just a few nights ago, it had seemed like a bad dream, a fear so distant it was barely worth thinking about. Then the impossible had become the inevitable so fast I didn't even have time to think of how to react.

I just... did.

The war had advanced further than I thought. The *Imperium* had advanced further than I thought. Rudu had been right—the minute they decided to *truly* pit their resources and strength against the Revolution, the Imperium would win this war. And once they did, they would have time. Time to find out, time to investigate. I didn't know how to say it but I knew that once the Imperium found out about Liette, they would come for her. They would tear her apart looking for the Scrath.

Torle's words flashed in my mind, the tales he'd told me of the knowledge about Scraths suppressed, of useful prisoners never dying until their minds were completely torn apart. My mind flitted briefly to an image of her, in a cage somewhere dark, surrounded by dark figures, unable to escape or flee or...

I feared that.

I feared Torle.

I feared what was about to happen. I'm not ashamed to admit that a Recivilizing scared me. Fuck, maybe if I had been more afraid of war than I had been of failure, we wouldn't be in this situation.

I was afraid. Afraid enough to leave here and leave whatever hope I'd found here behind. The others would understand. Liette would understand.

I couldn't afford to believe anything else at that time.

Soft voices met my ears. I followed them around to the back of a wine tent, where Agne stood, looming large over the servants who kept her plied with cups. Though she loomed even larger over her companion.

Riacantha spoke in soft words, sipping at wine. Her gauntlets and boots had been abandoned, traded for sandals and gloves. Their conversation—which, until not long ago, had consisted of them pulverizing each other into the dirt—was something I couldn't make out.

I noted the expressionlessness on their faces. Or on one of them, anyway. Agne's eyes twitched with restrained tears, her frowns deep and many. Riacantha's own was empty, void of emotion as they spoke plainly.

Much later, I would wonder if Agne saw what would become of her—of her feelings, her sorrows, her joys—in Riacantha. If I had known that, maybe I would have acted sooner. Or maybe I would have still messed it up.

But at that point, I wasn't thinking about that.

"Agne," I said. "We have to go."

"What?" Genuine ire flashed across her face. "I'm fine, Sal. You can take care of things without—"

"This isn't an option."

Agne could have done many things at that moment. She could have pouted, like she sometimes did. She could have rolled her eyes, which she did more frequently. Or she could have just come along, which I had hoped she would.

What she did instead was drop her glass and let it shatter on the floor, take three long, deliberate strides, and stand over me so close the top of my head almost scraped her clavicles. And through the coldest voice and the emptiest eyes I'd ever seen on her, she spoke.

"Are you going to make me?"

I'd never thought I'd have to fight Agne. Never thought I'd make her look at me like she did then. Never thought I'd forget how fucking big she was and how easily she could break me in half.

Today was full of surprises. All of them bad.

"Agnestrada."

Bad Neighbor had saved my ass a couple of times back in the Scar. Maybe it was habit that made her do it again.

"You should go," the little woman said, holding Agne's eyes with her own. "If it's true, what we talked about...you should see for yourself."

Agne spared another look for me, empty and cold, before she pushed past me and stalked out the tent. I moved to follow her.

"Salazanca."

Riacantha poured herself another cup, drank it. "You make shitty choices in companions, you know that? She isn't cut out for your life."

"She's a Siegemage and a Vagrant," I growled back. "She's strong."

"I didn't say she wasn't. I said she wasn't cut out for *your* life. For the shit you put yourself through, for the fights you pick. She wasn't meant to be your friend." She leveled empty eyes at me. "And you weren't meant to do what you're doing to her."

"Don't fucking lecture me," I snarled. "Don't you *fucking* lecture me while you're out here 'Recivilizing' this place. We are not the same."

"I didn't say we were," Riacantha replied. "I won't deny what we're doing. I won't deny that a bunch of dead nuls doesn't really bother me, either." She shrugged, turned back to her table, waved a servant over. "Maybe it's my Barter. Maybe I just can't feel it anymore. Or maybe I care about as much now as I did then, when we were both killing them left and right. Either way, I'll sleep at night, somehow."

She took another cup, sipped it.

"Agne won't. For now."

I had a thousand things I wanted to say to that—some of them questions, most of them curses. But I didn't have enough time for it.

Somewhere far away, the Lady sang a distant note. It held itself in my ears, a perfect sustained note frozen in flawless crystal. Everyone hears the song differently. But I remembered this one.

I'd heard it once, long ago. When my skin was unscarred and my name wasn't Sal the Cacophony. I'd heard that note when I flew far overhead and looked down upon tiny houses and their tiny people.

And five minutes later, I'd killed them all.

I spun on my heel, rushed out the tent.

High overhead, the clouds began to part.

...To be honest, I still have a hard time remembering a lot of it.

What happened next, that is.

With Torle and Bitterdrink.

I don't remember what I told everyone when we left. Or how far we'd run. Or what I was thinking when we finally got clear. So much of it is just...like I can't even hold the whole thing in my head all at once.

But I remember the sky.

The sky was a pale orange, the sun nearly disappeared behind the hills, not wanting to stick around for what happened next. I didn't blame it.

We were far away and on higher ground when I finally allowed us to stop. The crown of hills ringed the basin, painted dark by the fading sun, mourners attending a funeral. At their center, Bitterdrink's walls loomed large even from here.

From this vantage, it was easy to see how the Revolution had controlled this area for so long. The hills would make a natural maze to any invading force, making them easy pickings for the fort's long guns. Across the scorched grasses, I could see the burned-out skeletons of the villages that this fort had kept safe. The guns hadn't been as legendary as they thought.

But the walls had. Impenetrable, their gates were layered beneath metal and mechanics so dense that even a legion of Graspmages couldn't hope to wiggle it. Those who'd managed to flee had disappeared inside, along with all surrounding forces. They'd shut up tight, deployed their cannons, rallied their troops.

Revolutionaries ringed the fort's walls, gunpikes glistening in the dying light, plumes of severium smoke painting the sky as their cannons churned in anticipation of a charge. Their weapons rose and clashed, defiant chants tearing from their lips, daring the Imperial dogs to attack, blaring the Revolutionary anthem from their sirens.

I remember thinking how invincible it looked. Up there with all its soldiers and its huge guns and how all of them just kept calling for a fight. I remember thinking—maybe hoping—how it was so big, maybe even Torle couldn't bring it down.

But even then, I knew.

The many Embermages, tiny red ants assembled in a ring around the fortress, met the challenge with silence. The Imperial banners high on the other side of the basin hung still and flaccid.

The wind had fallen silent.

Purple flashed in tiny pinpricks of light across the basin. In tiny stars, the Embermages winked out through portals, disappearing back to their camps. The Revolutionary chants grew wild, drunk on victory as their cowardly foes vanished away with their magics.

None of them looked up.

None of them saw the tiny speck of an old man, flying high overhead, hands folded behind his back and eyes closed.

None of them heard the song.

But I did. I saw him. I saw Torle of the Void as he extended his hands. I saw his eyes open. I saw the burning purple light within them.

And then I remember... the earth moved.

A low groan at first. Starting on the outside of the basin, shifting beneath my feet and knocking me to the ground. That groan echoed through the earth, the shifting of a great old man that hadn't moved in a long, long time. Its great shudder tightened in a ring, pulling itself through every hill and plain as it came to a center.

Bitterdrink shook suddenly. The chanting died, unheard beneath the great cry of stone and earth. Some fell. Some screamed. The Revolutionary anthem kept playing.

It started slowly, I remembered.

Some bricks fell from the battlements. The walls began to crack a little. One of the guns tilted one way and started to fall, collapsing into the earth. The screaming got louder. More people fell from the walls, splattered across the stone.

The ground spat up great clouds of dust. They choked the field, rising up around the walls, obscuring what was happening. Great scars appeared around the fortress, the stone and dirt pulling itself apart, enormous gashes appearing in the ground. The walls shuddered. The fortress groaned. The people screamed. The Revolutionary anthem kept playing.

And by the time anyone realized the city was sinking... it was too late.

It all happened fast after that.

Maybe I just wanted it to.

But I remember how the walls collapsed in on themselves, like a paper being folded over itself. It pitched the Revolutionaries off, their screams vanishing in the great noises of the earth. The towers and their guns went crashing, collapsing in pieces upon the people below. I remember seeing them trying to climb the towers, maybe trying to get high enough to escape the rising earth. I remember them falling and pushing and screaming in panic. I remember the Revolutionary anthem kept playing.

Bitterdrink disappeared. It and all its people and all its weapons and all its houses and blacksmiths and lives slid beneath an earth that opened up to meet it. Its towers vanished beneath the rim of a great hole. The Revolutionary anthem continued to play, even as it disappeared farther beneath the ground. Were you there to see it, you would have just seen an entire fortress and all its people simply disappear, like a parlor trick.

But if you were Torle.

I wonder how you would feel.

Flying so high above it and looking down and seeing nothing but a great darkness.

A void.

He lowered his hands. The purple in his eyes burned brighter. The Lady's song rang pure and painful in my ears.

The earth began to close over Bitterdrink. The stone and dark pressed together. The screams went unheard beneath the grinding of the dirt and the hiss of sifting sand. The Revolutionary anthem blared in pitiful defiance from the swiftly disappearing grave. And when it finally fell silent, smothered beneath the earth, nothing of Bitterdrink remained but a flat, featureless plain.

A wink of purple. A servant emerged from a portal at the center of the plain. They planted an Imperial banner, saluted.

In the deathly silence that followed, I could almost hear the faint applause of his servants. They awaited him in a giddy throng as he descended from the sky, back onto the high cliff, and collapsed into their waiting arms. They took him gently, escorted him back to the comfort of their camp, turned their backs to the thousands slain in an instant and thought nothing more of them.

...Like I said, I know I'm not a good person. I don't always sleep easy. I don't always like what I do or what I am, even if I do it anyway. Maybe I didn't have a right to feel the way I did, seeing that happen like that. No fight. No escape.

But I still felt it.

I felt the numbness. The bloodlessness. The way my mind went blank to protect me from the truth of how close I'd been to this, how much I could have done to stop it. I felt myself staggering forward, felt my eyes swinging loose in their sockets.

I remember seeing Yria holding her brother, burying his face in her shoulder, begging him not to look, begging him to remember their mother as she stroked his hair and he struggled to breathe.

I remember seeing the tears fall down Agne's face, silver and sparkling. I remember seeing her look at the bare patch of earth, mouth hung open. I remember hearing her whisper to herself that it was all right, that she could still cry.

I even remember Velline, if you can believe it. She stood ghostly white on a nearby cliff, staring out over the earth. And I remember wondering, however briefly, what she saw when she looked at that banner flying there.

But most of all, I remember Liette.

I remember walking to her side as she stared out over the earth where people had once been. I remember standing beside her in silence and staring with her. And I remember the softness of her voice when she asked.

"If he took Eldest out of me," she whispered, "would the Imperium have him?"

I nodded, stiff. "They would."

"And if the Cacophony took it... would it be...?"

I swallowed hard, closed my eyes, told the truth.

"Worse."

At my hip, he seethed gently—indignant, but not in disagreement.

"Sal," she whispered, "would you go with me to Toadback?"

I took her hand. "I would."

"And would you stay with me in Toadback?"

I pulled her close. "I would."

"And would you promise not to let Eldest... let me... be used like this?"

And I lied.

"I would."

TWENTY-THREE

TOADBACK

You learn to live with it.

The horror, I mean. The pain. The stress. You know, all the bad shit.

That's not to say you ever really learn to get away from it. You drink, but booze runs out. You fuck, but people leave. You fight and sometimes you get lucky and die, but a lot of the times you don't.

The only thing that comes close is what I did, what we all did, after what happened at Bitterdrink.

We kept moving.

One foot in front of the other, eyes on the ground, tall as you can carry yourself and if that's not so tall, that's fine, so long as you keep moving. That's the only way you get away from it.

Kind of.

Because it always follows you. When you stop moving, it catches up. And when you start moving again, you can still hear it, that horror, screaming at you over and over of what happened and why didn't you stop it?

But if you keep moving, you can at least make it not quite so loud.

I needed to believe that.

We needed each other to believe that.

Or none of us believed it and we just chose not to acknowledge it.

Take your pick. It was probably all three that saw us trudging through the old marsh roads into the east. I led, Congeniality's reins in my hand and Liette riding her, the twins and Agne trailing behind. We exchanged glances occasionally—words, less often.

This, I thought, was a small mercy.

I did not know how to talk to any of them. About any of it. What we had seen—whatever it was that Torle had done, however close we had been to it—was something we all carried ourselves, too heavy to ask others to bear it with us. Or that's what it felt like, anyway.

How was I supposed to tell Agne that I was terrified when she wasn't even sure she still knew what terror was? How was I supposed to ask the twins to talk when Urda had to help his sister up whenever she rose because she'd spent too much of her magic on me? How was I...

How was I supposed to tell Liette that we'd had only one chance at getting that fucking thing inside her *out* of her and now I almost wish I'd never brought it up? How was I supposed to tell her I was out of fucking ideas?

Turns out, I couldn't.

I didn't know how.

So I stayed silent. And so did she. And so did they. The only sound that escaped our little group was the occasional discontented squawk from the bird.

And so it was that when the marsh gave way to river and the trees gave way to signposts and the road gave way to a stream of refugees, we found we fell right in: just more quiet souls, wearily trudging toward the distant town of Toadback.

As the bog smoothed out and became long shores, the Yuber River came sweeping into view. Its dark waters stretched broader here, as it flowed out to sea. Land fit for building was hard to come by. Spaces to trade, even rarer.

Toadback had the fortune to be both, which was why it was still standing.

The river city was actually two towns. The river pirates who'd settled these lands slowly traded their bases for towns and their weapons for trade. Bandit lords had become freehold barons as the two towns eventually grew big enough to be connected by a vast bridge of wood and stone spanning the river.

The bridge had brought trade. The trade had brought money. The money brought the armies.

Toadback wasn't the first freehold to realize that survival in the Scar often came down to whose colors you were flying. But they did perfect the art that other fliptowns would come to embrace: keeping a show force of an army to "surrender" with when a new power came to town and demanded it, happily greeting them as liberators before resuming business as usual, then doing it all over in reverse when another power showed up. The Revolution and Imperium were wise to the practice, of course, but the trade and base was too valuable to punish.

Personally, I found all this stuff fairly interesting but it turns out witnessing a massive magical slaughter has a way of really sucking the fun out of sharing local trivia.

What I found more interesting were the people.

The closer we got to Toadback, the thicker the refugees got. People who'd fled this far east had come hoping that the Yuber could put distance between them and the fighting. And if anywhere was safe from Revolutionary conscription or Imperial annihilation, it was a fliptown. Usually, anyway.

Some of the desperate faces I saw were ones I recognized. Meret's people—he took better care of them than I ever did. I was heartened, however slightly, but still kept my scarf pulled up around me.

A shudder ran through the stream of refugees. A brief cry rose and was settled as the people fell silent. Far away, there was the distant sound of a thousand locust wings beating, the crescendo of cannon fire. Somewhere nearby, one of the Ten Arrows sailed through the sky, raining fire and shrapnel on the world below. And on the road, everyone listened and waited to see if the noise would grow closer.

And when it didn't, they would go back to walking.

These people, even if they did recognize me, didn't need my shit. We both had problems of our own, after all.

Among the refugees, there were those I didn't recognize. People whose clothes were a little too nice, whose faces were a little too full, whose eyes were a little too intent on me. They hung out on abandoned wagons and on top of signposts, like crows grown fat on human carrion. Some were men, some were women, but I recognized all of them for what they were.

Ashmouths.

They wanted me to see them.

They wanted me to know they were expecting me.

I felt about as fine with that as you would expect me to. The Ashmouths were a deceitful, murderous bunch of cheats, liars, thieves, and professional assholes. They don't even do it for fun. Knowing that *they* were my best hope at making it out of this with Liette intact…

Well, I didn't fucking love it, I'll tell you that much.

But we'd spoken about it. She and I. In hushed whispers and desperate sobs. She couldn't go back to the Imperium; even if I could bear the thought of her ending up in a cage to be shredded for the Empress's library, she couldn't bear the thought of Eldest in the hands of someone like Torle of the Void. I couldn't blame her.

As for the Cacophony…

Well, let's not talk about the Cacophony just yet.

With no other options left, the Ashmouths made the most sense—terrible sense, but the most of it. The Three weren't lying: they could pay any price, find any expert, acquire any materials, knowledge, or means necessary to get what they wanted. I wouldn't even be shocked if one of the servants in Torle's entourage happened to work for them.

I didn't doubt that they *could* save Liette.

Only that we would come out of this together.

The closer we got to the city, the more they appeared. Now they loitered against walls and hung out lazily in the road. Some were dressed in peacekeeper uniforms, others disguised themselves in the stream of refugees, all had the same smug half-grin as they flexed in the middle of a sea of refugees just for my sake.

Which I understand. They are a professional organization. Sometimes they had to demonstrate their might. Fair is fair, after all.

Which is also why I felt perfectly justified in letting my scarf fall away from my hip to show the black grip swaying with my stride, the coils of steam escaping the sheath. He did so love being noticed.

The Ashmouths showed up on the road a lot less after that.

Fair is fair and all.

"Fuck me, I need a bath."

Yria was the first to speak when we made it into the town proper past the gates. All pretenses of keeping her shit together melted away as she visibly slumped, leaning hard on her brother's shoulder.

"Fuck me, I also need a drink. And a fucking bowl of stew thicker than your mother's ass." She paused, considered. "Actually, change that. Let me do the stew and drink first, bath later."

I couldn't say I disagreed.

Not even the part about my mother's ass. She was a proud woman and she'd carried it without apology.

"And unless Lord Greasemouth and Lady Flowerfarts over here"—she gestured vaguely to me and Liette—"have any objection, that's exactly where the fuck we'll be."

Urda looked at me with what he wanted to be intensity, what I wanted to be assuredness, and what ended up being desperate and pleading. I sighed, nodded toward them.

"Doov's Noodles is off toward the bridge," I said. "I had them last time I was here. Pretty good."

"First fucking favor you've done me." Yria slapped her brother across the back, possibly affectionately. "Now don't fucking make that face, I'll buy you some fucking tea."

Urda managed a smile. Weaker than I had hoped it would be. And as he and Yria left, I turned to Agne. She stared out over the refugees trickling in behind us as more of them cleared the peacekeepers at the gate.

I wondered what she was thinking about behind those eyes. Had they been brighter last night? Were they emptier now? Did she see these people with the same pity and compassion she once had? Or did she see simply more bodies that could be broken? Did she see them at all?

"Agne?"

Maybe I intended to ask. Or maybe I just wanted to beg her to talk to me. But I didn't and neither did she. She stalked off without a word, gliding effortlessly through the tide of misery. I watched her, made a move to follow.

Liette's hand found my shoulder.

"I...I think I need you more. Right now."

I sighed. She was right. There was no point in putting it off any longer. I took her hand in mine.

"Ready?"

She squeezed my hand. Rested her head on my shoulder, slumped into me.

"Do you think," she whispered, "I'm Lord Greasemouth and you're Lady Flowerfarts or the other way around?"

I grinned, pulled her close to me. "I don't think it matters." I kissed her on the brow. "Because obviously I'm Lord Greasemouth."

"I would love to hear your rationale for that." She smiled, pulled her arm over me as we started walking. "You lack both adequate lip coverage and lordly demeanors."

"If you're saying I'm thin-lipped, I'm going to let that go." I lifted my nose a little higher, sniffed. "Because I'm so regal and forgiving, you know."

"Forgiving," she repeated flatly. "Sal the Cacophony."

"Your implication impugns my honor, my lady," I replied, insufferably full of shit as I could possibly manage. "If I am devoted to retribution, it is only because my noble heart burns so passionately."

"I thought it was the booze and the fighting."

"Peasants drink booze and fight," I said. "*Lord* Greasemouth partakes of ambrosia and engages in passionate fisticuffs."

She looked at me. Her nose wrinkled. She did that thing where she laughed and didn't mean to laugh so it comes out as a snort.

This was nice.

What we had here. Walking. Joking. The kind of people who could be stupid on the street and not care about it.

The streets of Toadback were bustling. Refugees paused where they could, bartered for what they had with the merchants who were willing. But the town continued to work around them. Draft birds hauled carts between clean, respectable houses. Smithies burned, churning out spurs and bits and forks and other things people paid them for.

And, of course, the busy work of a coward never truly ends.

The distant sounds of Revolutionary airships had inspired a sort of haste in the local township. Peacekeepers were as occupied with changing local banners from Imperial to Revolution as they were with the refugees. Local people hastily pasted slogans and posters in their windows in anticipation of a coming occupation.

But even that couldn't diminish the feeling I had as we walked along the avenues. The feeling that we weren't people who needed to be here for darker purposes. The fantasy that we were here just to walk the streets and smell the bread.

I wondered where we'd live if we lived here. What kind of respectable, boring house we'd have. What would it feel like to wake up in a bed for more than a week in a row? What would it feel like not having to hunt or fight or threaten people? Would I be able to do it? Would she be able to?

The thoughts carried me off briefly. And I can't say I hated it.

Even if we weren't those kinds of people, even if we didn't get those kinds of endings to our stories, well...

Maybe it's just nice to think about.

I held her tighter as we rounded a corner down to a new street. I glanced up, found a sign hanging from one of the buildings of two rothacs butting heads over a bowl of rice. The smell of spices wafted out from its windows, steam carrying the sound of banging pots.

"Is here okay?" I asked her.

She looked up at the sign, adjusted her glasses. "Is the curry any good?"

"Best in the city."

"Then all right."

She turned to face me, hand on the door. I held her other hand for a moment longer. "Find a seat in a corner. Keep your back to a wall. If anything happens—"

"I can defend myself. For a little bit, anyway. And if anything happens to *you*..."

I shrugged. "I'm sure I can talk my way out of it."

I tried to be glib. But that time had passed. She didn't laugh now. We weren't that kind of people and we couldn't pretend we were. She slid behind the door, slammed it. I turned around, rested my hand on my hip.

"Ready?" I asked.

"Perpetually," he seethed.

Together, we searched.

I looked over the crowd, sought through the faces passing by. Here, a sweaty and exhausted refugee toting a heavy burden toward the bridge. There, a bored laborer hauling her sack of timber toward the harbor. And over there, a scrawny-looking girl reading a book on a porch. She yawned, covering her mouth with the back of her hand. Next door to her, a heavyset woman swept her steps with a rough broom.

Them.

I pushed through the crowd, stormed toward the girl on the porch. I put my foot down between her legs, hard sole clapping against the stone step. I leaned in, snarled a word.

"Where?"

"W-what?" The girl looked up, holding her tiny book like a shield. "I'm sure I don't know what—*hrk!*"

I grabbed her by the throat, hauled her to her feet. She slapped her waist, looking for something that wasn't there. I growled again.

"Where?"

"You're not supposed to talk to me," she gasped. "There's... someone that's going to be by soon and you're supposed to talk to—"

I cut her off. Slammed her against the wall of her house. She let out a groan as the wind and the sense were both knocked from her. She slumped, motionless, to the ground. I turned and scowled toward the dowdy women next door, asked more nicely.

"Where?"

Her eyes went wide. Her arm shot up. She pointed down the street. "Two streets down, two doors over. They're at a place called Kuron-Kurin. It's a teahouse. The jasmine is excellent."

"Thanks."

Now, don't get me wrong, I didn't feel great about that. Even if I did start off without even looking back at them. Obviously, when dealing with one's issues, one usually exhausts all possibilities before beating the shit out of someone and threatening someone else. *Usually.*

But I had my reasons. The Ashmouths had eyes everywhere. There was no sense in trying to hide Liette from them. They wouldn't make their move until they knew mine and a little show of force—say, picking out their informants and selectively beating one in public view—helped to remind them of that.

It may be Sal the Cacophony who came to speak to the Ashmouths.

But it was Sal the fucking Cacophony who was going to do the talking.

I found Kuron-Kurin exactly where she said it would be. In an assuming square, near the vast bridge. The teahouse had a view over the river, the waters pounding below. Refugees trickled through in a weary stream, crowding around the gates as they desperately tried to negotiate past the peacekeepers to get to the other side.

But despite the nearby suffering, the people here—families with noisy kids playing, elderly couples baking, a nearby butcher cutting and hawking fish from his counter—seemed mostly at ease.

Charming little place.

I might have liked it, even, if it wasn't fucking crawling with assassins.

I pushed the door open. A little bell tinkled. A charming hostess ran forward to greet me before showing me to a table at the back of the teahouse. Various patrons sipped and steeped in silence, barely glancing up at me as I arrived.

Rudu and Necla didn't stand to greet me.

They loitered instead beneath a cloud of silkgrass smoke and a dim paper lamp's light. Necla sat rigid, his hands on the table, fingers twitching, eyes unblinking. Rudu, significantly less crazy and significantly more high, lounged behind it, gestured with his pipe for me to take a seat.

"Tea?" he offered, pushing a cup and pot my way.

I glanced at it. "Is it poisoned?"

"Yes, dumbass, I just offered you poisoned tea." He rolled his eyes. "Look, not to be rude, but if you're going to suspect us of poisoning you like that, you shouldn't be fucking dealing with us like this."

Necla shot him a sidelong glare. "That is not helpful to the goals of the Ashmouths."

"What's helpful to the goals of the Ashmouths is being as honest as we, as a bunch of murderers dealing with a remorseless Vagrant who's killed more than a fucking few of them, can possibly manage." He looked between us. "Agreed?"

"Agreed." I poured myself a cup. Sipped it. That woman had been right—the jasmine was fucking amazing—kind of wish I hadn't threatened her now. "So you understand why I didn't bring her with me."

"We can find her," Necla hissed.

"And I can find you." I waved a hand at him and I hope he didn't like it. "I'm good on threats. What I want now is assurances."

"The Three has no reason to betray you," he replied.

"Except for all the reasons we know they have."

"And one big reason they won't," Rudu said. "The one thing they care about more than their people or their pride." He rubbed his fingers together. "The war makes decent money for them. But not enough as predictability. The knowledge they glean from our arrangement earns them money. Keeping you satisfied, happy, and out of their way until the end of your days earns them money."

He wasn't lying. It wasn't like the Three hadn't tried to kill me before. I'd done as much to them as to anyone else and I didn't doubt for a moment that they knew it was cheaper to stay out of my way than in it. They wouldn't betray me before I could figure out a way to hurt them worse, I was confident of that much.

I just had doubts about...

"How?" I whispered. "How are you going to do it?"

They held my gaze silently for a moment. Necla's left eye twitched, his lip curled back in the vaguest rumor of a sneer. Rudu took in a deep drag of his pipe, exhaled a shimmering cloud. It drifted beneath my nostrils, plucked at the strands of my mind.

"How do you want it to be done?" Necla asked.

"We can go to Ocytus and find out who you spoke to there," Rudu offered.

"Or we can ask a friend of a friend what you and Torle of the Void spoke of," Necla said. "If you believe this information to be of use, then the Ashmouths shall find it."

"You want to talk to the wisest sages in the Imperium? The most twisted devoted of Haven?" Rudu asked. "Done. You want researchers? Scribes? Equipment? Information?"

"All, likewise, are done," Necla said. "Anything you wish. Everything you wish. The most deranged rumor from the most depraved lips in the most remote part of the world, we'll follow up on, if you say it."

"And everything else you want to keep you and her in comfort for however long it takes," Rudu said. "A house? A fortress? A city? The Three can make it happen."

"This, too, you know."

They weren't lying. I did know. Nor were they exaggerating.

The Three had that power. The Ashmouths had that reach. They weren't making grand promises, merely statements of fact. Anything I wanted, they could give me. And though the temptations of research, equipment, whatever the fuck they said were many…

My mind kept coming back to that last part.

About the house. About life. About comfort. About what we could have. Not just not worrying about money, but not worrying about who was going to come after us or whether or not we were going to end up under someone else's heel. The Ashmouths could give me that.

I could give her that.

Even if it meant letting go of… well.

My list—I hadn't thought about it in days, yet it still hung in my vest like a knife in my heart. Even now, thinking about it, thinking of everything I went through in that dark place and letting go of the people who did that to me… letting them just… walk…

Well, I'll be honest.

It hurt like fucking hell.

Like I was going to tear my ribs apart trying to hold that thought in my chest.

But…

Fuck me.

"What now, then?"

There were some things that hurt worse than that.

I was expecting the tension to slide out of the room once I said that. We'd reached an agreement, or at least one tentative enough to move forward. I'd thought that they'd relax a little, like I was about to.

What I didn't expect, though, was for Rudu to hold his breath and for Necla to stiffen. What I didn't expect was for Necla to glance to a nearby patron and wave a hand. What I didn't expect was an ornate-looking box to be set down upon the table and for the two Ashmouths to look at me like they thought I was about to dig their dead mothers up and beat them to death with the corpses.

"There remains," Necla whispered, laying hands on the box, "just one more point."

I gritted my teeth. My body tensed. The box creaked open.

Within lay an ornate, elegant interior bedecked in silk and velvet. It was rimmed with gold and lined with exquisitely polished steel. In the center was a perfectly carved indentation for a gun.

With a dragon for a barrel.

"What the fuck is this?" I growled, looking over the box at them. "You told me they *didn't* want him."

"Sal," Rudu said, "let me explain."

Heat boiled at my hip. I felt his anger coursing through the sheath, into my skin. It mingled with mine, his indignation stacked on top of my fury. These fuckers, these absolute *fuckers* had just...

"No," I spat. "No explanations."

"Be reasonable," Rudu said. "Minds change. Hearts change. Deals change. Even if the Three could let this opportunity pass, the weapon is dangerous. It could be used for—"

"No."

"This is something the Three won't let go. I tried to tell them, but—"

My hand went to my hip. The entire teahouse froze. From beneath tables, the various patrons withdrew weapons and crossbows, affixing them upon me. Necla froze, swallowing hard. Rudu flinched back as I pulled out the Cacophony.

I laid the gun on the table. Steam coiled off his brass. Tea began to boil inside the nearby pots.

"You tell them this," I snarled. "That we made a deal, he and I. And that the next time they want to double-cross Sal the fucking Cacophony, they'd better send a higher grade of asshole than you two fucks."

Rudu tensed. The Ashmouths at the tables stirred. Only Necla remained unmoved.

He raised a hand. He spoke a word.

"Leave."

Rudu and the Ashmouth patrons glanced at him, curiously. He replied with a narrowing of his bloodshot eyes, a curl of his lip.

"I have this in hand."

If he did, I didn't fucking know about it. Neither did Rudu, by the look on his face. His lips twitched, like he wanted to say something. But instead, he shook his head, got to his feet, and emptied his pipe on the floor. He muttered a command to the Ashmouths, who silently filed out after him, glancing worriedly at us as we were left alone in the empty teahouse.

The lamplight flickered between us. The tea steamed in its cups, coiling up around my nose. Necla the Shroud leaned forward, steepling his fingers in front of his face.

"I did not want to do this," he said, "but I know now why I have to."

I tensed. The Cacophony's brass twitched. I lay my hand near his hilt.

"I was hoping to use it one day to settle an old score, or ease the banality of my retirement somehow," he whispered. "But retirement never came. When the war in the Valley began, the Three extended my contract. I fought. And I used magic. And I protected their interests. And I no longer dream."

"That's a fucking shame," I muttered. "Try the chamomile."

"But I'm glad I no longer do," he said, his voice soft. "I thought the nightmares that followed me were a curse, but in them, I've seen a great darkness. A future of corpses and eternal night after all has been burned to ash. And when I can't wake, it's you I see, Sal. You and that *woman* of yours."

My neck tightened. I made a move to rise. He held out a hand.

And ensconced within his fingers was a curved tooth stained with red. A harmless trinket. Useless and unnoteworthy but for the crimson paint. A Redfavor.

My Redfavor.

I'd given it to him long ago for the chance to speak to the Three. I hadn't even remembered doing that.

"You gave this to me once," he said. "I am using it now."

My breath caught. He wouldn't. The absolute fucker. The absolute fucker *among* absolute fuckers.

A Redfavor was the closest thing to law Vagrants respected. A Redfavor was the only thing that couldn't be rejected, that couldn't be refused. Whoever held a Vagrant's Redfavor could ask anything of them. That's what we agreed to, when we agreed to be Vagrants. Everyone knew it.

He and I included.

"You can't," I whispered.

"*You* can't," he replied.

And he was right. It didn't matter what it was, how outrageous the favor or how insane the cost. Redfavor was Redfavor. It wasn't given in haste and it wasn't taken lightly. And if you turned it down...

Then whatever safety from Vagrants your title might have carried was gone.

And you were just another hog to be slaughtered at their leisure.

Your name, your story, your presence—it no longer meant anything to them.

"Understand that I take no pleasure in this," Necla whispered.

And I didn't believe him. My blood boiled in my chest. My breath came hot and angry in my head. I could barely hear him.

"Understand that this is the only way forward," he said.

And I hated him for telling the truth. We were so close, *again*. And *again* I hadn't thought far enough ahead and *again* we were going to fucking lose everything.

"Understand that this Redfavor entitles me to anything," he said. "Your cooperation. The Cacophony. Liette."

My finger clenched.

"Everything."

Silence fell over the table. My body went cold. The blood seeped out of my head in one great, weary breath. My shoulders slumped. I didn't move for a long time.

Slowly, Necla placed the Redfavor—my Redfavor—on the table. And, with terrified reverence, began to reach for the Cacophony. His fingers had barely brushed the brass before he hesitated.

Because I'd grabbed his wrist.

"I understand, Necla. I remember what a Redfavor does."

I held his arm to the table. I pulled the Cacophony up. I pressed it to his forehead.

"And you remember what I said I'd do if you ever said her name again."

"Sal, wait!" he began to scream. "*YOU CAN'T—*"

I couldn't.

But I did anyway.

I wasn't there when it happened.

But I was told, later.

I was told that the square was peaceful. And then suddenly, that nice little tea shop exploded. The windows blasted out into a spray of shards, left behind jagged wounds. The door flew off, impaled itself in a nearby wall. The sign spun wildly into the air and landed on a nice old man's lunch through his roof three blocks over. The walls of the teahouse bulged out. A small river of steaming brown liquid poured from beneath the doorway and down the steps.

Rudu was there. Along with every Ashmouth that had been pretending to be a civilian. And all of them looked up, stunned and silent, as the dust began to settle.

I remember the next part, because I was there for it.

I came walking out of the teahouse, shards of shattered pots crunching beneath my feet. The Cacophony hung limply from one of my hands, steam peeling from his grinning maw. The box intended for him hung in the other. It fell from my hands, clattered upon the stones.

I reached up a hand, wiped the remains of Necla's skull from my face, my chest, my belly.

I flicked gore upon the earth, looked over the crowd.

"Deal's off," I said.

TWENTY-FOUR

TOADBACK

There is a thing in opera they do where, right before things get awful—before the lovers turn away from each other, before the hero is about to die—where a single note is played and left to hang for as long as possible before fading. The entire cast stays silent during this moment until the note fades and the play resumes.

They call it a *Vocca fui Fultho*.

The Voice of Sorrow.

It's said this started as an homage to the Lady Merchant's song and its often single, solitary notes. It's also said that this started when playwrights wanted time to let the atmosphere sink into the audience. But I like my explanation.

The reason they do that in opera is because that happens in real life.

There is a noise that rings out, just a moment before the shit sweeps right over you and you know in your bones that you've just fucked up something that can't be unfucked. And like in opera, it's different for everything. Different for each person, each moment, each situation.

Sometimes it's a glass shattering. Sometimes it's a door closing. Sometimes it's the little breath someone takes right before they're about to tell you the three words that are going to break your heart and ruin you forever.

For me, it was three noises.

The sound of Rudu's pipe falling from his lips, striking the stones of the street, bouncing twice and then falling. The hiss of ashes of his pipe spilling from the bowl, the embers glowing briefly before going gray and disappearing in the breeze. The tiny whistle of breath it took someone to whisper Necla's name.

Three sounds. One right after each other.

In an opera, you would know the hero was fucked.

Turns out that's also something that happens in real life.

I stood there, stained with Necla's remains, staring at the wide, empty face of the man who had just been sitting next to him not half an hour ago. Rudu stood there, his pipe on the stones, his hands hanging limp at his sides, every last hope he had for this ending well draining from his face.

And, of course, the Ashmouths stood there.

The people of the square—the patient parents and the bustling bakers, the laughing grandmothers and the complaining grandfathers, every smiling face and charming little personality right down to the fucking girl with a cat on her lap—now stood ready to kill me. Hand crossbows and alchemic flasks had been pulled out from under aprons and shirts. Vests parted to reveal tough leather beneath as kind-eyed men and happy women pulled long blades free from their clothing.

Rudu tried to say something. I could see the question boiling behind his lips, struggling to understand. I could see his eyes racing as he slowly realized it didn't fucking matter. And I watched as he leaned back and made ready to watch me die beneath a hail of bolts and blades.

I, personally, did not like my odds.

But between the two of us concerned, I was outvoted.

The Cacophony seethed in my hand. His steam coiled from between my fingers. His brass shivered, excited at the idea. Of course. What did he have to be worried about? He wasn't about to be full of knives.

I tried to remember what I'd loaded. Discordance, of course. Then what? Hellfire? Hoarfrost? Sunflare? What the fuck was useful here?

"In the name of the Great General, HALT!"

A distraction. Yes. That would be very useful.

If it were anyone else, that is.

The Ashmouths flooded to one side of the square as a great black fist punched through their ranks. Tretta appeared from the corner leading to the bridge, blade in hand and sporting a number of fresh cuts across her face. That would have been concerning enough.

But the Twenty-Second lined up behind her, unreadable behind their masks and their saw blades shining in the smoke-stained sun, made every scar on my body go numb.

I was relieved to see she'd brought only half as many—the ranks behind her were made up of regulars. Tough-looking regulars, many of whom I'd recognized from my last encounter with them, *many* of whom recognized *me* as the person who'd torn their friend apart with Steel Python—but still, regulars were handle-able.

Ashmouths were handle-able.

Rudu and Tretta were handle-able.

All at once was less handle-able and more—

"I don't need this fucking mess."

Rudu said it best.

"By the order of the Glorious Revolution of the Fist and Flame," Tretta bellowed, her troops snapping to attention. "And in the name of his Great Generalship's mighty retribution, we do so render judgment as to—"

"Okay, yes, very impressive. All hail his mighty cock or whatever." Rudu waved a hand, irate. "This is Ashmouth business. Fuck along."

"Do not *dare* speak of the leader of the Revolution in such terms," Tretta snarled, leveling her blade at Rudu. "And do not presume to ask of me respect for the business of criminals. The right of the Revolutionary Mandate of retribution supersedes the business of all, especially those of murderers and Vagrants."

Fuck. I was kind of hoping she hadn't noticed me.

"These brave soldiers saw the horrors of this animal's war firsthand." She swept her blade menacingly toward me before gesturing to the regulars. "And were so moved by the Great General's infinite vision that they joined immediately. And the refugees she made that could not take up arms told us where she lay. Their passions burn for the righteous fire of vindication!"

I had to admit, that hurt.

It hurt that the refugees I'd tried so hard to protect had turned on me like that. It hurt that I knew I couldn't bring myself to blame them for it. But there wasn't any room in me for hurt anymore.

My breath was hot steam in my mouth. My blood ran in cinders through my veins. The Cacophony burned at my hand and I didn't flinch. I didn't know what chance we stood. Neither did he. And neither he nor I had the good sense to calm down right then.

I could barely hear their words. But if I had taken a moment to breathe, I might have heard, somewhere far away, the sound of chains jingling.

"Then I'll stroke their hair and tell them they're pretty after I'm done here." Rudu narrowed his eyes. "Last chance. Fuck off."

And if anyone else had fallen silent, they might have heard the sound of heavy breathing growing louder. Closer. Above us.

"The Revolution cowers to no one. Mage, fiend, or criminal." Tretta struck a salute with her sword. "Retribution awaits the Ashmouths and all foes of the Revolution! *Ten thousand years!*"

"Ten thousand years!"

As it was, though, there was not much listening going on. A lot of chanting from fevered lips. A lot of stares from cagey, desperate eyes. And with the stink of all the violence and fear in the air, it's easy to see why none of us bothered to look up.

Not until a slender shape the color of night fell from the sky.

And punched into Tretta's throat.

Her chanting became a cry, her salute a flailing thrash as something wrapped itself around her and pulled blood from her neck in crimson flashes. Two of the Twenty-Second rushed forward, restraining her thrashing while a third soundlessly lunged to tear the thing from their commander's neck. Blood wept from the wound—not nearly enough to indicate a major vein had been hit, just my fucking luck—as her soldier hurled the missile to the ground.

Where it promptly rolled, got back to its feet, looked up with beady little eyes, and shrieked through a bloodstained mouth.

A kite viper is a horrid little thing. Picture the offspring of a snake that got obliterated on a small senate of illicit substances and subsequently, and in defiance of all logic and nature, managed to fuck an eagle and a shark at the same time and you'll have a decent idea. They come in a stunning variety, as well: venomous, paralyzing, stinging, or if you're really unlucky, saw-toothed.

Like this little fucker screaming on the ground.

They're a horrific scourge in the denser jungles of the Scar; massive swarms of them come flying out of the trees and leave behind skeletons. But there are a few upsides. Kite vipers are nocturnal, for one. They don't ever leave their forests. And you never, *ever* see them in cities.

Like this one.

So, as you can deduce, this wasn't a great development.

"Ordinarily, I wouldn't interfere with the squabbles of nuls."

A voice beckoned the kite viper back to the sky. All eyes followed it as it coiled, eel-like, through the air to perch upon a slender shoulder and curl adoringly about a slender throat.

Beneath a black veil, I could feel a pair of hateful eyes locked upon me.

"But, if you can stand some frank criticism, your posturing needs work." The woman spoke from beneath a shroud of lace that obscured her features—not that it mattered: I knew the voice, the veil, and the hate behind both of them. "I could not, in good conscience, permit you to control the stage further."

She ran long-nailed fingers across the kite viper's throat.

"Particularly when your concerns are with *my* quarry."

"Who the fuck are you?" Rudu demanded of the woman on the rooftop.

And I wish he hadn't asked.

The woman—slight as the kite viper nuzzling her throat—was seated, dressed in a long black dress to complement the black hat and veil, upon a towering armoire of polished redwood looking like it had been plucked straight from an antique store. Thin silver chains bound its doors shut. And carrying the whole horrid affair on his back was a thick, powerful-looking man, head bowed and knee bent as he came to a halt at the edge of the roof.

Beneath the veil, I could just barely make out dark lips curling into smile. Upon the pale skin of her chest, I saw a halo of violins arranged in an elegant tattoo. A Vagrant's ink. And it was ink I knew.

She fucking loved this part.

"I am the song of vengeance. I am the dirge all miserable women and wounded men sing before I darken their door." She slid from a sheath upon her hip a violin of a deep black hue, a matching bow in the other hand. "I am the storm that swallows the sun, the swarm that ends your crops, I am—"

"Oh, for fuck's sake, Chiriel, *can you hurry this the fuck up*?"

I know I shouldn't have shouted—it was just bad manners to ruin a fellow Vagrant's introduction. But then, it was also bad manners to blow someone's head off after using a Redfavor, so it's not like I had a lot to lose here.

Behind her veil, I saw her frown. Good.

"You profane everything you touch, Sal," Chiriel muttered. "And you *ruined* my introduction, you perverse philistine." She leveled her violin bow at me like it was a sword. "Your sacrilege alone would be reason enough to kill you. But a holier mission compels me here." She swept her veil across the Ashmouths and Revolutionaries. "And I must insist you leave."

"I have had enough of indulging the demands of fops and Vagrants." Tretta roared, directing her sword skyward, "*OPEN FIRE!*"

"Wait, you're not supposed to—"

Autobows whirred. Crossbows clicked. A hail of bolts flew toward Chiriel, shrieking as they sailed through the air. Through the whine of their flight, I could hear a faint, musical note.

In flashes of purple light, the bolts winked out of the sky, disappearing mere inches from Chiriel's face. The murmur of confusion that followed lasted only as long as it took for another note to play.

I hit the floor.

Light flashed. The bolts, still in flight, came back into existence. They streaked across the square in a haphazard burst, punching through Revolutionaries and Ashmouths and into the door above my head as I ducked.

I fucking knew it.

She had a Doormage.

"All right, you dicks, if that's how you want to play it."

Chiriel rose to her full, demure height. She stomped a gorgeous heeled shoe upon the top of the armoire. The burly man carrying it suddenly dropped it. The chains rattled, fell off. The doors trembled. A faint hiss emerged from inside.

Chiriel's eyes glowed bright purple behind her veil. She placed bow to string. The Lady sang a wailing, resonant note.

"Chiriel the Four-String will play the saddest song just for you."

She pulled the bow across her violin. A smooth, velvety note rang out. The doors to the armoire flung themselves open.

"Ocumani oth rethar."

She invoked the words—the same words all Vagrants invoke—in a screech.

And what happened next is a little difficult to remember. I remember seeing the darkness behind the doors. I remember seeing the hundreds of glistening eyes, the thousands of glistening feathers and scales.

And I remembered, very clearly, having a thought.

Oh, right. Chiriel's a Hivemage.

And then I started panicking.

But we all were by that point.

The armoire buckled with the force of their flight. They came vomiting out in a clot of glistening black ink, pouring in an endless font that bled into the sky. Chiriel's violin sang out a delicate tune and they danced to it. They twisted and curled in one sinewy mass, a writhing column that spun, twirled, bunched together.

And descended.

The screaming started immediately. Dulcet violin music accompanied the sounds of saw blades roaring and alchemics exploding, all to the chorus of the sounds of hundreds of kite vipers tearing into flesh.

Bursts of hot red blood flashed around the battlefield. The kite vipers tore into exposed throats, legs, arms, shredded through whatever they needed to get through to get to flesh. Revolutionaries and Ashmouths shrieked and fell in flailing heaps, going still as kite vipers swarmed over their fallen bodies to quickly dispatch the remains before flying off to seek new prey, leaving behind a shredded carcass. They grew fat on blood and flesh, gorging and vomiting and gorging again as they feasted over and over.

Whether it was their quarry's flesh or their own, they were not particular.

Kite vipers fell in sheets. Some flew recklessly into clouds of Ashmouth poison and fell dead and twitching on the ground. Some gnawed futilely at the armor of the Twenty-Second as they calmly swept their saw blades this way and that, bisecting the little beasts from the sky, even as their fellows shrieked and tried to pull gnawing fiends off of each other. Of Tretta or Rudu, I could see no sign.

Ordinarily, kite vipers would retreat by now. Ordinarily, they'd eat their fill and move on as soon as they could. But these were a Hivemage's vipers. They were not ordinary.

Chiriel writhed atop the armoire, lost in the frenzy of her own violin song. She thrust this way, the kite vipers followed. She struck a screeching note, the kite vipers flitted, found new targets. You might mistake them for expertly trained pets, if you'd never seen a Hivemage.

I'd never worked much with them when I was in the army. Neither did anyone else. Hivemages were creepy fucks. The Lady gave them the power to harmonize their consciousnesses with lesser intellects, bending them to their wills. If you read between the lines, the implication is that they could dominate *your* mind if they thought about it hard enough. And if you didn't read between the lines, Hivemages were still freaky fucks who sat around talking to roaches and teaching rats tricks.

Chiriel had been one of the best.

I knew because I had known her.

She was on my list.

And you might be wondering how I had the time or space to contemplate all this in the middle of a swarm of killer, magically controlled flying snakes.

To which I would say, if you didn't think I ran the hell away when I got the chance, your opinion of me is too damn high.

I took off running, pushing through the chaos best I could and bearing only a few nicks for it. I didn't know why Chiriel had shown up here. I didn't have time to think of it. I had to get clear. I had to get to Liette. I kept running, tearing around corners, heading for the curry shop where I'd left her.

Call it my good luck. Call it their bad luck. I didn't fucking care. I wasn't going to waste it, either way.

But luck is like wine. If you don't use it while you have it, it goes real fucking sour.

The Lady's note rang out in my ears as I pounded down the street toward the curry shop. Purple light flashed. The armoire, with Chiriel on top of it, fell down to crash upon the street with a thud. I tensed as the refugees and people of Toadback went fleeing, their panic filling the square. But Chiriel didn't even seem to notice them.

"I had hoped you wouldn't think so low of me to assume I came here solely to kill nuls, Salazanca," she said, her voice low and dangerous.

The doors to her armoire shuddered. I slid my hand beneath my scarf, kept it out of view as I fished something out of my satchel.

"I don't know why the fuck you're here, Chirielanthi," I replied, sliding a shell behind my back. "But if you're after Twenty-Two Dead Roses, I'm going to tell you the same—"

"I have no idea who that is," Chiriel snapped. "I am not here for you. For me. Or for anyone else but on the behalf of one."

She leveled her bow at me. She spat the name.

"Darrish the Flint."

I'd been hit a lot lately. I'd taken blows that left me reeling, cuts that left me bleeding and in so much pain that I felt like collapsing under the weight of my own scars some days. But until this moment, until I heard that name...

I don't think I'd been wounded.

"Darrish...," I whispered. "What happened with Darrish and me is no business of yours."

"DON'T."

Chiriel's bow trembled. I slipped the Cacophony's chamber open behind my back.

"Don't you fucking *dare* say that, you forsaken *animal*." Neither anger nor hate pulled those words from her mouth. They came on tears and sobs. "Don't you ever say that Darrish is not my business. She was *good* to us, Sal."

Chiriel the Four-String. Chirielanthi yun Vuinti. Who had served alongside me in the army. Who had done the bidding of Vraki. Who had sat in the shadows and snickered as I was betrayed, broken, and bled of my magic.

She wept. Unabashedly. Painfully. She wept.

"She was good to *me*," she whispered. "And you killed her."

I remembered Darrish. I remembered the day I left her. As that airship had begun to plummet out of the air, as a man I'd once thought my friend tried to kill her, as I couldn't bring myself to forgive her, even then...

"I didn't," I whispered, in a way that suggested I didn't really believe it. Because maybe I didn't. "I did not kill Darrish."

"Don't lie." Chiriel pressed her bow to her violin. "And don't move."

She struck a chord. My arms moved without thinking. The armoire's door burst open. The Cacophony's chamber slammed shut. Kite vipers came pouring out in a stream of teeth and beating wings. I raised the gun, looked away. I could feel their screaming in my skin. I pulled the trigger.

Funny thing about Hivemages.

The Lady gives them impressive powers. Chirielanthi herself had once put down a local rebellion with just a dresser full of her little friends. But she asks for a steep Barter. As a Hivemage communes with their swarms, their thoughts begin to leave them, their individuality plucked out of their heads, bit by bit, by the Lady's deal. Until one day, the consciousnesses are no longer separate.

Because you see, when you share thoughts, you share everything: strengths, speeds, skills.

And senses.

The Cacophony fired. Sunflare burst as it met the swarm. Bright light engulfed the square. I heard the confused terror of people who hadn't looked away as their sight was struck from them. But only barely.

Over the sound of Chiriel and her kite vipers, writhing in blinded agony upon the ground, I could hear nothing else.

"IT HURTS! IT HURTS! STOP IT! GET IT OUT OF OUR EYES!"

Individual deaths and wounds across their pets don't tend to affect a Hivemage—you needed to hit their swarm all at once to get a reaction like this. Usually, that's tricky. But Chirel was intent on killing me and that made her at least a little more predictable.

Lucky, lucky me.

Her wails were soul-deep, the agony of each of her little pets shared between them and delivered to her. Their anguish was profound and painful in my ears.

Not enough to get me to stop, though. I ran over them, crunching as many of the little fuckers beneath my heels as I could as I rushed past the armoire and Chiriel. I slammed a Discordance shell into the

Cacophony, looked at her writhing on the armoire, helpless for as long as it would take them to recover.

And then I looked at the people. The refugees. The citizens. Toadback. Paralyzed with fear.

And I sighed.

"DO YOU FUCKERS NOT GET IT?"

Sometimes I hate being such a nice person.

"*THIS IS A VAGRANT'S TOWN NOW.*" I aimed the Cacophony at a nearby house that looked the emptiest, hoped I was right. "*LEAVE NOW OR GET BURIED HERE. YOUR FUCKING CALL.*"

To their credit, they started running even before I pulled the trigger. But the resulting explosion of glass, wood, and—fortunately, for fucking once—no body parts, I hoped, would send the message home. And if the screaming was any indication, it had worked.

I didn't like doing that—particularly when I could have come up with a better line, I see that now—but I also didn't fucking want any more refugees. Whether I was going about it the right way or not, I'm open to debate. But I wasn't then.

"*SHE'S HEADING FOR THE SHOP!*" Chiriel found the mind to scream behind me. "*THE SHOP! STOP HER!*"

Her pets didn't respond, continuing to twitch. Ahead of me, the curry shop's sign loomed. The doors flung open, the people inside fleeing out into any direction but mine. All but one of them.

"Are you all right?" she asked me, breathless.

I wasn't, if I was honest. But I grunted.

"There was a noise and then everyone started running. What happened?" Liette demanded as she rushed up to me. "Where are the Ashmouths?"

"I don't know. Probably devoured."

She blinked at me. "Devoured?"

"Devoured."

"So I shouldn't ask?"

"Not yet." I pushed her toward the fleeing people. "We need to go. Keep your head down and don't stop moving."

We had begun to do just that when I heard another note of the Lady's song. Coming from somewhere close. A purple light blossomed inside the curry shop through its windows. I saw a massive shape emerge. And that's when I realized...

Chiriel hadn't been talking to her pets.

The front of the shop exploded. And not because of me this time. Glass and wood were launched in a spray as a huge silhouette emerged from within. Heavy feet thumped, making the fragmented foundation shudder. A great pair of curving, jagged antlers tore free the remains of the door frame as something very tall, very broad, and very heavy emerged from the curry shop and glowered down at me.

"Sal," he said.

"Grishok," I acknowledged. I looked across his bare chest, saw the broad tattoo of a weed painted across a great cask of a body. "Gone Vagrant?"

"Yeah. Same as you." A pair of meaty hands lazily swung a small tree that had been splintered into a large club. "But you knew that, right? I'm on your list, aren't I?"

"You heard about that, huh?"

"Yeah." He drew his club up over his head. "Can't say I'm happy about it."

I shouted, shoved Liette back as I pulled away. Grishok's club pounded a hole in the pavement, knocked both her and me to our asses, and sent stone fragments flying. I slammed a shell into the Cacophony, aimed.

"Yeah, well," I said, "maybe think before you betray me next time, you piece of shit."

And fired.

Hellfire swept over him. Gnawing, devouring, laughing. It savaged his body as surely as the kite vipers had savaged everyone else's. It swallowed him whole, chewed him in fiery teeth and spat out a glistening, skinless husk of burned flesh and charred, bubbling sinew.

A husk, I should point out, that was still standing.

"That's what I said." Grishok's skin twitched. Blackened flesh trembled, shrank. Scorched sinew pulled itself together. The wounds disappeared as his skin regrew, healthy and dark over his great muscle. "So I figured I wouldn't bother looking for you. Maybe not even fight when you came for me. I know I did you wrong."

He lumbered forward as I got Liette to her feet and backed up, keeping myself between us. He wasn't bothered by Hellfire. He didn't even look burned anymore.

But that was Mendmages for you. And among Mendmages, few were as legendary as Grishoktha ki Jurl. That's why the Empress had made him one of her chosen, after all. That's why he'd been there that night I'd lost everything.

He towered even taller than Agne, his shoulders almost scraping the eaves of houses as he pursued me, unhurried, through the streets. His chest and belly were broad, thick fat laid over thicker muscle. His arms were huge and powerful, his legs like tree trunks. He barely bothered to clothe himself, the only adornments upon him being a pair of tattered pants, a large sack, his tattoo, and of course, his antlers.

The Lady Merchant takes a Mendmage's blood in exchange for their powers. And the alchemic concoctions they quaff to replace it result in unusual growths. Some people get scales. Some people grow fins. And some people become horned, unstoppable killing machines the size of small barns.

She's a whimsical one, that Lady.

"If you want to leave now and wait for me to be done here," I said as I loaded the gun again and aimed, "I'll be with you as soon as I can."

The Lady sang. Light flashed. A shadow fell over me.

Ah, right. There was a Doormage, wasn't there?

Grishok and his huge fucking club appeared behind us. I shoved Liette away, tried to move myself. I avoided the blow, but not by enough. This close, even being near a weapon that size hurt. It clipped me as he swung, almost took my fucking leg off. I screamed at the hit as Liette helped me back up.

"See, that's my problem there," Grishok muttered. "I know I deserve to die for what I did to you, Sal. I made peace with that." His lips curled into a broad frown. "But Darrish didn't deserve that."

"I *didn't* kill Darrish."

"Yeah, I heard what you told Chiriel. I believe you. I believe you *think* you didn't kill her." He hefted his club again, held it high over his head. "But she was the best of us. Better than me. Better than you. She talked with me often. Gave me my Vagrant name, even."

He paused, smiled softly.

"Grishok the Dandelion. Like it?"

I swallowed. "I do."

"Yeah. So did I. I loved her, Sal." He sniffed. "*Ocumani oth rethar*, right?"

"*Eres va atali*," I replied.

And decorum was satisfied.

He roared, pulled his club high. I couldn't move, not with my leg fucked up like this. I shoved Liette, tried to limp away. I felt the club come down, falling onto the streets.

Behind him.

Which might be on account of the great, gaping, severium-smoking wound in his neck.

He blinked, uncertain as to what had happened. I didn't know myself. Not until I heard a hammer click. And when I saw the flash of Tretta's hand cannon, I put it together pretty fucking quick.

The severium charge unloaded into Grishok's face as Tretta came tearing out between the houses. His jaw flew off. His face became a spray of gore painted upon the walls of a nearby house. He fell, shaking the ground, as all of him—without half his skull—collapsed to the earth.

TWENTY-FIVE

ELSEWHERE

There is a story that I heard on the roads to Toadback.

The long dirt highways ran like veins through that part of the Scar. And in war, they bled people. Most were running from the war because they couldn't fight. But some were running from it because they could.

Deserters. People who'd been offered everything the Revolution had to offer and found they couldn't live off it.

They showed themselves rarely, only when the road had been bled almost dry of people. But I met them here and there. In the few darkest hours before dawn, they would appear at the cookfires along the road. Most had abandoned their kit—their uniform, their medals. More had hung on to their weapons—the gunpikes, the hand cannons. That which could keep them alive deserted with them, everything else could stay loyal for all they cared.

They told different stories. Some about the Valley. Some about Six Walls. A few about the town they'd grown up in before they were conscripted, a few about the life they'd lived beneath the unblinking eye of the Revolution. Many didn't speak at all, merely staring into the fire for as long as they needed before moving on.

But the ones that did speak told a similar story.

A story about the fortress of Bitterdrink.

Of the many people within, the ones who were ready to die and the ones who weren't.

And of a woman who couldn't save them all.

The details vary here and there, depending on the opinions and moods of the storytellers. But despite the differences, they all tend to start the same way.

With a fight.

The sky was on fire that day. The clouds had fled from the lightning arcs and boulders that had rained from above. The wind had stilled itself and died, afraid to attract the attention of the mages below. And behind a veil of black- and purple-tinged severium smoke, the sun cowered.

While I had been only a mile or two away, having tea with Torle of the Void, a battle had been raging on the other side of Bitterdrink's valleys.

Beneath the warring heavens, a silhouette picked its ungainly and desperate way among the battlefield. The earth erupted, craters blossoming like black and smoldering flowers in the gorge, cannon fire and magically hurled boulders retaliating against one another. Knots of soldiers loosened and bled out across the canyon, their formations shaken and lost beneath the onslaught of Siegemage charges and Skymage harrying. In a valley that closed like a choking throat, Revolutionary soldiers flooded away in full retreat as a wall of magical carnage pursued them.

Among them was a woman—wounded, bloodied, and battered. And draped across her shoulder was another woman, limp and breathless. The bloodied one, one eye sealed shut with the red that wept down her forehead, kept her one working eye focused on the line of tanks before her; their salvo of cannons fired over her head, signaling the only salvation she would see in that valley.

The woman pulled her comrade's weakened body past the line of Revolutionary cannons, the great machines' steady fire the only thing holding back the mages. She laid her comrade against the wheel of an idling machine and propped her up.

"Defiant," Tretta Unbreakable said, shaking the woman awake. "Keep your eyes open. Breathe. Don't fall asleep. You took a nasty hit. You need to stay up. Defiant? *Defiant!*" When the woman didn't respond, she roared over her shoulder. "*Proud!* Get over here!"

A man came rushing forward—a lean fellow with a bad eye and a Revolutionary coat a little too big for him. At Tretta's frantic gestures, he knelt down beside the woman called Defiant. He leaned toward her, shouted through the din of cannon fire.

"Ammoni," he said. "Ammoni, wake up. Don't fall asleep."

The woman stirred suddenly, eyelids fluttering open at the sound of her name. Her true name. She wasn't called Defiant until a few days ago. He wasn't called Proud. They'd come from the same town and when that town had fallen to the war, they'd joined the same stream of refugees heading east. The same ones that would follow a white-haired woman to Ocytus.

Some of them had gotten away in the chaos that followed her pulling the trigger. Defiant and Proud hadn't. They'd been taken to the same camp, given the same speech, drilled with the same propaganda, handed the same uniform.

They had left their town as Ammoni and Vilk, a tailor and a bookbinder.

They had been conscripted into the Revolution as Defiant and Proud.

"Vilk," Ammoni had whispered. She smiled softly at him. "Where are we?"

"We're all right," he said.

"We're not all right," she replied. "We were safer with the Cacophony."

He snarled. "She took everything from us. *Abandoned* us. How can you—"

"Defiant. Proud. That's enough. On your feet." Tretta imposed herself between them, seized Defiant by her wrist, and pulled her to her feet. "You were both exemplary in your service back there. The Great General smiles upon us all for your bravery. Well done."

Proud offered a hesitant nod of acknowledgment. Defiant stared at the ground. These were understandable reactions, given the circumstances.

Tretta's regiment had put a number of skirmishes behind them, but their nascent role as hardened veterans was quashed by their need to become rapid reinforcements. Bitterdrink, that noble fortress that controlled the entire region, was under attack by Imperial swine baying for scraps. The Imperium's mages harassed and harried the fortress, but showed no inclination to strike at the fortifications themselves. It was obscene, illogical, and appeared to be nothing more than a long waste of time.

Bitterdrink's commander had been right to be worried, Tretta knew.

Just as she knew that anytime you can't tell what a mage is up to, you should be worried. That knowledge had compelled her to haste—her shouts, commands, and orders had kept the regiment moving day and night until they finally arrived at the network of valleys and gorges that led to Bitterdrink.

It was there that they'd met the true resistance.

They'd been bogged down in fighting for hours, the Imperials displaying overwhelming force to keep the Revolutionary relief from arriving. And their show of strength only convinced Tretta more that she must reach the fortress before it was too late.

If she knew what "it" was, I wonder if she still would have hurried.

The remaining soldiers of her reinforcements—those that hadn't been crushed by Graspmages or torn apart by Maskmages stalking the field—stood in regrouping knots. Sergeants walked up and down their lines, bellowing orders to straighten backs and hold weapons tighter.

But Tretta had seen many battles and many, *many* soldiers. She could tell who was made of metal and who was made of glass. And I wonder, sometimes, when she looked over those flagging soldiers—those sad, desperate men and women who were miles from home fighting for a war they knew nothing about—if she contemplated whether the Great General cared at all that they were sending townspeople out to die in his name.

I like to think she did. Eventually.

But the people who told the story tell me different.

"I want to go home," Ammoni whispered. "I want to go home."

"You are home, Defiant," Tretta replied. "The Revolution is your family. We will take care of you now."

"No," she whispered, shaking her head. "No, this isn't home. Home was Lavont's Remorse. Home was *home*." She looked up at Proud, her eyes shining bright for a few fleeting seconds. "Remember, Vilk? Remember the drinks? Remember the *food*?"

"Ammoni..." Proud caught himself. "Defiant. Listen to the commander. She knows what she's talking about. Lavont's Remorse was destroyed by *mages*."

"The same mages that return to finish the job, Defiant," Tretta snarled. "The same mages that strain, in their *infinite* arrogance, to grind you beneath their heels. You are not their prey, Defiant. You are a proud daughter of the Revolution. You *will* survive and you *will* emerge triumphant."

I wasn't there. I don't know Ammoni or Vilk or even if those were their real names. I don't know how they would have reacted to hearing something like that. But I wonder if Ammoni's eyes were distant, full of the same fading emptiness that anyone feels when their survival depends on a lie. And I wonder if Tretta noticed. And maybe had held that same look in her eyes, once.

Ah, but that's just me wondering.

The people who told this story tell me that Proud stepped forward.

"Commander," he said, trying nobly and failing to put himself between Tretta and Defiant. "With all respect, she's not made for this. I don't think she's going to be helpful at all if—"

"*PROUD, DO YOU BELIEVE IN THE REVOLUTION?*" she shouted, loud enough to be heard over the sounds of magic, over the cannon fire, throughout that entire valley. "*Do you believe that it is not magic that makes a human, but a resolve that is unique unto a human? Do you believe that you are not the scraps of civilization to be fed to hogs? Do you believe that you have a purpose more important than fear, more important than magic, more important than anyone who would call you their lesser?"*

A chorus of burgeoning roars started in the ranks—slow, at first, but rising as the other sergeants fell silent and let her voice thunder across the canyon.

"I believe in the Revolution, Proud," she roared, seizing the two of them by their shoulders, her teeth bared like a beast's. *"I believe that it is worth fighting for because I believe you and I are the Revolution. And I believe that* you *are worth fighting for. I believe it was worth it to drag you out of that hell and it's worth it to drag any soldier here out of a hell a thousand times. I am the Revolution. You are the Revolution. And we are UNBREAKABLE."*

Ammoni nodded, finding her spine. Vilk helped her back to formation. The crowds roared, cried, screamed.

"Unbreakable! Unbreakable! Unbreakable!"

That part, everyone remembers. The roaring, the chanting of her name over the Revolution's. Each and every one of them told me the same thing, word for word. They all remember that speech. They always will.

And even the ones who came to curse her name said they felt the fire of her voice burning in them.

Everyone agrees on that part.

Not many people are sure what happened next.

"Commander."

Tretta had turned to see them. Long lines of soldiers, black-clad in their armored coats, masked behind heavy apparatus and thick glass lenses, wielding weapons of war so terrifying Tretta feared not being on the right side of them.

The Twenty-Second had appeared. Without request. Without even an indication that they had ever been in the area.

"We are here to relieve you," said their leader—or Tretta assumed, as she had no way of telling them apart. "Your presence upon this field is no longer necessary."

At this, she found her composure. And her anger.

"We have bled for every inch of this fucking valley," she snarled. "We have fought and died and fought again for this valley. I am *not* turning away for no reason."

"The interests of Culven Loyal, and thus the interests of the Great General, are concerned in Bitterdrink," the soldier replied, monotone and neutral. "Neither have requested your presence."

"*Bitterdrink* has requested my presence," she snapped back. "My soldiers have fought for that fortress and will continue to fight for that fortress. And unless you give me a fucking edict in the Great General's own blood right the hell now, none of us are going anywhere."

The Twenty-Second soldier stiffened. And, though some say it was just a trick of the light, some people swear they saw the other Twenty-Seconds stiffen in the exact same way at the exact same time, down to the briefest flinch.

"As you wish," the Twenty-Second said.

What happened next, they all know.

She returned to their formation. She stood beside the woman called Defiant. She laid a hand on her shoulder before drawing her sword.

"*Ten Thousand Years!*" she roared.

"*TEN THOUSAND YEARS!*" they roared back.

"Ten Thousand Years!"

The sky darkened.

"TEN THOUSAND YEARS!"

The tanks began to move.

"Ten Thousand Years!"

Fire rose in the distance.

"TEN THOUSAND YEARS!"

And they ran toward it.

The canyon echoed with the sounds of lumbering tanks wheeling forward, cannons blasting, and the retaliatory magical lightning flying back in response. The Revolution swarmed forward beneath a cloud of severium-tinged smoke, their howls on their lips and their gunpikes in their hands.

The Twenty-Second swept out in front of them, silently rushing forward to take the point. The line of mages began to collapse as withering autobow fire drove them back before their ferocious saw blades whirred to life and began to rend through skin and bone. Skymages were plucked from the sky with crossbow bolts. Siegemages were rendered into gore beneath whirling blades. The nul regulars were swiftly trampled by the surge of Revolutionaries swarming up behind.

Everyone agrees the counterattack was swift and brutal. Everyone agrees that the Twenty-Second led the way. And everyone agrees that the mages were about to break.

And while no one is quite sure why it happened, everyone knows what happened next.

The earth shook beneath their feet.

The line buckled. The retreating mages turned to many mages. Fire and frost bloomed around the Revolutionaries as they pressed forward. Resurgent mages emerged from portals, their powers bursting out of their eyes. One by one, body by body, the line began to fall.

Their advance became a melee. Tretta looked up from hacking at mages with her sword, searching the lines for the Twenty-Second. And, far behind, she found them.

The imposing soldiers stood there, as if they'd simply frozen in mid-charge. Their lensed eyes were turned toward Bitterdrink, all of their gazes focused on the same point in the sky. They stood there for a long moment, heedless of the battle raging around them. They twitched, all at once, as if arriving at the same conclusion.

And in unison, they turned and departed from the field.

Tretta shouted at them, but she could not hear herself over the shrieking of metal as the cannons were torn apart. Tretta pleaded with them, but she could not speak over the sound of the mages' terrible magic. Tretta cursed them, but how would they have heard her over the sound of the hand cannon going off?

A severium shot blasted past her head, hot metal and powder kissing the side of her face as it narrowly avoided taking her head off.

Too close to have been an accident—that shot had come from her own side.

She looked over her shoulder. Defiant stood there, the smoking hand cannon held in her hand, her eyes empty. Tretta didn't know where she had found the weapon, or when she had thought to pick it up and turn it on her. But neither of those questions, I like to think, bothered her as much as the bigger one.

How, in the midst of battle, could a nul have ever hated her more than she hated the mages?

Ammoni shuddered. Her body fell, bloodied. Vilk sobbed, stepped over her body with the gunpike he'd just run her through with, returned to fighting. The screams became thunderous in the canyon. It had to be a choking sound, a smothering noise, the kind that strangles all sense and reason out of a person.

And maybe that's why she did what she did.

She screamed. She charged. She struck.

She carved her way through the melee, through every mage and Imperial she could find, until she found the tank. The last machine stood, a Siegemage pounding on its hull, its crew pulped and leaking out of its hatch. She hacked her way to it, pulled the corpses of her dead comrades from the controls, hurled herself onto them.

No one knew what she was doing. Or how she expected it to work.

But when she hit the cannon and it blew a Siegemage apart, they saw. And when she drove the tank forward in a violent, haphazard path, they saw. And as she pulped mage after mage, heedless of the flame and lightning and everything else they hurled at her, the line followed.

The mages' line had only just begun to reassemble itself. It wasn't prepared to fight back against a tank driven by someone so desperate. As the mages struggled to either get out of its way or fight back against it, the Revolutionaries swarmed over them and started to tear them apart.

Bloody inches became bloody feet. The earth that had roared beneath them grew silent. Bodies burst across the canyon, drunk by a thirsty earth, as the tank carved its way through the smoke and the churned dirt.

Until finally there were no more enemies, no more bodies, and no more room to go forward.

She fell out of the tank as her regiment came up behind her. She staggered, breathless and limp, through the bodies. And she came to the edge of the valley that led to Bitterdrink.

I heard different things when people told me what happened next.

Some said they saw their chance to run—be it from the fact that they never wanted to fight for the Revolution in the first place or they just weren't ready to die to a mage—and took it. Some said they don't remember what happened and their escape became a blur in their head. But they tell me a lot of them did what Tretta did.

When she saw Bitterdrink sinking beneath the earth, the dirt rising up like an ocean to swallow it whole and the Imperial banner planted where it had lain, she fell to her knees. She felt the blood drain out of her face, her body, all of her. Her sword fell from her hand and the blood from Ammoni's narrowly missed shot wept onto her shoulder.

And though I don't think I'll ever know what she thought in that moment, I do wonder.

I wonder if she looked out over that long stretch of barren earth where a fortress had once been. And I wonder what she saw.

Did she see an injustice? A great grave where her comrades had been buried alive? Another wrong in a long litany of the Imperium's wrongs to one day be seared clean by the promised hellfire of the Great General?

Or did she stare over that barren earth that she had nearly died for and wonder why she even bothered?

I don't know.

And I think if I did, I wouldn't ever sleep again.

TWENTY-SIX

TOADBACK

Tretta Unbreakable, covered in bite wounds and wielding a blade slick with blood, looked toward me. "You did this."

I blinked, looked at Grishok's corpse. "No, I think that one is all you."

She shook her head. "No. This is yours. This blood. This city. The oath that brought my regiment here."

I backed up, kept the gun leveled at her. "Tretta, I'll tell you what I told him: I am in no mood."

"Did you recognize them, Sal?" she asked. "The men and women who were displaced by your war? Did you see them in Revolutionary uniform, the fire in their eyes? Do you know what I promised them to bring them here?" She took another step forward. "Your blood."

"I figured, yeah. I'm warning you, stay back."

Liette clung tightly to my shoulder. The emptiness of Tretta's expression, the absolute wear of the war, was a horrific thing to see up close. She spoke with the same conviction that makes us fear that madmen may be right.

"I will honor them, Sal," she said. "As I have honored every soldier who lost their life to you. As I will honor every soldier who shall ever serve the Great General by ending you."

She stepped around Grishok's hulking corpse. She glanced at him disdainfully.

"And ultimately, every Vagrant shall meet this fate." She sneered, kicked his body. "The Dandelion. A ridiculous name."

Grishok's corpse responded by swinging a hand up and smacking her so hard she skidded across the stones.

Liette screamed. I took her hand, ran around Grishok's carcass—which was now stirring, moving, rising. His body pulled itself to his feet. He glowered at Tretta through a skull that was now hardy and whole and was swiftly weaving sinew and skin anew over his face.

"It's because," he spoke as a regenerated jawbone clicked into place, "I just keep popping up."

That actually *was* a good name. If I was less terrified, I'd have praised it. But as it was, my thoughts were on my hand around Liette's and our feet pumping under us.

I said Grishok was legendary among Mendmages and I meant it. His magic was so strong it worked without him even trying. He'd been blown apart, cut open, run over, and incinerated—all by the same tank, once—and I saw him back on his feet in minutes. Wounds and injuries repaired themselves even while he was unconscious, even while he was...

Well, I mean, you saw his head.

It took time, as all magic did. But for as long as he was rebuilding himself, he wasn't chasing us. We ran, followed out of the alley by his baleful glower.

The streets were flooded by panic. People poured out of every rivulet, refugee and citizen mingling in a singular river of fear that flooded over the local peacekeepers. I pulled Liette into the tide with me, held her close as we waded through the jostle of bodies.

I saw Revolutionaries who had survived Chiriel's onslaught wading in, searching the crowd for me through savaged faces. I saw the Ashmouths creeping on the roofs, peering from the alleys. They'd find us eventually. I could outrun them. But running wasn't a plan.

I looked through the crowd. A gap had broken as they surged forward toward a distant landmark.

The bridge. To the other side. To safety. Or safer, at least.

The bridge wasn't a plan, either.

But it was better than this.

"Head down," I told Liette, pulling her tighter as we broke into a sprint. "Don't let go of me."

She clung to me. We rushed forward. Through the pounding of our own feet, I heard another note of the Lady. Bright light flashed overhead. A shadow fell over us.

The Doormage. Fuck me, the fucking *Doormage.*

A tree—yes, an actual fucking tree—came plummeting down from above. I stopped short, hauled Liette out of its way as it came to a thunderous crash in our path. The crowd behind us continued to surge forward, their panic not registering the obstacle yet. We had to move. Had to keep going.

I pulled her down an alley. I tried to go around. A note rang. A light flashed. A tree fell in front of our escape route.

And I had this creeping feeling that I was fucked this time.

But I couldn't let it settle on my shoulders. I couldn't slow down that much. I took Liette's hand. I looked into her eyes. She into mine.

Without words, I asked her if she would suffer with me.

And without hesitation, she agreed.

We tore off. Running through the back alleys of Toadback. We turned where we could, pivoting through the narrow corridors. But the Lady kept singing. And more obstacles kept cutting us off. It didn't take me long to realize we were being herded.

And by the time we'd pulled into another alley that curled around toward the riverbank, I realized who the Doormage was.

"DOWN!"

A single note. A portal opened at my left. I lunged forward, tackled Liette at the waist, and brought us both down.

A body came leaping from the portal, a tall and slender man dressed in tight-fitting leathers and silver jewelry. He cackled as he sailed over us, his hands just narrowly avoiding brushing against my back as he struggled to grab me. I pulled us down, forced us to the ground, covered her with my body.

I couldn't let him touch her.

He tumbled from one wall to another, disappearing into another portal. I pulled Liette to her feet, seized her by the shoulder, snarled into her face with a desperation I didn't think I was capable of feeling anymore.

"Run. Don't talk. Get clear. Find the others. Get to the bridge. Get out of here. Don't stop. Don't let him touch you." I held her by the face. "Do *not* let him touch you."

She didn't talk. I could see she wanted to, but she didn't. Good. I didn't want her to see this next part.

I shoved her. She ran. I heard her footsteps fade into the distance as she disappeared, unmolested.

Which made sense.

Since he was trying to kill *me* and all.

I slid the Cacophony back into his sheath, ignored his protest. I drew my sword, walked slowly down the alley, ears open, breath still. The gun was good for most mages. But against the man I was fighting, a sword was...

Well, to be honest, no weapon was of much use against him. But a sword was at least better for fighting someone who liked striking from behind.

Not behind, I thought as I heard a note. I looked to the street. *Below.*

I leapt away just as a portal opened up beneath me. A pair of slender hands wrapped in black gloves and adorned with thick silver rings shot out, groping feebly at where I'd just been. I lashed out with my sword, caught one across the forearm as they withdrew.

A shriek rang out from above.

The man appeared out of a portal on a nearby rooftop, clutching his wounded hand. Through a face fraught with silver piercings, he glared at me spitefully, looking more like I'd wounded his pride than his flesh.

"Fuck me, Sal," he hissed, "do you ever stop being such a poor sport? A more proper mage would have died by now out of courtesy alone."

"Quoir," I spat. "I fucking knew it'd be you working with those two."

"We became friendly after that torrid night when we listened to Vraki." He gestured, sarcastic. "What an incredible leader we had that he should be killed by the likes of you."

"You, him, and every other fucker there that night," I snarled. "You all deserve the same."

The fear had burned out in my veins. Now I was pissed. Pissed that they'd done this. Pissed that they'd struck out at me here. Pissed that they'd said that about Darrish.

. . . Pissed that they might be right.

But the beauty of fights is you don't have to work out complex feelings during them. So I spread my arms out wide, taunting.

"You couldn't kill me that night, either," I chuckled. "Quoirmuiro ki Thanthros. Empress's 'finest' assassin. And it took thirty-three of you to bring me down."

He sniffed, offended, and gestured to the tattoos across his biceps: hands adorned in fabulous jewels, clasped together in an endless chain.

"It's Quoir the Eternal Knock," he sneered. "And it only took one of you to kill Darrish."

"Don't say that," I roared at him. "Do *not* fucking say that unless you're ready to come down here and fight me."

"I intended to. Wholly. The moment I found out you had the audacity to put me on your farce of a list. But I put you behind me, moved on. Until Chiriel told me what happened." His face twisted into a grimace of metal. "Darrish deserved better than you."

He pointed to one end of the alley. A portal winked into existence. Grishok, whole and unharmed, lumbered out.

"You okay?" Quoir asked.

"I'm always okay," he rumbled. "I didn't deserve Darrish. She was outcast for us. Went Vagrant because of us. *Killed* because of us. We make that right."

I moved toward the other mouth of the alley. Another portal appeared. Chiriel and her horrid armoire appeared, violin in hand.

"Only in your arrogance, *Red Cloud*, could you think that you could hunt us and not be hunted in return." She pressed her bow to her violin. "Honor demands your blood. *Love* demands your death."

"You fuckers have it all wrong," I growled, backing up as much as I could. I drew the Cacophony, but what the fuck good would he do here? The moment I turned on any of them, the others would get me. "It's not what you think."

If they had called me a liar, I would have liked that. If they had cursed me and insulted me, I could have worked with that. Any time I kept them talking was time I could think.

Maybe they knew that, too. Maybe that's why they fell silent. I held my breath, raised my weapon in impotent warning. Chiriel played the beginning of a note. Grishok advanced. Quoir's smile grew broad. The armoire stirred. The Cacophony seethed, indignant. The Lady sang.

And *that* is what made them pause.

Because it hadn't come from any of them.

"Who is that?" Chiriel looked around. "Did you invite anyone else to—"

She fell silent. There was no need to finish the question. It was already answered.

Something appeared in front of her armoire—a shape wrapped in a cloak and wielding a dirty iron blade. They flung open the doors to the armoire. The kite vipers peered out, puzzled as the figure hurled a flask into their den. It exploded in a cloud of smoke. The figure hurled the doors shut and vanished.

The Quickmage.

The one from before.

"*CHOKING!*" Chiriel dropped her instrument, grabbed her throat as smoke wisped out from the armoire's doors, the furniture thrashing about as her pets bashed themselves against its walls. "*IT'S IN OUR LUNGS! GET RID OF IT! LET US OUT!*"

Grishok, unlike me, didn't waste time trying to figure out what was going on. The moment Chiriel started shrieking, he started running at me. He swung his club overhead, ready to strike. The earth shuddered with a heavy weight.

Which was his huge body collapsing. A great wound had opened in his tendon, hobbling him and bringing him low. He turned around, glared at the injury. A flash of darkness at his flank drew his attention. He swung. The Quickmage ducked under the blow, jammed the dirty iron blade into Grishok's armpit. He roared as his assailant vanished in an instant.

I would have acted. But I was stunned.

Usually, when someone else shows up like this, it's not to help me.

"Grishok!" Quoir snarled from above. "Walk it off, you big baby!"

"I can't," the huge man rumbled. "The complicated tendons take time to fix. She's got a fucking Quickmage!"

Quoir blinked. "That was a Quickmage?"

His eyes grew wide with realization. A shadow appeared behind him. The blade drew back, struck.

It only caught a hair from Quoir's luxurious head as a portal opened up beneath his feet. He dropped into it, vanished. Didn't reappear. He always had been cautious. And nobody wanted to fight a Quickmage.

Including me.

So when the shadow vanished and reappeared at my side, I put the gun in their face and I didn't feel fucking bad about it.

"Here to fight me?" I asked.

I caught a brief flash of a man's face beneath a hood—weary eyes, pursed lips, scraggly hair half-hidden in shadow. The Quickmage held up his hands, shook his head.

"Good enough for now."

I took off. He took off with me. We ran as far as we could.

I wouldn't stay up for much longer.

So when we got as far as my fear would allow me to believe was safe, I damn near collapsed and shit myself out of exhaustion. To my credit, I settled instead for collapsing against the wall and gasping for breath.

A flask was thrust toward me. And, for the first time in a long time, I was glad that this one was just water.

"Hurry," the Quickmage said—man's voice, didn't care, I was gulping down water. "We need to move again soon. They won't stay down for long."

"They won't stay down at all, dumbfuck," I gasped as I finished the flask. "One of them fucking *regenerates*. I need to get to the bridge."

"Too obvious. They'll head there next."

"I didn't fucking ask, did I?" I swallowed the last few drops of water, tossed the flask away. "They don't call you Quickmages for your brains, do they? Thanks for the water and the other part." I waved a hand as I limped off. "The saving me and shit."

He caught my hand. It felt warm on my skin. My eyes grew wide. My body went cold.

"It isn't safe, Sal!" he said.

He knew my name.

And I knew his.

I grabbed his wrist. I slammed him against the wall, felt the breath explode out of his lungs. I put the Cacophony in his face. By the glint of his burning brass, I could see the visage beneath the hood. Its sharp angles. Its wrinkles where a haughty grin pulled. Its eyes...

That I once looked into so lovingly before that dark night.

I swallowed hard. I looked into the face of Jindu the Blade.

I pulled the Cacophony's hammer back.

TWENTY-SEVEN

TOADBACK

Have you ever wondered where things went wrong?

Not just in general, but with people. Specific people. Have you ever had someone who you go back through every moment with them and run through it, breath by breath, wondering if you could pick out the exact point where everything got ruined? Wondering if maybe you could fix *that* moment and, in doing so, fix everything?

I do that sometimes.

Maybe more than sometimes, if I'm honest.

I think back to the times I said something I didn't mean—or something I did mean, but wished I meant it in a better way. I think back to the times I let things go that I shouldn't have, the things I buried down deep that I didn't want to. And I think back to them and their smiles and their eyes and their lying and their problems and the things I did to them and the things they did to me and...

Yeah.

It gets difficult to keep track of it all. Too difficult, honestly. The times that hurt get mixed up with the times that felt so good. It's hard to pry apart the times he roared at me with the times he held me gently after I'd seen something I hadn't wanted to and needed it. It's hard to separate the times where he said the things he couldn't take back from the times where he said exactly what I needed to hear without knowing it. The jokes he made get tangled up with the things he did with the way we fought with the love we made and so on and so on and...

Until you just get angry, I guess.

You get angry about the things that happened. You get angry about the things you can't have anymore. You get angry about how good it all felt and how bad it all ended. And then you just stop thinking about it because you feel your chest on fire and your breath stopped short like you're about to get your throat ripped out.

And that's all you feel. Until you can't remember feeling any other way.

Have you ever had someone like that?

Most of us do. That's just what happens. Unlucky. But most people are unlucky.

If you're truly lucky, you don't have anyone like that.

And if you have several someones like that—well, my condolences.

I had that. There, in that alley in Toadback. My arm on that someone's throat, my gun in his face, tears in my eyes. And I had that problem. When I looked into those eyes, the big dark ones that I used to love seeing in the morning, I went through it again. All of it. Every moment. Every breath. Trying to find out where it went wrong. Trying to find a reason not to pull the trigger right then and there.

I saw the first night we met, when my life in the Imperial army stopped being so lonely.

I felt the heat in my face from the first time I ever cussed him out, the rush of shame that followed saying it.

I heard the first time I'd made him laugh—*really* laugh, not the dignified airy noise he made when he was amused, but the ugly cackle he made when he was truly happy.

I remembered the cold wind hitting hot blood—my blood—the night I'd lost him, my powers, and the sky.

The night his blade had given me my deepest scar.

And I couldn't find a reason not to. A reason not to press my arm tighter against his throat. A reason not to let my finger curl around the trigger a little tighter. If he had just helped me, I didn't care. If I died because of killing him, I didn't care. It felt like I couldn't stop myself.

...*And* I couldn't make myself.

I didn't know why, then. Why I felt so conflicted. I still don't know, if I'm honest.

Though, if I had to guess...

"Say it."

Maybe I wanted it to not be my fault.

"Say it, you fucker."

Jindunamalar. Jindu the Blade. The man I'd loved, once. The man I'd fought with, bled with, killed with. The man who'd cut me deeper than I thought I could ever be cut and watched my magic bleed out. He wasn't fighting me. His arms, and their blade, hung at his side. His face, weary and pale, could not even muster enough to look scared. Or angry. Or anything, really, except just...

Tired.

"What do you want me to say?" he half asked, half gasped.

"Say it wasn't your fault," I all but spat at him. "Say you never meant to. Say you wish you could take it all back."

He stared at me. No pleas. No bargains. Just...those eyes. That exhaustion.

"Say it!"

"I can't do that," he said softly.

"Why not?" I wanted to know. I wanted to know why he couldn't just say something so fucking terrible I could pull the trigger and be done with it, him and every last breath between us.

"Because it was my fault," he said. "Because I meant to do it." He swallowed hard. "And because it doesn't matter what I wish."

Now how in the hell did he manage to say the one thing that managed to piss me off worse?

And how in the hell was it still not enough to make me pull the trigger?

My mouth quavered. My eyes got hot. My blood boiled. The Cacophony burned in my hand, begging me to do it, to give myself the release.

"Then why the fuck are you here?"

But something else in me couldn't do it. Not yet. Not like this.

Smashing him across the mouth with the gun's hilt, though? Yeah, I could do that.

And I did.

"Why the fuck are you here? Why the fuck did you do that back there if not to deny? If not to grovel? If not to tell me how it wasn't your fucking fault?"

And only then did his face change. Only then did the weariness, the exhaustion, give way to something else. Tears formed in his eyes. He shuddered, choked on them.

And I don't think I'd noticed until then how much he'd changed.

He was thinner now. Or maybe just hollower. He was still lean and muscular, but he no longer brimmed with the effortless energy I had once seen. His hair was still long and dark, but streaked more with gray and messier, evidence of where he'd trimmed it with his own knife—and sloppily. He was still handsome—time and stress couldn't take that from him, though from the hollow eyes and sunken cheeks, they sure fucking tried.

And the blade...his blade...the black blade that'd ruined everything.

It was gone.

The dirty weapon hanging from his dirty glove was barely fit to be called a weapon. In the hands of a Quickmage—let alone a Quickmage like Jindu the Blade—even a nail could be a weapon that kills hundreds.

That part hadn't changed, either.

"I don't know why," he said. "I just...didn't know what else to do."

Despite myself, despite the Cacophony, despite everything boiling inside me—I could feel my grip on the trigger loosening, my arm on his throat slackening. Maybe I don't know why I did that, either. Or maybe I knew all too well what it felt like to just act because you couldn't think.

He took in a deep breath and spoke.

I didn't stop him.

"After what happened with Vraki, after I listened to him, after I betrayed you for him, after you killed him..." He shook his head, shuddered. "I... stopped knowing. Stopped knowing what I was doing or what I was supposed to do. I just... stopped. And I couldn't figure out how to keep going after what happened, what I'd done. I just..."

His legs trembled. He fell.

I didn't stop that, either.

"I didn't know what else to do. I didn't know how to keep going without you, without Vraki, without anyone but this sword." He wrapped his fingers tighter around the hilt, the way we all hug things that stay with us when everyone else doesn't. "So I just... picked it up. And I started looking for you."

"Why?" I growled. "How did you think this was going to go? Did you expect me to break down into tears and forgive you?"

He sniffed, looked up at me with a grin I remembered. A grin that haunted my dreams long after I'd put his name on my list.

"Actually, I expected you to kill me."

I leveled the gun at him once more. "And if I did?"

He stared past the barrel, past the Cacophony's brass, looked at me. Not the gun.

"Then I die."

Have you ever had a moment? A breath? A single second where you can see everything going wrong right in front of you?

Yeah. Me too. A lot of them, honestly.

And I go over them a lot. I run them over and over in my head before I sleep and I fight them off when they come creeping back to me when I wake up. I wonder what I could have done differently, how I could have made it work. You do, too, probably.

And you also probably tell yourself, like I do, that each painful moment taught you something and that next time will be different.

What I'm asking is have you ever had a moment when you know you're about to do something really fucking stupid and you don't know why?

Yeah.

"And if I don't?"

Me too.

He slumped there, on his knees, and stared up at me.

"Then I want to help."

I held his gaze, and him, beneath the Cacophony. I watched the steam coiling off the gun's barrel eagerly, the narrowing of eyes, his grinning dragon maw. He'd been waiting for this. *We'd* been waiting for this. This moment. A very long time.

He was really going to hate this.

But I bit back the outrage he sent searing into my hand as I eased the hammer forward, pulled my finger from the trigger. And as I slid him back into his sheath, I found the heat tolerable enough. He was right to be angry. I knew it.

But shit, sometimes I'm just real stupid, I guess.

"How long have you been following me?"

Not so stupid as to help him up, though. I spun, took my sword in hand, started walking. I'd already spent too much time here—Chiriel, Grishok, and Quoir wouldn't be far behind. My ears were open, ready for the sound of feet behind me, of violins playing or whatever the fuck else they had.

What I expected to be able to do against them, I wasn't sure. I knew how fucked I was. But I'd be fucked twice before I made it easier on them. And so I kept walking.

And Jindu kept following.

"Months? Longer?" he replied. "I picked up the trail at Lowstaff, then I lost you when you headed north."

"You always were a shit tracker."

"I agree, but I was still able to find you after the Valley."

The Valley, I thought, *and Darrish.*

I swallowed back that pain. I had bigger agonies to worry about.

"Back with Velline," I said, "the Quickmage I fought, that was you, wasn't it?"

"Both times, yes. I tried not to intervene too often."

"Why not?"

"Mostly because I worried you'd kill me."

I grunted. "Reasonable."

"You have a lot of people pissed off at you, I notice."

"That's an interesting thing to say for a man I just decided not to kill yet."

We rounded out of the alleys and emerged on Toadback's waterfront. The shops and cafés had been emptied. What few patrons remained were busy fleeing for the bridge. The Yuber River roared beside us, its dark waters crashing against the streets. Its rushing tide was a match for the crowd of refugees ahead swarming over the bridge. A thick knot of them choked the passage as they fought to escape the carnage wrecking the town.

"Well, I'm sorry, but it *is* kind of pertinent to the situation," Jindu, who apparently had a hard time figuring out how not to get hit with things, continued. "I tried to warn you about Toadback. About Chiriel and the others. And when you went toward Torle, I thought you'd decided and I wouldn't—"

"Wouldn't what?" I interjected, annoyed. "Wouldn't have to face me?"

He fell silent for a moment. "Yes. Yes, I was afraid of that. This. I still am. But I don't think you can take on all of them."

"I could with the right shells."

"*And* the Revolution?"

"More shells."

"*And* the Imperium?"

"All right, fucker, I get it," I snapped. "I don't need this shit, either. I'm not here to kill anyone that's not in my way. I'm here to get someone across this bridge and then to figure out what to do from there."

"Right." He paused. "Someone. But doesn't it seem—"

And without thinking, I whirled on him. I grabbed him by his collar before he could act, slammed him against a nearby wall. Blood boiled behind my eyes.

"Don't," I snarled. "You don't get to talk about her like that. You don't get to talk like that at *all*. Not around me. Whatever the fuck you think you know about me and this situation, you don't. And if you want to help, you'll fucking help and not ask questions. Understand?"

He nodded slowly. "Should I help you right now?"

I furrowed my brow, snorted. "Obviously."

A faint whining caught my ear.

He inclined his head. "Okay, then."

He vanished out of my hands. I felt movement behind my back. Steel clanged and sparks flashed at the corners of my eyes. I turned, saw a harpoon-sized bolt clatter to the streets. Jindu stood before me, blade drawn and seared from where he'd just deflected it.

And out on the river, more were coming.

Black boats whirred up the Yuber. Far across the water, I could see dark-clad silhouettes raising monstrously sized bolts into massive crossbows sporting imposing pulleys and motors. Dragonkiller bows. You didn't typically see them outside of the Revolution, who crafted them.

But that's the thing about thieves like the Ashmouths.

They steal.

"Fuck."

I tore off running down the waterfront. Crossbows fired and the sky was filled with bolts. Jindu flashed at the edge of my vision, a shadow darting in and out. And wherever he appeared, sparks flew and another one of the massive missiles went flying harmlessly out of the way. Those that got by punched through storefronts and smashed through café tables, impaling themselves in the waterfront.

When I loved him, not a single one would have gotten past Jindu.

He was slowing down. Getting weaker.

I'd always thought that knowledge would make me happy.

"Fucking watch it, would you?" I shouted at him as I leapt over a bolt that went skidding across the stones.

"You're the one with the gun," he replied, between bouts of vanishing. "Shoot back."

"They're out of range, asshole! It's not magic!"

"It quite visibly *is* magic."

It was a good thing I had bigger problems because otherwise I would have shot him for that.

The chaos at the bridge loomed into view. From afar, it had looked like a disaster. Up close, it looked much worse.

The refugees had scattered in a halo, trying to pass through a skirmish that had broken out at the bridge's mouth. Agne stood there, snarling as she tore a saw-bladed spear from a Revolutionary Twenty-Second and jammed it through his chest. Severium smoke stained her skin from where gunpikes had, and continued to, open fire on her, explosive charges skidding off her impervious skin. A small pile of Revolutionary corpses lay around her feet, the rest of them quite alive and fighting to break forward against the one-woman bulwark.

Well, four-woman, two-man bulwark, I guess.

Yria lurked behind Agne, her eyes bright with magic. She spun portals here and there, vanishing Revolutionaries one way, refugees another. Liette and Urda were busily scribbling on various piles of debris that had piled up, spellwrighting them to explode, to turn to tar, to do anything to slow down the Revolutionaries. Amid all the carnage, Meret and Sindra bellowed to get befuddled and terrified people across the bridge. The few peacekeepers that had remained had joined with them.

They were at their limit. That much was visible. But they'd managed to keep things under control. We could still escape.

"Come on," I said as I pushed past the crowds and Liette and Urda's barricades. "We have to go."

"What?" Urda asked, glancing up from scrawling sigils. "We can't go now!"

"These people need us, Sal!" Meret shouted.

"The moment we turn our back, these Revolution fucks will conscript them," Sindra snarled, pushing a hesitant refugee through a portal. "We can't leave them."

"We have to," I said. "Things are about to get a lot fucking worse."

"Sal," Liette said, "we can't."

"And I said we *have* to," I roared. "There's no time to explain—"

"WE CAN'T LEAVE BECAUSE THIS IS YOUR FUCKING FAULT!"

Sindra's words cut through me like a blade. Her glare was alive with animal anger. Her sword was slick with blood. So were her hands.

"The Revolution is here because of you, the Ashmouths are here because of you, *everyone* is here because of you!" she screamed back. "We can't keep fucking running away from *your* shit!"

I'd been hit a lot that day. Harder than I thought I could be hit and still stay standing, if I'm honest. And, if I'm continuing to be honest, when I looked into Sindra's eyes and saw she meant every damn word that she jammed into my chest, I wanted to curl up and die. I wanted to just let it wash over me, drown me, quench the desires of everyone who had every reason to want to see me disappear.

Maybe the real reason I didn't is one I'll never know.

But at the time, I had one answer.

Spite's a funny thing. It's never spoken of highly—even the word is diminutive and flighty-sounding. But a lot of great things have been accomplished through spite. Empires have been destroyed and kings have been ruined by spite. People can call it petty and maybe that's true for some.

But if you're a special kind of person—a person with more anger than sense, a person who feels their teeth clench when someone tells them to have a good day and they don't know why—then spite is something else.

It's powerful. It's endless. And it's as easy as fucking breathing.

My mouth ran dry of curses, left only hot breath. My eyes

twitched as I swept them around the bridge-turned-battlefield, taking everything in—the alleys, the rooftops, the dramatic angles. The Revolution swarmed forward, struggling to wear Agne down. The engines of the Ashmouth boats roared ever louder. The refugees flooded past me in fleeting shadows.

I took a deep breath. I fished three shells out of my satchel, ran my fingers across the sigils on their casings. I drew the Cacophony, felt his indignant heat course up my arm as I flipped his chamber open and started loading.

"Yria," I said. "Stop the portals."

She looked at me like I was stupid. But she kept quiet like I knew what I was doing. And when I pointed to the rooftops, her eyes followed.

"Keep your eyes on the roofs there and there," I said. "When the kite vipers show up, take care of them."

Urda protested. Liette shouted something. But Yria just grunted. The portals stopped. The refugees tore across the battlefield with their heads down, desperate to avoid severium charges caroming off Agne's skin.

I ignored the screaming. I ignored the questions. I couldn't afford to listen to them now. After all, they were counting on me. I kept my eyes open as I glanced across the carnage. I kept my ears open as—

There.

A note. A flash. A portal opened above me. Grishok's massive shape came plummeting down.

"AGNE!"

I had the time to shriek a single word and pray that she knew what it meant. I aimed up, pulled the trigger twice. Grishok's body trembled, shuddered as two Discordance shells slammed into his chest and erupted. The walls of sound smashed off each other, and everything else, rending the pavement apart and knocking refugees to their asses.

The Mendmage did little more than grunt his displeasure. But his great bulk flew backward, hurtling toward Agne. Her hands shot up, caught him by his throat and his antlers. With a snarl and a note of the Lady's magic ringing in her ear, she whirled his body about like it was a toy and sent it flying into the Revolutionaries.

That was one good twist of fortune.

Another note played. I caught the flash of light. Chiriel and her armoire appeared on a distant rooftop. Her violin shrieked. The doors flew open. Her shimmering black pets came sweeping out in a screeching cloud.

A portal opened in front of them, swallowing them as they poured into it. I saw Yria's portal open again, miles away, the confused kite vipers swarming in a befuddled cloud as they pulled out far from the violin that directed them.

There was another good one.

"Fucking *well done*!" I howled.

"Yeah." Yria cackled—tried to cackle. Her voice faltered. Her throat tightened. "Yeah, it's...I...I can't..."

She teetered forward. Her legs all but snapped out from under her. Urda screamed, abandoning his tools as he rushed forward to catch her. He struggled to hold her weight, looked up at me with tears pouring out of his eyes.

"*SHE'S DONE TOO MUCH!*" he screamed. "*YOU FUCKING MONSTER, CAN'T YOU SEE SHE'S DONE TOO MUCH?*"

Another pain. More words to haunt me later. And later is when I'd deal with them.

"We're clear now!" Sindra shouted to be heard above the fracas. "Come on! *NOW, NOW!*"

The remaining refugees—mercifully, few—came surging forward to join the others as they rushed across the bridge. Urda helped his sister, Meret joining him in supporting her as they took off with the rest of them.

"Big lady!" Sindra snapped. "We're moving!"

Agne glanced over her shoulder. Not with contempt. Nor even with anger. I could have handled those. But the unbothered, casual displeasure with which she regarded us, narrowing her eyes as if considering whether it would simply be easier to kill us and everyone else.

In the end, she shrugged and started off after the others at a pace that was far too unhurried to be healthy.

"Nice work, shitface." Sindra seemed less bothered than I did, slapping me on the back like she hadn't just cut me to my core a moment ago. "Let's get the fuck out of here while we can."

The kite vipers wouldn't be away forever and Grishok would eventually get free. She was right. We took off running, bringing up the rear of the refugees. As we rushed across the bridge, I saw the white froth as the Ashmouth boats came roaring up to us. I heard the crossbows click.

I grabbed Sindra, pulled her back as a harpoon-sized bolt blew in front of us. I aimed the Cacophony as much as I dared, squeezed the trigger. Hoarfrost struck the water and erupted. Ice froze across the river, sweeping forward like frigid serpents as they rushed toward the boats. Ashmouths went screaming, launched overboard as great icicles punched skyward and splintered their boats into shards.

A shadow flitted in front of me. Jindu reappeared briefly, perched upon the bridge's railing, and raised an eyebrow.

"Out of range?" he asked.

Then vanished again.

"They were closer that time!" I spat to the empty air as I took off running in pursuit of the others, Sindra at my side. "Sorry. Old relationship."

"Oh, good. I saw him flying around and figured since he wasn't trying to kill any of us, he must belong to you." She glanced over her shoulder. "They aren't following." She chuckled, slapped at her prosthetic leg. "Good for fucking me, huh?"

"Yeah." I looked ahead, to the shrinking shapes of the refugees. "How many?"

"Huh?"

"How many do you think we saved?"

"Don't worry about it."

"How the fuck can I not?" I snapped at her. "This is my fault. You said so yourself."

"I did, it is, and you did the best you could cleaning up your mess." She glared at me sidelong. "And frankly, I've known you long enough to know a lot of the stories about you are birdshit. We were never going to help everyone. And if you worry about it, you'll drive yourself mad. It's just not possible. Not for me. Not for you. Not even for both us, the big lady, and the two shits."

"But Meret—"

"Meret has his mind on the people who still need him. Maybe if you could do a little more of that, you could— *LOOK OUT!*"

Just.

Give me a minute.

What happened next was...I still have trouble thinking about it. It's one of those moments I think I'll never really be able to look at. Or one I'll never be able to stop looking at.

I don't know what it was. Maybe I was too worried about the Vagrants. Or the Revolutionaries. Or the refugees. Or whether all the shit they'd said—about me, about Darrish, about all of it—was true.

I don't know. I don't think it does any good to wonder.

But I was distracted. I wasn't thinking. My ears weren't open. Neither were my eyes. I didn't see the air shimmering. I didn't see the light stirring in front of me.

But Sindra did.

And I only heard the Lady's song by the time she had already shoved me out of the way.

Quoir.

I had forgotten about Quoir.

He came leaping out of the portal, his smile alive with joy. He tackled Sindra head on, wrapped his arms around her, laughed. She snarled, shoved him off. He went caroming into me. I smashed the hilt of the Cacophony against his face. He screamed, staggered away.

Ten seconds. More or less.

That's all it took.

That's as long as Quoir needed.

He swayed, looked up at me, his smile white and red, blood trailing from the wound I'd just given him. And yet he smiled. He smiled at me like I had just walked into the punch line of the best joke in the world without realizing it.

His smile grew broader. His eyes sparkled. He held up his hand. Something dark and fleshy, glistening with blood, sat plain in his palm. An organ. I couldn't recognize it. But I knew who it came from.

"Oops." He tossed it into the river. "Missed."

He laughed, tumbled over the edge. I moved to chase him.

"Sal?"

Sindra stumbled forward. She clutched at her belly. Her skin grew incredibly pale with every breath she took. She stared at me, fear and pain in her eyes.

"I don't... feel..."

Blood trickled out of her mouth. Then burst. Bile and fluid splashed onto the ground. She collapsed to her knees, looked at me through a face pale with terror and illness. I ran toward her. I grabbed her as she fell. I pulled her close to me.

I don't know why.

I already knew it was too late.

No one had ever used magic like Quoir had. No one ever thought you could target an individual organ and teleport it out of a person's body. It had made him feared among his enemies and his allies, revered by his Empress. It was a precise art. Left no room for error. He had to be close to pull it off.

He had to touch you.

I learned later it was part of her lungs that Quoir had taken out of her. Not the whole thing. Just enough to make it messy. Her entire body had broken down within seconds. She'd choked on what remained of it. It was a horrific way to die.

And I couldn't save her from it.

When the air shimmered next to me again, I saw it. When Quoir's hand came reaching out for me, I saw that, too. I just held Sindra there. And I closed my eyes. And I waited for it to happen.

"Stop it."

But it didn't.

"Let go!"

Quoir didn't touch me.

"LET ME GO!"

He screamed.

I opened my eyes. I saw Quoir, not far away, his arm caught in his own portal, desperately trying to pull it back out. Beside me, that arm extended from another portal. It held there, rigid and trembling in the air, as if against his own will.

A note rang out.

Not the Lady's.

Not anything I'd recognized. This one was deeper. More rolling. Like an old, ancient bell.

I followed the sound to its source. And she stood twenty feet away.

Liette's hand was extended. Her fingers were outstretched. Her eyes were dark and alive with stars.

She clenched her fist. There was a loud snapping sound. Quoir's deadly limb contorted into unnatural shapes. On the other side of the portal, he screamed.

"STOP! STOP IT! STOP!"

It did not stop. Liette took a step closer. The skin of Quoir's arm rippled. A step closer. It began to unravel, like cloth. A step closer. It got worse—the flesh peeled back, desiccated, and became Dust. The sinew of his arm was untangled, strand by strand. The veins were dissected, string by string. The shattered bones grew visible beneath it.

She was taking him apart. Layer by layer.

"LET ME GO! LET ME GO! GET OFF!"

Quoir felt it. All of it. His screams tore my ears apart, as surely as Liette tore him apart. He struggled to get free, but she wouldn't let him. He thrashed, trapped there as the unraveling continued down his arm, past his elbow.

I heard a note. There was a scream. A splatter. The half-unraveled arm flopped to the ground, severed and twitching like a fish half-skinned.

He'd closed the portal. Severed his own arm to escape.

I stared at it. But I could barely see it. I could barely think or remember where I was or remember anything, for that matter, but the cold body in my hands. I looked down at Sindra, at the horror seared across her face, at the words that she couldn't say trapped behind her eyes.

I didn't weep.

Not then.

Not until the sounds of everything—all songs, all fears, all pains—went soft. And I felt Liette settle down beside me. And I felt her wrap her arms around me and pull me close to her.

And I cried.

And I let her hold me.

Until I could remember how to walk again.

TWENTY-EIGHT

NEW VIGIL

This was the one part about people that Ozhma was no good at.

She'd once been assigned to deliver a case of Avonin & Family batch 182, "The Wedding Whiskey," it had been affectionately called, owing to how often it was requested for such occasions. So her impending delight had been dashed when she'd arrived and found a feast gone cold, a party gone quiet, and an old man sitting where his daughter should have been getting married.

He'd said nothing. Never explained what had happened. But the wedding had clearly not gone as planned. And the old man had only a few words to thank her before he started sobbing. She hadn't left—she wasn't a complete monster—but the truth was that tragedy sat unwell with her. People's pain was terrifying to her, sometimes.

How could it not be? Pain was wild, unpredictable. You never knew what someone in pain was going to do or ask of you or how to give it to them or if you even wanted to.

She'd simply sat there, silently, trying her best not to say anything.

As she sat here, silently, trying to avoid the sound of Sal's quiet sobbing.

The Vagrant wasn't calling attention to it, of course. She'd simply leaned away from Ozhma, covered her eyes with a hand and just... stopped. Stopped talking, cursing, drinking. Everything except shuddering softly as a quiet, pained noise escaped now and again.

What *was* the protocol here, after all? Offer consolation? To Sal the fucking Cacophony? Tell her it was all going to be all right, when it was obvious to everyone that came within six feet of her that it was *not* going to be all right? When she had just spent hours upon hours explicitly explaining how things had become so incredibly not all right?

Offer scorn? Harsh criticism? Tough love? That seemed like an *excellent* way to get smashed in the mouth with a tankard, so maybe not. And even if it didn't, Ozhma found she couldn't bring herself to do it.

So she sat, awkwardly, and waited as Sal's voice went steadily softer until it went quiet.

"Sorry." Sal wiped her eyes, sniffed. "Sorry about that. What did you say?"

"Oh! Um." Ozhma fumbled around with her notes, not quite sure what to do. "I was going... well, do you need, like, a minute? That sounded like it was... um..."

"It was," Sal said. "It really was." She sighed, shrugged. "But it's not like it's going to get better anytime soon, so we might as well keep going. What'd you ask earlier?"

"Right, right." Ozhma flipped through her papers, squinted. "I wanted to know about Quickmages. I'm still not quite sure what they are, despite *two* of them featuring in your account. Velline and Jindu." She paused, looked embarrassed. "Um. Am *I* allowed to talk about him? He seemed a touchy subject."

"Yeah, it's fine. He's—" She stopped, touched a scar. "Anyway, a Quickmage's magic enhances their speed and reflexes to unbelievable degrees. They can move so fast and react so quickly that the rest of the world slows to a crawl."

"That explains why you couldn't see them fighting."

"It also explains why there's not many of them and the vast majority of them work for the Imperium," she said. "How do you fight a guy that can see you pulling a sword and cut you in half before you've even thought about touching the hilt?"

"Well, I mean, you tell me," Ozhma said. "You seem to have held your own against a few."

"I've gotten lucky a few times," Sal replied. "I've never fought Velline alone. If I did, she'd have torn me apart."

"But she didn't." Ozhma thumbed through her notes, muttering to herself. "In fact, a number of your foes seem to forgo killing you to confront you first. Chiriel, Tretta, Velline." She caught herself. "Those are all women examples, I realize, but your ability to enrage people across genders is truly remarkable."

"Fuck, woman, go easy on me, would you?" Sal half winced, half grinned. "And you've noticed mages are dramatic. Vagrants love making speeches before they fight. *I* love making speeches. We try to do each other that courtesy."

"If that were true, you probably wouldn't have killed Necla," she said. "And it's not just mages who do it, either. I have a theory." She paused, looked up over her papers timidly. "That is, um, if you'd like to hear it."

Sal sighed, rubbed the bridge of her nose. "Go ahead."

"Well, have you noticed it's very rarely about the people who you've pissed off?" Ozhma glanced through papers, reviewing her notes. "Like, I'm sure it happens, but most of the people who claim to need to kill you are also claiming they're doing it in defense of someone else. The Revolution, the Imperium, um... Darrish."

Sal tensed. "Yeah."

"Do you ever wonder if they do that because they worry they're too much like you?"

Sal glowered. "I didn't. But go on."

"Well, you're pretty destructive, don't get me wrong, but it's not like the Revolution or Imperium is known for restraint. And it doesn't sound like these Vagrants particularly cared about the people, either. But you at least tried to get people across the bridge."

"Well, yeah. It was my fault. I had to."

"Right. Because if you didn't, you would be something of a monster, right? Not saying you *are*, just saying—"

"Yeah, I get it. What's your point?"

"So, it's not like destroying a bunch of shit in the name of protecting people is exactly *good*. But if you're destroying a bunch of shit and not doing that, it's worse. I think your enemies need to make it clear that they're fighting for someone else because they worry that, otherwise, they'd be like you. Just killing and breaking and burning with no purpose."

"Well, thanks for that, asshole."

"No, I mean they *think* you do that. So they want to *not* be like you. If that makes sense."

"Not really. But I'll confess that I haven't spent a whole lot of time contemplating it." She smacked her lips. "I'll also confess that I'm probably not going to spend a whole lot longer contemplating it. Maybe another minute or so."

"Well, it *might* be useful for figuring out how to avoid conflict."

"You can't avoid conflict. You can only face it when it comes."

"I..." She was about to say that made no sense, but after a while with the woman, Ozhma could see how it *could* make sense. "Well, that seems like a pretty awful way to live."

"I completely agree."

Ozhma furrowed her brow, her mouth hanging open. "Has anyone ever told you you're fairly cryptic for a woman famously ill-tempered and foulmouthed?"

"Does cryptic mean 'incredible ass'?"

"You know it doesn't."

"Then you know no one's told me that before."

A knock at the door mercifully smothered this line of dialogue in the crib. It creaked open to reveal Cavric, face creased with weariness.

"There's been a situation up top," he said.

"The kind that needs me?" Sal asked.

"Yes, hence why I called it a 'situation' and not anything else," Cavric sighed. "I hate to interrupt but could you..."

"I don't mind," Ozhma chirped. "I can wait."

"You don't have to if you don't want to."

"She probably should," Cavric interjected, his voice just a touch too chilling. "Really."

Sal didn't miss the warning in his voice. Neither did Ozhma.

"All right, then." Sal's large chair groaned as she pulled herself out of it and stomped toward the door. "Stay here."

She faltered in mid-stride. Ozhma froze as Sal stood beside her, the shadow cast by the flickering light falling over her. She flinched when Sal raised a hand. But when it landed on her shoulder, it felt... like it belonged there.

"Thank you, Ozhma."

She squeezed Ozhma's shoulder gently. And then she was gone.

The door slammed. The two of them disappeared. And Ozhma was left alone in the room. She touched the warm spot where Sal had squeezed, found that without the Vagrant's presence, she was getting slightly anxious.

What was going on upstairs? she wondered. What had Cavric meant by what he said? What could be bad enough that it required Sal to be up there herself? Had the emissaries returned? Did they have more time? Were they about to attack even now? Should she be running? Staying? *Crying?*

She exploded out of her chair, started pacing, started pulling at the collar of her shirt. It was too hot down here. She'd spent too long here. Too long in this room. This room that shouldn't even be here.

That last thought sank in, slowed her feet as her shoes clacked across the hardwood floor. She found herself contemplating her surroundings—the pelt rugs, the nice tables, the exquisite chair Sal herself took. The polished wood and moody furnishings would be out of place anywhere in the Scar, let alone the cellar of a war-torn city. And yet here they were. Sal's throne stood in the middle of a beautiful living room deep underground with perfect furniture, perfect lighting, and...

One door.

One plain, boring door at the very back of the room. So ordinary and unassuming that Ozhma had barely looked at it throughout this entire time. But now, her eyes fixed on it, its ordinariness too glaring to ignore.

She stared at it. And the longer she stared, the bigger it seemed to grow. And the more certain she felt about what was behind it.

She took a step forward.

Sal would kill her for this. Maybe slow. Maybe quick.

But she kept walking.

She didn't know if she was ready to face it, if she'd even survive.

And she kept walking.

But so much had died for this door, so much had bled for this door, she had to know. For herself. For everyone she was trying to help.

She put her hand on the knob. The knob put its hand on her. She couldn't explain how—the metal shifted, grew warmer, *reached* back for her. And when she held it, she found she could hear it. Like a heart beating. Like a voice whispering.

Inside her.

She should turn back, she knew. She should run back to Rudu and tell him to take her far away from here. She should try her hardest to forget everything about this place.

But there were a lot of things she should do that she would never end up doing, she knew.

This was one of them.

She opened the door. She stepped inside. Her hand left the knob. The door shut itself gently.

Darkness swept over her. It crawled like a living thing, reached for her with great sheetlike hands and drowned her in a lightless, soundless space. She held her breath, realized after a time that she no longer needed it. A silent wind blew across her face from nowhere.

"Hello?" she asked.

It echoed a hundred times over. She shut her hands over her ears, winced at the sound of her own voice reverberating back against her. And then, just as suddenly, it stopped. She dared to release her ears. She looked around the darkness, so painfully silent without the sound of her breath.

"Hello," something replied.

She swallowed hard, reached behind her, and found the doorknob was no longer there. Neither was the door. There was no point in turning back now, though the option to do so *had* been nice. But without that, she found herself walking.

This room should have been no bigger than a closet, but she counted at least forty paces. Then four hundred paces. Then four thousand. Then she lost count. Both of her paces and of time. How long had that taken? A few seconds? A few hours? She couldn't remember. Or tell where she was. A cave? A forest?

Grass crunched beneath her feet. But that was impossible. She looked down and saw only darkness. Until she blinked. When she opened her eyes, she stood upon a bleak field the color of ash. Far away, hounds bayed and loped beneath roiling clouds on human hands. Lightning in brilliant prismatic blues and oranges clove the sky, their electricity twisting into the shapes of living creatures. They reached for each other, shrieking as their light burned one another. The sound echoed into Ozhma's bones.

She started running. The field of gray grass beneath her rippled with every step. Her feet began to get caught in it. She sank into the ground, struggled to escape, found herself plunged into a brackish sea. She descended, breathless, through liquid that flowed through her as surely as she flowed through it. In the abyss surrounding her, she saw faces of ancient creatures calcified into baleful frowns peer out of the darkness, regard her with disinterest, and fade.

She opened her mouth to scream. The sound that emerged was a wailing shriek that tore through the ocean, split it apart, and left only empty darkness behind. She tumbled through the void, landed hard on stone. Angry cliffs rose up around her in fierce crags of deep, offensive purple. Great masses crawled through valleys the size of continents, their mutable flesh quivering and shedding itself over and over to birth horrific monstrosities that became more gruesome with each stride, faces both human and inhuman emerging from liquid shimmering flesh to speak a word or make a face before returning back into the mass, cysts reclaimed by the body.

Panic surged through Ozhma. And as though she'd just screamed at the top of her lungs, the creatures in the valleys stared up toward her. Millions of eyes opened across a sea of living darkness. Mouths opened and screamed back at her.

The earth collapsed beneath her, disappeared. She plummeted into a void of echoing screams. Her body felt like it was shattering just by being here, like every time the land changed, it took part of her with it. She shut her eyes. She shut her ears. She curled up tightly and drifted and hoped it would be over soon.

Something flickered past her.

Small, shimmering, and eel-like in its undulation. A ribbon of pale light, alive and writhing purple and pink through the infinite dark. She found herself fascinated by it. And, soon, found herself following it. She hurried to keep up as it sped through the endlessness. More joined it, until the dark was alive with these creatures, these living lights, coiling and writhing and dancing in a whirlpool.

"Beautiful," she whispered.

And, to her surprise, she heard her own voice.

"They are."

And someone else's.

A woman had appeared before her. Short. Small. Dark eyed, dark haired, dressed simply with her hair hanging loose around her shoulders. Her small hands rested on her knees. Her face was expressionless. And her eyes were locked on a box.

A simple brown box. Its lid closed. Unadorned with anything, even a lock.

Yet Liette stared at it as if it were trying to kill her.

Perhaps it was.

"Oh." Ozhma's voice came out as a whisper. "I'm—"

"Ozhma Tenstead. Child of Ozhvur and Kesme. Born in a quiet room to a midwife. Her name was Seletha. She feared that she would die alone and she did. She was buried at the edge of town in a grave whose headstone fell away. When people walk over her, they feel an intense regret and don't know why."

Ozhma stood still, watching Liette as she remained there, staring at the box still. The lights dissipated and rejoined overhead, like a school of fish being plucked apart by a slow and lazy predator.

"Apologies," she said. "That was not me. It's just what happens in this place. Knowing one thing means knowing many things."

"I don't understand."

"I am aware. I would explain, but that would end poorly for both of us. I hope you understand that, at least."

"I believe you," she said, because she had no other choice.

"You should not be here," Liette said. "But I knew you would come."

"I had to." There was something wrong with her voice here, Ozhma thought, something wrong with her mind. The trepidations and fears that normally danced on her tongue with each word were leaking out of her, a glistening purple ichor that bled out of the corners of her mouth. "I had to see for myself."

"Whether this was worth it? All the blood? All of Sal's story?"

She did not want to say it. But the ichor bled dry and she found she couldn't lie. She couldn't remember what a lie was. "Yes."

"Whether *I* am worth it?"

A pause. An eternity.

"Yes."

"And?"

"And I don't think it matters."

"I agree."

Liette's left eyebrow twitched. A city sprang up around them: houses and people and bustling talk. A moment passed. It exploded into flames, blackened bodies fleeing through the streets. Another moment, it became a placid lake. Damp soil blossomed beneath Ozhma's feet.

"Where are we?" she asked. But even that felt strange. She should have sounded more desperate, shouldn't she?

"It does not have a name. Nor do the people that live here. Not really. The one we have for them isn't the right one. It is not big enough to contain them." Liette kept her voice slow, even, neutral. "You should be careful here. They hear every feeling."

"I'm not sure what that means."

"Does that bother you?"

"It doesn't." But it should have.

"This place takes away things," Liette said. "Curiosity is one of the first to be lost. You should leave."

"I should, but—"

Something stirred inside her. The darkness rippled, recoiled, inched forward—a slug drawn to water.

"Do you want me to stay?"

Liette stared silent at the box for a moment. "Yes."

Ozhma stood beside her, hands folded behind her back, and looked to the box. And within the box, she could feel something looking back at her. And she knew who it was.

"If it isn't safe for me, it isn't safe for you," she found the courage to say. "Sal needs you. She's breaking herself for you." She looked at the box again and cringed. "But maybe you're breaking yourself for her, too."

A pang of regret stirred within her at her words. Just a fleeting feeling, born and dead in an instant. And in that instant, she became aware of something—something terrifyingly large, something terrifyingly old—stirring in response to it.

Somewhere far away. Something turned its gaze toward her.

A hand shot out, clasped her wrist. Liette's focus with the box remained unbroken. Her voice went frighteningly soft.

"They hear *every* feeling."

She released Ozhma's wrist, placed her hands on her lap.

"I once thought I was breaking myself for her, too. I don't think I realized that wasn't true until I came here." She focused on the box. Resentfully, it focused back on her. "I called him such a burden, spoke of him so dismissively. He caused her so much pain and she refused to get rid of him and the solution was so obvious to me I couldn't understand why she didn't just leave him behind."

She smiled softly. Something far away stirred. Her face fell again.

"So I ignored him. I pretended he didn't exist. That he was just an inconvenient tool I would find my way around, like any other. I thought I was doing what was best for her. But that wasn't true, either. I ignored him because I was afraid of him, of what he did to her, of how little I knew about him. I ignored him because *I* didn't want to face him and how much he was a part of her. And he just kept hurting her. And he just kept growing."

Ozhma looked to the box. Only briefly.

"You can hear him?"

"Only in this place."

"What does he talk about?"

"Himself, mostly," Liette observed. "He doesn't boast as much as I thought he might. He is emotional. He talks of pain and fear—often his own. He speaks of things he's terrified of and the things he's prepared to do to escape them." She blinked. The box stirred. "It scares me knowing how much I agree with him."

"You couldn't have known. From what she's told me, no one could have."

"Maybe that's true. Or maybe I could have tried. Maybe I could have learned more, saw more about what it did to her. Maybe I could have been less afraid of him." She closed her eyes briefly. The box rumbled. "Maybe then he wouldn't have gotten so strong."

"I don't think it matters."

"I agree."

Ozhma let her eyes linger on the box. Too long. Every now and then she saw it move—or did she? Sometimes, when she unfocused her eyes, she could almost see it opening, almost see a brass-colored hand reaching out from an impossibly small space, to snatch one of these twinkling lights, writhing in its grip, before dragging it back into the box and letting the lid snap back shut.

Then she would blink and it would be just a box again.

"Is he really getting stronger?" she asked.

"He is."

"Is it as bad as Sal said it would be?"

"It is." Liette glanced at her briefly. The box whispered. "Does that frighten you?"

"Yes." Ozhma swallowed hard. The fear was muted inside her, and without animal panic, she found she could look at it clearly. "I'm scared of what will happen because of me. Because of what will happen because of what I didn't do. And I'm scared of what will happen to me."

"I am, too."

Something quivered inside Ozhma's throat. "Is it going to be okay?"

"I don't know that."

"But Sal said you were smart. She sounded so sure of whatever you were sure of. If anyone would know, it'd be—"

"Be careful," Liette whispered. "They're listening."

"I'm sorry!" she all but shouted. The panic came crawling back, wailing and trapped inside her. "I'm sorry but I'm really scared and I need to know! Please, can you tell me—"

A great groan coursed through her, a pressure coming down from all around her—as though existence itself had just sighed. Somewhere, so far away she couldn't even contemplate the distance, clouds began to roil. Painful prisms of colors swirled within. Hateful stars winked into existence.

Within the flashes of color, she saw a massive silhouette stir. A colossal head turned toward her. A great and ancient eye opened.

It heard her.

It heard her fear.

"You can't stay here anymore," Liette said. She was looking at Ozhma now. And Ozhma felt herself frozen in place by her gaze. "It knows you're here."

She tried to protest, but couldn't speak. The thing in the darkness took one miles-long stride toward her. Liette raised a hand.

"I need you to tell Sal something for me. Tell her that it doesn't matter and to keep going. You'll remember that much, at least. And tell her..."

She paused, smiled.

"Never mind. She knows. Goodbye, Ozhma. I don't dare hope to see you again."

And Ozhma was flung. Liette, the box, the thing—all of them shrank before her as she was hurled backward at impossible speeds. Worlds raced around her as she went flying—the burned-out husk of a once-great city, the frenzied skies alive with airships, the walls of flame where people shrieked and screamed—and on and on, flying through lifetimes in the blink of an eye, until she arrived.

Precisely back where she was.

Back in the room at New Vigil. Back at the closet door. Back with her hand on the knob, thinking she should turn away.

And, without knowing completely why, she did.

Something about the door—its offensive ordinariness, perhaps—made her feel unsettled just touching it. Whatever was behind there, Sal clearly meant to remain behind there. Wiser to leave it be, Ozhma thought.

And while she didn't always listen to her wisdom, this time she did.

Which was fortunate, as the other door slammed a moment later.

"Hey. You aren't poking around my closet, are you?"

Sal stood, a tray with pitcher, glasses, and assorted food tucked under her arm, a furrowed brow locked on her.

"Oh." Ozhma backed away, her hands held up. "No. No, I wasn't. I was just—"

"Trying to see what kind of smallclothes I wear. I know." Sal stalked over to her, leaned down low, and sneered. "Well, I'll tell you what I tell everyone who goes poking around in Sal the Cacophony's forbidden closet. I don't wear any."

A chuckle. A slap on the back that sent Ozhma sprawling a couple of feet. Sal jerked the door open, revealed a heap of dirty clothes and discarded boots.

"I'm just fucking with you. It's where I put my old shit."

"But..." Ozhma started to protest, but why? What had she really expected to find there? "Wait, where have you been? What did Cavric have to say?"

"Important things. Here. Eat first."

Sal dropped the tray. Wine and tea sloshed in their pitchers. Cheeses—*expensive* cheeses, and Ozhma fucking knew—and tasty-looking dumplings in bowls of sauce quivered alongside desserts and confections as it hit the table. Sal plucked up a dumpling, popped it in her mouth, talked through it like that wasn't something only an animal does.

"You seemed like a girl who likes sweets, so I grabbed whatever we had of that," she said. "No judgment, of course. Cheese gives me gas, but I figure why not?"

"Wait, wait." Ozhma rubbed her temples; something about this felt not right. "Where is this food coming from? Don't the soldiers need it?"

"No. It's just going to go to waste if we don't eat it. So don't sweat—"

"Sal." Ozhma interrupted, held her gaze. "Tell me what happened."

Sal's face twitched, like she wanted to punch her. Then it screwed up, like she tried to come up with a lie that just wasn't coming together in her head. Then it finally fell as she sighed.

"Torle of the Void is here," she said.

Ozhma held her breath.

"Or he will be here. Tomorrow. And..." She held out her hands, helpless. "I mean, do *you* know how to fight him?" At the silence that followed, she grunted. "Exactly. So we might as well eat up. We're fucked." She ate another dumpling, spoke through another full mouth. "I'm fucked, anyway. You can still leave."

"Wait, what?" Ozhma shouted. "What does that mean 'you're fucked'? What are you going to do? What do we do now?"

"There is no 'we,' you dumbfuck," Sal said. "You and I are going to eat whatever makes us almost happy, then you're going to go with

Rudu and get the fuck out of here while I do what I always do when I fight someone with limitless magical potential." She plucked up another dumpling. "That is, I'm going to die horribly and be buried alive beneath the earth with everyone else. Fuck, these are good."

"But what about the plan? The gun?"

"I didn't ever have a plan. Just a hope that shit would work out," Sal replied, chuckling in the way people chuckle when things aren't actually funny. "And it didn't. The gun was just—"

"But Liette!" Ozhma continued to protest, not quite knowing why. Nor really knowing why Liette's name came to mind. "What about her? What about everything she's doing? You can't just give up while she's not!"

Sal's eyes went wide, as if she'd just been struck. Ozhma honestly never thought she'd see the Vagrant make such a face.

"Who told you what Liette's doing?"

"It doesn't matter," Ozhma replied. "Keep going."

Sal narrowed her eyes. "Who told you to say that?"

"You know."

Ozhma knew that was true. And nothing else. She didn't know who had told her to say that. Or even what she had just said. The words had simply fallen out of her mouth on reflex. As easily as any other word.

Only these felt right. Impossibly right.

"Keep going, huh?" Sal shrugged, popped the dumpling in her mouth. "All right. Well, I guess I should tell you how we came to New Vigil, then."

TWENTY-NINE

THE NAILS

We took a day to bury Sindra.

We found a nice, dry patch of earth on the other side of the river. We laid her to rest beneath the eaves of a tree that was bent and tired-looking—it just felt right. We rested beside her grave and we drank and ate.

And I wish I could tell you it was good.

I wish it could have been like the operas, where we sang and danced and lived because Sindra would want us to live. But it wasn't like that. It was like everything else in real life—it was awkward, it was painful, and no one spoke because nothing that could be said would do anything but hurt.

Neither the Vagrants nor the Revolution pursued us to the other side. Either they had their own wounds to lick or were too preoccupied with their own machinations. Or maybe they knew we were already beat.

It'd taken too much. That fight. That whole thing.

Yria could barely walk anymore. Her legs were so numb that she had to be carried the last part by Liette and her brother. Agne said nothing to any of us. She wept briefly at Sindra's funeral, though for her or for some other pain, I didn't know. They'd burned up too much Barter, given up too much of themselves to fight the Vagrants and the Revolution.

My enemies.

My problems.

My price. And they were paying it.

I drifted often between wanting to talk to them and wanting to never talk to them again. Whenever I ventured near Yria, Urda would look at me with that heartbreaking stare that begged me to stay away. Whenever I ventured near Agne and faced the possibility of her empty, emotionless stare…I panicked and retreated. And Liette…

She hadn't said anything. She wouldn't. But I knew that what she'd done to Quoir had done something to her. It had given too much of herself to Eldest, to the thing inside her. She'd lost something to it. Something she might not get back. All to save me.

I couldn't face her, either. Couldn't ask her to look me in the face and wonder whether it was a fair trade. I couldn't help any of them. Just like I couldn't have helped Sindra…

…or Meret.

"I don't think I can keep doing it, Sal."

He'd come to me that night.

"I don't think any of us can. The people, they're scared of you. They're running from you as much as from the war and you just…"

I hadn't bothered saying anything. I knew it was coming. And I knew he was right.

"It's hard, Sal. Because what they say is right. You are dangerous. I know that. But…it feels wrong leaving you. It feels like you need…"

I don't know how true that was. I wasn't going to help him figure it out, either.

"There are low roads that lead into the east, into the desert. They're hard to find, but they're safe from monsters and armies and…yeah. The people want to take it. And I want to go with them. Sindra was…"

He'd paused to cry. I let him. I tried not to look. Tried not to share his tears with him.

"Once we're that far east, there's nothing out there, Sal. Nothing but the deserter camp in the Nails. You've heard of it. New Vigil."

Even then, I hadn't liked the name.

"I don't know if you'll head there, too. But I know we can't go together. I'm sorry, Sal. If this is goodbye..."

Dawn had started creeping over the hills by the time he spoke again.

"Sal, please. Please say something."

I didn't.

"What happened with Sindra... it destroys people, even to watch it."

I didn't have anything to add.

"Sal. Are you okay?"

Nothing that wouldn't make it worse.

Dawn came and went. And so did Meret and his people. I let them go without a glance or a word. And when the others rose, I went about my business the same way.

We used Liette's money to buy mounts and supplies. This far east, the badlands made it hard to go it on foot. Agne had picked a thick-legged Crested Strut, a pair of sprightly Yellowheels for the twins, and Liette had chosen a stately riding crane. Congeniality had led the pack that left Toadback that day.

Toward what, I didn't know.

And I didn't know after the next four days of travel, either.

For all the prices they'd paid, for all the destruction I'd wrought, I was no closer to figuring out what to do than I was at the start.

The Ashmouths were clearly no longer an option—even if they *had* intended to be true to their word, they weren't going to overlook me killing their emissary. And when word got out about how I'd killed someone who called in my Redfavor, no one else was going to overlook it, either.

I'd thought about bringing up Torle of the Void with Liette again. But I didn't get far. What we'd seen, what we'd felt over these past months—well, it was pretty fucking tempting to give it all up to the Imperium just for the chance to get away from it all. But Liette knew—and I did, too, eventually—that a Scrath in the hands of the Imperium would lead to more of the same. More death. More war.

And I couldn't disagree with that. So, I let that thought go.

Or I tried to.

But the farther we rode, in the hours and days that turned to silent, wordless conversations with my own brain, the more I kept coming back to the same inevitable questions.

What the fuck could I do that *wouldn't* turn to more blood? Who the hell could we give a Scrath to that *wasn't* going to use it for more horror? The Ashmouths were never going to be straight with me, I knew, but I was willing to accept whatever foul purposes they used. The Imperium would never honor their word, because that's for people who *don't* have magic, but I was willing to accept that, too.

And the Cacophony...

I could barely even think of him. With the Scrath in him, there'd be no controlling him. An assassin saw people as money and a mage saw them as inconvenient, but those both at least acknowledged people.

A weapon? A weapon didn't acknowledge a person. You point it at a beer keg, it'll blow it to pieces as surely as a human—the weapon doesn't care. The weapon just wants to be used. And whatever else the Cacophony was, he *was* a weapon.

And I knew how he saw people.

I would accept more war. I would accept more blood. I would accept anything to free Liette of that thing consuming her.

I tried to avoid looking her way as we rode silently. I tried to avoid meeting her eyes and remembering how I'd let another chance to help her slip away. But it was impossible. Every time I even looked in her direction, I found my eyes fixing on her eyes and wondering if they were a little darker than they were the day before.

And whether it was still going to be Liette behind those eyes the day after.

A wise woman would have figured something to do or say to help this. A brave woman would have at least tried, even not knowing what to do. Maybe I'd been one of those women, at some point on the road. But this one, the one riding, was neither wise nor brave.

She was clinging to the reins, her eyes fixed ahead, trying just to think of how to stay upright for a few hours longer and not collapse and wait for everything to go dark.

If there were answers in the road, though, I couldn't find them.

And the farther we went, the less I could find of anything.

The marsh had dried up way back in Toadback. Trees and grass had vanished, their rolling greenery abruptly halted by harsh baked badland and looming plateaus. Sand and hard-packed earth made for difficult travel as roads turned to dust and bird trails became the best means of progress. Gloomy gray skies wended through the chimney-straight rocks, painting menacing shadows across the badlands.

For as many people who were willing to go to war over it, there wasn't that much in the Scar, especially this far east. Resources were scarce out here, which meant people were, as well. Even in times of relative leisure, the powers of the Scar had never been that interested in this land.

That didn't mean that there were *no* resources, mind you.

Just that the resources tended to fight back.

The animals out here were bigger, meaner, and braver. Cacuarls big as wine casks luxuriated with feline curiosity upon cliffs, eyeballing us as we passed and wondering if we might be worth the chase. Miles-long serpents coiled lazily around the great stones, requiring us to navigate our way around their snoozing bulk. Those few trees that remained here that we passed would open great yellow eyes and whisper horrific promises through tongues of bark and leaves.

There were some people out here. *Some* people. And they called this place the Nails, as in "what you hang on by when you live here." Which is pretty clever.

I thought "The Forsaken Lands" would also have been nice, but nobody asked me, did they.

My companions and I were uneasy. For different reasons, of course. They, like sane people, were concerned about being eaten, mauled, stung, or excreted. I, like a still-sane-but-in-a-different-way person, had to resist the urge to pick a fight. It would at least occupy my mind for a bit. And hey, I might get lucky and die.

Wouldn't that be nice?

"Ah, fuck. Here comes another one."

As it was, the only creatures interested in meeting my challenge were also the only creatures I didn't want to fight.

I glanced up at Yria's mutter and saw the bird immediately. It came stalking around a nearby stone, tall and powerful, muscles apparent beneath thick tufts of red and black feathers. A mottled wattle dangled from a sharp black beak, a match for the glinting spurs adorning a pair of long, muscular legs. A proud coxcomb swayed back and forth as it surveilled us through a pair of blood-colored eyes.

"Lovely." I sighed, spurred Congeniality forward. I pulled my sword and gun out, banged them together at the bird. "Shoo! Get out of here, bird! You don't want this!"

The bird didn't seem intimidated. In fact, much like the last one and the one before that, the noise only seemed to irritate it and make it charge.

In theory, I liked Banters.

In theory.

They were considered a fairly rude bird by the various militaries and most of decent society. Ill-tempered, untrainable, and incredibly aggressive, they refused to fear humans or beasts and thus pecked out existences in places rough as the Nails. I felt I had a lot in common with the Banters. But, just like *some* people might find my presence a little grating, I fucking hated dealing with the things.

They were an impressive breed, by my standards. One of the few birds capable of handling the beasts out here, they were famous for pecking away the carcasses of much larger prey they'd felled. You saw them roaming around in herds, dozens of the big, angry fuckers being escorted across the badlands by bigger, angrier fuckers.

Like this fucker.

"Don't do it," I warned the Banter as it crept closer, its crest and tail rising in an intimidating bristle of feathers. "You're not ready to be dinner, big boy. Go home to your family." I gestured with my sword. "Go! Get out of here! You're in the way and you smell bad!"

That did it.

The Banter let out a crowing shriek. It came rushing forward, wings furiously beating and spurs shining as it came leaping toward me. I had a moment to appreciate it—the legendary muscle and spurs that had torn so many Cacuarls and Kelpbrides apart, the vibrant plumage and coloration. In that moment, I respected it not only as a beast, but as a foe.

In the next moment, Congeniality killed it, so it didn't last long.

She caught the beast's neck in her beak and swung the bird down to the earth. She planted a taloned foot in the bird's back and pushed down as she pulled its neck up. The Banter squawked and shrieked, lashing out with wings and spurs in an attempt to get her off. Bones snapped under her thrashing, the Banter went limp, its fury turned to fear as Congeniality closed her beak and pulled.

I felt my heart sink.

Not for the bird—because fuck that guy—but because I knew what happened next.

Congeniality's beak pushed past the ribs she'd just broken, started tearing organs and flesh out, swallowing them whole. I gave her a limp ankle kick to try and spur her forward, but I knew there was no moving on.

I would have insisted, but in my general experience, interrupting a lady's dinner was one of the more effective ways to end up bleeding.

"All right, take a break."

I sighed as I slid off the saddle, knuckled the small of my back in a vain attempt to smooth out the pains the road had inflicted.

"Again?" Urda chirped up, a note of panic creeping into his voice. "We've stopped three times today. My sister needs to get to a place where she can—"

"I KNOW."

I didn't intend to scream at him. Didn't intend to make him flinch like that, either. But I did and he did. And I found that when I tried to stop myself, to apologize...

"I know your fucking sister needs help."

I couldn't.

"And I know you fucking need help and I know the refugees need help and I know *everyone* fucking needs help because everything is fucking on fire." I grabbed the hilt of my gun—everyone stiffened. "*This* is what I have to do that. *This* fucking thing. *This* is how we get help right now. Do you have a problem that would be solved by me pulling him out?"

Urda didn't say anything. He couldn't. He sat there, freezing under my gaze, his hands curled so tight around his reins I thought he'd break his wrists. Yria reached over to him, put a hand on his shoulder.

"It's all right," she grumbled. "We'll wait here." She glowered at Congeniality's backside. "My fucking leg's asleep, anyway."

I didn't miss the worry in her voice, even as I turned away and started stalking off. In fact, I couldn't help but hear it, ringing in my bones like a gunshot. Yria needed somewhere to recover. Urda needed to help Yria. Agne needed not to fight so she wouldn't burn any more of her emotions away. Liette needed the otherworldly being of immeasurable strength torn out of her and—

See what I mean?

It's not that walking away was the right thing to do. It was just the only thing I could think of.

"Where are you going?" Liette asked as she slid off her crane. "It isn't safe out here."

"Oh, shit, really?" I asked, gaping. "Thanks for telling me. I had no fucking idea it wasn't safe out here. I mean I guess I saw the gigantic fucking snakes and said 'you know what, that's a little concerning,' but good thing you spelled it out for me. Guess we can just pack up and go, then. Where would you like to visit next?"

She blinked. "I sense you are in a mood."

"Farmwives get in moods. I burn down cities."

Liette removed her spectacles, rubbed her eyes, let out one of those sighs that feel like my fault. "I understand that this is a stressful time for us."

"For *us*? I'm talking about—"

"For. Us." She held up a single finger, spoke shortly and severely. "For everyone." I started to speak, but she kept that finger rigid, that voice sharp as an axe. "*And because I know you*," she said, "I know you're trying to think of ways to fix this. And I am giving you my professional and personal opinion as someone who is *also* going through this shit—as well as someone of such *staggering* genius as to make scholars weep with envy, you *ass*—that snapping at the twins and storming off is not going to help anything."

"Then what the fuck am I trying for?" I leaned forward, loomed over her, spat through clenched teeth. "If you're such an amazing genius, why the fuck aren't *you* figuring out how to get out of this?"

It wasn't Liette's emotions I feared. I hated to see her cry, I groveled when she was mad, and I stood in front of her whenever she got scared. But I didn't fear those emotions. It was this face that I feared, this perfect evenness of expression she wore, this casual, disinterested scrutiny with which she surveyed me.

When she looked at me like she could peel back every layer of skin I had and see what was inside and decide that nothing there was all that impressive, after all...

When she looked at me like that, I wanted to run.

"Because I am trying to hold you up."

People say they get so mad they can't think straight. But that's only half true. When they feel so mad, so scared, so cornered that the only thing they can think of is how to get away from that, that they need to fight, to hurt, to make something bleed just to stop feeling their own pain, but they *don't* do that...well, sometimes that's the straightest thing you can think.

Or maybe that was just me.

That's why I didn't say another word. Why I took my many weapons and things that hurt and started storming off. I heard her shouting after me—heard a few of them, actually—but I didn't stop or look back. I couldn't. If I did, I'd have to think. And if I had to think, I'd have to realize how much of what she was saying was true.

Which I would, later. Much later.

But right then? Honestly, being eaten alive by a beast sounded more pleasant.

I made my way around one of the giant chimney rocks. Unmercifully, no monster awaited on the other side. And since no one was going to eat me, I decided to start walking. Nowhere in particular, just wherever I could get a fight. Or a drink. Or a nice hole to crawl in and die.

I don't know when it became too much, when my shoulders became so heavy and my legs so weak. When I collapsed to my knees and started crying, I didn't know why. And when I told myself to get back up, to keep going, to keep fighting... I didn't believe myself.

The wind whispered behind me. I whispered back.

"Fuck off."

I don't know if the wind actually did, but the guy who came with it didn't.

"I wanted to see if you were all right," Jindu replied softly.

"As you can see"—I paused to wipe my nose with the back of my hand—"I'm fine."

He fell quiet. I remembered this, this moment of when he didn't believe me but was afraid to say so. I'd always hated it when he and I were...

Anyway.

"You don't sound like you're—"

"*You* don't sound like you're dumb enough to be the motherfucker at the top of my list, yet here you are."

"That is true," he said.

I can't explain why I leapt to my feet and stormed over to him. Nor why I pulled the Cacophony out and leveled it at his face, my finger on the trigger. Or maybe I just didn't want to.

"Yeah, it's fucking true," I snarled, pressing the brass to his forehead. The Cacophony seethed, excited at the prospect. "It's true that you betrayed me. It's true that you took my magic. It's true that you did it all for some skinny motherfucker who died like a fucking pig squealing on the cold hard ground and the same thing should happen to you."

"That is also true," he said. "And it is also true that I helped you in Toadback."

Now if you asked me why I hit him just then, I *could* explain that, but I trust I don't need to.

"You piece of shit. You *utter* piece of shit." I slammed him against a rock, jammed the gun under his chin so hard that his neck almost broke. "You think that makes up for anything? You think that does anything for what you took from me? You took my magic. You took my life! *YOU TOOK* EVERYTHING *FROM ME, TELL ME RIGHT THE FUCK NOW WHY I SHOULDN'T PULL THIS TRIGGER.*"

He didn't tell me, or beg me, or even flinch away. He stared past the brass and the coiling steam and the voice hissing at me to do it, to pull the trigger and watch everything inside him paint the walls. He just kept looking at me.

"I can't."

"Then why come back? Why say you helped me? *WHY HELP ME?*"

"Because it is also true," he answered. Not calm. Calm people sounded different. His voice was choked and wet. "All of it. Every part of it. I did betray you. I did take everything. And I did come back to help. None of it makes up for any other part of it."

He held his hands out wide, far from the blade at his hip, far from me.

"But I am here, Salazanca. I want to be here. I want to help you. And if the only way I can do that is by standing here while you pull the trigger, then that's what I'll do."

The heat coursing up my arm was unbearable, the impending ecstasy coursing through the Cacophony making him twitch in my hand. He'd been waiting for this day, for the day I would finally kill the name at the top of my list and we'd be one step closer to killing the next. We'd killed many Vagrants, he and I. But he'd been building his appetite for this one for a long time.

The angry sear he shot through me when I lowered him damn near made me scream with pain.

I released Jindu's neck. I sheathed my gun. The Cacophony's heat shot through my veins, but I didn't care. Not right now. I turned, made to start walking, but whatever anger had been fueling me had just ebbed away.

I was too angry to think, too tired to be angry, too afraid to be tired. I walked as far as I could muster before my legs gave out. I found a rocky outcropping and sat down on it. Jindu appeared beside me, also sat down. I didn't tell him to go. I didn't tell him anything until the sun had sunk low for an hour.

"I'm not going to forgive you."

He knew that. I could tell by his silence.

"And I'm not going to thank you."

"You never thank anyone," he replied.

"Fuck you, I say thank you all the time. *I'm* nice. Now shut the fuck up before I tear your teeth out through your dick."

More silence followed. Probably wise, considering that actually doing what I just said would be really hard to do, but I wasn't about to be called a liar.

But silence is a funny thing. Wise people call it strength, bold people call it weakness, and the rest of us call it fucking miserable. When no words found their way to my mouth, my head was full of all the words I couldn't bear to have there. Angry demands. Furious curses. Images of that dark night, of his blade jutting out from my skin, flashing over and over in my head until they all blended together in a bitter poison that coursed out of my head and into my veins, the shame and anger and pain all roiling through me.

It hurt.

It hurt worse than the Cacophony.

It hurt so bad I had to say something just to spit it out.

"Why?"

I didn't know that was going to be what I said.

I looked toward Jindu. "Why did you do it?"

Jindu blinked at me. "Does it matter?"

"No."

"Would it make you feel better to know?"

"No." I snorted. "But I want to anyway."

Only then did he start to look uncomfortable. More uncomfortable than he ever had beneath the barrel of the Cacophony. He stopped looking at the horizon and started looking at the ground, at the trees, at anything but me.

I don't know if you've ever seen a man who can move faster than the wind realize he has no way out, but it's something. I might even have felt bad for him, another time.

"My Barter."

I furrowed my brow. "What?"

"My Barter. A Quickmage's Barter. What the Lady takes from us."

"Your *Barter* made you do it?" I didn't intend to reach for my gun, but then I didn't expect to hear that kind of birdshit falling out of his mouth.

"*No*," he snapped, defensive. "It just..." He paused, pursed his lips. "But yes. And still no. And..." He gave up, sighed, rubbed his temples. "She took time from me."

"Huh?"

"Time. She takes time from you. From Quickmages."

"That's just called getting older, you dumb fucking—"

"You fucking asked, now are you going to let me finish?"

I admit, I didn't expect that tone of voice. I didn't expect him to be capable of sounding like that. But I didn't say anything.

"She takes your place in time. The moments you're in, the moments you've *been* in, the moments you're going to be in." His mouth grew dry, his eyes grew wet. "It starts slow. Sometimes you wake up and you don't know when you are for a few minutes. Then it gets worse. Sometimes I'm years ago, when I was a kid, before my powers came to me. Sometimes I wake up and I'm yesterday, back when I said something or did something or..." He swallowed hard. "And sometimes... sometimes I'm in the future.

"And I don't know what I'm seeing. People that I knew are dead. People that I didn't know are somewhere else. And sometimes..." He swallowed hard. "Sometimes you're there. Sometimes you're dead. Sometimes you've killed everyone else. And I can't tell if it's real or..." He shook his head. "The Lady takes it all. My moments. My life. And when she finally takes it all... I don't know what I'm going to be."

He tried to smile and failed. He tried to speak and failed. He tried to hold back tears and then he stopped trying. And he just... sobbed. Sobbed like the kid I knew from the academy when he was frustrated with his powers, like he had when he brought me a present I didn't like.

"I didn't know how to tell anyone what was happening. I didn't know how to tell *you*," he whispered, "or even if I could. You were..." He paused, frowned. "The war over here was hard. Hard on you. After Vigil burned. I didn't want to add to that. So when Vrakilaith asked me what was going on, I just..." He held out his hands. "I told him. Everything. And we talked. And I trusted him. And I believed him when he said that the futures I saw, where you were..."

He closed his eyes, remembered. The way his body shuddered was something I'll never forget.

"I believed him. Believed him when he said it was necessary to betray you. Believed him when he said we needed a new emperor, that we could make one, that it was the only way to stop any of it from happening. He was lying. Or he thought he wasn't, but he was. Or he wasn't, but..." He held out his hands, empty and impotent. "Well, I guess it doesn't matter."

I stared at him. "And so... what? You regret it? You want to help me to make up for it?"

"No. Or... maybe? I don't know. Is it so bad to regret it? To want to make it right?" He looked at me. "Salazanca, I want to do right by you. I love—"

I didn't hit him. Not this time.

And if you were hoping for some two-piece back-alley opera shit where I forgive him and kiss him or something, I'm sorry to disappoint you there, too.

I didn't do anything but get up and run.

My heart thundered in my chest. My breath ran my throat raw. My muscles pulsed with a fearful life they hadn't had a moment ago. I don't fucking care if it looked childish or stupid. I just couldn't be there. I couldn't hear him say that. I couldn't *let* him do that to me.

Not again.

So I ran. From him. From the others. From all the people whose lives I'd ruined and who had ruined mine. I couldn't take it anymore and I didn't care how I got away from it. I ran until my breath gave out and my lungs gave out and my legs gave out and I collapsed to my knees.

And the poison came back. The images of his smile and his laugh and all the ways I'd wanted to make him happy. The feeling of what he'd done to me and of his blade and the way he'd whispered that apology that hadn't done anything to keep me from bleeding on the floor of that dark place. The pain, the happiness, the fights, the reconciliations—they all swirled in my head, in my body, into my throat.

I opened my mouth, tried to vomit them out, tried to scream them out, tried to be the fucking hard killer of men and destroyer of cities Sal the Cacophony was meant to be.

But I wasn't any of those things just then. And I couldn't do anything but sit there and let the tears fall out of me until I didn't have any more.

The sun fell lower in the sky. Long shadows cast themselves over me. The wind plucked at my hair. When I didn't have anything left in me, only then did I bother looking up.

A long chasm wound its way through the cliffs. The dirt had been beaten down by carts and bird tracks, even paved in some areas. I won't lie—I *was* curious about who had managed to build a road this far into a place as forsaken as the Nails. Or who would even *want* to.

Then I glanced up at the cliffs and got my answer.

Uniforms looked down at me. Thick coats in Revolutionary blue, their fur trim whipping in the breeze. Purple silks of Imperial mages, their ostentatious adornments and masks bright, even in the fading sun. Hundreds of uniforms, side by side without regard for faction, staring down at me from shadows on the cliffs.

I would have been pretty fucking worried if any of them had any soldiers in them.

As it was, though, there were no bodies to fill them—not human ones, anyway. Crude scarecrows had been constructed out of shattered shrapnel and broken weapons, the wonders of the Revolution's machinery and the Imperium's magic alike both broken down to make ill-fitting frames. As my breath slowed, I could see the burns and tears and bloodstains ravaging the clothing.

Imperials had been here. Revolutionaries had been here. Someone had killed them both. And they didn't want more.

This was a dangerous place. And I was pretty fucking happy to be in it, if I'm honest. Danger, I understood. The other shit—Liette and Jindu and Agne and the twins and everything I'd ruined—I didn't want to deal with that. I wanted to hurt people. I wanted to hurt. I wanted to drop everything I was carrying on my shoulders and pick up a sword again.

I wanted to *fight*.

And, kindly, I got one.

I don't know when he'd spotted me. Probably about the same time I'd noticed one of the uniforms wasn't a scarecrow. A man slipped out of the Revolutionary coat he'd been hiding in, clad in garb I didn't recognize. The crossbow he raised at me, though, I did.

The Revolution called it a Hand of Splendid Harmony: a fancy word for a killing machine that fired armor-piercing bolts. This one looked a little weirder, I admit—it had some modifications to it I didn't recognize. But I'd faced enough of them to know them. Nasty things—shot straight, shot far, and had a very distinctive *twang* sound when their triggers clicked.

The same sound that echoed through the chasm as he aimed his weapon at me and fired.

THIRTY

THE NAILS

I probably should be used to ambushes by now.

I know, I know—the whole point of an ambush is that you don't see it coming. But given that this is the Scar and I am Sal the Cacophony and we don't have the *best* relationship, I still felt kind of stupid for assuming I'd be safe in the Nails.

Or at least, safe from one kind of danger.

The Nails were, after all, not named because of how pretty they looked when painted. No one was intended to be out here. There was nothing out here worth fighting over, or so I thought. What had compelled enough Imperial and Revolutionary forces out here to be killed in such numbers? And who was out here in enough force to even *want* to challenge them, let alone succeed in killing so many?

All good questions.

Good questions that would be better asked when someone wasn't shooting at me. I see that now.

The bolt streaked toward me, got close enough that I could see the glistening barbs of its head before I heard the Lady sing a note. The wind shuddered. A shape appeared in front of me. The bolt fell to the ground in two pieces.

"Who's that?" Jindu asked, glaring up at the cliff.

"I don't fucking know," I snapped. "Kill them."

"But why are they here?"

"I don't know. Kill them."

"But shouldn't we—"

"*Now* you want to think things through?"

He looked past me, over me, above me. He vanished, reappeared in the air behind me, sword swinging. He landed on the ground, along with three other bolts. I drew the Cacophony, slammed a shell into his chamber, aimed upward, and looked for my target.

Despairingly, I found I had a few.

They slipped between the scarecrows, shadows moving in and out of the rows of desecrated uniforms. They would appear between them like mice from a field, squeeze off a few shots from intimidating-looking autobows, and disappear back behind the effigies. Bolts flew out in swarms, flurries of black bladed insects flying across the orange sky toward me.

I took off running, leaping for the nearest cover I could find. Bolts followed me, punching through rocks and scrub as they struck and impaled themselves into the earth, quivering in frustration as I dove beneath the saddest rock I'd ever seen. It put up a brave front as I ducked behind it, but the bolts chipped away at it with every strike.

Organized ambush—not good. Enemies that knew what they were doing—even less good. Weaponry you didn't see outside of the hands of proper militaries—much, much worse. This was bad. Who were these people? What did they want out here?

Those, too, were good questions.

Good questions that I would feel better about asking *after* I had killed them.

I sprang out as my cover split into fragments. The bolts followed me, were already tracking me. I paused for as long as it took to figure out which cliff had the most of them on it. I aimed the Cacophony at a big chunk of rock, pulled the trigger.

I was running, breathless, panicked. It was a shit shot. I winced, made ready to fire again.

But I didn't have to.

The shell trembled in midair, almost like it was deciding. It curved around, altered its trajectory to punch right into the middle of the pack of sharpshooters. The explosion of noise was bigger than anything I'd ever seen—the sound of Discordance shattered the cliff side like a teacup in a bar fight.

A great cloud of dust swept out, a vomit of earth and sand that blasted chunks of stone and humanity across the chasm. The noise of the entire cliff face collapsing, of the people hurled through the air to smash against cliff walls and falling rocks, was lost in the wail of the shell's sound. The other sharpshooters disappeared in the roaring cloud of dust, screaming as their comrades' shattered bodies were thrown from on high to break and splatter across the rock, fleshy birds cleaved from the sky by an angry god.

The Cacophony had never done that before.

The Cacophony *couldn't* do that before.

A chorus of clicks behind me. The sound of restless wind. I whirled and saw the bolts shrieking toward me. Jindu appeared a moment later, his sword plucking them from the sky like overfed mosquitoes. But the wildness of his eyes told me the same thing I already knew.

Even for him, even for both of us, there were too many.

My body protested, my muscles screaming as we took off running. It would never get used to all this retreating. And there was only so long my fear could smother my exhaustion. But I wasn't thinking about that right then.

The numerous crossbow bolts flying at me seemed more pressing.

I darted and dodged where I could. Jindu deflected and parried where he could. But neither of us could hold them back. Bolts whizzed past my hair, nicked at my clothes, even bit a chunk of flesh out of me as they grazed my arm. Crossbows—even *those* ones—couldn't aim like that.

A trio of bolts came falling down in front of me. I skidded to a halt.

So did the bolts.

The bolts hung in midair for but a moment before sharply pivoting, aiming, and spitting themselves at me as if of their own volition. I screamed, fell to the ground as they shot overhead and punched into a nearby looming rock.

Crossbows *definitely* couldn't do that.

"Magic."

Jindu's hand was extended. I only hesitated briefly before taking it. He helped me up, ran with me as we rounded a corner, heading back to our camp.

"They have a mage with them," he said, breathless.

"Vagrants," I growled. "Bandits."

"Bandits don't fight like this," he replied.

"All right, dickwipe, why don't you go ahead and ask them about their motivations while I keep not dying." I leapt over a rock. The familiar figures of birds and people greeted me. "Mount the fuck up!" I spat at my companions. "We're getting the hell out of here."

"What? Why?" Urda asked, glancing up.

"Stay here and find out," I snarled.

If there was any hesitation after that, I didn't pay attention. I pushed Liette up onto her crane, hopped into Congeniality's saddle. With a firm kick to her sides, I took off, leading the others as we rushed forward, seeking to disappear into the ravines and rocks of the Nails. Wherever the sharpshooters were, more rock between us and them wouldn't hurt.

I searched the cliffs. The sun was going down. Shadows were growing longer. They'd be up there, I knew, trying to find the best shot to take before night fell and put us on equal footing. And, for the record, I'd like it known that I was probably right. There probably *were* sharpshooters up there.

"SAL!"

That didn't mean there weren't other things to worry about.

At Liette's cry, I pulled the reins up short. Congeniality squawked, distressed. Possibly because of the sharp jerk on her reins. Or possibly because of the legion of bloodthirsty birds arrayed before us—honestly, it could have been either.

In a thick line of red eyes and red spurs, the Banters stood in squat, ornery formation. The sight of twenty of them would be enough of a reason to worry. But these ones wore sharp blades on their wings and adorning their spurs. These ones wore reins and thick saddles. And seated atop each of them was a rider in the same green dirty coat as the sharpshooters.

One of them approached. A bloodred bastard of a Banter streaked by scars and naked patches of feathers strutted forward, wattle and coxcomb flapping arrogantly. Its rider, her hood doffed back, wore a pale woman's face twisted into a frown. They were a perfect match—the same fiery red hair, the same scars of hardship and battle, and the same pissed-off expression.

It was kind of cute, in hindsight. But at the time?

"Listen," I tried shouting, "we don't want trouble."

The woman replied by unhooking a massive axe from her belt and leveling it at me. The angriest howl I'd ever heard tore free of her mouth in a spray of spit and fury. The Banters took it up, one by one, crowing angrily at the sound. In a shudder of earth and the rattle of metal, they were rushing.

"Come on, come on, *come on*."

I wasn't sure if I was talking to myself, my mount, or my companions—fortunately, it worked for all of them. We whirled our mounts about, taking off at a sharp rush. Congeniality pushed to the fore, her huge stride eclipsing the other birds.

We led the retreat, turning corners sharply, rushing through whatever twist or turn we could find. Deadfalls and barricades impeded our progress, forced us to keep moving deeper into the ravines.

We were being herded.

The Banters crowed and shrieked behind us. They were made for this land, agile and fleet—but fifty of anything, no matter how agile, is a pain to take around a sharp corner. I kept running, kept pivoting, kept our retreat as haphazard and unpredictable as I dared.

I don't know if I really believed this would shake them, but I forced myself to.

I couldn't think of anything else.

The sound of metal and spurs rattled in my head. My eyes darted between the path before us and the cliffs above us. They were behind us, over us, they might even be beneath us for all I fucking knew. But that was fine. I let that fear fill me. I let it smother the only other thought I had.

Even here, I thought, for the briefest, most heartbreaking of moments. *Even fucking here. I led them all here to die.*

I gritted my teeth, forced my fear to the front of my mind, let it smother my despair. So long as I kept running, I could keep those thoughts from my head. So long as I kept them out, I could keep going.

That's what I'd always thought, anyway.

But the deeper into the ravines we went, the more the sound of our pursuers faded. Their distant, frustrated calls rang off the canyon walls, but they grew no closer. We'd managed to find a moment to breathe, if nothing else.

"Thank fuck," Yria gasped, almost collapsing off her bird's saddle. "Thank fucking fuck, we lost them."

"Not for long," I muttered. "Keep moving."

"We can't," Urda protested. "I was just about to take care of her when—"

"Then don't move," I said. "Stay here and fucking die." I sneered as I spurred Congeniality forward, around an immense pillar of stone. "But have the decency not to blame me when they tear you apart."

I wish Urda had been worse. I wish he had been an asshole or a murderer or even just mildly irritated. I wish he had told me off or cussed me out or something I could fight back against.

When he sullenly fell in line behind me, along with the others, it felt worse than a fight. A punch in the face or a knife in the ribs was something I understood—an action was made and a response was given. When he simply fell silent, when all of them did, I knew they did it because they trusted what I said was right.

They trusted *me*.

And that didn't feel right. Because I wasn't the kind of person you trust.

And that hurt a lot worse than a knife.

The canyons opened up as we went in. The ravines got big enough for the ground to have been pounded flat and made into a road. I assumed that was what happened, anyway. Largely because the things that had pounded it flat were still here.

Tanks. Righteous Marchers of Farts or Indisputable Speakers of Whatever-the-Hell—I forget what the Revolution called them. But there were many of them. They stood abandoned across the field, the earth still bearing the blackened scars from their cannons. The great metal beasts lay dormant—a few had been reduced to soot-colored husks, bombed out by explosions, a few others had sunk into the earth and remained there, as though someone had started burying a grave for them and simply lost interest halfway through.

Revolutionary machines. Out here, where no one else should be. That was bad. Not as bad as the half-mad roosters trying to run us down, though.

I glanced at the others, grunted a warning, started off. Congeniality took the lead, picking her way through the graveyard of machinery. The tanks and their cannons stood in smug silence, as if mocking me for thinking I was going to make it through here when they and all their armor and guns couldn't.

Or maybe I was just thinking that because I hadn't slept in a while. Either way, I wasn't about to let these metal assholes have the last laugh.

The canyon floor swept upward the farther in we went, the sand giving way to scrub grass and hills. That was good luck. Not great luck of course. In fact, pretty bad luck—fleeing into a bunch of hills in the dead of night while pursued by rampaging murderbirds wasn't what most people would call a "good" idea. But it would at least get us clear of any sharpshooters and allow us a chance to disappear into the hills. Bad luck and a bad idea to go with it.

But when you've been doing this as long as I have, any idea better than curling into a ball and crying counts as a good one.

We'd made it halfway through the canyon when I heard it. Faintly, at first—the rattle of metal and the shuffle of sand. I glanced behind—nothing but the husks of dead machines looked back at me.

"Come on," I whispered to Liette as her crane caught up. "*Come on.*"

She didn't ask why. None of them did as they went hurrying past me toward the hills. I kept my eyes on the tanks, watching them as they sat still and silent. So still and silent I only barely noticed.

One of the cannons was moving.

"Agne!" I shouted as she came forward, bringing up the rear. "*AGNE, MOVE!*"

She looked up just in time to see the tank's cannon leveled at her. She had just enough time to raise a hand before the flash. Fire lit up the night sky as a severium shell struck her; a burst of purple-tinged flame erupted where it struck. Agne disappeared in the fire, shrieking along with her mount as they were both swallowed.

I saw her bird blacken, burst into fire, and crumple into a dead silhouette behind the flames.

Then I saw her.

She burst from the fire without a word. Her arms and legs pumped mechanically, her face empty of fear or rage or anything but a wide-eyed focus on the tank. I heard people within shouting, heard the machine whirring. The cannon fired again, the shell bouncing from her forehead and caroming off to explode against a rock face.

A hatch opened. There was a panicked attempt from the greencoats within to escape. One almost made it out before Agne lowered her shoulder and struck the tank's hull. It all but shattered beneath her, crushing the escaping greencoat in the hatch and severing him at the waist. The screams within grew more panicked as the remaining ambushers struggled to claw their way past their mutilated companion.

The panic turned to terror as Agne's fingers punched through the shell. She hoisted the tank out of the sand, ripping the metal into a shrapnel as the others came tumbling out, scrambling to find their wits and feet enough to get away from her. The shadow of the tank, and the woman holding it over her head, fell over them like a shroud.

I saw her, then.

Not Agne the Hammer, the woman who had fought with me, protected me, pulled me out of the Valley. Not Agnestrada, the woman who wept in my arms because she feared losing her emotions, the woman who told me at quiet moments in the night what she wished her life had turned out like. The woman holding up that tank was empty. Empty of remorse. Empty of pity. Of anything but the great strength in her body and the magic burning out of her eyes.

I cried out. At the time, I didn't know for what. I thought it was for the violence unfolding before me or for the fear pumping through my veins. But now I know what I did it for.

I cried out for her.

For the woman who'd given everything to me.

Including herself.

The greencoats made a last feeble attempt at defense, holding up pitiful arms to protect themselves as they failed to get back to their feet. It did not save them. Either from her or from the tank she brought down upon them.

She crushed them beneath it, striking over and over. The first strike killed them. The second one turned them into greasy stains. By the third time, she wasn't even listening as I cried out to her.

And I know now that I was too scared of what she'd become to face her.

A bolt flew past me. The sound of rattling metal filled my ears again. I spat a curse, pulled Congeniality around, took off. I left her behind. The crossbows didn't even need to find me—I already felt like I was bleeding.

Congeniality picked up speed as we made it to the hills. Liette and the twins were still fleeing when I caught up to them. I glanced over my shoulder, saw the canyons emptying as the Banter cavaliers came pouring out, flooding back into the hills after us. The bloodred woman with the bloodred bird was at their head, her axe held high and a war cry on her lips.

Fuck. Fuck, fuck, *fuck*.

I spurred Congeniality forward. Her legs were already straining against the steep hill. The Banters scaled it with ease behind us—by the time we were halfway up, they were already almost on us.

I searched the hills for anything—any cover, any terrain these strutting fucks couldn't just leap over, *anything*. And I saw nothing. Nothing but grass and trees and—

There. Far ahead. I could barely see it against the collapsing sunlight. A small depression in the hillside—too small to be a cave, too big to be a hole. Cover enough...but not for all of us. It could fit maybe two people, either the twins or me and Liette or me and...

"*Yria!*" I screamed, the idea I just had slapping her name right out of my mouth. I spurred my bird up to her. "Yria! I need you!"

"Oh, great news," she snarled. "I was really hoping we were going to talk about *your* problems right now. Thanks for not disappointing, really."

I chose to ignore that. "I need you to put me on that bird."

"You're already on a bird, dumbfuck. Why are you in charge, again?"

"*That* bird."

I pointed behind me. To the bloodred Banter. And its rider.

"*What?*" Yria screamed. "You want me to portal you onto a fucking *moving* target?"

"Can you do it?"

"Yeah, sure. Just whip off your pants and I'll lick your butthole and make you tea while I'm at it. Anything fucking else? A cheeseboard for m'lady?"

"She can't!" Urda protested. "You *can't*, Yria!"

Yria pursed her lips, snarled at me. "You got any other ideas?"

"No."

"Yeah, I figured," she sighed. "All right, all right. Give me a second."

She kept her eyes over her shoulder. Her face screwed up in what I thought was concentration but quickly realized was pain—it was taking everything in her to even think about this. I tried to ignore it as I heard the Lady's song, saw the pinpricks of light born into existence—one right ahead of me and one right behind me.

The portals burst open a second later. A swirling door of purple light blossomed across the hillside. I let myself fall from the saddle, tumble off and into the portal. I closed my eyes, felt that unsettling feeling of my guts being torn out of my belly and then crammed back in.

When I opened them again, I was airborne. I plummeted out of the other portal, flailed briefly in midair as I fell down, legs first. I'm not religious, of course—no one with a big enough gun is—but I almost wanted to let out a prayer of thanks just then.

It fucking worked.

I landed rudely in the saddle. The Banter buckled as the weight of another ride suddenly fell upon it. Its rider, the woman with the red hair, let out a cry as she felt someone appear behind her. She glanced over her shoulder.

Just in time for me to hit her.

The Cacophony's hilt smashed into her jaw. I'd hoped that'd crumple her, but to her immense credit, she refused to go down—the asshole. Her elbow snapped back, caught me across the cheek. She swung her axe, struggled to dig it into my ribs. But it was an unwieldy weapon, we were fighting on the back of a bird, and I was really, *really* irritated.

Suffice it to say, the next three blows I rained down upon her subdued her.

As she slumped in my arm, I seized the Banter's reins and jerked hard. It let out an irritated squawk as it was jolted to the side, its path suddenly veering sharply to the tiny cave I'd seen. The thunder of the Banters behind me changed as cries of alarm went up.

"*Commander!*" someone shouted.

They liked this woman, apparently.

Which was good for me. Pretty hard to take a hostage no one wants back.

I saw Liette and the others disappear into the hills as the remaining cavaliers altered their course to pursue us. I snarled, pulled the reins harder. The Banter tilted sharply to the left. I could feel the blades affixed to its wings brushing against my legs, cutting through my clothes.

I pulled the woman against me, hurled both of us from the saddle. We hit the ground with a grunt, rolling across the dust. I hauled myself and my captive to our feet. The Banters came barreling forward as I pulled us into the cave, hunkering down behind a thick rock. Bolts and thrown axes ricocheted off my cover, narrowly bouncing away. The woman was starting to regain consciousness; I only had a few minutes to work.

I slammed a shell into the Cacophony—I didn't see which one—aimed it over my shoulder, and fired. Hoarfrost erupted out in a gale of frigid wind and ice. I heard trees and scrub grass crackling as frost swallowed them. I heard Banters shriek and topple over as the slippery ice beneath them broke their charge.

Caught the little fuckers that time.

The chaotic chorus lasted for a moment before an unsettling silence descended. My captive stirred back to life just in time to see the Cacophony's grinning barrel pressed into her face, wisps of frost peeling from his maw. She struggled a little, but only enough to preserve her dignity. We both knew which way this would end if my trigger finger got restless.

"Easy," I muttered to her. "Easy, easy. You and I are both too pretty to feel good about me splattering my face with the remains of your face, so if you just sit still for a bit, I'll make this quick."

"Fuck you," the woman snarled, struggling against my grasp.

"The Nails aren't surrendering and neither are we. Crawl back to whatever dog you serve and—"

She stopped talking because a punch to the mouth will do that.

"All right, I apologize for that," I said as she spat blood onto my knee. "I know I didn't say *specifically* 'no impotent posturing threats,' but I really am in kind of a hurry right now. That's on me."

She didn't offer a response to that—which I would normally call rude, but I did just take her hostage, so I guess we were even. Just as well, anyway. It wasn't her I wanted to talk to.

"You still out there?" I shouted over my shoulder.

A moment of terse silence. Then, someone shouted back.

"The Nails will never surrender!"

"Yeah, no, I heard that one from..." I looked back to my hostage. "What's your name, madam?"

"Fuck you," she snarled.

I pressed the Cacophony to her temple. "You want that on your grave?"

She swallowed hard, spat through clenched teeth. "Ketterling."

"Ketterling what?"

"Ketterling Eat-My-Snatch-You-Fucking-Dog."

"I heard that one from your very ill-mannered friend here, Ketterling," I shouted out to the soldiers. "I don't give a fuck about your land or you. I'm just trying to find..."

Find what? A place to do something that wouldn't work? A place to hide from enemies that would never rest?

This is the problem with talking instead of stabbing and shooting everyone. Once you start realizing how insane everything you want to say sounds, the more you realize you shouldn't even bother with nonviolence.

"I'm not opposed to letting your friend—"

"Commander," Ketterling grunted.

"I'm not opposed to letting your *commander* go, sorry," I shouted back out. "And once I see no bolts, birds, or bastards out there, I'll be happy to consider it."

A long silence followed.

"I don't hear anyone being smart out there," I shouted again. "If we all want to be stupid, then I'll be happy to be stupid with you, but it'll end messily."

And then, a noise.

Footsteps. Not the sound of dozens of people retreating, like I wanted. Just one.

Coming closer.

"That better not be someone thinking they can get close to me," I snarled. "This isn't opera, motherfucker. You try any shitty dramatic rescue attempt and I'll turn her into scenery."

They didn't stop. The same pair of heavy boots crunching across the ice got louder. They didn't even hesitate. The poison came back—the thoughts, the failures, all the pain I'd put everyone through and how it was all about to come crumbling down for nothing. Like Ocytus. Like Toadback. Like *everywhere.*

"*DID YOU FUCKING HEAR ME?*" I roared. I pulled the hammer to the Cacophony back. He seethed with barely restrained joy. "*Who the FUCK do you think you're dealing with?*"

It wasn't going to work. This whole thing wasn't going to work. We were going to die here. We'd given up everything and it was all for nothing. I couldn't keep the poison out of my head anymore, I couldn't keep it out of my throat, I wanted to cry, I wanted to scream, I wanted to—

"Sal?"

A voice. Male and familiar. Deeper than I remembered, more tired. But it wasn't hate or fear or scorn in his voice. There was something there, something soft and tender and concerned.

It cut me deep to hear it again. Just like it'd cut me before.

"Is that really you?"

I didn't want to believe it. I didn't want to hear his voice. I didn't want to come out from behind my cover.

But I did.

He wore a green coat now instead of his old blue one. Stress and time had made him heavier, burlier. His boyish face was hidden behind a thick beard. And he had way more scars than I remembered—or maybe he always had and I hadn't noticed.

He was bigger now. Stronger, too. But I saw his open posture, the way he carried himself like he knew I wasn't going to kill him. And so did I.

"Cavric?" I whispered. "Cavric fucking Proud?"

He smiled at me. Wearily. And sighed.

"Sal the Cacophony," he said. "Would you mind terribly not murdering my wife?"

THIRTY-ONE

THE NAILS

There is a story about a man.

Which may not sound so surprising. There are many stories about many men. Fewer in the Scar than in other places, but enough that you wouldn't stop to hear this one if someone offered to tell it to you.

I probably wouldn't have, either.

But this one is worth sharing. This one is something you never hear of in the Scar.

This is a story about a town called Hightower. You might have heard it. You might not have. A long time ago, someone was supposed to be executed there. A Vagrant woman with a big gun. She wasn't. Hightower burned, like many places in the Scar burned, and in the fires that followed, two people left that city.

One was the Vagrant. You know her story.

Another was the man who set fire to the city.

They spoke briefly that day before parting. She left to her own stories and her own troubles. And he left to his, turning his back on the burning city. For as long as he could, anyway.

It's said he got almost a mile away from the city before he stopped, cursed himself, and turned back. Despite being the one that had set fire to things, he walked right into the city without anyone noticing.

It was a Revolutionary city, they were Revolutionaries, and he was one of them.

Or had been, before that day.

He did as many others did. He took buckets of water to burning buildings. He helped people get away from the fire. He ensured no one did anything stupid like rushing into a building he had made certain was empty before he lit them ablaze.

It's said that the fires took an hour to set and two days to put out. He stayed for every last moment.

When it was done, there were celebrations in the traditional Revolutionary fashion. Praise was heaped upon the Great General, the Great General's choices in commanders, the Great General's wisdom. Those who had participated in the rescue efforts were offered promotions within the Revolution, as was the man.

He accepted it. As they all accepted it. For to turn down the opportunity to serve as the Great General's will was to disrespect the Great General—the only crime the Revolution had, for which all offenses described and which the punishment was always the same.

Then, that night, the man left Hightower again.

This time, he had gotten about two miles from the city when he realized he was being followed. He reached for a weapon he no longer carried as he turned to confront his pursuers. But there was no need. His foes had no weapons, either.

The people who had also been praised for their efforts, who had been handed their medals and the unspoken promise of pain that awaited them should they disgrace it, had followed him into the night. Defectors from the Revolution were not uncommon—he was one of them, after all—and he told them to find their own way to whatever destiny they sought.

They claimed they feared the Great General's wrath. He told them he did, too, but he told them that the Great General would kill them whether they left or stayed, and so it was better to go.

They claimed they did not know where else to go. He told them he didn't, either, but he also told them that anywhere in the Scar would be as dangerous as anywhere else—people would kill them for ideals and glory, beasts would simply kill them for food.

They made many claims and many reasons and he found none of them reason enough to let them accompany him. Until finally he grew so frustrated that he asked them.

"What the fuck do you see that makes you think I know what the hell *I'm* doing?"

They say he said something else, of course. Something more dramatic and compassionate. But I know the guy and I know what he sounds like.

"You stayed," they said simply. "And then you just left."

He had stayed to put out the fire. He had stayed to help the people. He had stayed to make sure no one had to die. They had watched him do all of this. They had watched him keep his eyes on the fire, instead of looking for approval from Revolutionary commanders. They had watched his eyes glaze over with boredom when the Great General's dogs heaped praise on him. And when he had departed that city in the middle of the night, they watched as he left without even looking back over his shoulder, completely unafraid of the pain that awaited him should he be caught.

When he stayed, he commanded their attention.

When he left, he commanded their respect.

He did not want respect. Or to command anything, really. He was weary. That, too, is not uncommon in the Scar. Everyone is weary out here—weary of beasts, of bandits, of the danger bearing down on them at all points. But he was weary of a thing few other people were weary of.

He was tired of seeing people get hurt for no reason.

He had a choice. As we all do. If he had left them to their fate, to be eaten or killed or robbed, he could have slept soundly. Tragedy was tragedy, but no one ever stopped for tragedy. But he knew that if he did truly leave them, not many would die. Few would even be hurt, in all honesty.

But they would go back. Back to Hightower. Back to the

Revolution. Back to being terrified of who was ready to kill them for the pride of a man they would never see with their own eyes, back to hurting each other to avoid being hurt themselves, back to the same empty victories and hollow triumphs he had seen that had made him leave.

He could live with tragedy. Anyone could.

But that would be a betrayal.

And he found he could not live with that.

He began to walk. And they began to follow. There were problems, of course. They were not hard people who followed him. Many were old, many were weak, all carried scars. Scars that came not from blade or lash, but from fears and paranoia and quiet voices of panic in the backs of their heads that they feared were madness.

He knew they weren't.

The whispers at the backs of their heads hadn't simply blossomed there one terrible evening. They'd been planted, they'd been watered, they'd been tended to. Years of threats, of coerced obedience, of being told what would happen to them if they ever even *questioned* the Great General had left them unable to be free of him, even in their sleep. Not merely him, but the *idea* of him, the singular obsession with pleasing him and his Revolution under the threat of death.

It consumed them, that fear, that obsession, those scars.

The man who led them out of that city knew what those scars were.

He'd known someone like that, once.

But even with those scars, they followed him. He helped them back up when they fell. He fed them what he could when he could. And when they found new towns, new homes, new people to call their own, he wished them well and hoped he'd left them a little better at handling their scars.

Like he hadn't been able to do before.

Many left him, then, and he was happy to see them go to better places than he was going. But when he left their new towns and their new homes, he would often look behind him and find that some still followed him.

"Where are you going?" he asked them.

"We don't know," some of them said. "Where are you going?"

He furrowed his brow and opened his mouth to chastise them. But when he did so, he realized he didn't know, either. He stopped and he pondered and scratched a chin that was starting to grow a beard, until he eventually spoke.

"I don't know," he said. "Somewhere that's not so fucking terrible, I guess."

Again, they said he said something more dramatic and poetic, but this was the gist of it.

It was a good enough reason for him to keep going. And so it was a good enough reason for them to follow.

And more of them did. It wasn't like the Scar had any shortage of people who wished they could be less afraid or who wanted to be somewhere else. Many of them followed him as he went farther east. Many dropped off here and there—returning to their homes or finding new ones or simply disappearing in the middle of the night with whatever they could take. But many stayed with him, still.

There was no shortage of pains, either. As the weeks dragged on, along with the journey, there were beasts to reckon with and bandits to fight off and infighting and shortages and maladies. It was frequently hard—hard enough to make people leave, or be left behind, either beside the road or underneath it.

He tried hard not to let those times cause his own scars to hurt.

Frequently, he failed.

And those times became more and more frequent the more people started to follow him. They took up arms to protect him and the others and he winced that they had to. They visited brutalities on their enemies that had been visited on them, and it was hard work stopping that. He lost many—some to the violence, some to the joy of it—and the nights he stayed up worrying whether he was just leading them into another kind of hell were more than the nights he slept.

And then something happened one day.

One night, he used liquor and smoke to sleep, as he sometimes did. And when he woke up in the morning and stumbled out of his tent, nude and unwashed and still reeking of intoxicants, he was dismayed to find someone flying in the sky waiting for him.

"You are the man they're talking about?" the man hovering in the sky asked.

A mage, he knew—he'd fought them before, didn't care for them. His own band had been unfortunate enough to have had to fend off Vagrants, the only kind of mage worse than every other kind. So when he saw this mage, hovering over him in full Imperial uniform, he looked for a weapon to fight off the imminent Imperium reprisal that he was certain had been coming for him.

Finding nothing to wield but his own cock, he scratched the growing beard on his face instead.

"Uh, maybe?" he said, in the sort of way you wouldn't expect a man leading hundreds to sound. But then, you probably wouldn't expect that sort of man to show up to talk to an enemy while nude, either. "Who wants to know?"

"Galvarang ki Anathoros," the mage replied, offering a bow in midair. "I have heard it said that you lead this rabble."

"Well, I wouldn't call them 'rabble,' but I suppose I do have some sway here."

"You are unclothed," the mage pointed out.

"You *did* show up unannounced," he replied.

The mage leveled a glare, sharpened by magic and war, upon the man. He hissed ruefully through his teeth. "How do you hope to lead them like this? My regiment stands not ten miles away, ready to strike should they even get the faintest *whiff* of your excursion. How do you intend to deal with them should they arrive and find you, who has taken their loyal subjects from their Imperial homes?"

"Depends." He scratched his ass. "Am I still naked when it happens in this hypothetical?"

The mage narrowed his eyes. He sighed.

"I don't know. I guess I'd ask those subjects if they wanted to stay here with me." He gestured over the roughly put-together camp. "With all of us."

"And if they did not?" the mage asked.

"Then I would wish them well."

"And if they did want to stay?"

The man, tired and sweaty and naked and reeking of foul substances, looked up at the mage flying over him in his regal uniform. The man sniffed once, scratched his beard, and spoke.

"Then I'd stay with them."

The mage quirked a brow. He descended and landed upon the earth. Words were exchanged. And continued being exchanged as day turned to night. The others huddled around the man's tent as he spoke to the mage inside, waiting for the violence to happen.

It did.

A week later, the mage's regiment did arrive. And they did take umbrage at this man who had led so many of their loyal citizens astray from their secure Imperial homes. They attacked, as the mage said they would. And the man stayed with his people, as he said he would.

And when they took up arms to fight back against the Imperium, it was Galvarang ki Anathoros who led the charge against his own people.

The battle ended swiftly. The talking that followed did not. More words, more weeks, more walking followed. And when the man and his people finally left that region behind them, it was mages and soldiers that walked with them.

There was still hardship. In the Scar, there always would be. There were vengeful Imperials that pursued and hampered them. There were fanatical Revolutionaries that fought them. The battles were hard. Many died. Not everyone wanted to hear words.

The man bore those hardships over many hard nights, as well.

But he found it was easier, even if it was never easy. The people they picked up from one town knew how to tend wounds and treat infections. The Revolutionaries who had defected from another regiment knew how to fix machines. The Imperials who had come from another city knew how to cook.

It's said he learned from them, and I don't know if that's true.

But it's also said that his curry is delicious and that, I can say for a fact, is *mostly* true—I don't care for raisins in mine, personally.

But for as many as joined them, there were more that fought them. The Great General would not have it said that his people feared him so much they would prefer to face the wilds than live under his laws. The mages of Cathama were infuriated to hear that a band of ragged refugees continued to thwart their advances.

There were fights. More than he could ever keep track of. And the nights that had become easier grew harder as he grew to realize that there was no place safe for them. That this truly *would* be it: this endless fleeing from one threat to another, losing too many people to sleep comfortably, gaining too many people to ever be able to leave them all behind.

I sympathized with that, when I heard it.

He grew desperate, and they along with him. Desperation was different than fear. Fear made you more sensible. Desperation didn't. It wasn't a fearful man who pointed so far east they don't make maps for it and suggested they go there. It wasn't a fearful people who decided to follow him.

But not a single one of them would have called themselves brave when they went into the Nails. And when they got there, they called themselves insane.

The brutal sun, the hostile terrain, the freezing nights, and the endless monsters made them question their decision to follow him. And, more than that, they questioned his decision to lead them out there.

So he sat down one evening while he was making his curry and he spoke.

"It is a bad place out here," he said. "And it's going to be a bad place no matter where we go."

"My bed is back in my house in my town," one person grumbled.

"My farm needs me," another one said.

"At least the Great General provided for my family," another said.

"But it wasn't your bed," he replied. "It wasn't your farm. And, I'm sorry to say, it wasn't even your family. It was the Imperium's bed. The Ashmouths' farm. The Great General's family."

"Birdshit," someone snapped.

"Then go back," he said, barely looking up from his curry. "Go back to your bed, your farm, your family. But answer me this. If the big people with the big guns and the big spells show up at your house and say it's their house now, do you think it'll matter to them that you built it yourself or that you raised your children there?"

At that, no one said anything.

And in the morning that followed, there were a few that had turned back.

But more had stayed.

They followed him to the middle of that horrific place. They set up their tents. They started building. They started making. They started cooking and growing and hunting and living. And though they were not free of the hardships of the land, they were at least free to carve from those hardships themselves without someone bigger taking it from them.

Which did nothing about the Banters.

Their biggest source of frustration turned out to be the birds. Not merely the birds, but their riders as well. The Nails were home to a lot of terrible creatures, and some of them were human.

When Banter riders harried them across the plains, they found themselves ill-equipped to deal with them. They could fight off bandits *or* build, but not both. Even the mages and Revolutionary defectors they picked up were no match for the birds.

So the man, one day, walked out to the middle of the plain without a weapon. And he waited.

It took a long time before the Banter riders showed up—long enough that he'd started cooking some soup. And when the birds and their bandits had surrounded him, he barely looked up. If they were going to kill him, he knew, they would do so when they felt like it.

"It's not like I wanted to die having made shitty soup," he had told me, when I asked him about it.

The riders—remorseless, relentless, their faces weathered and hardened by this land and its dire cost for survival—merely glowered at him. It wasn't until one of them, a pale woman with red hair, stepped down and approached him that any words were exchanged.

"You're on the wrong side of the Scar," she said.

"I agree," he replied. "This place is fucking awful."

"Then you can be on your way," she replied harshly. "Leave your metal, weapons, and any fighting aged people behind and go. The Nails aren't a place for weaklings."

"I agree with that, too," he said. "Honestly, this place doesn't seem like a place for anyone."

"It's a place for us," she said. She pounded her chest. "*We* fight. *We* ride. *We* live. And I lead."

"What is your name?"

She paused. "Ketterling. Killer Ketterling."

"Why 'Killer'?"

"Because I'm in charge."

"Could you be in charge with a different name?"

"No. They follow me because I'm the strongest."

"I believe it." He ladled something into a bowl, offered it to her. "Soup?"

She responded by kicking it out of his hand. "Leave."

"I'd prefer not to."

"I didn't ask."

"You didn't," he replied. "But if you don't want to ask, then you'll have to remove us by force."

"I *just* told you I was the strongest."

"You did. And I told you I believed you. And if you told me you were going to kill us all and leave none standing, I'd believe that, too." He glanced back to the collection of tents his people crowded in. "But if you did that, you'd have to fight all of us. We have nowhere else to go, so we'd have no real choice but to dig in and fight. And you'd kill us all, for sure, but then you'd lose some people, too."

He glanced over the riders, pointed to them with his spoon. "How about him? What does he do?"

"That's Machlan. He's the fastest rider we have."

"If he died, would you still be able to talk without a fast rider?" the man asked. He slurped his soup, pointed to another rider. "What about her?"

"Vechita can hit harder than anyone out here."

"The beasts here have hides like iron, I can see why you'd need that. But if she died, how would you fight them? How long would you last out here if all your best were killed by us before your best killed all of us?"

"I see what you're doing. I'm not stupid."

"You probably wouldn't be if you were in charge, no."

"But regardless of who you killed, you'd still all be dead and we'd still have all your stuff."

"I get that, too," he replied. "But you'd be dead for no particular reason, since I'm sitting here offering you stuff I have to begin with." He ladled another bowl. "So I ask again . . . soup?"

And Killer Ketterling, before she decided to just go by Ketterling, paused and glared at him. And she glared harder at her riders who might doubt her. And she got off her mount and sat down and held out her hand.

"Fine," she said. "Give me the soup."

"Gladly," he replied. "But pick up your bowl first. I'm not fucking getting you another one."

She did not kill him for that. Or for any of the other things he said while they talked that night. When her riders got bored and started howling for blood, she merely told them to go back to their camp. A day and a night passed where her axe, big and broad, did not leave her side, never discarded but never drawn.

On the second day, Killer Ketterling and her riders came to the man's camp and met his people.

On the second week, Killer Ketterling and her riders began to trade with the people from the man's camp.

On the second month, Killer Ketterling and her riders had begun to move their camp closer to the man's camp.

And, sometime after that, Ketterling and the man were wed.

I asked for more details about that—because who wouldn't?—and no one has any real idea when it happened and none of the rumors I heard about it were at all interesting.

You know what happened next.

The woman with the gun who left Hightower in flames found her way to the Borrus Valley. She made some choices there and some mistakes to go with them. And, after all was said and done, there was another war. It was a grim time for almost everywhere in the Scar.

But not for the people in the Nails.

The riders, the refugees, the defectors and the deserters were, for once, left free of the interference of the powers that were now concerned with destroying each other. And with their new freedom, they began to build. The riders became hunters, the refugees became builders, the defectors became leaders, and the deserters became protectors. Yet none of them forgot the pains they had carried before—their weapons, their powers, their scars—but they were *their* pains now, in service of their own fates.

And none of them forgot the man who led them to that.

The man himself continued to build. And cook. And talk. It was exhausting work. Work that I wouldn't have survived. But he kept going. Just like he always had. Just like he always would.

And the more he kept going, the more people began to arrive. More deserters. More refugees. More people.

He asked them to help him build. And they did.

Camps became houses. Houses became a village. A village became a town. Though not until the Imperial defectors insisted on an opera house did they call it a city. It isn't truly civilized, some very intelligent and attractive people say, until there's opera.

The man didn't quite understand but, thankfully, he didn't question it.

And one day the man looked over his city, its many houses and its many people and their many problems. And he believed he had gone far enough. This dead earth, these desperate people—he wanted nothing more than them.

He stopped walking.

He stopped looking.

He found what he wanted.

And he gave it a name.

THIRTY-TWO

NEW VIGIL

New Vigil." Cavric glanced over his shoulder at me with too much intent to be considered merely a glance. "Not bad, huh?"

I looked up at the city looming over the horizon and bit my tongue. In the middle of the vast, blasted plain of the lowland Nails, crowded around by mountains and looming peaks, lay a...

Well, it was a nice wall, at any rate.

Heavy sandstone bricks stood in resilient formation, an imposing wedge set defiantly against the hostile landscape. A pair of massive iron gates hung open—not invitingly, but at least a little more warmly than they would appear shut and barred. But it was the wall's workers that truly caught my eye.

Situated upon the battlements, I could see Graspmages hovering in repose, waving a hand to beckon heavy stones up great heights. Repurposed Revolutionary machines and tools whirred and buzzed as the stones were set into position and the wall grew taller, brick by brick.

It was lower than it ought to be—clearly, the work was slow-going and difficult—but it was already more impressive than most cities' defenses. A stern warning against the forces that would seek its ruin. A defiant position against the wilds of this world. A good, fine wall.

Not quite sure why they were going to so much trouble to protect a pile of shit, but I suppose that's one of many reasons why I don't work on walls.

Once we joined the stream of weary, weatherworn people entering the city, the buildings got significantly less impressive. Most of them were skeletons, the bare bones of homes they had only just begun building. Others were ramshackle and scavenged, torn apart for their precious lumber and stone. Only a scant few were whole—a handful of homes here and there, a tavern, and in the distance, I could see the domed amphitheater of an opera house.

Not a Cathama opera house or an Anchylus opera house. Not even a fucking Genzire opera house. But I applauded the effort, nonetheless.

All in all, I found New Vigil to be mostly a ramshackle mess of a town with a big fucking wall.

But I had also burned the old Vigil to the ground, so it wasn't like I could say shit.

"Not bad," I agreed as we rode farther into town. "Not great, either."

"Hm. I suppose it does look a little shabby." From high atop his steed—an enormous Badlander that he no doubt learned to appreciate the merits of—Cavric stroked a long worry of a beard that he hadn't had when I last saw him. "Oh, well. If you don't like it, you can always fuck back off into the desert."

"Don't fucking tempt me, you dumb—"

"It's a fine city." Liette rushed her crane forward, cutting off both me and my retort. "And we are grateful for the opportunity to have some reprieve." She glanced far ahead, to where Ketterling and her riders pointedly rode. "And *apologetic* with regard to the circumstances that led to our otherwise-fortunate reunion." She glowered at me behind her glasses. "Are we not?"

"Yeah," I grunted. "Sorry about your wife, Cavric."

Eyes that had been way less tired the last time I had looked into them pricked open. "Is that a 'sorry I made your wife bleed, Cavric' or a 'sorry you're married to your wife, Cavric'?"

"Both, I guess."

Admittedly, the answer to that wasn't polite. But in my defense, it wasn't polite of him to give me the option, either.

"Then I guess I'm only a little offended." Cavric let out a weary sigh that still cut me, even today, and waved a hand. "You're right, though. The city is shitty. It has shitty amenities. It's in a shitty place."

Liette surveyed the various inhabitants in the dirt streets as they went about the business of hammering houses together, doling out sustenance to hungry lines of workers, or sometimes rooting out various venomous creatures from holes cropping up around the city.

"While I can certainly accept your frank appraisal of your city's array," she said, adjusting her glasses, "I question whether you should do so with such... volume. Your people seem to be somewhat demoralized."

"I appreciate your concern, but I'm sure they're fine." Cavric pointed down from his bird at a nearby citizen hauling a dead carcass of what looked like a spider with a *truly* unacceptable number of legs. "You there. How's your morale?"

"I'm hot, I'm thirsty, and every time these things sting me, I start hearing the voices of my dead parents," the citizen replied. "If you wouldn't mind kindly fucking off, sir?"

"See?" Cavric said, resuming our walk. "He's fine."

"He didn't sound fine," Liette said.

"He sounded like he was living a shit life and had no illusions about it," I interjected. "He wouldn't sound fine if he were happy about that."

Cavric tapped his head and winked at me. "New Vigil may not be the best city, or even a good city, but it's the most honest city. Life is hard. You will be buried here in a deep hole dug into cold earth. I would do no one here any favors by pretending otherwise." He smiled, broader than he'd ever smiled around me. "But at least you die with the satisfaction of knowing you died for yourself and not for a general or an empress."

"Uh-huh." My nostrils quivered. "Or maybe some people just really like the odor of birdshit baking on the earth."

"Maybe." Cavric tilted his chin upward. "You can ask your friends there if the smell bothers them."

I felt my body tense even before I looked. As the small section of the city that was actually built gave way to the hills and plain of the rest of it, I saw the country dotted with tents. Familiar bodies gathered around them and the many cookfires—bodies that were bent, tired, and familiar.

The bodies I knew. The faces I didn't recognize.

I knew they were the refugees—the same that I'd walked with for months. I recognized their worn clothes and their meager possessions. But their faces, the icy masks of fear and anger that they'd worn, had begun to thaw. They were sitting there, laughing, talking, looking...well, not happy, but something closer to it than what I'd given them.

"When did they get here?" I asked.

"Ketterling found them a few days before you," Cavric responded. "She brought them back here before heading out to see if anyone was looking for them." He glowered over his shoulder. "Not that I *necessarily* believe you're here for them, but I should warn you that they aren't going anywhere they don't want to."

"It's rather rude to suggest I'm here to kidnap people, Cavric," I replied.

"You kidnapped *me*," he snapped back.

"Yes, and I'm a little sensitive about it, thank you."

"*I truly hate to interrupt*," Liette interrupted in a way she was clearly not unhappy about, "but given that I *have* just come in from a *very* long ride that culminated in being pursued by several unruly persons atop several unruly birds, I must preemptively reiterate my level of exhaustion at the moment." She removed her glasses, wiped them off. "To this end, Cavric, if you *do* still hold a grudge over the situation that led to your imprisonment, I insist you execute me and I insist on it being done swiftly, as I would find the promise of death preferable to riding for even just one more minute, but only if it came promptly so as to spare me more of this conversation."

Cavric blinked, his mouth hanging open briefly. I didn't blame him. I would have, too, if I wasn't trying desperately to keep the color from rising to my cheeks.

Don't judge me. I couldn't help it. I love it when she gets all *wordy* like that.

"I've got a place, yeah." Cavric rubbed his eyes, gestured vaguely in a direction. "Ost's Grave is just up the road. Tell them I said to give you a room."

"I will inform Ost that I am fully capable of paying for my own room." Liette pulled on her crane's reins. "Given the rather ungainly state of your nascent civilization, I would expect that the mere presence of money would elicit a sort of primitive uproar as we see when rain relieves drought. Were I so tempted, I expect I could purchase the entire city from you and still have enough left over for noodles. I mean this not as an out-and-out criticism, merely a frank appraisal of the situation."

She looked over her shoulder.

"It's good to see you again, Cavric," she said, like anyone would know that's what she meant.

And she was off, her crane picking its way elegantly through the streets. Cavric deflated, his heavy frame looking several pounds heavier as he sighed.

"Glad to see Liette hasn't changed," he observed. "Even if I've gotten dumber. I think I understood even less of what she said than the last time, but I still got that she was insulting me." He furrowed his brow. "Or...was she?"

I was only barely listening to him. I stared out at the distant refugees, at the people who had followed me and been chased for so long. What did they speak of me now? I wondered. Did they fear me? Hate me? I was afraid to know. And because I was afraid, I was angry. And because I was angry, I found myself moving Congeniality toward them.

"Hey."

Until he spoke.

Cavric shook a heavy head, sent his heavy beard swaying. "Don't, Sal."

"I'm not going to do anything."

"I believe you," he said. "I believe you when you say that, anyway. But what they need right now isn't you."

"I know that," I snapped, more defensively than I intended. "But I... I don't know. I fucked things up for them. I feel like I owe them..."

Don't I?

"You don't," Cavric said, as if in response to my thoughts. "You got them this far, one way or another. However they got here, they're here now. What they need now is something in their bellies and something to do with their hands. You can't give them that." He smiled softly. Not weakly. His smile was the itchy comfort of a threadbare blanket—harsher than I'd hoped, gentler than I'd feared. "You're a different kind of person."

I observed him flatly. "You haven't changed, either, Cavric."

"Yeah?" he chuckled. "Glad to see that?"

"I didn't say that."

"Yeah, you didn't." His smile didn't diminish, though it did grow a tad itchier, so to speak. "You sure you don't need to be with her right now? Or with your other friends?"

My mind drifted back to the moments before we'd entered the city. To the brief, hurried words I'd had.

"No, I'm sorry, but... no."

Urda's voice. It had been soft—it was always soft, of course. But when we arrived here, it had been softer than I could ever have imagined.

"Yria's been putting it off for so long, trying to pretend that she's strong enough to withstand it, but she's my *sister. I can't let her keep being dragged into this... this...* all *of it. Whatever you need to do at this city, please just... don't include her. Please. Let me take care of her. Just for a while."*

Had he always sounded like that? I was so used to him sounding afraid and nervous that I didn't notice when he started sounding weak, his voice so hoarse he could barely get a word out without wincing. Had he always been that pale? That thin? That sick-looking?

"No, no, NO. I'm not *going to do that. It's* not *just for a while. She can't do this anymore, Sal. She can't do portals for you. She can't do* anything *for you anymore! She's killing herself for you and you don't... you don't even seem to care that she is. And even if you did, it wouldn't be okay."*

Had I always made him shake like that?

"I... I can't stop you. I know that. But if you care about her, Sal, if you ever really did... please, just leave us alone."

I couldn't remember what I said. If I even said anything when I let them go. But I remember what I said to Agne.

"Can you believe this?"

My voice had felt like hot iron in my mouth. Something painful and burning on my tongue.

"Finally get a moment to stop shitting ourselves in fear over what's trying to kill us and Urda starts... starts just... ah, fuck it. Fuck it and fuck him. He said... he said..."

I'd tried to forced it out, but it hurt too much. I'd looked to Agne and she didn't even bother staring back. From atop her bird, her eyes were distant and her expression was empty. Even as I felt like I was about to start bleeding from my mouth, she barely seemed to notice.

"He said it was my fault. He said Yria is killing herself for us. For me. He said it like... like nothing else we did mattered. Like all that we did for Liette and everyone else was just... just..."

It burned on my lips. It hurt to speak the words. But it hurt worse to hold them in. And neither hurt as bad as seeing Agne's vague disinterest play across her face.

"I don't know what to do here, Agnestrada. I thought I did. I thought I fucking knew, but now I don't know if I ever did. What if she did kill herself for me and we have to run again? What the fuck am I going to do with that? How... what am I supposed to do? How do I fix this?"

Short, hushed, and rushed—I'd spit the words out like poison. Every second they lingered on my tongue, I felt sick. Yet even for all that, for all the churning in my stomach and the queasiness in my throat, I couldn't bring myself to ask what I really wanted.

"Do they hate me, Agne? Do—"

I couldn't finish it.

Not when she looked at me, that beautiful woman who was once so afraid of spiders and had once wept in my arms when she heard a song on a voccaphone that reminded her of someone. And when her shoulders rose and fell in a bored shrug, I felt like a moron for even asking.

When she drifted off to find something else to do, I didn't stop her.

I didn't cry, either.

"They'll be okay," I said, feeling no less sick.

"What about him?" Cavric asked.

I looked down the street he gestured toward. Jindu sat with a group of other people who, despite being war-torn refugees, somehow looked better dressed than his shabby ass did. They silently sipped tea from a kettle, muttered softly among themselves. He only glanced toward me once, as if to check I was still there.

He'd been the only one I hadn't spoken to on the road.

The only one I was terrified of.

Not of what he'd say. But of what I'd do when I heard it.

"Him, too." I let my eyes drift toward Cavric's mount, the big gray Badlander adjusting himself beneath Cavric's frame. "I see you found some good taste in mounts."

"Yeah, well." Cavric nodded approvingly toward Congeniality. "I liked the one I met once. And they're good for terrain like this."

"Uh-huh. You figured out how to make them stop puking when they're mad?"

"No. How do you do it?"

"I was asking you."

"Great. Good talk." Cavric sighed, pulled his bird back down the street from which we'd come. "Given that the conversation has turned to vomit, I assume that we're probably finished here. You can find Ost's on your own. Nice to see you, Sal."

I don't know why he kept walking. I don't know why I felt like I needed to call out to him.

"You sure you should leave Sal the Cacophony alone in your city?" I asked. "I...I burned down Vigil, you know."

"I know," he said without looking back. "And if you decide to burn this one, I know I probably won't be able to stop you, either. But, like I said, if you hate the city, there's always the desert."

"Do you want me to leave?" I shouted at him.

"I don't want you to burn down my city," he replied, shrugging. "Past that, I don't really know what you want to do."

The poison came swirling back to my tongue, the bitter words that made me sick to hold them again. The words I'd wanted to say to Urda, to Agne, to everyone else. I don't know why I chose to say them, then. I didn't even shout them. They came tumbling out of my mouth, soft and delicate like a candle flame. And when they fell to the earth, they were snuffed out before anyone could hear them.

"What if...I want to stay?"

Or so I thought.

Cavric pulled on his reins. He sat there atop his mount, not moving a muscle. He drew in a long breath and I saw his broad shoulders puff up.

"Do you want to stay?" he asked.

The words choked in my mouth. I couldn't bring myself to speak them. I couldn't ask him to hurt himself like Yria and Agne and every other poor bastard had. I didn't say anything. I waited for him to keep walking.

He didn't.

He turned his bird around.

And he looked at me with the same wide eyes that I remembered—as big and bright and full of that naïve, stupid hopefulness that had made me think he was a fucking moron and I was a fucking terrible person for thinking it.

"Sal," he said, "do you need help?"

My mouth hung open. My breath was labored. I tasted copper and blood in my mouth and my nose. The poison words, the terrible words that seemed to ruin everything, burned on my tongue. I felt a tear trickle down the length of my scar.

"I need," I said, "a drink."

And he didn't roll his eyes. Or laugh like it was a joke. He just nodded and he beckoned with his chin.

"Come on," he said. "I know a place."

He waited for me to come along. He slowed his pace to walk with me. He said nothing, barely even looked at me. But he didn't have to.

He was there. Just sitting there. Like I wasn't the most dangerous thing in the world.

When I'd met Cavric, I'd thought he was a buffoon. He served the Revolution like it was a good organization, he talked to people like they weren't bastards, and he believed me when I said I didn't want to solve all my problems with violence. I'd thought him an idiot. A good idiot, a brave idiot, but just one more idiot destined to become one more plot of black earth in the Scar.

Maybe he had never been an idiot. Or maybe he still was and I just never knew how good a thing that could be. I didn't know and right then, I wasn't about to question it.

For once, it felt like someone was around me that wanted to be around me.

And I was hoping to ride that as long as it lasted.

THIRTY-THREE

NEW VIGIL

"All right, in my defense," Cavric said, approximately thirty minutes later, "I didn't say I believed Sal *would* murder us all in our sleep, I only said that *if* she did, I wouldn't be surprised."

The feeling of hopefulness I'd had when we entered had been nice while it lasted. The feeling of creeping irritation that had been crawling up my back ever since was decidedly less nice. But the feeling of cheap whiskey filling my belly evened me out to a vaguely disgruntled.

"Oh, my apologies, then. So long as she's *only* a *potential* slaughterer of masses, it's fine. We can't go around being wary of people with magic fucking guns, can we? Wouldn't want to be rude."

Which, given the circumstances, was a nicer feeling than I was anticipating.

"I didn't say that, either," Cavric replied. "There's an answer between waiting for death and inviting it in."

"Not in the Nails, there isn't," Ketterling snarled.

"We're not in the Nails," he replied. "We're in New Vigil."

"There's no difference."

"If there was no difference, we wouldn't have bothered building the city." Cavric held up a hand to preclude any objection. "That is *not* to say you're wrong to worry." He looked at me and frowned. "Or to be suspicious."

"You think I'm lying?" I asked, taking a fighting swig of whiskey. "You think I wouldn't come up with something better for a lie than *that*?"

"Cavric thinks you're lying," Ketterling replied. "*I* think you're a fetid pile of birdshit we should throw off the wall."

"*Not* lying," Cavric interjected before I could deliver my stunning retort. "I just want to be sure that nothing is being left out." He leveled his eyes upon me. "You asked for help. Technically. So if you want it, it helps if we know everything, correct?"

I wanted help. I also wanted no one else to die because of me. And because those two thoughts were hard to think about at the same time, I wanted to finish my drink and fight them both instead of thinking.

But there were probably many reasons why that wasn't a good idea.

"Correct," I sighed.

"So, then, let me make sure I've got it straight," Cavric said. "There is a Scrath inside Liette. A being that has the power to potentially kill us—a being you yourself believe is slowly growing stronger inside her—and you believe that the best chance of saving her is to draw that Scrath out of her using..."

A long, awkward silence. He didn't want to say the weapon's name. I didn't blame him.

"The Cacophony," I finished for him.

"Using the Cacophony," he said, "a gun I know for a *fact* can kill us all. And because you're being pursued by the Revolution and the Imperium—"

"And the Ashmouths."

"And the Ashmouths, yes, thank you. Because you're being pursued by all three of the most dangerous powers in the Scar, you want to use the city I have labored long and lovingly to build to do this extraordinarily dangerous thing, which you're not sure will even work and you can't guarantee that it *won't* end horrifically."

"I don't recall saying it was *extraordinarily* dangerous," I replied, swirling my drink. "But yes, that's the gist of it."

"Okay, excellent. I was worried that you hadn't gotten to the crazy part yet."

I sneered at him. Mostly because I would have rather hit him and it seemed rude to do that when he'd just invited me into his command center.

Or his tavern.

One building served both functions in New Vigil. The "historic" tavern, made so by way of the fact that it was technically the first building finished in this burg, was where the soldiers of the city worked, worried, deliberated, and plotted. And, when you're doing all of that in a land that's trying its best to destroy you, that tends to involve a lot of drinking.

"I'm sorry," Cavric sighed. "I don't mean to be flippant. I just… that's a lot. A lot on top of a lot."

He finished his long sigh by draining his entire flagon of beer in one go. Suddenly the heavier weight on his frame made a lot of sense. There were worse ways to cope with the stress of leading a city than drinking and eating, after all. I preferred drinking and drugs, but to each their own.

It's not like I could fault him, either. I'd told him everything—about the Valley, about Eldest and Liette, about Ocytus and the Ashmouths and Toadback and the Vagrants and Torle and…

Well, who wouldn't want to drink after hearing all that?

But seeing the defeat seeping through his face, the utter helplessness brimming through his beard at the situation, I almost wished I hadn't bothered. It's not like I could blame him for that, either. What could he do? What could anyone? I and the whole-ass Cacophony hadn't come up with anything.

"You think I don't know that?" I sighed myself, trying admirably to keep up with his drinking. "I've heard about this place. I didn't want to come here for the same reason she doesn't want me here." I gestured to Ketterling with what I hoped was an adequately offensive gesture. "You've got your own problems."

"It's not that Ketterling doesn't want you here," Cavric said.

"It is that," Ketterling retorted. "It is *exactly* that."

"All right, fine, it's not that you *need* to not be here," he said, sparing a glower. "New Vigil *had* been doing well enough up until a while ago. Neither the Imperium nor the Revolution want us here, but we'd been able to build without them attacking us. In part because of their war."

"You're welcome."

From the unblinking offense present on the faces turned my way, I gathered that was probably the wrong thing to say.

"Well, I mean, if *any* good was going to come out of it," I tried to offer before draining my glass and pouring another. "Why would they even bother with anything out in the Nails? There's nothing out here but beasts and badlands."

"And us," Cavric said. "All of us. Traitors, deserters, defectors, and everyone else who turned their back on the powers that run this place."

"Lots of people think the Imperials and Revolutionaries are shit."

"Yes, but who else has told them that to their face and lived?" Cavric said. "We have. We have for a long time. And neither of them are pleased about it."

"You don't seem to be too thrilled about them, either," I observed. "I saw the handiwork you left of them on the cliffs."

"Warnings," Ketterling growled. "Let them know that they aren't welcome here. It worked before."

"Before, it was just bandit clans out here," Cavric said. "Bandits can only steal their stuff and kill their people. *We* can refuse to kneel. Of those two offenses, only one is intolerable to a ruler."

Ketterling spat something angry, but formed no other objection. From the way she folded her arms, I gathered this was a conversation they'd had many times before and it had ended badly each and every time.

"The war is drifting toward us," Cavric said. "And every inch it gets closer, the harder it is for them to find a reason to tolerate our presence. We've rooted out Revolutionary spies and agitators trying to win our defectors back. We've found Scrymages and Maskmages slipping in and observing us. The Vigilants have been able to find them all, but—"

"Vigilants?" I asked. "That's what you call your soldiers?"

"Yeah. Because of New Vigil. Not bad, right?"

"Why not Vigilantes? It sounds nicer."

"Well, anyone can be a vigilante."

"Why not New Vigilants?"

"*Point being*," he interrupted with a bellow, "we're not able to fight them off like we used to. We've got mages and Revolutionaries of our own. But we don't have training of our own or the vast, vast, *vast* resources that two gigantic sprawling empires have. It's slow going. We're being whittled down. And eventually, the Imperials and Revolutionaries will catch on that we can't keep them out."

He became aware, at some point after that, of how tight his hands curled, of how hot his breathing had become, of how stiff his chest had grown. Ketterling shot him a concerned glance, visibly restrained herself from reaching out. Cavric paused, drew in a deep breath, let it out, took another drink.

"It helps if we know everything, doesn't it?" he asked through a heavy sigh. "And if you want our help, you need to know what we'd be giving up to help you." He ran a hand through unwashed hair. "So, I'll ask again... do you want our help?"

I didn't.

I know that sounds weird to say, given all that I'd been through. But in that moment, I didn't want their help. I didn't want to be worrying about what I owed them for it. I didn't want to take another drink each night to try to forget the ways I hurt them for helping me. I just... didn't want that. I didn't want that so much that I just wanted to throw my drink in someone's face and storm out.

"Yes," I whispered. "I do want your help."

But I knew I couldn't have what I wanted. Not this time.

Cavric held my gaze for a long moment, as if he were waiting for me to throw a punch or an insult or something else. And I won't lie—sitting there, holding his eyes with mine like that, knowing that he could see the urge in me to run just as keenly as I felt it...

Well, fuck. Let's just say I've had a lot of bad hits I'd take again before this one.

He rolled his tongue around in his mouth. His eyes drifted agonizingly slowly to his right, over his shoulder toward a distant table.

"What do you think?" he asked.

A figure at the other end of the room stirred. A silhouette rose from a table and walked over. And by the time I caught the glint off of Meret's glasses, I was already looking away.

I take it back about that moment with Cavric being the worst hit I'd felt. That was just the windup. This was the punch.

Meret slumped down into a chair. The coat he wore now—in the Vigilants' green—looked ill-fitting on him, even though I knew I'd seen him wearing that size before. He'd grown thinner. And the brightness in his eyes that war, walking, and loss had failed to diminish now looked dimmer. Duller.

"Meret," I whispered, finally mustering the nerve to face him. "I...you made it."

"He arrived with the others," Ketterling said, inclining her head toward him. "He found them space, brought them into town, even got us some help from them. We're damn lucky to have him." She glanced at me, snorted. "Or we were."

"He's done a lot to win us the help of the refugees," Cavric said, folding his hands together. "And he's earned a place at this conversation, both for his help." He looked back at me, intently. "And for his insight."

All eyes turned toward Meret, even as Meret's eyes were fixed dully on his hands. I wondered if what was running through his head was the same as what was running through mine, if he was also wondering how it was that he'd managed to see so much suffering and stay unbroken. Until we met.

"Then share it," Ketterling said, eyes drifting toward me. "All of it."

"I... I don't know," Meret said softly. "I believe Sal." He smacked his lips, swallowed something dry and painful. "But I believed her when she led us to Toadback. And everywhere else. And everywhere, we've lost more people. I can't even remember them all, some nights, no matter how hard I try and..."

He took his glasses off, rubbed dark-circled eyes with the heel of his palm.

"I'm good at believing people. I'm good at thinking they're good. And Sal didn't have to lead us, but she did. But I'm not always right. And when I needed to know, I'd ask Sindra and..." He shut his eyes tight, but not tight enough to keep the tears from coming. "She's gone now. And I don't know. I believe Sal needs our help. I believe we should help her. But I... I don't know if I'm right."

Whatever pain he swallowed, it cut him deeply. It made him wither in his seat, almost fall over. Cavric sighed, clapped him lightly on the shoulder, or as light as that heavy hand could manage. Ketterling sneered, slammed her hands on the table.

"And you know what I think," she said.

"Yes," Cavric replied, "I do."

"*Well, I'm going to fucking say it again because someone has to.*" Ketterling leveled a finger at me. "Do you fucking know what you're entertaining? Even without the shit about the Scrath, that is *Sal the Cacophony.* She doesn't destroy cities with her big evil gun, she does it just by *visiting* them. I don't believe the shit her stories say, but I know how to fucking count." And she did so, on each weathered finger. "Lastlight. Lowstaff. The entire fucking Borrus Valley. Six Walls. Toadback. We're out in the fucking *Nails* and we know how many she's destroyed."

"Don't fucking blame me for Six Walls," I snarled, rising out of my chair. "That was the Imperium."

"Fighting the war *you* started!" Ketterling shot to her feet, hands curled around the haft of an axe she wished was there. "And they'll fucking chase you here. If it's the Revolution, they'll execute every mage who worked with us and conscript the rest."

"And if it's the Imperium, they'll incinerate us all for looking at them funny," Cavric sighed, rubbing his head. "We knew that was true, whether or not Sal is here."

"Then admit that we *don't* need the extra risk," she snarled, leaning over him. "Have you already fucking forgotten what this city is supposed to be about?"

"HAVE YOU?"

Cavric burst to his feet, sending the table shifting and the drinks spilling. His broad frame quivered, his brows thick and knitted over a pair of wide, wild eyes.

"I remember every risk I've taken to get here," he bellowed. "I remember the first Revolutionary defectors I accepted, knowing they'd be trouble. I remember the first mages that joined me, knowing *they'd* be trouble. I remember because this place, this whole fucking city, is *supposed* to be for people who want to take that risk. To live whatever life they want that the people with the guns and magic won't let them have. New Vigil is supposed to be a place for people like that. Like me and you."

He pointed a finger angrily in my direction.

"AND HER."

Ketterling's mouth hung open in rage. She stepped forward as if to strike him. He held himself tall, as if to let her. She curled her hands into fists, clenched her teeth so hard I could hear the ivories cracking. He planted his feet, snorted, and sent his beard shuddering. She let out an angry snarl in his face, slammed the table with her hand multiple times, then turned and stormed out.

When the drinks stopped spilling and the lamps stopped swaying from the force of her slamming the door, I was left with two dour-looking men and an awkward silence.

"So," I said, "at least with that kind of energy, the sex must be great, right?"

In hindsight, I probably shouldn't have tried to break it.

"That is none of your business," Cavric replied. "And she's entitled to be angry, even if she agrees with me."

"*That* was agreement?"

"You didn't see a weapon come out, did you?" I could tell he was trying to joke, but it was difficult with a tone that defeated. "And I agree with her, even if not about everything. What else could I tell her? There are no celebrations when you come to town, Sal."

That was true of everywhere but Keverly's Last Woe, but now wasn't the time to bring that up.

"You could tell her what you know about me."

I felt the weight of my steel and brass hang on my hips. My footsteps thundered in that soft space as I stood before him and rested a hand on the black hilt of the Cacophony.

"That you don't know anyone better at handling the Revolution, the Imperium, Haven, the Ashmouths, or any shithead with a dream and a sword better than me." I tilted my head back, looked down my scar at him. "If you want me to, I will. And if she wants that in writing, I can borrow a pen."

Cavric glanced me over briefly, before his eyes settled on that large gun on my hip. A flash of worry creased his brow, a pang of regret lit up his eyes. The Cacophony burned with a low and gentle pleasure at his unease.

But the big man took a big breath, let out a big sigh, and smiled at me.

"Why would anyone need a promise from you?" he asked. "After all, how would you live with yourself if it was said that Sal the Cacophony accepted help and never returned it?"

I grinned a little. "It's nice to see you again, dickhead."

"Likewise," he replied, his smile falling as he turned away. "Let's see if it lasts."

He shut the door on his way out, leaving me alone. Almost.

I wanted to run from that room, from Meret. Failing that, I wanted to let him spit whatever hatred he wanted, whatever anger he held at me. But he would never do that, I knew. And I knew that this time, I couldn't run.

No matter how badly I wanted to.

"I'm sorry."

My whisper was funeral-soft, fearful and timid. I didn't know my voice got that soft. Maybe it didn't before then.

"I know you probably don't want to hear that. I know it... it doesn't bring Sindra back. Or make it hurt less that she's gone. Or... or..."

The words hurt to say. Same way it hurts to do anything you're not good at. You don't like being reminded of all the ways you aren't a complete person. You don't like knowing you can't do what it seems like everyone else can.

"I don't know why she did it, Meret. And I'm sorry she did. I wish I..."

I laid a hand on his shoulder. Maybe that was the best I thought I could do.

"I'm sorry, Meret. I'm sorry."

I started walking away.

The sound of my feet on the hardwood filled my ears.

I didn't hear him.

"Sal."

Not until he was right behind me.

I turned. He threw himself at me. His arms wrapped around my chest. His face found my neck. I felt his tears burning hot on my scars. And nothing else. My chest went tight. My breath went short.

"Thank you," he whispered into my ear. "Thank you."

"I didn't—"

"You did. You got us this far. And we got the rest of the way. Sindra chose to protect you." He squeezed my neck. "She chose you, Sal. She knew you needed to be here." He laughed, just a little. "I mean, did you ever know someone as mean as her to do anything she *didn't* want to do?"

I felt myself laugh a little, too, the tightness in my chest replaced with something else. Something that hurt just as bad, maybe worse. But I didn't want to run from it.

"No." I found my hand on his shoulder. "Who the fuck could make her?"

"No one could," he said. "And she'd tell us to stop acting like such weepy assholes if she were here."

"She would."

He pulled me closer. "You don't mind if I'm a weepy asshole for a little longer, do you?"

I wrapped my arm a little tighter, shut my eyes. "No."

And for a little longer, it didn't hurt as bad.

THIRTY-FOUR

NEW VIGIL

It's not that I'm insensitive.

I *did* cry, after all, at all three versions of *My Queen, My Killer.* Even the Quelsing and Vrost–directed version.

I can have feelings, same as anyone else.

But I can also die, same as anyone else.

And while I'm sure it sounds terribly dramatic to say, sometimes the two are closer than you think. I don't mean in a tough-girl "feelings are weakness" way, though sometimes they are. I mean more that fear and sorrow can wear a woman away as surely as blades and bolts can.

The terror of a thing can swallow you, inch by inch, over years until you see it in every shadow cast by every light. People can bleed out from battles they escaped without a scratch, some part of them weeping out so slowly they don't realize until they're empty.

It's like having a knife in your chest. One that hurts to pull out, to even touch. So you get used to it there and you get used to the hurt and somehow it eventually feels like you've always had it in your chest, that taking it out isn't even possible, let alone desirable.

And when you one day pull that knife out—even if it's just by an inch or two—it bleeds like hell, hurts like hell, makes you wish like hell you hadn't done it for a while.

But eventually, you start breathing a little easier.

That's not to say I necessarily *was* breathing easier when I left the tavern with a bottle of cheap whiskey and took to the streets of New Vigil. If I had been, I probably wouldn't have been swigging out of it every time I smelled Meret's tears on me.

My problems weren't gone, after all. Nothing Ketterling had said was a lie. New Vigil was an insult to the powers of the Scar that wouldn't stand for long, with or without me. But it wasn't like anything got easier when the Cacophony and I showed up. And the Cacophony and I showing up with the intent of performing an incredibly risky process that I wasn't even certain about the specifics of…

Well, anyway, maybe worrying about the Cacophony feeding off an entire city would be a refreshing change of pace from worrying about the Imperium and Revolution consuming them.

Ha.

I joked, of course, because I was a little drunk. And I was a little drunk because I was still quite worried about…well, everything: Liette, Agne, the twins, everything. But at least when I passed refugees I recognized in the streets of New Vigil that night, I found my breath came in deep and clean.

And that was, at least, enough to keep me going.

Night had fallen on the streets of New Vigil—my chat with all three of the best and brightest the city had to offer had run longer than I thought. There was a noble attempt at alchemic lamps lining the main avenue of the city, but the rest of it was lit by whatever torch, campfire, or pyre could be found.

The earth of the dirt road crunched under my feet. The few buildings constructed stood dark, their residents hard at work somewhere else in the city. When I'd entered, I found the whole thing to be something of a joke—a house of sticks behind a big wall waiting for a fart of sufficient force to knock it over. But I had to admit, it had charm.

Rougher and uglier than even some of the borderest border towns out there, but the earth had been taken care of, the houses were built sturdy and, aside from the occasional scavenger bird hurriedly rushing between shadows with a fresh piece of offal, it was clean and safe. I could see why Cavric felt so strongly about it.

I couldn't quite agree with dying for it, of course. But there are only two people and one restaurant I feel that way about.

"Madam! *Madam!*"

I was snapped from my brief reverie by the sound of someone doing something terrible to something expensive. A woman, short and stout and clad in the fineries of Imperial Cathama, came shuffling toward me. She carried a sheaf of papers in one arm and a mask in the other depicting a pair of operatic characters, neither of which seemed perturbed by the *very* fancy dress dragging in the dirt behind her.

"I must chastise you, madam, quite thoroughly, though I know you to be innocent of all crimes," she purred in an *incredibly* refined Imperial accent. "For how could you know that you simply *must* introduce yourself to Lady Mjorille upon entering New Vigil?"

"Lady... who?" I asked.

"She of Sainted Taste? The Refined Palate of Cathama? The *Pinnacle* of Culture?" she chortled. "Oh, it's quite all right, darling. You seem a touch removed from the capital. Hardly your fault for not recognizing me. But I assure you I will take the *most* grievous offense should you not hear of me now."

Before I could ask, she shoved a paper into my hands. A very expensive illustration had been printed on extremely cheap paper, depicting a woman very like the one standing before me onstage. In boldly printed letters, a title and cast read out.

"Opera?" I asked. "New Vigil has an opera company?"

"Well, we have an opera *house*, don't we?" Lady Mjorille chuckled, waving a hand. "We can't profane it by leaving it empty. And the people of New Vigil can't *possibly* labor as hard as they do without leisure. It should be a personal duty to support them through art, don't you think?"

"I mean—"

"Of course you do. I can tell you're a woman of refinement. And I *know* women of refinement. Even out here. So, *do* come to our debut, won't you? I'll simply perish of embarrassment should you abstain and you couldn't do that to me, could you?"

Lady Mjorille spun neatly on her heel and spared nothing more than a playful bat of her eyelashes before shuffling away. The thought hit me barely a moment after.

"Hang on," I cried after her. "Why the fuck is there an opera house here?"

"Because I built one, obviously," she replied.

"For what? You're from Cathama. Why the hell would you be all the way out here in the Nails?"

She blinked at me in a way that made me feel like I had a dick drawn on my forehead. "What a ridiculous question. Why *wouldn't* you need opera in the Nails?"

Now, see, that *sounded* stupid but I couldn't think of a smarter response to her. Not that she was listening to me, anyway, her lyrical beckons already fixated on a nearby pack of people surrounding a cook fire. I glanced down at the playbill she'd given me, looked it over.

O My Darling Tailor.

A saccharine mess of dramatic monologues, bad fight scenes, and cheap sentimentality.

One of my favorites. We put on three productions of it while I was in the military. And, not to brag, the one we did where *I* played the role of Ichiligo the Boastful Chef got a standing ovation.

I found myself drifting through the lyrics in my head, going over each line I could remember. I was still doing it when I found the dingy little two-story building at the edge of the finished part of town called Ost's Grave. I'd seen worse inns—and even slept in a few of them—and barely even noticed the sawdust odor, the oppressive atmosphere, or the half-finished floor when I came in.

"What will you have?"

Liette's voice drifting from around the corner, though, I noticed.

I slowed down as I approached the common room. The dim light of a dying hearth and insufficiently oiled lamps greeted me, the odor of cheap food nobly masked by cheaper drinks assailed my senses.

"Tea," another voice replied.

And when I realized it was Jindu, I stopped entirely.

"Tea?" Liette asked. "You drink tea?"

"Lots of people drink tea," Jindu replied.

"I'm aware of that, I simply always thought you were a wine drinker."

"Why wine?"

"In my head, whenever I heard your name—albeit rare as the occasion was—I would picture a man ensconced in a throne sinisterly swirling a glass of wine. I confess I am uncertain why I came up with this image."

"Ah."

"Possibly because I intended to kill you many times."

"Ah."

My hand was reaching for a weapon. My body was tense. Yet I felt no urge to rush in. They certainly didn't sound like they were about to kill each other—despite their last interaction nearly ending with him cutting through her like wheat. Maybe I just wanted to be sure of what was happening before I acted.

Or maybe I was feeling insecure and wanted to know what they were saying about me.

It's good to be honest with yourself about these things.

"How many times did you hear my name?" Jindu asked.

"Four, that I can recall," Liette replied. Porcelain clinked as a pair of glasses were filled. "Two cried out in her sleep. One when she assumed I couldn't hear her crying. One more when I read your name aloud."

"And you thought of killing me each time?"

"No. I thought of killing you much more often than that."

"Huh." Jindu didn't sound fazed by that, which was nice of him. "How?"

"I am uncertain of what you mean."

"How would you kill me? In your mind? Was it different each time or was it always the same?"

Liette paused. I heard her sip something. "I had never thought about it."

"How strange."

Yeah, that *was* strange.

"I don't think...you dying was ever the point," she said softly. "Not in my head, at least. I wasn't thinking about you as anything other than a...problem. Something that I just had to solve and then..."

A moment. "And then what?"

"And then I'd fix it. Fix whatever it was that you had done to her. Whatever it was that kept getting between me and her." A faint squeaking sound as someone dragged a finger around the rim of their cup. "Because I kept believing there had to be one. A solution, I mean. A fix. One action I could do, one thing I could make that would solve everything. Make her hurt less, make me easier to be around—I'm not sure what, exactly, I thought it would be. But I knew it was out there."

An empty glass hit the table. "When did you know it wasn't?"

She snorted—I couldn't tell if it was disdainful or amused. "I'm not sure I have yet. Not fully. Maybe I never will." She chuckled—ruefully or hysterically, I didn't know. "You know how often I boasted about my own intellect?"

"Aren't you a Freemaker?"

"Yes. I am a Freemaker. I am the *best* Freemaker within six hundred leagues of here. I am capable of bypassing any form of ward, translating any language, and rewriting the entire nature of a thing, if I so choose." She sighed. "And I can't make her stop hurting. I can't do what a fucking *bottle* can do."

A pang of heat in my chest shot through my legs. Even if I wanted to interfere, I couldn't feel them under me anymore. I felt...I don't know, I couldn't tell if it was pain or joy I felt upon hearing that.

Probably both. I had been trying to save her from the thing inside her this whole time and she couldn't even bring herself to worry about that more than me.

She was an asshole. And I loved her dearly.

"It's difficult to realize, isn't it?" Jindu asked. "I could cut down as many nuls as I could count and the wars never stopped. I could win every challenge the Empress set before me and my friends didn't stop dying. Everything I was good at was only making it worse."

"And what you're good at has solved everything so far," she sighed. "And so you think you just need to try harder, work harder, think harder and you can make it work. You can make people stop hurting. You can make them happy again."

A painful pause.

"When did you know?"

Jindu didn't answer. She pressed.

"When did you know you couldn't make it better?"

A long sip. Tea sloshed out of a kettle and refilled a glass. His voice came fleeting as steam off porcelain.

"The second I tried to," he replied. "The minute I... when I cut her, when I thought I was going to save her from the things I had seen, from the Imperium that betrayed us both... that's when I knew I couldn't. I never could."

"But you kept working with Vraki even after realizing that?"

"I did."

"How?"

"I wonder about that often. Even now, I'm not sure. Same as you aren't. But at the time, all I could think about was... not stopping. Whenever I stopped—stopped running, stopped fighting, stopped *moving*—I would see them. The images. The moments in time. Working with Vraki wasn't a good idea. But it was something to do."

The moment stretched out, a painful silence.

"What do you see now?" Liette whispered. "Is it happening?"

I could almost hear the length of his blink.

"It is," he whispered. "It happens when I slow down. One moment,

I'm here. Another moment, I'm somewhere else—somewhere with dark skies and endless fog, somewhere consumed by flame and her shadow is staining the sky—it changes every time. Sometimes it's for seconds. Sometimes it feels like a lifetime. And I wonder..."

His voice choked.

"I wonder if one time," he said, painfully soft, "I'll disappear into another moment that lasts forever."

The silence stretched out, long and sharp like a blade. "What will happen to you here if that happens?" Liette asked.

"I don't know." The sound of a chair moving. "But I know I need to finish what I started before it does. The moments, my Barter... they're just moments. They might be real. Or they might not be. But I know I am real. I know she is real. And I know I can do something for her."

Feet shuffled.

"I don't know how to help her." The words tumbled out of Liette's mouth. "And I don't know how to fix her. And I don't know how to do anything else but *try* to fix her, even when it's not working and I..."

She let out something choked, a silk scarf tightening around a throat.

"I know," Jindu said, gentler than his name could ever dare to be. "But maybe we can try something different."

His heels knocked on the stairs. The sound of porcelain clinking fell smothered beneath the crackle of the hearth's fire. I lingered there, at the edge of the common room, wishing that either I had left sooner or that the whiskey I carried had been less watered down.

I took a step backward, intending to rectify both of those by escaping this heat in my chest.

"Come sit with me."

But she had to go and ruin that.

"Please."

I contemplated running anyway. Or pretending I was drunk. Or any number of things that, now that I'm saying them aloud, seem kind of silly. In the end, though, I didn't find any of them compelling enough.

"You knew I was here, then," I muttered as I stepped out into the common room. "You could have said something."

She pushed a chair out from the small table she sat at. A teapot and two half-drunk glasses sat upon it, both of them dingy and well-worn. A match for the rest of the common room, devoid of anything with more life than another dingy table and a sputtering hearth.

"I was having a conversation," she said.

"With him," I growled as I tossed the contents of one of the teacups out and filled the rest with whiskey. "With *him*."

"Does that bother you?" she asked.

I hesitated to answer before I drank. And I hesitated to drink before I'd had another drink. When both of them settled weary and warm in my belly, I sighed. "It's your sparkling wit. I can't tell you who to waste it on." I pushed a drink toward her. "How did it come up, anyway?"

"How could it not?" She accepted the drink, sniffed at it, cringed, drank it, regardless. "Wouldn't you want to know? Wouldn't you want to know what they knew? About what they'd tried? What they'd failed at? Wouldn't you want any information, at *any* cost, if it would help someone that is to you what you are to me?"

I blinked, poured her another one. "Well, I meant how'd you end up meeting, but sure, I guess that's also true what you said there."

"Oh." Liette looked at the drink before hastily downing it. "He arrived an hour ago while I was here reading. I noticed him, we spoke briefly, and then..." She leaned into her hands. "Did you hear all of it?"

"Not much."

"Liar."

"You got me."

We sat there for a long moment. I poured another pair of drinks. We raised them in toast to each other, set them back down on the table, did not touch them again. I folded my arms, stared at the worn wood of the table, as if I'd find an answer in there.

"You're a real asshole, you know that?" I asked.

"I don't, but I'm willing to entertain new evidence."

"I've been fighting, I've been killing, I've been running from every asshole with a cause and a slogan across this fucking forsaken land so I can get you somewhere where I can fix this mess," I muttered, "and you've been worrying about me. That's quite rude, you know."

"I apologize."

Her hand slid across the table. Her fingers found mine. She smelled of flowers and ink.

"But I can't help it."

I squeezed her fingers. They coiled between mine. Sweat from her palm glistened upon mine.

"I am terribly fond of you."

I smiled without meaning to. "I can't." I choked without realizing it. "I can't forgive you for that. It's my fault you're here. Me and my fucking war. My fucking list. My fucking scars and guns and..." I shook my head, scratched the scar on my cheek. "You can't be worried about me."

"Do you believe that you have somehow fallen in love with an imbecile?" she asked. "Or would you presume that the greatest Freemaker in the Scar could safely assume what she can and cannot worry about?"

"The greatest Freemaker in the Scar is still full of a fucking Scrath, whether I love her or not." I didn't want to tell her this. I wasn't ready. But I never would be and it's not like I could stop. "There's nothing left, Liette. I can't think of anything left to do but... but..."

I didn't finish. I didn't speak his name. I didn't want to.

The Cacophony burned, regardless. He coiled and writhed inside his sheath, alive with desire. He was enjoying this, the realization that we had no other option, the noose tightening around our throats, ready to choke his name from my throat.

"Then we'll do that."

But of all the things I had expected to hear, that one wasn't it.

Nor was I expecting to see her eyes firm and unafraid when I looked up at her. There was no bravado in that stare, no false bravery. Only the unassailable certainty of the woman who had told me she could do anything and made me believe it.

I couldn't betray that.

"You know what it entails?" I asked. "Because I don't. I know it *can* be done, but I'm not sure how. And even if there's two of us, I'm not sure—"

"Then we'll find out," she said. "We'll think of something. And we'll try."

I glanced up at her. "We could die."

"We could."

"It will be bad, even if it succeeds."

"It will be."

"You're sure?"

"No," she replied. "I'm not. I don't think I ever can be. But I can try. And if I can't..." She smiled, shrugged softly. "Well, if the world's most brilliant Freemaker can't do it, it can't be solved, surely."

I smiled, drew my thumb over the tips of her fingers, felt their length, their softness. On the night I'd met her, I'd thought them beautiful—soft skin, delicate nails, clean and smelling lightly of flowers. A pretty girl's hands that I'd held in my own and kissed gently. I never imagined what they could make, what they could do. I never imagined I would one day weep at the idea of them never making anything else again.

"Okay," I said. "We'll try."

"We'll try," she said. "And we'll figure it out. All we need to do is figure out where to start."

I ran my hands over hers. I slid something papery into them. I turned them over, showed her the playbill with Lady Mjorille in all her round, short glory.

"Want to see an opera with me?" I asked.

THIRTY-FIVE

NEW VIGIL

If you can get past the crushing inequality and the fact that your life can be snuffed out with one magical thought, life as a nul in the Imperium can be all right.

I mean, you'll still never be as well-treated as a mage and your life is still subject to their whims, but certain prestige is afforded to those magically uninclined individuals who demonstrate exceptional merit.

That Spellwrights and engineers and other practical arts are desirable goes without saying, but a nul who excels at any craft or art can earn repute as a Master. Be it skill in poetry, an exceptionally good talent at pottery, or even rave reviews in the Intimate Arts, a recognition of Mastery affords someone certain privileges.

Masters are permitted to trade and travel freely between Imperial holdings, for example. Masters are always first on the list of nuls to be considered for promotion within the Imperium's imposed hierarchy. And Masters are granted protections under both the law and society—it is considered quite poor taste, as well as illegal, to bludgeon a Master to death.

Say, for giving you a bad suit, for example.

"I tell you, Konz, you're lucky they decided to call you a Master," I said as I surveyed my ass reflected back to me many times in the tailor's mirror. "Because aside from making my already-splendid ass look positively magical, this suit is bad enough to warrant physical retaliation."

Konzillius yun Navamada glowered at me from the pile of other suits I'd already tried and discarded, which he was attempting to put back on his meager racks. A quiet gentleman of clear Cathama poise and polished pate, I hadn't thought his kindly old face capable of the sneer he gave me.

But excuse me for having taste.

"My shop is back in Cathama, along with my good clothes and everything I couldn't get out," he replied. "With Imperial silk and a needle, I can do anything. With what I've got, I can do what I can." He gestured at the mirror. "But I can do nothing for the criminally insane. Look at yourself. You look *stunning*."

"Stunning? *Stunning?*" I whirled at him, gestured to the silk shirt with a collar that came up *criminally* high on my chest. "I'm a war crime!"

"You're a delight! The modest look is very popular right now in the capital."

"We're not *in* the capital, you clod, we're in the *Scar*. I need to make a *statement* with my clothes." I gestured to the shirt, lamented at it coming up almost to my neck. "What am I saying with this? I'm not saying 'here she comes, bold and brave,' I'm crying for help, I'm begging someone to put me out of my misery."

"I've seen that body-baring mess you were wearing," he snapped. "Don't try to convince me you couldn't benefit from a little mystery."

I cast a glare over a shoulder dressed in an admittedly *very* nice short jacket. "Konz," I said, "you better either grab your scissors or your knife, because one of us is leaving with a neckline and one of us isn't."

Konzillius was, as all Masters were, concerned with two things: reputation and principle. The two, as all Masters knew, were responsible for each other: a Master's principles were his reputation and his reputation was his principles. A tailor as reputed as Konzillius would have to have principles to match, if he hoped to be called a Master.

So, while *some* people might have been alarmed to see Konzillius slowly slide his scissors back into his apron and purposefully draw a long knife, I wasn't.

What good, after all, is a tailor that *won't* fight for their work?

I left Konzillius's with a very nice suit and only a little less blood.

Which, by anyone's standards, is a damn fine bargain.

Of course, were you to tell me that you found it positively unacceptable to engage in a brief knife fight over a difference of opinion on fashion, I would accept that. I would find it terribly sad, but I'd accept it. And normally, I might agree with that. After all, even if the Scar *weren't* a place with innumerable concerns to address before style, it's slightly unreasonable to fight people over a neckline.

In most cases, anyway.

But that night was not like most nights. That night when I left the tailor and walked through the dusty streets of New Vigil was something different from the sleepless evenings and the liquor-laced comas I'd been alternating between. That night, when the smoke of cook fires wended against the starry sky, I was someone else.

Someone who hadn't done the things I'd done, killed the people I'd killed. Someone who looked like they could walk without the weight of metal on their hip. Someone who could have been walking down the streets of Cathama or Weiless or any other city—just another person in nice clothes out for a lovely time.

I didn't know, then, if I really was that person—somewhere, buried beneath the scars and the steel—or if I was just pretending. I still don't know, if I'm honest. I like to think that was me. That the lightness in my step and in my breath was really my own and not just a desperate bid to pretend I wasn't a killer.

But back then, I wasn't thinking of anything but holding on to it as long as possible.

I wended my way through the streets, into the dingy rooms of Ost's Grave, and rapped upon the shitty door of a shitty room.

I could spend any other night worrying. That night, I owed to someone else.

The door creaked open. A dark eye peered out from behind it.

"Erm," a soft voice drifted out, "yes?"

I blinked, tugged at the sleeve of my jacket. " 'Yes'? What the fuck do you mean 'yes'? What do you think I'm here for?"

That eye narrowed into a glare. "Given that we agreed this was intended to be a romantic overture, I assessed that you were intending to put slightly more ceremony into your arrival. I would further cite your multiple allegations of being an opera lover as evidence for a higher standard."

I squinted. "You want me to woo you."

She glanced away. "Maybe."

"All right." I held up a hand, backed away. "Close the door and I'll try again."

The door shut. I slid up beside the door. I rapped gently upon it. When it creaked open, I extended my hand gently and unfurled it, letting it linger before the door.

"In Cathama," I said, "you're supposed to touch the madam before you lay eyes on her, so that you and she might know the touch of each other before you know anything else." My fingers twitched. "Let me know you, madam. And I will give you everything."

A moment of hesitation.

"Is that true or did you just make that up?"

"I don't know," I replied. "Did you like it?"

I could almost hear her cheeks color through the door.

A delicate hand wrapped in a silk glove set in mine. Fingers I remembered the first touch of wrapped around my own.

"Yes," she said, "damn you, I did."

I turned toward her. And I know it's something of a cliché to say my jaw fell open and all I could muster was a breathless gasp, but fuck you—if you'd have seen the dress, you'd get it.

Imperial silk, hugging her like it was born worshipping her, in the elaborate stitch and cut of the court style—plenty of suggestion, little implication. Short-cuffed gloves matched the sash cinched about her waist—though both clashed aggressively against the wrapped sandals, you'd barely fucking notice. A short shawl trimmed with fur clung to her bare shoulders, her hair falling in coiling black cascades, framing a face adorned with short jade spectacles.

On someone born to wear it, that was the sort of outfit that armies fought each other over.

On someone shy as her, it was the sort of outfit I'd fight all of them over.

"I should inform you that, even among smugglers, New Vigil is lacking," she said. "What little I could acquire I had to pay dearly for and required significant adjustments, physical and spellwritten alike." She tugged self-consciously at the dress. "So... you know, if any part of it is awry, I did the best I could with what I had."

I smiled. "I can bear my disappointment."

Her lips curled into a furtive grin beneath rapidly reddening cheeks. "Shut the fuck up."

I did.

I didn't say a single word as I laid one arm on the door and curled the other around her waist. I said nothing as I pulled her against me, felt her bare skin, warm and trembling against the silk of my shirt. I spared not a breath for anything but my lips upon her neck, my hand upon the small of her back.

She pushed back, pressed me against the door frame. I felt her hand on my chest, fingers at the edges of my scar. Her grasp sought me hungrily, fingers running across the frame of my shoulders, down the muscle of my back, searching the expanse of my side beneath my jacket. Her lips found mine, the taste of her filling my mouth.

It had been too long.

Too long since I remembered her like this—not something to fix, to guard jealously, but someone to be smelled, to be tasted, to be held. Too long since we'd done something this close, this breathless, this hungry. Too long since we'd been anything but our names, our deeds, our spilled blood, and our burned homes.

That night, we needed no names. No memories. No apologies and no forgiveness.

That night, I needed nothing else.

But her.

"And who is this who calls himself bold? Who polishes his valor to such sheen that it claims to reflect upon all others?"

I'd asked around and heard about three different theories as to the origins of Lady Mjorille of Cathama.

The first was that she was a diva in exile, a torrid princess of the opera whose endless affairs in the marriages of powerful people were so outrageous, so scandalous, so *brazen* that they necessitated not just fleeing the capital but disappearing to the farthest reaches of the Scar.

"And who is this who calls his sword his world? Who knows no victories but through blood? Does he not know that steel can teach nothing of love?"

The second was that she was a fraud and a criminal who had crossed some powerful people and fled with her embezzled fortunes to the Nails where she could disappear and be reborn as an eccentric opera lover funneling her ill-gotten money into a farce of an opera house.

"Though my tailor's needle shall never bring low a foe, it can do the only thing your sword cannot. No sword shall ever win a heart as the stitch of needle and thread can."

The third was that she was of regal blood and a hopeless addict of a litany of pleasures and, after blowing her entire inheritance on any number of illicit drugs, received what she thought was a divine vision commanding her to build an opera house in the middle of fucking nowhere.

"Now, behold love's truest craft!"

Honestly, I could believe any of them.

But it didn't matter. She played one fucking *great* Fearsome Tailor.

The orchestra—a humble affair mostly consisting of weary-looking men and women playing workhorse instruments—nonetheless rose to a crescendo as Mjorille, playing the Tailor herself, broke into song.

Her pitch was flawless. Her projection was masterful. And anyone whose lyrics can stir inside me the ugly sobbing that I could feel boiling up inside my chest, I would forgive damn near any crime. Even the weird ones.

"Isn't it a *touch* short-sighted to say that a sword can't teach love?"

Others, of course, disagreed.

"After all, it feels like there's enough evidence out there to suggest that some people find power attractive." Liette adjusted her glasses as she surveyed the performance over an imperiously crossed leg. "The commentary on violence seems rather narrow when it excludes themes of protectiveness and passion that are also associated with it."

I was in a delicate situation here. Because the audience was sparse enough that her commentary probably wouldn't bother them, but thick enough that someone would notice me screaming at her how wrong she was. I chose, instead, to scoff—which, I think you'll agree, was admirably restrained of me.

"You're completely missing the point of it," I said. "The Fearsome Tailor isn't talking about what the sword *isn't*, but what the needle *is*. The Tailor is proving that her clothes are more important to kings and queens than swords, because society values appearance over substance."

"Even if I *were* to exclude the fact that she very *pointedly* said what the sword *wasn't*," she counter-scoffed, pedant that she was, "which I will not, it's not missing the point to say that there's value in violence that the script is woefully lacking in addressing."

"Hypocrite," I said, sneering. "You lament violence all the time. I wanted to fight the usher for better seats, but *you* said—"

"That's real violence," she replied. "*Stage* violence, I want it acknowledged, is powerful in its eroticism."

I smiled, leaned back in the uncomfortable seating. "I know. I remember when you asked me to leave the sword belt on."

You'd think I'd get tired of embarrassing her, but she just kept turning redder and redder and it was adorable. When she half playfully, half murderously swatted at me, I caught her wrist in my hand.

"You're an asshole for bringing that up," she growled at me. "Especially when I've *never once* commented on your... proclivities. I let the mask incident go without a single complaint."

"You shouldn't have. I worked hard on those masks."

She tried to pull away, I tried not to let her. At some point, my grin got too big or her cheeks got too red, because she simply gave up. She fell, warm and soft, against me. The stray curls of her hair plucked at my nose as she pressed her chest into mine.

Below, the songs unfurled into one another. Mjorille's Fearsome Tailor continued to mend and boast and stitch her way from one situation to another. The orchestra tried their best and the supporting cast's relative lack of experience struggled to weigh the performance down, but that woman carried it through sheer force of will.

Some unbearably pretentious assholes say that art is proof of humanity and I like to think I'm one of them. As I watched the Fearsome Tailor's travails, I wasn't thinking about wars or fights or disasters yet to come. I wasn't thinking about anything but the feel of my chest rising and falling as she lay her head and hand upon it, the smell of her hair in my nose and the feel of my arm around her shoulders.

I didn't feel any of the burdens—the blood I'd spilled, the fires I'd started. I didn't feel my scars or my aches or my fears. I felt like those things had slowly drifted off my shoulders, melting away like snow, and left behind this.

This night. This feeling. This person I felt like I might be, one day.

Maybe it was the opera. Maybe it was her. Maybe both.

I didn't question it. And if it ever happens to you, I suggest you don't, either.

"I always used to wonder something in opera."

Her voice drifted up to me softly around the end of the second act. Mjorille's Fearsome Tailor was in the throes of her death soliloquy, the empires to whom she was so important finally finding her too important to allow to live—proving the entire point of the opera.

"I always used to wonder," she whispered, "why they didn't just talk their problems out."

I felt myself tense beneath her. Like I was about to get knifed. "Well, there are lots of reasons why."

"I know," she replied. "I know that now, at least. I only used to wonder." She watched the play continue. "But I do sometimes think it might be a good idea."

"People in operas aren't supposed to have good ideas."

"Why not?"

"Because people out of operas don't have good ideas," I said. "If an opera hero did something sensible, it wouldn't be satisfying. There'd be too much unsaid and undone, no one would believe anyone could be at peace with that. So they have bad ideas and fuck up a lot. Otherwise it would be too simple."

"Why?"

"Because how else would they become heroes if they didn't start as assholes?"

She paused, nodded. "That's why you like it so much."

I would have taken offense to that if it weren't completely true.

"But what if..." Her voice came and went, soft and hesitant. "What if they don't talk about their problems not because it's too simple, but because it's too complicated?"

"What do you mean?"

"What if they don't talk about it," she said, "because there's too much? There's too much to say, too much to hear, too much to ask and answer?" I felt her swallow hard. "What if... what if they don't talk because they're afraid of what they might hear?"

I wanted to argue with her there. I wanted to block it out and just keep listening to the opera. I wanted to do anything but what we did.

"Liette," I whispered, "what are you saying?"

She held me a little tighter. Her fingers curled around my chest. I felt her shudder against me.

"I want...," she said, "to talk to the Cacophony."

My heart caught in my chest. And even though I'd left him far behind, buried beneath as many things as I could find just to feel free of him for one evening, I could still feel him.

His burning smile searing into me. Thrilled to hear his own name.

"No," I whispered. "No, that's not a good idea."

"It isn't," she said. "But it's the only idea I've got."

"We can think of another idea."

"We can't. None that makes sense. Neither of us knows how the weapon can remove Eldest from me. But I can hear Eldest and I can—"

"It doesn't matter. The Cacophony isn't what you think. He's—"

"And I can hear the Cacophony," she said. "I've tried so hard not to. But ever since..." She winced. "I know he's alive. I know he's thinking. And I think..." She held her breath, fearing to say the rest of the words. "I think I can talk to him."

My blood ran cold. A scream beat itself bloody against my lips, desperate to be free, desperate to tell me to run, to curse, to start fighting or do anything but listen to this.

"Nothing has changed."

But I listened anyway.

"Nothing," I repeated. "Putting that thing...Eldest...in the Cacophony..."

"It won't end well."

"No. It won't. It will be worse than Torle. Worse than the Valley."

"I know," she said. "But it's going to end badly, no matter what we do."

"That's not a good reason to try it."

"It isn't." She closed her eyes. Her breathing slowed. "You are."

Her warmth seeped into me. The searing heat of the Cacophony felt numbed beneath her—her breath, her scent, her touch. My heartbeat slowed. My breath came warm and easy.

Lady Mjorille collapsed onstage, a fake dagger plunged into her breast. The audience gasped, wept at the agony. The opera stretched on. The moon continued to climb into the sky.

Nothing had changed. I knew that. Nothing was less serious than it had been. We weren't different people with different problems. Tomorrow I'd awaken and still worry about Agne and the twins and Cavric and the Cacophony and every other thing that could go wrong.

But for that moment, that long dying note from the Fearsome Tailor's lips, my breath was clean and easy.

And I didn't question it.

Midnight and I met each other in the coarse sheets of a cramped room.

Beneath pale light seeping through the shutters and the heat of her breath.

I fumbled for my clothes, my fingers unsure of what to do with something made of silk instead of metal—she took my wrists, steadied them as I pulled each button free. I laughed nervously, made some kind of joke, some vulgar pun—she took my face in her hands, pulled my lips to hers. I reached for the whiskey bottle, just to loosen us up a little—she caught my fingers, squeezed them before they could find the bottle.

"No jokes, no whiskey," she whispered to the space between my ear and my jaw. "Give me you."

Her hand found my arms, held them above my head. Her tongue found my mouth, my neck, my chest. Her fingers found the length of my jaw, followed to the hollow of my throat, splayed flat against my belly and pressed against me as she drifted lower, below my waist and beneath the sheets.

My hips bucked. My legs arched. I felt her warmth seep through me, crawling up my body and into my throat. My voice came breathless and soft, lost in the rustle of sheets over her wrist and the sound of her lips upon my neck.

My eyelids fluttered open. Strands of white hair clung to my sweat-slick brow, and her own dark locks fell around her face, her eyes glittering bright and her mouth full of warmth in the dark.

Her lips trailed over my cheeks, plucked lightly at the edges of my scar. She found my lips, coaxed my breath from them—it came like steam, a rush of hot air that carried everything else out of me with it.

I lost everything to that night: all sense of time, all sense of space. I couldn't imagine another world beyond this bed, these hands, those lips. I didn't need to, then. I didn't need a name, a story, anything but her.

I think about that night often.

I think about the sound of my voice as I called out her name, and the things she whispered to me as her lips trailed down the center of my chest, and the feel of every thought and ache fleeing my body on every breath that escaped me.

And I remember the feel of my back arching, my body pressed against the bed, the great, smoldering exhaustion that settled over me when she lay against me, weary and warm—and the thought I had between the moments where my breath found me again.

I wondered if I'd ever fight for this feeling like I fought for my list, my weapon, my name—anything else. And I wondered how badly it would hurt if I lost.

It was that thought that stirred me awake, I think. Hours after she'd fallen asleep. I slipped from her grasp, heard her mumble a question after me that I mumbled an answer back to.

The bottle of whiskey slid into my grasp. The door slipped shut with a whisper.

I found my ways downstairs to the darkened common room. The embers of the hearth lingered on their very last legs, anyone who might tend to them having since departed. I didn't mind the absence of light or of people.

My body and my brain were both feeling heavier with every passing moment. Memories of my problems and my worries and my fears came creeping back up my spine. I poured myself a cup, brought it to my lips, set it back down to the table, still full.

I didn't feel like drinking. Or like forgetting.

I reached for a cold teapot, poured myself a cup, took a sip. It tasted foul and stale. I smacked my lips, took out another cup. I set it upon the table, filled it, slid it across.

"It tastes awful, but it's rude not to offer a drink." I smacked my lips. "Jasmine, I think."

A pair of hands folded themselves neatly on the tabletop. A warm smile beamed back at me.

"Jasmine," Torle of the Void said, "happens to be my favorite."

THIRTY-SIX

NEW VIGIL

I suppose the correct thing to do was panic.

To feel my blood go cold, to let my mouth hang open, to fumble for the words I needed for the sight before me. Or, at the very least, it would have been good manners to raise an alarm and go shrieking through the streets.

"How did you like the opera?"

But monsters are a funny thing.

Think of a beast that hunts you through the forest or breaks down your door and you've got something to fear—something that can run faster, hit harder, and go longer than your puny human frame can handle is scary. But think of a beast that can slay you without any effort at all and it somehow seems...less impressive, doesn't it? If it can always kill you whenever it wants, there's no real reason to be afraid of it, is there? After all, it's not like you can do anything about it.

Torle of the Void, who'd slain thousands with a thought earlier, could just as easily kill me. He could make my head explode or turn my guts to acid inside me or transform me into a toad...maybe. I thought I heard he could do that.

Besides, I'd been a Prodigy, too, once. They aren't *that* impressive.

"You knew I was watching?" Torle of the Void asked me.

"I assumed you wouldn't miss it, if you knew it was there," I replied. "And if you knew I was here, you probably knew everything else about the city, too. So." I gestured to him. "I ask again. What did you think?"

"I have seen better, if I am being honest," he replied, absently glancing into his untouched cup of tea. "The role of the Fearsome Tailor is meant to have at least a modicum of timidity—the boldness of this diva's portrayal was refreshing, I will agree. However, I can't help but lament the slow death of the classic."

"A classic is only a classic until you forget it." I sipped my tea. "What's refreshing today will be classic tomorrow and what's classic today will be forgotten."

"Mm. A bleak commentary." He smiled at his teacup, poetic. "Perhaps comforting, too, to know that all greatness is eventually consigned to the ashes of history, no matter how long it takes. The Imperium, too, shall one day fade from memory. As shall we."

I drank my tea, poured another.

"I must commend you," he added, "I confess that few people would be able to engage with a Prodigy of the Imperium so calmly."

I glanced at the table. "You haven't touched your tea."

I tapped the cup in front of him. In the tea, his reflection did not stare back at us.

"But how can you if you're not actually here?"

He grinned, winked, like a grandpa whose grandchild just learned how a charming little trick worked.

That made my blood go colder.

"Curious, isn't it? I *am* here." He tapped his temple. "I am simply *here.* My consciousness projected upon yours. Interesting trick, no? I did not learn how to do it until long after I had retired."

I grunted, poured another cup of tea.

"I often wonder what you would have learned, what gifts you could have shared with us all, Salazanca," Torle said, smiling gently. "How far could you have taken the Imperium, had your powers never been robbed from you? How far could you have gone?"

I paused. There was a time when that sort of talk would make me happy. Make me think of days where I flew. But now, it felt like his words were thick, cloying honey funneled into my ears—sticky, smothering.

"I know how you aren't here," I said, "so why don't you tell me why you are? Because I sure as shit know it wasn't to talk about the Fearsome Tailor."

"Oh, come now. Surely, there is no reason we can't—"

"Torle." I met his gaze, clasped it in mine. "You either respect me or you don't."

His face fell swiftly this time. The warmth and charm did not so much drain away as flood out, leaving behind something cold and hard as the dark creeping in through the windows. His posture straightened severely. His hands folded together.

"If you wish."

The room became darker. Closer. The furniture felt as though it crowded around, grew hateful consciousness and leveled it toward us. I kept my breath steady, my mind clear—it was him, I told myself. He was in my head.

"You know that I am aware of your location." He stared over his folded hands at me. "As I am aware of this great snub of a city. An insult to the Imperium."

"What snub? They're out here clinging to a dry, acrid asshole of a land."

"And they claim that this atrocity of a realm is preferable to the embrace of the Empress," he replied. "They claim that the battles you and I bled for were for nothing, that all the efforts to tame this land were for nothing. The service, the *sacrifice* we have given the nuls and they reject it, all of our efforts, to go play opera in the desert." His eyes narrowed. "I would not suffer this insult were it given to my lowest servant, let alone my colleagues and my Empress."

A smile tugged at the corner of my mouth. "Yeah? Is that why you're pissed? Or is it because they don't have to dedicate their lives to an Imperium and we did?"

Generally, it's considered not wise to tease people whose thoughts are in your thoughts. But I couldn't help it. It was like a joke I just now got.

"I would advise you to focus on another implication," Torle said. "You have no doubt understood that the Imperium is aware of this city. And that my focus has been turned on it."

I said nothing, poured another cup.

"The Empress tires of distractions. She wishes the Recivilizing to be a message to the entirety of the Scar, including this city." He let those words weigh heavy on my shoulders. "You, likewise, understand that this city has little chance against me, no?"

"Almost none."

The barest, coldest smile plucked at his lips. "Then you understand the futility of defiance. This can end well, Salazanca. You can help it end well. The Empress is willing to show mercy. Simply help the people of this city see—"

"No."

If you ever want to know how a person stronger than you feels about you, tell them that word. If they love you, they'll cry hot tears over the fear that they've hurt you. If they hate you, they'll sneer and laugh and pretend they don't care. But if they're like most people, they'll do what Torle did.

He simply sighed, like he was speaking to a stupid child.

"Be reasonable," he said. "You are a collection of deserters. You stand no chance against the Imperium."

"Or against the Revolution," I agreed. "Honestly, a team of motivated people with sufficiently harsh language stands a fair chance of taking this city apart."

"Then you see the futility."

"I do, yeah."

"Then you also, no doubt, see the wisdom in surrender."

"I take exception to that 'no doubt' bit, but I agree."

"Then what is the debate?"

I admit—I took just a *little* bit of joy in the frustration creeping into Torle's voice.

"You can no doubt compel this city to submit. You can save *thousands*."

"There's three problems with that," I replied, holding up a finger. "First and foremost, this isn't *my* place. I'm just visiting. So, it'd be kind of rude for me to come in and start telling them how to do things, wouldn't it? I mean, how *awkward*."

Torle sighed. "Salazanca..."

"Second, since you're so smart, you also know the Revolution is gunning for this place," I said, counting off another finger. "And while I have no doubt the Imperial asshole is a little chafed at the idea of New Vigil, I can't believe that a rabble of nobodies is of more concern to the Empress than the Great General."

People like Torle—people whose strength comes from only one place—aren't great liars. They have no need to be. He didn't bother cajoling or denying. His face simply fell, frozen, as I spoke.

"So I have to wonder why you're not concerned with that, either," I continued, "since, if you know I'm here, you must also know they're around." My scarred eye twitched. "So you either think I'm too stupid to have forgotten that or you just hoped I didn't notice. Either way, I'm a little insulted."

He recoiled, looked like he'd be happier if I'd kicked him between the legs. "I would never stoop so low as to insult a fellow traveler, Salazanca."

"Then don't," I said. "Tell me why you're not worried about the Revolution."

Torle scares me. I don't feel any shame saying that and I don't think anyone would disagree—anyone would fear a man who could sink cities. I was scared when he did that, no doubt.

But not as scared as I was when he started smiling, delighted that I was finally catching on.

"Did you know there are scholars among the Revolution?" he said softly. "We're all told that they have no culture, no education, no curiosity—for the nuls' sake, I presume. But after I retired, I found that they, too, had their thinkers as any society does. And they were no less interested in more... obscure subjects.

"Did you know they know about Scraths?" His voice grew more excited. I'd never heard that before. "More than even I knew. The Revolution has such intimate knowledge about them, more than we ever gave them credit for, including their feeding."

His smile grew cold, morbidly fascinated, like a quiet kid with a dead bird in the road and a sharp stick to poke it with.

"Emotions, you see," he whispered. "Doubt. Fear. Passion. Lust. The errant thoughts that torment the mortal mind so easily are their meat and milk. They crave it. They're drawn to it. To us. Even you or I, the earth-shattering power we command—they care for none of it. It's so trivial to them, they don't even notice. They left everything behind when they became what they are, every concern and worry and desire. Everything but the hunger."

I held his gaze, though I wanted desperately to blink. I held up a third finger, though my hands shook terribly. I spoke the words, though I wanted nothing more than to say anything else.

"Three," I said, "why are you talking to the Revolution about Scraths?"

And if you ever truly, *truly* want to know what a person stronger than you is thinking, see what they look like when you ask them something like this. Not about Scraths, just about something they're interested in enough not to pretend to be humble.

And when you do, if the smile that creases their face looks anything like the one that creased Torle's, you have my truest sympathies.

"Now, then, I should really be asking you something like that, shouldn't I?" he asked. "After all, don't you feel just a little remorseful hiding a secret like Eldest from me?"

My eyes narrowed. My jaw set. My pulse quickened.

"One of the children, accompanying your companion," he said, shaking his head. "It was mere *feet* from me back at my encampment. I could have learned so much."

"Stop," I growled.

"Does she feel it inside her? Does she hear its thoughts? What does it feel like when it begins to consume her?"

"Torle, stop it."

"Aren't you curious? Aren't you *fascinated*? Secrets beyond anything we've known, beyond the reaches of what even the Imperium can teach us, and it all lies within—"

"*DON'T.*" I slammed my fist on the table. Cups upturned. Tea splattered onto the floor. "Don't keep talking. Don't finish that fucking sentence. *Don't* say her fucking name."

Torle stared at me, scrutinizing me with an expression that suggested I'd said more than I wanted to. But he stayed silent, at least. For one merciful moment.

"The limit of the Empress's curiosity has proved something of a difficulty in my research," he continued, after a time. "I am certain she will be quite cross to understand that the Great General and I have come to something of an understanding regarding this city and our mutual intentions toward it."

"An understanding?" I asked, sneering. "Torle of the Void won't stoop so low as to insult a Vagrant, but he'll commit treason?"

"When it comes to knowledge," he said, "there are no factions. No nations. No cultures. The Empress may one day strike me from her graces and my name from our history. The pain of that will be intense." He stared at his own hands. "But I will have taken my seat at the black table by then. And the pain of not knowing... of being so close and not knowing... it's worse. It is a pain deeper than anything I could ever know."

"Then you know even less than you thought you did."

So, don't get me wrong—Torle of the Void is an unstoppable mage. He could destroy me with a flick of fingers and a nasty thought, if he wanted. He still might have. But when the record of how he killed me comes out, I want it noted that, after I said *that* to him, he looked like he was about to cry.

Make sure you tell them that when they're sweeping up my ashes.

"Your antagonism is unwise, Salazanca."

"Oh yeah? What are you going to do? Kill me worse than you already were going to?" I sneered at him across the table, folded my arms. "Why are you even bothering telling me? Why not just come in and kill us all?"

"Courtesy and compassion," he replied. "I am still recovering from my last expenditure. You still have time to save lives here."

"Birdshit. If you wanted something this bad, you wouldn't let that stop you. And you have more than enough strength to come get what you want. You're not holding off out of charity."

My eyes widened as the realization struck me like a brick to the face.

"You're holding off," I whispered, "because I'm not the only one who knows you're here."

The room grew darker. The last traces of the light and heat—the embers from the hearth, the lone candle on the counter—were snuffed out. And though a cold wind rapped lightly on the windowpanes, the room began to grow warm.

Papers left on tables began to crinkle and smoke. Tea began to boil in its cups and pots. The candle's wax began to melt. In the distant dark, from somewhere far too close, a gaze peered out and settled upon us. An unseen smile, brimming with cinders, split open in the dark somewhere.

The Cacophony did so love it when someone talked about him.

"You're afraid of him," I whispered. "You're afraid of the gun."

Torle said nothing. His form grew hazier, insubstantial—as though his body were a tapestry that someone had just plucked a stray thread from.

"See reason," he whispered, urgent. "You cannot win this. Not with every weapon, not with any weapon. I can help you. *You* can help everyone."

"I agree with that, too," I replied. "I can't win."

"Then you see—"

"I don't think I even know what 'winning' looks like, at this point," I continued. "And when I try to picture it, I can't. All I've been trying to do is survive and I'm not even sure I can do that." I stared at him across the table. "But I know what losing looks like. I know what will kill me. Giving her to you, that'll kill me. Giving up, that'll kill me. But coming after me?"

I rose out of my chair. His body continued to warp and diminish, steam coiling off his body. The Cacophony was reaching out for him—and even through this mental magic, he could touch him.

"That'll kill you, Torle," I said. "That'll kill everyone you love, everything you ever held dear. If you come after me, after this city, after *her*...then all your service, all your knowledge, all the questions you don't know, I will turn to ash. Whether I'm alive or dead, I don't fucking care and I won't let that stop me."

He sneered through a fading face. "You are exaggerating."

"Then say her name," I said, "and see for yourself."

He stirred, as if to do just that. But even that movement attracted too much attention. He winced with the effort. Smoke continued to rise off of his image—the Cacophony's burning fingers tightened around him, reaching through his spell, his very thoughts, to covetously seize him.

A projection. A simple mental image. No more than thoughts and memories. But the pain on Torle's face was real enough. As was the horror to learn that there was something out there in that big wide world that could hurt him.

"I am disappointed, Salazanca," he hissed as his form continued to smolder away. "I had hoped we could be civil about this, as colleagues. I had even concealed your presence as a courtesy."

I furrowed my brow. "Huh? Concealed it from what?"

"I had intended to take care of it for you as a kindness. Alas." His body began to fade, a bad dream leaving behind only a smoky stain. "A final courtesy. He is a Doormage. I would advise you to be aware of your surroundings."

"What the fuck are you talking about?"

I was talking to ashes by that point. The ghost of Torle's spell ignited, the remains of it burning away like cheap paper. The Cacophony's growl, frustrated at being denied a taste, filled the room.

And between the notes of his anger, I heard the barest echo of a noise.

A single note of the Lady's song. Crystalline. Clear.

Right above me.

THIRTY-SEVEN

NEW VIGIL

I heard Quoir's laughter as he came plummeting out of the portal. I only barely managed to stagger out of the way as he, arms extended and hands searching, fell into the floor. Another portal yawned open, swallowing him whole. I had barely enough time to breathe before I heard another note.

Behind me.

I scrambled forward as two tiny portals burst to life. Quoir's reaching hands lashed out, furiously groping at the empty air. Just one touch was all he would need to pull something out of me that needed to be in me.

Beneath me.

I used a chair to haul myself to my feet as a hand reached out from the floor. Another portal appeared on the table beside me, reached around for me. I snatched a fork off the table, jammed it into the back of his palm. Somewhere close by, he screamed.

Good.

I took off running. If Torle had *really* wanted to be courteous, he would have waited for me to get a weapon. My bare feet padded across the hardwood floors and up the stairs of the inn. Winking purple lights burst in and out as hands came reaching above, behind, out of the floor and walls. He had only two—wait, hadn't it been just one last time I saw him? Didn't matter—he was so quick he might as well have had a thousand.

My ears and eyes open, I ran down the hallway, slammed myself shoulder-first into the door to my room. I leapt under a grasping hand, plunged my hands beneath my bed. I hauled out the leather bags and the clothes and everything else I'd buried him under until my fingers wrapped around metal.

Hot brass. Cold steel.

Reliable.

I pulled away from the bed, tearing my sword free from the scabbard. A portal blossomed in the wall beside me. Quoir's hand came lashing out, fingers stretched taut. I fell back and struck instinctively, my sword catching his palm. The blow cut past the first two fingers before he pulled his bloodied limb back. His scream was closer this time. Above us.

He was on the roof.

Now, don't get me wrong. New Vigil had been kind to me. I'd come to appreciate this place. The people were good, the opera was lovely, and the drinks were just terrible enough.

I owed them a debt of gratitude.

And after that night, I owed them a debt of gratitude and one roof.

I grabbed the shell out of my satchel, aimed skyward, and pulled. Discordance wailed, hammering through the roof to send planks and shingles and windowpanes careening through the sky in a thousand destructive stars. The open night greeted me. No Vagrants in sight.

For the moment.

I belted my satchel and pulled on my boots and I swear if I had the time I would have apologized to Konzillius for ruining his suit but at the moment someone was trying to kill me.

I burst into the hall. Liette, similarly hastily clothed, was already there, her ornate jade glasses exchanged for her broad, serious-looking ones.

"We're under attack!" I shouted.

"*You don't fucking say!*" she snapped back.

Which, fair enough.

"Who is it?" she demanded. "What do you need me to do?"

"Get the fuck out of here," I said.

"Except that," she replied firmly. "I am going to help you, Sal. I *can* help you."

"I completely believe you," I replied as I hastily slid another pair of shells into the Cacophony's chamber. "And you can absolutely help me by getting the fuck out of here and *thinking of something better, for fuck's sake,* you're *the smart one.*"

Her eyes said she understood. Her mouth said I didn't know what the fuck because I was running again.

She broke one way out of the inn, I broke another. In the only favor I'd get that night, the sound of the Lady's song followed me instead of her. I saw portals glistening on rooftops as I ran down the streets of New Vigil. Quoir was on my trail, trying to pinpoint where I was heading. I made my way straight to the biggest, openest, un-bystander-est space I could find. I wanted his eyes on me—no sense in making it difficult for him.

I slowed to a jog when I saw the portal wink open ahead of me, coming to a stop as the shape of Chiriel's armoire came slamming down into the road, blocking my path. And when Grishok came lumbering out of another portal behind me, I took comfort in the fact that I had succeeded in one thing, at least.

All eyes were on me.

I kept the Cacophony in one hand, ready to train on them. Chiriel's violin was pressed against her chin, her bow dangling from twitchy fingers. Grishok hefted his club, sent his antlers rattling with the effort. Quoir appeared on a rooftop ahead of me, staring me down as he clutched a bleeding hand.

"Growing your hand back," I observed, sneering at him. "*Very* unsporting, Quoir. Some might call it rude, even."

"What would truly be rude is declining the attentions of someone as renowned as my colleague," Quoir replied. Even now, Grishok's magic wended its way through his hand, pulling the skin taut. "Yet I could do a thousand things a thousand times worse and not come close to the insult you've rendered, Sal."

"And you followed me here," I spat, "all the way to the fucking *Nails* to answer it?"

"For Darrish, I would have gone farther," Chiriel hissed behind her veil. "For Darrish, I would go to any length."

"Any of us would," Grishok rumbled. "And if it has to be all of us that avenge her, then it will be."

"And is this what she would want?" I forced fire into my voice, jerked the gun around. I had to keep them back, though for what purpose and for how long, I had no idea. "This killing? This bloodshed? All these people dying?" I narrowed my eyes. "She was a Vagrant, but she never enjoyed blood."

"No, she never did," Quoir agreed. "But you put her on your little list, regardless."

"She was there," I snarled. "You were *all* there. You worked with Vraki. *Against* me. Don't fucking tell me you all deserved mercy."

Quoir's face hardened to pale, beautiful stone. "No. Not all of us. I didn't."

"I didn't," echoed Chiriel.

"Not me, either," Grishok said. "But Darrish did, if any of us did. Darrish deserved better than being food for your fucking little toy."

The Cacophony seethed in my hand. "That's not how it happened," I said.

"Don't lie." Chiriel leveled her bow at me. "Don't you fucking dare profane her by lying, Sal."

"Someone with a gun like this doesn't need to lie," I snarled back. "Now lower that bow before you do something you regret."

"Is she dead because of you? Yes or no?" Quoir pressed.

The memory flashed through my head. The airship plunging to earth, in flames. The look on Darrish's face, the last words she spoke to me. What she chose to do and why she chose to do it.

"Yes," I answered. "She is. But—"

"But nothing," Grishok rumbled. "We deserve to die for what we did to you. She didn't." He lowered his head, prepared to charge. "She never did."

"You don't want to do this," I warned them, backing up.

"You and I will never know that for certain." Chiriel pressed her bow to her violin. "Darrish will, though. And that will be enough."

I tensed, readied for it—Grishok's antlers plunging through my belly, Chiriel's vipers gnawing me to the bone, Quoir plucking something precious out of me. Any of it. All of it. I didn't have enough shells for them. Not all of them.

Bad situations like these aren't impossible, despite the odds. All three of them together would kill me, they knew. Same as they knew that I'd take one of them with me—maybe even two, if I got lucky. But while they knew and accepted that not all of them would make it out, no one accepts which one of them is going to be the first.

Not usually, anyway.

This was different. This time, they weren't afraid. This time, they were fine with two of them dying, fine with all three of them dying if it meant I'd go to the black table with them. They looked at me with the same face I made when I read my list.

I'd been in bad situations before. I knew bad situations. This was worse—they didn't come worse than this.

But you know what they say about bad situations.

"STOP!"

Even if they can't get any worse, they can always get more complicated.

The mage appeared atop a nearby roof, levitating to a stop just above it. The green coat of a Vigilant hung around his slight frame. A large axe hung from one hip, a thick hand cannon from the other, and he drew both in short succession.

"Whatever grudge you have, whatever oath you've sworn, whatever business you came here to do," he said firmly, "you won't do it here."

"This doesn't concern you," Chiriel hissed.

"And which regiment taught you manners?" Quoir demanded. "It's terrible form to interrupt a duel."

"Seriously," Grishok rumbled. "Did they not go over that with you before you went Vagrant?"

"I serve no regiment and I am no Vagrant," the mage retorted. "I am Galvarang ki Anathoros, second among Vigilants."

"Tuh." Chiriel sneered. "Imagine boasting about being the *second*."

That was an incredibly cruel and a little true thing for her to say.

"My rank is irrelevant to my duties," he continued. "Which is to keep the streets of New Vigil safe from lunatics like you." He raised his sword commandingly. "Now, if you'll see reason and lower your weapons, we can solve this without further issue."

A tense moment passed. Chiriel cleared her throat.

"That's a lot of words to say 'please, kill me,' but I got the gist of it."

She ran her bow across her violin. A wailing song filled the sky. The armoire shuddered, flexed.

Burst.

The kite vipers came streaming out in a torrent of glistening scales and feathers. They coiled out of the armoire and pivoted in the sky, plunging like a spear toward Galvarang. The mage responded—a note of the Lady's song ringing out faintly as he reached toward the roof he stood upon.

A Graspmage. I had wondered.

Shingles and timbers shuddered, were torn out of the roof in a great heap of debris. It swirled in a sphere of carnage for a moment before he hurled it in a great spray of rubble at the cloud of kite vipers flying toward him. Some of them were struck from the sky by the blow—some were not.

As the kite vipers swarmed over the mage and began to gnaw, I saw him fumble with his weapons before raising his hand cannon and pointing it skyward. He pulled the trigger and a bright flare cleaved through the night sky, illuminating the darkness of the streets in a bright, phosphorous cloud of light.

Far away, on the wall, I could see a flash of light, hear a note of the Lady's song. Close up, right beside me, I could hear the sounds of portals opening.

The Vigilants came silently. No war cries or shouts of thunder. They burst wordlessly from the portals, a flurry of scavenged weapons and well-worn coats that rushed toward the Vagrants.

I had to admit, that was pretty impressive.

Almost as impressive as the carnage that followed.

"I hate, hate, *hate* uninvited audiences," Chiriel hissed as she spun on top of her armoire and faced the interloping Vigilants.

She played a few short, staccato notes on her violin and the kite vipers whirled—those stunned on the ground stirred themselves to life, those haranguing Galvarang pulled themselves off of his bleeding, gnawed-on body. They coiled together in a column of feathers before dispersing and swarming over the Vigilants.

No screams. No shocks. Not even a cry of alarm. Every man and woman on that field waded in, weapons held high, as if they genuinely expected to be eaten alive by flying snakes that day. That kind of tenacity was hard not to admire.

Whether it was effective or not was a different conversation.

Repurposed gunpikes swung wildly, trying to fend off the incurring swarm. Vigilants fought, fell, and were dragged off by their comrades. Chiriel's wailing song continued to compel her pets to dance and ravage and feast, even as the Vigilants continued to cleave them from the sky.

A stirring sight of defiance in the face of overwhelming aggression.

Almost made me wish I had stuck around to see it.

Now, you might think me a coward for turning and running after seeing so many people show up to offer resistance. You might think me tactically unwise for letting them handle Chiriel while I took off. You might even think me downright stupid for leaving the field of battle like that.

To which I would say the following.

For the first point, the Vigilants were defending their own territory their own way—we couldn't coordinate when we had entirely different goals, my own being more along the lines of "*don't* get your marrow sucked out by snakes." For the second, the Cacophony isn't a weapon that makes situations *easier* to control, so I highly doubt they'd appreciate me being there, blowing things up.

And for the third, *I* was the one being chased by a giant, immortal killer mage, so I didn't really give a shit what you fucking thought, you judgmental prick.

"Why are you bothering with this, Sal?"

Grishok, for a bigger guy, was actually quite athletic. He could talk while running, which was impressive, and he could keep up with my frantic retreat, which was impressive *and* obnoxious as hell.

And, most importantly, when I ran through the skeleton of a half-finished house, ducking under beams and leaping around piles of debris, he didn't even slow down.

"Why run? Why fight?" Grishok's voice boomed as he crashed through wood and metal in pursuit of me. "All the stories, all the talk about your list—and you can't even face revenge when it comes for you?"

"You loved poetry, not logic, Grishok." I broke clear of the house, whirled on him. "Why are *you* fighting? You said you deserved to die." I aimed the Cacophony. "Prove it."

Pulled.

Hoarfrost sped out, burst into a cloud of white that coalesced, shaped itself into a shimmering lance of ice. It punched through sky, wood, and flesh, plunging through Grishok's chest and bursting out the other side. He let out a grunt—a fucking *grunt* for all that—and fell to one knee.

"Asked myself that quite a bit, if you can believe it." His breathing was a little more labored, what with the *giant fucking icicle* impaled in him. "For a long time, I didn't have an answer. What we did with

Vraki was worthy of death. I accepted that. And when I heard you were looking for us, I just sat and waited for you to find me."

He reached into his chest, *past* the wound that the icicle had carved. He gripped it in one massive hand, tore it free in a spray of red crystal. His blood froze to the icicle, frost crackling as the sinew and bone in his chest began to regrow like weeds.

"Turns out you found Darrish first."

I pulled the trigger again. Shockgrasp exploded against his body, sending coursing electricity over his skin. The shards of metal—the shattered tools and nails and struts of the home—quivered and flung themselves toward him, twisted shards embedding themselves in his temple, his chest, his kidneys, and his thighs. Blood wept from his wounds, pooled in his footsteps.

As he continued to lumber toward me.

"I didn't think I'd be that bothered by what you did to her, either." His magic continued to course through him. His body pushed the shards out of his skin, the wounds closing right before my eyes. "But I was. I didn't think I'd miss her, but I did."

"You should have thought of that before you stole my magic."

I aimed the final shot. Pulled the trigger.

Hellfire exploded, raked his flesh. It burned, crisped, sloughed off, and fell from his bones. He became a conflagration on two feet: blackened bones and skin stark as shadows against the fire devouring him in hungry jaws.

And he didn't stop coming.

"I should have, yeah. I should have done a lot of things different." Grishok continued forward. And by the time he was out of the remains of the house—devastated as they had been by the Cacophony—he was extinguished. And whole. "She came to me, you know. Darrish. Before she died."

I paused in the middle of reloading. Mistake.

"What?"

"We talked. We talked about you, about Vraki, about that night."

"What did she say?"

"A lot. A lot that made me realize how important she was to me. To all of us." He hefted his club over his shoulder, his eyes fixed on me. I backed up, but in these streets, there wasn't much room to navigate. "See, she was the only one from that night to come looking for me. She was the only one who still could stand to look at me. Even if I couldn't stand to look at myself."

"What did she say, Grishok?" I pressed again, not knowing why. "What did she *say*?"

"They were beautiful words, Sal. I wept." He took his club in both hands. "I'll tell them to you when you're dead."

He lunged at me, brought his club down in a huge swinging arc.

Had he been clever to talk to me about Darrish or was I really that much of an idiot that I listened? I leapt away, caught my heel, and fell. The club missed me, but the power of it coursing through the earth as he struck was enough to keep me off my feet as he turned and swung his club again. I ducked, narrowly avoiding it taking off my head, tried to scramble away.

A massive shadow fell over me.

The wind split with his club's blow.

I shut my eyes, waited for it to hit. And I wondered, in that moment, if Darrish would hear what I said when I died, too.

Metal jangled. The earth rumbled. A bird shrieked.

When I opened my gratifyingly not-pulped eyes, I saw Grishok looming over me, his body twisted awkwardly against the chains encasing it. A pair of hooks were embedded in his skin, metal links tangled in his limbs, struggling to restrain him as he pulled on it.

"Could you fucking move?"

A question. Strained with effort. And directed at me.

I saw Cavric nearby, atop his Badlander, both of them struggling to hold the chain keeping the killer Vagrant from pulping me.

"Like right now?"

Ketterling chimed in, holding on to another chain from atop her Banter. The two birds strained, squawking with effort as they struggled to contain Grishok.

"Smart," I grunted as I pulled myself clear, started loading again.

"Yeah, I thought so," Cavric spoke through grunting. "If you can't kill a Mendmage, you can slow them down, right?"

"Yeah," Grishok rumbled. "What's your plan for after this?"

"I hadn't thought of one yet, so—"

"Good to know."

With a roar, Grishok pulled on a massive limb. Cavric was jerked from his bird, dragged along the ground screaming as Grishok went rushing at Ketterling. She dropped the chain, kicked her bird's flanks. The Banter pivoted, flapping away as Grishok swung at him. The bird launched itself at him, its spurs raking at his skin as it climbed onto his back and pecked angrily at his throat.

Tiny wounds. Ones that closed as soon as they were open. But it was a distraction.

And distractions, when paired with giant women, help quite a bit.

The Banter leapt off of Grishok just in time to allow a *significantly* large piece of timber to connect with the Mendmage's jaw. Agne came rushing forward, swinging a beam the size of a small tree. It connected with Grishok with such force it damn near spun his whole head around.

With a chorus of sickening cracking sounds, he righted his skull, his spine and his rib cage from the blow.

"Rude."

He swung his club. The fragments of it, along with Agne, went crumpling to the ground. Grishok's foot came down hard on her back, stomping her into the earth again and again and again. Her hand shot up, caught him by the ankle, swung. Grishok went tumbling across the earth.

The woman that pulled herself out of that half-dug grave wasn't angry. Wasn't anything, really, besides a pair of empty eyes and a vaguely bored expression.

Whoever had been put into that hole, it hadn't been Agne the Hammer to come back out.

It bothered me more than her. She didn't even stop before

launching herself at Grishok again. I moved to intervene—to help? To ask if she was okay? What the fuck was I expecting to accomplish? It didn't matter. Cavric found my shoulder.

"I heard there were three of them," he said, heedless of the light winking open over his shoulder. "Where's the other one?"

I shoved him to the side. Quoir came leaping out, hands extended, eyes alive with vicious laughter. We split apart as he went sailing through us to disappear into another portal.

I scrambled to my feet, found my sword. A portal opened up beside me, Quoir's hands shot out, shrank back as I lashed out at him with my blade. I heard something behind me, whirled with my blade out just in time to ward off another hand.

Again and again, he came at me. Sometimes he leapt, rushing in before opening a portal beneath him and disappearing. Sometimes it was just his hands, reaching and seeking and deadly. Again and again, I beat them back, warded him off, scared him away with a wild slash.

But with every cut, the steel in my hand got heavier and my arm got weaker and my breath got more ragged. He was wearing me down, bit by bit, waiting for the right moment to tear my heart right out of my chest.

But, when I saw the air shimmer as a portal was born in front of me, I had a thought. And as I heard the Lady's song reach a discordant note behind me, that thought became a terrible realization.

He had two hands.

Why couldn't he just hit me from both sides at once?

It's a cliché to say that time slows down when you're about to die, but it's true. Poets call it the proof of the divine, evidence of a just deity who stretches out your final moments so that you truly appreciate the idiocy of the life that led you to this disastrous end. I'd believe that. I'd certainly done enough to offend any and all divine figures for that to be true.

I had already started lunging away from his grasp as his hand came lashing out in front of me. I had barely a moment to look over my shoulder and see another portal behind me, Quoir's hand reaching out, fingers twitching eagerly as I fell toward it.

It took an eternity for me to fall into his grasp. An eternity of a pounding heart and breathless lungs. And when I finally fell close enough to see every twitching muscle in that horrible hand, it only took a second to be over.

The air shimmered in front of me.

A silhouette darkened my vision.

There was a scream. Blood. A body falling. Quoir reappeared upon a nearby rooftop, a handful of something red and glistening in his hand.

"Oh, for fuck's sake," he snarled, "how many times are you going to let people die for you, Sal?"

I only barely noticed him. My eyes were on the body beside me. The man on his knees, coughing up blood, clutching his side. And before I knew it, I was beside him, the man who'd taken the hit for me. My hands were on his shoulders, holding him steady as he swayed and fell against me, unmoving.

He felt cold.

Jindu felt cold.

"Fuck you."

It had been instinct that made me reach down to Jindu and hold him, reflex.

"FUCK YOU!"

It was something else that made me leap to my feet and scramble for my gun.

"Stay right there," I snarled. *"Stay right there, you piece of shit!"*

Quoir flexed his fingers, considering it. But I could see the stiffness seeping in, I could see the way he swayed a little on numbing feet. Even the most powerful mage could use too much of it. His Barter was kicking in.

"Mm. I think not." He glanced out over New Vigil. "I see Chiriel has already quit the field, the little minx. So I think we'll have to call this one a stalemate."

He glanced over to where Agne and Grishok were squaring off. His eyes flashed. A portal opened beneath the massive Mendmage, swallowing him whole with a grunt of alarm. Quoir looked back at me and batted his eyelashes.

"See you next time, Sal. *Love* your suit."

He dropped the gore from his hand. Whatever he'd pulled out of Jindu made a grisly sound as it splattered on the ground. He smirked, winked, waved.

Disappeared.

Just like that. He'd done it again. He would *always* do it again.

He'd struck, killed, and run.

Or so I assumed.

The Lady's song rang out. A portal opened. Quoir was dumped on his ass, looking quite confused as he was deposited right in front of me.

It took me a moment, too, before I raised the gun at him. He screamed, vanished through another portal.

...And reappeared two feet away with the biggest what-the-fuck on his face I'd ever seen.

I admit, I was also puzzled. Especially when he attempted on unsteady legs to leap into another portal and only made a short little hop into nothing.

"You want to hurry the fuck up, Duchess Dithercunt?"

Yria stood nearby. Her outstretched hand was covered in sigils, barely keeping it aloft. Liette and Urda stood on either side of her, propping her up. Her face was contorted in effortful agony.

"I can't fuck up his portals forever."

"Asshole," Quoir snarled, catching on about the same time I did. "You utterly, *utterly* rude asshole."

He rushed toward her, hands outstretched. A massive hand caught his wrist. He looked up into Cavric's baleful stare.

"Let's see you jump around now, you little bastard."

His axe flashed. Bone cracked. A spray of red and a ripping sound.

Quoir screamed, fell to his knees, cleaved from collarbone to rib cage.

He fell, he spat blood, drew ragged breath.

Still alive. For a few painful moments more.

"Fuck," he rasped through blood. "Fuck, fuck, fuck. You win... again..."

"I didn't win anything, asshole," I snarled back at him as I approached, sword in hand. "You killed people. *My* people."

"Not enough," he rasped. "For Darrish... I wanted more..."

"You were a monster in the army and you're a monster now, Quoir. Darrish loathed you."

"Not true." He tried to crawl to his knees. "She never looked at me like I was a monster." He spat blood onto the ground. "For that—for *her*—I'd have killed every last one of your people."

His words twisted in my chest. Cold steel knife scraping on bone. "And now you're dead. For no fucking reason."

"Not true again."

He pulled himself to his knees. Bone and sinew glistened from his gaping wound. The blood pumping out had run dry. His skin was bone white, his eyes fading.

"I was on your list," he said, smiling through a mouthful of red. "And you didn't get to kill me."

"Does that comfort you?" Cavric muttered. "As you die here?"

"Yes."

His voice came breathless, desperate.

"Yes."

He fell to the ground, his eyes rolling back in his head.

"Yes."

He died with a smile on his face.

The red stain that had been Quoir leaked out upon the city streets. Debris from shattered buildings and collateral destruction lay this way and that, haphazard offerings scattered before an unimpressed god of destruction. Yria slumped, bloodless, between Liette and Urda. Agne stood, staring at the spot where her foe had just stood, numb and unmoving. Vigilants, ravaged and bitten by kite vipers, came limping in.

A hacking cough caught my ear. Without realizing it, let alone thinking of it, I reached down for Jindu. I pulled his arm over my shoulder, steadied him as he spat blood onto the ground. His heart beat against me—faint, weak, but there. He tried to wave me off. I tried to convince myself to let him.

But...fuck me, is it wrong that I didn't want to?

Cavric approached, surveyed the carnage slowly before looking to me. Not saying. Not judging. Just asking.

I licked my lips. I pulled my hair out of my eyes. I sighed.

"So," I said, "I have some bad news."

THIRTY-EIGHT

NEW VIGIL

So the Imperium and the Revolution both have their eyes trained on the city. They are aware of Liette, the Scrath, everything, and they want it. And they, being two ancient and implacable enemies, have discovered that this is the only thing they want more than killing each other and have, thus, decided to cooperate in destroying us. At least a little."

Cavric leaned back in his chair, stroked his beard thoughtfully. After a long, quiet moment, he shrugged.

"Well," he said, "that's not the *best* news, I admit."

All eyes in the command center where everyone also got drunk turned slowly, incredulously, toward him. He blinked, held up his hands.

"What? I *said* it wasn't good."

"It's...*possibly*...worse than not-good." Meret adjusted his glasses. "This city is full of Revolutionary defectors and is a bruise on the Imperium's ego. We should probably assume that surrender would mean conscriptions for the lucky and executions for the unlucky. Or the other way around, depending on how you look at it. If Sal's associate...this..." He glanced to me. "Sorry, what did you say it was? A ghost?"

"No, Torle of the Void appeared to me as a mental projection cobbled together from my own memories and layered on top of mine so that he *appeared* to be there and was in communication with me from across great distances," I replied, rolling my eyes. "There's no such thing as ghosts, Meret."

"Oh. Um." He looked away, sheepish. "Yes, of course."

"I suppose we should thank you for it, then," Ketterling muttered, folding her arms. "I'm just so *pleased* that you could tell us two armies are rolling toward us."

"I actually am, though," Cavric rebutted. "This doesn't change anything we didn't already know. We knew they'd be coming. And if they are, I'd rather know than not."

"We aren't ready for them," Ketterling said. "The wall's the only thing that's even *close* to being finished."

"It's not perfect," he sighed, "but it's better than where we started."

"You're the one in charge. Tell us what to do, then."

Cavric hummed. He opened his mouth to say something, reconsidered, picked up a tankard of beer, and took a sip. He tried to speak again, reconsidered again, picked up the tankard and finished the entire beer. He slammed it back on the table.

"Well," he said, smacking his lips. "I suppose we'll fight."

"Are... are you sure?" Meret asked.

"Fight? *Fight?*" Ketterling all but laughed. "Do we fight them with our wall? Or our birds? Or should I have my riders put together some unkind lyrics about their insecurities and we can try our best with that?"

I stood up in the chair, laid my hands on the table.

"They're right," I said. "You're all right. It's my problem that brought this to your door and it's me they're looking for. If I leave, we might stand a chance of—"

"Oh, for fuck's sake, don't start with this shit now." Ketterling chuckled—and for once, it almost sounded like it wasn't the spiteful, derisive kind. "We got our asses kicked for you. You owe us."

"It's considered quite rude to interrupt them when they're monologuing," Cavric said before glancing at me. "She's right, though. We already bled for you. We're not kicking you out." He leaned back, folded his hands over his belly. "*But* it might be nice if you chipped in here, considering you're the one with the massive gun and all."

I suppose I must have looked pretty stupid standing there, dumbstruck. But you have to appreciate how rarely this happens to me. If it ever has.

I'm used to the stories that follow when I leave a city: the tales of Sal the Cacophony laying waste to an entire township, the frightened whispers of her passing, the curses that chase her back when she finally moves on.

People wanting me here? Even after I'd brought ruin to them?

That was new.

And it felt...

"What do you need me to do, then?"

Well, it felt like that.

I slid back down into the seat. Cavric's eyebrows rose—he hadn't expected that. I'd have taken offense, but Ketterling already seemed like she didn't have a lot of patience for dialogue right then.

"I'll take my riders out," she said, rolling out a sore muscle. "Try to keep eyes on them, reset traps, maybe harry them to slow them down."

"Not wise," Cavric said. "Hard to harry tanks and mages on birdback."

"Torle will have Scrymages watching you, too," I chimed in. "If you move in small groups, they'll have a harder time finding you. Good for evading detection..."

"Bad for fighting." Ketterling spat onto the floor. "Fuck. This was way fucking easier when it was fighting other clans and robbing people." She rubbed her temples. "All right, no harrying. Just traps and...and...I don't know, I guess I can *hope* real hard that they get rocks in their shoes and have to stop every few steps?"

"I'll take whatever you can give me," Cavric said. "Hope and rocks, included."

"I'll have *one* of them for you by the time I get back." Ketterling plucked her coat off her chair, draped it over her worn leathers and strapped axes. "I'll do what I can. You do the same." She started moving for the door, paused, called without looking up. "Hey, Cacophony."

I looked to her. She spared the narrowest sliver of a glance for me.

"I heard you once took out one of the Revolution's tanks with that gun," she said. "That true?"

"No," I replied. "I took out several of the Revolution's tanks with this gun."

She paused, grunted, flung the door open.

"Let's hope you ruin them as much as you ruin everyone else."

The door slammed. Drinks shuddered on their shelves. Cavric looked to me, beaming with delight.

"Oh, she *really* likes you."

"I was going to say," Meret agreed, "I haven't seen her warm up to anyone like that before."

"That, uh"—I cleared my throat—"didn't sound like she does." I smacked my lips. "In fact, it *sounded* rather like she hated my guts."

"Yes, but *yesterday* she hated your very existence," Cavric said. "It's all about perspective." Without waiting for me to respond, he laid a hand on Meret's shoulder. "Not to overstate the obvious, but we're outnumbered." He furrowed his brow, thought. "Actually, let me overstate the obvious. We are *severely* outnumbered. Whatever force they send is going to be bigger than ours."

"I can find volunteers," Meret said. There was a grimness in his nod that hadn't been there before. But there was a sadness in his eyes that would always be there. "People who can fight. Or at least, people who can't sit and wait."

"We need more than fighters," Cavric said. "We need food, we need medicine, we need people who can clean shitters, even."

"I can find them, too." Meret plucked up his coat and spared a smile for me. "Feels kind of familiar, doesn't it? You and I, about to face disaster together."

"Yeah," I sighed. "It didn't end so well last time, as I recall."

"Disaster never does." He draped his coat around him, headed for the door. "But if it's going to happen, I'd rather be with you."

The door shut. Cavric and I were left without a word exchanged between us. I could feel a thousand things to say swirling in my throat, but couldn't get them out. There was a pain in my chest that wouldn't let me speak.

He, not being similarly moved, could not speak a word because he had already begun eating from a plate of meat skewers.

He paused, suddenly aware of me watching him, spoke through a full mouth.

"What? If you're hungry, you should have brought food, too."

"You're optimistic," I said, "and you shouldn't be. Traps aren't going to slow them down. And no matter how many volunteers you find, they aren't mages. They aren't cannons. They aren't—"

"Yes, I'm aware," he interrupted, tearing off another piece of meat. "As I am aware of the fact that you're about to attempt to draw out a Scrath in my city. As I am aware that we just fought off a trio of Vagrants out for your blood. As I am aware that I've got one—one of *two*, I should mention—of my *very* hardworking Mendmages trying to keep your creepy friend with the sword alive."

I fell silent, my eyes heavy in their sockets. There were about a hundred different sharp, pointy objects I'd rather have been hit with than that. I didn't want to think about Jindu. What he'd done. Who he'd done it for.

"And you're aware, too."

I looked up, saw the plate of meat skewers slid before me.

"Someone is hurt because they chose to protect you. And I chose to use my people to help him. Just as I chose to come out to the middle of nowhere to die. He chose you. I chose you." He slurped the last traces of fat from his skewer. "Not everyone is afraid of you, Sal. Some might even like you, no matter how badly you wished they didn't."

He pulled himself out of his chair, began to fasten his coat around his shoulders. He hesitated, briefly, as he did.

"It's not optimism."

"Huh?" I glanced up.

"It's not optimism," he repeated. "It's resignation. I have no expectation of getting out of this. None of us do. It's the first thing we made peace with when we moved here. The other powers would one day come and wipe us out. We knew. We always knew it would happen one day."

He picked up another skewer from the plate. He took a bite of it.

"But to live out here, as we want... it's worth making peace with that," he said. "It always was."

"Where are you going?"

"I have people to see about the wall, about the mages, about our strategies. I'll keep you informed, tell you where you can help the most. Do as you will until then." His boots clomped toward the door. "If I were you, though? I might go see one of those people who you wish didn't like you."

He didn't wait for me to respond, choosing instead to leave and shut the door behind him. Which was quite rude, since now I had nothing to distract me from his words, weighing down on me. Nothing but the skewers he'd offered, anyway.

I picked one up, chewed on it.

It was good.

But not good enough to keep me there.

She had chosen a quiet section of the city to reside in.

A humble square of half-finished homes surrounding a well. Amid the barrenness of the rest of the New Vigil, a small scar of greenery had blossomed around the well's base. The grass there was soft. The dandelions grew tall and their shaggy heads shuddered off buds to offer to the wind as it blew.

Even here, nestled between approaching war and unending nothing, she found the one place soft and green.

She belonged in a place like that. A place where she could be surrounded by beautiful things. A place where the wind smelled of growing things and not smoke.

My hand trembled at her door, hesitant. It wasn't courage that made me knock.

She didn't answer. That was probably wise. Wiser still would be me turning around and abandoning this plan, leaving her to her evening.

Wise isn't what I'm known for, though. And wise wasn't what I needed to be that night.

"Agne?"

I whispered into a softly lit room as I eased the door open. A cozy skeleton of a home greeted me: a barely finished roof, walls that needed more wall, a ladder where a staircase would one day be. My eyes were drawn to the softest corner of the room, where the orange light of a small band of candles flickered softly.

I found her there. A glass of wine sat before her, full and untouched. She sat at a small table in a small chair. Her hands were clasped together in her lap. She did not look up at me as I approached, as I sat down beside her. Her eyes were empty, unblinking, fixed on the glass as though it were a thousand miles away.

My eyes drifted around the room, from the blankets she'd draped here and there, to the careful way her clothes had been arranged atop a nearby crate. I searched for some observation to make, some joke to crack, *anything* to break the silence.

But I didn't.

I believe in no god. Not many in the Scar do. But the silence seemed somehow sacred in that room, something mournful and respectful. It felt cruel to speak. As though I'd be wounding something that needed to be protected.

"Do you like wine?"

It was her that spoke. And she spoke so gently that it did not stir the silence, that reverent softness.

"I've never seen you drink it."

"Not as much as whiskey," I replied. "But I like it."

"Do you want this one?" she asked.

I looked down at it, not so much as a fingerprint on the glass. "You don't like it?"

"It's my favorite."

"Have you had enough?"

"I haven't had so much as a drop."

My eyes drifted to the candles she'd left here and there. They'd burned down to thin pools of melted wax, quivering and threatening to consume the flames that danced precariously on their wicks.

"Agne," I whispered, "how long has it been since you poured that wine?"

"Hours," she replied. "I poured it hours ago." She stared at the glass. "I used to love doing this. Lighting candles. Pouring wine. Reading poetry. Trying on silks."

"Do you not love it anymore?"

"I don't know if I do or if I don't." Her voice changed not even a little. "I used to enjoy perfumes. And today I realized I haven't bathed in days. And I wondered... do I still like wine?"

She stared down the wineglass like it could stare back.

"And then I wondered, if I don't like it... if it doesn't taste right, will I weep? Will I still have the capability to weep?" Her face remained empty, her voice painful soft. "And then I think how strange it is to let a glass give me so much trouble when I could simply break it. Just with my little finger. Like so many things. I could simply break them all and be done."

The silence descended between us again, this time not so reverent. This time, it was the silence of crickets when a monster prowls, the silence after you say the wrong words to the wrong people. It was the kind of quiet that twisted between my joints, made it hurt to move in, let alone speak.

And when I did, it was agony.

"There are armies coming," I said softly. "The Revolution and the Imperium have... well, it's hard to explain, but they're both coming for this city. They know about Liette and the Scrath. They know we're here. And they're coming."

She stared vacantly at the wine, barely even noticing the words I spoke. War had become rote to her.

"We don't know their numbers or their strength," I continued, "but we know that Torle of the Void will be with them. Whatever plan we have... if we have a plan... will involve an incredible amount of fighting. It'll be—"

I choked on my own words. I saw Agne's face begin to fall.

"It'll be hard fighting, Agne." My chest felt tight. It hurt to speak. "It's going to be some of the hardest fighting I can imagine. If we're going to come out of this alive... if there's any *chance* of us coming out of this alive..." I shut my eyes, forced the next words out. "The cost will be incredible. And that's why I needed to tell you."

I forced myself to look at her, forced myself to look past the tears that began to cling to the corners of her eyes, forced myself to still my voice and speak the words I'd known I'd have to speak all this time.

"Agne," I whispered, "you have to leave."

Siegemages are some of the most revered mages in the Imperium. Both for their incredible power and for the sacrifice of their Barter. They gain strength, endurance, invulnerability. They lose sorrow, laughter, love. In the end, they become hollow people, empty of everything but the power and the need to use it.

Agne had lived in fear of that.

And to see her shut her eyes tight and watch tears slide down her cheeks, I was grateful to have at least spared her it.

She could still weep.

"No," she whispered.

"Yes," I replied. "They'll be here soon and when they arrive, you'll be far away."

"I can't leave you. You need me. You all need me."

"We do, yes," I said. "But you need you more than we do. You aren't made for this."

"I'm a Vagrant," she said, her breath halted with tears. "I've fought. I've killed. I'm no flower."

"You aren't. You're Agne the Hammer. You fight, yes. But this isn't the fight you're meant to be in. This isn't the death you deserve to have. You're supposed to be in someone's arms, surrounded by people, in a comfortable bed with a beloved pet—I don't know. But you aren't supposed to die out here, ground into the dust, until everything in you is so spent you can't even feel it when you're bleeding out."

"I would, though. I *would* die for you."

"I believe you would, if I asked you. And I'm asking you to do the opposite of that."

"I can't abandon you. Not now, especially. I don't *want* to. Don't you believe *that*?"

I stared at her.

"If you can look me in the eye and say it, I will."

She opened her eyes, thick with tears. She met my eyes, her face trembling. Her lips parted, made a sound. But no words. The more she tried to speak, the harder the tears came.

"Can you?" I asked. "Can you say it?"

"No," she whispered. "I can't."

"You can't," I repeated. "Because you can still feel. And that's how you know I'm right."

I pulled my scarf around me. I stood up. I laid my hand upon hers.

"Goodbye, Agne," I said. "Thanks for coming with me this far."

I turned to leave.

I couldn't.

Her hand was around my wrist. On my shoulder. She turned me around to face her as she stood up, loomed over me. Her entire body trembled with barely restrained sobs and between her hands, I could feel that if she wanted to break me, it'd take no more than it would to break that glass.

She pulled me into her, against her. Her arms wrapped around me. Her tears fell hot and freely upon my shoulder. Her body shuddered against mine as she began to sob and did not stop.

"I'm sorry," she wept into my ear. "I'm so sorry, Sal. I should have... I should—"

"You have nothing to be sorry for." My arms found her shoulders. "Nothing. Everything you gave to me, you gave because I asked you."

"No," she whispered. "I've been trying to pull away. Trying not to feel. Trying not to get close to anything so I wouldn't even notice when it…when I couldn't—" She bawled into my shoulder. "I'm sorry. I could have done more. For you, for Sindra, for—"

"Stop that." I tried to laugh, almost succeeded. "What you gave me, I was lucky to have. But what it took from you killed me. And it'll kill you, too, if you don't leave while you've still got what you have." I held her by her shoulders, dried at her tears with my scarf. "This isn't where it ends for you."

She took my hands, held them in hers, pressed them to her cheeks. Her tears felt warm on my fingers.

"Thank you, Salazanca," she whispered. "I love you dearly. I would have given you everything."

I smiled at her. "If I didn't feel the same about you, Agnestrada, I would have taken it."

We held each other as long as we could.

Agne the Hammer, one of the most tenacious Siegemages I had ever had the pleasure to meet, left the city that night, freshly bathed and with the taste of wine on her lips. I like to think she rode far that night. I like to think she didn't look back.

But I know she did. Because I know who she is. And I have no regrets about sending her away before she could become something else. If I'd had the time, I would have stood upon the wall and watched her disappear over the horizon.

But I had someone else to see that night.

"*Fuck me*, is it too much to ask that you try *harder* not to kill me? I'm your sister, dickwipe! How can you do this to *family*?"

"If you wouldn't *move* so much and, frankly, if you didn't raise your voice at me so much, I could be a *little* more precise. It's *very* stressful."

"Oh, *you're* stressed, are you, you little shit? I'm the one with the dead fucking arm, aren't I? *I'm* the one that can't feel her own asshole. You think that's relaxing, Captain Cockstink?"

"And if you'd let me work, you might actually get the chance to retain some function in it. The sigils are *incredibly* precise, though, which requires *incredible* concentration—which, I will point out, is not helped by you cursing so much."

"Sure, blame me. See how that goes for you. You hear what they say about me in the streets? About how I trapped that Vagrant? I'm a fucking *hero*."

"That was very reckless. *Very* reckless. I didn't like that, Yria. It was wildly dangerous and the work I have to do to repair it is going to make my hands shake for a week."

For the first time since I had walked in, they stopped talking. There was an uncomfortable moment before Yria let out an uncomfortable noise.

"Yeah, well," she grunted. "Sorry. I didn't mean to worry you."

Urda took a deep breath. "It's okay. I'm happy to help. Just try to go easier on my work."

He returned to his work, tending with quill and loupe to the sigils he was painstakingly scrawling across her numb arm. She returned to her tankard, leaning back in her chair and drinking deeply.

The twins had staked out a room at the only other inn that wasn't Ost's Grave—which was, allegedly, just a room in a home owned by an elderly woman. And, in short order, the tidy, cozy room had been consumed by ink stains and loose papers and an odor that wasn't quite alarming but was far from unconcerning.

Almost every part of their abode had been centered around the massive, cobbled-together chair Urda had finagled to accommodate his sister's needs. She lay reclined across it, her dead arm laid out on a work surface for her brother to scrawl upon, her other arm concerned with the hefty tankard she held.

At some point, she seemed to remember I was in the room. Her eyes popped open, she set her drink down and licked foam off her upper lip.

"For fuck's sake, *say* something next time," she spat. "I fucking forgot you were even here, let alone what you were saying."

"I said Agne's gone."

They shot me each their own distinct glance. Urda's was hopeful. Yria's was suspicious. Both of them unsettled me.

"She left not long ago," I continued. "I don't know where she's going."

"If she's got any sense that doesn't go to dice, she'll go away from here," Yria mumbled.

"She has. Wait, what do you mean about dice?"

"Agne and Yria have—or had, I suppose, given this revelation—an ongoing dice game," Urda answered. "I don't approve."

"What? When did this happen?" I asked.

"When you were off doing your own shit? I don't know," Yria snapped back to me. "I have a life outside of you. And I was just about to win back everything I'd lost to her but now I guess I won't, so *thanks for that*, shitmouth."

"You're not listening to what I'm saying," I said.

"Unless there's something crucial I'm missing, it sounds as though Agne chose to part ways with us," he said with a note of bitter satisfaction. "Good for her."

"And it sounds as though you're telling me you didn't bother to stop her so I could win my money back." Yria rolled her eyes as she drained her ale. "So I'm out metal and you're still an inconsiderate dick. What's new about that?"

"I'm saying I told her to leave," I said. "And I'm telling you to leave, too."

They both fell silent. He stopped working, she stopped drinking, they both fixed me with a stare I wasn't used to. I was used to their anger, their contempt, their fear, and even their occasional begrudging admiration. But this...

This was the first time they were listening to me.

"Agne was going to lose herself," I told them, trying to swallow down the painful sensation crawling up into my throat. "Everything about herself. Just like you're losing yourselves. *Both* of you are losing to her Barter. This war is going to take everything. From both of you. And I can't ask you to do that. I can't let you do that.

"The Imperium and Revolution are coming," I said. "And we don't know when they'll be here. But when they arrive, there won't be any getting away. Even with portals. But there's time for you to go now. And you should take it."

The silence was stunned. Or maybe stupefied. The twins exchanged a look before Yria turned a long glower back toward me.

"Help me up," she grunted.

Urda hopped off his chair, took her by the shoulders, helped her to her feet. She thrust her tankard toward him.

"Hold my shit."

He took the cup from her, set it aside. She draped her arm over his shoulder, her legs shook numbly beneath her, ready to give out should he not support her.

"Get me up in her face."

Together, they hobbled toward me. He propped her up as she leered into my face, the tattoo on her chin twisting wildly with the strength of her contempt. Her eyes narrowed to the thinnest, cruelest slits I had ever seen.

"Do you know who the fuck we are?"

I sighed. "I know who Yria the Cell is. You're a Vagrant. No one says you're not strong."

"No, I mean do you know who the fuck *we* are. Him and me. Urda and Yria. We're not just Vagrants, we're brother and sister. We're family. We have..." She caught herself. A tear danced at the corner of her eye. She snarled it away. "We *had* a mom."

"She was...she was killed in a war. One of the earlier ones. There were so many." Urda breathed heavily as he spoke, the words like iron as he pulled them out of his mouth. "Yria helped me...helps me with it, but it's still...it's still..."

"And another war is coming," I said, "and that's why I want to—"

"*Fuck what* you *want*," Yria roared at me. "We've given you *months* of our help, so you're going to fucking listen to *us*."

I didn't speak. Not another word. I stood there. And Urda swallowed hard.

"But I can't," he whispered. "I can't keep the sounds out of my dreams. Not without Yria. I can't... I can't..."

He couldn't finish. He fell into her, turned away from me. With her one good arm, she pulled him close, held my gaze.

"I've always been an asshole. Since the day I was born," she said. "But he didn't use to be like this. He used to be..." She clenched her jaw. "It used to be easier for him. Big people with big guns did this to him. Made him this way. Made *us* the way we are. It was hell without Mom. She took care of us." Her jaw tightened. "And I take care of him now."

They turned toward me again. And for the first time, their eyes were full of the same tense resolve, the same furious ire, the same desperate aggression that they saw in each other.

"And now the big people with the big guns are coming this way, to do what they did to him to everyone," she whispered, "and you think we're not going to stay here and stop that?"

I admit, that wasn't what I was expecting her to say.

And I wasn't expecting to be left speechless by it.

"You can't stop it," I said. "None of us can. The Imperium *and* the Revolution are—"

"She heard you," Urda said. "We both did. And we heard from Cavric. When he asked us if we would help." He nodded, shakily. "And we said yes."

"What?" I asked, agog.

"Well, don't look so surprised, you selfish ass," Yria snapped back. "If you ever bothered to sit down with me like a civilized human being, you'd know I've got a rich inner life."

"I wanted her to leave," Urda said. "I wanted to protect her. But we talked and... she's right." He shook his head. "I don't want more people to end up like us. I don't want them to lose what we lost."

"But your Barter," I said. "Your arm is—"

"Is *my* fucking arm to do with what I please, thank you very much." Yria grunted with effort, made the barest wiggle of her numbed arm. "And his work is fucking shit, but Urda helps."

"Excuse *me*," her brother protested. "Applying sigils to flesh is considered *extremely* dangerous. Frankly, we should be astonished that it's working at all. If we weren't twins—"

"Well, we *are* twins, so shut your fucking mouth. You're making us look stupid in front of this moron."

"Are you sure you know what's happening?" I asked. "What I'm going to ask of you isn't nothing."

"You aren't asking anything of us and we aren't doing anything for you," Yria spat. "You just happen to be in the same city *we* are choosing to apply our numerous and splendid talents to."

Urda cleared his throat, glanced sheepishly toward me.

"That said, uh," he whispered, "since we *are* in the same city... I'm glad you're here, too, Sal."

"Yeah, yeah." Yria sniffed, looked away. "I mean, better behind the Cacophony than in front of her, right?"

"Right." Urda winced a little. "Though, I think a cacophony doesn't necessarily have an implied directional force, does it?"

"I'll consult my glossary while you get me another beer," his sister said, grimacing as she stiffened up. "Now help me to my chair so we can finish. This shit itches like hell."

It was me who took her this time, hoisting her weight onto my shoulders as I helped her to her chair. Urda tensed, but let me help. And as I lowered her back onto her seat, I squeezed Yria's shoulder.

"I'm glad you're behind me, too."

She grinned, shoved my hand off her shoulder. "Yeah, we're just a real pile of feelings over here, aren't we? Now get the fuck off me and get the fuck out. I know what you do with those hands, you sick fuck."

I did as she asked, Urda offering me a smile as he went back to work applying the sigils to her skin and I went out the door and back into the streets.

Now, don't get me wrong—I don't think I'm a *total* bastard. But I also didn't expect to find myself in the situation I did that night. You hear about it in some stories, see it in operas sometimes.

Making amends, exchanging final words before a great and terrible battle. It felt like the sort of thing I'd never do. The sort of thing that better people than me ended up doing. And the things I'd received in return—the warmth of Agne's embrace still on my skin, the twins' smiles still bright in my eyes—were the sort of things meant for people better than me.

People who fought for better things than lists.

And as I walked and the moon began to sink in the sky, I found my steps slowing until I finally came to a stop under the halo of a dimly burning lamp. Vigilants patrolled slowly, the final shapes to grace the streets before dawn.

It would be morning soon. And then another morning after that. And another and another until...

I turned down a nearby street, started walking toward a distant building.

The people who nights like these, talks like these, were for—the people in operas and stories, the people who fight for great and good things—wouldn't have gone there. They would have gone to sleep, justified in the moments they'd shared.

But I was a different kind of person.

And there were some words I couldn't leave unsaid.

I never forgot the first time I held him.

I wanted to. I tried to. There were a lot of memories of him I tried to rid myself of. Some of them I did. Some of them I didn't. That one—that night—I tried very hard to be rid of.

We were young. Young enough that the academy felt less like a duty and more like a life. He and I and everyone there had only known a scant few years of life outside its walls. And in only a scant few more, we'd come to accept that our lives would be spent in service of the Empress and our sprawling Imperium.

We'd even started to enjoy it.

They trained us, honed our powers in ways that made us feel powerful, more capable than we ever thought we could be. They celebrated us, praised us as the future of the Imperium and the answer to the Revolution's upstart aggression. They gave us all we ever asked and more.

How could we not fall in love with ourselves?

It was four nights after our graduation. Service in the Scar was still distant, a concept so far in the future we couldn't even conceive of it. But we were strong, we were young, and we were amazing.

We'd fumbled around before, struggled with each other's mouths and bodies, let our hands wander across each other. But that was sex. Sex is very good. But it's not the same as holding or being held.

When I disrobed him that night, I expected him to be strong. He had always been so capable: in training, in sparring, even in learning we'd thought he'd be the best of us. But when I pulled the cloth away and beheld him in the pale light, I remember noting how very fragile he looked.

His body was lean and strong, but he didn't carry himself that way. He was shy in my arms, trembled in ways I didn't think he would and guided my hands slowly across his skin. When we kissed, it wasn't hungry or wild, but as deliberate as a poem. When we made love, it was as long and gentle as all good conversations should be. But when I held him, when I saw the things he flinched at and the things that made him melt, that's when I thought I knew him.

When I realized I didn't—and maybe I never did—it cut me as deeply as his blade had.

That was long ago—lives and scars and wars ago—when he was slender and strong, when he melted in my arms.

When I looked at Jindu now, he looked... smaller.

He lay sprawled out across a wood cot, one of many in the tavern that had been commandeered into a makeshift infirmary. Cavric claimed the abundance of sterile alcohol made it a natural choice for treating wounds. Personally, I just think putting the liquor near the place where important decisions are made was good sense.

The morning found the ward quiet. Only a few Vigilants remained in the room, slumbering off the alchemic concoctions that had eased the pains of their kite viper bites. One weary-looking Mendmage walked the rounds, checking on her patients. Pale light crept in through the shutters, painting macabre shadows across half-empty alcohol bottles and numbed bodies.

"Her name is Antilo." Jindu's eye lazily followed the Mendmage as the morning light cast her into silhouette. "She was from a regiment out toward the coast. A good, easy post. She did nothing more than heal injuries from bird riding and tend to the sick children of nobles."

"No combat," I said. "Not bad."

"That's what I said. But she thought differently. She wanted to see action, to put her magic to real use." He stared at her for a moment. "After she did, she deserted. She followed rumors to New Vigil. Started working with Cavric within a week of setting foot in the city."

"A week?"

"He's a charming guy. Did you really kidnap him at gunpoint once?"

"Yeah."

"For what?"

"So I could find you and kill you."

"Ah."

It got slightly awkward after that. I glanced around for something to comment on, found his wound. His body, once strong and slender as his blade, now resembled something of a shiv: a crude, sharp implement hardened and cobbled together. There was a visible dent in his body, a hollow in his skin where sinew was supposed to go.

"Does she do good work?" I asked. "Antilo?"

"I'm not dying, if that's what you're asking," Jindu said. "She does her best. She kept me from succumbing to... whatever the fuck Quoir did to me. But what he pulled out, she can't put back in."

"What does that mean?"

"That's what I asked."

"What did she tell you?"

"Same thing you tell anyone who runs afoul of Quoir," he said. "It doesn't matter."

"Did she tell you he died?"

"She did."

"Painfully. It was a mess."

"I imagine."

"So, yeah." I stared at my feet, scratched the back of my head. "We got him back for you. If that's any comfort."

He rolled his head to look at me. "Was it? It wasn't my list his name was on."

I hadn't even thought about it.

But the moment he said it, I felt it like a stone upon my chest. I reached into my vest, pulled out the folded-up scrap of paper and a piece of charcoal. My eyes drifted down the various names on the list until I found the one.

~~Quoir the Eternal Knock.~~

I put the line through his name. Stared at it as it sat nicely there, only a few lines down from Jindu's own name. I was searching through my head and my heart for the joy that was supposed to bring me. What had I imagined it would feel like when I killed him? Had I even imagined it or had I just...forgotten at some point? When I'd penned his name on the list, along with all the others, I wanted him dead. I wanted them all dead.

Now he was. He, whose ghoulishness was feared even among mages. He, who'd been the cruelest and most dangerous among us. He, who had killed Sindra and made her die in my arms...

And I hadn't even been the one to kill him.

At my hip, I could feel the Cacophony stirring, as if in sympathy. He had wanted it to last longer. When I made the deal with him, so had I.

Revenge for ruin.

The list was the closest thing to a contract our bargain had. The pact we struck to carve his name across the Scar until he was feared and to give me all the names on that paper. I'd clung to this list, let it keep me warm at night when I had no other comforts.

And here it hung in my hands.

A simple piece of paper. A few smudges of ink.

It was uncomfortable to think about. Hard to think about.

"You shouldn't have done that."

Getting angry, though? That was comfortable.

"You shouldn't have fucking thrown yourself in front of me like that," I growled. "It was stupid."

"I preferred looking stupid to seeing you die."

"Birdshit. If that were true, you wouldn't have done what you did back in Cathama."

Jindu winced. "I won't deny what I did but I can't change it, either, Sal. And whatever I might have done, what I'm doing now I do by my choice."

"For what?" I demanded. "For *me*?"

"No!" he protested, then winced again, deeper. "And... yes. It's for me. And for you. And because of you. And because of a lot of things. I don't know. But... is that bad?" He raised his eyes to me. "That I want you to... to..."

A hundred battles, a betrayal, a pound of flesh plucked right out of him by Quoir—in all the struggles I'd seen him fight through, I never saw Jindu look as pained as he did then. His lips struggled to form the words, struggled to ask the thing I knew he wanted to, struggled to keep the pain of the words in his mouth.

I offered him nothing. No words. Nothing more than the eyes I couldn't get to blink.

Say it.

I wanted him to. I wanted him to ask for it. To beg for it.

Ask for forgiveness.

And I didn't want him to. I didn't want to have to hear the pain in his voice.

You piece of shit.

I wanted to deny him everything, to crush whatever hope for it he had.

You took my magic.

And I didn't want him to. I didn't want to see how his face looked when I said it.

I loved you.

I wanted him to carry the pain in his mouth forever...

I loved you so much.

...and I wanted a world where him doing that would have helped anything.

I didn't have that world. I didn't know what I did have. I didn't know what I wanted, what I couldn't bear to hear, what I couldn't bear not to say. I struggled to hate him as surely as I struggled to listen to him. I struggled...and I failed.

So I stared.

I stared at him as he tried and failed to speak.

I stared at him as his face fell, as he looked at his hands and I looked at my feet.

And in the last silent moments between us, we shared not another word, not another look, as morning found his bedside empty and my boots in the dirt as I walked into the dawn without looking behind me.

THIRTY-NINE

NEW VIGIL

What did Agne say?"

Sal glanced up at Ozhma. "When?"

"When she left," Ozhma said, leaning over the table. "You glossed over that part."

"I glossed over it because there was nothing to say." Sal shrugged, leaned back and, conspicuously, glanced away. "She left that night, I watched her go, I wish her well. That's all."

"Birdshit."

Sal recoiled at that statement, curious, irritated, and—maybe?—a little bit impressed. And, to be honest, Ozhma was a little surprised she'd said it. She had one of those faces that wasn't made for cursing, the kind of smile and eyes that made any vulgarity from her sound unusual.

"Excuse me?"

"Birdshit."

But she wouldn't let that stop her.

"Everything you've told me about her, about the twins, about *Liette*," she continued,. "and you expect me to believe she left without a word?"

"Why does it matter what she said?" Sal shrugged again, reached for another drink. "Hardly relevant to what you're here to do, is it?"

"What I'm here to do—" Ozhma caught herself, choked suddenly beneath the weight of the realization. "I know what I'm doing here isn't going to do anything."

"Or help anything," Sal offered, rueful.

"That's *not* true," Ozhma countered.

"Oh yeah? You think we're going to save this city, these people, if I tell you what Agne told me?"

"Well... no, obviously. But—"

"Is it going to make the Imperium stop? The Revolution stop?"

"No, but—"

"So we both agree that it's pointless."

"*NO!*" Ozhma leapt out of her chair, slammed her hands onto the tabletop. "No, no, *no*! It is *not* pointless to ask that because what she said is about what you did and what you did was about how you felt about her and how you felt about her and *everyone else* is the whole reason why we're here, right now, in this city, about to be destroyed. What she said means *everything*."

Sal's brows knitted together. "Huh?"

Ozhma admitted to herself that this line of thinking might have been hard to follow, possibly because of how red-faced, out of breath, and wild-eyed she looked right now. She hadn't expected it to come out like that. She hadn't expected that to come out at all.

She let out a hot breath as she sat back down. "You chose to tell Agne to go, right?"

"For reasons I already told you, yeah."

"Just days before today? Before the Imperium and Revolution struck? A Siegemage would be *incredibly* handy to have around for that, right?"

The confusion on Sal's face began a leisurely stroll into irritation. "That thought had occurred to me, yes."

"But you didn't ask her to stay."

"What would have been the point? There's no fighting the enemies we've made."

"I don't... *disagree*. But you were all right with the twins staying. You're all right with Liette staying."

"They *wanted* to stay," Sal retorted hotly.

"And Agne would have, had you asked," she said. "And you would have asked, but something stopped you."

"I already told you, I—"

"So you *chose* to let her go," Ozhma pressed on, undeterred. "You *chose* to ask her to go. And because of it, you don't have a Siegemage. And here we are."

"You're trying to point out actions have consequences." Sal rolled her eyes. "Are you sure you want to sell liquor for a living? You could easily be Chief Lector at the Academy of the Fucking Obvious."

"*NO!*" Ozhma shouted. She caught herself. "Well... *yes*, actually, actions *do* have consequences. But so do feelings. So do fears. So do hates and loves and... and *everything*. The things you're afraid of are the reason you're here and I'm here so I *think* that I *fucking know* what I'm asking for when I want to know what she said before she left." She plopped back down in her seat, threw up her hands. "*THANKS* for listening."

Ozhma wasn't sure what kind of reaction she was expecting from Sal. She sat there, clinging tenaciously to her chair, as Sal surveyed her with a look of fury. Or of perplexity. Or sorrow? Or... was it all of them? Ozhma thought it might have been all of them.

Sal tensed, her body drawing taut as a crossbow, her jaw clenching like she were physically chewing on Ozhma's words. Her brows knitted together, her eyes narrowed, she slammed her fists down on the armrests of her chair. She shot to her feet and let out a floor-shaking groan.

Or... wait. That wasn't Sal.

The noise reverberated through the room, seeped in through the walls, as though it were the wooden throat of a great and ancient creature through which an eons-long tired sigh was expelled. That noise flooded up around her like a tide, pushed itself into her skin, into her bones.

She *felt* it.

The floor began to tremble and warp. The walls began to shake.

In the wood of the walls, patterns began to emerge—faces of men and women forming in the lines and warping of the timber, their faces twisted into impossible shapes and mouths gaping open in screams. Sal's chair twisted, its armrests and feet becoming limbs from which an agonized creature was born, writhing and taking hideous, cracking shape within the wood.

They looked at Ozhma.

The faces. The shapes.

They recognized her.

She looked to Sal, breathless and unblinking. Sal slowly turned around to face her, swallowed hard.

"You should go."

The door slammed open. Rudu appeared, alarm in his eyes that the *truly* impressive amount of drugs in his pipe was doing its best to smother. Beneath his sandals, the floors began to grow fingers and reach for his ankles.

He exhaled a massive cloud of smoke. "Do I have to fucking say it?"

He didn't. When he snatched her by the wrist and started pulling her forcibly out through the doorway, she didn't question it. They hurried over the shifting floor, fingerbones cracking beneath her heels. The walls of the cellar began to flex and glisten, taking on a grotesque and fleshy scene. They rushed up the stairs, heard it echoing with depraved and manic laughter coming from the air as leering faces began to emerge from the walls, whispering to her with horrific familiarity.

"Do you worry what their last thoughts of you were? Mother and Father? Do you want to know which one hated you?"

"Nothing. You accomplished nothing. A glorified barmaid. Pitiful. You squandered everything everyone ever gave you."

"Where are you going? What are you running from? The sickness is inside you."

She screamed. She wailed at them to stop. She begged Rudu to make them stop. The stairs continued to stretch out beneath them, as though they'd been running for miles and hadn't moved an inch. She pounded on the walls, on Rudu's wrist, on her own chest as the voices and this terrible *sound* wended itself inside her.

It knew her. And in some way she couldn't explain, she knew it—this feeling, this sound, this *presence.* It reached out to her with envious need, a desperate desire to claim her again, to hold her close like a treasured object and never let her go. She felt it coiling around her, ready to pull her back—down the stairs, across the floor, into the closet and the horrible things she knew, somehow, that lived there.

She felt her lungs giving out. She felt the stairs stretch impossibly far away. She felt herself begin to slide backward into a dark place she had never seen before and yet knew all too well.

With her last breath, she shouted.

"STOP."

And it did.

But not because of her.

The stairs stopped growing. She felt herself stop falling. The cellar's warping stilled. The faces ceased their incessant whispering and slowly began to look back toward the room where Sal remained.

They were straining to hear the same thing she was. A noise. Distant. Wailing. The sound of bent brass trumpets and ringing bells of glass pounding themselves to dust. It came roiling up, a great noise that struck her like a blast of wind and knocked her to her ass.

It got hot.

Sweat beaded on her forehead. By the time she got back to her feet, her clothes and hair were soaked. Every ounce of moisture was wrung out of her like a bar rag. The air shimmered with heat.

"Hot."

The wood began to smoke.

"Too hot."

The faces in the walls contorted in pain.

"Help."

And began to blacken.

"Come the fuck *on*."

Rudu's voice was hoarse from exhaustion as he snatched her hand and hauled her up the remainder of the stairs. They burst out into the stale air of the tavern, kept running into the night air. They took deep, grateful breaths together—though the smell of cook fires, however faint, still made Ozhma feel nauseous.

"What...what..." She struggled to find the breath to ask, "What the fuck *was* that?"

"Don't know," Rudu said as he fumbled for his pouch. He poured the remainder of his silkgrass into his pipe, lit it, and smoked hastily. "Don't know, don't know, don't fucking care. We're getting out of here."

She couldn't find the will to resist that statement, nor even the sense. Her lungs were straining for breath. Her blood ran hot and wild in her veins. Panic—true panic, animal-in-a-fire panic—raced through her mind as she numbly followed Rudu through the streets of New Vigil.

She'd had many chances to leave. And each time she stayed, she regretted it. But now, after what had happened down there, after she had...*felt* that presence, she knew there was no choice any longer. It was too much. It had *always* been too much. Too much for Sal, let alone her.

Sal.

She couldn't do anything for anyone here. Not with *that.* Whatever the fuck it even had been.

"Look out."

Rudu grabbed her by the shoulder, snapped her out of her reverie as a swarm of Vigilants came rushing past her. They didn't look to be in any shape to be rushing anywhere—the most hale among them was limping and missing an eye. But they charged toward the wall, regardless, their weapons in hand.

"Morons," Rudu muttered as he walked in their wake. "Morons and their fucking toys."

"What are they doing?" she asked.

"Defending. Or pretending to."

"From what?"

"It doesn't fucking matter what they're doing because they're not going to do it," Rudu mumbled. He waited a moment, spoke breathlessly. "Torle of the Void is hours away. He'll be here by dawn."

"What?"

"You didn't fucking expect him to wait, did you?" Rudu stormed up to a door on a nearby building, banged on it. "Hey. *HEY.*"

It creaked open after a moment. Yria, clad in nothing but a coat and a cigarillo dangling from her lips, answered it.

"You fucking mind?" she asked. "We're all about to die and I'm trying to be fucking comfortable for it."

"I need a portal," Rudu replied. "For two people. Out of here."

"I need a handy and a backrub," Yria snapped back. "We all got needs."

"Is that the unwashed-looking fellow with the drugs?" Urda called out from within. *"Will he share his drugs?"*

Yria furrowed her brow, shrugged. "You got any drugs you can share?"

"I'll smoke you like a side of meat," Rudu said, grabbing Ozhma and shoving her forward, "if you can get her out of here."

Ozhma had no hope of protesting that. No reason to, really. He was right. She needed to get out of here. Torle of the Void was the most lethal thing in the Scar right now and even the knowledge of his presence felt so... insignificant.

She could still feel it, the noise inside her. She could feel its hideous familiarity, the grasping desire with which it had reached for her, *known* her. Torle of the Void could merely kill her, make her just one more casualty among thousands.

That noise... that *thing*... she didn't know what it could do to her, but she couldn't bear to know it. She wasn't Sal.

Sal.

"Yeah, fine." Yria staggered to a wall, her body numb as she leaned on it and drew a thin square with a piece of red chalk. "Only because I like her, though." She snapped her fingers. A portal yawned into existence. "Nothing fancy. This'll get you out of range and no farther. I don't like you *that* much."

Rudu stepped toward the portal, held his hand out toward her. She had no reason not to take it. No reason to stay here. A thousand reasons not to.

It had known her. It had known her *feelings.* It knew her mother and father, it knew her fears, it knew every trauma and every misery and every heartbreak she'd ever had. She could feel it, the same way one feels the executioner's axe over their neck. She could feel it still down there, still looking at her, still reaching for her.

She couldn't face it again. She couldn't face those fears, those traumas, whatever else it was going to pry out of her insides and lay on the floor for her to see. She couldn't do that. Not for anyone. Not for New Vigil. Not for...

Sal.

She stared at Rudu's hand.

She placed hers in it.

She held on tight.

The cellar door creaked open with a lonely sound. The odor of sulfur and burning things wafted up. Faces twisted in pain, their last moments of agony forever seared into faces of blackened wood.

Stairs and floors crunched and turned to kindling beneath fragile footsteps. Ashes hung in the air like a veil, drifting tranquilly through acrid air. Blackened hinges screeched as a door opened.

Sal the Cacophony sat in the middle of a scene of soot-stained carnage. Bodies wrought of the room's furnishings sat charred and twisted in a halo around her. A hunk of sturdier debris served as a stool as she sat, leaning on her knees and staring at the only thing not left destroyed.

A door. Simple. Wooden. Looming in the middle of the room and leading nowhere. It had no reason to be there, unattached to anything. Yet she stared at it, unblinking.

And when Ozhma pulled up another chunk of debris to sit beside her, she started staring at it, too.

Silence hung between them. A sound long and painful enough to ring in her bones, same as the feel of that awful sound had been. She could still feel it—even under all the ash and charred wood, it was still there, that sound that knew her. And it still reached out for her, even faint as it was now.

It still made her want to run.

"Was that there before?"

It always would.

"No," Sal answered after a moment. "It just showed up a minute ago."

Ozhma stared for a long minute. "Have you opened it?"

Sal stared for a longer one. "No."

"Do you want to?"

"No."

"Are you going to stay until it opens?"

Sal swallowed hard. "Yes."

Ozhma smiled faintly. "Can I stay, too?"

Another long moment. This one, not so painful.

"Yes."

The silence descended again. Neither the relentless dirge-like quiet that followed a great tragedy, nor the tense drawn-knife silence of a tragedy yet to occur. It was a contemplative silence, the kind that follows the death of an old great lie or the birth of a new one.

"Was it Liette that caused that?" Ozhma asked.

"Yes."

"And...Eldest?"

"Yes."

"And that heat, was that the—"

"Yes."

"What does that mean?"

Sal let out a long breath. "We'll know before long." She glanced at Ozhma. "Torle of the Void?"

"By dawn."

Sal nodded. She stared down at the ruin that had been the room.

"Sorry about your notes."

"It's okay," Ozhma said. "I remember most of them."

The door hung there—impossible as a dream, unflinchingly real. It stared at Ozhma, as surely as she stared at it. She did not know what lay behind it. But it knew her, in a way that no one else did. It terrified her. It made her want to run.

But something else made her want to stay.

"Do you think," Sal whispered softly, "you could remember a few more for me?"

Ozhma smiled. "I think I could."

FORTY

NEW VIGIL

Dawn found us the same way it finds us all.

Cruelly.

We'd done everything we were supposed to do. We scouted the forces arrayed against us. We fortified, laid traps, gave all the impassioned speeches, and received all the roaring support that such speeches were awarded, if they were any good. We did everything to prepare, just like you hear in the stories.

What you don't hear in the stories is how little that seems to matter.

When the pale light washed across the great flatlands sprawled before the gates of New Vigil like a dusty, broken carpet, they were revealed to us. A thousand shadows, teeming between the shafts of light pressing through the towering columns of rock.

Their anthem reached us before any of them did. An electric warble of voices blaring lyrics of incomprehensible loyalty and obedience. The smoke came next, flickering purple with severium as their machines rumbled forward. We only knew their numbers when they came into the light, counting the glints of their gunpikes held ramrod straight.

The Glorious Revolution of the Fist and Flame.

I must have put a hundred of them in the ground over the past year, at least—more, if you count incidentals. Somehow, I'd managed to go this long without being terrified of them.

Not a bad streak. Unfortunately, it came to an end when I stared out over the fields leading toward New Vigil, along with a number of my hopes for how this day was going to go.

The sound of snarling engines and groaning metal wheels echoed off the mountains, belches of severium smoke shrouding their approach. Marchers—great towers bristling with cannons and seated upon whirring metal treads came rolling forward, the thunder of their machinery rivaling the chorus of the Revolutionary anthem blaring from the crowns of sirens they wore at the top of their looming battlements.

Lesser machines—the iron beasts and mechanical monsters of their armies—rolled between the shadows cast by the line of the looming Marchers. Mortar teams hauled their stout cannons. Mobile ballistae platforms rolled forward, chariots pulled by explosive chambers brimming with great spears. Tank-like Iron Boars brought up the rear on churning wheels, Revolutionaries hanging off the transport's metal hides like quills on a porcupine's back. Suits of mobile Paladin armor rolled to the front, their engines churning as they toted massive cannons in huge mechanical gauntlets.

I could count ten Marchers, which was bad enough. The smaller machines and Paladins, I lost track of after twenty. There was plenty to be terrified of in either of those numbers, but if I had even tried to count the soldiers, I probably would have screamed until I passed out.

Thousands? More? How are you supposed to count droplets in a river? Because that's what they looked like, flowing in between every spare inch of land left by the machines. In thick battle squares, in rolling columns, they came flowing over. Sergeants and commanders on birdback rode this way and that, barking orders and propaganda to keep the massive force of humanity moving toward New Vigil's gates.

I couldn't see their faces from here. I didn't know how many were veterans and how many were fresh-faced. Nor did I know how many were conscripts pressed into service and how many were there of their own will. And though it wasn't healthy, I wondered how many of them down there I had known, how many of them had walked with me across the Scar as refugees before they ended up there.

And maybe some of them down there, clutching their gunpikes, were looking up at New Vigil's walls and wondering if I was up here.

That wonder festered as my eyes settled upon a thick knot at the rear of the formation. The black uniforms of the Twenty-Second stood at unmoving attention, their weapons bristling. I saw a blue-coated figure conversing heatedly with them, saw black hair and dark skin and a *very* familiar angry flailing.

I resisted the urge to ask for a spyglass to see if that was Tretta.

Honestly, if she had to come and see how many people besides her also want to kill me, I would have just been embarrassed.

"That's... well, that's not great."

Cavric hummed into the spyglass as he surveyed the approaching Revolutionaries. When he lowered it, I saw his face twitch briefly beneath his beard—a flash of nerves he swiftly smothered beneath a steely calm he hammered into his eyes. With every eye on that wall trained upon him, he knew he didn't have the luxury of fear.

"But it's not unexpected." He cast a glance down New Vigil's wall. "We have what we need to deal with it." He fought down a grimace. "Just not enough of it."

It was true. The wall would be an imposing sight in any other circumstance. Vigilants, each one with the familiar poise of a veteran, stood armed with salvaged weapons. Unruly-looking cannons that had been scavenged and repurposed by defectors dotted the wall at regular intervals. The few mages on the city's side were stationed in positions of strategic support. It was a good defense, better than most.

But that's one of the first and harshest of life's lessons.

Better rarely beats *more.*

"That said, it could be worse."

A number of people, myself included, looked to Cavric with an expression that was equal parts curiosity and what-the-fuck.

"Torle of the Void claimed to have an agreement with the Revolution," he observed, surveying the field. "We can probably assume that to be true. But it can't be *too* true." He gestured to the Revolutionaries. "They aren't marching together. Our scouts tell us the Imperials are holding position far from the battle in that valley over there. Makes you wonder how solid this agreement between them is if they need to be separated." He stroked his beard, thoughtful. "We could use that to our advantage."

It wasn't a terrible observation. Torle's charisma was one thing, the Revolution's ability to follow orders was another—neither was as big as the many years and many corpses the two powers' rivalries had left behind in their history of animosity. Pain like that doesn't go away just because two people want it.

I *think* he was expecting some murmurs of approval or curiosity. At the blank faces that met him, he produced a sigh so fierce it almost knocked me to my ass.

"Then again," he said, "a magic fucking gun would be a pretty handy advantage here, too."

The blank faces turned toward me. And they weren't so much blank as pissed off. Honestly, it was hard to blame them. But I tried to anyway.

While they had been listening to their impassioned speeches and getting each other all excited to go die, I had been somewhere else. With someone else. Soft hands had fallen into mine. Large eyes had looked up pleadingly, full of stars.

"*It knows*," she had whispered. "*Eldest knows.*"

But they didn't know that. They couldn't know that. All they knew was that Sal the Cacophony, the walking disaster that was at *least* supposed to come with her namesake, was here with all the disaster and none of the gun.

They could be pissed off.

If they wanted to see if I was in the mood for fucking around.

"Yeah?" I leaned, resting a hand pointedly on the hilt of my sword. "Would it make things easier if I *weren't* here? Because I can go relieve myself while you all die, if that's what you want. I had a big breakfast."

Cavric nodded, held up a hand. "All right, yes. I understand. We all do." He looked down the wall at his soldiers. "Because we all understand that, even if we survive this, it won't be the last time. And next time, we won't have a magic gun, either, will we?"

That made the faces go from pissed off to...mostly resigned? That was an improvement, right?

"But if you want to help, then help me now," Cavric said. "You know Torle of the Void. When he gets here, what can we expect?"

I would have said "*besides suffocating and agonizing death?*" but I didn't want to be seen as not a team player.

"It knocks the shit out of him to do what he does, that much I remember." I leaned on the crenellations of the wall, stared out over the approaching blue tide. "He needed a team to survey the land to be able to pull it off without killing himself. They needed..."

The realization crept upon me as I remembered the sight of Torle flying high over the cliffs overlooking the fortress. And it struck me so hard it damn near beat the wind out of my lungs.

"A view," I whispered, breathless. "They needed high ground to see the city."

Cavric was already searching the field. His eyes settled on a nearby cliff face that loomed close, a ridge dotted with trees coiling like a great serpent toward the city's walls. He pointed a thick finger toward it.

"There," he said. "There's forest on those cliffs. We use the logging trails to bring timber down. But you couldn't move a force through those woods."

"Yeah, you're right," I said, "these are probably the kind of mages that get discouraged by difficult terrain as opposed to just burning it down."

I knew my tone wasn't helpful. I wanted to be a team player, but I also wanted to be not-dead. So...

"Point," he muttered. "And from there, their Doormages could get forces into our city." He gestured to a nearby Vigilant. "Get word to the other end of the wall. I want eyes on the ridge at all times and people ready to defend it, if need be."

A swift salute and the soldier was off. I couldn't help but be impressed. Cavric couldn't help but notice.

"What?" he asked.

"Nothing," I said. "It's just...you've changed a lot since we met, haven't you?"

"You choose very inconvenient times to show interest in people, Sal."

"Look, I just mean..." I sighed. "You have less reason to help me than I have reason to ask. And I just...just..."

"Yeah." He smiled at me. "Well, this was always going to happen, eventually. And I like Liette enough to try."

I found the strength to scoff. "It's *my* fantastic ass up here fighting for you."

"It is." His face fell briefly as he looked toward the impending force. "They'll be here very soon. It'll be too loud to hear." He looked at me. "You got anything to say before then?"

I felt a painful twist in my belly, the kind you get whenever you hear words you needed, but didn't want, to hear. I pulled my scarf up around my throat, stalked toward the stairs leading off the wall.

"How'd you know?" I muttered.

"Because you haven't changed," he replied.

"When did it find out?" I asked as we pushed our way through the command center.

"I don't know," Liette whispered. "I don't know, I don't know." She held herself tightly, pressed her body against mine, refused to look up. "It just...I *felt* it. Eldest is afraid. It...it doesn't want to die."

I wouldn't normally blame it. Except *it* was a Scrath.

It was impossible to know how long Eldest had been aware of

what we planned to do, how long it had been *thinking*. Maybe it had waited until today in hopes of the battle distracting us away from it. Or maybe it was scared. Or maybe it was an inscrutable creature of impossible creation and it didn't matter what the fuck it thought.

We came to a halt, her legs going out as we came to the stairs leading down to the cellar. Her breath caught in her throat. She fell, sending me struggling to pull her back up. She flailed out with a hand, pressed it against the wall for purchase.

The wood of the staircase shuddered and flexed, a great rippling wave washing out from where her hand had rested. I blinked—the wood had formed great grins that splintered apart with grotesque laughter. I blinked again—it returned to normal.

"Sal."

I looked down.

Eyes pitch black and full of stars stared back at me.

No more words. No more worries. No more fears. I didn't have those luxuries, either. I took her up against me, carried her bodily the rest of the way into the cellar. The cold darkness of the room assailed me, the sudden lack of noise and warmth and light a subtle but welcome change.

"Over here."

Meret waved me toward the end of the cellar, where he held open a door. He gestured into a sparse cell of a room, a cold spot deep below the earth full of fermenting barrels.

"This is where the beers are stored," he said. "It's...a little crowded, I admit. But, in my defense, you only *just* now told me to find somewhere dark and quiet."

I helped her into the room, glanced around before easing her down onto a barrel. "Is it quiet enough?"

"It is," she whispered. Her eyes shut, her head swayed as though she were ravaged by fever. "I can hear them. Both of them now. They know each other." She touched the barrel beneath her, winced. "So uncomfortable here, though."

I sighed, looked to Meret. "Can we get a pillow or something?"

Meret's eyes widened at the request. Or... wait, not at the request. At something behind me. I turned to see. Then my eyes went wide, too.

I had only looked away for a second. Yet when I looked back, the tiny cell had exploded out into a room. A well-furnished room of polished timber, with moody lighting and subtle, cozy décor. The barrel she had been sitting on was suddenly a large, ornately carved chair.

I recognized the chair.

This room.

We had dreamed it before, she and I, in a whispered conversation late at night the very first time we met. This room. And the house that had gone with it. It was where she—

"Sal."

She stood up. Her eyes stared at me. Brown and wide behind her glasses. Her eyes. Her own.

"It has to be now."

I nodded. I drew back my scarf, revealed the empty leather sheath at my hip and the heavy wooden box I carried under my arm. I set it warily into her hands. Behind the wood, I could feel the heat, the bemused seething whispering between the planks.

He was ready. He was eager.

"Are you sure about this?" I whispered to Liette.

"No." She took the box from me. "But I am sure I can do it."

I put my hands on it. The pain that shot through me—was it fear? Or just separation?

"He's dangerous," I said. "He's more dangerous than you. Even if this works, I'm not sure if—"

"I am sure you can do it, too." She prised my fingers off it. "Even if you don't know what it is yet."

I reached out again. This time, it was her hand I took. Her fingers I pressed to my lips.

"Come back in one piece," I whispered.

"Keep in one piece for me to come back to," she replied.

She walked to the end of the room that shouldn't be. She opened a door to somewhere that couldn't possibly exist. She spared one look for me before her eyes began to shift and darken. She flinched, held the Cacophony tight against her, and disappeared behind it.

Just like that.

It had been only a few seconds.

It hadn't been long enough. There was more I needed to tell her. More I needed to say. I had to go after her, I had to—

"Sal?"

Another voice. Meret's. When I looked at him, his eyes were no longer wide with fear. Now they were empty.

"It's started," he said.

But by then, I could barely hear him over the sounds of cannon fire.

FORTY-ONE

NEW VIGIL

The stairs shook beneath my boots with every step.

I held the wall for purchase as I climbed my way to the top of the battlements. It shuddered, like a living thing, with the reverberation of machines firing and smoke belching. When I crested the top of the wall, I was greeted by bouquets of fire and smoke, tossed affectionately from the walls of New Vigil to adoring masses below.

The long flatlands were scarred by patches of black cannon fire, sporadic shots falling well short of the columns of Revolutionaries. Who were, not to make *too* big of a deal of it, close enough that I could count their boots.

So you might wonder, as I wondered, why it was, what with the enemy so close, the cannons on *our* side were shooting like they were drunk?

"What the *fuck*, Cavric?"

But that was a lot to convey and there wasn't a lot of time, so I just went with something else.

He didn't answer me. Nor did he even seem to notice that his cannons—of which, I should point out, the other guys had *many* more of—were firing off what appeared to be *very* limited ammunition at ground unoccupied by soldiers.

Only when the wall's cannons were answered did he even bother to move.

A chorus of cracks roared from the field. Mortar fire streaked from below, painting arcs of smoke and ash across the sky. Most fell short of us. A few sailed overhead to crash elsewhere. Two struck the wall, their explosions throwing Vigilants through the air like burned toys.

"*Cavric!*" I shouted, grabbing him by the shoulder. "Whatever you're doing, it isn't working. You have to—"

"DON'T."

He didn't so much cut my sentence off as tear its head from its shoulders with his teeth. Dark brows knitted as he glared at me.

"I trust you to do what's right for you and good for my city," he said, his voice going soft and urgent. "Trust *me* to do what's good for you and right for my city."

I'd seen more than a few battles in my day—as Sal, as Red Cloud. I'd seen more than a few battlefield commanders, too, broken under the weight of their own command. Some panicked, some froze, but more did what he did—bet every last piece of metal he had on one strategy, whether it worked or not. Whether it even looked sane or not.

In the Imperium, we relieved such commanders. Always after they broke. Usually before they could ruin everything. Often by force.

And part of me wondered if that was the right thing to do here. There were many reasons to fear it was—Cavric's inexperience in wide-scale battle, the fact that his cannoneers were apparently high—and few reasons to fear it wasn't.

So if you told me I was stupid for trusting him, for releasing his shoulder and standing back, I wouldn't say you were wrong.

Hell, at that point, I was agreeing with you.

A cannon fired. And in the aftermath of its echoing rumble, I heard the sound of boots tromping, of gunpikes rattling, of a voice breaking over the sirens and blaring with a cry from a hundred sirens at once.

"Ten Thousand Years!"

And taken up ten thousand times over.

"TEN THOUSAND YEARS!"

The war cry was torn from every throat and spat bloody into the air. The flatlands thundered as Revolutionary regiments broke into a charge, their bird-riding sergeants leading them in a howling rush across the blackened field.

I cursed inwardly. They were emboldened, these attackers, encouraged by the fact that the cannons were shit. They'd seen an opportunity to crush the defense and had been smart enough to take it.

I'd have cursed outwardly, too. But I had to duck, at that point, as crossbow bolts came arcing up over the wall.

Vigilants squatted behind barricades, popping up to offer retaliatory fire in volleys. Sheafs of bolts were run between each squadron—far too little to keep up any sort of withering fire. The Revolutionaries' bolts damn near darkened the sky, forcing us to keep our heads low.

When the locust-like hum of bowstrings ebbed a moment, I dared to peek through a crenellation. And at that point, cursing inwardly *or* outwardly no longer seemed sufficient.

Teams of Revolutionaries came rushing toward the wall, four of them to each squadron, a heavy piece of bizarre-looking equipment in their grasps. They flicked their wrists, shields unfolding with metal whirrs to protect them as they toted their machines toward the wall. Not all of them made it across the field. But too many did.

They jammed their machines at the base of the wall. I strained to see, but watched as two of them carried their burden just a few feet from where I hunkered down. I saw them seize a thick cord and give it a jerk. An engine roared to life. Pistons shot. There was a burst of severium smoke.

And then a ladder came out of fucking nowhere.

I'm still not sure what kind of machine that was, but I know it was birdshit. Collapsible ladders came firing out of the machines, shooting up to punch grappling spikes into the walls to cling to them with a ferocious *thunk* of a noise. It was the second-worst sound I could have heard that day.

The *worst* sound was the echo of that *thunk* as dozens more ladders shot up and punched into the wall's stone. In a matter of seconds, the only defense New Vigil had was bristling with immovable siege ladders. And in a matter of minutes, they were swarming with soldiers.

Revolutionaries came rushing up over the ladders, shields deployed in one hand and gunpikes strapped to their backs. Their howling cries echoed off the metal of their own equipment, became thunder in my ears as they swarmed up over the wall.

Including the part right next to me.

I tore my sword free of my sheath, came rushing to join the Vigilants as they, too, rushed to meet the Revolutionaries. I watched one of them fold under a gunpike blast, face scattered to the wind. I went low, under the arc of the pike and caught its wielder in the belly.

In, out. My sword cut through the Revolutionary. He gasped, only half sure of what had happened but entirely sure he was dead. I caught him by the collar as he flopped backward, took his sputtering deadweight against me and rushed forward. His body shuddered as gunpikes and blades struck off his carcass.

I ran until I hit a body, pushed until I heard a scream. My feet scraped up against the crenellations of the wall. I held my dead partner close for a minute as I found the ladder before pushing him over it. The carcass caught his comrades as he tumbled down, knocking three of them from their perches and sending them tumbling back to the fields.

Three. Plus the one I'd killed. I looked over, saw the Vigilants wiping up the remainder, the corpses of five other invaders lying at their feet. Nine dead Revolutionaries. Tens of thousands to go.

Not a bad start.

Not a *great* start, either.

"Cavric!" I shouted. "*Cavric!* Is this the fucking plan?"

"No." He pulled his hefty axe out of a Revolutionary's shoulder and a hand cannon from his belt. "*This* is the fucking plan."

He angled it upward, pulled. The flare streaked into the sky.

And was answered with a flurry of bolts.

Ballistae rang out from behind the walls. Lit fuses crackled as massive bolts painted smoking arcs over the wall. They punched down into the crowd of Revolutionaries, some skewering enemies, some clattering harmlessly away. But in another moment, they all met the same fate.

The fuses ran out. Explosive charges strapped to the ballista bolts erupted, spraying shrapnel and splinters in massive clouds. They carved through the Revolutionary onslaught, blossoms of hewn gore sprouting across the crowd.

Admittedly, that was a better plan than what I thought.

But it still wasn't—

"Vigil! To the ends of the earth!"

Cavric's cry cut through the carnage.

"TO THE ENDS OF THE EARTH!"

And was answered.

With a little more enthusiasm than a rallying cry that unimaginative deserved, if you asked me. But no one did.

Vigilants came swarming up from below. With great autobows and spears. With explosives and spellwritten clothing. With every scrap of weaponry, armor, and fortune they'd been able to scavenge from this vile land, they came rushing up.

And with the pain of all those battles, they got to work.

Axes were deployed, hacking and hewing through the invaders and bashing them down. Vigilant alchemists rushed to the ladders, carrying heavy barrels on their back from which they poured thick, sticky tar down the metal rungs. The cannons began to aim a little less drunk and a little more like they wanted to win.

Cavric.

You magnificent prick of a human.

I'd have kissed him if it wouldn't have been all weird.

He'd served in the Revolution. And served with zeal. He'd heard their propaganda, the legends of their own destiny, and believed it. Until he didn't. He knew what made them confident. And how to punish it.

Now those fanatics were clustered together so tightly you couldn't miss one even if you were trying to.

Ballistae and crossbows continued to pepper the backline as archers fired blindly over the wall at their Revolutionary foes. The cannons continued to fire and return fire, even as one or two of them smoldered on the wall. The Vigilants continued to hack and hew their aggressors from the wall.

But every bolt fired saw a hundred returned. Every Revolutionary machine that fell was replaced by another. And every soldier that fell in his assault of the wall had fifty more waiting to replace him—and they were only getting angrier.

I fought where I could, cut what I could. But it was clear that even with the alchemists' interventions slowing them down, time was on their side. Numbers were on their side. And, most notably, the big fucking mobile towers with huge fucking cannons were on their side.

Had I known Cavric had a plan for that, I probably would have fought less hard.

Through the haze of the battle, I could see the bushes stirring on the edges of the flats. I saw a Banter come stalking out of the underbrush, surly as the angry woman on its back. It threw back its head, let out a braying crow, took off running.

The underbrush shuddered as the rest of the flock came running, a bright red scar painted across the flatlands, hurtling toward the Revolutionary columns. The Vigilants astride the Banters were fewer in number than the birds themselves, riderless birds stampeding instinctively along with the remainder of the flock.

With an angry crowing and a clash of flesh and feathers, the wisdom of this became clear. Banters aren't particularly smart, or good-mannered, or reliable for much of anything except two tasks: shitting and being incredibly foul-tempered. Those birds who had riders continued to rampage up through the ranks of the Revolutionaries. The wild ones remained behind in the throngs of Revolutionaries, furiously lashing out with sharp wings and sharper spurs.

The riders pulled free of the affray, charged toward the Marchers. I saw the scramble of sergeants and commanders as they struggled to command defense to the siege machines. I saw riders get cut down by lucky shots and fanatical guards. I saw one of them leap from the back of their bird and cling to the side of the tower. I watched her scramble up into the Marcher's tower, disappear behind the window.

I never caught a glimpse of the explosives she was carrying.

I only knew she had them because of what happened next.

The tower's walls buckled outward, strained for a moment before erupting. Stone and metal struts were launched everywhere, crashing across the field. The severium charges inside the tower exploded in a burst of purple flame.

I learned later what it was. A concoction of alchemic runoff and various spellwritten scraps cobbled together into an incredibly unstable, incredibly dangerous mixture that reacted to almost anything and almost always with explosive properties. A dangerous and grotesque weapon, one that left no victors and nothing but fire behind.

The Vigilants called it Worst Impression, I was told later. A joke.

I wonder if that comforted them at all when it exploded and took them with it.

I doubted it.

The other Marchers continued to roll forward, undaunted by the collapse of their fellow. The success was short-lived; I saw explosions erupting prematurely across the fields as the Revolutionaries struck down the riders carrying them before they could reach their targets.

Bloody swathes had been carved in circles around where the Banters had died. A Marcher tank lay in smoldering ruin. But when the remaining Banter riders broke free of the affray and disappeared back into the brush, they had left far too few alive for how many of them had died.

I had to believe they knew that would happen.

I still have to.

I had been breathing for several moments before I realized I'd had room to do so. The battlements had been cleared, for the moment.

Revolutionaries lay dead by the score, fought back by blade and bow and blast. But the dead Vigilants among them stood out more starkly. And their absence would be felt much more, I knew.

The Revolutionaries continued to teem, innumerable, below. I heard sergeants reestablishing order and feet marching back into siege positions as I ran across the wall. I found Cavric helping his troops beat back the last of a wave over the ladder.

"How's it looking down where you were?" he grunted, gasping for breath.

"Clear, for the moment," I replied. "But not great. Ketterling's riders, they—"

"They did what they could," Cavric said firmly. "It's up to us now." He swept his eyes over the field. "We keep the cannons clear, we stand a decent chance of taking down those Marchers."

"Do we stand a decent chance of keeping the cannons clear?" I asked.

"Great question." He shook his head. "Let me worry about that. I need you to worry about other things."

"Like what?"

He pointed a broad finger skyward.

"That."

Over the wooded ridge high above, I saw the light. A flare flew into the sky, sputtering for a few desperate moments before vanishing pitifully. I sighed deeply.

It really *had* been going too well, hadn't it?"

"Only one flare," Cavric said. "Not as many Imperials as we expected. They either sent too few—"

"Or they're very confident in who they sent," I muttered.

"For your sake, I hope it's the former." He nodded at me. "You know what to do?"

"Whatever I can?"

"Ideally, better than that. But you know mages better than I do. So whatever you do..." He placed a big hand on my shoulder. "Do it *now*."

He didn't need to tell me twice. He didn't need to give me a shove to get me going, either. But since this was a stressful situation and I *was* actually kind of terrified, I let it slide.

Fighting mages was never something you looked forward to, even if you were lucky enough to have a magic gun. Since all I had to fight them with was what everyone else had to fight them with, I can't say I was excited to go.

But I was running, all the same.

Others joined me, summoned by the flare—Vigilants, some carrying weapons, some looking like they'd spent time in the Imperium themselves, started swarming toward the end of the wall. Cavric's picks, I assumed. The best chance New Vigil had of surviving. Them and me. Less than fifty people, by my count.

I tried not to let my chest tighten at that thought.

"Well, look who fucking decided to show up. Give me a second to get the fancy silver out."

Despite the cannons bursting and the sirens blaring and the sounds of people screaming and dying, the dulcet sounds of Yria's uncouthness carried. She stood at the edge of the wall, smugly poised in the center of a large chalk square she'd drawn; her brother was furiously busy dividing his time between placing sigils around that square and eyeballing his sister for any sign of her pushing herself too hard.

Despite the fact that she heavily favored one side over the other and one arm hung barely usable, despite all the carnage and horror raging around her, she appeared in good spirits.

Or... maybe she was in good spirits *because* of the carnage and horror?

"Ridge," I said, breathless. "Get me to the ridge. The Imperials..."

"Yeah, yeah, I heard all about it," Yria grunted. "And we're working on it."

"What?"

"I don't fucking know. Ask Little Lord Pencilpuss here."

Urda barely looked up as he continued on his hands and knees, scrawling sigils on the ground. "I'll have you know that there is an *extremely* problematic number of Doormages present right now and it's making portals touchy."

"Like what you did to Quoir?" I asked. "Is that an issue?"

"Normally, not an issue," Yria grunted, picking up her numb arm and letting it drop. "Lately? An issue."

My body shook with the scream I swallowed. Adrenaline had been the only thing keeping my nerves from fraying. Forced to wait while Urda continued with whatever birdshit he was doing made me aware of the nervous energy in my legs and hands, the way my fingers twitched and searched for a weapon that wasn't there.

It had to be done. I knew it. He had to be with her for now. I knew that, too. But my body didn't. My body needed a weapon. My body needed the—

"Cacophony?"

A voice from behind me. I glanced—a Vigilant stood, trying to look less scared than she was.

"They say you killed a lot of mages in your time," she said.

What the fuck did she mean "in my time"? There's no age limit on killing mages.

"Do you have any advice?" she asked. "For fighting them, I mean? I've battled plenty of Revolutionaries, but not as many Imperials."

"Yeah," I grunted. "Don't let them corner you, don't let them pin you down, don't let them *think*, if you can help it."

"Don't let them... what? How do I do that?"

"Tough question, isn't it?" I sighed, turned around. "Just keep moving and try to keep them moving, too, and you'll—"

I paused as I beheld the long weapon she held in her hands.

"Like it?" she asked, beaming. "I found it off of one those masked bastards. Like I said, I've fought a lot of Revolutionaries."

"Yeah... you did say that." I admit that there was possibly a little *too* much breathlessness in my voice to be tasteful. "Do you know how to use that thing?"

"A little. I'm better with something smaller, but I figured we should learn the enemies' weapons, shouldn't we?"

"Absolutely. Hey, here's another lesson about mages: they take what they want and act fast."

"That's good to— HEY!"

Now, technically, I only *used* to be a mage, but I figured I gave her enough warning. Certainly enough that she had no business being so upset when I jerked the weapon out of her hands and took it myself. She cursed at me, had to be held back by her fellow Vigilants, but I didn't notice. I only barely noticed it when a note of the Lady's song rang out and Yria's portal opened.

As I walked toward it slowly, my eyes were on the horrific thing in my hands. Its haft was long and polished metal, its grip adorned with a small lever. At its head, a small engine ready to be called to life lingered, a perfect complement for the glittering ebon blades on its saw head.

I touched the lever. The engine purred. The blades whistled, thoughtfully.

"I'm going to call you," I whispered to the weapon, "Reginald."

I took Reginald by the hand.

Together, we walked through the portal.

We had company to meet.

We emerged onto the ridge, the portal winking shut behind us as the last Vigilant got out—an open escape route would have been nice to have, but given Yria's limitations, I realized the unfeasibility of keeping a portal going the entire time. I would simply have to trust in her ability to look out for me.

Which didn't do much to calm my nerves.

Nor did the lone Vigilant I saw come bursting out of hiding and running toward us, breathless and bloodied. He said something about slowing them down as much as he could, something about numbers, some other things.

I didn't hear him. I couldn't. Not over the sound of dozens and dozens of notes crashing off of each other in an otherworldly and unsettling chorus.

The Lady's song. Mages. A *lot* of them.

And then, against them, a single solitary note that I recognized. No matter how much I didn't want to. The wind shifted beside me. A shape appeared, clad in dirty rags and carrying an iron sword.

"They're coming." Jindu coughed, swayed, tried to pretend he was okay. "Plan?"

A twitch of ire tugged at my mouth, begged me to hurl an insult or tell him to go back to the infirmary. A pang of pain in my chest bade me not to listen to that urge.

"Keep them unsteady," I said. "If you see a commander, go for a kill. Otherwise, we're trying to keep them busy." I glanced around, surveyed the area—dense forest, rocky outcroppings, irregular terrain. Impossible to fortify, but difficult to fight in. "Terrain is on our side. Try to keep them in it."

"Ah," he replied. "Like the holdout at Hagtown." He flicked his sword briefly. "We took that one handily, if I recall."

"Hagtown was a long time ago. We had troops, I had magic, and you had a bunch of meat that hadn't been teleported out of you."

Jindu blinked. "All right, well, sure—if you look at it like *that*, it looks pretty—"

A cry went up. The woods shuddered. Reginald's engine roared to life.

"Later," I said.

"Right."

But he wasn't wrong. My nerves steadied as I walked forward, Reginald in hand and Vigilants at my back. I breathed deeper as he vanished, a comforting shadow at the corners of my eyes, watching the spots I couldn't. It was like old times. Times when I felt invincible.

For the briefest of moments, I wondered if this was what it would have always felt like. If he'd never cut me, if his name had never been on my list—would we still be doing this? Moving so easily, so readily around each other like we had during all those years and all those wars ago?

Maybe.

But that wasn't important now.

Maybe it hadn't been.

Metal flashed in the darkness. The underbrush shuddered. Imperials came sweeping forward—long and lean and each of them wearing the same kind of pale, vaguely human metal mask. Swords burst into flame as spellwritten sigils erupted across the blades.

Soundless but for the rush of their feet and the cackle of their fiery weapons, they swept forward. I darted out of the way of a blazing arc, veered away from lashing, laughing tongues as my attacker lunged at me. They struck, over and over, forcing me back with each fiery strike. I knew this tactic.

I'd often ordered it, in fact.

My foe struck at me. I struck back. Their fiery blade caught in the teeth of Reginald's saw blade, the flames roaring impotently against the black metal. I pulled the trigger. The blades whirred to life, shattered the sword in two.

My attacker fell back, holding up the hilt of their shattered weapon. For the briefest moment, I could see the flash of terror in their eyes behind their mask. They saw the Vigilant coming too late, went down beneath a blade that punched through their flank as one of Cavric's soldiers charged into their side.

The ridge was dotted with their bodies, bellies bleeding out on the dirt even as their swords sputtered. I could see a few hasty Vigilants getting excited at the victory. They hadn't fought enough mages. They didn't know.

Imperials always sent in whatever unlucky or foolish nuls they'd drafted into their legions first. Mages preferred to watch their foes fight their underlings to better gauge their strength. The nuls almost always died, of course, but not without the dubious honor of having given their masters precious information.

This was nothing to be excited about.

The first Vigilant to die taught that lesson to the others.

A wave of frost came swirling out from the woods, cold mist

accompanying a flurry of icicles. The biggest of them took a Vigilant in the chest, sent her corpse flying over the ridge.

Another two fell before the rest of them found cover. They took up their crossbows with seasoned aim, picking their targets in the woods before firing. When the other mages emerged, Embermages bursting out in fiery explosions and Sparkmages sending lances of lightning striking from the darkness, the Vigilants did not break, barely flinched.

They merely wore a new kind of resignation on their face, ready to shovel this birdshit as surely as any other. They kept moving, firing where they could, striking where they dared, preventing the mages from pinning them down. There were few killing blows, but we took more than we lost. And, if nothing else, a mage occupied with staying alive is *very* different than a mage occupied with killing you.

Had it been down to mettle and nothing else, things might have turned out different.

But, by now, you know enough about magic to know it doesn't give a shit about mettle.

The ridge shuddered. Trees trembled and fell in great swathes. The darkened woods that had been our battleground was cleared in just a few short moments. When the last of them fell down, scythed like wheat, I beheld the little woman who had brought them low.

"Salazanca." Bad Neighbor didn't *sound* thrilled to see me as she tossed aside the massive tree she'd used to smash the others out of the way. "I am surprised to see you here."

"You don't sound so good," I observed, both for my own information and just to be a dick, if I'm honest. "You've used a lot of magic, haven't you?"

"I have." Her heavy boots crunched earth and rock beneath her feet; her eyes were empty. "Your war has been costly. When I retired, I could still cry. I have lost that, now."

I met her gaze. "I'm sorry."

"I do not believe you," she replied. "Where is Agnestrada?"

"Gone," I said. "I told her to go. Told her not to spend herself out here."

Bad Neighbor's face shuddered. The echo of an emotion, a flicker of relief, flashed across her face. It lingered for as long as it could, a candle flickering on an open window as a storm approaches, before it was snuffed out. What remained was a face as empty as the masks of the mages that came charging in behind.

"That was good of you, Salazanca," she said.

I raised my weapon. "I believe you."

The Vigilants rushed forward to intercept the mages that appeared. Graspmages hurled great chunks of debris, trying to track the Vigilants that swept through the battlefield. Doormages vanished here and there, struggling to find cover from the crossbows that hunted them across the carnage. Mendmages fought to keep themselves standing even as Vigilant gunpikes tore at their flesh.

The battle swept up around me like a tide.

Bad Neighbor, like a wave.

She came crashing down, her metal gauntlets echoing as she struck at me. I darted away from the heavy blow, but it only barely mattered. The shock of the strike resonated in my bones, made it hard to stay standing as she came charging forward. I pivoted out of the way, pulled Reginald's trigger, and thrust his whirring saw blade into her back.

The blades all but skidded off of her flesh, scant more than a scratch left on her skin. Terror caught in my chest—she'd used too much magic, she was all but invincible now. But then, it wasn't like I'd had much chance against her anyway.

I stilled my breath, forced myself to focus on staying alive.

Goodness knows there were enough mages there focused on the opposite.

Bad Neighbor pointed a metal finger, barked a command. A thick spear flew toward me. I caught sight of the Graspmage, a halo of spears levitating around her, as she continued to hurl the weapons with unseen hands. I was forced to pivot, to run, to retreat and re-retreat as her weapons continued to track me.

Until they didn't.

I heard her cry out. Looked up quickly enough to see Jindu's blade being pulled out of the Graspmage's chest. He met my eyes briefly before nodding and vanishing.

Like old times.

Cold hissed at my side. I saw a pair of Frostmages appear, casting their hands toward the earth. Patches of glistening frost crept toward me, slicked over the ground, trying to trap me on the freezing mirror. Jindu appeared behind one. The other looked to see his companion vanishing in a spray of gore before he, himself, was likewise bathed in a spray of his own as Reginald carved through his belly.

I pulled away. Jindu vanished. Bad Neighbor struck, seizing the corpses of her underlings and hurling them after me as though they were boulders.

I ran, found my retreat cut off by walls of flame and hurled obstacles, the Imperial mages fixated on me at their commander's behest. The Lady's song rang out as Jindu appeared at my periphery, striking down Embermage and Graspmage. I ran again, found myself narrowly ahead of Bad Neighbor as she pursued me without a word.

No time to figure out how many mages, what kind. No time to do anything but trust in Jindu. No time to reflect on how fucked up things must be for me to do that.

It was everything in me just to escape Bad Neighbor. Her every movement made the earth shake. No obstacle so much as slowed her down. My breath ran short, but she'd grown too strong to feel things like exhaustion.

I saw my chance as the magic thinned out. No more flames, no more obstacles, no more mages to hinder me. I heard her growing closer, felt the shudder of the earth under me so strong that I was certain she was right on top of me. That's when I whirled. That's when I struck.

I thrust Reginald into her face, pulled the lever. She caught it, growled as the blades whirled and bit into her cheek. It barely even annoyed her, let alone slowed her. It didn't occupy her for more than a handful of seconds.

But that's the thing about Quickmages.

Seconds are all they need.

I couldn't kill Bad Neighbor. I didn't know where to cut a Siegemage to hurt her. But Jindu did. Jindu appeared behind her in a flash. Jindu raised his sword. Jindu brought it down.

Sparks flashed.

The wind shuddered.

I blinked.

When I opened my eyes again, Jindu was skidding away, his blow suddenly deflected. Reginald barely stayed in my hands as Bad Neighbor ferociously shoved me away. I tumbled over debris and dead bodies, struggled to my feet. The wind shifted—Jindu appeared beside me, helping me up. Together, we looked across the battlefield at what had just fucked up everything.

And, across the battlefield, Velline scowled back.

"I knew it," she hissed, her voice desperate with panic barely contained behind a cackle. "I *knew* you would be here. It was too perfect. Torle of the Void, the Revolution—with so much violence, how could you stay away?"

"Velline," Bad Neighbor observed, dispassionate. "You are in violation of duty. You were instructed to keep your regiment away from the Revolution."

"And I refused that mad instruction," she snarled. "Do you understand how many have *died* here, Riacantha? How many mages? How many of *us* have given our lives in this horrific land, so far from the Empress? An order that commands me to show mercy to the upstart nuls that killed them is madness." She leveled her sword at me. "An order that commands me not to avenge their deaths at *this* monster's hands is an insult."

I backed away, tense, glanced over my shoulder. The way back to the ridge was as clear as it could be—the Vigilants continued to pin down the mages, but I saw too many bloodied green coats on the ground to feel good about it. Things were getting bad.

"No chance of holding them both off," I hissed to Jindu as I edged back toward Reginald. "We make a break for it while we still can."

I wasn't sure if he liked that plan or not. Mostly because he didn't seem to be listening to me. He stood up and called out to Velline.

"You're a Quickmage, right?" he said. "Have you seen them?"

Velline stiffened, her eyes narrowed.

"Seas of fire, skies without sun, a single figure looming over disaster?" his voice was breathless, almost achingly so. "Have you seen it? Have you given enough of your Barter for the Lady to show you it? That future?"

"Shut up," she snarled. "Don't speak the Lady's name in my presence, Vagrant."

"I've seen them, too," he said, undeterred. "I *still* see them. I woke up there this morning. I think you did, too."

"Silence."

"But they aren't real. You *need* to realize they aren't real. They're not the present. They're not where we are right now. You don't have to try to stop them. They aren't real."

Velline's face shuddered.

"We don't have to fear them."

And then, it shattered.

She screamed, vanished in a shriek of anger. Jindu disappeared. I saw them reappear across the field, right next to me, six feet behind me. Moving so quickly I couldn't see them but for the moments their blades clashed as they struck at each other. The Quickmages became shadows, so swift I could only feel them as rushes of wind against my skin.

A Siegemage, though? I could feel that in a different way.

I could also feel the giant rock she hurled at me.

Or I would have had I not already started running, anyway. The great boulder smashed into the earth behind me, then smashed into rubble as Bad Neighbor came breaking through it, the rock offering no more trouble than a twig.

Bodies fell around me. The earth shuddered and groaned under me. And at the periphery of my senses, I could feel the dueling Quickmages intensifying. Blood spattered the ground here and there as they cut wounds on one another. Depending on whose, the situation was either shit or fucking shit.

I wasn't going to wait to find out which.

I came to the ridge, my scarf wrapped around my arm and flowing. I waved it at the wall of New Vigil below. I had to hope that was Yria down there scrambling to get a portal ready. But I didn't have time to see.

I whirled and saw the mages sweeping forward. An Embermage erupted toward me in a gout of fire. I pushed Reginald through the flames, let them wash over me and lick at my skin as the saw blade bit through the mage. I cut down the Frostmage that came after, narrowly catching the jagged blade of ice they thrust at me, too slow to keep it from leaving a freezing gash across my ribs before the mage's blood froze on Reginald's blades.

I was slowing down. So were the Vigilants. Those not smart enough to get out of her way found themselves ground beneath Bad Neighbor's boots as she rampaged toward me. Those smart enough began to pray or weep or simply run as she swept forward, a blood-soaked killing machine.

Fuck. *Fuck.*

I knew we weren't going to win. I knew our chances had been low. But it's one thing to think you know it and another thing to see it. To see the broken bodies, your enemies surging forward, all the things you thought you knew burning or crushed. I had nowhere to run. And no way to hold them off.

When Bad Neighbor came rushing forward, I had no hope of stopping her.

And I didn't intend to.

I made a move as if to run, backing away toward the edge of the cliff. She pivoted to intercept me, eyes narrowed. I didn't duck out of the way when she came. I set my feet, held Reginald before me, and let her come.

I leapt at her, roaring along with Reginald's engine as I jammed the whirring weapon in her face. It caught her at the shoulder just as she caught me around the middle. The blow knocked the wind out of me, would have killed me if I hadn't twisted. I could barely hold on to the weapon, but forced myself to keep it whirring, keep it in her face.

Keep her from seeing where she was going.

We flew off the edge of the ridge together. I felt the cold air buffet me, take me from her grasp, and pull me into the wind as I went plummeting into nothingness. I was aware of the battlefield below rushing up to meet me. I was aware of the voices of the battle above vanishing in the rush of wind. I was aware of Bad Neighbor's body plummeting, right along with me.

I'd slowed her down. Maybe hurt her bad enough to keep her out of the battle. Sure, I'd be dead. But at least I'd done that. At least I'd given Cavric, Yria, Meret...

...Liette...

She'd have time now. More, at least, to get clear.

And if she didn't...well, I tried my best, didn't I?

I tried to feel that comfort as the sky held me out and let me go.

FORTY-TWO

NEW VIGIL

So, to be clear, I never found out if that stuff Yria said about Doormages interfering with her portals was true or if she was just being a prick.

Point being, she *did* manage to grab me out of the sky.

Eventually.

And her portal ended up spewing me out somewhere *other* than where I wanted.

I know I sound ungrateful, since she *did* actually save the entirety of my ass back there. But I was under a lot of stress. And she *was* a prick.

When I crawled out of the bushes, I had scrapes across my body, leaves in my hair, and a couple of splintered branches embedded in places they ought not be. However bruised I was from the portal dumping me was by far preferable to the cold realization settling on my neck like an axe blade.

We'd lost the ridge. We'd lost the fucking ridge. Were Torle's surveyors up there even now? Searching New Vigil's structures for weaknesses? How long did we have before it joined Bitterdrink and Six Walls beneath the earth?

Breathless with stress, I searched the horizon for the ridge. But I couldn't pick it out among the cliffs. As my senses slowly recovered from the fall and the portal, I realized Yria had launched me clear across the fucking battlefield.

So either that shit she said about Doormages was *really* true or she was *really* a prick.

I'd ask her later. I had bigger problems then.

I had no idea where Jindu was. Or Bad Neighbor or Velline. And since it's generally ideal to know where your allies *or* your enemies are—preferably both, but we can't be picky—I wasn't sure it could get much worse.

Until I noticed Reginald didn't make it through the portal with me.

I cursed under my breath, took as much comfort as I could in the sword still scabbarded at my hip—Eric, reliable as always—and made my way toward the screaming.

When I found the battlefield, my mood didn't improve. Neither did our odds. The walls of New Vigil still held, but pockets of Revolutionary incursion had popped up across the battlements. Steady streams of ravening soldiers came flowing up their mechanical ladders, undeterred by the bodies of their comrades plummeting off the wall above them.

The cannons still held, trading fire with the Revolutionary machines on the field below. The charge of the Banters had stalled the towers, and the few that had managed to regroup did their best to harry what remained. But the ending to this farce of a defense was written in a language everyone could see.

By cannon, by magic, or simply by the fists and hands of thousands—New Vigil was on its last legs, and the first few hadn't been as strong as they'd seemed.

Things being what they were, I wouldn't even make it there in time to see it fall.

The Marchers loomed before me—Yria's portal had dumped me out behind their line. Getting to New Vigil meant getting through them and a whole-ass war. Which was impossible enough.

But then, wouldn't you know it, shit got worse.

My ears quivered at the sound of the Lady's song. Faintly—only a dozen or so notes, couldn't be more than a handful of mages. But to find them here? Behind the Revolutionary line? That was curious enough to compel me to follow it.

I picked my way among the earth torn up by the march of the machines and the rocks of the canyons. I had enough wit left about me to hurl myself behind a nearby mound of churned rubble at the sight of purple light flashing.

The Doormage that appeared didn't notice me. Neither did the next ones that appeared. In their stealthy Imperial uniforms, they crept forward and began advancing toward the Revolutionary line. I held my breath until they passed. And when I was certain they couldn't hear me, I made to follow.

"Hey."

Until someone stopped me.

I glanced over my shoulder at the sound of the whisper. In the crush of the Revolution's march, I saw only the barest flash of red hair and green coat. Ketterling caught my eyes, shook her head to discourage me from following the Doormages. With her chin, she gestured for me to follow.

Which was very impressive, because her chin was positively caked in blood.

She must have noticed me staring, because she gestured to the large mess of gore covering her and shook her head.

"Don't worry. Most of it isn't mine."

"All right," I replied. "Is it okay if I'm still worried?"

"Probably smart." She beckoned again as she kept low and picked her way to the edges of the jagged earth. "We were supposed to take out more of those towers. We *needed* to, but—" She stopped in the middle of cursing herself, found her breath. "It's worse than you know. There are mages."

"Yeah, I met them," I replied, rubbing a sore spot on my back.

"No, there are *more* mages." She pointed over my head toward the Doormages. "Those ones have been coming and going, keeping an eye on the Revolutionaries, then reporting back." She turned her finger toward a canyon. "There's an entire fucking army in there. Waiting."

Velline.

Cavric had mentioned the Imperial army being held in reserve; Bad Neighbor, too. It seemed Velline ki Yanatoril trusted the accord wrought between Torle of the Void and the Revolution as much as she trusted anything else that wasn't her sword. Was she plotting betrayal? Or did she fear it?

But then, she was trying to kill me, so I suppose it didn't make much difference.

Ketterling sneered. "I can't fucking tell mages apart, but there's a lot of them and they look mean as fuck. If you want to stay and catch up with them, you're welcome to. But if you'd rather not risk a lightning bolt up the ass, you'll come with me to my bird."

Instinct screamed at me to follow her. But something heavy and painful kept me in place.

"What are you going to do?" I asked.

"We can find a break in the battle, make our way back behind the wall. It'll be tricky, but we can—"

"And then what?"

Ketterling paused, hesitated to answer. "Pick up an axe, start fighting until we're dead, I guess."

My eyes drifted toward the Marchers again. My heart sank at the sight of their imposing stature, how easily they'd roll over New Vigil. But the longer I looked at them, the more I started feeling less depressed.

"You sound ready to die," I observed.

And perhaps slightly more insane.

"I am," Ketterling replied grimly. "And if you aren't, you have no business coming with me."

As she started to stalk away, I called after her. "Because if you are ready to die, maybe you're ready to die in a better way than you're planning."

She didn't bother slowing down. "Death is death. How it happens doesn't matter."

This is why people need opera.

"Don't be stupid," I replied. "You go back to New Vigil, you die under a pair of boots like everyone else and nothing changes." I slowly pointed toward the Marchers. "You go toward those big tower-y shits there, you still die. And I do, too." I swallowed hard. "But we maybe do a little bit more for your city before we go."

She stopped. She looked over her shoulder.

"You have a plan?"

"I have a desperate, half-thought-out scheme that I think *might* work, if we're lucky, but will probably still result in our gruesome deaths."

Ketterling shrugged.

"Close enough."

Here's the thing about plans involving stealth.

They're hard to do while riding a giant bird.

That was the overriding logic behind why I was on the back of a saddle, a bird's bristling feathers between my legs and my hands wrapped around Ketterling's waist. And when the Banter let out an aggressive crow as we rushed headlong toward a column of Revolutionaries, alerting them to our rush, I didn't mind.

I was trusting Ketterling's bird to play to its strengths. And me to mine.

I couldn't help New Vigil with stealth. Or a sound, well-thought-out strategy. We didn't have time for those. And I was never very good at them anyway. But making shit incredibly difficult for everyone around me?

That, I could do.

"*Go, boy!*" Ketterling kicked her Banter into a higher frenzy, its wings spreading wide and its feet thundering across the plain as we rushed toward the enemy. "*Gut them, Bloodthirst!*"

"Bloodthirst?" I shouted. "You named your bird Bloodthirst?"

"Yeah!" Ketterling shouted, excited. "Great name, right?"

"Absolutely," I said.

It was a good thing I was riding behind her. It would have hurt team morale if she saw me roll my eyes that hard.

The Banter, at the very least, lived up to his incredibly stupid name. His wings beat past the gunpikes that met us as the Revolutionaries struggled to form a firing line. His spurs tore eagerly into coats and flesh. Anger and raw animal instinct kept him from fleeing from the carnage.

It also kept him from getting out of it, stupid fucking bird.

But I didn't need him anymore. Ketterling's job wasn't to kill them all, it was just to get me this close. And I wasn't here to fight Revolutionaries.

I was here to steal a big fucking gun.

I pulled my sword free, leapt from—*ugh*—Bloodthirst's back. The Revolutionaries were busy with the wild, thrashing bird, leaving me free to run toward the rumbling engine looming before me.

The treads of the Marcher's base stood taller than I was. The soldiers crewing it shouted out alarms, struggling to be heard over the roar of the tank's engine. Too late to be of help to the Revolutionary guarding the hatch—my sword caught him in the throat and my hand caught his gunpike.

I pushed the machine's door open, scaled through its guts as engines and gears rattled around me, the stink and heat of severium assailing my senses. The path led upward, toward another hatch door. I aimed my stolen gunpike up, pulled the trigger.

A blast of smoke and fire punched through the wood. I followed. The Revolutionary I had caught in the blast recoiled, bleeding. Her comrade was still trying to figure out what happened when I burst through and jammed my gunpike into them.

I looked up. The hollow interior of the Marcher's tower stretched above me, iron steps spiraling upward. And at the top—the cannon.

If I lasted long enough to get up there, I might have a chance at making things worse. In a good way. It was hard to explain.

I drew my sword, fought my way up the stairs. My scarf took what blows it could, the blood pushing through my veins took care of the rest. When the last soldier fell, I pulled myself onto a platform where an enormous cannon stared out over the battlefield, an array of levers and devices beside it. And standing in front of it was a *very* nervous pair of cannoneers.

They fumbled for their weapons. I didn't waste time. I ran forward, shoved one of them hard enough to send him flying off the tower and plummeting to the hard earth below. The other one screamed as I grabbed her in weary hands.

"Tell me how to use the cannon," I snarled.

She glanced around, nervous. "I...I don't—"

I cut her off by smashing the hilt of my sword against her face.

"How about now?" I shoved her toward the controls, spat. "Turn it west. Toward that canyon. *DO IT.*"

Shaking, nervous and bloodied, she did as I commanded. Thank fuck for propaganda—makes you great at obeying orders, not so good at the opposite. The platform began to rotate, the cannon aiming toward the canyon Ketterling had indicated. Now I had to hope that her information was right, that the angle was correct, and that this wouldn't fail spectacularly.

"How do you fire it?" I snarled, trying to keep up the menace in my voice. "*TELL ME.*"

"N-no!" she screamed. "I won't!"

I smashed the sword against her face again.

"How about *now*?" I snarled.

Which was a waste of time, as it turned out I had inadvertently bludgeoned her unconscious. Which was always a possibility when you did this sort of thing.

I dropped her, turned toward the assembly of controls and mechanisms that operated the cannon. I searched my mind for what I knew about Revolutionary machines, recalled what Liette had told me about their devices, remembered what the cannoneer had been doing. I took a deep breath, made my best, most informed guess, and pulled a lever.

The cannon started rotating.

Which, uh, wasn't what I wanted.

So I did the other thing I could think to do and just started pressing everything.

The Marcher shook under me as the cannon erupted with an explosion of sound and fire. I was knocked to my ass, my ears ringing as I got back to my feet to watch the cannon's shell paint a fiery arc across the sky to fall toward the canyon. I winced, spat curses as I saw the explosive projectile drift away from the canyon.

I missed. I can't believe I fucking—

I was interrupted by the sound of a faint explosion. The shell collided with the wall of the canyon. The cliff side began to crumble, jagged boulders tumbling from its face. I winced, then winced harder as the soft earth and dirt of the rest of the cliff gave way, a great rush of earth sliding into the canyon.

I watched a great plume of dust rise from the canyon. I held my breath. I squinted, waited, so long that I felt fear grab me by the neck and start to choke me.

And then, almost imperceptibly, I saw it.

A faint, slender silhouette—black against the dust cloud rising from below—drifted into the sky. Followed by many, *many* more. They turned and flew toward me, the sashes of their uniforms painting a colorful riot across the sky.

Skymages.

Imperial Skymages.

It had worked. They took the bait.

By the time I made my way out of the Marcher, I could already hear the sound of their songs. I saw purple lights flashing, portals opening. I didn't bother waiting to see what came out of them.

I found Ketterling fighting to calm her bird. When I climbed back onto the saddle, she didn't need telling to kick Bloodthirst into a full sprint.

"What the fuck was that?" she spat. "I thought you were going to use it on the Revolution!"

"Then I could only take out one tower, at best," I replied. "Whereas if I use it to antagonize the Imperium, I can let them fight each other."

"Oh. I get it." Ketterling paused. "But won't they still kill us? And won't more people die if we're caught between them?"

"Possibly?"

"So how is that better?"

"I DON'T FUCKING KNOW, KEEP RIDING!"

She wasn't wrong to criticize me. But it's not like I could think of any kind of rebuttal then.

We pulled away from the tower just before the Skymages hit. Over twenty of them flew low, in a precise formation. They sped overhead, rushing toward the Revolution's siege. There was a momentary stillness after they flew over us before the wind caught up. An enormous rush of air followed, almost knocking the bird to the ground.

I knew this tactic. I remembered this strategy.

"Pull clear," I snarled at Ketterling. "Pull *clear.*"

I was happy she didn't care to argue. There was no need to. The reason became readily apparent in a few moments.

As soon as she pulled the bird toward higher ground, the portals began to sing. Hulking Siegemages lumbered out of doors of light. Imperial Graspmages accompanied by levitating panoplies of arms came gliding silent across the land. Mirrormages walked forward, first as one, then as a hundred.

And Embermages. And Nightmages. And Songmages and Mendmages and Hivemages and seemingly every last fucking asshole with a Barter in the Imperium. They came rushing forward in an organized charge, silent but for the notes of the Lady's song ringing out—unheard by the Revolutionaries they descended upon.

But not for long.

The Skymages leading the charge suddenly swooped low. The rush of wind that followed sent the Revolutionaries into disarray, readying them for the impact of the Siegemages. The brutes waded into battle, callously swatting aside soldiers and shrugging off gunpike blasts. The other mages descended—with flame and blade and all the force of their magic—and began to go to grisly work.

Imperial tactics. The same that had won a thousand battles. And they carried them out with thoughtless, blood-hungry efficiency. I would expect no less from those who served under Velline ki Yanatoril.

The Revolutionaries scrambled to respond. Squadrons were spun about by the frantic cries of bloodied sergeants. Ground machines—their cannons and autoballista—were upstaked and turned to fire bloody reprisal into the encroaching Imperials. Paladin armors that had been carrying huge cannons dropped their burdens to turn and take up arms against their oldest foe.

"Yes, *yes, YES*!"

Ketterling's shriek was wild and jubilant, both elated and astonished. Her bird rushed along the edges of the battle, clear of the fracas as disaster turned to catastrophe.

"Oh, fuck *me*," she exclaimed. "When you said you had a plan, I thought you were just talking out of your ass. But you fucking did it, you magnificent bitch, you *did it*!"

I hadn't done shit.

It wasn't *just* luck that my plan had worked—it didn't take a whole fucking lot to make Revolutionaries and Imperials fight, after all. But in truth, I hadn't done much more than buy New Vigil a little more time.

The fighting between the two powers roared and the Revolutionary tide swept away from New Vigil's walls. But even the best case here had New Vigil being conquered by mages instead of machines.

Still, that was time. Time for Cavric to breathe. Time for Yria and Urda to recover. Time for Liette to . . . to . . .

I tried not to think about it. Thinking about it meant worrying about it. Worrying about it wasn't helping. This—however fucking worse or better I'd made things—was the closest thing to helping I could do.

For all of us.

"Bloodthirst is at his limit." Ketterling patted her weary bird's neck. "We'll get close to New Vigil and make our way in when the fighting's stopped. There, we can see what Cavric wants our next move to be."

That was all sensible. I'm sure if I had been listening, I would agree. But as she talked and as we rode, my eyes were drawn skyward.

In all that had happened, I'd barely noticed the clouds rolling in, the sky darkening. But there was one particularly dark cloud that moved a little swifter than the others. It seemed to coil and curl through the sky. And, if I squinted, I could almost see it arcing and coming right toward...

Ah, fuck.

By the time I'd thought to shout anything, she couldn't even hear me. A column of glistening black feathers and scales speared into the bird's throat with a hundred tiny, gnashing jaws. Bloodthirst was all but knocked out from under us by the blow, sending us tumbling to the ground as he disappeared beneath a cloud of the shrieking, writhing things.

Kite vipers.

I found my footing, and my senses, long enough to realize what the fuck was happening. And when I did, I had the wit to utter only one word.

"Fuck."

"Yeah," Grishok the Dandelion said, "I agree."

I turned, looked up.

And a great slab of wood came crashing down to meet my face.

FORTY-THREE

ELSEWHERE

There is a story that only very certain people know.

It's not that the story is rare. It's just that the story is somewhat hard to believe. Only a handful of people tell it, only a handful of people think it's true—and both of those are the same people.

It's hard to blame them, of course.

When four Vagrants arrive in a town, it's never for anything good. Unpredictable natures combined with incredible power rarely makes people comfortable. One Vagrant in a town was enough to set people on edge. Anything more than that means they're either there to fight each other—which is bad—or to get along—which is worse.

So who would believe that, one evening, a quartet of colorful murderers showed up in town with weapons sheathed, attended dinner and had a lovely meal, and paid and left without a single incident?

The people of Grund's Curse did.

Because the people of Grund's Curse had been there to see it.

They'd seen the four of them coming from miles away. The Vagrants had made no particular effort to conceal themselves. And it was easy enough to tell they were Vagrants—the tattoos, the air of menace about them, the fact that one of them was traveling by riding on an armoire carried by a hulking man.

And they'd had plenty of time to run. The Vagrants hadn't been in any hurry, taking well over an hour to make their way down the road to the humble little burg that stood in the shadow of a lonely mountain, somewhere at the edge of the Husks. Perhaps the people thought the idea of facing Vagrants was preferable to running out into the magic-blasted, windswept wastes of that dark place.

Some didn't. They left. But others remained.

They debated what to do—to beg for mercy, to offer tribute, or to put up some feeble defense. They were still debating when the Vagrants arrived. The elder of that town—a pleasant little old lady with a nice hat, they told me—was sent out to speak to them. It was agreed that the Vagrants might show deference to an elder and that if they did kill her, she had lived a rich, full life.

She came out of her home, waddled quietly over to the four of them, and exchanged words. Then she went back inside and cleared her throat and informed the anxious people who had barricaded themselves inside that the Vagrants had asked whether or not the place with the good soup was still here.

And she had told them where it was.

"Huh," Grishok the Dandelion rumbled as he ran a big finger around the rim of his bowl and sucked the last of the broth from it. "When you're right, you're right. That *is* good soup."

"What did I tell you?" Quoir the Eternal Knock said, smirking. "You can't turn up your nose at these little towns. A *true* connoisseur knows that the real gems are hidden in the most unexpected places."

"Merely an extension of your own pretentiousness," Chiriel the Four-String had replied. She held a bowl in a small gloved hand, a kite viper coiled around her neck and flicking its tongue in and out of the broth. "We could find a thousand soup shops on a single avenue in Cathama. Back in the capital—"

"We aren't *in* the capital anymore," Quoir hissed. "And we never will be again. How long will it take you to make peace with that?"

"How long will it take to get another bowl, too?" Grishok asked. He glanced around, rumbling at the collection of servers and cooks who stood warily in the corner. His brows knitted, his great antlers lowered. "Or is this one of those uncivilized places where you have to get up and get it yourself?"

The people cringed away as Grishok looked to rise. A tiny hand rose from the table and took him by his. And a woman a mere fraction of his size pulled him back into his seat. She looked up through weary eyes, smiled warmly at the restaurant's staff.

"My friend wants another bowl." She pulled out a glistening golden piece of metal the length of a human knuckle and put it on the table. "Sorry for the trouble." She glanced at Grishok. "You okay with waiting?"

"I'm always okay," he grumbled back.

Quoir sighed as the staff went nervously about their business. "You're only going to encourage them, paying them like that. When I was here, I recall all my meals being compensated."

"Because they were terrified of you and you were an asshole," Darrish the Flint replied, glowering. "I haven't seen you in so long, Quoir. Would it really kill you to make it nice for me?"

Chiriel giggled at her companion's visible embarrassment. "Agreed, Quoir. It would hardly be an effort to be slightly more civil, would it?"

"Like in your precious city?" The Doormage's mood soured, along with his face. "Groveling at the feet of the Empress, waiting to be crumpled up and disposed of, like... like..."

The others—even Chiriel—huddled around the table to conceal him from sight. It wouldn't do to let nuls see him. A Vagrant couldn't be seen to weep.

"What happened?" Darrish asked.

Quoir wiped his eyes, looked away. "Oanthe is gone."

"Oanthe?" she whispered. "How did it happen?"

"Imperium? Revolution?" Grishok asked.

"It was *her*, wasn't it?" Chiriel hissed beneath her veil. "Her and her fucking list."

Darrish shot her a glance. Neither a warning nor an agreement. Merely a request. And Chiriel acquiesced, averting her eyes.

"No," Quoir said. "It was his..." He choked briefly. "His Barter."

"He is... *was* a Graspmage, wasn't he?" Darrish winced, sympathetic. "Ah, fuck. The Lady Merchant takes their memories, doesn't she?"

"How does one die from that?" Chiriel asked. "Forgot to look where he was going?"

"He isn't dead," Quoir replied.

"But you said—"

"I said he's gone. I spoke to him just a few days ago. And he..." He made a face like he was swallowing a knife. "He didn't know me. Didn't recognize me. After all these years, all the time we spent in the army together, he just..." He held out his hands. "I barely recognized him, either. He's been using his power to fortify himself inside that dingy little cave of his. He was paranoid, ravening, barely even..."

A mourning silence had fallen across the table, the fear and pain shared wordlessly between them. It was a rare fear for a Vagrant to confront—an end like that. It was no tragedy for a free mage to die beneath a nul's guns or in proud defiance of the Empress and her false emperor son. A death like that was dramatic, poetic, maybe even beautiful.

But a death by Barter... to be claimed by the Lady Merchant so utterly, every ounce of your body and mind given to her...

They knew it could happen to them. It *would* happen to them. Quoir's limbs would one day be lifeless. Grishok's blood would run dry. Chiriel would lose her mind to her thralls and lose all sense of identity to her brood. Darrish would forsake all sense of safety and certainty and wither away into a cowering creature.

Doormage, Mendmage, Hivemage, Wardmage—it never seemed to matter how much power you had, whether you used it right or not. In the end, a mage faced either a death in combat or a death by their Barter. There was not a mage, Vagrant or otherwise, that did not meet their fate the same way.

Panicked. Tortured. Consumed.

"What was he hiding from?"

Quoir looked up. "Huh?"

"Oanthe." Darrish leaned onto the table, her weary eyes probing. "You said he was fortifying himself. What was he fortifying himself against?"

He deliberately looked somewhere else. "It was hard to tell."

"Quoir."

Darrish's hand was on his. And while he knew there was no such thing as a safe life for a Vagrant, holding hers made him think that maybe there was.

She'd had a real talent for that.

"Tell me."

"The list." His voice became a conspiracy—dark, quiet, terrified. "He heard about the list. About the gun."

"*Her,*" Chiriel rasped behind her veil. "It's *her*. I knew it. I *knew* she would be coming for us. Zanze told me as much and *you* said he was a fool."

"Zanze *is* a fool," Grishok grunted. "And so is Oanthe."

"You dare." Quoir's wounded eyes turned into a scowl. "You *dare.*"

"Yes, I dare," the Mendmage rumbled in response. "Listen to you. Frightened and quivering like a child. All because of what? A list? A piece of paper?"

"She's coming for us," Chiriel snarled. "She'll kill us all." She clutched her head, her breath heaving—the stress of hundreds of tiny hearts beat in her chest. "*She'll kill us all.*"

"And why are we waiting for her to?" Quoir's nails raked against the table. "Are we going to let ourselves wither away? Like him?"

"Better than meeting her," Grishok said. "Better than meeting that gun. But if it has to be one or the other..." He laid a massive hand on the table. The bowls shook. "Why wait?"

"You're right, of course," Chiriel muttered. "We can't go on like this. We can't *wait* like this."

"It's torture," Quoir agreed. "It's *torture.*"

"We can't let ourselves be hunted down," Grishok growled. "Not like animals."

"Then we shouldn't have betrayed her."

Darrish's voice was different. It always had been. Not a growl or a rasp or any kind of proud, booming noise a mage ought to make. She always spoke softly, incisively. Every word she said was like a single stitch tearing in a fine dress.

The eyes that turned toward her were wild, angry, incensed. But voices did not follow. This part, everyone agrees on. How could you forget the sight of three Vagrants choosing to hold their tempers and listen to the smallest and softest of their number?

"It's terrible what happened to Oanthe," she said, her hand never once leaving Quoir's. "It's terrible what it's done to us. And it's terrible what we did to her."

Not a word was uttered in disagreement. Even if eyes turned away.

"We knew her. We trusted her. And she trusted us. And we took away from her something that..."

Darrish hesitated at this part, I like to think. Darrish remembered us—what we had together, the softness I found in her and the heat she found in me—and spoke with something in her throat.

"She's killed Oanthe. Maybe she'll kill us. Maybe she deserves to. Maybe..." She closed her eyes. "Maybe there isn't another way. For her, at least."

"Then join us," Grishok said. "Between the four of us, we can't lose."

"No."

"What?" Chiriel growled. "Don't tell me you're still loyal to her."

"No."

"Then what is it?" Quoir said. "Do you think she won't come after *you*?"

"*No.*" Darrish sighed, all but collapsed on the table. "That isn't what I'm saying. I'm saying I...I..." A tear slid down her cheek. "I'm tired. I'm so tired. I was tired of the wars so I listened to Vraki, like all of you. I was tired of the Imperium, so I became a Vagrant, like all of you. And I'm tired of being scared." She swallowed hard. "Like all of you."

"I am *not*—"

"You are," Darrish cut Grishok off. "You are scared. And I'm scared. I'm scared of what she's going to do, what the Imperium is going to do, what *everyone* is going to do. I can't just keep doing things because I'm tired and scared."

Her other hand reached out, clasped tiny fingers around Grishok's massive paw.

"There are things happening in the Scar," she said. "Things that can change all this, all the endless wars. I don't know if all of them will work out, or even if any of them will. But I know it's not running. It's not fighting. It's not waiting."

"You can't be serious," Chiriel whispered. "You can't change the Imperium. The Revolution. *Or her.* Think, Darrish."

"I am," she replied. "And you're right, I can't change them. Or her." She smiled at Chiriel. "But I don't want them to change me, either. I want to feel something...other than scared." She looked around the table. "And I want you to have that, too."

"Darrish...," Grishok started to complain, couldn't find the will to finish it.

"Her being dead would make me feel *quite* bold," Quoir muttered.

"No, it wouldn't. If she dies with you scared of her, you'll be scared of her forever."

"So, what?" Spite dripped behind Chiriel's veil. Her kite viper hissed. "Are we to simply wait for her and roll over when she comes to kill us?"

"No," Darrish said. "But there has to be more than waiting for her to come." She gathered their hands, pulled them closer to hers. "We gave all our years to the Empress. To the war. I don't know how many I have left before my Barter takes me. I don't want to spend it afraid. I don't want any of us to."

What happened next is where things start falling apart.

Some say there was more arguing, that they all grumbled and parted ways. A few say they got violent, chasing out the remaining staff. But there are one or two that say something that I wish were true.

Even if it doesn't sound very likely.

They say that the four Vagrants that night laid their hands quietly in the middle of the table, that three of them touched her own soft fingers. They say that the four of them quietly made a promise to each other, to try something different than killing. For as long as they could.

It's not that it makes me feel better.

Knowing that things could have been different.

Knowing what they wanted instead of what we all got.

But I like to think that on that night, before they paid their bill and left, that she was still thinking of me. And them. The woman whose name was on my list, who sat with all those other names at the soup table, and loved all of them. I like to think she had happy memories of that night.

She deserved them.

FORTY-FOUR

NEW VIGIL

Why are you running?"

Someone was talking to me. I couldn't hear them. My ears rang, blood dribbling down the side of my face. The sounds of carnage—of fires bursting and of bodies falling—was muffled in my ears, smothered beneath a thick blanket along with any words.

"This is what you wanted."

I didn't know how I was still alive—I didn't know how bad I'd been clipped. My bones shook in my skin. My blood hurled itself against my skull. I had sense for nothing but forcing myself to breathe. My legs pumped numbly beneath me. I felt a prick at my shoulder, searched with unfeeling fingers. I felt a strange puckering sensation, like pulling away from a kiss, and jerked a writhing beast whose teeth were slick with blood.

My blood.

"You can't run from it."

Sound bled back into my ears. Explosions hammered the sky around me. Severium-tinged fires bloomed across the battlefield, a macabre garden of orange-and-purple blossoms. Machines churned, roared, belched smoke and flame and metal. Gunpikes cracked and roared. Paladin armors, their engines their own anthem, tore through the battle with hulking, mechanical weaponry.

Shapes in metal masks and silk uniforms responded. Notes of discordant songs, unheard by half the battle, rang out. Skymages rent the air apart with great gusts of wind. Embermages and Frostmages carved paths of red and blue across the field. A great towering Marcher tank tilted, shuddered, collapsed as a pair of Siegemages upended it, watching emotionlessly as the crew inside were crushed.

The bodies were everywhere. Broken. Burned. Shattered. Skewered. Swarmed over and carved apart as if by ants. The happiest among them were dead and unmoving. The unhappiest weren't.

"Turn around. Look at me."

The voice. Behind me. Above me.

I turned. I saw Grishok's massive silhouette. I saw the sparkle of the chains shackling an armoire to his back. I saw Chiriel, tiny upon his shoulder. And then I saw the club rising.

"She deserves that."

And coming down.

I managed to hurl my numb body out of the way in time to avoid it. I went low, scrambled through a small forest of legs and weaponry and over a corpse before I managed to find my footing again. Grishok and Chiriel turned their glares toward me.

"They both do," she rasped beneath her veil. "Darrish. Quoir. If you won't say their names, then you'll hear them."

Grishok loomed over the battle. The wounds he took—and continued to take—were already closing, his skin pushing out crossbow bolts and sealing shut over gunpike cuts.

He took his huge club in both hands. And with barely a notice for the desperate battle raging around him, began to wade toward me, trampling the fools who tried to challenge him.

And I was already running.

There was nowhere to go but the battle. They'd run me down out on open ground. Trapped between an incredibly stupid plan and an incredibly futile one, I chose the obvious one and fled deeper.

I picked my way around the thickest knots of fighting as best I could. I batted stray blows away with my sword where I could, suffered as much as I was able where I couldn't. I darted beneath explosions as cannons tore through mage legions as autoballista churned bolts into their ranks. I swept around the passionless, destructive gazes of Siegemages as they wandered through the throng looking for new targets to add to their piles, bored by the triviality of war.

Any time I came up long enough to catch my breath, I saw them. Coiling in a halo above the battlefield, an onyx crown of feathers and scales. When I glanced up, the kite vipers saw me—and because they did, so did Chiriel. She played a riotous chord and they dove, carving like a knife into the fracas. Mages and Revolutionaries alike collapsed, tearing at their flesh as the frenzied serpents sought a target, any target.

I swung wildly at them as I took off running again, trying my damnedest to beat them off and disappear back into the melee at the same time. Soldiers went down beneath the clouds of overeager serpents, the beasts unbothered by bursts of fiery magic or roaring engines.

Even in the thick of the fighting, it was easy to see how things were going. Revolutionaries swarmed mages, hacking them to death beneath a flurry of gunpikes. Revolutionary machines churned bolts and bombs into the melee. Revolutionary chants filled the air above the screaming and fighting.

But it was Revolutionaries who died by the score under sheets of flame. Revolutionaries whose machines could only annoy the Siegemages who tore them apart. Revolutionaries who screamed and panicked beneath the sound of their chants and songs.

And for every mage that fell, damn near forty fanatics lay dead around them.

They were devoted as they could be. But the attack from behind had taken its toll. And the Imperium was slowly and steadily chipping away at their numbers, their bodies and their spirits.

It wouldn't be long now before the Imperium stood victorious, the Revolution lay dead, and New Vigil…

The walls of the city were far. Impossibly so. I could barely see their battlements, let alone know how it was going for them. Had the Revolutionaries taken the wall? Had they fallen back? How the *fuck* was I going to get back?

Hard to think, breathing as hard as I was. I needed to slow down. I needed to keep running. I needed... I needed...

I needed *him*.

His burning brass in my hands. The scent of his anger in my nose. The feel of his weight at my hip. I'd worn the Cacophony so long that I couldn't remember what it meant to be without him. I'd always dreamed it, but that was just a dream. It wasn't supposed to be like this. I wasn't supposed to feel like this. I wasn't supposed to feel this *terrified*.

I needed a weapon. I needed an escape. I needed him.

But he's not here.

My mind crept to those thoughts, slowly, as if it was afraid to do so.

He can't help you. He can't help her, either.

And I found something not quite courage, nor quite wisdom.

So why don't you take a fucking breath and get to work?

But, when you can't get either of those, anger will do for a little bit.

I looked over my shoulder. Grishok continued to follow me through the combat, only noticing the battle long enough to swat an upstart Revolutionary or indignant Imperial out of his way. Chiriel's swarming kite vipers kept the combatants at bay, her violin furiously playing note after note as she directed them through the bloody work.

I needed to shake them. Long enough to think of something better. I needed a better plan, a better weapon, a better *chance*.

But since I had none of those, I settled for a distraction.

I found a black stain of Revolutionary pride amid the crimson-stained earth. The Twenty-Second stood in a tight knot, the engines of their saw-bladed weapons whirring as they ably carved through the Imperials who desperately struggled to get close enough to tear them apart.

The earth shuddered beneath me as a hulking Siegemage, her face unbothered by the gore coating it, waded into the knot of the Twenty-Second. They reorganized to face her, leaving one of their number at the edges.

There.

I came up behind them, jammed my sword through their back, felt the apparatus on their uniform splinter as the tip of my blade burst through their chest. The body of the Twenty-Second soldier stiffened, their saw-bladed weapon falling from their hands and into mine. Their breath ran short as steel emptied their lungs. Their body went still.

So why weren't they dropping?

There was an uncomfortable grinding noise as the soldier's head slowly turned to face me, their bones contorting. From behind the lenses of their helmet, I saw a pair of eyes twinkling in a smile that was painful in its familiarity and serenity.

"Hello, Cacophony," they spoke to me in a voice that ran cold in my veins. *"I am pleased to see you here."*

I knew that voice. I felt it in my sinew. Just as I'd felt it so long ago, when that woman had come to me with the same voice in her throat.

Loyal.

Culven Loyal.

Revolutionary. Lieutenant. Scrath.

I shoved the corpse off my sword, picked up my new weapon, tried to pull free of the throng. Black flashed at the corner of my eyes. A saw blade whirred. I pivoted aside too late, felt the spinning blades bite into my leg and pull out a spray of red.

Fire lanced down my limb. I screamed, fell, whirled onto my back. The Twenty-Second soldier stood over me, my blood on their weapon. Their empty lenses were trained upon me. Their voice was in my bones.

"I have come to see my sibling." Their head canted to the side, curious. *"Tell me, where is Eldest? Or shall I simply go find out for myself?"*

The soldier glanced up, leapt away as the Siegemage came through. In one hand, she clutched the battered corpse of another black-clad soldier, swinging it around like a club. And as she swept it up over her head, the carcass's head tilted and looked at me through its pulverized helmet.

It spoke.

"If you want to prolong it, that is fine, too," the corpse said with Loyal's voice. *"I have lived this moment before. I have seen how it ends. I have time."*

I hauled myself to my feet. My leg was ablaze with pain. I struggled to bite it back, to smother it under the adrenaline still rushing through me. I tried to pull myself clear as the Twenty-Second surged forward to attack their new foe.

I had only just begun to put them behind me when the screaming started. I glanced over my shoulder, saw both mage and nul being hurled aside as Grishok waded through the throng, scything through bodies with sweeps of his giant club.

The Twenty-Second regrouped as he pulled through, their empty lenses training on him even as his scowl trained on me.

Chiriel cursed, kicked the chains securing her armoire to Grishok's back. It fell to the ground and she hopped atop it from the Mendmage's shoulders. She plucked a few strings on her violin and her kite vipers responded, swarming forward to occupy the Twenty-Second.

"I will tend to the nuls," she rasped. "Go make Quoir proud."

Grishok rumbled his agreement, started after me.

I was gasping for air. It took too much breath to haul my body and my wounded leg across the battlefield. Too much strength I'd left scattered across the earth in red stains. My lungs burned, my body ached, my vision started to go blurry.

Fields of the dead and the dying stretched before me—blue coats pounded into the earth, machines left empty with idling engines as their crews were scattered like fallen leaves. The battle had turned. Grishok and Chiriel had provided the disruption the Imperium needed to break the Revolutionary ranks. The remaining fanatics stood in tight knots circled by mages who hung back with predatory arrogance. It was clear to everyone but the most unhinged who would emerge from this battle in victory's colors.

I looked to the walls of New Vigil, finally able to see them without soldiers crawling all over them. They were empty. The ladders had been dislodged, the invaders repelled. My plan had bought them a little more time.

That was something, at least.

The wind shifted behind me. I saw Grishok closing in, as aware as I was that my body would give out long before his. There was no more running. I took up the weapon I'd pilfered in both hands, gave it a squeeze to summon its engine to life.

His name was Gerald. And it was my pleasure to face the end with him.

Grishok closed the distance wordlessly—everything left to say between us had already been left in the dirt. He swung his club, watched me pivot away. Gerald lashed out, whirling blades eating a chunk out of Grishok's arm. The Mendmage glanced at the gruesome wound left behind.

"Revolution got themselves some new toys?" he asked.

"Yeah," I said, breathless. "Scared yet?"

The Lady's song flittered through my ears. The wound sealed itself shut. Grishok shrugged his great shoulders.

"A little, yeah."

He swung again, and again, and again. I dodged each time, retaliated each time, but none of that bothered him. He was seeing how much I had left in me, figuring out how much more I could go. Once he knew how to corner me, he'd make his move.

And it was coming. Each time, my feet left the earth and came down a little heavier. Each swing left my lungs a little more breathless.

The wound in my leg seared angrily with each step, the skin threatening to tear, as if any movement would rip it further and—

There was a tearing sound. A leg split wide open. Blood wept out in an ugly red mark. A body hit the earth forcefully.

Made me glad it hadn't been mine.

Grishok staggered to one knee, suddenly struck down. Annoyed, he glared over his shoulder. A great wound had appeared in his hamstring, bringing him down as it started knitting itself together slowly. He swept his irate glare up, muttered something.

"I knew you'd try some birdshit."

Made me glad he wasn't talking to me.

The wind shifted. I blinked. And he was there.

Jindu flicked Grishok's blood from his blade. He pulled a lock of dirty hair from his face.

"Sorry," he said to the Mendmage. "I'd hoped it wouldn't come to this."

"It hasn't." Grishok pulled himself back to fully healed footing. "Not yet. She's after you, too, Jindu. You knew Darrish as well as I did. You don't have to defend her."

"I know."

Jindu steadied himself. He readied his blade. He drew a sharp breath.

"But I want to."

A note rang. And he struck.

Grishok's eye disappeared in a spray of blood, pulled itself back together a moment later. The hulking mage glanced to his left, and a great wound appeared in his liver. He looked to his right, something carved into his shoulder blade.

The wind rustled around him. Shadows flashed as Jindu appeared, struck, disappeared, struck again. Blood sprayed from Grishok with every blow, every wound opened. But each blow slowed him down for only a moment, nothing more than a pause as he glanced around, trying to pin down the Quickmage.

I had to do something. Jindu couldn't hold him off forever.

Neither of us could. I had to find something to slow him down, something to stop him long enough for me to get away from him.

But what? The fields of devastation offered nothing but corpses, metal, and blood. I had to run. I had to find something. I had to—

I heard something behind me. A crack. Grishok had gotten lucky. Or Jindu had slowed down, spent too much power. I didn't know. I didn't know how the club had caught him, or how he ended up in Grishok's grasp, flailing desperately as a massive hand began to tighten around his throat.

Fucking Quickmages. Swift as the wind, so fast they can't be tracked. But grab them and they're like every other sad, fragile bastard on this spit of land.

"*Sal*," he gasped.

I didn't know a damn thing except how to move my legs.

They pumped under me, numb and bloodless, as I rushed toward my target. An autoballista, its crew draped dead over its metal, lay idling nearby. My muscles went numb as I grabbed its stern and pushed it around.

"*Sal*." His voice. Weak. Soft. I could still hear it. "*I wish I...*"

I tried not to listen, tried not to wonder if I was even really hearing it. I could see his face going blue, his flailing growing weaker, Grishok's fingers closing tighter around his throat. I leapt on top of the machine's platform, searched its myriad controls and apparatus for some indication on how to use the damn thing. Panic coursed through my veins. A scream clawed at my throat.

I heard only two more words.

"I'm sorry."

And I screamed.

I brought my fists down on a lever. The platform shuddered beneath me. The barrel of the machine shrieked as a massive bolt went flying through the air. It streaked across the field, over corpses and broken earth, before it found its target.

Grishok had narrowly enough time to look up before it took him square in the chest.

Jindu fell from his grasp. The bolt punched through him, smashed through bone and sinew to burst out the back. The angle of it bore him down, embedded itself into the earth, pinning him with it. He growled, less bothered by the bolt in his chest than the fact that it slowed him down. He pawed at it, the annoying piece of wood and metal keeping him trapped to the earth. He would break it and be free in seconds, he knew.

And so did we.

He wrapped a hand around the bolt. The wind shifted. His fingers fell off, cleanly severed at the knuckles. He snarled, glared up at Jindu. Which was useful, since it distracted him from me jamming Gerald six inches into his flank.

Spinning blades flensed his flesh, tearing jagged wounds when I pulled away as Grishok tried to swat me. His attentions on me, Jindu appeared at his neck, hacking a deep cut. He swung his club at Jindu, left himself open to me and Gerald raking down his back.

He struck at me; I darted away and Jindu struck. He reached for Jindu; I leapt in and tore him up. The Lady's song rang out in our ears alongside Gerald's engine. Grishok's torn flesh continued to try to mend itself.

But something was happening.

It was too much blood. Too many blows. Too much for his body to handle at once. Wounds were appearing on his body faster than they were closing. His body swayed under the weight of his injuries, the limits of his magic suddenly apparent. And under the relentless punishment, it wasn't long before his furious flailing turned to a desperate attempt to shield himself from our blows.

Jindu's blade, then mine. Cutting. Carving. Tearing. My arms went numb from the shock of the engines. Gerald's whirling blades slowed as they became thick with gore. But I didn't relent. I wouldn't.

And neither did he.

It became familiar—a dance that only we knew the steps to. Like the old times, the times when we felt invincible, like war was just a game for us to win at our leisure. Our harmony was agony, every strike an ugly note in a sad red song.

And Grishok screamed.

He didn't snarl. Didn't shout. Didn't curse. The noise that came out of his throat was something I felt lodge in my chest. It was the sound of fear, the first fear, the very first time you ever felt yourself be afraid. It was the terror of the priest of a false god and the mother who raises a cruel child.

The sound of a man who never thought he could be killed suddenly afraid to die.

I'd never heard a sound like that before. I hoped I never would again.

But I did.

Grishok's cry was met with a wail. A screeching chord was played across four painful strings. With agonized clarity, it rang across the battlefield—a song penned at the end of a cruelly sharp quill by a hand withered by sorrow and shaking with rage. It cut above the roar of slaughter, a noise that made no sense to me.

But then, I knew I wasn't the audience.

"Run."

I didn't see why I bothered warning Jindu. It's not like I gave him a choice. I grabbed him by his wrist, started pulling him toward the autoballista I had hijacked. I slid under its platform, took him with me.

The horror began a second later.

Chiriel's armoire began to shudder, swell. The doors burst open. A nightmare of kite vipers escaped. Thousands of the screeching things went flying into the skies, an impossible number of beating wings and screeching maws. They coiled and writhed in a panicked dance.

Chiriel's fingers frenziedly played. Her violin wailed its desperate song, her body jerking with the force of it, matched only by the sound of the Lady's own chorus. Chiriel's eyes burned purple beneath her veil. The kite vipers screamed and surged in response to her magic, plunging from the sky to swarm over soldiers and mages and anything they could find to rip and chew and gnaw and devour.

It was a horrific sight. It sent mages fleeing through portals. Revolutionaries disappeared beneath clouds of the winged beasts. To anyone else, Chiriel's anger must have seemed a terrible thing. And maybe it was. But it wasn't anger that she played with.

It was fear. She was using magic from panic, burning incredible amounts to control that many kite vipers. Her body was breaking down with the fervor of her song, the magic tearing her apart, but she couldn't help herself.

And no one could help us.

A hand found mine. And, as I knew in my bones I would never do, I took it. I took Jindu's hand.

"Sal," he whispered, "I need to..."

I couldn't hear him over the sound of the vipers. Over the dying. It was too much. I shut my ears to it. I shut my eyes to it. But the sound continued to punch through me, shaking me from the inside out so hard I felt as though my teeth would break.

I don't know when it stopped. Or how. Or what made me open my eyes. My ears were ringing faintly, the screech of kite vipers still coursing through my brain, but the air was still and the sound of the violin had stopped.

I dared to creep out. Carnage met me. Bloodied combatants moaned and rolled around on the ground, clutching at bite wounds that savaged them. A few had been stripped damn near down to the quick by the beasts. And the kite vipers themselves...

Were nowhere to be seen.

At first, anyway.

My eyes drifted up to the sky. There, beneath the dark clouds, I saw them swirling. Not with purpose, nor with frenzy. Glutted and idle, the beasts sailed in a lazy cloud, like any other creature would. It was as if they had never even known the song of Chiriel.

The reason why became clear. No matter how badly I didn't want it to.

Chiriel the Four-String stood on the ground, far below her pets. Her violin had fallen from her hands and lay on the ground. Her face was turned upward behind her veil, watching the creatures. Numbly, arms at her side, she walked in slow circles, a mindless mimic of the monsters she had used to command.

And who she had now joined.

"NO!"

Grishok's wail broke the silence. He came rushing forward. His magic had caught up, the gaping wound where a bolt had been now closing. But his club was gone. There was not a thought for his weapon, for his foes, for anything but the woman walking slow circles around the field.

"No, no, no, *no*," he whimpered, as much a plea as a denial. He rushed toward Chiriel, reached out for her with massive hands, recoiled away as she continued to walk in numb circles. "Chiriel, why'd you do it? Why'd you fucking do it? *WHY?*"

Chiriel didn't answer.

Chiriel couldn't.

Chiriel didn't exist anymore.

"I would have been okay," Grishok wailed. *"I'm always okay.* Chiriel..."

It was a painful toll that the Lady Merchant extracted from her Hivemages. Every bit of their magic came at a cost, one that few of them were ever ready to pay. The control they exerted over their swarms was a treacherous magic, causing them to blend senses and sympathies with their charges. The Lady takes their individuality, their sense of self, in exchange. If they're careful and use their powers sparingly, they can escape with only a little trauma.

If they're not... they become hived.

Bereft of anything that made them human. Joined forever with the swarm they once commanded. Nothing more than a primitive bestial mind trapped in a body no longer fit to house it.

"Chiriel. *CHIRIEL.*" Grishok's voice was thick with sorrow. He took her gently in his arms. "Look at me. Please."

He pulled back her black veil. A face, pale and pretty, looked back—totally empty. Chiriel looked around vacantly, no more understanding for her surroundings than any kite viper would have. And when her eyes settled on Grishok's face, there was no recognition in them.

I don't know what happened to Grishok.

I don't know if he survived or escaped or died outside the walls of New Vigil.

I only know that I didn't kill him.

Grishok's howl came torn out of the deepest part of his chest. The despair in his voice was too heavy for his mouth to hold. He collapsed over his friend, the last one alive, and sobbed. He clutched her to him, heedless of how she tried to bite and scratch out of his grasp. He sobbed like a monster shouldn't be able to. Like a killer ought not dare.

Like people like us had no right to.

"I would have been okay..."

That sob followed me. Like an angry thought or a bad dream. It followed me.

As I turned on my wounded leg.

And limped away.

FORTY-FIVE

NEW VIGIL

Heavy.

That word was the first to come back to me, wending its way through the memories of carnage and the pervasive exhaustion and the echo of my enemy's despair. I felt heavy. My arms felt too heavy to carry a weapon. My head felt too heavy to carry these memories. My legs felt too heavy to carry me.

But I kept going.

One foot after another. Legs shaking, knees threatening to give out beneath me. Wound in my leg burned, no rush of combat to keep it numb. Every breath I took had to be clawed out of my throat like an infection.

But I kept going.

My blood fell in soft patters upon the churned earth, coalesced in droplets beside cold fingers and empty eyes. I trudged through the battlefield, surrounded by stained blue coats and shattered machines. The sound of pocketed resistance to the battle's conclusion only barely registered—the fight was over, even if not everyone had heard about it yet. The Revolution and all its promises lay shattered on the earth.

I tried to ignore it. When that didn't work, I tried harder. The scent of death isn't like others—it gets in your nose and turns to lead, makes your head heavier and your limbs weaker. I couldn't focus on the dead, couldn't focus on the battle, couldn't focus on anything else.

But the gates.

The walls of New Vigil loomed in the distance. A mile? Two miles? Hard to tell. No matter how long I felt myself walking, whenever I looked up again, they seemed just as far away as they were when I started. I had to keep going, had to get to the gates, had to get behind them.

But was I even going anywhere?

My breath ran out. I stopped, hands on knees, breathing hard. The dead eyes of the soldiers around me seemed to look upon me with pity, lamenting this one poor dope among the dead who didn't realize she belonged down there with them yet.

"Fuck you," I growled to a particularly smug-looking carcass. "*Fuck you.*"

The carcass started laughing. A long, whining sound came out of his mouth, amusement at a joke so funny he came back from the dead just to laugh. But as I watched, the laughter became something else. The sound turned from whining to droning, the sound of metal wings beating together like...

Locusts.

The sky shook overhead. I looked to the clouds and beheld a dark shape.

It had been months since I'd seen the Ten Arrows, the airship fleet of the Great General and his Revolution. Months since I'd been aboard one of those flying monsters of metal and smoke and sky. I'd seen them injured. I'd seen them die, like any other monster.

And still, even seeing one of them was enough to make what little sense I had left start panicking.

I wasn't the only one. The Imperium forces broke off their casual slaughter of the last remnants of Revolutionary resistance, began to redeploy themselves into formation at the sight of this new mechanical monstrosity and its many, *many* cannons.

The great ship came down on metal wings, the earth shaking as it drew closer to the ground. Its engines roared as it hovered there over the earth like a bad thought that wouldn't go away. The bay doors began to rumble open, ladders falling down to the ground. It was far away—too far to see its crew or the soldiers it was expelling from it.

"Hello, Cacophony."

But nowhere was far enough to escape Culven Loyal's voice.

I could see him—*him* and no one else. The crew upon the ship's deck was impossible to make out from this far away. But him, the bent old man with the dark eyes standing at the railing... I could see him clear as fucking day.

He didn't say another word. Just beamed a cruel, dark smile that I could see for miles, reveling in the carnage. The fear. The agonies. Torle of the Void's words came back to me.

Scraths crave emotion.

Another sound caught my ear. A wail so strong and powerful that it cut across the slaughter. I saw a figure descend from the airship—striking blue coat, dark skin, dark hair done up in a severe cut. I would have recognized her anywhere.

"Ten thousand years!"

Even before I heard her.

Tretta Unbreakable began to walk among the devastation. She searched the dead with fervent eyes, seizing the wounded and the living by their shoulders and pulling them back to their feet. She shoved weapons into their hands, took them by their faces, shouted into their eyes.

"Ten thousand years!"

No one said it back.

I turned, holding on to what little breath I'd managed to claw back into my lungs. I kept myself going. Couldn't be out here for this. Whatever the fuck was going on—Culven's arrival, Tretta, I didn't need any of it. I needed to get free, get back behind the walls, back to a place I could breathe.

Breathe.

It became less a word and more a command in my head as I realized I wasn't. It felt like I was being choked—by the stink of death, by the sound of Grishok's despair still resonating inside me, by the memory of Culven Loyal's cruel and twisted smile.

Breathe.

It was too much. Too much in my head. Too much death, too much pain, too much—

Breathe.

I couldn't. I slumped to one knee. I tried to remember how to do it. I couldn't.

A dim note played in my head. The wind rustled at my side. As I started to collapse, a hand caught me, steadied me, held me up.

"Breathe," Jindu said. "Please."

I tried.

I did.

We kept going.

He started by holding me up. Then he started shaking and it was my turn. I didn't know where he'd been, what he'd done, only that it had hurt him. He was bloodied, worse than I'd ever seen him. Cuts lined his face, as he tried valiantly to hold back the exhaustion.

"Are you leaving?"

Loyal's voice. In my bones. It followed us as we limped toward the gate.

"A pity to be limited by such a fragile shell, isn't it? We had the same thought, my siblings and I. Eldest, Strongest, Cleverest—all of us gave up our bodies to be free of pain, like Mother. And like Mother, we missed it."

"Ten thousand years!"

A few scattered chants rose behind me, applause for the worst joke ever told. Tretta continued to walk among the dead, finding the survivors and hauling them to their feet. There were a few more this time, but nowhere near the number of dead. And Loyal continued to watch, transfixed.

"You cannot see it? The beauty of the struggle. The energy of their

anguish. It's nourishing. Maddening. You are so afraid to be hurt, so afraid to be afraid, that you bury yourself beneath bravado and stories. Such amazing gifts you have been given and you seek only to run from them."

We kept going. The gates got a little closer now. I could see people on the wall. Could they see us? Did they know we needed help?

"Had I the ability, I would weep for you, Cacophony. All you've devoted toward escaping your fears and your loves, all for protecting Eldest. And it will still mean nothing. I require my sibling. You cannot stop this. You have no right to."

We kept limping. I saw people on the wall flailing, making a commotion. Had they seen us? What were they talking about? I tried to cry out, couldn't find the voice.

A faint note played in my ear, settled right beside the sensation of Loyal's voice.

"Do you not feel it, Cacophony? The despair at the futility? The agony of knowing that everything you did was for nothing? Come. Let me feel it. Share it."

I gritted my teeth, set my eyes on the wall, kept going.

The note played again, louder.

"Ah, well. I suppose I cannot blame you for withholding. You have already given me so much, haven't you? And Mother does so love her bargains. Very well. Let me repay you with a warning."

The Lady's song was ringing in my ears.

"You are about to die."

The wind shifted. Steel rang out, inches from my ear. Sparks kissed my cheek. A body flew past me, skidded to a halt.

Velline stood there—her uniform was shredded, her body was trembling, her skin was red with life. But her blade stood, rigid and unblemished, in her hands. A match for her eyes.

Both her blade and her gaze were sharp as ever.

And trained on me.

"No more," she whispered. "No more blood. No more wars. No more Vagrants."

"Sal."

Jindu's voice was weary to the point of breaking, his body shuddering with the effort it had taken to deflect her blow. He stood beside me, his sword in hand, eyes on Velline. He took in the longest, slowest breath I'd ever seen him take.

"Keep going."

Two notes played.

Two winds shifted.

And two blades met.

FORTY-SIX

ELSEWHERE

There is a story that not many people know.

A story that I heard myself and even I'm not sure if I know it.

It's not a story you hear, really. It's a story you collect—in bits and pieces scattered across so many tongues and seen through so many eyes—and try your best to fit together. And even when all the pieces seem to fit, you're still not sure if you're looking at it correctly.

I pity the people whose stories are like that. The story is the one thing we all get in life, the one thing that *we* know even if no one else does. People whose stories are fragmented like hers was...

Well, it must be a special kind of pain not knowing if your own life makes sense to you.

This story is about a woman who was born under bright stars, even if she didn't know it. She grew up in a splendid city, far beneath the Empress's gaze, in its dire slums and alleys. Her family's misfortunes weighed on her, as they weigh on all children whose parents think they don't know what's going on. But when she turned a certain age, she ran a package for her mother across the city.

In eight and a half seconds.

From the day she was recognized as a Quickmage to the day she graduated from the academy, she led a charmed life. They told her that she would do great things and perhaps that was true. They told her that her days of suffering in darkness and filth were over. They told her she would be seen as something great. But they didn't tell her that the cost of being recognized would be deep.

And it would cause her to live that life in ways she could never have expected.

"Velline ki Yanatoril."

She blinked. And they were saying her name.

A chorus of them surrounded her, a thronging symphony of applause and reverent cheers from the soft hands and painted lips of the Imperium's elite. In their stately garb and in the shadows of regal statues of mages long dead, they watched her walk the long violet carpet of the Imperium's finest academy.

Graduation day. One of the defining moments of any young mage's life. By the time she finished walking that carpet and ascended the steps to where her instructors stood, beaming, she would be revered in Imperial society. And a few days later, she would be sent to the Scar like so many others.

On that day, she hadn't thought about that—the horrors that awaited her on those forsaken shores. Nor had she been able to keep her eyes on the steps before her. Her gaze searched the crowd of the dignified and the pompous until she discovered the thin woman hopping up and down and screeching with joy.

Shenazar. Skymage. The only person she'd managed to go through this entire ordeal with and still call friend. There was no honor like this awaiting Shenazar—all mages were revered in the Imperium, but not all were revered equally, after all. But her friend never cared about that, never cared for the decorum or ritual or metaphorical masturbation that dominated so much of Imperial life.

She was here. Smiling and laughing and cheering instead of acting reverent. She was the whole reason this ceremony was bearable. Velline smiled when she saw her, smiled the entire way up to the steps.

"Her magnificent gaze has beheld your progress with deliberate interest. A surge of certainty courses through her hand as she extends to you this honor."

The robed minister said as much, but the Empress, seated high above her on her throne and looking down through her metal mask, betrayed no such interest nor certainty. She sat completely apart from the proceedings in her name, giving not so much as a gesture to the woman about to become her champion.

"It is with the promise and legacy of all the emperors that have come before that she now awards you this great honor. This blade granted to your open hand entrusts to you all the honor and authority of Imperium and Empress. May we follow the tip of your sword to a bloodless era. Alocari ancemori. Imperium Eternal."

"Imperium Eternal!"

The cheer was taken up again, by her instructors, by the crowd, by Shenazar. Everyone in that cramped, overwrought hall was cheering. Except for Velline herself.

Why would she?

It wasn't real, after all.

She blinked. She was back in the Valley.

And fire was falling from the sky.

The tundra of the Borrus Valley stretched out before her, sodden with smoke and the dead. Revolutionaries lay dead by the score, their faces still twisted into whatever fanatic vigor made them think they could oppose her. Her friends, too littered the earth—mages she'd known and held and consoled over their Barter.

Both were pitilessly swept aside beneath the rain of red and purple falling from the sky.

Mortar fire from their trenches. Echoing flame bursting out of their cannons. The droning locust-like sound of their airship's engines overhead accompanying the fire that fell cinder-like from the great mechanical leviathan. The Valley's snows whipped and its winds howled, but neither could tame the roaring laughter of the fire that fell from everywhere.

She was running. A sword was in her hand. Blood was running down her cheeks. She cleared miles in seconds, rushing across the battlefield at speeds so great she disappeared from sight. But she hadn't vanished. To her, everything simply slowed down.

The furious charge of the Revolutionaries became as a sluggish, plodding march. Their ferocious war cries turned to dull, witless sounds in their throats. Their bursting, roaring engines looked flimsy and broken. She rushed through the weird, slowed-down world, her eyes fixed on the distant walls of Terassus and the woman that stood before them. She dropped her sword, her pace growing frenzied—even as fast as she knew she was, she felt too slow.

She couldn't stop it. Every time she lived this moment, she couldn't stop it.

She found Shenazar standing there, the flowing material of her uniform whipping in a cold wind. Her face was numb, her mouth without breath, her eyes struggling to take in the impossible expanse of flame before her.

"Shenazar!" Velline cried out, as she had cried out that night. "*Shenazar!*" She appeared beside her friend, grabbed her by the arm. "I'm sorry, I shouldn't have left you—"

"Nothing."

Shenazar's voice came soft and wracked with sobs. Her tears reflected gold firelight as they fell across her cheeks. She couldn't close her eyes to the sight of the city, its many homes and many buildings drowning beneath the fire that rained from the sky.

"There's nothing here," she whispered. "It was already burning. There's nothing here to fight over."

She looked at her. Velline knew what she was going to ask, knew she didn't have an answer, knew it would hurt just as bad this time.

It always did. Even when it wasn't real. Even if it didn't feel real.

"Velline," Shenazar whispered, "what the fuck are we doing here?"

She blinked. She was somewhere else.

It was cold and dark, a land blasted black by fire whose sun was a memory, vanished behind hundreds of years of ash. The people crawled gray and wormlike beneath trails of broken banners, a graveyard of every power that had ever fought to avoid this fate. Those not broken by misery shrieked and wailed from behind sheets of flame, reaching out from ever-burning pyres with limbs that blackened but would not die.

Over it all, the clouds of ash swirled, becoming a halo of cinders and soot about the crown of a single figure. A body of brass and heat burned at the center of the world, the last burning heartbeat of a dying land. The figure looked down upon the ruin with delight and the people wailed and shielded their eyes, terrified to behold that burning smile.

Velline's heart raced. She drew short, rapid breaths and choked on the taste of ash.

"Not real," she whispered to herself, "it isn't real."

She told herself the same thing every time it happened, every time she saw this place. But it was the same fear each time, the same pain in her chest and the same terror racing up her spine. And every time she returned, she told herself again.

"It isn't real."

And every time, it sounded more and more like she didn't believe it.

She blinked.

Shenazar was dying in her arms.

Another fight. Another battle. Which one was it, even? Bluegallows? The Ivakian Heights? How many had it even been? How much time had they served together? Why did it have to end after all that?

The dead lay around them—the Revolutionaries and Imperials and civilians becoming one tangled mess scattered across the town. The fighting had gone street by street, the pavement painted with the human toll and its buildings torn apart by magic. She barely noticed. All of it seemed so insignificant against the blood shining on her hands.

"Velline."

A wound in her friend's chest. A lucky shot. Some Revolutionary upstart that didn't know when to stay down. The gunpike had been overcharged. Or the Revolutionary had been feigning death. Or...or...

Every answer she came up with didn't make it stop. The fear in Velline's chest. The pain in her throat. The blood on her hands.

"Velline, please. Look at me."

She couldn't. Not again. She couldn't see Shenazar's face like that again—she was supposed to be smiling too much, laughing too easily, refusing to take anything seriously. She was supposed to look like she did that day when they'd finally graduated.

But Velline looked. Because she always looked. Every time she came back here.

And Shenazar did not look like Shenazar. Blood was flowing out of her mouth, painting her skin, her throat glistening red. Her wound twitched as she coughed, her eyes going dimmer. Her hand reached out, took Velline's own.

"Velline," she whispered, "what the fuck am I doing here?"

"No."

A denial. A plea? She didn't know. Every time she came here, she knew less.

She blinked. She was watching thousands die.

Bitterdrink was trembling, a great city rendered into a frightened child. Torle of the Void hung in the air like a bad omen. She wondered if he had once walked the same long carpet she had. Had he walked through the same ceremony, beheld the same emptiness on the Empress's mask?

Who had he looked out to, she wondered, in that crowd? Or had there been anyone there at all?

Bitterdrink continued to shake. The world opened up wide beneath it. Its walls disappeared beneath the earth. It hadn't lasted long, she knew. Not as long as she felt like it had.

To her, it all moved agonizingly slowly, as all the world did. She watched the walls disappear, brick by brick. She watched the faces of the people who chose to hurl themselves from the battlements rather than be buried alive. She watched the horror play across the face of Sal the Cacophony.

The woman who had started this whole thing. The woman who

had no right to look horrified at this, to act like the Imperium—the Imperium who had given so much in the name of the war *she* started—was villainous here. The woman who was alive right now only by the grace of Torle of the Void, that miserable cur.

She was tempted to strike me down, then. I knew that before I ever found this story.

But before she could, she blinked. And she was in that dark future under that forgotten sun. And then she blinked again, and she was back at her graduation. And she blinked again and she was fighting alongside Bad Neighbor.

She blinked. And she vanished. And she appeared elsewhere.

A battle here. A war there. She found herself a child again, running carefree through the Imperial streets. She found herself an old woman, weeping over a grave that never shed a tear back. She found herself with sword in hand, with friend in hand, stained with blood, then clean, then clashing against someone else. And none of it was real. And all of it was real.

And she couldn't make any of it stop.

I've never really forgotten that I met Velline ki Yanatoril as a friend and have had her as an enemy ever since. And sometimes I wonder what things would be like if we hadn't ended up on each other's bad sides. And sometimes I wonder if she does, too.

But then I think to what Jindu told me about Quickmages. I think of their Barter, of all the moments and places in time they give up to the Lady Merchant for whatever purposes she needs them for. I think of the tragedies they relive over and over, the things they can never change that they wish they could.

And I think back to Velline. And I think how many of those pains she's doomed to relive will feature me in them.

And I wonder if there was ever a chance for us to be anything but what we are.

FORTY-SEVEN

NEW VIGIL

I knew their battle only in suggestions: the rush of wind where Velline's blade aimed for my throat, the spray of sparks where their weapons clashed, the notes of their songs rising and falling as they moved, struck, parried, moved again faster than any eye could ever keep up.

And I kept going.

I trudged across the field, biting back the pain, the exhaustion as much as I could, forcing my eyes to stay open and fixed on the gates. They continued to fight around me. In blurs and flashes, I saw them strike at each other. I heard the echoes of their voices on the wind—him pleading with her, her scorning him, them cursing at each other.

The world moved slower to Quickmages. So slowly that they lost their place in it, on occasion. I wondered what their battle might have looked like then, what words they might have shared that were spoken too quickly for me to have ever heard. What did they tell each other as they fought past me, painfully slow and mortal?

I think back about that, sometimes. Even now, after everything, I find I want to know. But at the time, I couldn't afford the luxury of that contemplation. I couldn't spare a single thought for anything but the gate.

"TEN THOUSAND YEARS!"

There were more of them now. More wounded Revolutionaries finding their feet, more defeated Revolutionaries finding their voices. More soldiers pouring out of the mighty airship's seemingly endless hold. And at the center of it, Tretta continued to pick up pieces, continued to shout, continued to have her shouts answered.

The Imperials were regrouping still, rallying to face the new threat. I had to keep moving. Had to get out of here before they could fight again. I wouldn't make it if they—

"Ah. I apologize, Cacophony."

Loyal's voice. In my bones. In my wounds.

"I had hoped to take a little more time."

Far away, on the deck of the airship, one of the great cannons swiveled and groaned as it turned toward the field. It was loaded without question by a crew that would never truly understand why Loyal had ordered it.

"But I feel Eldest waning."

It fired with the sound of thunder.

"I am sorry we did not get to see it end together."

Fire painted a red arc as the severium charge flew hot and screaming across the sky. I watched it up above like a great red-and-purple eye fixated upon me. I watched it hang there for a moment, almost pensive. And then I watched it come plummeting down toward me.

Fire filled the sky. The sound of metal and severium shrieking filled my ears. I watched it fall, my body too numb with pain and horror to flee. I blinked. I saw the shape of a man flash in front of my eyes.

I blinked again.

I was on my back, far away from the inferno that had blossomed where I was just standing. A shadow fell over me. Jindu stood there, breathless and exhausted from the effort of getting me clear. His eyes met mine. He swallowed hard. His body trembled.

A drop of blood fell onto my leg.

The sound of steel singing.

Of a body splitting.

And a song dying.

Jindu let out a breathless gasp, stiffened spear-straight. Velline's blade twisted, its glistening tip jutting from his chest. Steel scraped as she pulled her sword free. Crimson spread across his shirt, the linen soaked with the grotesque flower that bloomed there.

He pitched forward. I reached to catch him. He landed in my arms.

Jindu. Jindunamalar.

Who had met me the night I wept with loneliness in the academy and waited with me until I stopped.

Who had held me as I had held him and told me that we would be happy, even if the world burned to ashes.

Who had cut me so deeply and so cruelly that I wished more than once he had just killed me then and there.

Jindunamalar.

Jindu the Blade.

Jindu.

Growing colder in my arms.

"How does it feel, Sal?"

Velline stood with a rage she struggled to turn to composure. Her eyes were cruel, cold, imperious. But her hands shook as she wiped her blade clean. Her breath came ragged as she spoke. And her words fell as an overheated blade: hot, brittle, seething.

"How does it feel to lose everything to your war?" she asked, voice shaking. "How does it feel to lose everything, as I have? How does it feel? How does it *hurt*?"

She clenched her fists. She shut her eyes. She shouted.

"Answer me, you fucking piece of—"

I didn't wait for the end of that.

I was far too busy punching her in the mouth.

Velline recoiled—somehow, in the vast number of ways she expected me to answer, a fist in her teeth wasn't it. Which was unfortunate, because if she was surprised by that, this next part would be real uncomfortable.

Here's the thing about Quickmages. They have incredible power that borders on obscene, they are fearsome opponents and invaluable allies—all of that is true, but like anyone, it's only true of them on their best day. When you cut them, they still bleed. And when you grab them?

Well, they don't fucking jump around anymore, I'll tell you that.

I rushed her without a word, without a howl of rage or a snarl or even a curse. I tackled her about the waist before she could think, pulled her to the ground, and crawled on top of her. She didn't know how to get out of my grapple as I straddled her, pinning her arms to her sides. She'd learned to fight wars, but she'd never learned how to fight an asshole.

Which she should have considered.

My fists felt numb and hard as I smashed them against her jaw, her cheeks, her temples—sledgehammer weights at the end of my arms, fit for nothing but violence. She sputtered and shouted and cursed as I did, but I didn't hear them. Or anything, really. Not the crunching of bone as her nose shattered or the spatter of her blood on my face.

If I'm honest, I didn't feel much of anything.

I wasn't feeling sorrow or rage or something like that. I wasn't thinking about her or me or what we'd done to each other. I wasn't thinking anything but a single word. A word I thought had no meaning for me anymore.

Jindu.

In my head.

Jindu.

Down my arms.

Jindu.

At the ends of my fists as I beat her, over and over and over, until I was numb to everything. All angers. All pains. All scents. All sounds.

"TEN THOUSAND YEARS!"

Almost all sounds.

The earth began to shake.

The sound of thunder filled the sky.

I looked up.

I talk a lot of shit about the Glorious Revolution of the Fist and Flame, I'll admit it. Their machines are impressive, sure. Their fanatic loyalty is remarkable, to be certain. And their leadership is ironclad in their resolve, which is nice. But none of that is what really makes the Revolution powerful.

It's easy to forget that. I've forgotten it before. The Imperium never bothered to remember it in the first place. But every now and then, you get a demonstration that the Revolution's true strength isn't machines or Relics or propaganda.

"UNBREAKABLE!"

It's that they outnumber everyone else a hundred to fucking one.

An ocean of blue coats, gunpikes, and noise came rushing across the field. Endless. Surging. Not a scrap of bare ground between them, they were packed so fucking tight.

The sound of their feet struggled to compete with the roar that collectively tore itself out of their throats. The sound that had begun as chanting and slogans devolved with every step until all that came out was just one long torrent of noise, a river of fanatic anger that swept aside everything in its path.

They stopped for nothing—not for their own dead, not for those that fell in the mad rush, and certainly not for their enemies.

The Imperium rallied, formed up as best they could. Skymages swooped. Siegemages planted their feet. Embermages conjured great sheets of flame.

It looked to be a sound defense.

At first.

Engines wailed to life, roared mightier than even the Revolutionaries. From within the ranks, a trio of Iron Boar transports burst free of the charge, their drivers mowing down their own in a mad bid to get to the front. Smoke poured out of the windows of their vehicles, iron wheels tearing the earth apart as they surged ahead of their comrades and drove heedlessly into the Imperium.

It appeared foolish, at first.

But then, most dangerous things do.

The transports plowed into the line of mages. Their engines let out one final frenzied metal howl. The smoke pouring out of them became purple flame. The severium charges inside caught.

Exploded.

Pillars of smoke and flame erupted across the Imperial battle line, the machine drivers consumed along with their foes as their Iron Boars and the severium they carried exploded. The Imperials were cast into disarray, struggling to get clear of the fires and erupting debris.

From the wall of smoke left behind, they came. The Revolutionaries exploded from behind veils of cinders and soot, screaming through the fire with ashes in their lungs as they met their foes in battle.

Not in formation. Not in machines. Not with slogans or chanting or the names of their leaders.

They came in one great, sweeping wave. Swift. Ferocious. Endless.

The Revolutionaries surged over their foes. The Skymages were hauled from the sky and dragged down into a carving flurry of gunpikes. The mighty Siegemages were swarmed, Revolutionaries climbing over them to defiantly jam their daggers in their eyes. The Embermages and Graspmages and Doormages were simply crushed where they stood, trampled.

The howling did not stop. The blood did not stop. Nothing could stop either of them.

Certainly not me. There would be no escaping them.

Which was fine. I was past feeling fear. Past anything but the need to keep punching.

So I did. I punched and struck and hit until I drew back my arm and felt it get stuck.

"For fuck's sake, is killing her worth dying?"

Four hands clutched my wrist. Urda and Yria held me, desperation in their eyes. Meret was behind them, struggling to put Jindu atop a bird. Congeniality stood beside them, glowering expectantly. All of them kept glancing up toward the approaching tide of Revolutionary fervor.

"We need to go," Urda said. "We need to go *now*."

"Go," I said. "I'll be fine."

"When he said 'we' he meant all of us, you dumbfuck," Yria snarled. "Don't you fucking get that we need you, too?"

It's not that what she said made sense. Not a lot did when I was like that. But rather, what she said...well, I guess it felt different. Maybe it was because she cussed with a little less vigor. Or because he pulled with a little more. I didn't know.

I still don't, if I'm honest.

But I don't question it now. And I didn't question it then. I let them help me up. I let Velline vanish. I let myself follow them back to the birds.

I mounted Congeniality, pulled the twins up behind me, ran a hand along the folds of her skin. She let out a squawk of alarm as the sound of Revolutionary fury grew louder in our ears. I put the spurs to her, trotted toward the waiting gates.

Shouts of alarm and the frenzy of motion greeted us as we passed into New Vigil. Vigilants swarmed forward to slam the gates shut and ascend the battlements. The cannons on the wall rang out as a new defense was taken up.

I wasn't thinking about that. I wasn't thinking about anything when I fell off my bird and ran up to Meret's. I still wasn't when I pulled Jindu off the bird, felt him cold and still in my arms.

I pulled him out of the way of the commotion, pulled him away from Meret as he shouted for help. He knew as well as I wanted to not know that there was no help for him. He didn't need that.

"Sal."

He needed something else.

"Sal."

His eyes were glassy. His voice was soft. He grew paler and colder with every fading breath.

"I don't think... I'm here anymore."

"What?"

"My Barter... I'm...," he gasped. "I'm not here. I'm back... back then. Back in the academy. When we were young."

My mouth hung open. There was something caught in my chest. It hurt. Even thinking about it hurt. It spread so far through me, I couldn't get any words to my mouth, couldn't get any air to my lungs.

"Am I there, too?"

I could barely speak. Couldn't think. How could I talk to him like this when he was on my list? How could I have fought alongside him all this time? I had always thought there would be time to deal with that later, I had always thought...

"You are... you're so small, and so am I, and we've never even heard of war and..." His eyes drifted to that place, that time he had disappeared to, even while his body was trapped here. "You're crying."

I suppose it didn't matter how long I had. Maybe I didn't know what to say then because I had never known what to say. Because I never thought this would ever happen. I never thought he'd ask for forgiveness. And I never thought I'd...

"It's okay."

Jindu was staring at something else. His smile was faint and manic, as if he were looking at something I couldn't see just yet. His breath came shallow and wet.

"It's going to be okay," he said to that place he vanished to. "I'm going to take care of you, Sal. My name is Jindunamalar. I love you. I love you so much."

His fingers fell.

His face fell.

"I think this is the one...," he said softly, "that's going to last forever."

He let out one great sigh, a sound so soft and vast it smothered the violence behind me. His head lolled on his shoulders, his body went limp. The sound of his final breath drew out forever, stretched from day into night, as he disappeared to another place, the moment that would last forever.

Jindu left.

And I couldn't go any further.

FORTY-EIGHT

NEW VIGIL

Life isn't like opera.

I know I keep saying that, but that's because I keep forgetting it. Because I want it to be like opera. I'm not ashamed to admit that. I want everyone to be charming and vibrant, I want romance and overtures, I want stories that end neatly and with no words left unsaid.

I want that. Desperately.

I think a lot of people do.

A lot of people love opera, after all.

But those who don't also have a valuable perspective—if you never believe in those things in the first place, you never have to be disappointed. You never have to learn that heroes are also often murderers. You never have to find out that sometimes things just end and no one is happy. You never have to learn that leaders aren't dramatic and often have no more idea of what they're doing than you do.

"Well, I'll be honest, I didn't actually expect us to survive this long, so I'm not quite sure where to go from here."

As I was saying.

"That's...I mean, that's not *exactly* encouraging to hear." Meret wanted to say something a little swearier than that, I could tell. But to his credit, he kept it together. He leaned in closer, whispered, "But given that you're the leader and all..."

"Right, right." Cavric's sigh escaped like steam as he stroked his beard. He glanced over our heads. "I admit, I'd find it easier to think if I weren't hiding from my own soldiers."

It couldn't be helped, honestly.

The tavern that had been turned into a command center had been turned into an infirmary. The wounded—countless in number, gruesome in injury—lined the walls; every space that wasn't occupied by a table was occupied by a cot, leaving precious little space for an overworked Mendmage and a handful of scurrying medics to work among their numerous charges.

The mood was bleak, despite the day's reprieve. The unexpected clash between the Imperium and the Revolution—or, shall we say, improvised provocation—had broken the siege, but the breathing room had only given everyone a chance to realize how close they were to being overrun. The two forces had retreated, regrouped, reorganized—or so we suspected, scouts being in short supply after the day's carnage.

To know that the Imperium and Revolution had been wounded might have brought some much-needed morale.

To see how easily they could shrug off such a wound brought no comfort in those cramped quarters.

The mood was tense. Morale was bleak. I admit, it wasn't good for the soldiers to see their commander and his associates huddled in a corner like a pack of thieves. But I also agree that it was probably better that they not hear the dumb shit coming out of their leader's mouth.

"Maybe they've had enough. We could strike a truce."

Yeah, like that.

"I was off the wall, so I didn't see. Did you hit your head in the battle?" Ketterling, still dirty from her desperate escape from the battle, snarled. "Because that's the only thing I can think of that might explain the big puddle of stupid you just dribbled on the floor. Do you not know who's on the other side of that wall?"

"I fucking know who's on the other side of that wall," Cavric replied, ire creeping into his voice. "Just as I know that we somehow, through whatever birdshit Sal pulled—"

It would have been rude to interrupt.

"You're welcome, by the way."

But I wasn't feeling polite just then.

"We *somehow* managed to beat them," Cavric persisted, glaring at me, "we bled them on that field and we buried them by the score and we *still* lost. They tore us apart on those walls and that was just the Revolution. They might have fucked each other up for now, but they'll recover. We won't." He took a breath, held up a hand. "They're bastards and they don't deserve it, but a truce would be the best option for—"

"You dumbfuck," Ketterling interjected angrily, "it's because they're bastards that we *can't* treat with them."

Cavric opened his mouth to reply.

"She's right."

But I beat him to it.

"And she's right because you're right." I leaned heavily on the wall, tried to keep weight off my bandaged leg. The medics had done the best they could, but there were more pressing needs for their talents. "The Imperium and the Revolution *will* recover. And we won't recover. And they know that just as well as you do." I smiled, but it wasn't happy. "Why would they agree to something like a truce when they could just as easily wait a few days and try again?"

The anger that flooded his face didn't alarm me. I knew it well—hell, I'd worn it myself just a few moments ago. It was the heaviest kind of anger to hold, the kind struggling to hold back something true. And like it had done with me, the fury on his face gave way to sorrow, then defeat, and then he wore the same unhappy smile I did.

"Yeah," he sighed. "You're right. Both of you. Nothing has changed." He looked at us. "Nothing. New Vigil has always stood for more than they could give us. It has since we built it." He let out a slow breath. "It will when it gets burned to the ground, too."

Life isn't like opera, like I said. Pithy, inspiring statements don't inspire the same kind of courage. The bravest last-ditch efforts don't always change anything. And the plucky underdog still ends up getting crushed.

"Commander."

But then again.

"Commander!"

Sometimes it is like an opera. For example, sometimes when you think things can't possibly get any worse, some asshole comes in with a new development.

In this case, it was a scout who ran breathlessly to our huddle, saluted briefly. "Commander," he gasped to Cavric. "Revolution, sir. At the gate."

We tensed, made ready for action. The scout shook his head wearily, held up a hand, caught his breath.

"Only three of them, Cavric," he said. "Diplomats. They want to meet."

"Meet," Cavric repeated flatly. "As in... surrender? Or..."

He shook his head. "She wouldn't talk to me beyond demanding to speak to you." He glanced toward me. "*And* you."

My brows rose. Cavric's brows furrowed.

"Me?" I asked.

"*She*," Cavric grunted.

"Yes, sir," the scout nodded. "She introduced herself as Cadre Commander Tretta Unbreakable. Said you used to be friends."

So, just to get something clear, it's not that I'm *un*diplomatic.

I had my fair share of negotiations when I was in the army, after all. I was familiar with the protocols of it: the etiquette, the techniques, the pageantry. It's just that I was much *more* familiar with what followed after diplomacy.

You know, the burning and such.

Which I guess is what diplomacy is meant to avoid.

So, I take it back—maybe I am bad at diplomacy.

I was fairly sure I wasn't alone in that realization. If the spear-straight postures of Cavric and Ketterling were any indication, anyway. We rode out from the gates atop our birds, Ketterling carrying New Vigil's banner, the sigil of a rearing Banter flapping in the breeze. The tension settled on our shoulders as we made our way, each of us worried at least a little about my presence here.

After all, it's not like most people asked me to make things *less* complicated.

But, then again, my presence had been personally requested.

We were met on the field by a trio of envoys. The passing hours had not been kind to the battle's aftermath. Many bodies had been recovered by their respective sides, but not enough to discourage the numerous scavenger birds and beasts that braved the presence of armies to get a bit of food.

If the morbidness bothered Tretta, she didn't show it.

She stood in a dirty coat, grimy and bloody from battle—she'd been there, leading the charge. Impressive woman. Wish she didn't want to kill me all the time. Her face was restrained admirably into an expression of mild distaste. Her escorts—a pair of faceless Twenty-Second guards—stared emptily into space.

"Cavric Proud," Tretta said. "I am pleased to see you alive."

"I go by just Cavric now," he replied as we pulled our birds to a stop. "And no, you're not, Tretta Unbreakable." He sniffed. "Congratulations on your promotion."

"That is..." Tretta's face screwed up in restrained fury for a moment before she let out an unhappy, defeated sigh. "That isn't fair, Cavric. I don't want you dead any more than I want anyone in this city dead."

"Could have fooled me," Ketterling muttered, "what with you killing us and all."

That twitch in Tretta's left eye at that comment was *just* severe enough to make me finally like Ketterling.

"Those are Revolutionaries behind your walls," Tretta said, holding her ire behind her teeth. "Derelict in their oaths, traitors to the Revolution, which has given them everything." She let out a sigh.

"And even still, neither I nor anyone with wisdom wants to see more dead today."

"Wisdom, huh?" I muttered.

My eyes drifted skyward, to the airship hovering bloated over the field, and the creature posing as a man poised at the railing.

"At the behest of the Great General," Tretta continued, "his most esteemed hand, Culven Loyal, has, in the interests of preventing further bloodshed and in providing sanctuary for all the Revolution's wayward and disaffected, requested an end to the strife."

"Outstanding," Cavric said. "The road out is back the way you came. Don't look in any holes on your way out."

She narrowed her eyes. "A wise leader listens, thinks, and *then* acts."

"Of course, of course." He glanced out over the field and its strewn bodies. "We wouldn't want anyone to get hurt now, would we?" Cavric sighed. "So, then. What does the general want me to hear?"

"The *Great* General"—Tretta's face soured so fiercely I felt my ass pucker—"has deemed that all interested parties should be present to partake of his font of wisdom."

All parties?

A note of the Lady's song caught my ear. A portal winked into existence not far away. An Imperial Doormage emerged, an Imperial banner clutched in their hands. They stood aside, expectant, as another shape emerged.

She looked like Bad Neighbor, sure enough. But the woman that emerged from the portal wasn't her. Riacantha ki Camathusula had always been brusque, maybe even a little bit of a prick. But her eyes had always held light. Her lip could still curl into a smile.

This woman, whose eyes were empty and whose face was as still as the mask her Doormage wore, was no one I recognized.

"Huh, so it was true," Cavric observed. "Imperium and Revolution working together."

"To kill us," Ketterling grunted. "We should be flattered."

"No such alliance exists." Bad Neighbor's voice was as empty as her face as she spoke. "The Imperium's interests were better served by nonaggression."

"Until they weren't," Tretta observed sharply. "Had *I* been there to offer counsel to Loyal, I would—"

"You didn't." Bad Neighbor didn't even bother looking up as she folded her gauntleted arms. "Whatever you could have done, you did not. Whoever you could have saved, you did not. And now we are here." She snorted. "May the regrets of Torle of the Void console you."

"And Velline?" I interjected.

Bad Neighbor's face hung still for an ominous moment.

"Torle of the Void extends his regrets regarding her, as well. She will not be attending."

"What a pity. I would have offered tea." Cavric rolled out his shoulder, tried his best to shake the weariness from him, failed. "Is there anyone else 'attending'? I can send for some, maybe a couple of cookies to go with it?"

"Proud—" Tretta caught herself. "*Cavric*, you serve your people ill with your flippancy."

"Then you know they're my people," he replied. "And this is *their* city. They want nothing more than this forsaken spit of land to call their own. We need nothing from you, we want nothing from you."

"The Empress disagrees," Bad Neighbor said. "You took her mages. You took her people. This city's presence stands as an insult to her, her people, and all that our blood has built."

"She's got plenty of blood left," I said, which was probably not *particularly* helpful. "A whole fucking Imperium's worth."

"The Great General likewise will not tolerate a city that provides haven to counterrevolutionary thought," Tretta said, forceful. "Nor should those most vulnerable be left to the insufficient protection of..." She narrowed her eyes at Cavric. "*Dissidents.*"

"Torle has exchanged words with the Revolution," Bad Neighbor added. "We have arrived at a conclusion that will limit the bloodshed."

"To what?" Ketterling scoffed. "A few lakes' worth?"

"To nothing," Tretta replied. "There shall be no retribution. No punishment. No occupation of territory. Nor even executions of leadership." Tretta's eyes lingered thoughtfully on me for a moment. "The Great General's fury is exceeded, it seems, only by his mercy."

"The Empress finds the terms amenable," Bad Neighbor said. "She will permit all leadership to remain in this"—she glanced over our heads, to New Vigil's walls—"this very fragile city to remain, uncontested. She merely insists on her right: the return of her mages and all pertinent citizenry."

Cavric stiffened. Ketterling's eyes went wide.

"The Great General likewise demands that the proud and loyal people of the Glorious Revolution of the Fist and Flame be returned immediately to be escorted to the nearest Revolutionary stronghold for education." Tretta's back stiffened. "You have my solemn word as cadre commander and emissary of the Great General that none shall be harmed."

"Harmed?" Cavric straightened in his saddle. "*Harmed?* Have you even heard the shit that comes out of your mouth, Tretta?" He burned behind his beard, broad shoulders trembling. "I know what the Great General's education is. I've *lived* it. It's nothing more than torture with a quiz at the end."

"You speak unwisely, Proud," Tretta growled.

"His name is fucking *Cavric*, you greasy bird-mouthed motherfucker." Ketterling's Banter bristled beneath her, encouraged by the anger flowing out of her. "*This city* is New Vigil. It isn't here to spite you. It's here to get the fuck *away* from you." She spat at the feet of Tretta, then took a quick swig of water and spat again at the feet of Bad Neighbor. "And we'll sooner die here on our terms than live under the 'protection' of yours."

Bad Neighbor's eyes drifted to me. "You're quiet, Salazanca," she observed. "You know what's going to happen if you don't speak up. You were there. With Torle of the Void." She blinked, vacant. "So was I. You saw what happened there. You know it'll happen here."

I did know. So did everyone else. Tretta's face screwed up at the memory of Bitterdrink, the muscles in her neck straining to swallow the rage. Cavric's and Ketterling's own anger was stiffened by the fear crawling up their spines at the mention of Torle. Silence fell over us, as their gazes fell over me.

I closed my eyes. There was a pain in my neck that I couldn't seem to roll out. It followed me as I pulled my scarf up a little higher over my throat and spurred Congeniality forward.

"Yeah." I knuckled the small of my back as I approached—not to seem nonchalant or anything, my ass just hurt. "Yeah, I know what'll happen. You'll kill us all. You'll bury us under the earth." I paused, considered. "Or you'll incinerate us all. Or electrocute us with lightning." I glanced at Tretta. "Or, hell, maybe you'll just do it hand-to-hand. I know you're going to kill us all." I gestured with my chin to Cavric and Ketterling. "So do they. So do you. So does everyone in that city."

"You disgrace this meeting with your empty bravado," Tretta said, sneering. "Don't act like retribution doesn't frighten you."

"It scares the piss out of me," I said, "if I'm honest. I wouldn't take odds against everyone else in this city feeling the same, either."

"Then stop acting stupid," Bad Neighbor said. "See reason."

"Oh, I am, I am," I said. "I'm just considering all angles." I smiled gently. "But then, I'm always the only one doing that, aren't I?"

The silence deepened from uncomfortable to desperately uncomfortable. Bad Neighbor's face fell the barest inch it could manage. Cavric shifted in his saddle behind me. Only Tretta took the bait.

I could always count on her for that.

"What is it," she said, "that we aren't considering?"

"You're out here." I pointed back to the walls. "And I'm in there. And there isn't anyone in this little circle that doesn't know how much worse I can make this and isn't hoping I don't decide to."

There's an art to shit-talking.

You never want to be too detailed in your threats, because that just makes people want to see it more. And you never want to be too vague, or you'll sound like you're scared. The trick is to be *just* specific enough to give them an idea, then let their imaginations run wild.

Which, if the twitch across Tretta's face was any indication, she was doing. I could count on her for that, as well.

"So here's our counteroffer," I said. "You leave. You go home and have a drink. You never return to New Vigil, never speak its name, never even dream about it. And none of us will have to worry about what I'm doing behind those walls."

"You're full of—"

"Ah, ah, ah," I cautioned. "Listen. *Think.* Then speak."

I turned Congeniality around, trotted back. The silence didn't last as long this time. And when a word was spoken, it was fraught. Fraught with fear. Fraught with fury.

So I *might* have just made things worse.

Bad Neighbor snorted at Cavric. "It won't be long until Torle arrives. This city won't last the night."

"If that," Tretta agreed.

"Are you sure you want to let her speak for you?"

Cavric took a deep breath. "No." He let it out. "But I'm sure that surrender can't be done. Not like you want." He set a hand upon the haft of his axe. "You do what you have to do, and we'll do..."

His voice trailed off. His eyes did, too. A little rude to do while you're delivering your defiant last stand, but I didn't blame him. I was looking, too.

Across the chaos-riddled field, a single wagon pulled by a single bird came trotting. Completely unbothered by the macabre horrors surrounding it, neither the bird nor the charming lad driving it seemed to even notice the many bodies they picked their way through. A merry bell jangled a tune as the wagon approached us, pulled around, and came to a halt.

The hay in the wagon's back rustled as a shape emerged. A shabby shape in shabby clothes, eyes sunken and face unwashed, *reeking* of drugs, booze, and grief.

It's not that I was being mean to Rudu, it's just that he looked a little rough as he pulled himself out of the wagon. He handed a piece of gold to the boy and packed his pipe as the wagon rode off. His smoke arrived before he did, a cloud of silkgrass reek heralding his return.

"Sorry I'm late," he said through puffs. "Takes a bit to find a ride out here." He glanced around the assembled, who regarded this stinking newcomer with a mixture of indignation and curiosity. "So, what'd I miss?"

"What?" Tretta snarled. "Who dares to—"

"Rudu the Cudgel," he said. "Representative of the Ashmouths and the Three."

"The Ashmouths are a gang of criminals and murderers," Bad Neighbor observed. "They have no interests to represent here. And a Vagrant is no emissary."

"Well, good thing I said I'm a *representative*, then, isn't it?" Rudu took another puff. "And, as the Three see it, they've got a fairly vested interest here." He made a lazy attempt at a bow to Bad Neighbor and Tretta. "Your war has been difficult to manage, let alone profit from. The Three believe that they are owed a say in how this plays out. Call it recompense for losses."

"I'll call it fucking stupid," Tretta snapped. "You and your criminal mistresses should fear the conclusion of this, because once we're done here, we're coming for—"

"Yeah, yeah, very intimidating, I'm both scared and a little aroused, whatever." He reached into his robe, produced a pair of envelopes. "I'm a little pressed for time, so if you'll skip to the end of your threats, I'll skip to the end of mine."

He approached and handed one to each of the women. They glared at him, but made no move to reject them—or kill him. Each of them tore the envelopes open. Bad Neighbor unfurled a letter and began to read. Tretta furrowed her brows in confusion as a dull metal item fell into her hands.

"This is a medal." Her eyes widened. "This is *my* medal. My *first* medal. It never leaves my quarters." She turned her gaze to him. "How did you get it?"

"One of your soldiers owed me a favor," he said.

"Which one?"

"The one that knows where and when you sleep."

"Impossible," she said. "*Impossible.* The Revolution does not have spies in its midst."

"Probably not, no," he replied, shrugging. "But you've got a lot of people with a lot of needs that you can't satisfy. And all the Ashmouths ask in return is a little favor. Done quietly." He took another puff. "You know, a leader stabbed in the night here. A trade route sabotaged there. We have all sorts of people willing to do us favors. Maybe we're popular."

She narrowed her eyes. "You cannot hope to stay the hand of the Revolution with pathetic threats."

"Wouldn't dream of it," he replied, glancing at me. "Nor would I dream of getting in the way of whatever back-alley heroism is going on here. But there's a lot of people in that city, a lot of material, a lot of interest the Three want to make certain are secure before they let any mage or cannon bury the place."

"I don't blame thieves for wanting to pick our pockets while we're down," Cavric said. "You *are* assholes, after all."

"All right, listen, I just met you."

"And I'll be fucked before I invite them into my city," he finished, forcefully.

"Okay, fine, we won't go in ourselves," Rudu said, sighing. "What if we just sent a representative?"

"The Revolution will *not* permit the Ashmouths unfettered reign of the city," Tretta interjected. "If they send an emissary, the Great General demands one present, as well."

"Oh, fuck you," Ketterling snapped. "You want us to set the table for you while we're at it?" She elbowed Cavric. "This is pointless."

He shook his head. "It isn't." He held up a hand. "We'll agree to three emissaries. One for each of you. No more. But while they're in the city, you don't so much as raise a weapon against our walls or we're back to doing this the hard way."

"A bluff to buy time," Tretta said, sneering.

"For what?" Rudu asked. "Looks like they're not going anywhere. But I'm kind of busy today, so if you could just go ahead and tell me if you're in or not..."

She seethed for a moment. "Fine. The Revolution shall send an agent."

Rudu glanced to Bad Neighbor. "And the Imperium?"

The little woman hadn't said so much as a word since she opened her envelope. And when she lowered the letter she'd read, the last traces of emotion were wrung out and splattered across her face. Her eyes were misty, her throat heavy as she swallowed hard.

Whatever the Ashmouths had on her... it was all she had left.

"Fine," she said. "Whatever."

"Then we're all in agreement," Tretta said. "For the moment. But there's only one way out of this, Cavric, and it is through the Great General."

"It always was," he replied, terse.

The silence lingered for only a moment before Tretta and her guard turned smartly and left. Bad Neighbor didn't look up, clutching the letter to her chest as she returned to her portal and vanished. Rudu stood, hand in pocket, exhaling smoke into the sky.

"What was in her envelope?" I asked.

"Don't know," he replied. "They have another guy for that." He licked his lips, snorted smoke out his nostrils. "I'd wager the big boys here can keep themselves entertained for... what? A day? Maybe longer?" He clicked his tongue. "Not a lot of time, is it? Best to make the most of it."

I didn't miss the implication. No one did. I wasn't sure if Rudu was simply bluffing or if the Ashmouths actually *did* have business there. I still don't know, if I'm honest. But I liked to think that maybe...

Well, hell, maybe he was tired of killing, too.

"Thank you," I said. "For that."

"Yeah," Rudu replied.

"And I'm sorry... about Necla."

Rudu was quiet for a long, long time.

"Yeah."

He turned on his heel, started to wander off, a cloud of smoke trailing him. I watched him go, unsure whether to speak to him again or not. But curiosity overwhelmed me.

"Where are you going?" I asked.

"Well, shit," he replied, "I've got to go find an emissary, don't I?"

FORTY-NINE

NEW VIGIL

It was a full minute after Sal had stopped talking that Ozhma realized she was staring.

"What," she asked, pausing to take in a breath, "happened next?"

Sal didn't look away from the door standing in the middle of the room, the door that went to nowhere and had nothing behind it. A sad grin pulled at the corners of her mouth.

"What happened next," she said, "is I found a few nice bottles of whiskey, came down to this room, and made myself comfortable."

"But what happened after that?"

"I just spent hours telling you. If you weren't listening, I'm going to be really pissed."

Those words did not so much strike her as pick her up and throw her off a tall cliff.

It was over.

She knew the rest of the story. Rudu found her, she found her way here, and then...

It was over. There was no more story to tell. No more time to take. When they'd started talking, she'd thought a lot of things—that she couldn't be here, that she couldn't do anything, and then finally, that she couldn't leave. How odd, she thought, that not once in those many thoughts it had occurred to her that it would end.

Had her mind simply not grasped it or... or...

Or, on some level of rationale she couldn't believe and feared to question, had she felt ready to stay here with Sal?

Right to the very end?

"Ask me," Sal said, "what you really want to ask me."

Ozhma didn't know what she was talking about.

No, Ozhma corrected herself. *You know. You just don't want to ask it.*

She shut her eyes. She swallowed hard. She tried to think of something else.

But you have to.

"What," Ozhma said softly, "happens now?"

Sal tore her eyes from the door to nowhere for a moment. She turned that cool blue stare onto Ozhma. And Ozhma herself wondered if this was the same stare, the same smile, the same scars that Liette and Jindu and Agne and all of them had looked into.

"Would you hate me," Sal asked, "if I said I had no idea?"

Ozhma felt the correct reaction was at *least* some irritation. Instead, though, she found herself wearing the same weary smile as the white-haired woman.

"No idea? Nothing?" Ozhma asked. "You have no plan?"

"Well, I didn't say that, did I? I certainly *had* a plan," she replied. "Somewhere along the line, anyway. But the further I went, the more I realized that..." She sighed, shrugged. "Look, I'm trying my hardest, okay?"

Ozhma nodded—that sounded reasonable. It wasn't like she had any better answers. Silence fell over them as they both returned to watching the door. Long moments of quiet passed—not painful, not awkward, just the comfortable feeling of not needing to say anything else—before Ozhma thought to ask.

"How do you want it to end?"

Sal seemed to think about this for a long moment. She opened her mouth to say something, but nothing came out. Her eyes twitched briefly. Tears rimmed them. A droplet fell, trailed down the scar as it hung from her jaw for a brief moment.

"I want—"

Three knocks.

Faint. Polite. Hesitant.

Sal paused. The tear fell, vanished. She got to her feet. She came to the door. She reached for the handle, hesitated, as if she feared to touch it and find out it wasn't real.

Three more knocks.

Louder. Stronger. Desperate.

Sal didn't wait this time. She took the knob. She pulled the door open. Inside a frame that should be empty, there was a vast field of darkness, a night sky yawning for eternity. And in that gloom, something twinkled—some faint and distant star, so far away as to be even the barest fragment of a dream, the kind that's forgotten immediately upon waking.

But Ozhma recognized the star. And the star recognized her. And it looked at her with a sort of regret, as if to say...

I miss you.

A shape appeared in the darkness, a silhouette that filled the door. It stood in the frame, hidden by night. It shuddered, trembled. And fell.

Sal cried out, leapt forward.

She caught the shape, stumbled to the floor.

And Liette fell into her arms, exhausted and weak.

The name weighed heavy in her mind. The woman Sal spoke of had seemed so powerful, so invincible. The woman in Sal's arms looked wearier. Her hair was disheveled and messy. Her face glistened with sweat plastered on top of dry sweat. Her clothes hung worn around her, her body looked as though it barely had the strength to tremble at all, let alone as fiercely as it did.

And yet... this didn't look unfamiliar to Ozhma.

"Hey," Sal whispered. She pulled Liette closer, smoothed hair out of her eyes. "Hey. Look at me."

The woman shook gently. Sal stroked her neck.

"Please."

Liette turned upward. Sal tensed, fearing what she'd see when that shaking, trembling head looked up, what horrors would be scarred in her eyes. When Liette looked at her, her eyes were heavy with sadness.

But not stars.

Not darkness.

The sorrow in her eyes was deep. It was pained. But it was hers. It was all hers.

"Hey," she whispered back, breathless. "I did it."

"I knew you would," Sal whispered.

"You didn't."

Sal took her gently by the chin. "Are you all right?"

Liette tried to smile, shook her head. "No. No, I'm not. Not yet. I…I spoke to him, Sal. I heard him. I felt his voice. He is so angry. He's so…so…" She swallowed back pain, failed to swallow back the tears. "And you've been carrying him all this time. Listening to him. And I never…I never helped you."

She weakly reached out, took Sal's fingers, pressed them to her lips.

"I'm sorry," she whispered. "I'm so sorry, Sal."

Sal didn't say it was okay. Sal didn't tell her not to worry. She just sat there as Liette spoke. And she nodded weakly. And she pulled Liette against her for a long time, kissing the top of her head and holding her there.

The moment stretched out. For as long as moments like those could.

"What did he say?"

Liette shuddered at Sal's question. But Sal didn't relent.

"What did he tell you?"

Ozhma noticed, then, that Liette was clutching something to her chest. A box of charred wood, warped and split from heat in places. Her hands trembled as she raised it, turned her face away from it, and held it out.

Sal stared at the box as though it could stare back. And so did Ozhma.

"Did he take Eldest?"

She didn't mean to blurt it out—in fact, she was quite mortified to have interrupted the moment between them. Curiosity compelled her. But courtesy condemned her.

"Sorry!" she said. "Sorry, sorry, I didn't mean to ruin the mood. My name is—"

"You didn't ruin anything, Ozhma." Liette's voice was weary, but the gratitude in her words still came through. "Thank you. For staying with her."

Ozhma furrowed her brow. "But... we haven't—"

"Is it bad?" Sal interrupted, pulling Liette closer. "The answer... is it bad?"

Liette shook her head.

"Worse."

Sal slowly reached out and took it from her hands. The wood splintered as she did, the char beginning to smolder. The fragments of wood caught ablaze as they fell, becoming fiery petals that turned to ash on the floor. An object remained in her hand, wrapped in cloth that began to smoke. A fire caught, swept across her palm—she did not flinch.

Trappings fell away and became kindling on the floor. What remained in Sal's hand was a black wooden grip, a thick brass barrel forged in the shape of a grinning dragon, a heavy trigger. The room was lightless, yet the metal was so bright that Ozhma could see every detail in its design.

Ozhma stared, breathless, at the weapon.

And the Cacophony stared back at her.

The gun's metal was moving. Breathing. Alive.

And pleased.

Ozhma could feel the heat of his contentment radiating out from him. She could feel him reaching out to her with unseen hands; a fever rose behind her eyes the longer they lingered on that weapon. Images of fire, of blackened hands groping out of seas of flame, of screams so innumerable they swallowed the sound of wind, flashed before her eyes. She felt her chest tighten. She felt her legs go weak. She felt—

"Ozhma."

Hands. Hands on her shoulders, picking her up. Hands on her cheeks, waking her up. Her eyes flitted open, her vision restored. Sal stood before her, the weapon in his sheath and burning at her hip. Ozhma felt her gaze drifting inexorably back to it.

"Hey."

Sal grabbed her face, forced her to meet her stare.

"I'm sorry to ask this of you," she said, "but I need a favor."

Ozhma's mouth hung open. "W-what?"

"I need you to go."

Ozhma's focus returned. Her eyes snapped wide open. "You said you had no plan."

"I didn't say that," she replied. "I always had a plan." She smiled sadly. "I was just kind of hoping I wouldn't have to do it."

"I don't understand."

"Yeah. I know." Sal took her hands in her own, squeezed them. "But you listened to me, anyway. Thanks. For that."

"You're . . . welcome?"

Sal shook her head. "Ask me what you really want to ask me."

Ozhma looked away. Only for a moment.

"What do you need me to do?" she asked.

Sal released her hands.

"Yria will be waiting upstairs," she said. "She'll get you out of here. Somewhere very high and very safe. You'll be able to see the whole thing."

The whole thing?

Ozhma didn't have time to speak the thought before the realization hit her.

The Imperium.

The Revolution.

The legions of soldiers, cannons, magic, and worse arrayed out there against New Vigil. Still waiting. Still ready to bury this city.

Nothing had changed. She hadn't saved anyone. She hadn't helped anything. She—

"Hey."

Sal's voice grew a little irritated. She glared at Ozhma as she helped Liette to a chair.

"I'm trying to tell you what I need you to do before we all fucking die," she said. "You mind listening?"

"R-right," Ozhma agreed weakly. "Right. I'll see..." She took a deep breath. It didn't stop her chest from hurting. "I'll see the whole thing."

Sal nodded grimly. "I want you to see it, Ozhma. I want you to look at as much as you can. I want you to remember as much as you can. I want you to get out of here alive—and when you do, I want you to go to every town with more than two people in it and tell them what you saw here. Tell them what I did here. And tell them I'll do it again if any army comes back to this city."

Ozhma swallowed something hard and painful. "Is that all?"

"No," Sal said. "There's one more thing." She reached down, took Liette's hands in her own. "When it happens..."

Liette looked at Ozhma. Etched in her eyes was a fear, a fear as deep as night and endless as the oceans. And when she spoke, it came out in her words.

"Cover your ears."

"Not to be rude, but that sounds pretty fucking stupid to me."

Rudu didn't sound rude. Honestly, he didn't sound wrong, either. This *did* seem like a bad idea. It *was* a bad idea.

But then again, most of the past day or so had been.

"I used to *be* in the Imperium, lady," he muttered, a little more forcefully, behind her as he took another light. "It's not all pageantry. We did horrible shit. The kind of shit I shouldn't have seen. The kind of shit I have to keep smoking just to stay ahead of." He gestured out over the field. "Torle of the Void is a thousand times worse than *any* of that shit. Look away, you don't want to see this."

Ozhma agreed. Everything she'd heard about Torle of the Void was horrific—and even so far away, on another cliff far from his own camp, she could see the fanfare of his arrival. Trumpets played and banners flew in the Imperial encampment that had been erected on the ridge.

No more delays. No more tricks. No more threats.

Torle of the Void was here. And ready to end this.

And even if, by some miracle, he wasn't, it wasn't as if there wasn't another, equally horrible end awaiting the city. The airship of the Revolution hovered over the field, its engines muttering and its many cannons fixed upon New Vigil's wall.

The fields had been cleaned of the dead and now stood brimming with soldiers. Imperials. Revolutionaries. It was hard to tell the difference, sometimes, there were so many. And it wasn't like it mattered if she mixed them up, either—they were both ready to destroy the city.

Buried. Burned. Broken apart brick by brick.

New Vigil would fall, one way or another.

And she knew it.

"I'm serious," Rudu said. "Are you listening to me?"

"Yes, I am," she replied, looking plaintively to him. "And I am *really* grateful for your concern and the efforts you've made to take care of me thus far. I really, truly am and I'll be happy to spend more time telling you that. But until then, if you could maybe *FUCK OFF*?" She snapped. "I made a promise to watch. And that's what I'm going to do."

"But it'll—"

"Even if it hurts." She turned back to face the field. "Go if you want. But I'm going to stay."

She heard him scoff, then snort, then smoke, then smoke a considerable amount more, and then stomp off.

And, after a few minutes, she heard him smoke again and come stomping back. He took a position beside her, his sullen look evaporating under a cloud of smoke cloying at his face.

"You don't have to stay," she said.

"Yeah, I know," he sighed. "But I can't leave you here after asking you to do me a favor like you did." He smirked at her. "What would they say about Rudu the Cudgel if I did?"

She smiled back at him. He took a deep inhale, passed her his pipe. She took a drag of her own, coughed a lot, handed it back.

"It's... *so good.*"

Her lungs burned too much to say anything else. And that was fine, honestly. There didn't seem to be anything more to say. So they didn't say anything as they stood there.

And they watched.

Until the gates of New Vigil creaked open.

And a woman walked out.

Sal looked tiny on the field as she came striding forward slowly, unhurried, as though there *weren't* endless soldiers, machines, and mages standing by to destroy her. She took her time as she sauntered away from the gates and the walls of the city.

She paused there, between the city and its conquerors, and took a long look up at the sky. Ozhma squinted; she could make out the woman reaching down to her hip, pulling a weapon free and holding it.

And then, she set it down upon the ground, took ten paces backward and sat down.

Nothing else.

No plan. No great gamble. No legendary luck.

Even the Cacophony could not destroy empires. Sal knew it as well as anyone else did—and no matter how badly she wished she didn't, Ozhma knew it, too. Whatever resistance Sal was intending to offer here, she knew it was all she could do. All that she was doing right now.

Sitting.

Waiting.

Watching.

A trumpeted chorus blared from the ridge. A faint silhouette rose from the camp, like a wisp of smoke from a fire. Black robes fluttered as the shape sailed into the sky, hovering high. The Revolution's airship did not move to challenge this new arrival to the skies—why would it?

They had the same goal.

Torle of the Void looked different than she thought—at least from here. She was expecting someone more terrifying. The man that hung in the sky there could have been her grandfather.

She held on to that impression for as long as it took him to raise his arms, for his eyes to flash purple. She wondered now if the Lady's song was playing. She was not a mage. She couldn't hear it. But she wondered how it sounded to Sal down there. Was it sad?

Or was it just tired?

Torle of the Void spread his arms wide, as if in invitation. And, as if in acceptance, the earth began to rumble.

Slowly, at first, like the sound of stone grinding on stone—an ancient groaning of earth that was never meant to be moved like this. Then, the lines started to appear—black scars spreading at the edges of the city, clouds of dust and earth exhaled from the cracks forming in the ground.

What was it like in there now? she wondered. Were Yria and Urda still bickering, even as the world came apart? Were Cavric and Ketterling and Meret still trying to get people out?

The groan of the earth became a roar. The bricks of the city's mighty walls began to shake free of their standing. The ground shook, all the way to beneath her feet. She felt the breath trembling out of her, the despair sinking in even as the shudder of the earth reverberated through her bones.

She wanted to look away. She tried bargaining with herself, reasoning, trying to find the courage to look away. But she forced herself to ignore them. She forced herself to watch.

She told Sal she would.

And so she would watch. As the cracks continued to open. As the city started to sink. As the great void opened up beneath it.

She told herself this. She prepared herself for this.

She waited for it.

The earth started to split open. The clouds of dust became walls. The stone and dirt screamed as they were forcibly split apart. The city shuddered visibly, as if bracing itself for its grim fate.

Torle of the Void spread his arms wide.

Wider.

Wider.

Until they snapped.

Ozhma didn't notice until the earth began to calm and pull itself back together. She looked back up to Torle of the Void. The man hung there in the sky, writhing and screaming as his arms were pulled backward by some unseen force until his shoulder blades split.

Sirens blared in warning. Soldiers stirred in their ranks. Something was happening. None of them knew what.

Except her.

His legs followed, bending forward to snap at the knees and twist unnaturally. He hung, spinning in the sky, limbs bent like the toy of an especially cruel child. Even from here, Ozhma thought she could see the agony on his face, the fear and confusion as he struggled to comprehend what was happening.

Maybe the people of Bitterdrink had worn the same face.

She didn't have time to reflect on that. Not as Torle of the Void's spine snapped backward, folding the mangled mage in two. Not as his body shuddered in the air and then sped toward the gates of New Vigil, plucked from the sky by an unseen hand. She didn't have time for thought anymore.

Or anything beyond three words.

"Cover your ears," she said as she put her hands to her head.

"Huh?" Rudu asked.

"COVER YOUR EARS!"

FIFTY

ELSEWHERE

There is a story that only one woman knows.

It was not told to her. She picked it up in pieces and snippets and frustrated arguments over years of traveling with the only other person who knew it. The person it happened to.

It is a story about a young man who was born to do great things.

And what he ended up doing instead.

He was born to a great family, this young man. One child of many born to an emperor and empress, who smiled at each of their children and told them they would do great things in their lives.

And they did. The Imperial children were born to great power and great destinies, each of them.

One became a great leader of wars and breaker of rebellions, who carved a path of obedience and terror across her father and mother's territories.

One became a scholar of arts and magics, whose research and studies would be hailed as enlightened by the people who started the wars his sister ended.

Another became a diplomat. Another became a minister. One became one great thing, another became another great thing.

Except the young man. Who, most agree, was nothing particularly offensive, nor anything particularly special. His magical talents were subtle, but by no means unimpressive. His aptitude was great, but his ambitions were low. He was interested in telescopes and stars when such things were considered frivolous in the face of so many wars to fight and people to slay.

He was decently liked by the few who could tear their eyes away from the accomplishments of his siblings. Not many noticed him; he noticed not much beyond the lenses of his many telescopes—and for a time, both he and the world were content with this.

But two were not.

The emperor and empress had hoped their child's aptitude would turn him into a great scholar or a shrewd tactician. They did not bother to hide their disappointment in his love of the stars. Nor did they hesitate to remind him of the accomplishments of his siblings, to impress upon him the duties of being their child, to express how grievously they were wounded when he failed to live up to expectations he had never agreed to and never knew how to navigate.

The emperor and empress told themselves they were doing it for his own good, for the betterment of their people, for the strength of their line—the reasons changed, or so the young man thought, but the reactions were always the same. Their children agreed with them. Their ministers agreed with them. Their court agreed with them.

Only the young man did not. He tried to—tried to apply his shrewdness to something bloodier than he was used to. But he wasn't fit for such things. He knew it. And no matter how much he tried to pretend otherwise, the emperor and the empress knew it, as well.

He became accustomed to no longer being invited to functions and balls, accustomed to not being present for matters of state, accustomed to being ignored in the halls of their great palace. Slowly left behind by his family's glorious march across history.

And accustomation turned to resignation. And resignation turned to sadness. And, as it sometimes does, sadness became bitterness. And, as it always does, bitterness became anger.

And so it was that the anger became the young man's companion, along with his telescopes, for many years. When the emperor and the empress died, his anger at the things he'd never been able to say to them only grew. These feelings grew as the nights became years and passed unhappily and alone for the young man.

They grew until one dark night.

The evening before the coronation of his brother, the great scholar who would become the great emperor, was spent much as it always was: in his lonely observatory in the company of his telescopes. He stared, ruefully, into the lens of his biggest one, trying to find something in the stars that would help him avoid the pain, the anger, and the ugly thoughts that came with them.

He found a distraction as he spotted something in the night sky. A star he'd never noticed before. A tiny, tiny speck in a great field of emptiness. It was nothing more than a faint light of an unusual color, yet he found he could not stop looking at it.

Not when it was looking back at him.

"Hello."

Speaking to him.

"What is your name?"

With a voice that he could feel in his heart.

He gave the star his name, and asked for the star's name in return. The star gave it to him and he found that he knew it already. They continued to speak to each other, the star and he, long into the night. He told the star of his pains and his angers for an hour, then of his sorrows for six more. He wept to the star, whispered to it, and the star listened to every word he spoke.

The star offered him an exchange. The pain of his anger for the light of the star. A simple exchange. And he needed only to accept.

Old magic.

The Oldest Magic.

A bargain. A barter. A trade.

He hesitated.

And then he accepted.

"What is it you desire?"

The star asked him a question, at the end of the long night, and he considered it. And though his sadnesses had been many, it was his anger that he answered with. And in exchange for his many pains, the star gave him what he wanted.

And on the day of the coronation, after the many rituals and honorary operas and feasts and festivals, he took it.

He left his brother's body on the floor of the imperial hall in a pile of quickly cooling cinders.

The death of his sibling brought him no joy. And he said so to the star.

"What would bring you joy?"

The star asked.

And he answered.

One by one, his siblings perished at his hands. The few that defied him were slain instantly by an onslaught of magical power that none could explain the sudden appearance of. The many that tried to mollify him were accepted, at first, but as his resentment and fury grew, so too did his unhappiness with himself. He slew them, too. And many others in a quest to escape the feelings.

And it led him to a throne. And a crown of brass thorns resting upon his brow.

The people accepted him, as did the ministers and the courts. Surely, they reasoned, his mysterious surge of magical power must mean that it was he who should have been ruling the entire time. He took lovers and sired children, as was expected of an emperor. He put down rebellions and killed a suitable amount of people, as was also expected. In time, he began to be respected... but not in the way he wanted.

They called him mad.

They feared him.

They feared to fail him, as he had feared to fail the emperor and empress.

This, he told himself, made things fair. Now everyone felt as he had once. And yet the rushes from obedience and terror were fleeting. And with his siblings gone and his children hiding from him, he felt a profound loneliness, an emptiness that he found he could not escape, no matter how much he tried to avoid it.

"What would make it better?"

The star asked him.

And he answered.

The truth of the Mad Emperor's name only grew as he spent increasingly more time in his observatory, muttering to his telescopes. Yet, so too did a fear—for as often as he was mad, he was also often right. Rebellions dwindled, fortunes grew, the Imperium prospered, guided by the star's whispers and the Mad Emperor's relentlessly hungering emptiness.

Until one day, he received a vision of a land he had never seen. It was a land of monsters, of strange minerals and forests, and of ancient ruins left behind by a forgotten people. The vision grew in intensity, plaguing his dreaming and waking life in equal amounts.

He knew that the star was trying to tell him something. And he stopped trying to escape the visions and instead studied them. The ruins, the great land left behind—he recognized it, even though he had never seen it. He put things together slowly, over many sleeplessness nights.

That land, that forsaken land, was where the star had been born.

Where the star had gained such power.

Where the star had risen, shining brightly over a vast emptiness.

As he yearned to do.

It was not easy to put together an expeditionary force—objections were raised by those concerned, until those concerned started to disappear in the night. Forces were difficult to persuade to go, until they were offered instead remote positions on the farthest, most desolate reaches of the Imperium.

The nuls were the ones that suffered most. Worked to death in the assembly of a vast flotilla of ships. Requisitioned from their comfortable homes by right of Imperial decree. Assembled in vast forces like livestock for the journey to come.

Their suffering went as disregarded as everyone else's.

Slowly, the Mad Emperor put together his ships, his mages, his nuls.

And he sent them over the sea.

When they returned, two years later, they were fewer in number and greater in riches. They came back with tales of monsters and fiends, of ores with incredible powers and lands rich in resources they'd never even seen before. The tales spread like wildfire, as did the knowledge that the Mad Emperor rewarded those explorers handsomely on top of their already impressive hauls.

Forces flowed to that scarred land like water. Explorers returned regularly with new tales and new wealth. The Mad Emperor saw his visions, the obsession with stars that had always earned him scorn, suddenly propelling him to worship among his people.

Until there was a rebellion he could not crush.

The nuls rose up against their Imperial overseers. A general, some fool nul, had led their trifling revolution. Their machines and explosives threw the mages from the land. The days of glorious exploration turned to intractable warfare as conflict swept that land.

Despite his great powers and all his accomplishments, he began to be looked on not with fear and respect, but with terrified, silent loathing.

The years stretched on and his anger ate him. It consumed his sinew, his heart, his mind. No conquest or triumph or accolade or worship could make him think differently about his pains. His anger ate him spitefully, bit by bit, until the magic diminished and his strength failed and he was left with nothing else.

And he realized, even that anger was fading.

The star had taken so much of him. It had grown bored with the taste of his fury. His visions began to fade, his body began to waste, but the anger endured just long enough.

Long enough to decide that he knew what he really wanted now.

To be like the star.

Eternal. Perpetual. Escaped from this horrific world and into a vast, peaceful emptiness.

He wanted it. And as his anger had given him everything he wanted, it gave him this, as well.

His most loyal servants sought the most skilled practitioners of the most forbidden sciences and most ancient magics. As he clung to life, they plotted and researched and planned and dreamed of the rewards promised to them. Until, from the oldest tomes in the darkest parts of the Imperium's most forsaken libraries, they uncovered a solution.

A solution to prolonging his life.

To rid him of this weak body that crumbled under the weight of his anger.

To give him a new vessel that would see him live long enough and consume enough to become like the star.

He slept one last time in his body.

And awoke in a cage of brass.

And there he waited, in that dark place, for a day he knew would one day come.

A day he would meet someone with an anger to match his.

FIFTY-ONE

NEW VIGIL

The world started ending thirty-two minutes after Sal had put her weapon down.

Torle of the Void, the greatest terror of a terrible war, hung helplessly before her. His body was contorted into weird and painful shapes as he twitched in the air, suspended by unseen strings like some macabre marionette. His face was twisted into the kind of horror that wise people think they'll never have to face; his mouth struggled to form words he'd never thought he'd have to speak.

Sal stared back into his begging eyes, pleading for understanding. Her only answer was her stare drifting down to the gun on the ground. The Cacophony's metal pulsed, rippled—a heart of metal and flame, beating.

There was a gruesome popping noise, a grinding and a snapping. Torle of the Void was wrung out like a cloth rag, and from his broken husk, a pale purple light emerged. It slithered out of his eyes and his mouth, a wispy and pale light that coiled through the sky. And his body fell, cold and stiff, to the ground.

She knew this light. She remembered it.

Though she had thought the light that came out of her was a little more vibrant than what came out of Torle of the Void.

It trailed on smoky vapor through the sky, drifting upward for a moment. There was the sound of a great yawning, a vast emptiness opening. Inhaling. The light was pulled out of the sky, writhing as it disappeared into the metal of the weapon.

The beating heart became strong.

Healthy.

Whole.

The metal of the weapon rippled like the surface of a pond. Fingers of brass reached out, pulling themselves out of the gun. A metal arm, strong and lean, followed. A pair of broad, brass shoulders. A thick and sturdy neck of metal. A head of barbed hair. A long and powerful back.

A body hauled itself out of the weapon, drew itself out of impossible space. Steam peeled off of his shoulders. Cinders fell from his mouth. He turned a pair of burning eyes out over the field, at the airship and the mages and the many soldiers of the many armies arrayed against him.

The Cacophony smiled through brass lips.

"Truly," he said in a burning voice, "I am honored to be welcomed with such spectacle."

A siren blared. The airship's wail cut across the field, a wall of noise punctuated only by the shattering sound of cannons firing. Severium charges flew from the airship, streaking through the sky to come hammering down in fire and smoke upon Sal.

They exploded on the ground. Fire raced across the field, scorched the blood from the sand. Veils of flame swept around her, blackened the stones and the earth, swallowed the air in great fiery jaws of red and purple.

And she felt none of it. Her skin bore not a trace of soot as the flames whirled around her.

He burned with a greater heat than their cannons could.

The Cacophony held out a brass hand. The flames swirled around them in a vast pillar—then, like birds to seed, they came rushing eagerly into his palm. In seconds, the great swathes of fire had become a single burning cinder in his hand. He squeezed his fingers together, quenched the conflagration with a little pressure.

"Magnificent." The Cacophony watched the tiny plumes of smoke drifting off his metal fingers. "To think that nuls could make such fire and pain from ore and metal." He turned eyes of burning brass over the armies, stirring with alarm at seeing the Revolution's greatest weapons snuffed in moments. "I've seen it so many times. But to actually *feel* it is... different. Exhilarating."

He turned to face her. Brass thorns jutted from his regal brow. A mane of barbed and bristling hair fell around his shoulders. The Mad Emperor's smile leaked cinders as he spoke.

"I have so much to thank you for, Salazanca," he said. "And so much to experience."

She stared at him, numbed. Perhaps she was horrified into silence by the display. Perhaps she was still struggling to comprehend what terror she had just unleashed upon the world. Perhaps something else.

She offered him no gratitude, nor any welcome. She stared silently at him as he turned his burning smile to the sky.

"Ah. Convenient." His gaze settled upon the airship as it began to veer wildly away, its engines roaring with the effort of turning the mighty ship around. "I have been so curious what speaking to Culven Loyal would be like face-to-face."

He extended a long, muscular arm.

"Haven't you?"

There was a faint humming sound, like the vibration of a bowl. The Cacophony tightened his fingers. From far away, there was the splintering of wood, a cry of alarm. A figure came flying through the air—indistinct, at first, as it was pulled forcibly from the airship's railing. It grew rapidly closer and, in two breaths, a frail figure wrapped in a Revolutionary coat was writhing in his grasp.

"Stop." Culven Loyal's throat was collapsed, but his voice echoed in her body without one, all the same. *"This isn't your magic. She doesn't share it. What you think you're doing, you're—"*

"Huh. I admit I'm disappointed by the tediousness." The Cacophony's eyes narrowed, mouth gaped open. "We have waited centuries to meet, and you greet me with *that*?"

Culven Loyal—the husk that housed the Scrath inside—writhed with a ferocity not possible in a body that frail. But even the power inside that weak frame couldn't escape from the Cacophony's grasp as he tightened his fingers, opened his mouth a little wider, and breathed deeply.

Loyal's body stiffened. A twisting light was pulled forcibly from him—like Torle of the Void's, like her own, except this one was vibrant and glittering with thousands of colors, colors that she'd never seen before. It shrieked with a voice of light and shade as it was pulled, writhing into the Cacophony's maw.

It vanished behind brass teeth. Steam peeled off of the Cacophony's metal flesh.

"Still. I can't say it wasn't a pleasure."

The Cacophony turned toward the armies—the mages and their nul servants, the fanatics and their machines—with mounting delight. They were in full panic now. Regiments shattered, lines broke, Revolutionary and Imperial alike were joined in their desperation to escape.

"Nor can I deny that this will be."

The Cacophony inhaled deeply, his mouth open and baring brass fangs. He exhaled a great breath across the field, and from his burning throat came a wall of noise. A great rush of blistering air swept over the earth. A great sound of thundering brass and wailing trumpets and shattering bells followed.

The sound struck the soldiers. Shook the limbs from their bodies. Peeled the skin from their skulls. Pulled blood from their ears and throats. Machines shattered. Bones were pulverized. Bodies fell.

Their screams were deafening as they collapsed, their skin sizzling and turning a cooked, glistening pink beneath a great heat. Coils of smoke peeling off their burning faces veiled the rest of the armies' flight as they fled, shrieking, into the canyons.

The mightiest armies the Scar had ever seen. Arrayed alike against a common foe. And they had both turned and fled, leaving behind their dead, a road of meat and blackened bones, to tell the tale of their defeat.

The echo of the Cacophony's anger faded. The sound of cooking flesh abated. The wail of fear disappeared into the rocky gorges and pits. The silence that fell over the field was morbid, unnatural, painful.

It was the silence of the torturer's delight when he discovers what makes his victims beg. The quiet of the condemned when they know there is no way off the gallows. The great deep stillness between two siblings the moment they realize they hate each other. It was a silence of pains yet to come.

Pains that would make this seem pleasant.

"I apologize that I leave you here." The Cacophony's footsteps left searing, blackened tracks as he began to stride away. "I apologize, too, that you shall be alive to see what happens next." His smile betrayed no regret. Nothing but sadistic joy. "May it console you to know that the suffering of your enemies shall be endless."

He looked to the sky, to a distant star visible only to him.

"It's agony that draws them," he whispered. "The fear of war. The pain of loss. The suffering. They crave it, for they cannot feel it. Envy is all they know. If that envy demands pain, then so be it."

He took another step forward.

"Worry not, Salazanca," the Cacophony said. "Their pain will be great. And the ending I pen for this wretched earth shall be an unhappy one. Such is needed to get their attention. But rest assured, I will—"

"Oh, for fuck's sake, I *get* it."

The Cacophony halted. He turned, slowly.

"Great suffering, oceans of blood, pain and misery and suffering for all—yes, you're scary, I fucking get it."

And the woman stood there, a sneer on her face as she picked her teeth.

"All that time trapped in a fucking gun," she said, "and you couldn't come up with a better monologue than that?"

The Cacophony stared at her for a moment. His eyelid twitched. Then, his smile grew wider. He shrugged his broad shoulders, let flames fall from his mouth as he laughed.

"You wound me, Sal," he said. "But I take your point." He held up one hand, placed the other over his heart. "I do solemnly vow to come up with something a little more poignant, no matter how many I must go through."

She snorted, spat something out. He grinned, extended a hand.

"Permit me to reward you a final time," he said, "by sparing you the horror of what's to come."

His brass fingers tightened. Steam coiled from his palm. Cinders burst from his mouth as he hissed, his anger narrowed to thin, burning slits. Heat wrapped around her, assailed her as the fire had, clutched around her with burning fingers.

So it was a little surprising when she still stood there, unhelpfully not dying.

"*That* was better, I have to admit." Sal started to walk toward him. "But I think there's a problem with it. With killing me at all, if I'm honest."

The Cacophony's metal brows knit together in confusion. His mouth hung open. His face of proud brass struggled to convey an emotion as humble as incomprehension. He tried to tighten his fingers again.

They would not bend.

His burning eyes widened. He tried to take a step back.

His foot would not move.

"You remember what we did the day we met? You remember what the man who made you told me?" She chuckled. "He said you needed magic to work. Not just any magic. The first magic. The Oldest Magic." She pointed at him. "We made a deal, you and I. Revenge for ruin. Ruin for revenge."

He looked down. He was sinking. His feet were growing softer, melting beneath his own heat. His eyes raced with a predator's quickness, struggling to see the magic that assailed him so as to undo it. But the realization grew dire on his face as he began to see the shape of a foot slowly transforming into a grip, a kneecap twisting to form a hammer.

"You had a taste of your ruin."

He looked at her. She looked back.

With an infuriatingly shit-eating grin.

"But we've still got business."

Realization turned to horror turned to fury in a frighteningly short amount of time. Flames burst from the Cacophony's mouth as he lunged for the woman that had once wielded him. But his hands stopped short of her throat as a sudden weight caught his other foot and pulled him undignifiedly to his knees.

He looked behind him to see his body disappearing, falling back into the gun, back into the bargain he had sworn to fulfill.

"That's not fair." He threw his head back, spewed fire with his scream. "*THAT'S NOT FAIR!*" He roared, lit up the sky with gouts of flame, as he struggled to keep hold of his fast-fading body. "I killed for you. I killed *so many*! I fulfilled our bargain."

She glanced over him, rapidly reverting to a weapon again. "Seems the arbiter of our bargain disagrees."

"How? *HOW?* I killed *everyone* you asked me to. *All* names from your petty little *list*. I gave them the pain they deserved!" His face contorted with fury. "*HOW HAVE I FAILED?*"

"Jindu," she replied, her voice soft in the face of his anger.

His eyes narrowed. "What *about* him?"

She smiled a knife of a smile. Small. Sharp. Painful. A tear plucked the corner of her eye.

The Cacophony's brass face fell. Then, it erupted. He lashed out with a hand, reached for her, found himself scraping at the ground as one hand disappeared back into the gun.

"You can't," he snarled. "You *can't*. We made a deal."

"We did," she replied. "You and I are bound together until I get my revenge. Nothing has changed. Except..."

She reached into her vest, pulled free the scrap of paper with the names, all of them. She unfolded the parchment, let her eyes glide over the names, the ones she'd crossed out, the ones she hadn't. The one in red.

~~*Chiriel the Four-String.*~~

Kothi the Scrawl.

Jindu the Blade.

She closed her eyes, let them run through her mind one more time.

And she let it go.

And, for all its weight, all the parchment and all those names became one more cinder on the breeze. A single fiery note singing and extinguished in the wind.

"Ah, shit. Butterfingers," she said. "Well, fuck. I'm sure I'll get around to fulfilling the rest of that revenge bit." She clicked her tongue. "Eventually."

"You cannot," he roared, cinders pouring from his mouth like saliva from a slavering cat. "You *cannot. YOU CANNOT DO THIS TO ME!*"

The Cacophony's eyes burned with a hatred not possible in mortal eyes. The Cacophony snorted and exhaled a cloud of steam so searing as to bleach the earth white. The Cacophony took a deep breath, looked at her.

And smiled.

"And you cannot do this for yourself, either."

She hadn't liked it when he'd done that as a gun.

She definitely didn't like it now that he had a face.

"The fuck are you so happy about?" she asked, sneering.

"Nothing," he replied, his voice softening to a dim hiss. "Because nothing has changed. I have been with you all this time, through all this blood. I am the first thing you think of when you wake and the closest thing to your heart when you go to sleep. And when you feel your blood burn, it is my heart beating in your chest. I know you, Salazanca. As you know me."

His body continued to disappear into the gun, his brass face melted. His proud crown of thorns, his arrogant gaze, his burning smile—all took on a misshapen morbidity that could not conceal his smug pleasure.

"You will never forget their names. The list is written on your heart and it will ache with every breath you take. Forgive who you want. Pretend you are not who you are. May it comfort your pains for as long as it lasts. You can pretend you are beyond this, beyond me..."

His brow grew horns. His face became a dragon. His smile became leering and full of teeth. And his delight was no less for it.

"But we made a deal, you and I."

His voice diminished on the wind.

"And you will hurt forever."

And became a single rasp of smoke and steam.

"But when you want it to stop..."

Until that, too, was taken to the wind.

"I will be there for you."

And faded upon the breeze.

FIFTY-TWO

THE SCAR

Are you sure you don't want to wait?"

Ozhma shielded her eyes as she glanced back down the road. The marching pillars and canyons of the Nails still loomed large, the narrow road winding through the great rock formations stayed empty.

"I'm sure that Cavric would want to say goodbye," she said, frowning. "Wouldn't he?"

"He might," Sal answered without looking up from her work. "But he's got more important things to do."

Ozhma felt her frown deepen. "What could be more important than saying goodbye to an old friend?"

"Explaining to a terrified citizenry the fiery heap of crazy birdshit that took place on their doorstep?" She grunted as she hoisted another crate and stacked it in the wagon. "I mean, *I* personally would prioritize saying goodbye, but I suppose that's why I'm not leading any cities."

Ozhma's face stiffened a little. She supposed that was true.

New Vigil had survived. Survived the onslaught of the Imperium and the Revolution. Survived that horror she had seen unfurl at the gates of the city. Few cities in the Scar could boast such a record of triumphs. And no others could claim to be witness to the Cacophony's terrible strength.

But there was not always joy in surviving. The scars did not hurt less just because you lived through getting them. And sometimes, walking away alive was as painful as falling down and giving up. She knew that now.

She'd learned that.

"You don't want a goodbye."

Sal's voice was weary as she hefted another box and loaded it into the wagon. The aging draft bird yoked to it let out a low squawk of resentment as its burden increased. Congeniality, nearby, let out a hiss and snapped in response. The wagon bird squawked, snapped back. The two seemed a decent match.

That hadn't been intentional. New Vigil had spared as much as it could for the woman who had both saved them and nearly destroyed them. What it could spare amounted to some food and supplies, a bottle of whiskey, and a run-down wagon with the run-down bird it had come attached to.

It felt a little like an insult, to Ozhma. Or a shakedown. Sal had been happy just to have the whiskey.

"You want reassurance." She paused to take a swig of water, wipe her brow. "You want him to come and say he isn't angry or afraid. At me. Or you."

Ozhma swallowed hard. "Yeah. Yeah, I kind of do want that."

"Yeah." Sal swirled water in her mouth, spit. "Feels like shit to not get it, doesn't it?"

She sighed. "So... what do you do when you don't?"

"Suck it up. Move on. Make peace. Or get so fucked up you can't remember what it was you were upset about it. All of those work. Some longer than others." Sal picked up another box, set it down on the wagon. Her hands lay atop it, hesitant to move it any farther. "Do it enough times and you get pretty good at it."

A simple box. Thick, sturdy wood around dull iron. A heavy lock with a heavy key to go with it.

That was all that kept the most terrible weapon known to humanity in check.

That and Sal, anyway.

"What are you going to do with him?" Ozhma whispered her words—she feared to attract the gun's attention. "You can't... destroy him, can you?"

"We made a deal, he and I." She closed her eyes. "I can't get rid of him, and he can't get rid of me. And I'll live with that. And with him." She pursed her lips. "And I guess we'll see which one of us is right."

She let out a long sigh. Then she shoved the most terrible weapon known to humanity in between a sack of rice and a couple of pairs of old boots.

"But, fuck," she said, "I'm tired of his birdshit."

She kept stacking, burying him under more luggage, more supplies, more food and other things, until he was just one more part of a collection. She rolled her shoulder out, knuckled the small of her back. Ozhma kept silent until she could no longer.

"I just... have to ask something, sorry."

"If you have to ask, you're not sorry," Sal said.

"It's just that..." Ozhma almost hesitated to say it. "When did you realize your plan would work?"

Sal shrugged. "I don't know. Maybe five minutes after it did?"

Her eyes widened, her heart caught in her chest as the answer slammed into her.

"What? *What?*" she gasped. "You didn't know? We were so close to... to..." She flailed, as if she could pluck the words out of the air. "And you didn't even *know*?"

"Well, obviously I *thought* it might, or I wouldn't have done it, would I?" Sal scoffed, hands on her hips. "But I'm so terribly sorry if my magic gun that can turn into a man that kills a lot of people is so *complex*, madam. It was the only thing I could think of at the time."

"But... what would have happened if it hadn't worked?"

Sal blinked, shrugged again.

Ozhma's mind struggled briefly to consider all of this, gave up. Sal smiled as she walked past, laid a hand on her shoulder and gave it a gentle squeeze.

"But, hey, you're not dead, are you?" she said. "Why not go enjoy it for a bit?"

Sal went to soothe Congeniality, in the midst of a heated squawking argument with the wagon bird. Completely oblivious to how infuriating she was. Ozhma didn't necessarily feel *great* about thinking that, but the thought was unavoidable.

It had been a guess? They had come so close to sharing the same fate as all those bodies seared and stained on the ground by the weapon's power because of a *guess*? She felt the need to protest, to press, or maybe just to shake Sal and scream for a little bit.

"Insufferable, isn't she?"

She whirled around like a startled cat. Liette, to her credit, didn't point that out as she walked past, bundles of parchments, quills, and books cradled in her arms. She set them down on the wagon, took a moment to sneer before she went about rearranging Sal's haphazard stacking.

"She almost destroyed everything and herself," the Freemaker huffed, "*and* she's complete shit at packing."

"I... yes?" Ozhma bit her lip, winced. "I'm really sorry. I mean *really* sorry to ask, but... should you be walking around?"

Liette turned a familiar smirk toward her. "You really are quite charming in situations that adhere to the laws of time and space, aren't you? I'm sorry we didn't get to talk more."

Ozhma just smiled. She'd long since stopped trying to figure out what the Freemaker meant with statements like that and simply decided to enjoy the conversation—it hurt her head too much otherwise.

"I suppose I'm just worried," Ozhma said, rubbing the back of her neck. "I... don't know exactly what you went through. And I heard a lot of it. Are you... going to be okay?"

Liette paused, stared into the distance.

"I am going to try."

She resumed her work, meticulously arranging each piece of luggage in the wagon. Though she did not move the box containing the weapon. She did not so much as touch it. Perhaps she was afraid of it, still. Or perhaps it was simply Sal's decision where it was moved.

"And so is she," Liette said. "I wanted so much to protect her. To make everything stop hurting so much." She smoothed a stray lock of hair back over her ear. "I don't think I ever thought there was another way." She swallowed hard, bit something back. "But I think... I know a little more now. Enough to try, anyway."

Ozhma blushed, looked at her feet. "Where are you going to go?"

"I don't know," Liette replied. "Elsewhere, I suppose. Somewhere where it's easier. Or at least quieter."

"In the Scar, that could be a long way away."

"Yes, well, the few—and I emphasize, *few*—heralds of culture New Vigil can boast saw fit to donate some reading to pass the time." Liette plucked up one such book, adjusted her glasses as she studied its spine. "*The Pomegranates of Her Garden.*" She wrinkled her nose. "Smut. Of the cheapest, trashiest kind. Ugh. Reading it for a forty-fourth time will be *agony.*"

Congeniality let out a squawk from the front. Her fight with her surly company resolved, both of the great birds rustled their feathers, eager to get on their way. Sal pulled at her reins, wheeled her about, and extended a hand to Liette.

"Well, then," Ozhma said, "I guess I'll let you—"

Her breath caught in her throat. A rush of warmth caught her cheeks. Liette's arms tightened around her, pulled her close. Her voice was a soft, wet whisper.

"Thank you," she said, "for staying with her."

It didn't last long enough for her to even register what happened, let alone respond. But as Liette hurried off and took Sal's hand, pulled up onto the back of Congeniality, she smiled. She watched them turn and go, the wagon rumbling behind them.

She watched the dust rise from their wake.

She watched them disappear up the road.

She followed their tracks, for a time.

Sal the Cacophony had ridden here. The woman who had started a war. The woman who had beaten the two greatest nations the world had ever known. The woman who carried a weapon—her namesake, the most terrible power to have ever laid searing gaze upon this land—in her luggage, next to her spare boots.

There would be stories of what happened here, Ozhma knew.

There would be stories told by the survivors of this battle, of how Sal the Cacophony and her terrible weapon had slain Torle of the Void and Culven Loyal, two powerful people who served other, more powerful people. They would whisper her name with terror and learn to fear her and hate her more than they already did. They would make their grudges, swear their oaths, and feel the same cold fear that all boastful people pretend they don't feel in their bellies.

And there would be stories told by the people who saw it happen. Of how Sal the Cacophony, a Vagrant who stood with only a handful of people against two great nations, could not be shaken. Of how she dispersed the strongest armies with one terrible sound from her awful weapon. Of how New Vigil stood against its enemies and their overwhelming power because of her.

And there would be stories told by those who saw the devastation. They would talk of the fields littered with bodies and the ruins left in her passing. They would talk of the savaged towns and the sleepless people she had left behind her. They would hear a loud noise, see a fire burning too brightly, see the flash of brass and feel their chests tighten and fear the name of Sal the Cacophony.

But no one would talk of Sal and Liette. The two women who tried their hardest not to hurt each other. The woman who loved whiskey and the woman who loved books and the lengths they went to for each other. The loud, obnoxious one and the soft-spoken, obnoxious one, who left behind a war and tried to find something better.

Ozhma would, from time to time, she knew.

To those close to her. Or those who should know.

But those who walked along that road, who counted the tracks of two birds and a wagon being pulled through the Scar, would never know who had passed by. No one would but her.

And when their paths finally diverted and she took another road, she found that when she looked back, she could no longer tell whose tracks they were, either.

Ozhma found her bird roughly where she had left her. The stout draft bird was nearby, grazing on some tall grass as she seemed to have been doing all this time. And her wagon was nearby, mostly untouched. The barrels and crates of whiskey she had been carrying in the back were gone, but she'd accepted that might happen. It *was* Avonin & Family, after all.

She found everything more or less where she expected to when she returned from the road.

More or less.

The man sprawled out in the back of her wagon was new, though.

"Hey." Rudu, his arms draped on the railings of her wagon, glanced up through red-rimmed eyes. "How was it?"

"It was...harder than I thought it would be," Ozhma replied, cocking a brow as she walked to her bird. "Um, sorry, but have you been—"

"Waiting long?" Rudu interrupted. "Yeah, kind of. But it's all right. Your shit had been mostly picked clean by the time I got here—I would have stopped them, but I was...well, you know, you were there for it." He grinned. "It's all right, though. There was one bottle left."

"I suppose that's not the entire shipment, then," she said as she got her bird and led her back to the wagon. "That counts."

"Sorry." Rudu let out a belch, tossed an empty bottle out. "There *was* one bottle left."

"Right." Ozhma sighed. "Okay."

She yoked her bird to her wagon, crawled into the seat. Her body felt stiff suddenly, as though she wasn't used to sitting this still anymore. She rolled her shoulders out, took the reins of the bird, gave them a crack, and started the wagon rattling.

"I'll replace the whiskey." Rudu sparked his pipe behind her, began to puff deeply. "How much was it?"

"Fifty femurs' worth."

"Fuck me. Silver?"

"Gold."

"*GOLD?*" He took an especially long drag. "Okay, fuck. The Ashmouths will cover it. Just get me as far as..." He paused. "Where's the next town?"

"Harld's Wake."

"That's far." He groaned, fell back in the wagon. "Fuck me, that's far."

"It is. Could be days away, honestly, if the weather gets bad."

"All right, shit. Well, then...what do you want to talk about for that long?"

A smile crept across Ozhma's face. She reached a hand back. Rudu handed her the pipe. She took a deep breath. It tasted foul. It set her lungs ablaze. She coughed it out, handed the pipe back.

"I've got a story."

ACKNOWLEDGMENTS

Through the angry and desperate times in which this book was born, both it and I were able to make it thanks to the support of my mom, my dad, my dogs, and my amazing fiancée, Danielle.

I have more scars than I did when I started writing this. And maybe you do, too. Hope this helps us both ache a little less in the morning.

meet the author

Libbi Rich

SAM SYKES—author, citizen, mammal—has written extensively over the years, penning *An Affinity for Steel*, the Bring Down Heaven trilogy, *Brave Chef Brianna*, and now the Grave of Empires trilogy. At the time of this writing, no one has been able to definitively prove or disprove that he has fought a bear.

Find out more about Sam Sykes and other Orbit authors by registering for the free monthly newsletter at orbitbooks.net.

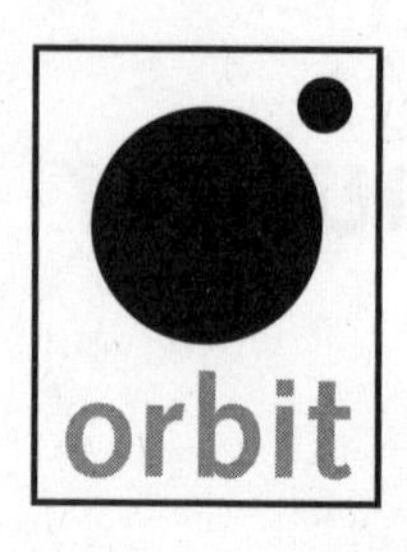
orbit